PRODUC... NY

PUBLISHED BY IMAGE COMICS BERKELEY, CA

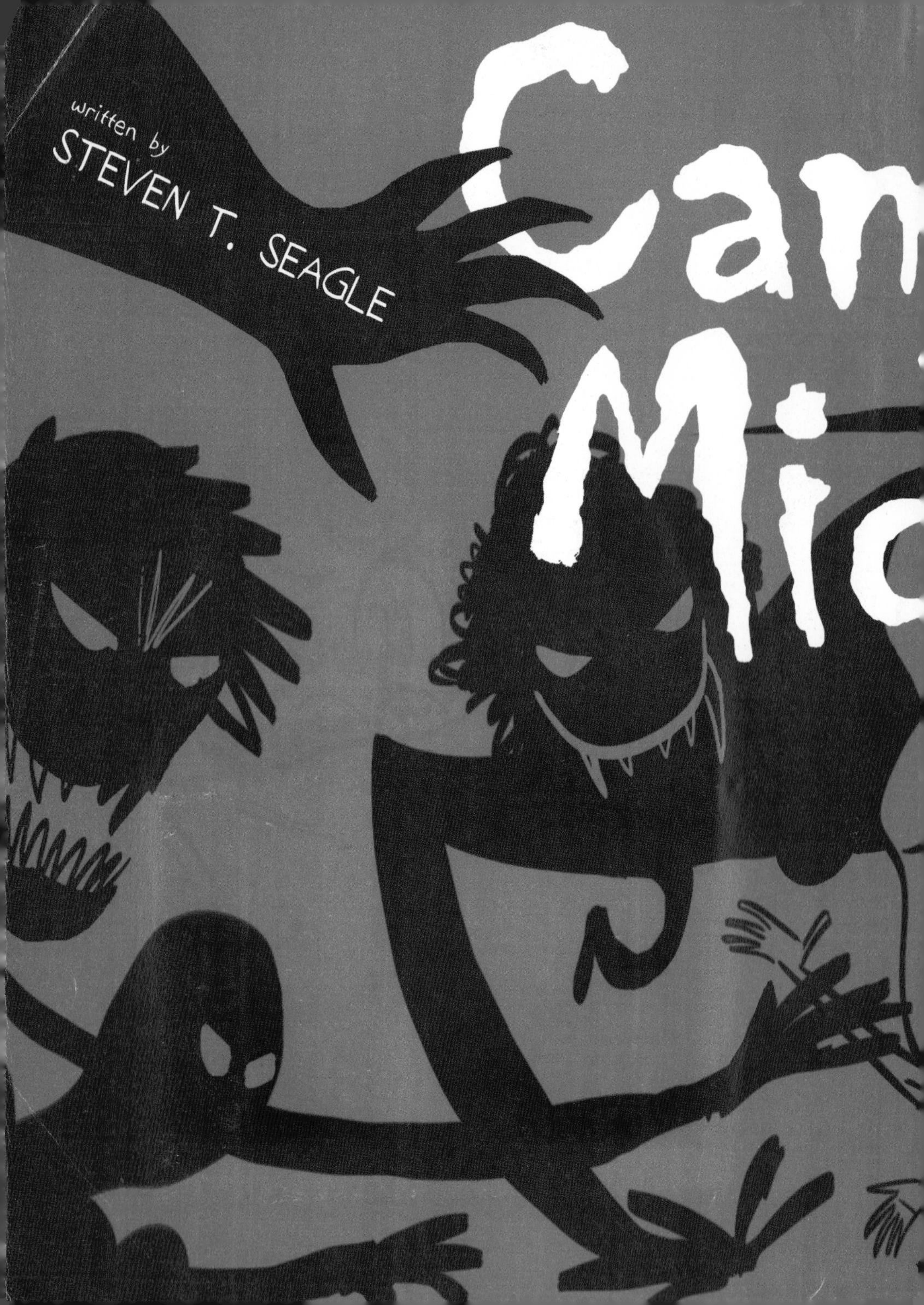
written by
STEVEN T. SEAGLE

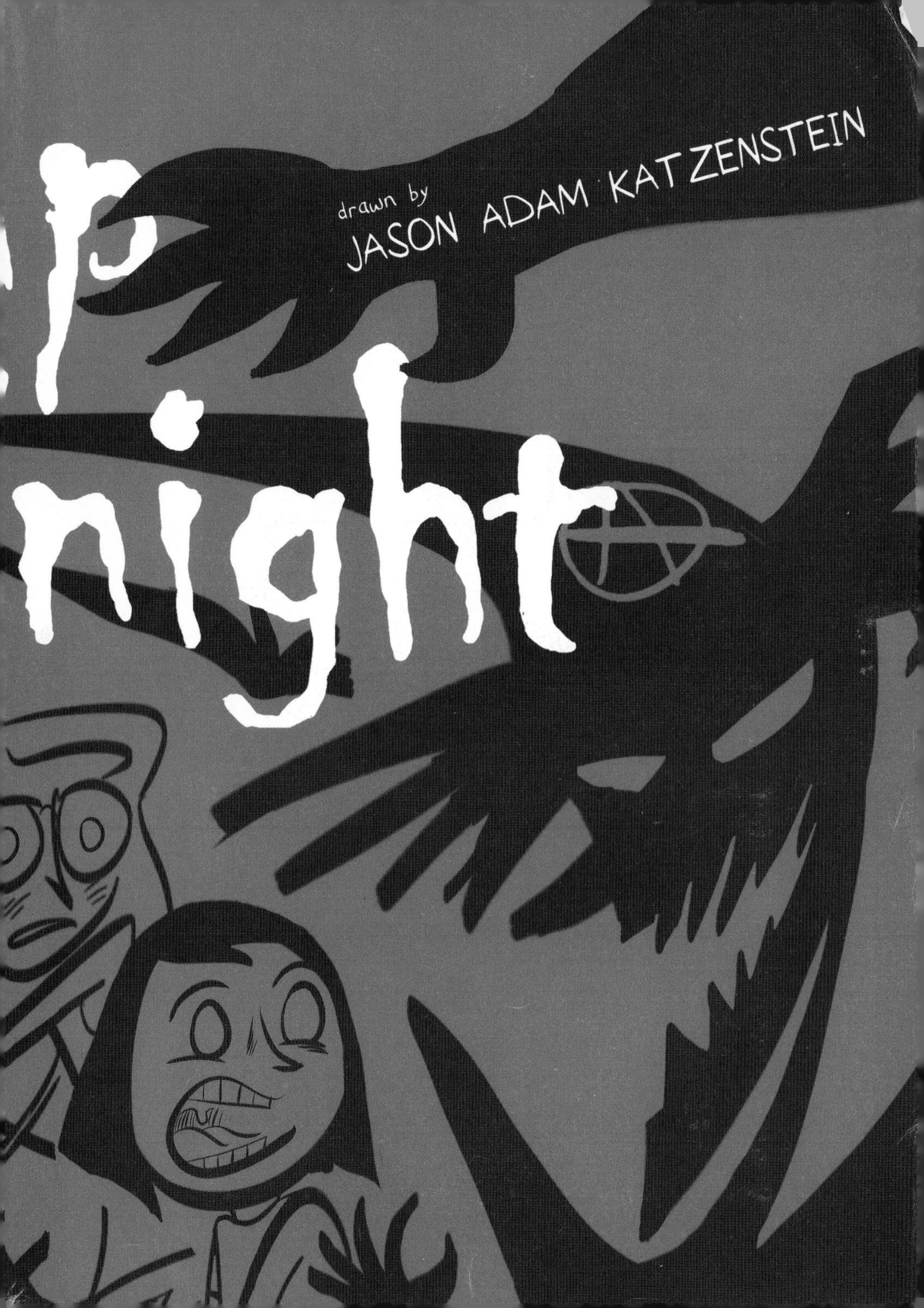
drawn by
JASON ADAM KATZENSTEIN
night

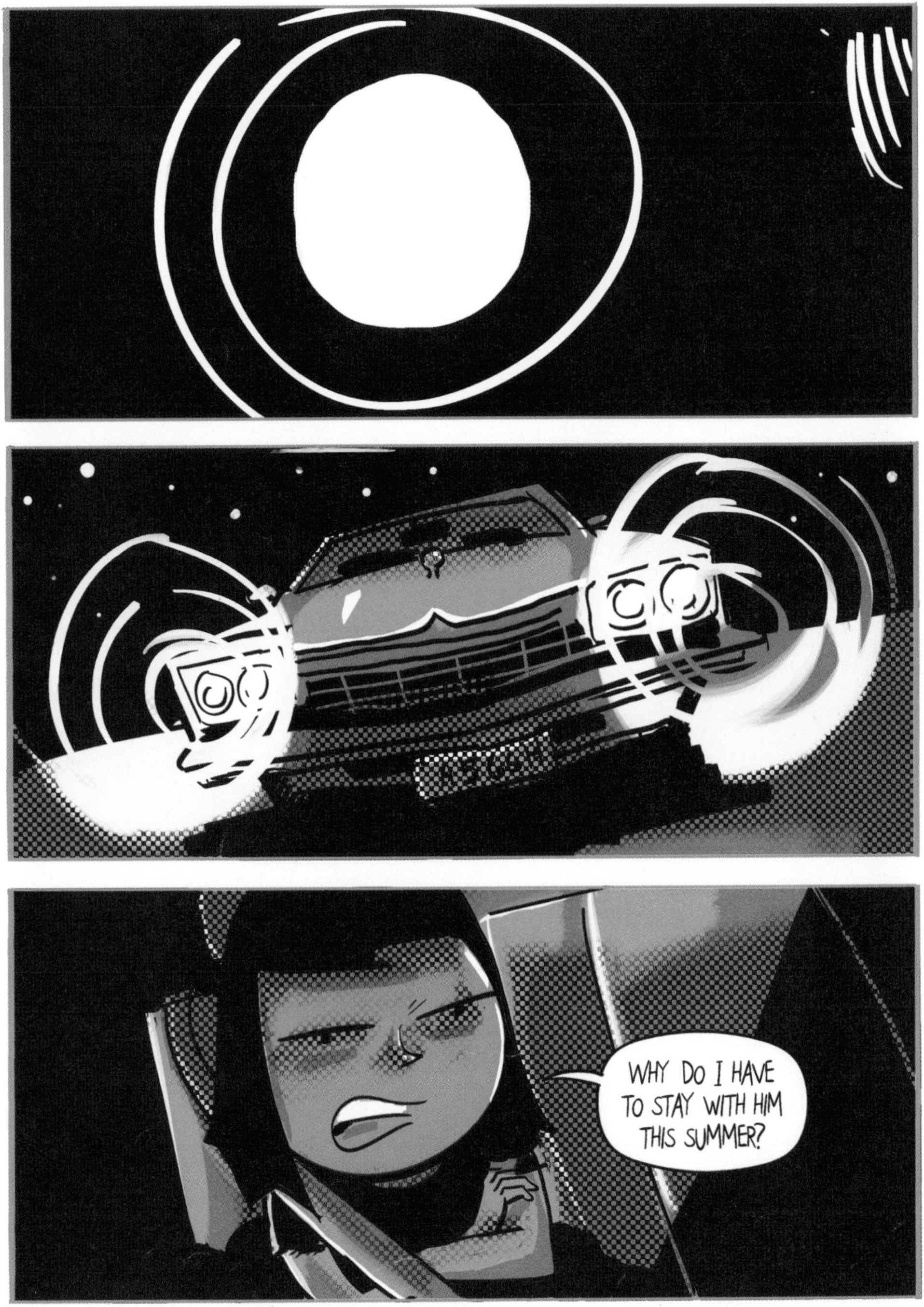
WHY DO I HAVE TO STAY WITH HIM THIS SUMMER?

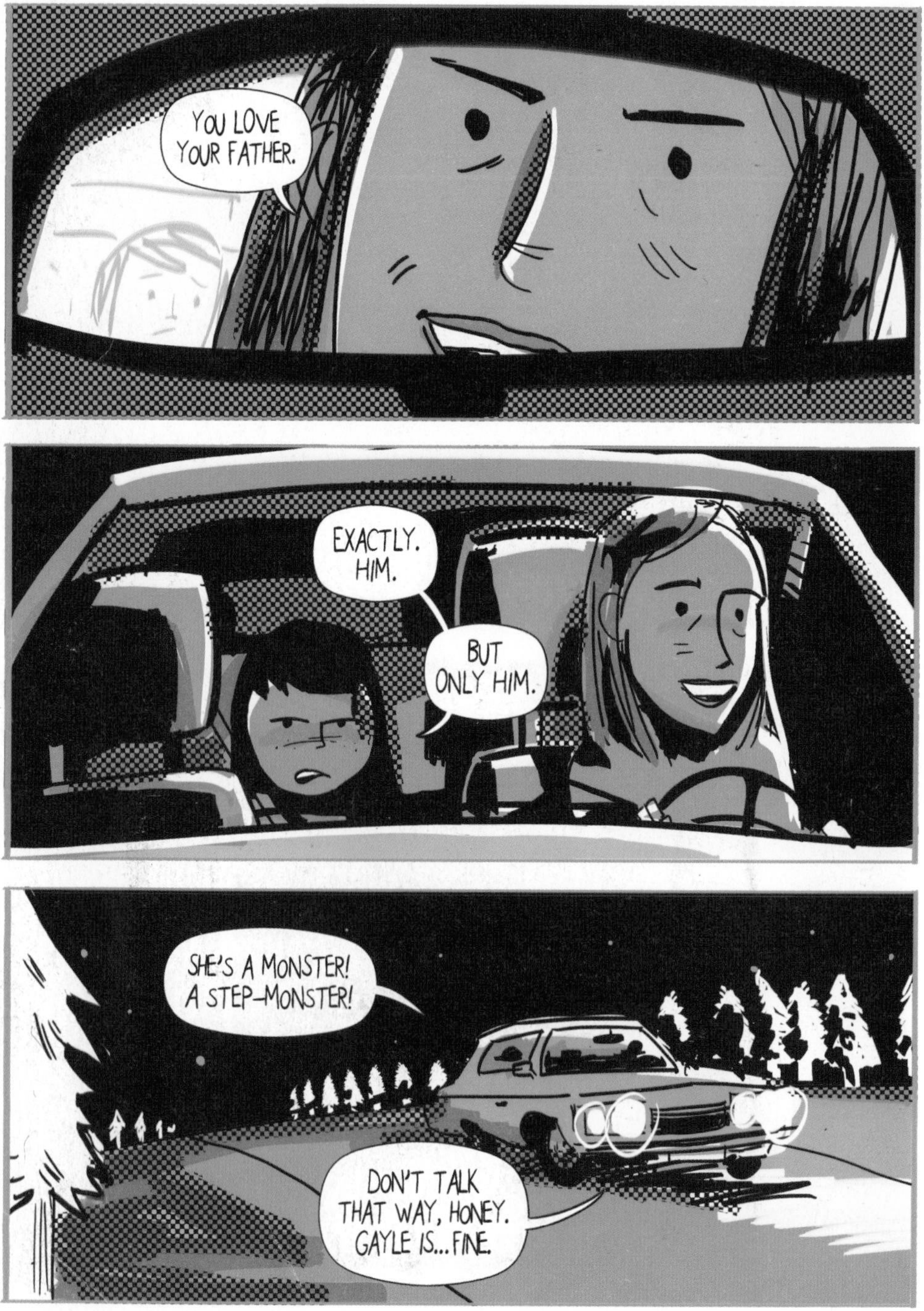
YOU LOVE YOUR FATHER.
EXACTLY. HIM.
BUT ONLY HIM.
SHE'S A MONSTER! A STEP-MONSTER!
DON'T TALK THAT WAY, HONEY. GAYLE IS... FINE.

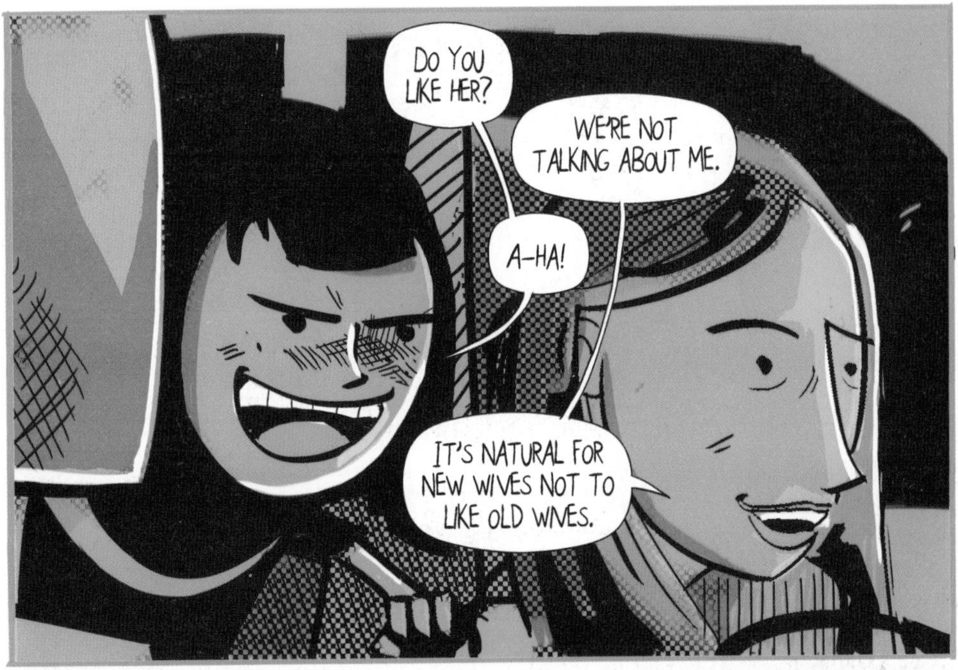
DO YOU LIKE HER?
WE'RE NOT TALKING ABOUT ME.
A-HA!
IT'S NATURAL FOR NEW WIVES NOT TO LIKE OLD WIVES.

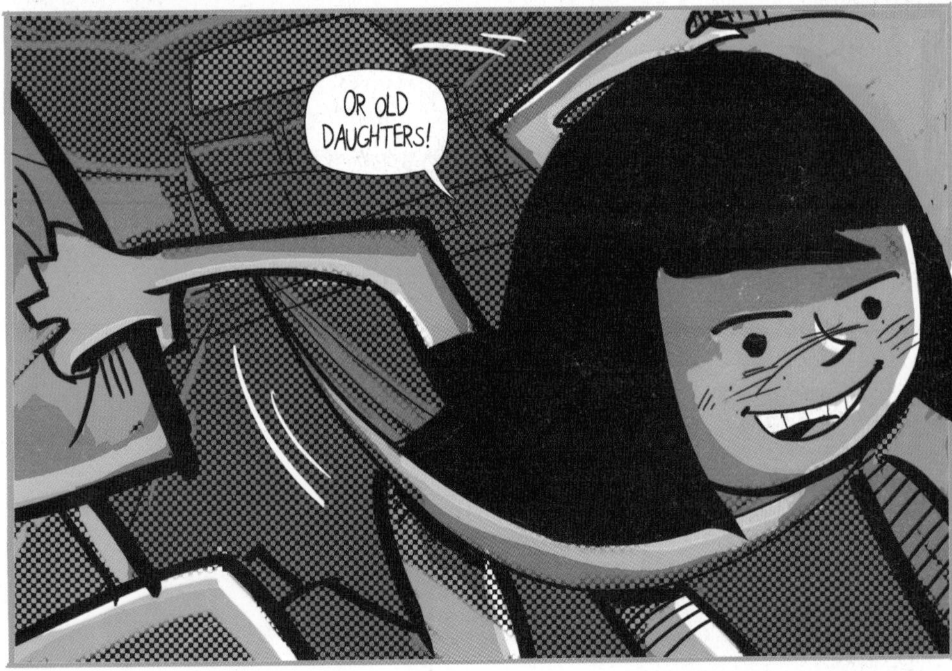
OR OLD DAUGHTERS!

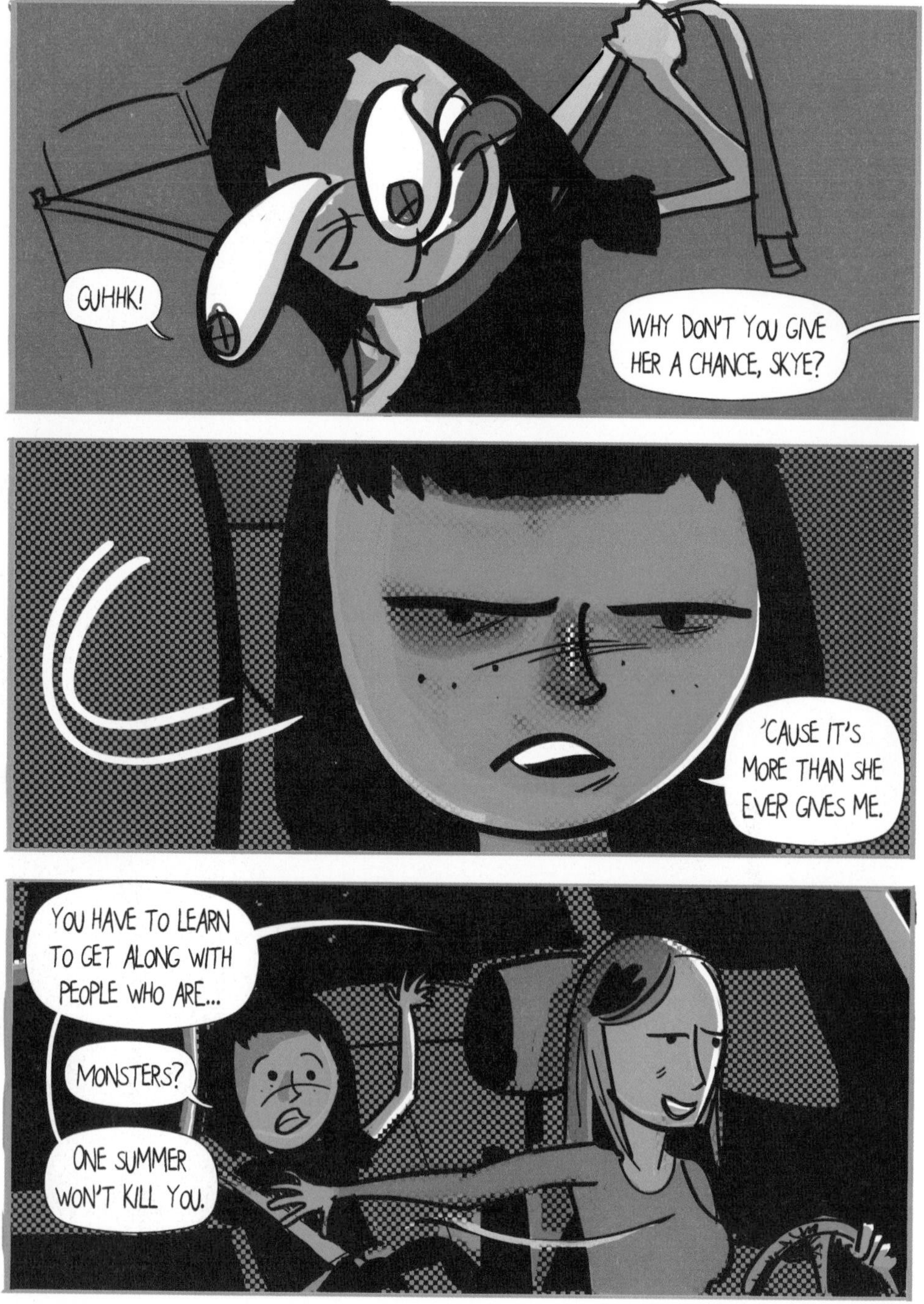
GUHHK!
WHY DON'T YOU GIVE HER A CHANCE, SKYE?
'CAUSE IT'S MORE THAN SHE EVER GIVES ME.
YOU HAVE TO LEARN TO GET ALONG WITH PEOPLE WHO ARE...
MONSTERS?
ONE SUMMER WON'T KILL YOU.

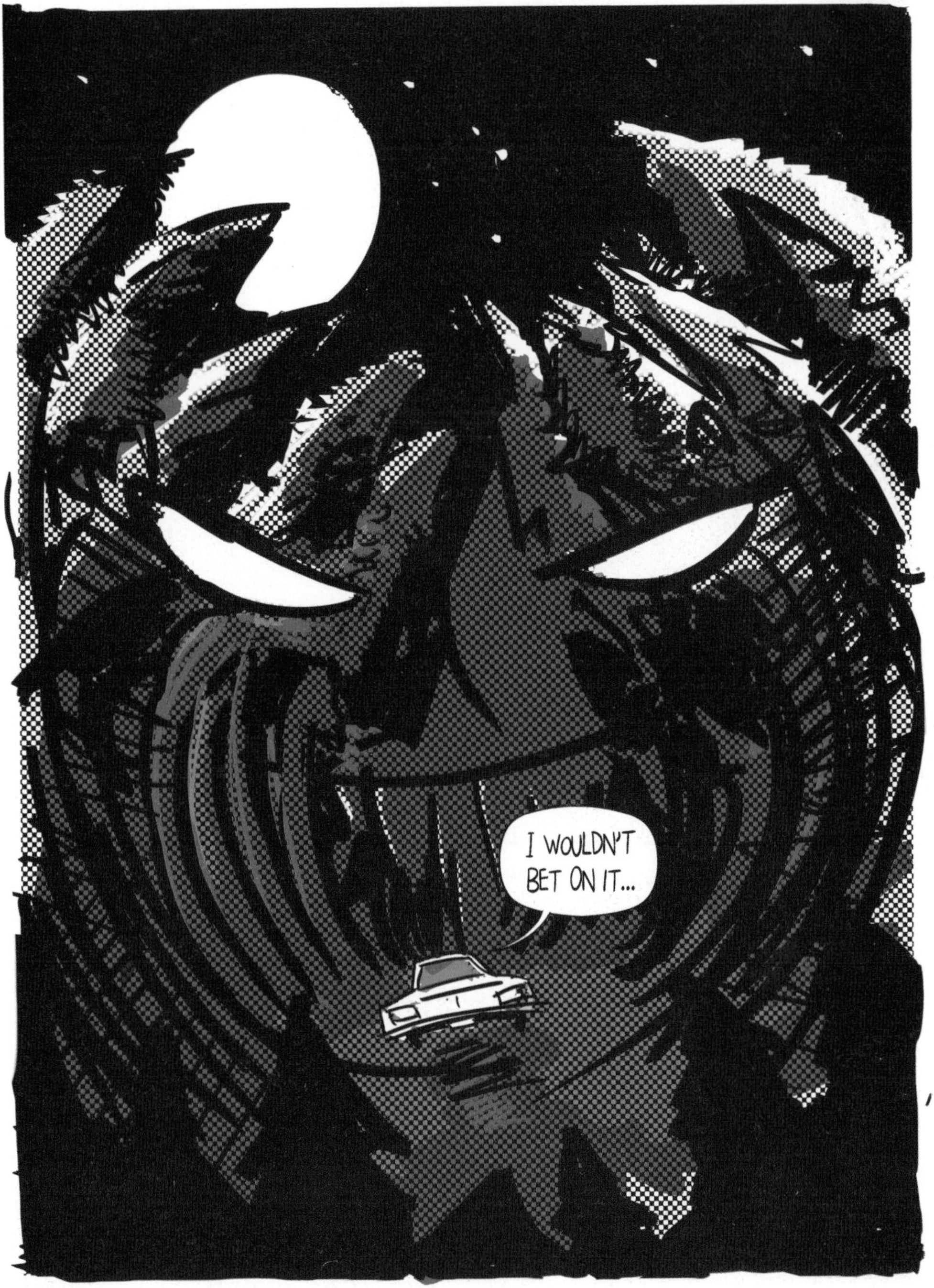
I WOULDN'T BET ON IT...

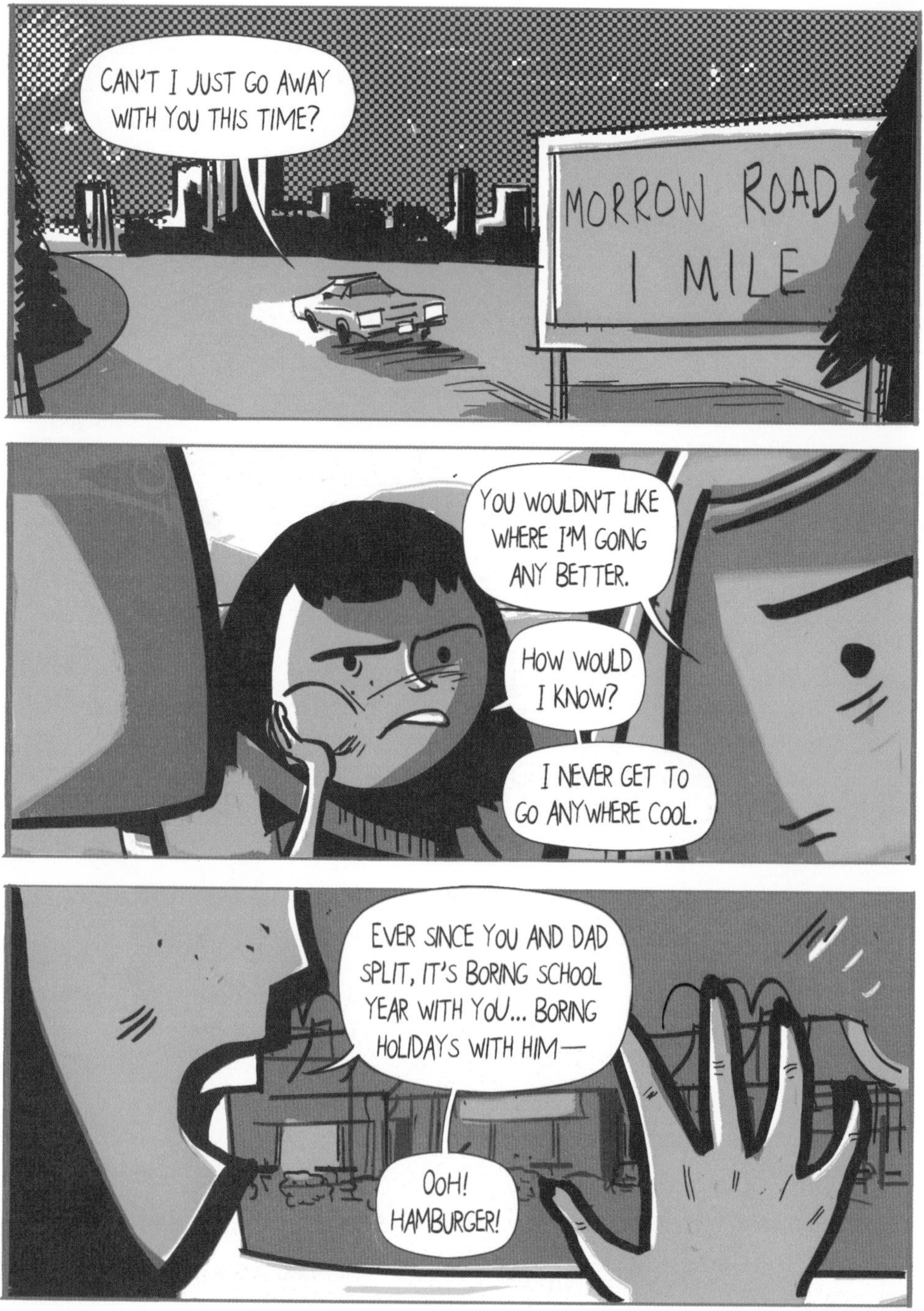
CAN'T I JUST GO AWAY WITH YOU THIS TIME?
MORROW ROAD I MILE
YOU WOULDN'T LIKE WHERE I'M GOING ANY BETTER.
HOW WOULD I KNOW?
I NEVER GET TO GO ANYWHERE COOL.
EVER SINCE YOU AND DAD SPLIT, IT'S BORING SCHOOL YEAR WITH YOU... BORING HOLIDAYS WITH HIM—
OOH! HAMBURGER!

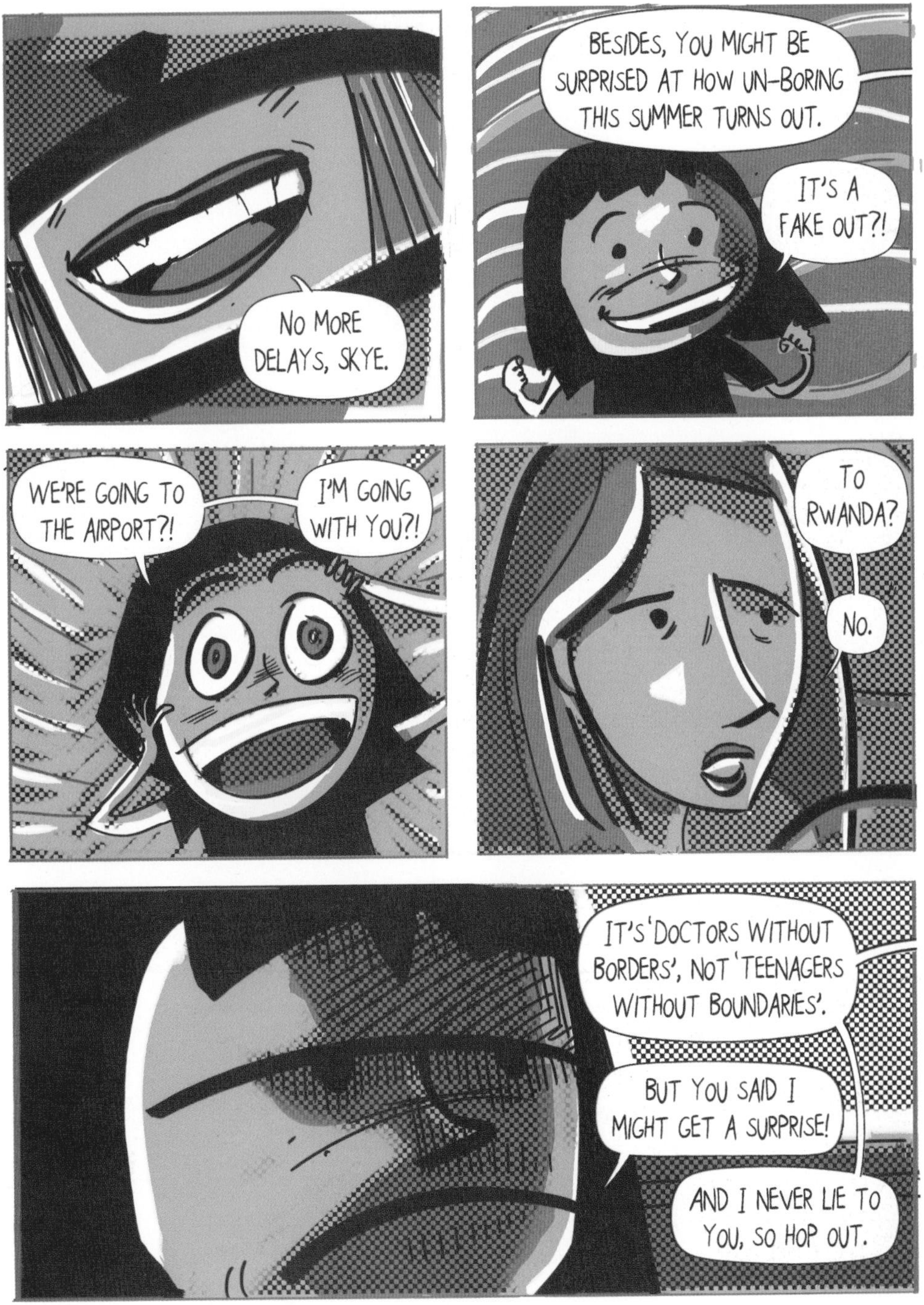
No more delays, Skye.
Besides, you might be surprised at how un-boring this summer turns out.
It's a fake out?!
We're going to the airport?!
I'm going with you?!
To Rwanda?
No.
It's 'Doctors Without Borders', not 'Teenagers Without Boundaries'.
But you said I might get a surprise!
And I never lie to you, so hop out.

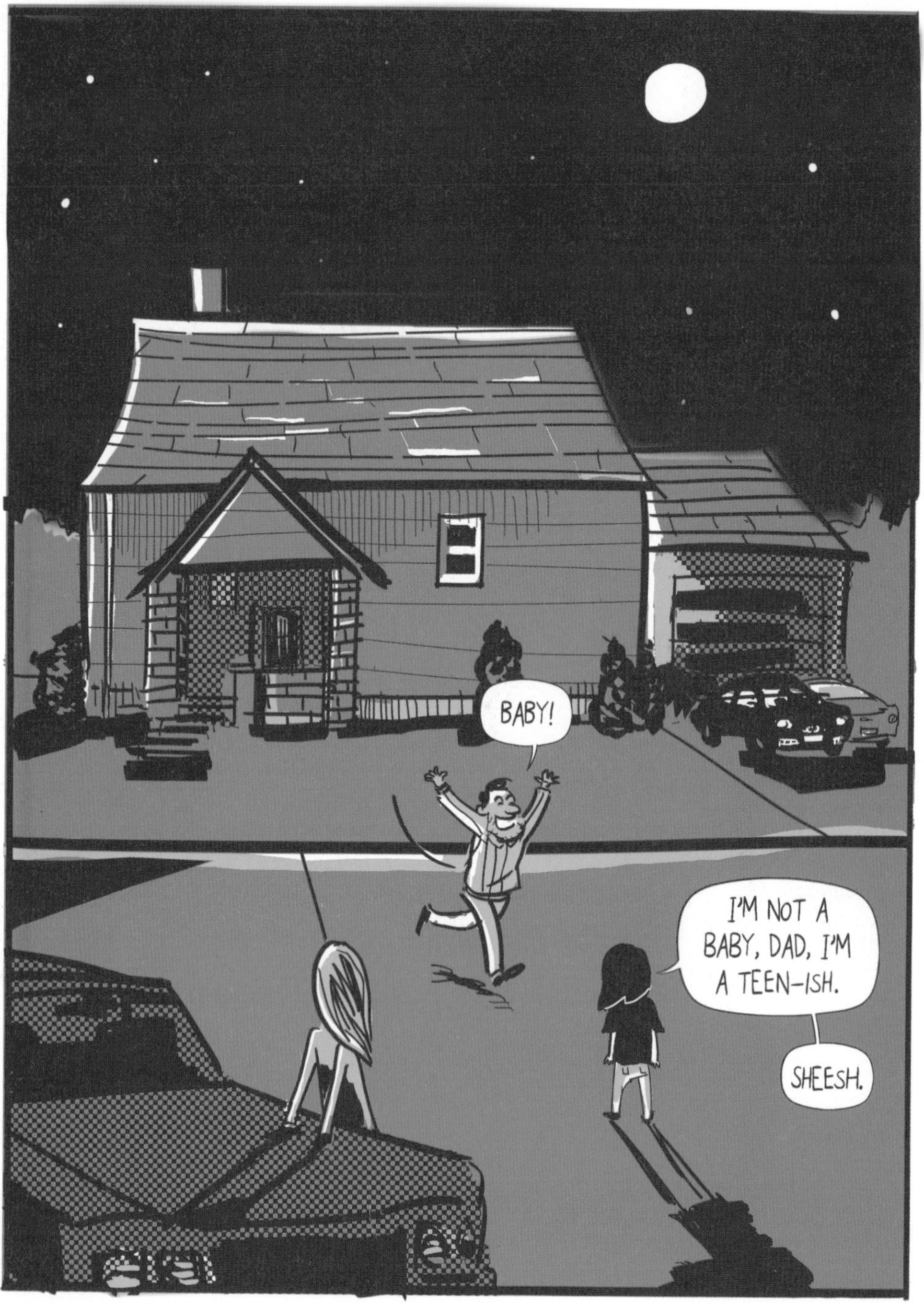
BABY!
I'M NOT A BABY, DAD, I'M A TEEN-ISH.
SHEESH.

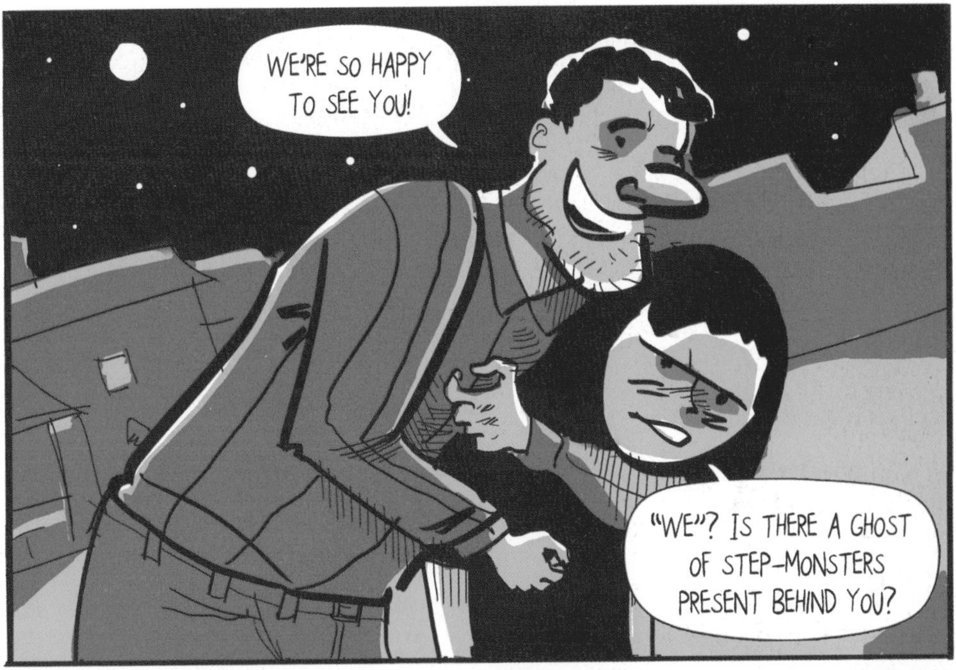
WE'RE SO HAPPY TO SEE YOU!
"WE"? IS THERE A GHOST OF STEP-MONSTERS PRESENT BEHIND YOU?

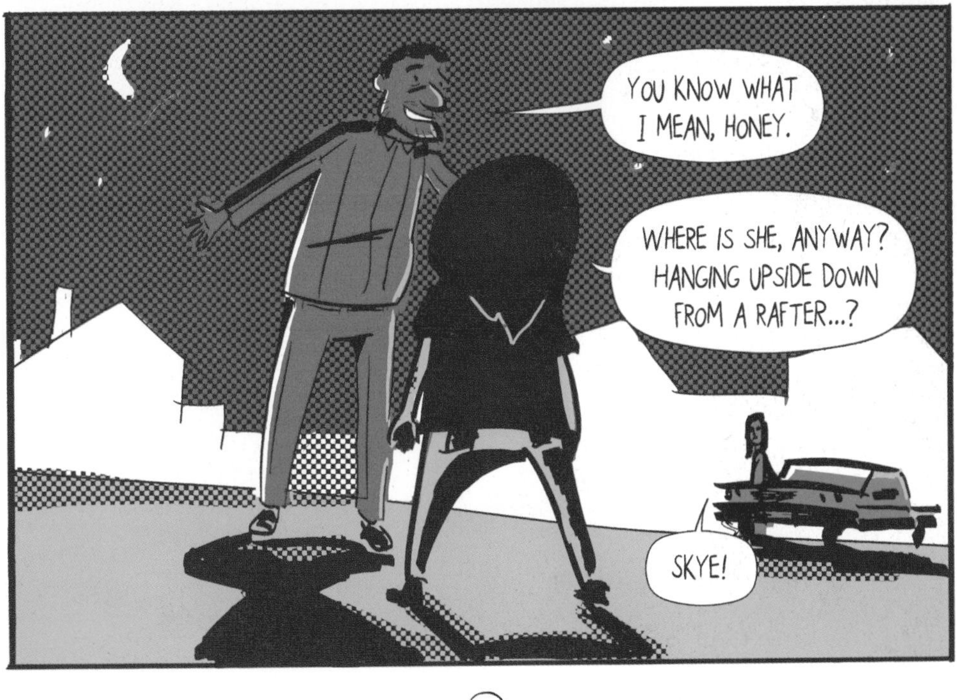
YOU KNOW WHAT I MEAN, HONEY.
WHERE IS SHE, ANYWAY? HANGING UPSIDE DOWN FROM A RAFTER...?
SKYE!

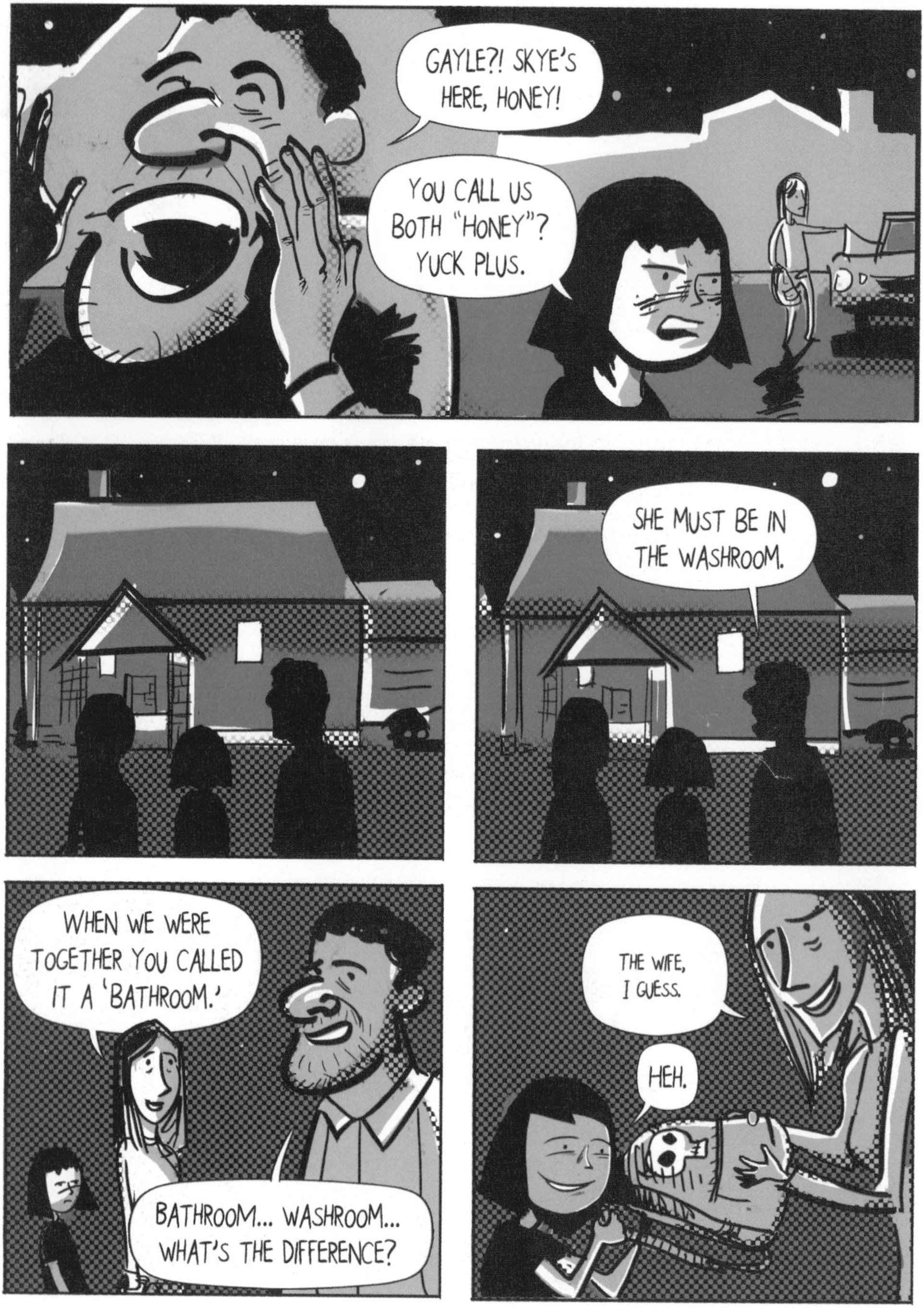
GAYLE?! SKYE'S HERE, HONEY!
YOU CALL US BOTH "HONEY"? YUCK PLUS.
SHE MUST BE IN THE WASHROOM.
WHEN WE WERE TOGETHER YOU CALLED IT A 'BATHROOM.'
BATHROOM... WASHROOM... WHAT'S THE DIFFERENCE?
THE WIFE, I GUESS.
HEH.

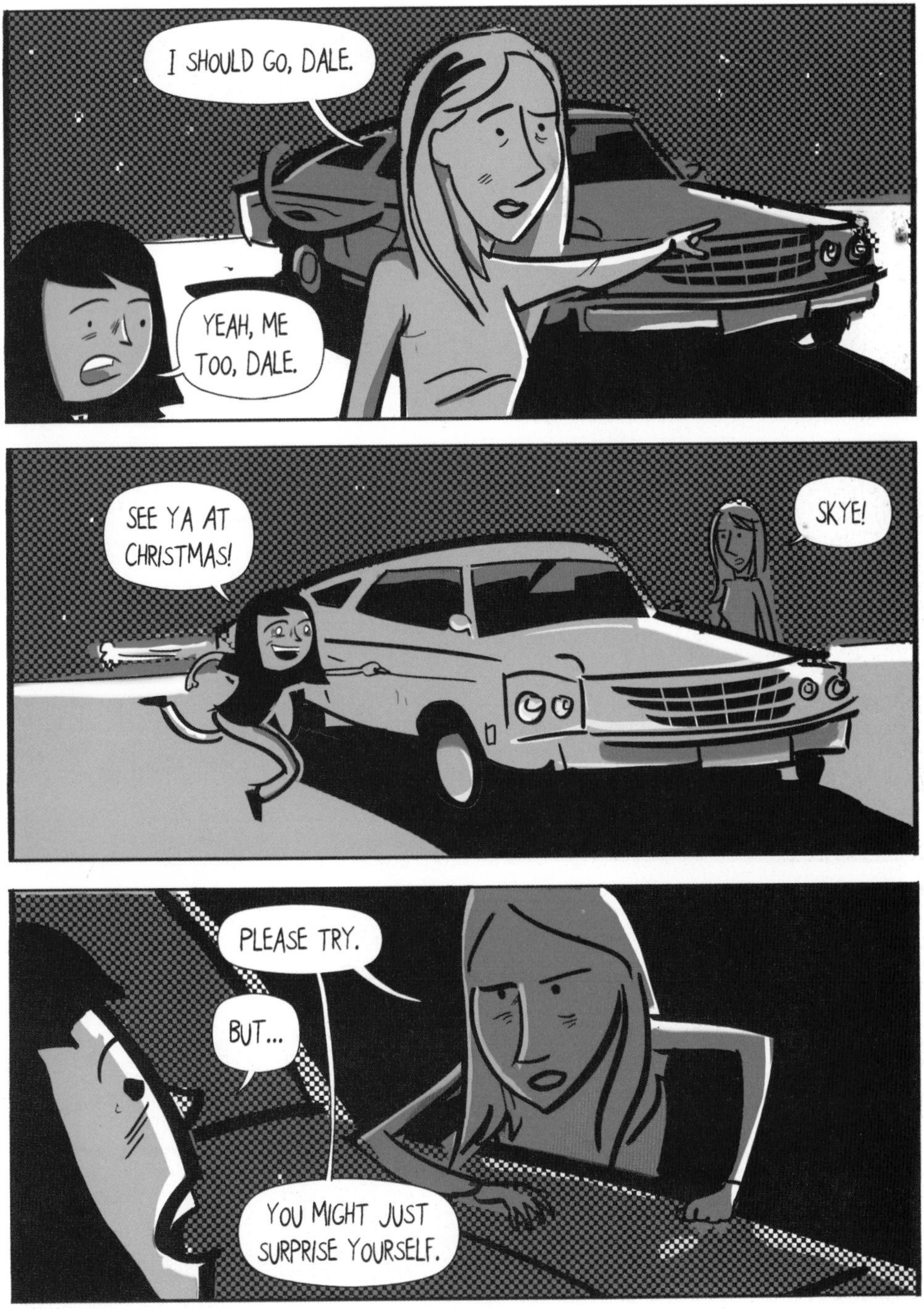

I SHOULD GO, DALE.
YEAH, ME TOO, DALE.
SEE YA AT CHRISTMAS!
SKYE!
PLEASE TRY.
BUT...
YOU MIGHT JUST SURPRISE YOURSELF.

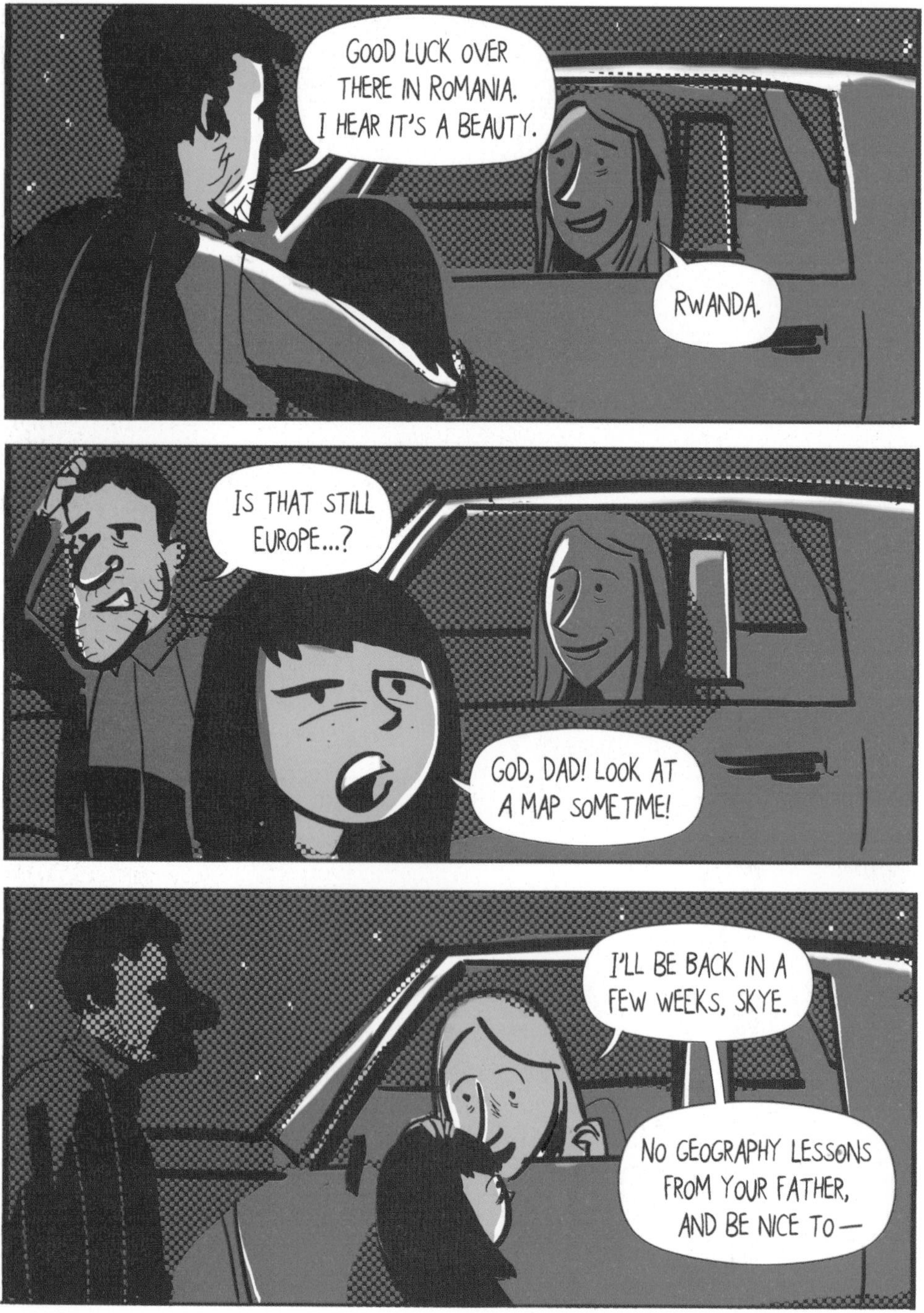
GOOD LUCK OVER THERE IN ROMANIA. I HEAR IT'S A BEAUTY.
RWANDA.
IS THAT STILL EUROPE...?
GOD, DAD! LOOK AT A MAP SOMETIME!
I'LL BE BACK IN A FEW WEEKS, SKYE.
NO GEOGRAPHY LESSONS FROM YOUR FATHER, AND BE NICE TO—

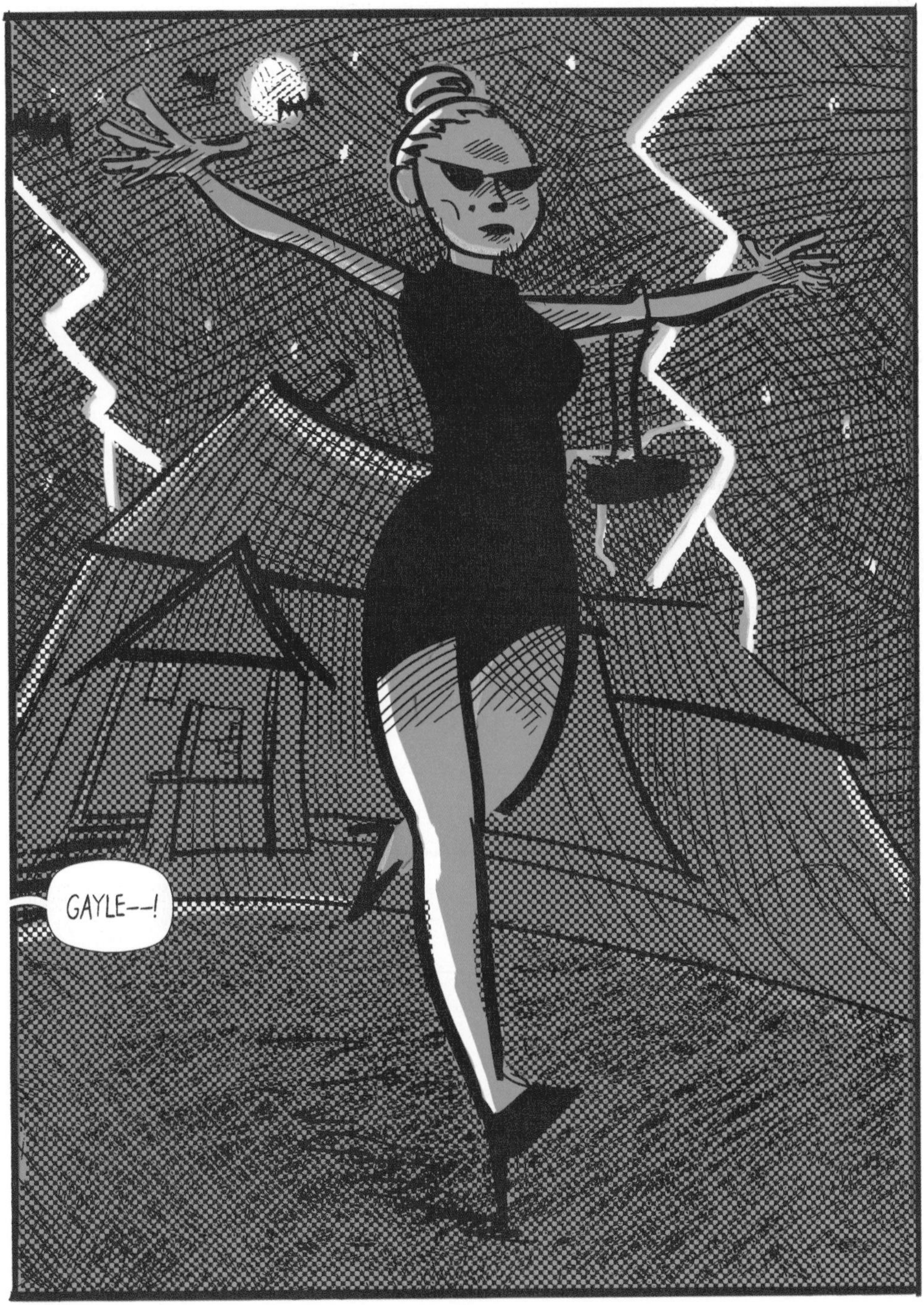
GAYLE--!

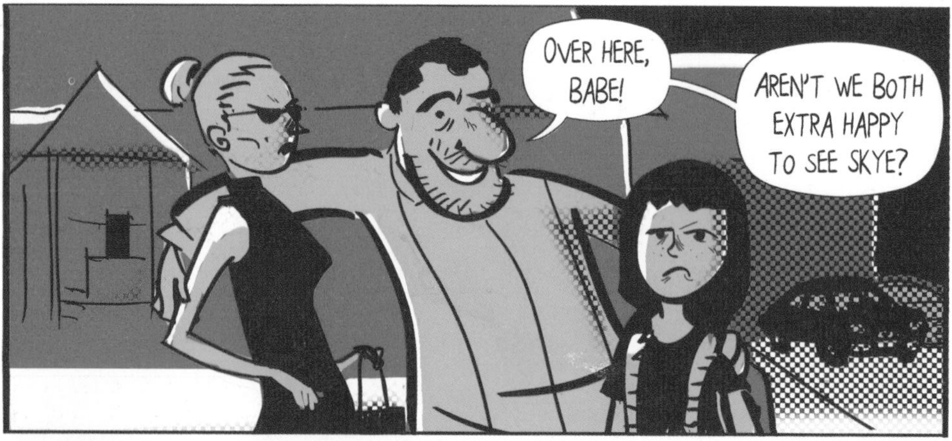
OVER HERE, BABE!
AREN'T WE BOTH EXTRA HAPPY TO SEE SKYE?

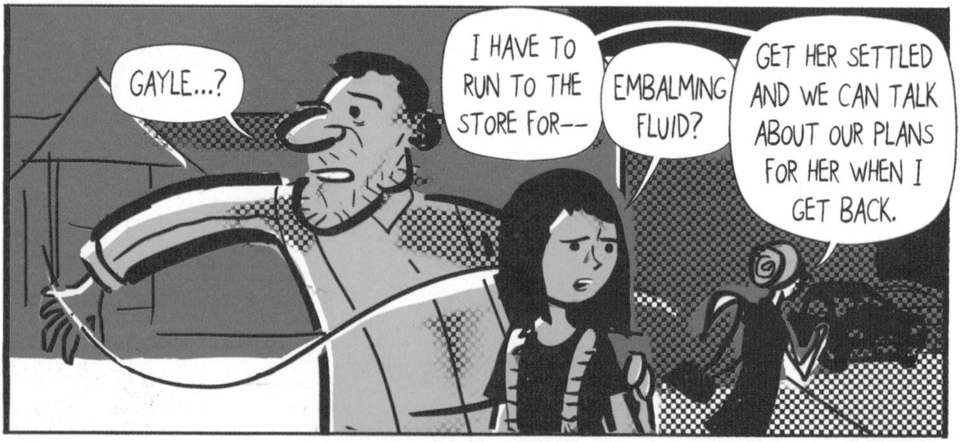
GAYLE...?
I HAVE TO RUN TO THE STORE FOR--
EMBALMING FLUID?
GET HER SETTLED AND WE CAN TALK ABOUT OUR PLANS FOR HER WHEN I GET BACK.

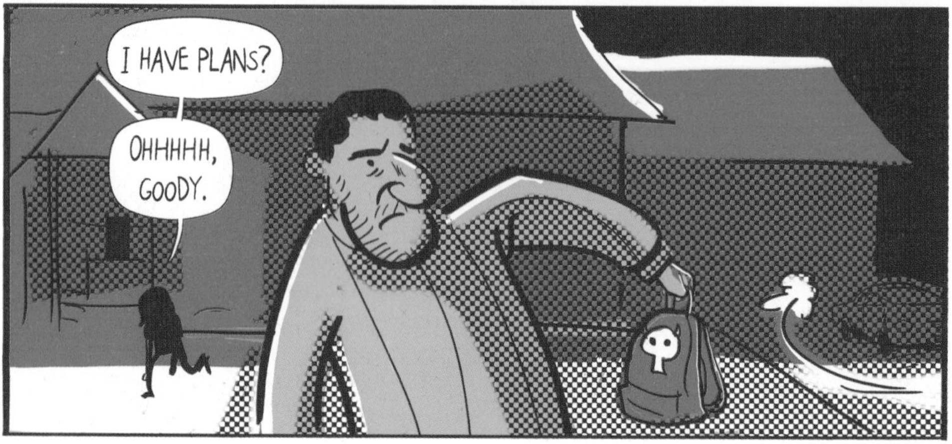
I HAVE PLANS?
OHHHHH, GOODY.

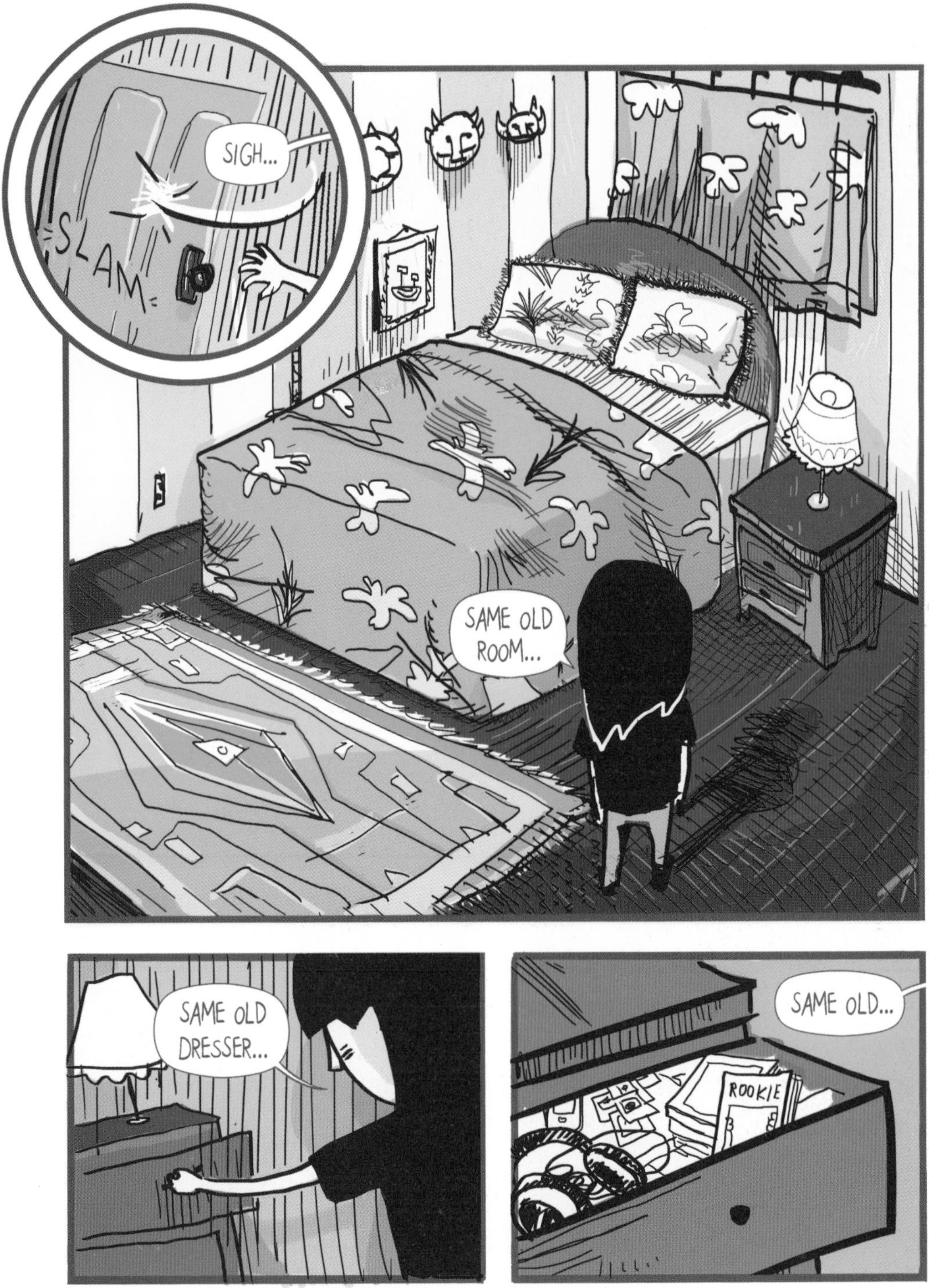
SIGH...
SLAM
SAME OLD ROOM...
SAME OLD DRESSER...
SAME OLD...
ROOKIE

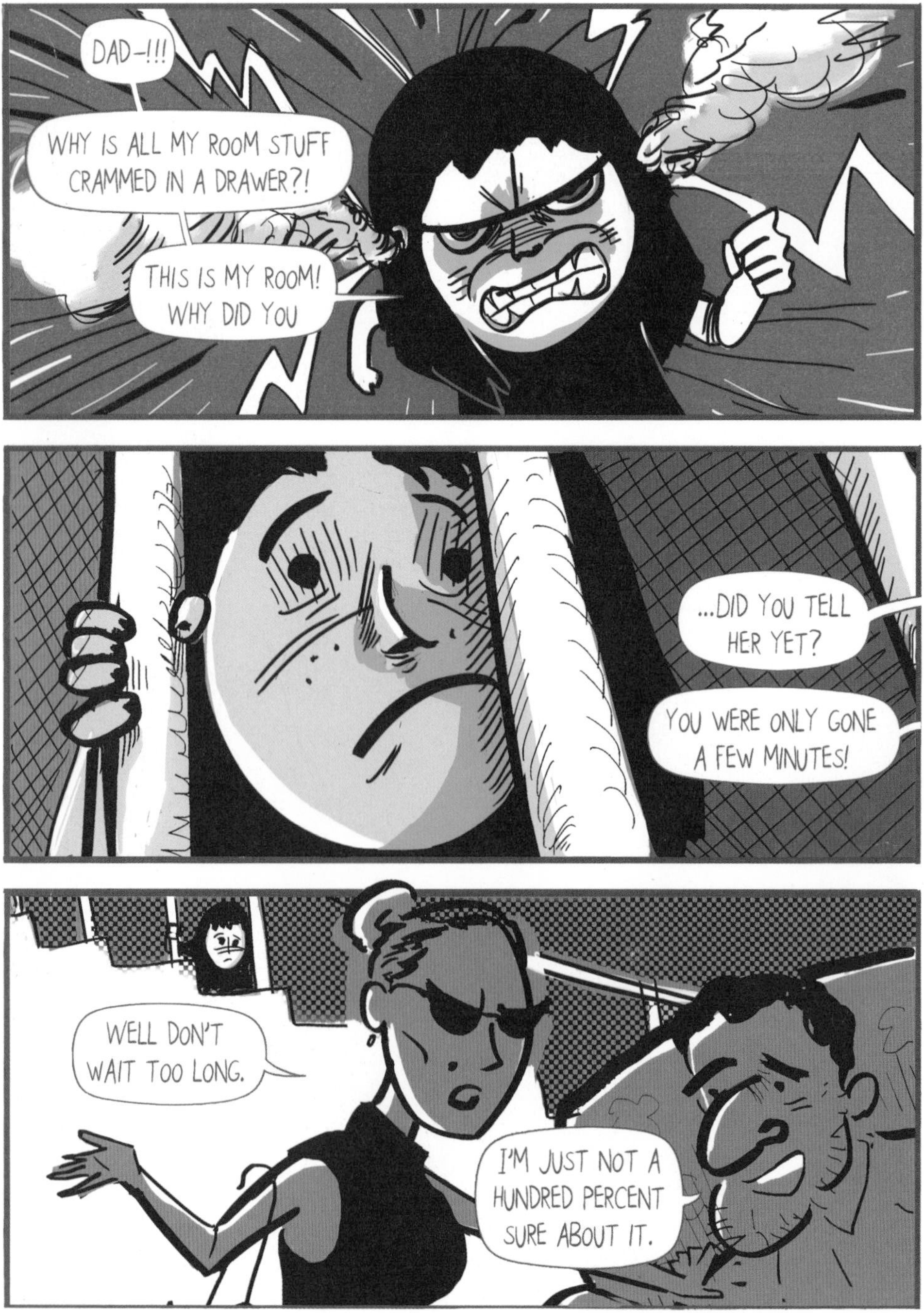
DAD-!!!
WHY IS ALL MY ROOM STUFF CRAMMED IN A DRAWER?!
THIS IS MY ROOM! WHY DID YOU
...DID YOU TELL HER YET?
YOU WERE ONLY GONE A FEW MINUTES!
WELL DON'T WAIT TOO LONG.
I'M JUST NOT A HUNDRED PERCENT SURE ABOUT IT.

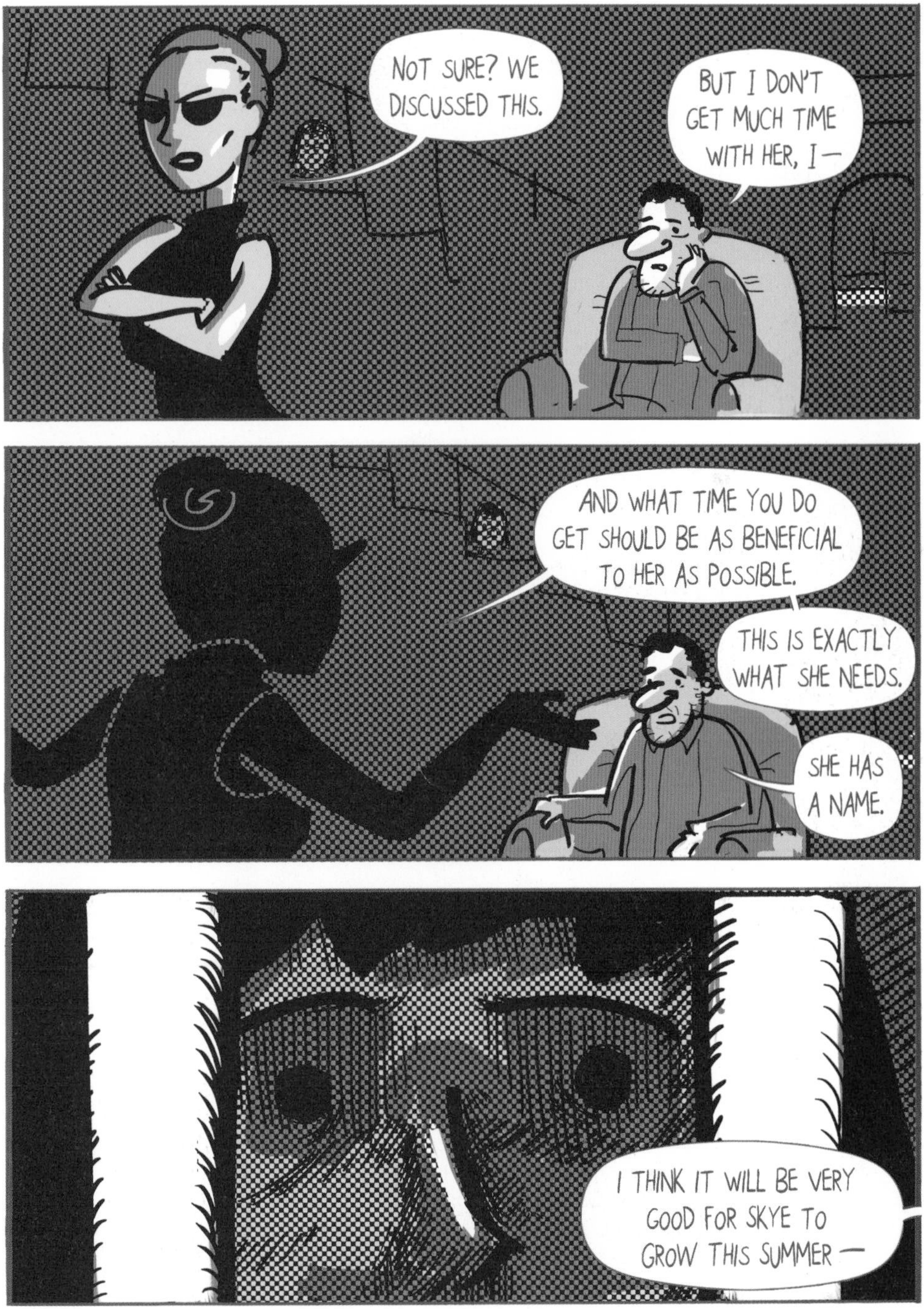
NOT SURE? WE DISCUSSED THIS.
BUT I DON'T GET MUCH TIME WITH HER, I—
AND WHAT TIME YOU DO GET SHOULD BE AS BENEFICIAL TO HER AS POSSIBLE.
THIS IS EXACTLY WHAT SHE NEEDS.
SHE HAS A NAME.
I THINK IT WILL BE VERY GOOD FOR SKYE TO GROW THIS SUMMER—

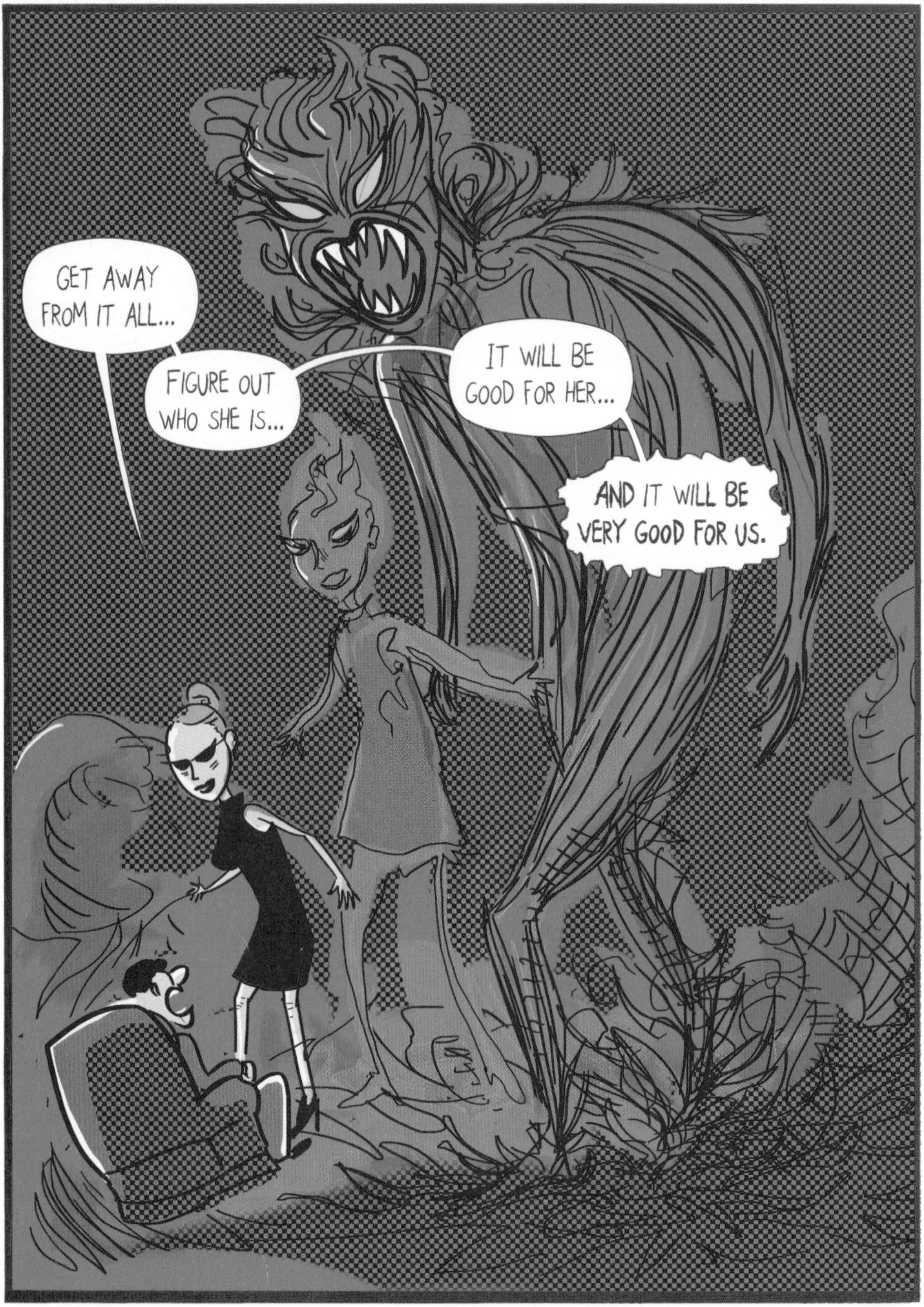
GET AWAY FROM IT ALL...
FIGURE OUT WHO SHE IS...
IT WILL BE GOOD FOR HER...
AND IT WILL BE VERY GOOD FOR US.

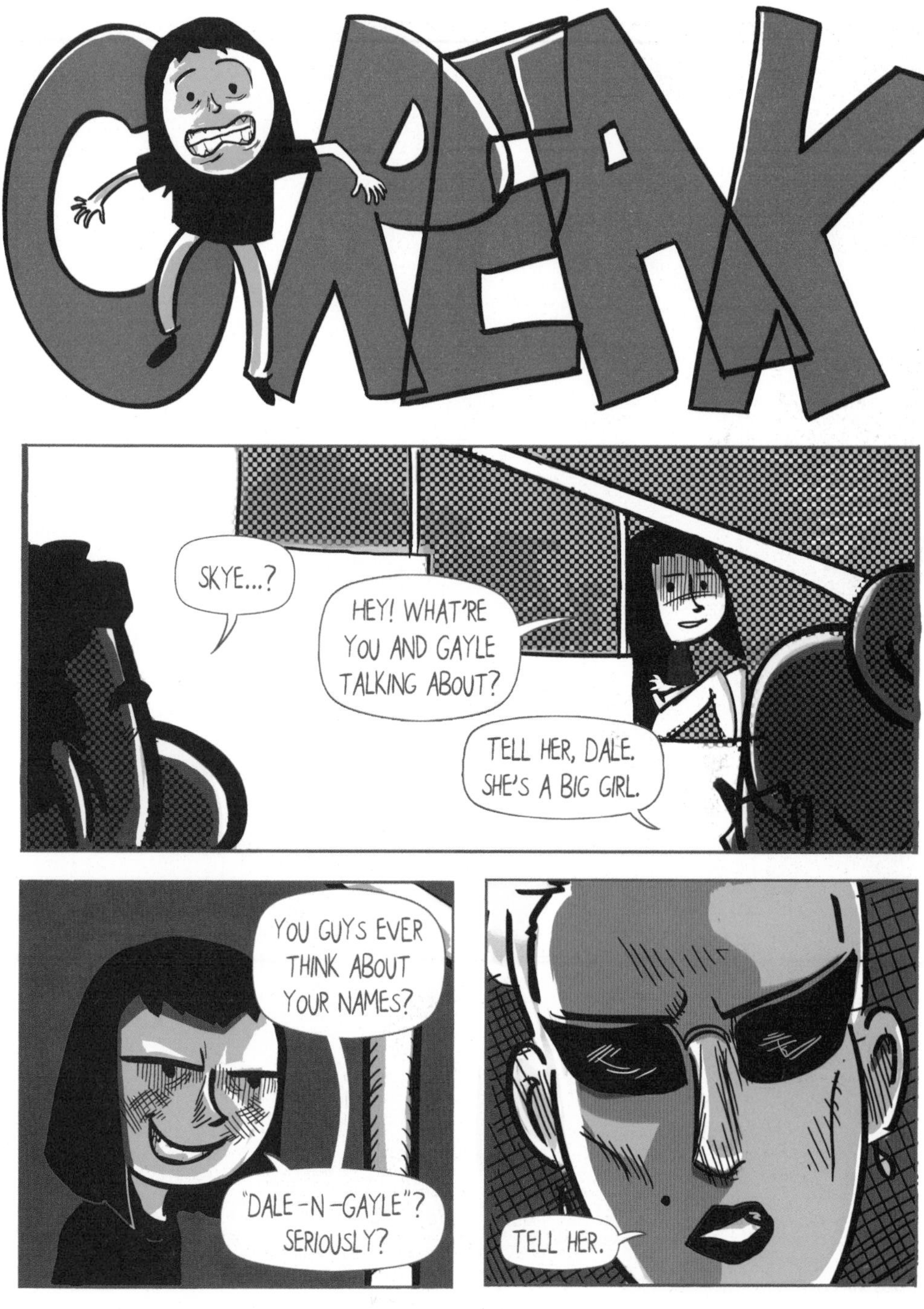
CREAK
SKYE...?
HEY! WHAT'RE YOU AND GAYLE TALKING ABOUT?
TELL HER, DALE. SHE'S A BIG GIRL.
YOU GUYS EVER THINK ABOUT YOUR NAMES?
"DALE-N-GAYLE"? SERIOUSLY?
TELL HER.

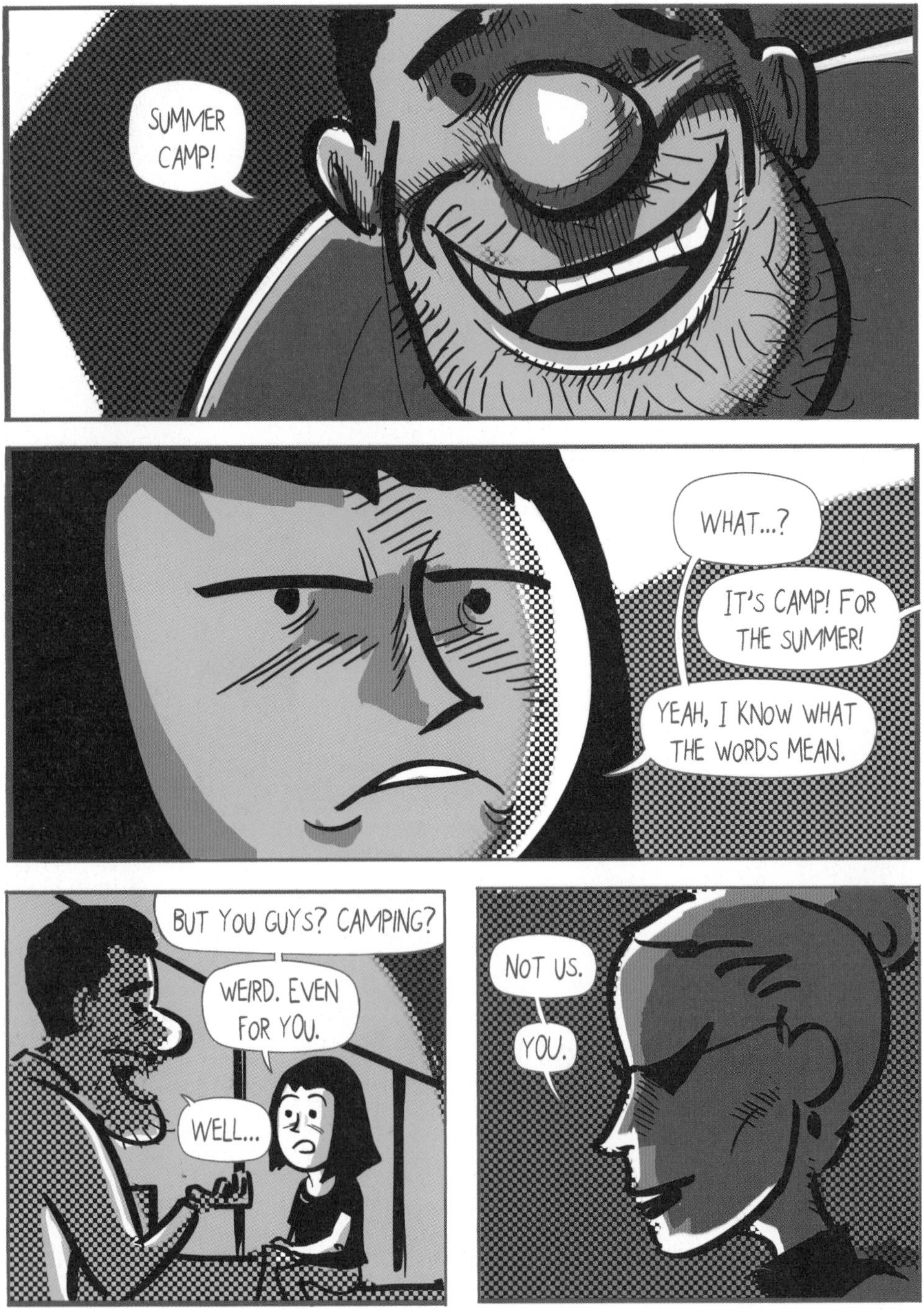
SUMMER CAMP!
WHAT...?
IT'S CAMP! FOR THE SUMMER!
YEAH, I KNOW WHAT THE WORDS MEAN.
BUT YOU GUYS? CAMPING?
WEIRD. EVEN FOR YOU.
WELL...
NOT US.
YOU.

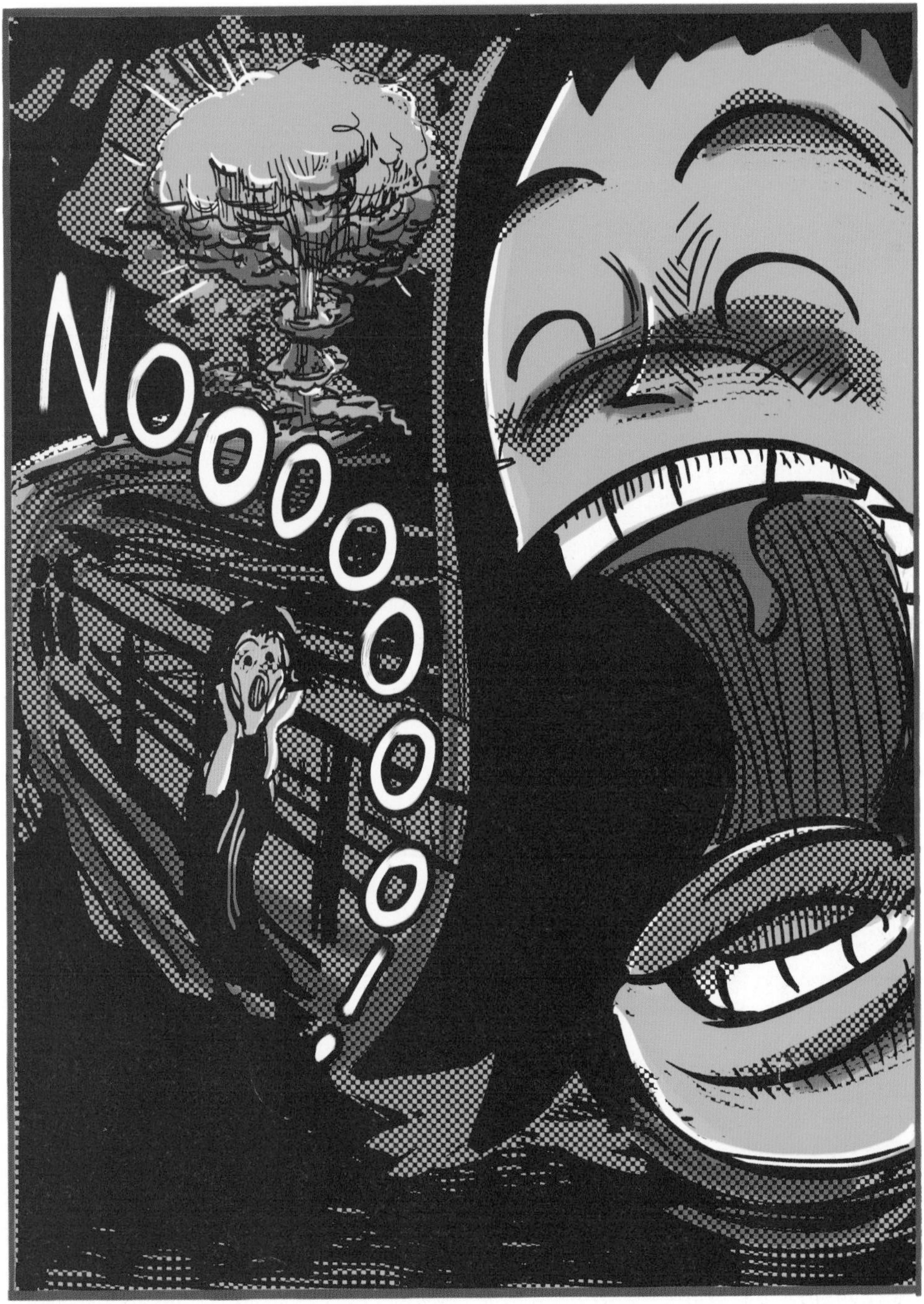
NOOOOOOOOOO!

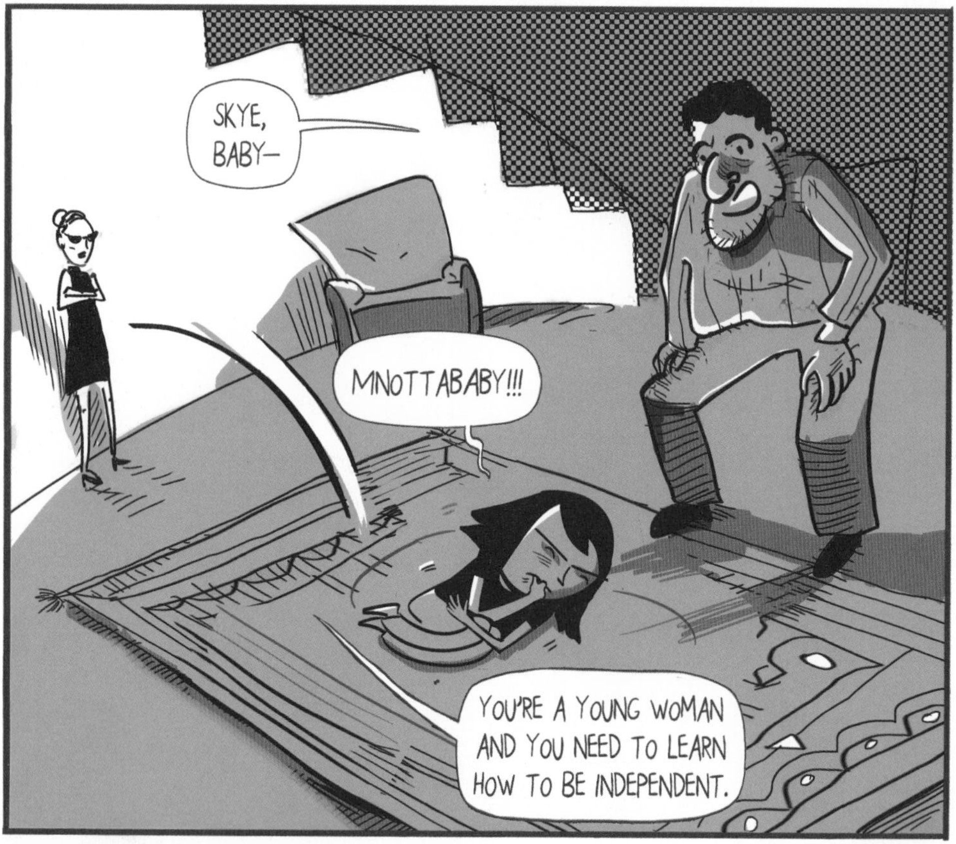
SKYE, BABY—
MNOTTABABY!!!
YOU'RE A YOUNG WOMAN AND YOU NEED TO LEARN HOW TO BE INDEPENDENT.

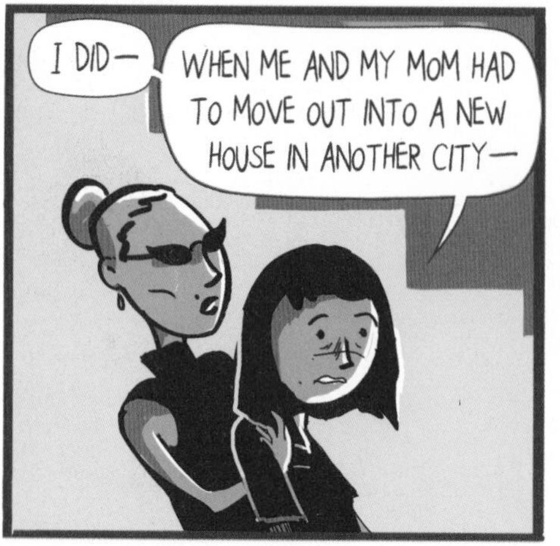
I DID—
WHEN ME AND MY MOM HAD TO MOVE OUT INTO A NEW HOUSE IN ANOTHER CITY—

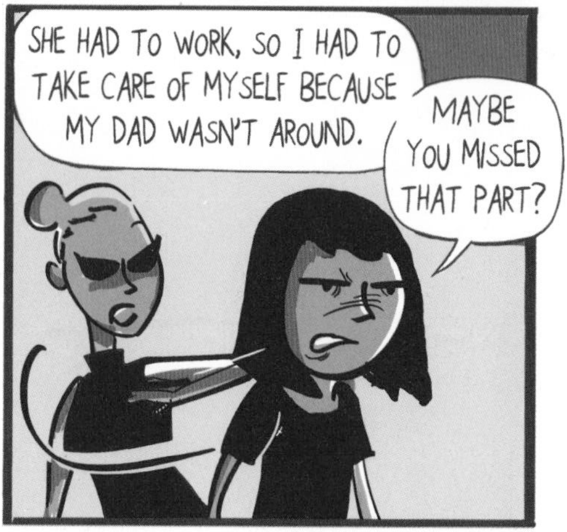
SHE HAD TO WORK, SO I HAD TO TAKE CARE OF MYSELF BECAUSE MY DAD WASN'T AROUND.
MAYBE YOU MISSED THAT PART?

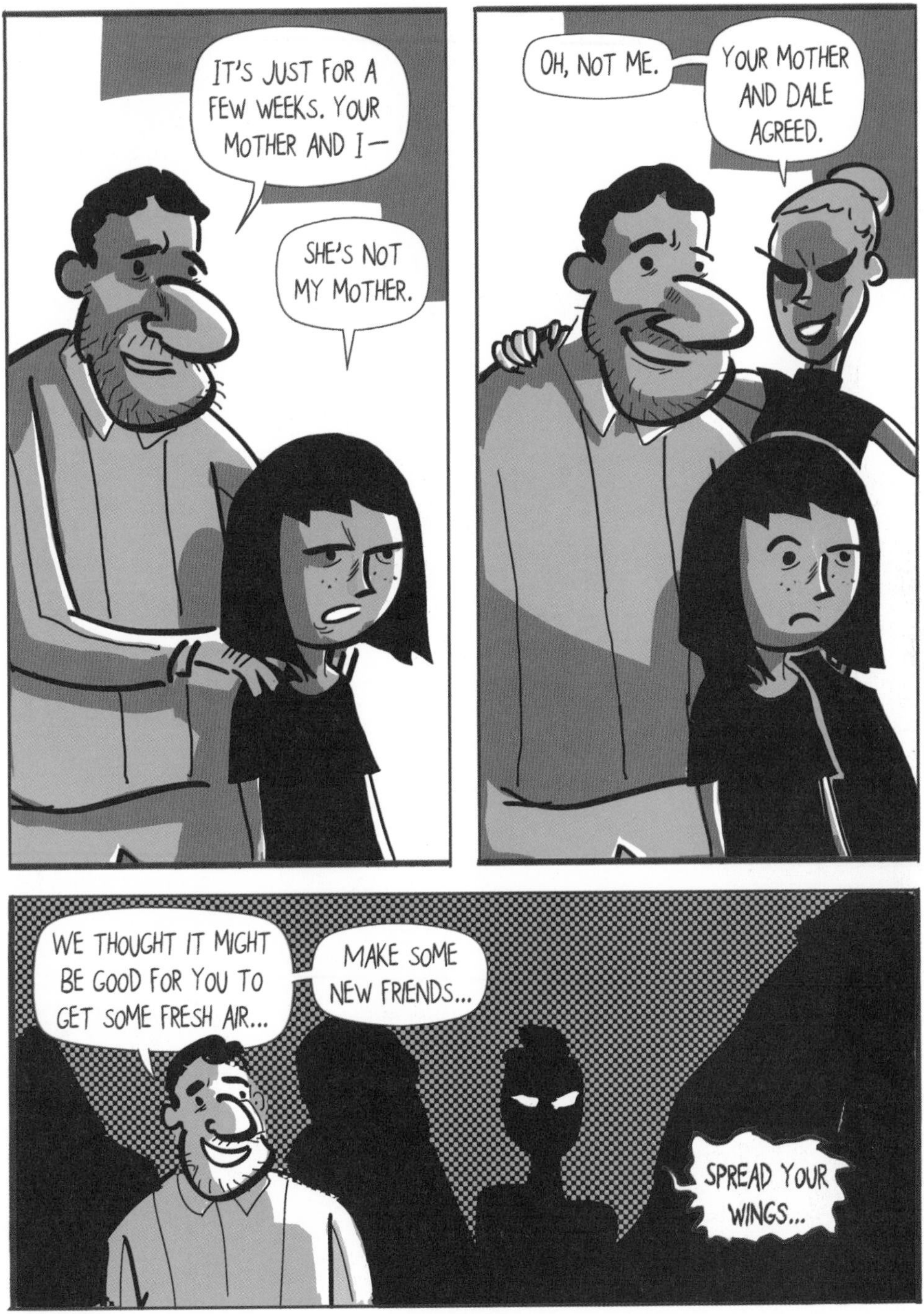
IT'S JUST FOR A FEW WEEKS. YOUR MOTHER AND I—
SHE'S NOT MY MOTHER.
OH, NOT ME.
YOUR MOTHER AND DALE AGREED.
WE THOUGHT IT MIGHT BE GOOD FOR YOU TO GET SOME FRESH AIR...
MAKE SOME NEW FRIENDS...
SPREAD YOUR WINGS...

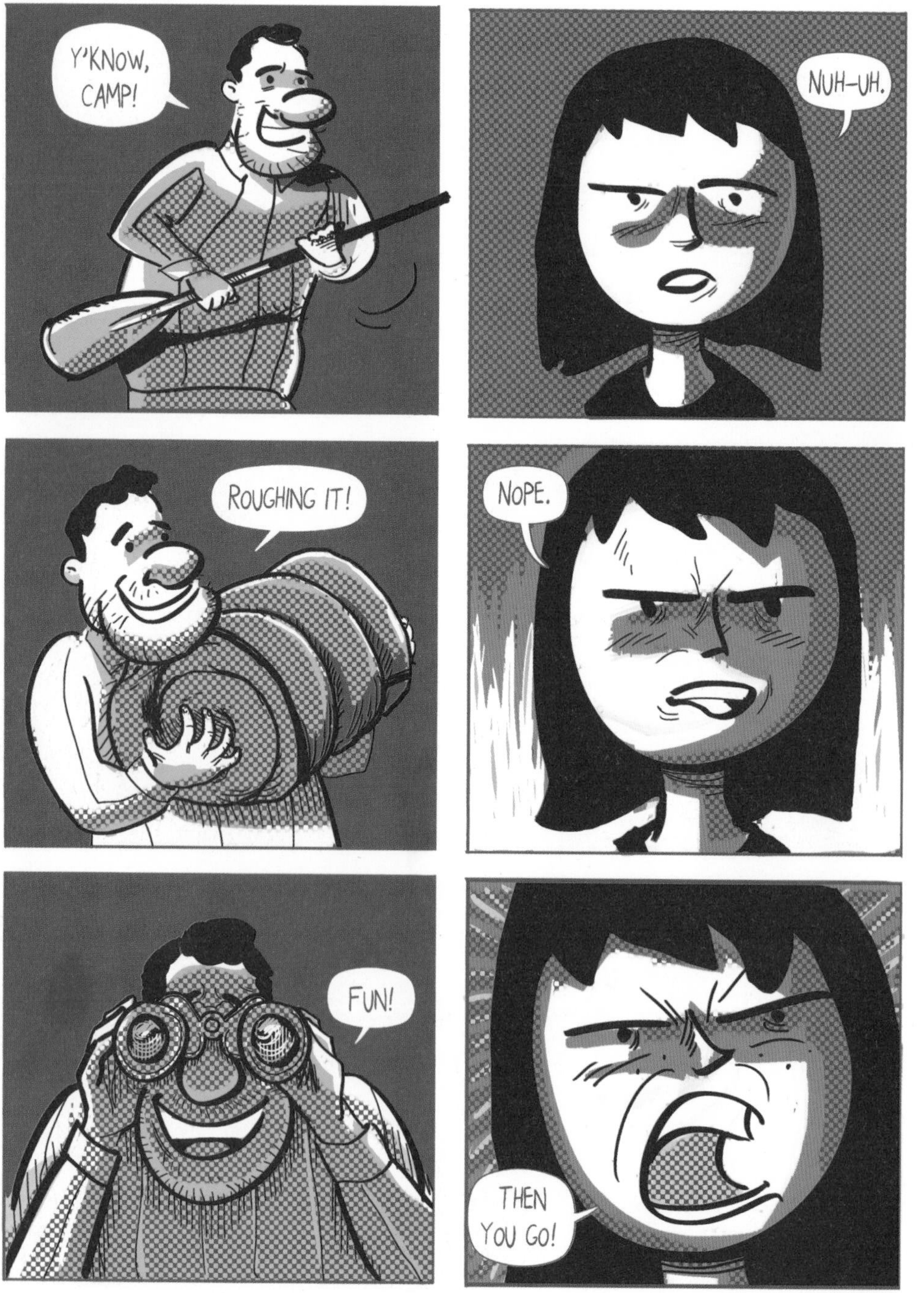
Y'KNOW, CAMP!
NUH-UH.
ROUGHING IT!
NOPE.
FUN!
THEN YOU GO!

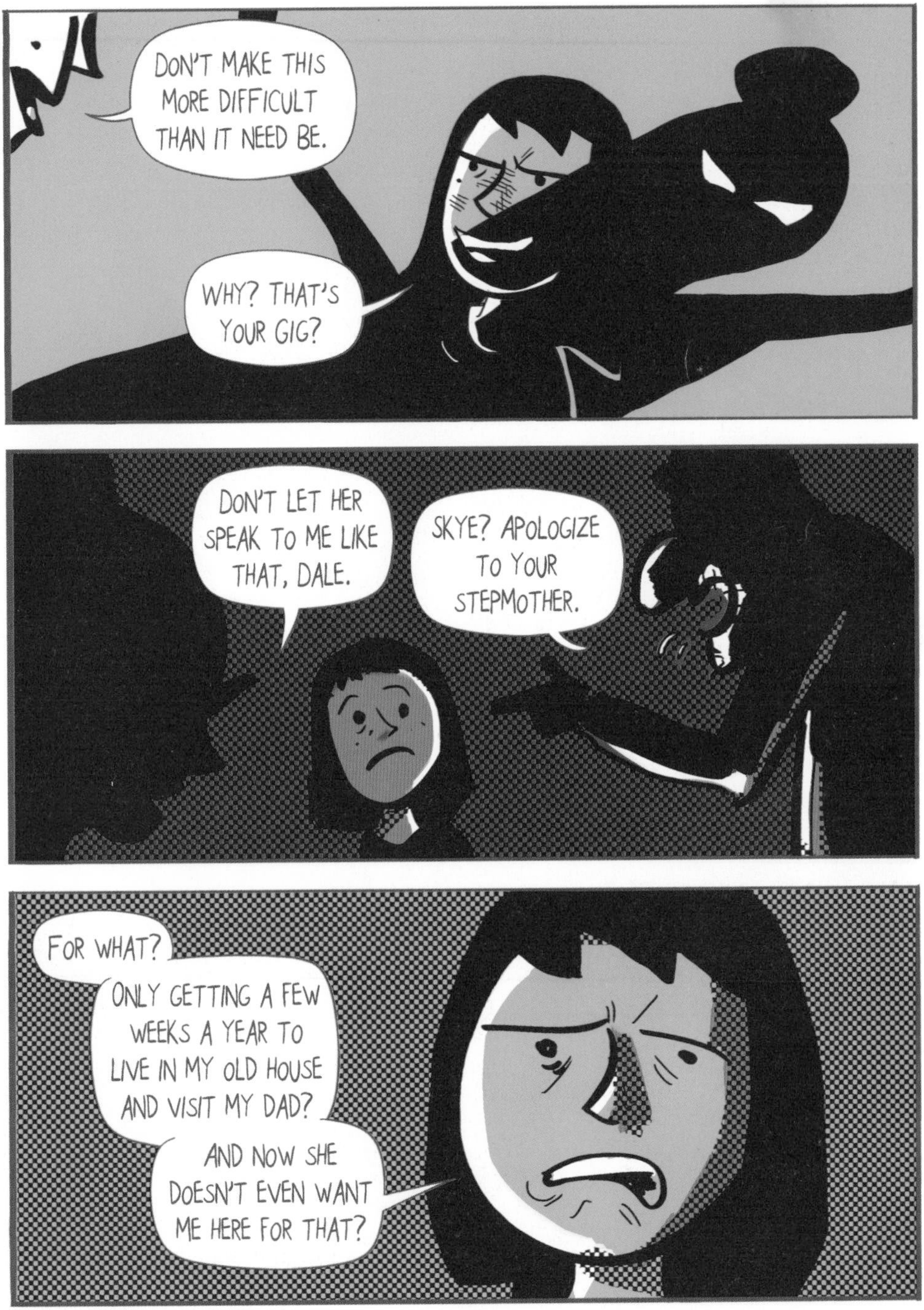
DON'T MAKE THIS MORE DIFFICULT THAN IT NEED BE.
WHY? THAT'S YOUR GIG?
DON'T LET HER SPEAK TO ME LIKE THAT, DALE.
SKYE? APOLOGIZE TO YOUR STEPMOTHER.
FOR WHAT?
ONLY GETTING A FEW WEEKS A YEAR TO LIVE IN MY OLD HOUSE AND VISIT MY DAD?
AND NOW SHE DOESN'T EVEN WANT ME HERE FOR THAT?

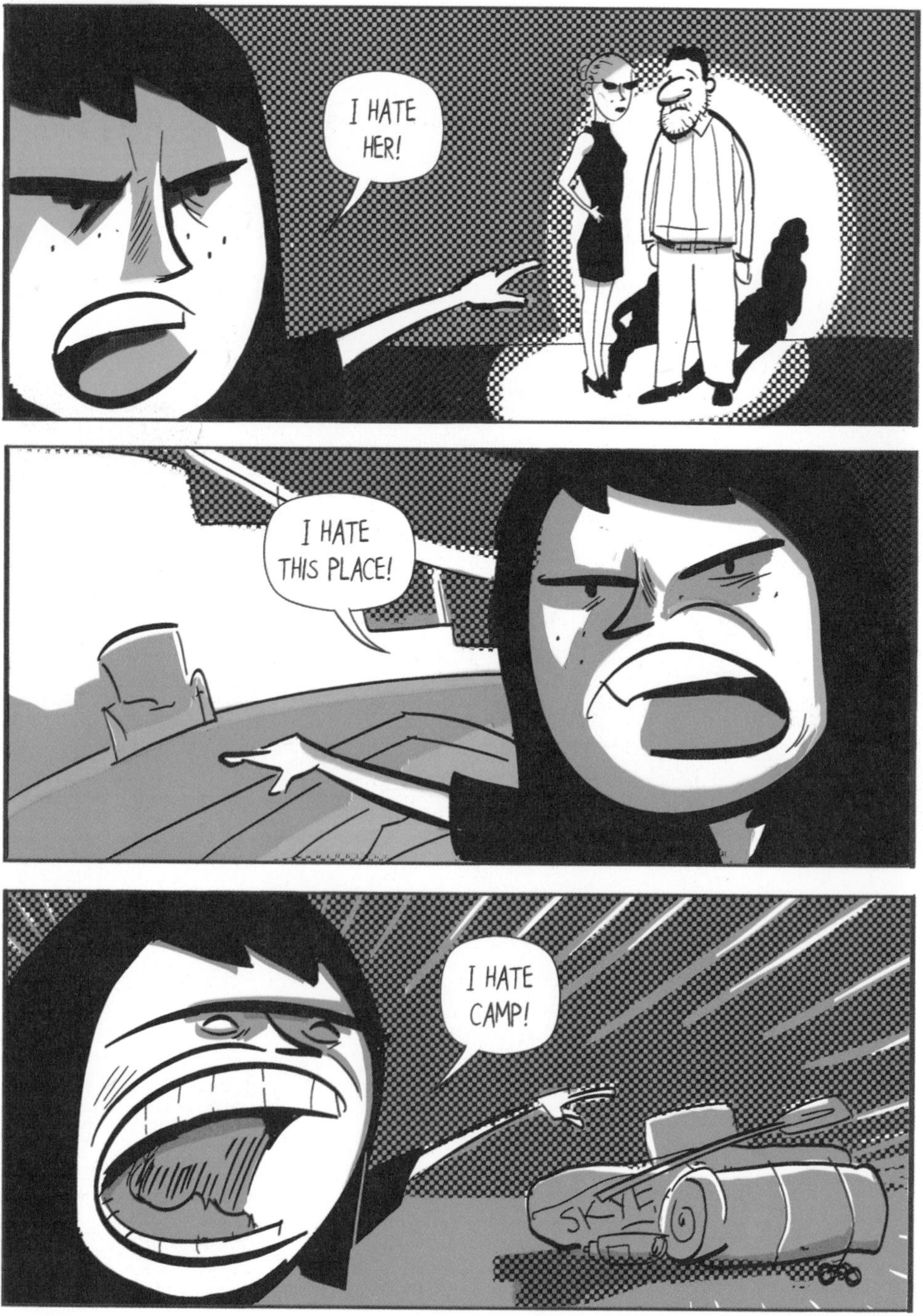
I HATE HER!
I HATE THIS PLACE!
I HATE CAMP!
SKYE

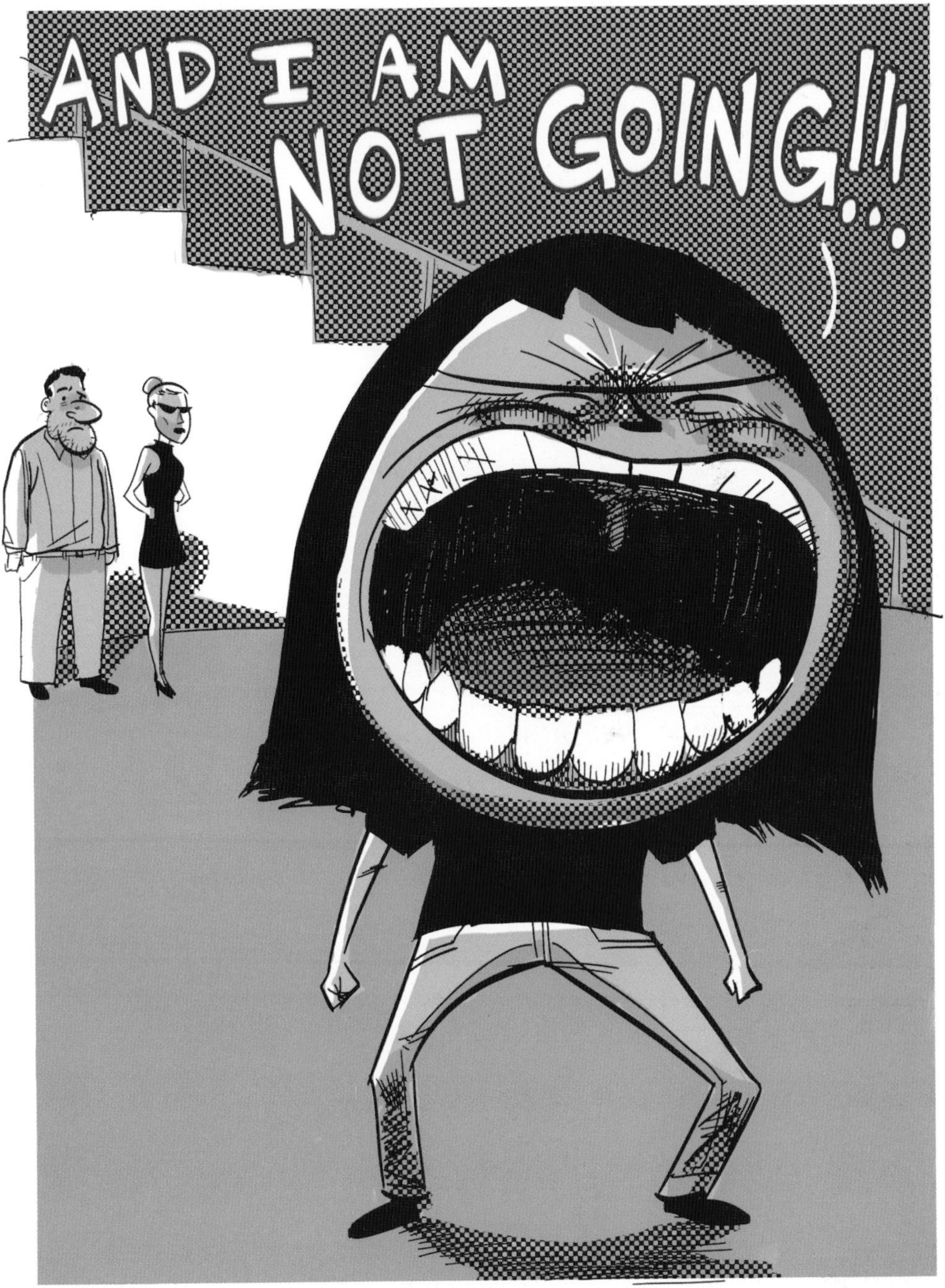
AND I AM NOT GOING!!!...

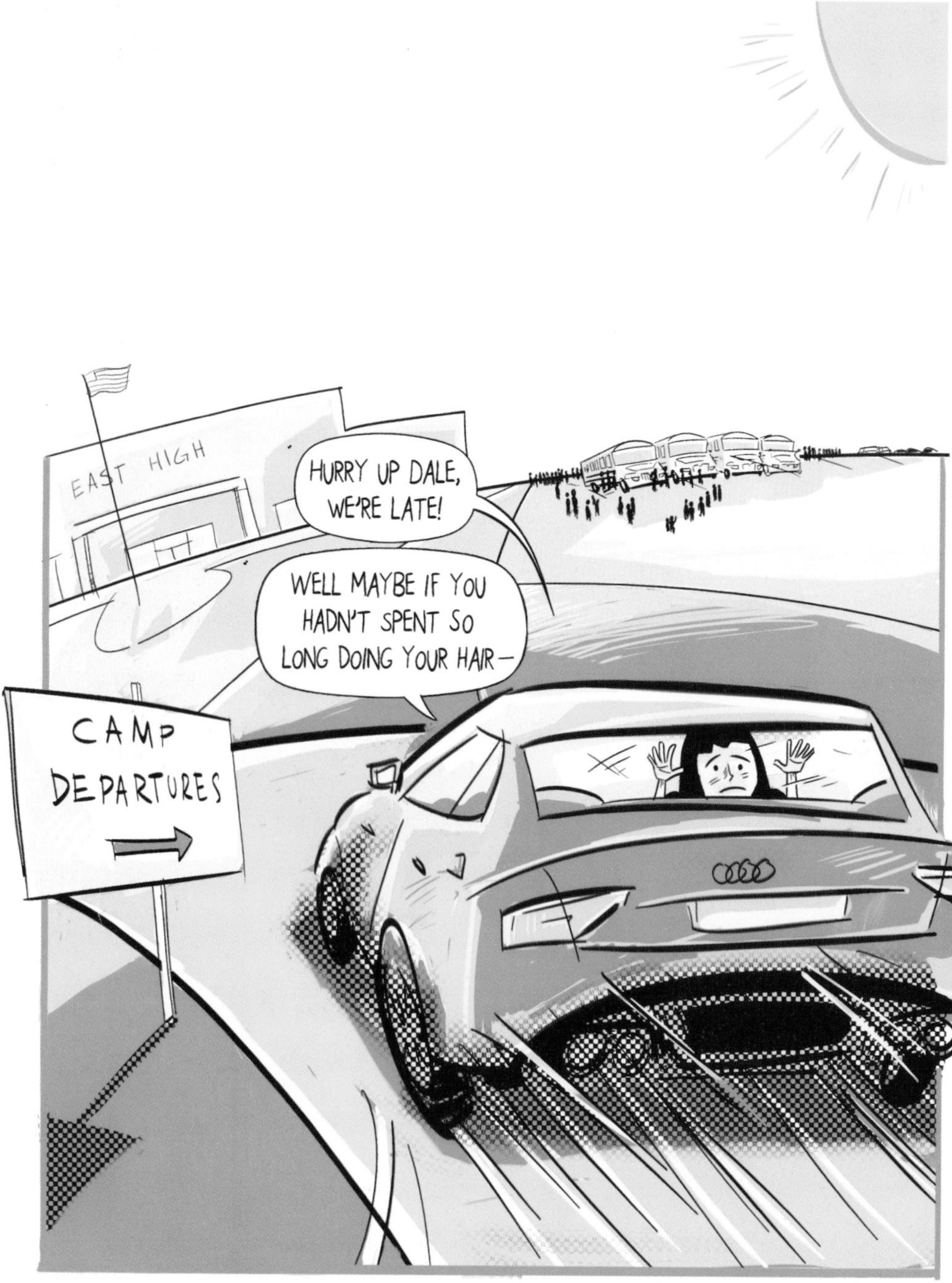
EAST HIGH
HURRY UP DALE, WE'RE LATE!
WELL MAYBE IF YOU HADN'T SPENT SO LONG DOING YOUR HAIR—
CAMP DEPARTURES

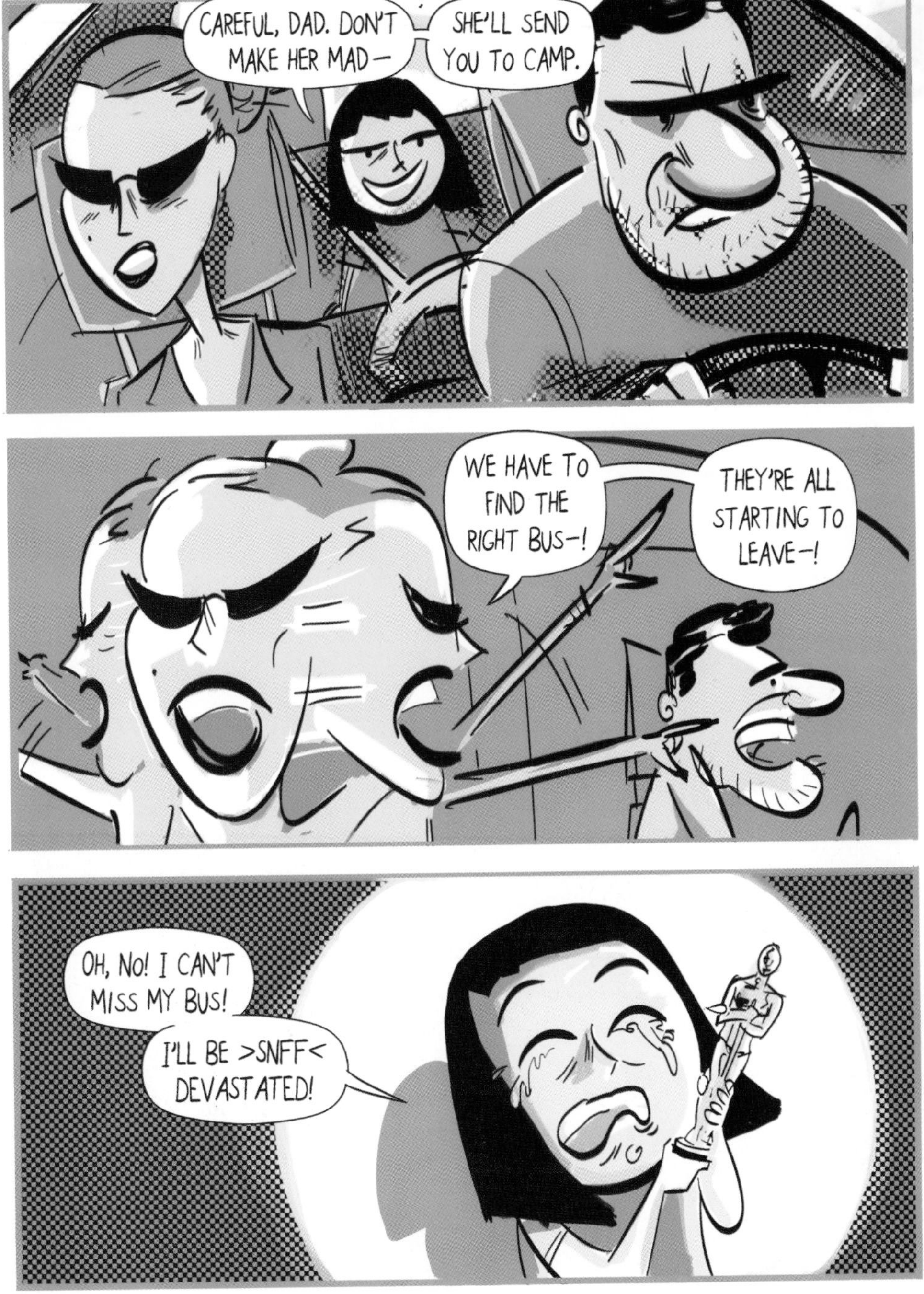
CAREFUL, DAD. DON'T MAKE HER MAD—
SHE'LL SEND YOU TO CAMP.
WE HAVE TO FIND THE RIGHT BUS—!
THEY'RE ALL STARTING TO LEAVE—!
OH, NO! I CAN'T MISS MY BUS!
I'LL BE >SNFF< DEVASTATED!

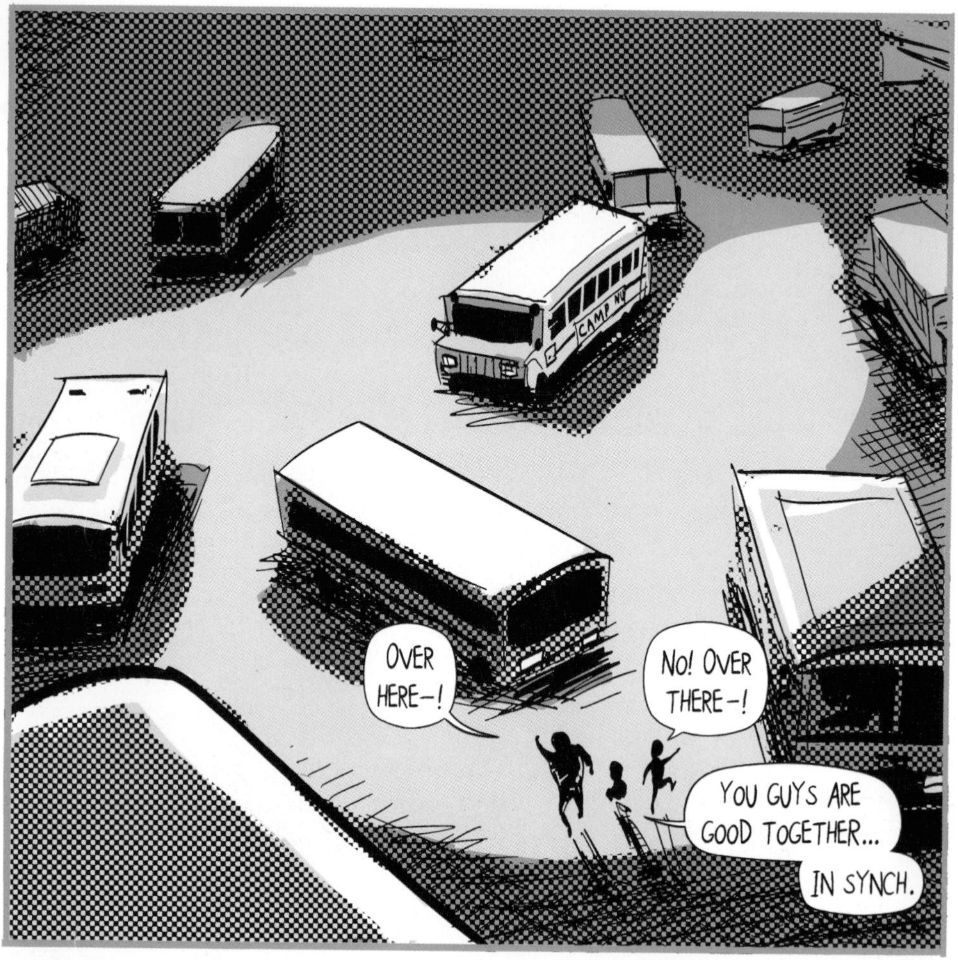
CAMP NO
OVER HERE–!
NO! OVER THERE–!
YOU GUYS ARE GOOD TOGETHER...
IN SYNCH.

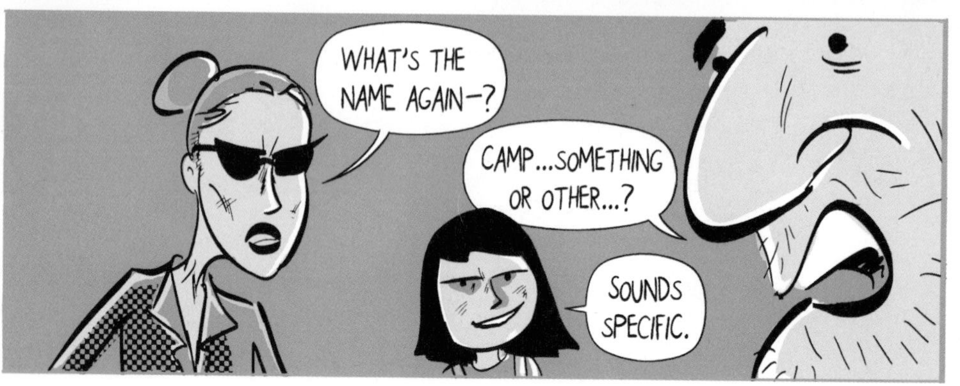
WHAT'S THE NAME AGAIN–?
CAMP...SOMETHING OR OTHER...?
SOUNDS SPECIFIC.

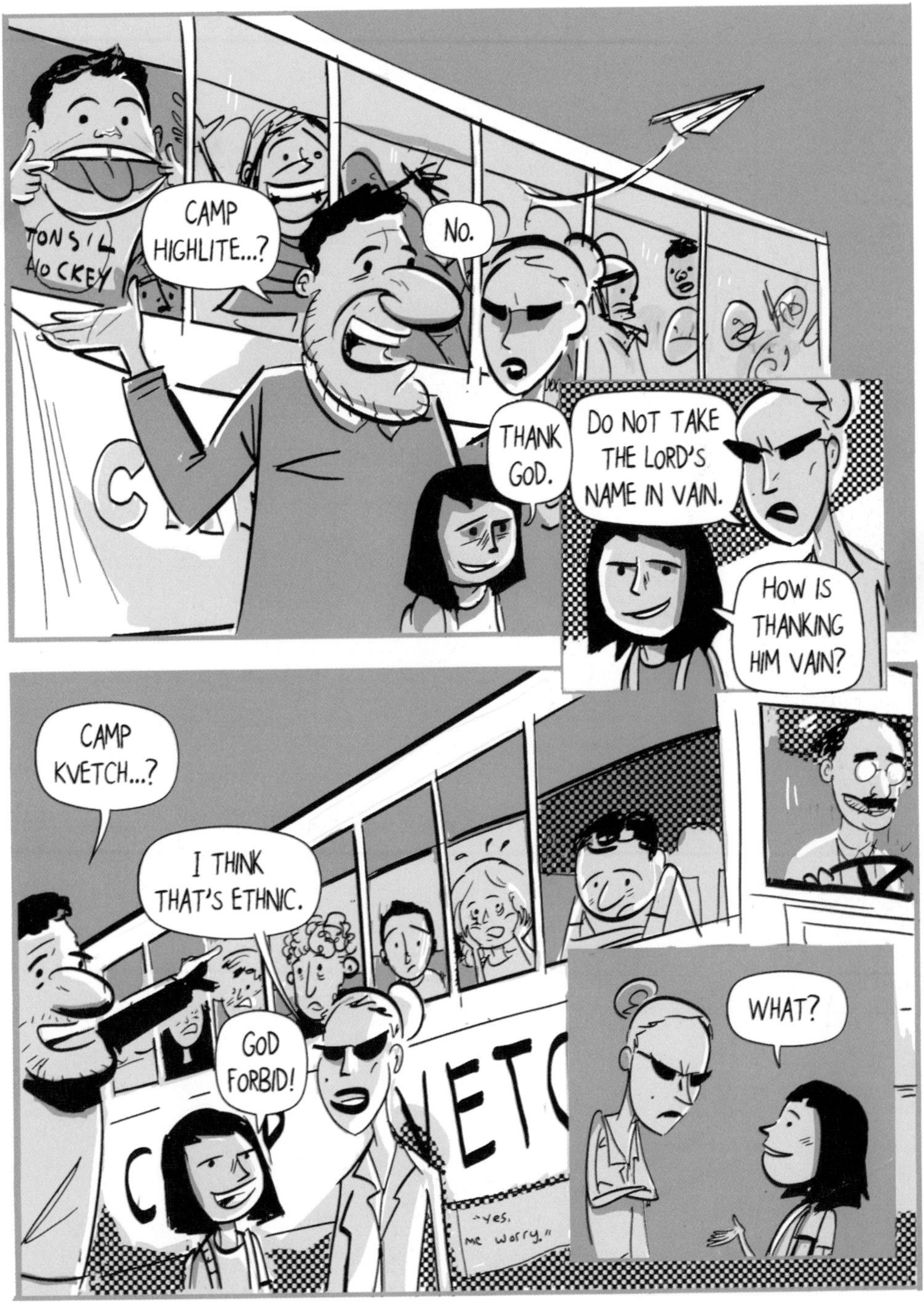
TONSIL HOCKEY
CAMP HIGHLITE...?
No.
THANK GOD.
DO NOT TAKE THE LORD'S NAME IN VAIN.
HOW IS THANKING HIM VAIN?
CAMP KVETCH...?
I THINK THAT'S ETHNIC.
GOD FORBID!
~yes, me worry."
WHAT?

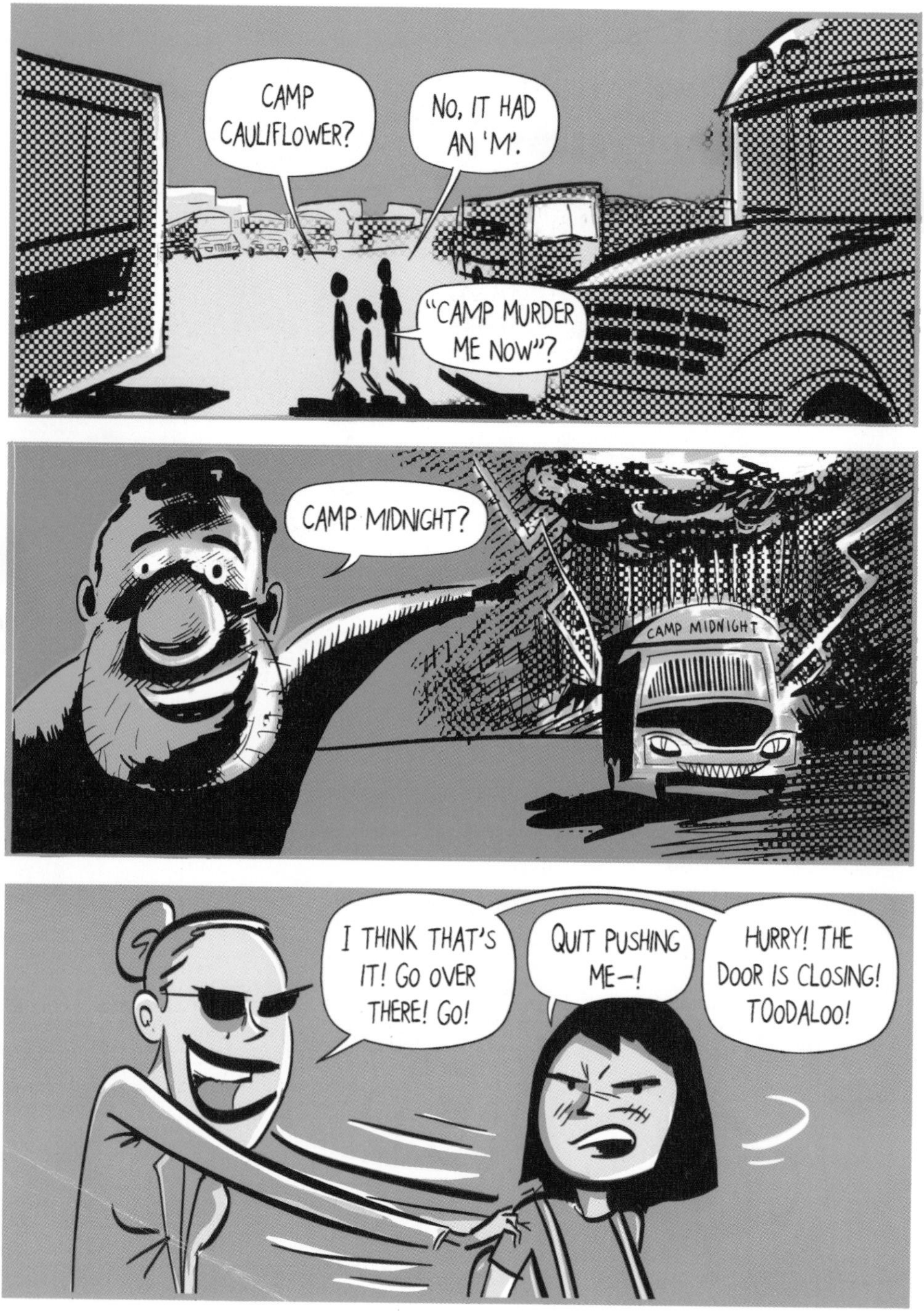
CAMP CAULIFLOWER?
NO, IT HAD AN 'M'.
"CAMP MURDER ME NOW"?
CAMP MIDNIGHT?
CAMP MIDNIGHT
I THINK THAT'S IT! GO OVER THERE! GO!
QUIT PUSHING ME–!
HURRY! THE DOOR IS CLOSING! TOODALOO!

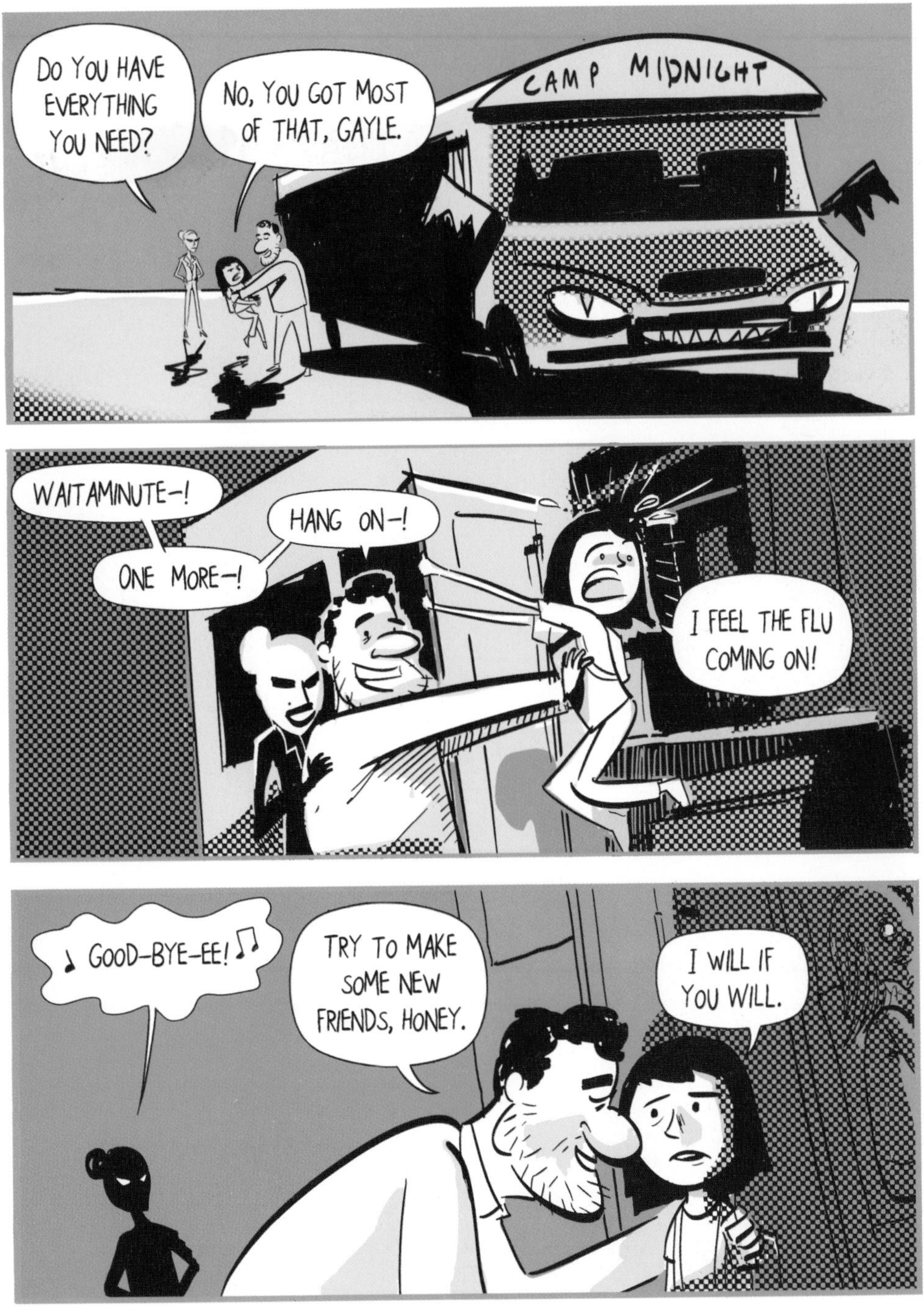
CAMP MIDNIGHT
DO YOU HAVE EVERYTHING YOU NEED?
NO, YOU GOT MOST OF THAT, GAYLE.
WAITAMINUTE—!
ONE MORE—!
HANG ON—!
I FEEL THE FLU COMING ON!
♩ GOOD-BYE-EE! ♫
TRY TO MAKE SOME NEW FRIENDS, HONEY.
I WILL IF YOU WILL.

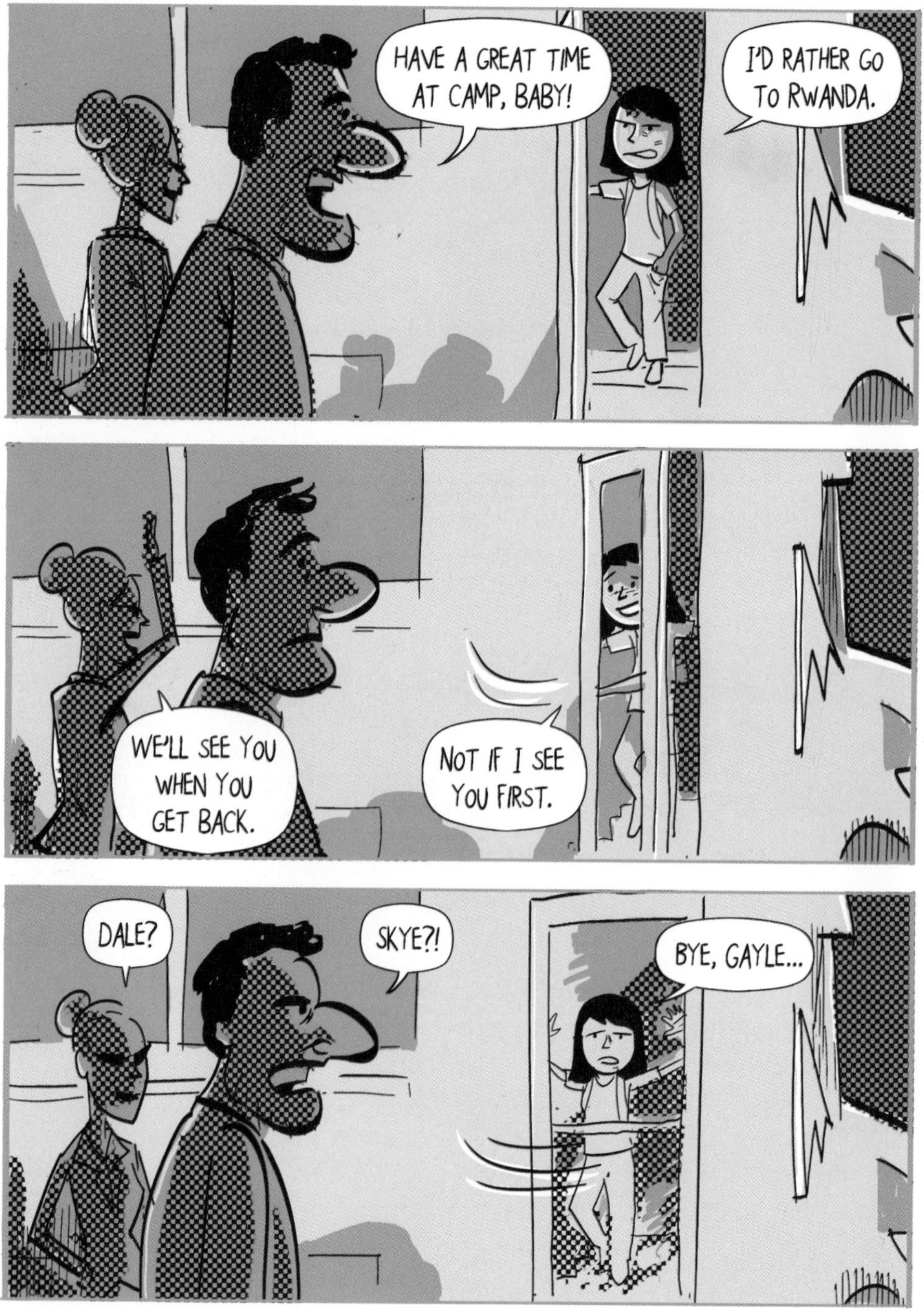
HAVE A GREAT TIME AT CAMP, BABY!
I'D RATHER GO TO RWANDA.
WE'LL SEE YOU WHEN YOU GET BACK.
NOT IF I SEE YOU FIRST.
DALE?
SKYE?!
BYE, GAYLE...

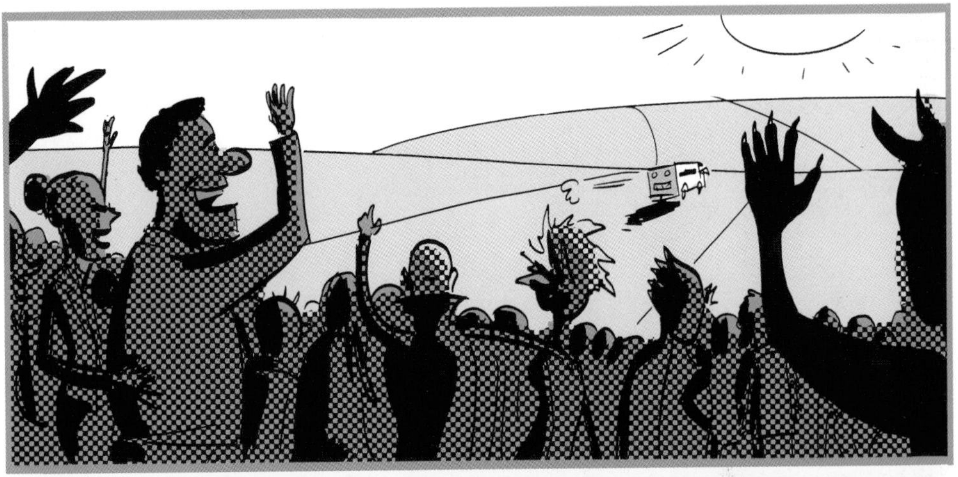

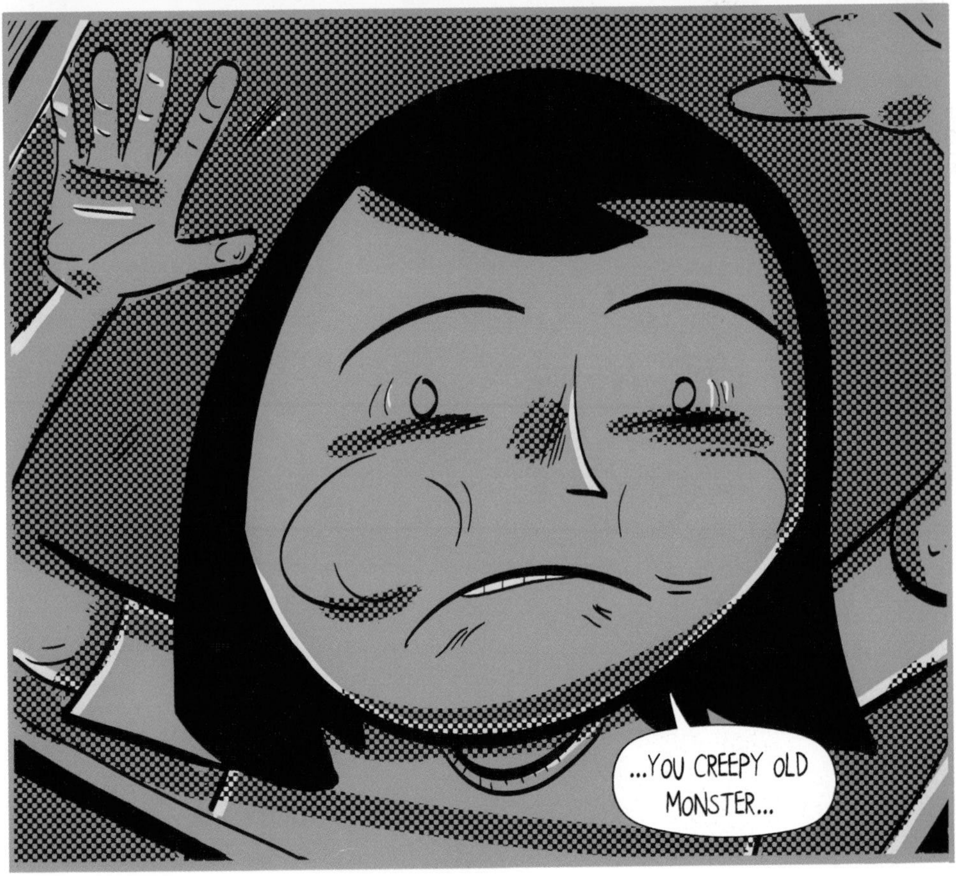
...YOU CREEPY OLD MONSTER...

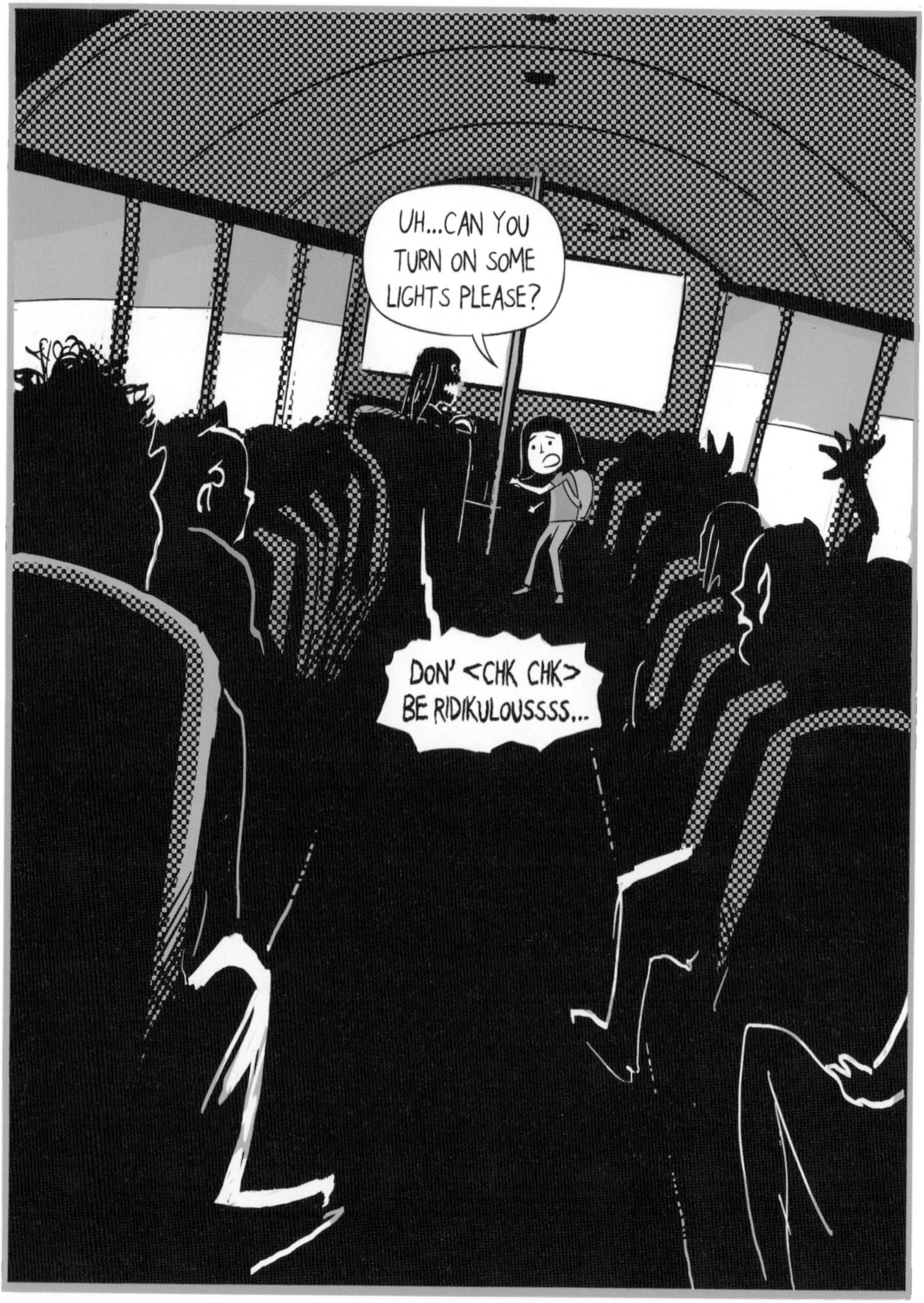
UH...CAN YOU TURN ON SOME LIGHTS PLEASE?
DON' <CHK CHK> BE RIDIKULOUSSSS...

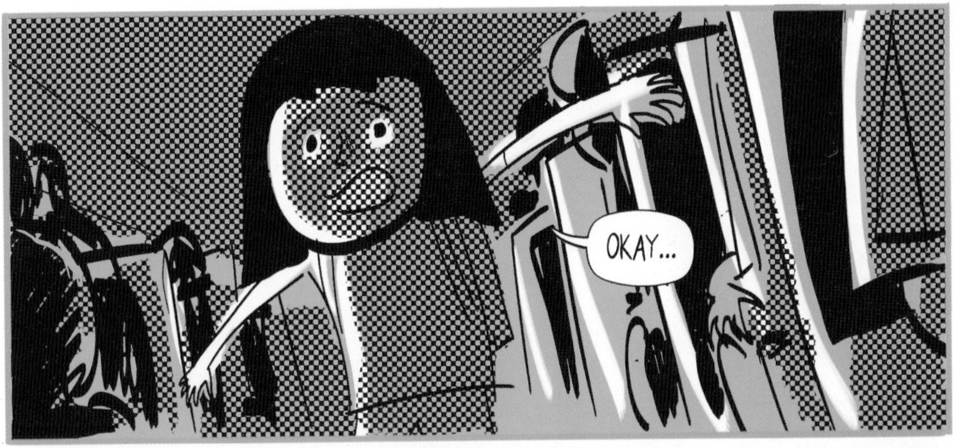
OKAY...

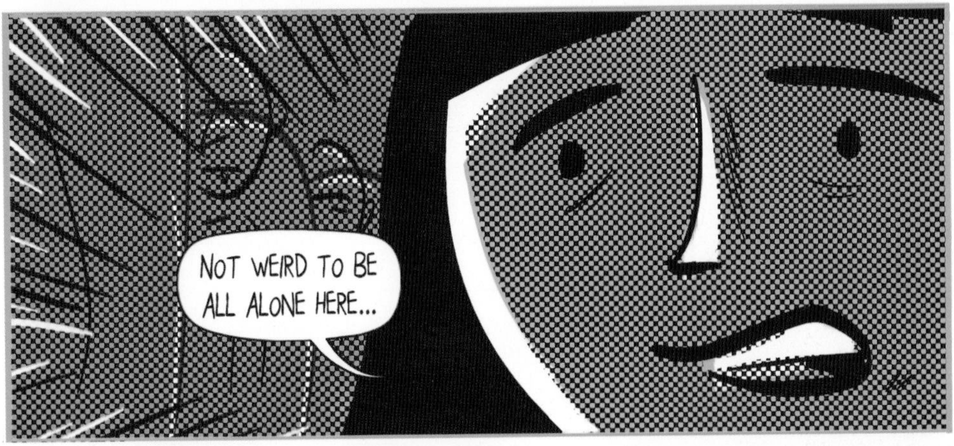
NOT WEIRD TO BE ALL ALONE HERE...

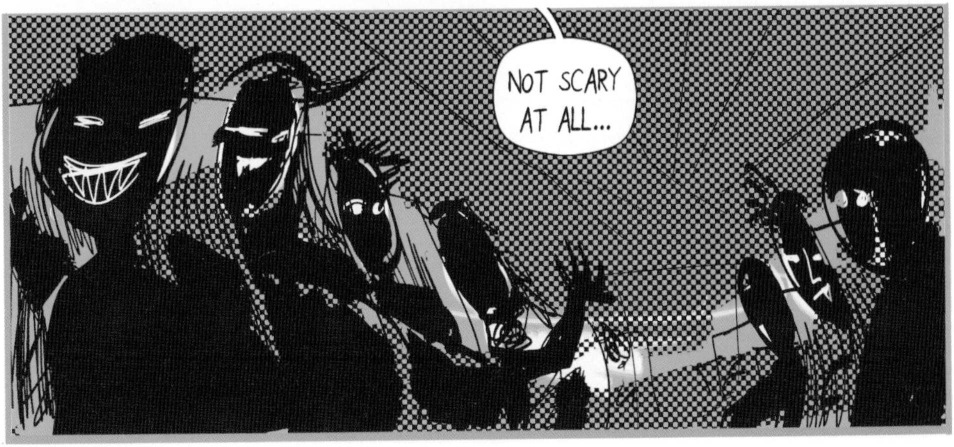
NOT SCARY AT ALL...

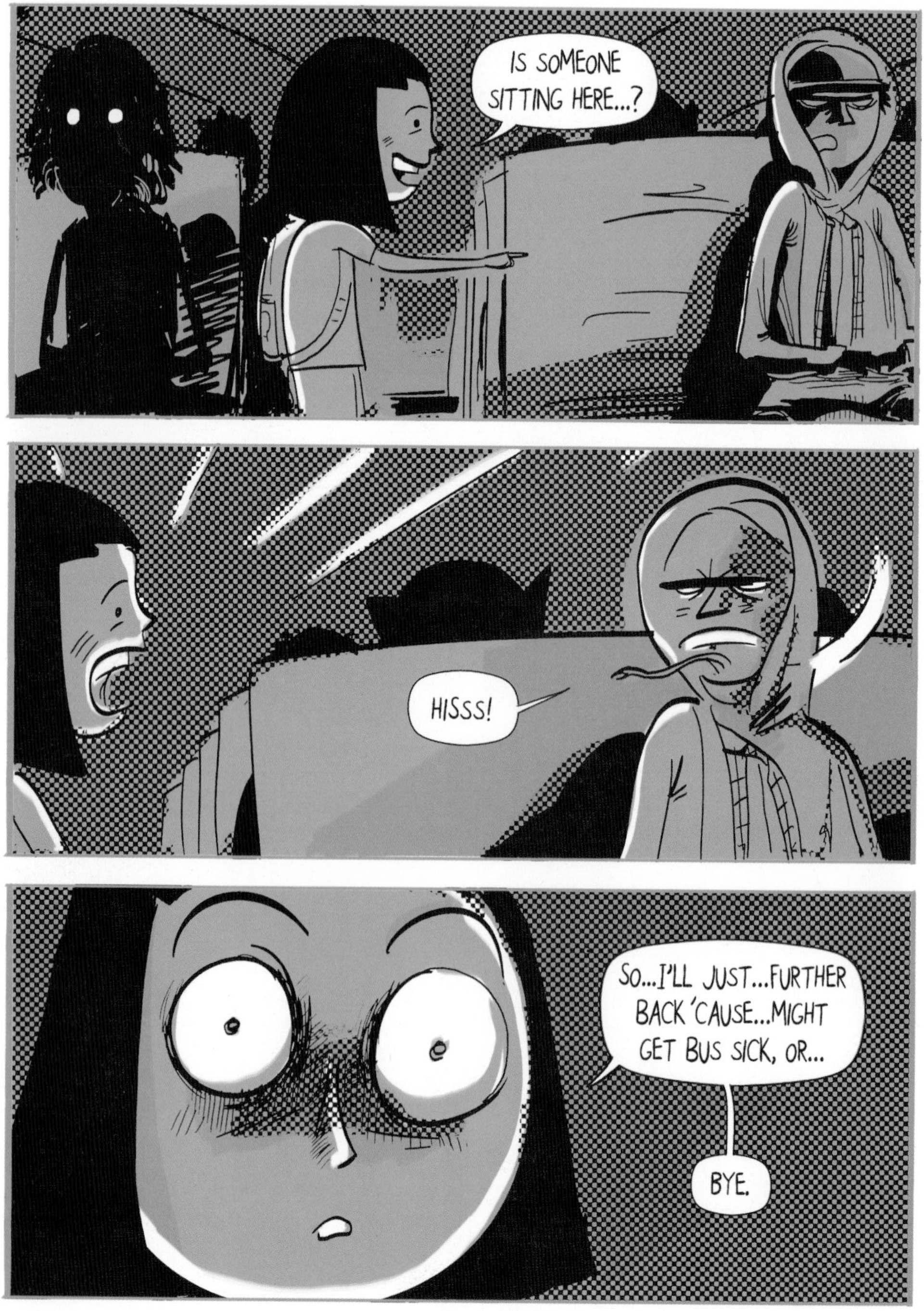
IS SOMEONE SITTING HERE...?
HISSS!
SO...I'LL JUST...FURTHER BACK 'CAUSE...MIGHT GET BUS SICK, OR...
BYE.

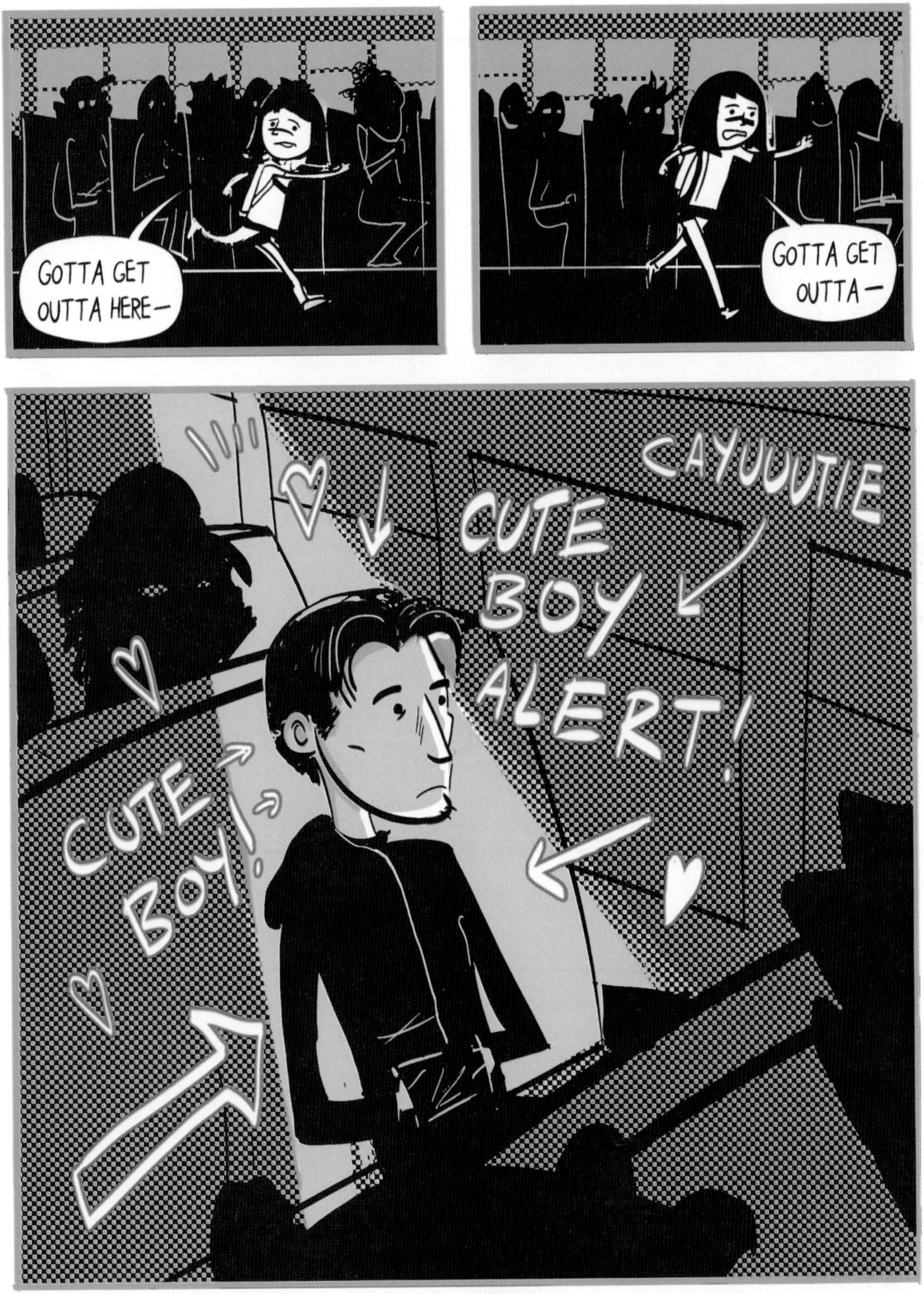

GOTTA GET OUTTA HERE—
GOTTA GET OUTTA—
CUTE BOY ALERT!
CAYUUUTIE
CUTE BOY!

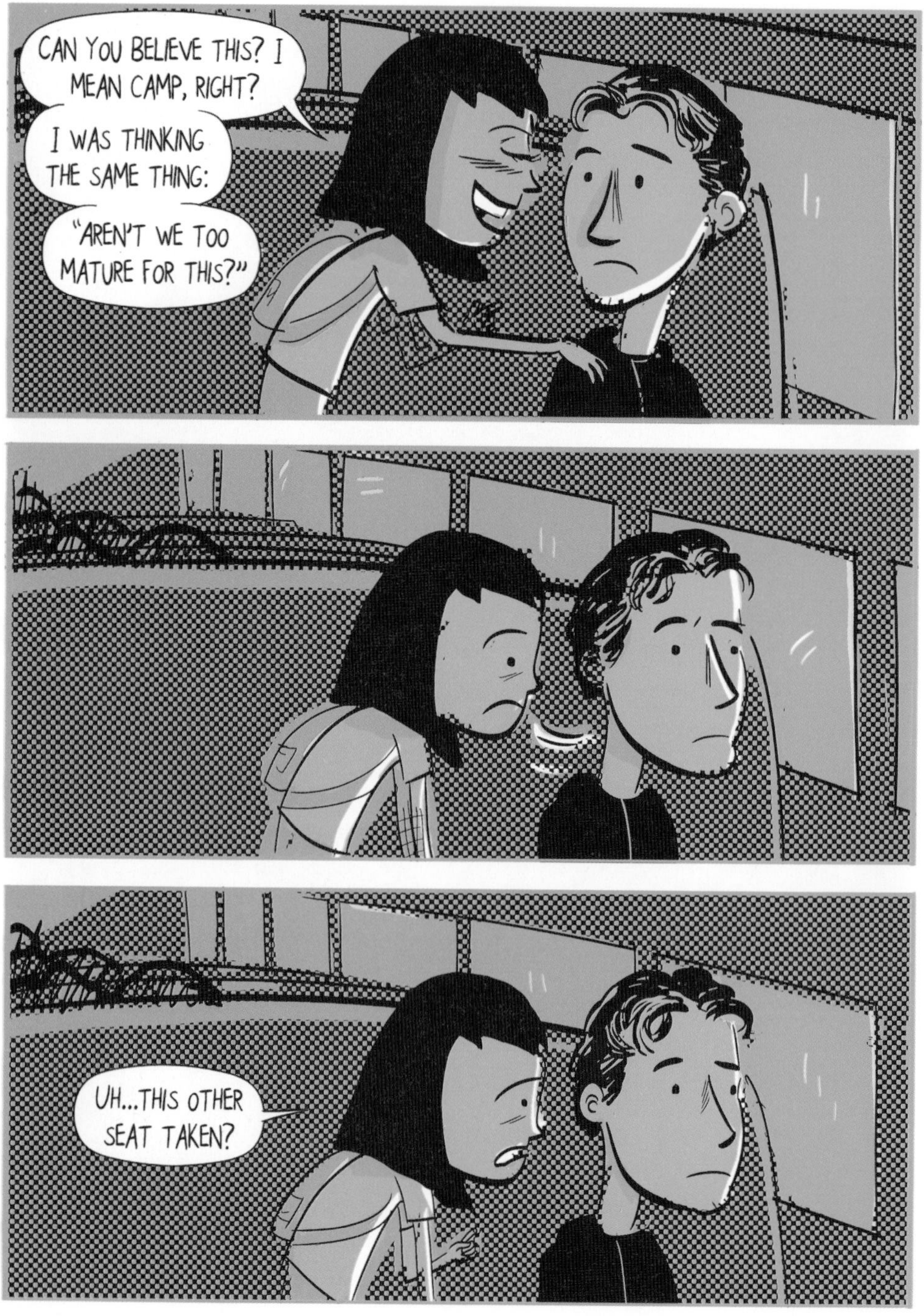
CAN YOU BELIEVE THIS? I MEAN CAMP, RIGHT?
I WAS THINKING THE SAME THING:
"AREN'T WE TOO MATURE FOR THIS?"
UH...THIS OTHER SEAT TAKEN?

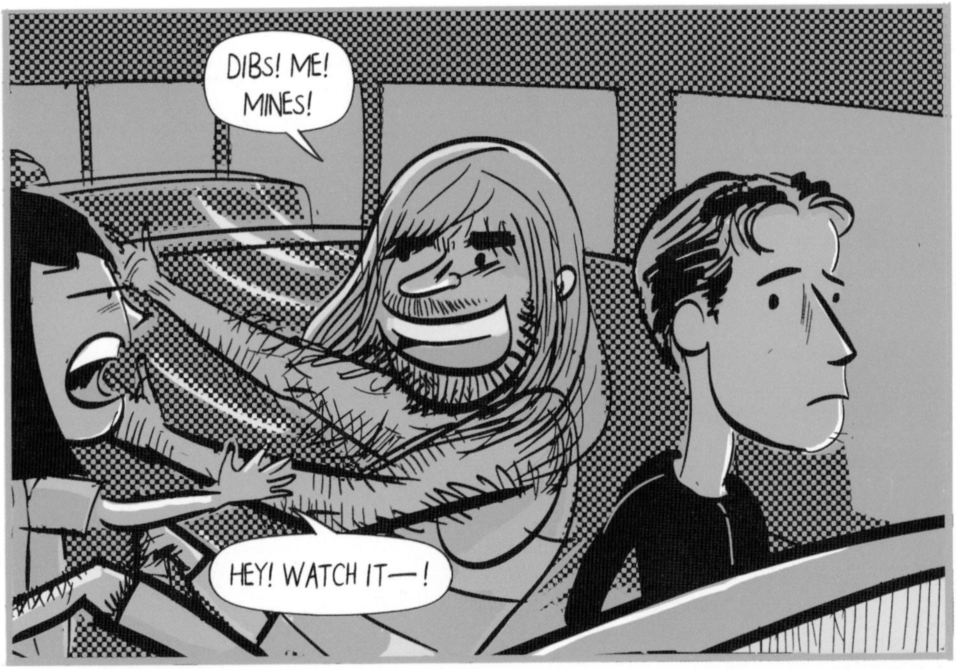
DIBS! ME! MINES!
HEY! WATCH IT—!

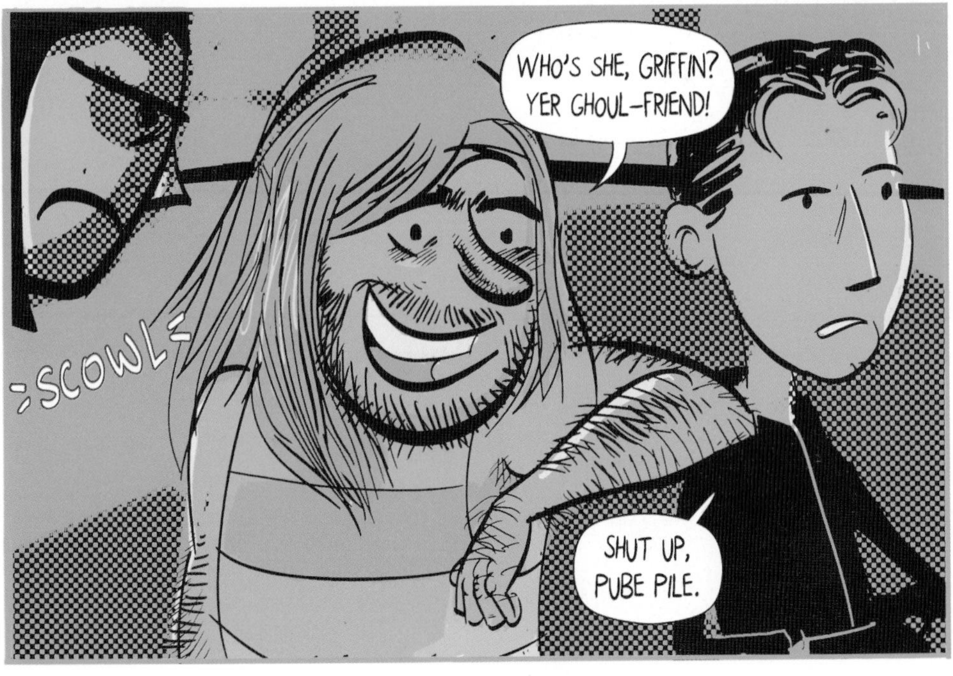
WHO'S SHE, GRIFFIN? YER GHOUL-FRIEND!
=SCOWL=
SHUT UP, PUBE PILE.

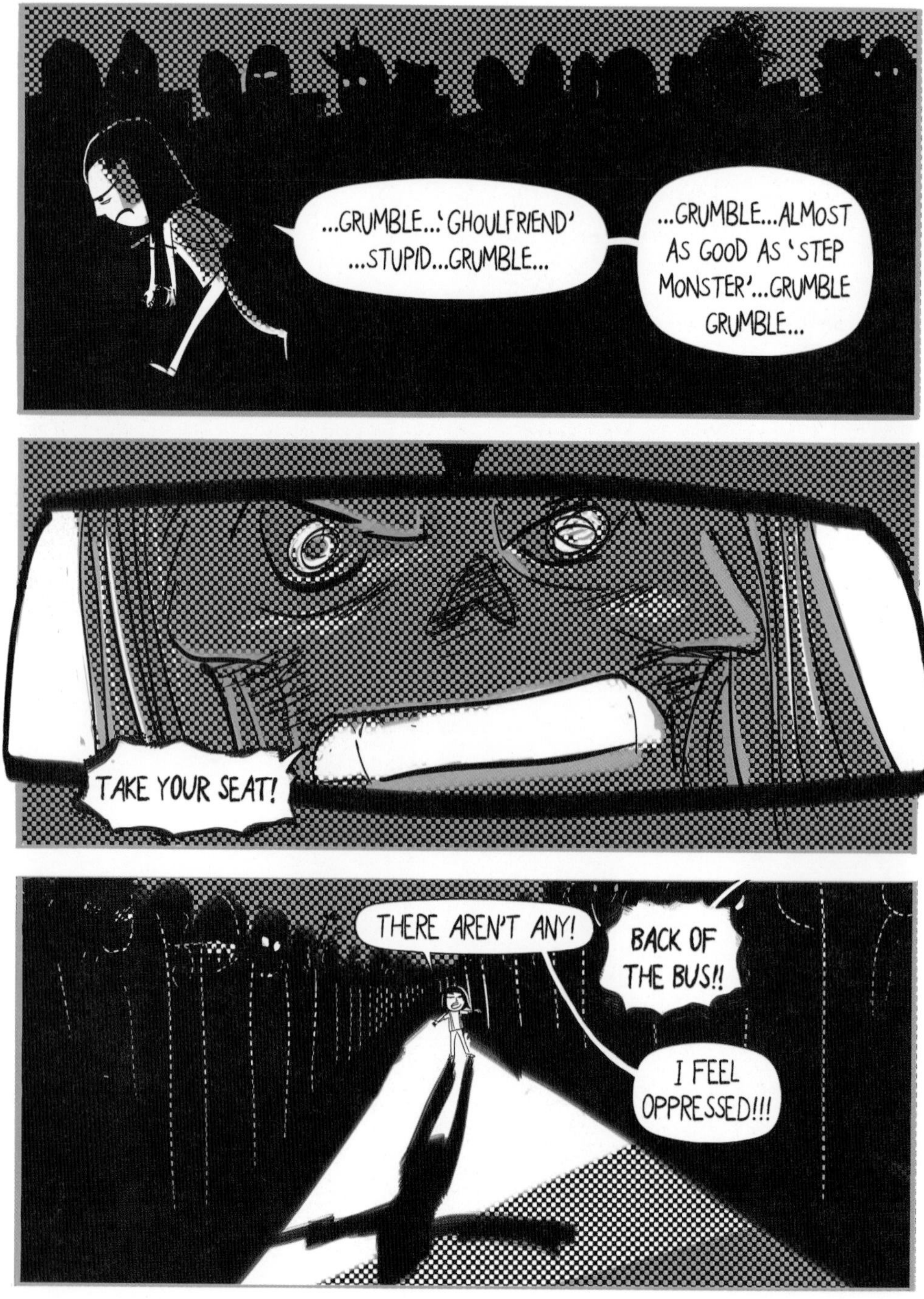
...GRUMBLE...'GHOULFRIEND' ...STUPID...GRUMBLE...
...GRUMBLE...ALMOST AS GOOD AS 'STEP MONSTER'...GRUMBLE GRUMBLE...
TAKE YOUR SEAT!
THERE AREN'T ANY!
BACK OF THE BUS!!
I FEEL OPPRESSED!!!

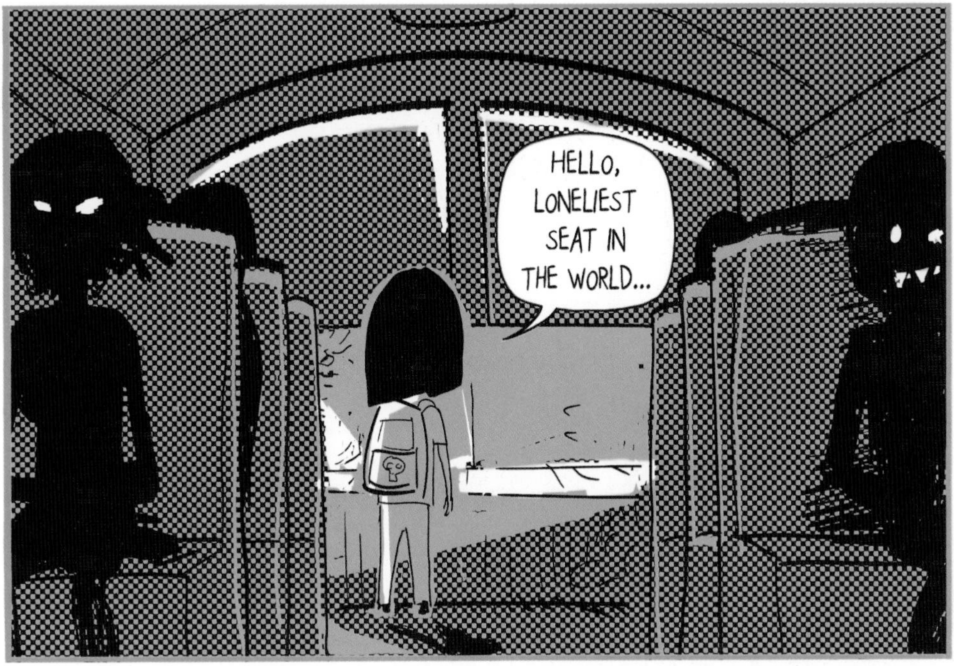
HELLO, LONELIEST SEAT IN THE WORLD...

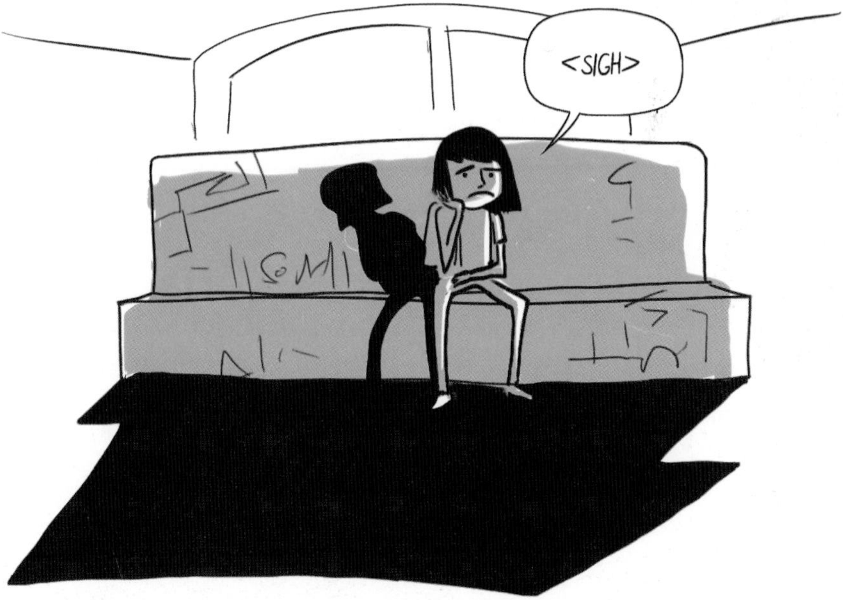
<SIGH>

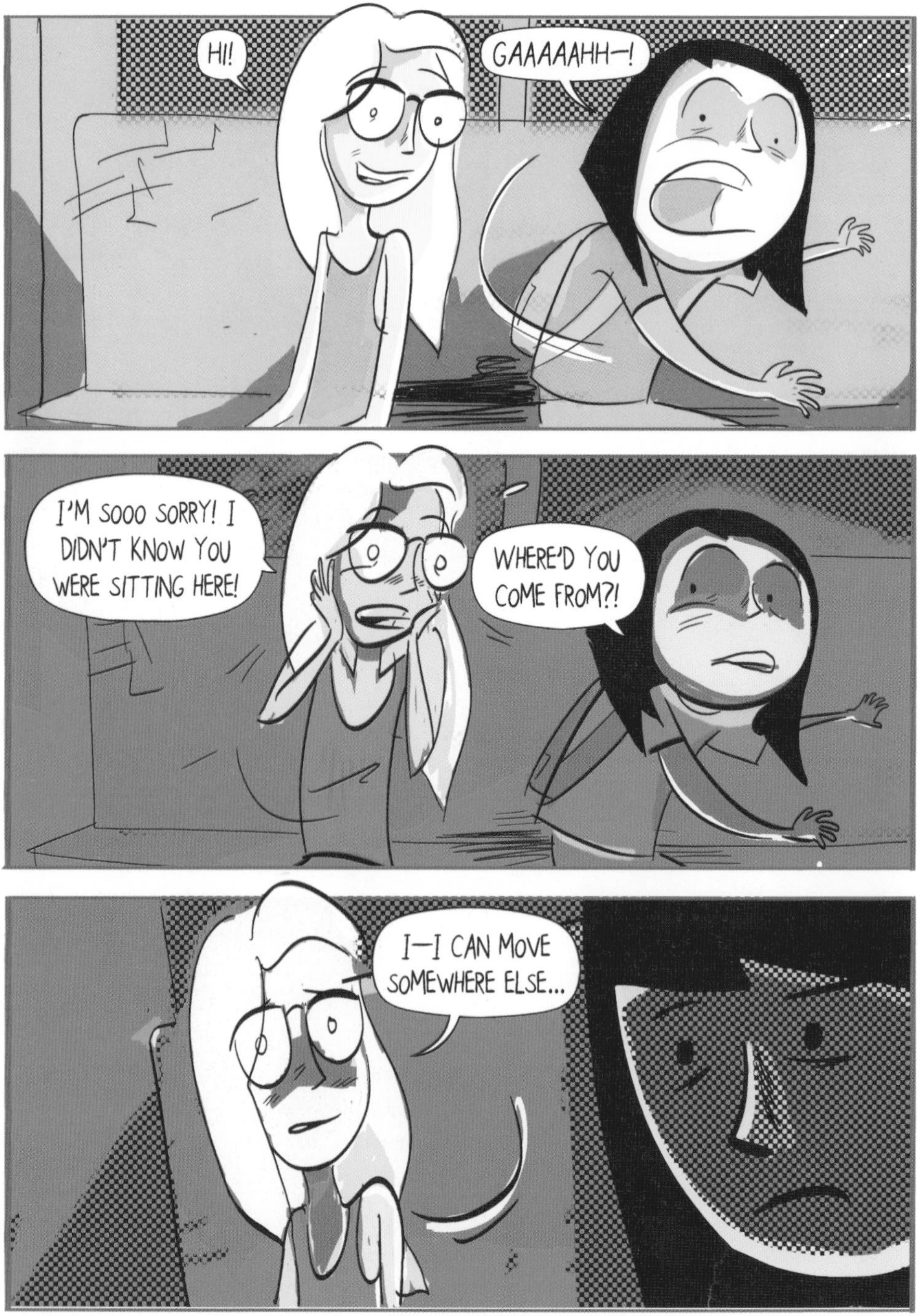
HI!
GAAAAAHH—!
I'M SOOO SORRY! I DIDN'T KNOW YOU WERE SITTING HERE!
WHERE'D YOU COME FROM?!
I—I CAN MOVE SOMEWHERE ELSE...

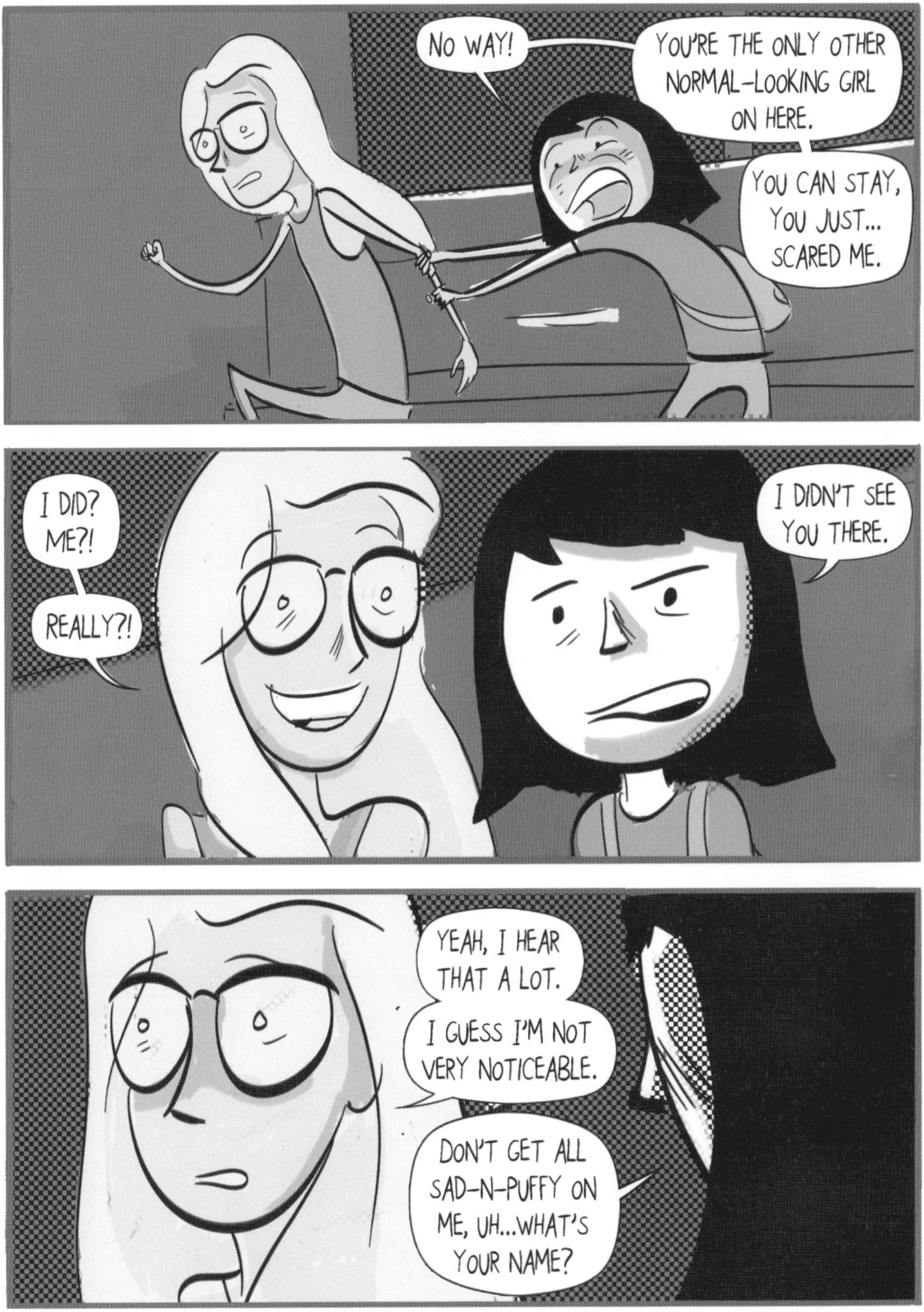
NO WAY!
YOU'RE THE ONLY OTHER NORMAL-LOOKING GIRL ON HERE.
YOU CAN STAY, YOU JUST... SCARED ME.
I DID? ME?!
REALLY?!
I DIDN'T SEE YOU THERE.
YEAH, I HEAR THAT A LOT.
I GUESS I'M NOT VERY NOTICEABLE.
DON'T GET ALL SAD-N-PUFFY ON ME, UH...WHAT'S YOUR NAME?

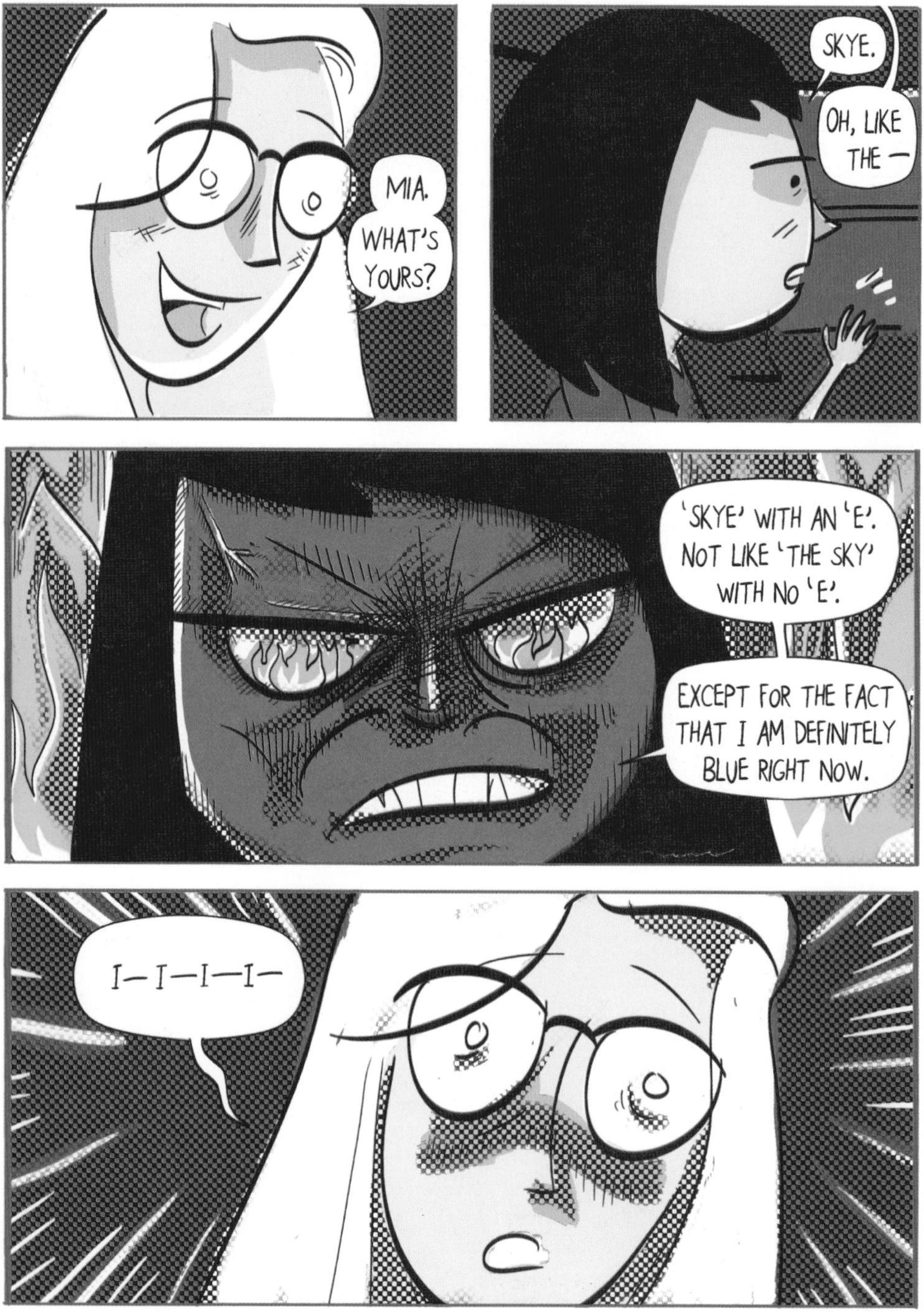
MIA. WHAT'S YOURS?
SKYE.
OH, LIKE THE —
'SKYE' WITH AN 'E'. NOT LIKE 'THE SKY' WITH NO 'E'.
EXCEPT FOR THE FACT THAT I AM DEFINITELY BLUE RIGHT NOW.
I—I—I—I—

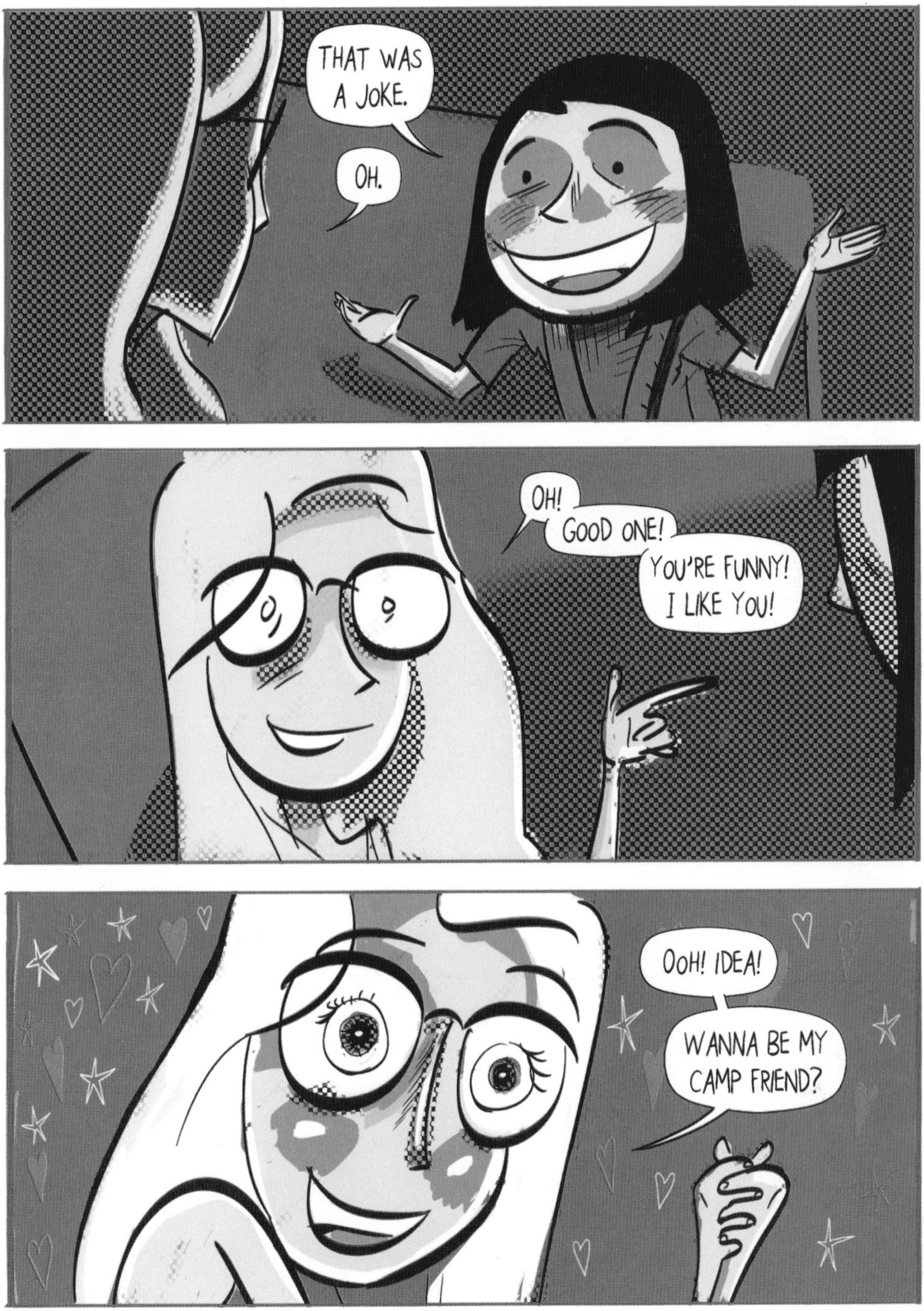
THAT WAS A JOKE.
OH.
OH!
GOOD ONE!
YOU'RE FUNNY! I LIKE YOU!
OOH! IDEA!
WANNA BE MY CAMP FRIEND?

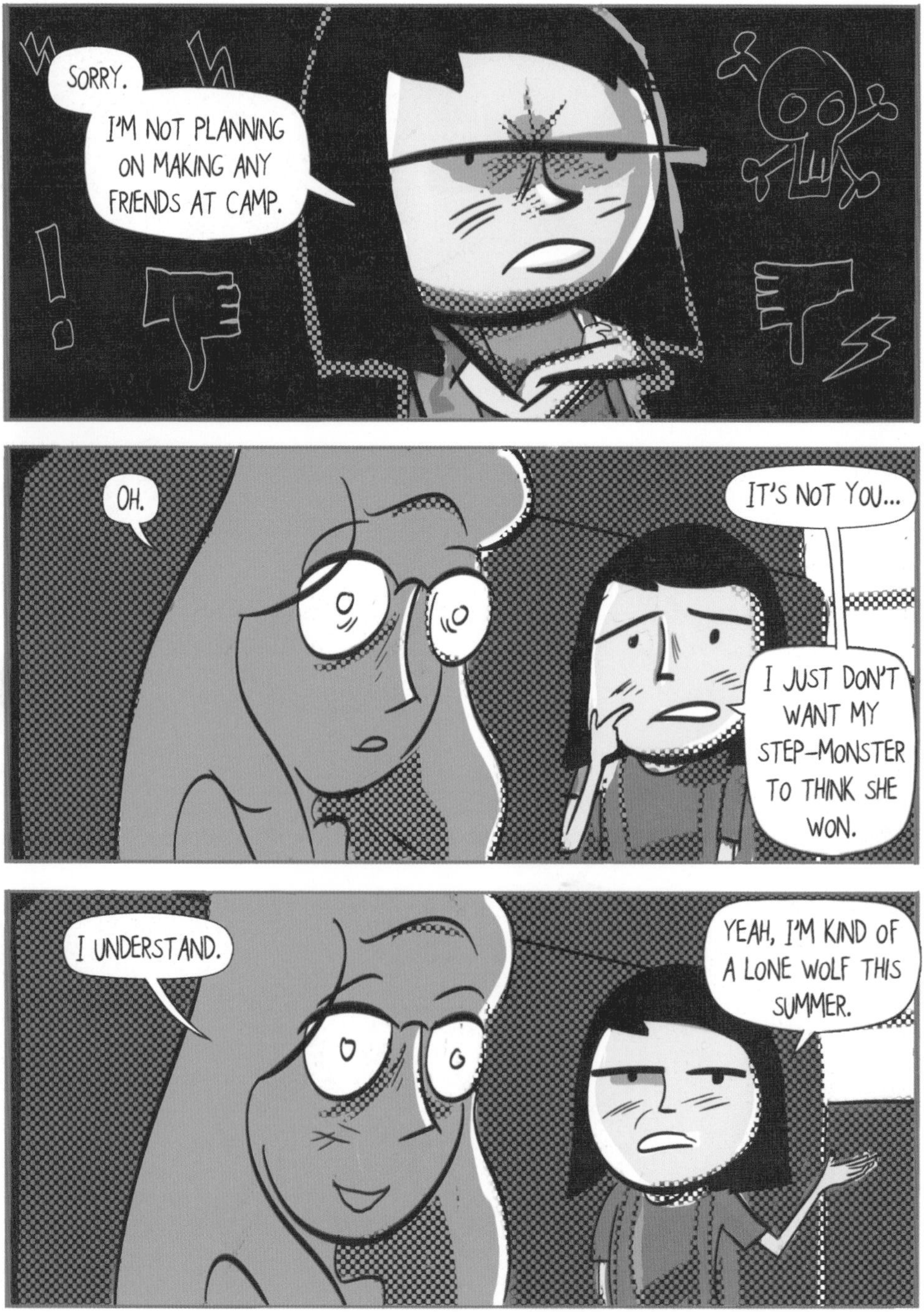
SORRY.
I'M NOT PLANNING ON MAKING ANY FRIENDS AT CAMP.
OH.
IT'S NOT YOU...
I JUST DON'T WANT MY STEP-MONSTER TO THINK SHE WON.
I UNDERSTAND.
YEAH, I'M KIND OF A LONE WOLF THIS SUMMER.

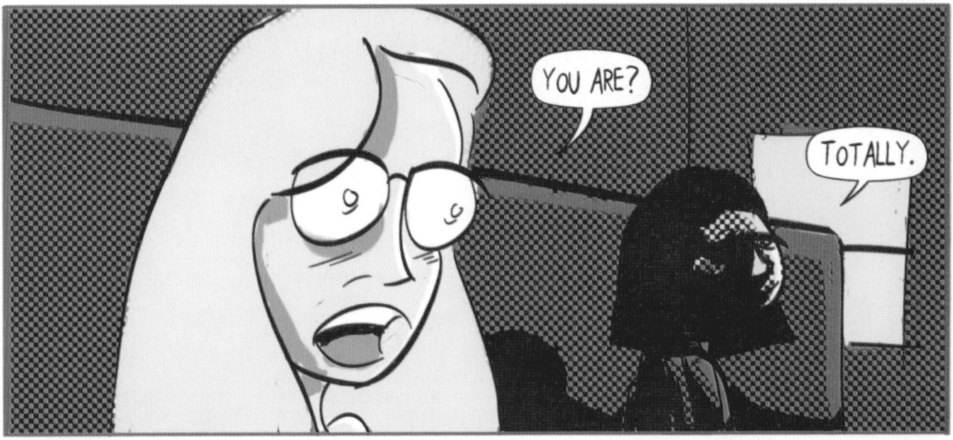
YOU ARE?
TOTALLY.

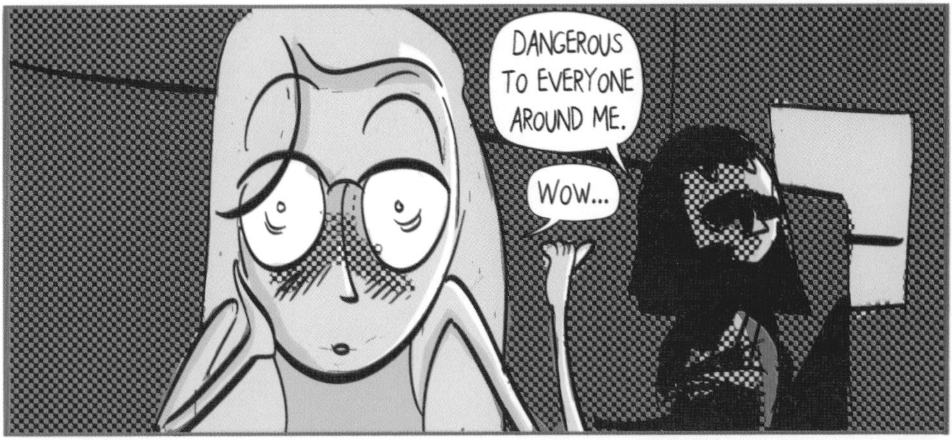
DANGEROUS TO EVERYONE AROUND ME.
WOW...

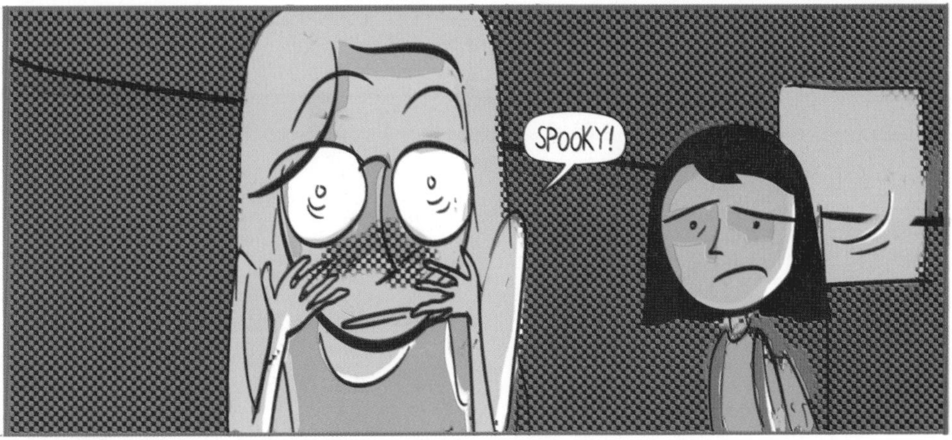
SPOOKY!

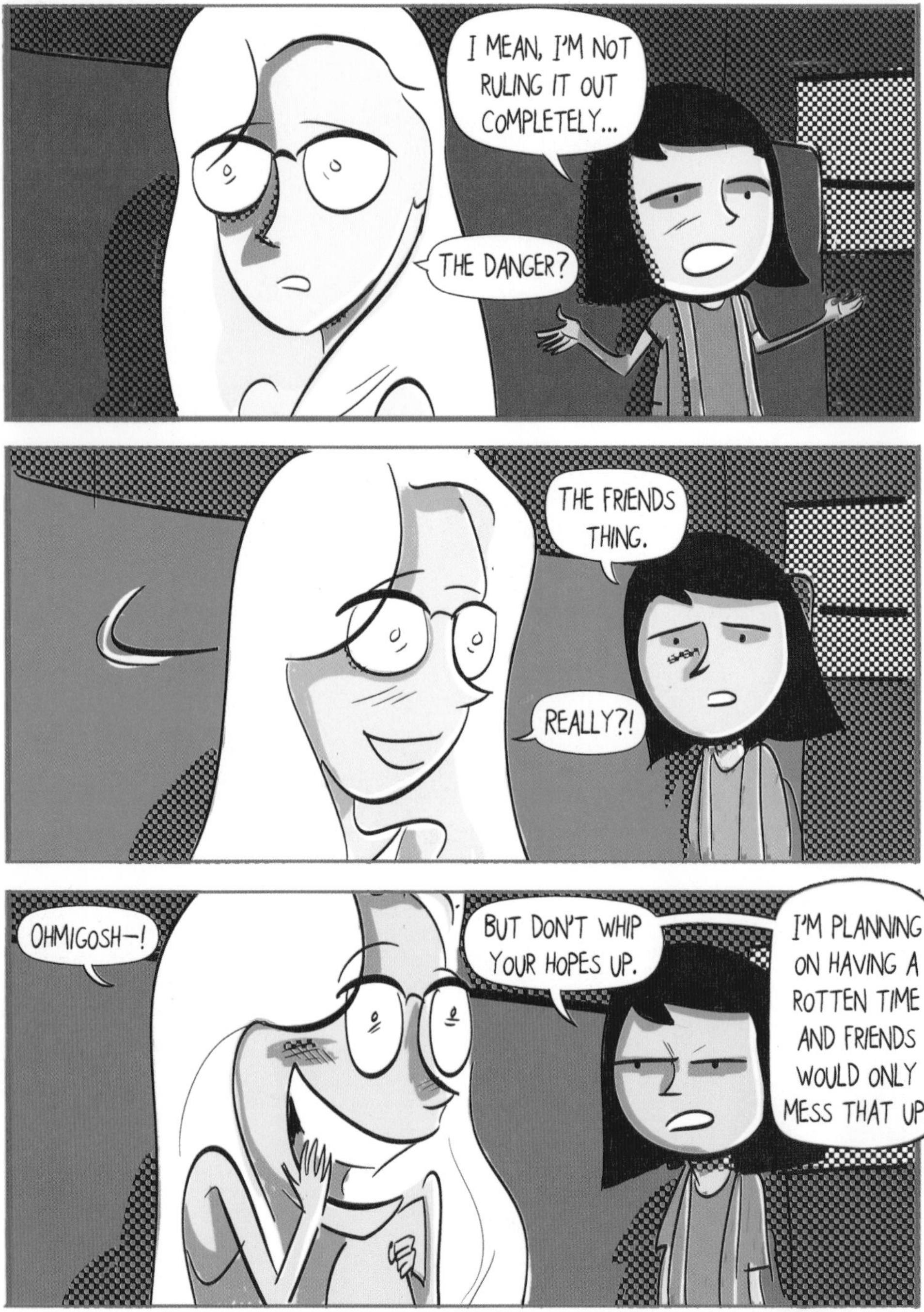
I MEAN, I'M NOT RULING IT OUT COMPLETELY...
THE DANGER?
THE FRIENDS THING.
REALLY?!
OHMIGOSH—!
BUT DON'T WHIP YOUR HOPES UP.
I'M PLANNING ON HAVING A ROTTEN TIME AND FRIENDS WOULD ONLY MESS THAT UP.

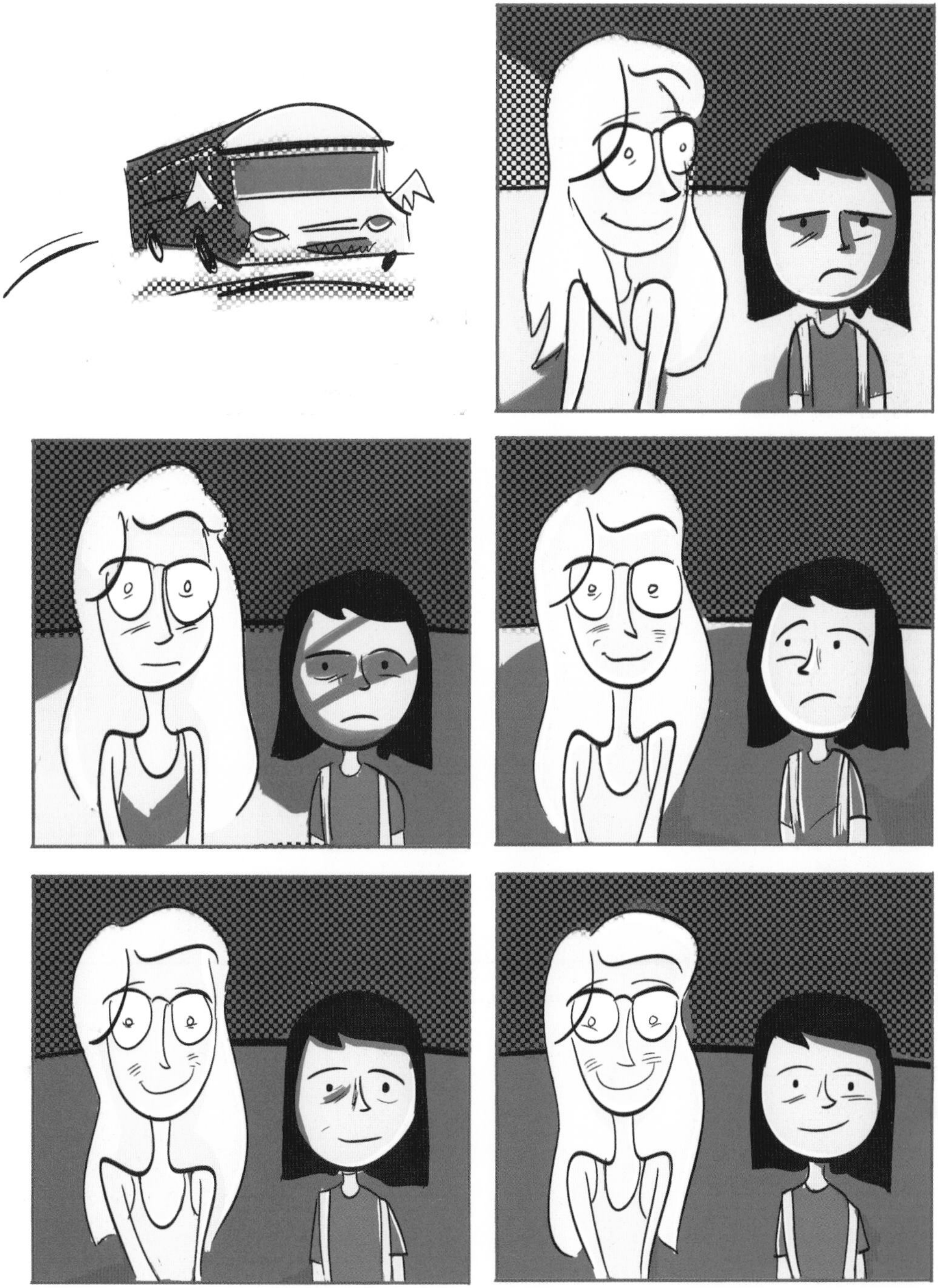

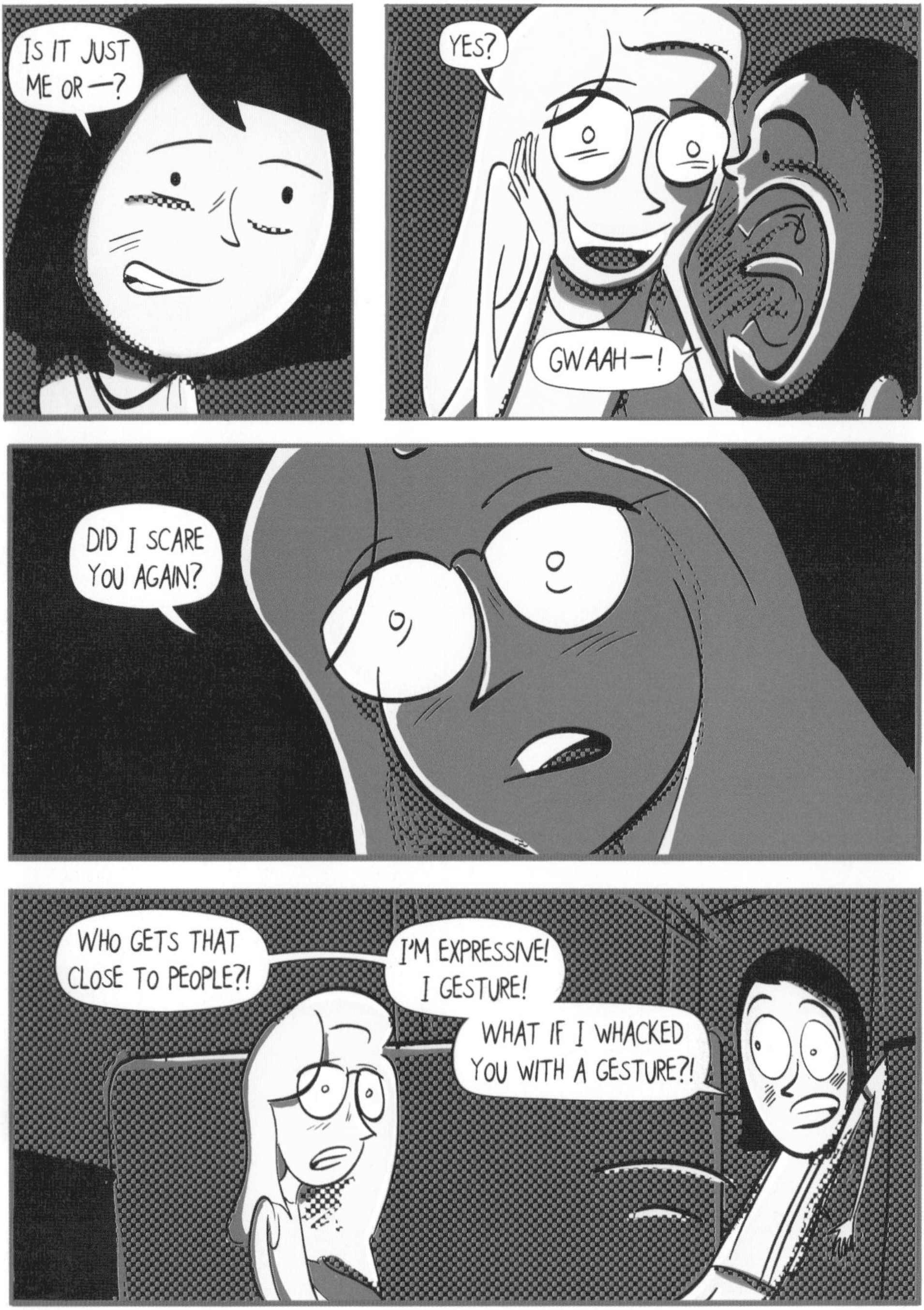
IS IT JUST ME OR—?
YES?
GWAAH—!
DID I SCARE YOU AGAIN?
WHO GETS THAT CLOSE TO PEOPLE?!
I'M EXPRESSIVE! I GESTURE!
WHAT IF I WHACKED YOU WITH A GESTURE?!

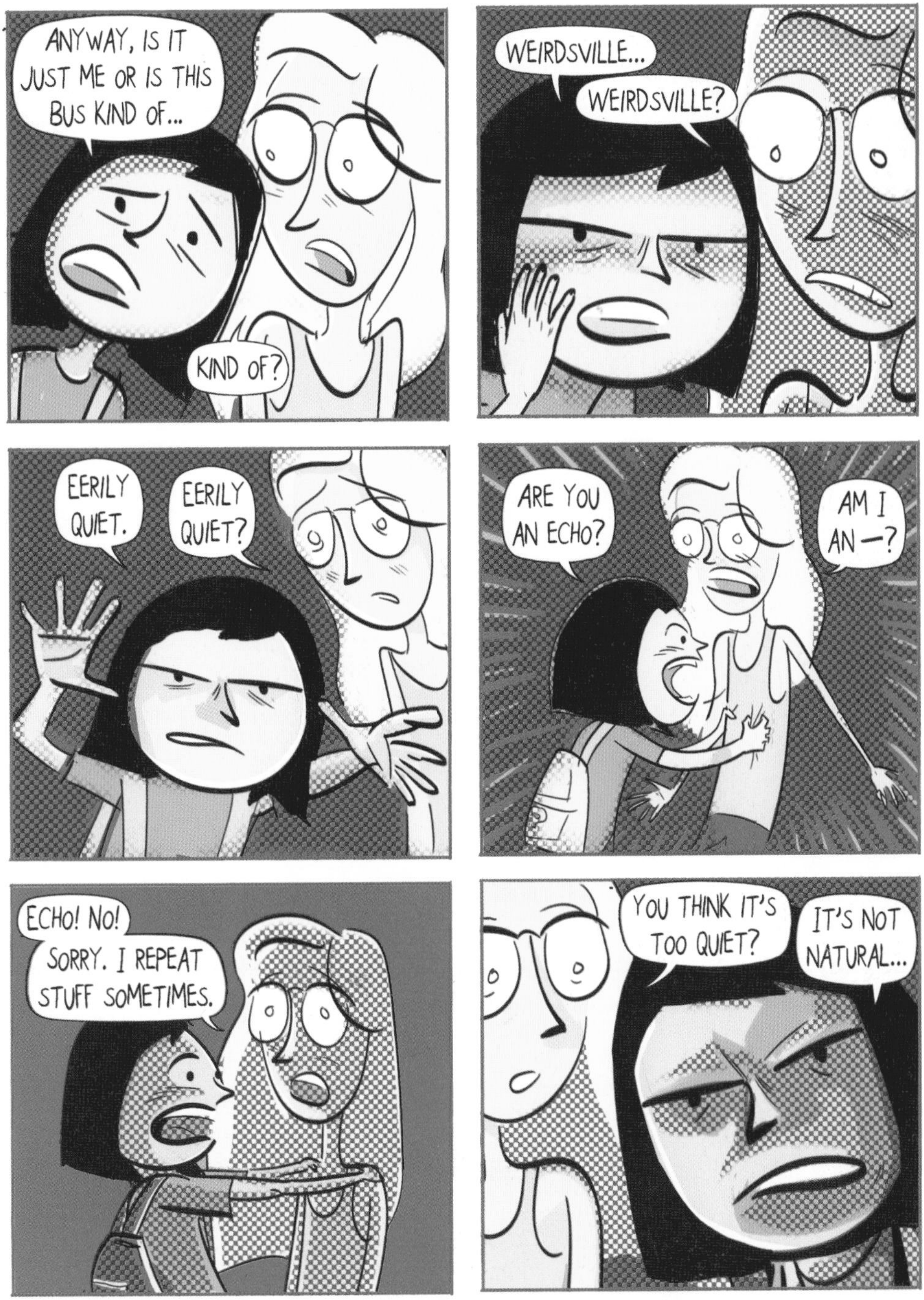
ANYWAY, IS IT JUST ME OR IS THIS BUS KIND OF...
KIND OF?
WEIRDSVILLE...
WEIRDSVILLE?
EERILY QUIET.
EERILY QUIET?
ARE YOU AN ECHO?
AM I AN—?
ECHO! NO!
SORRY. I REPEAT STUFF SOMETIMES.
YOU THINK IT'S TOO QUIET?
IT'S NOT NATURAL...

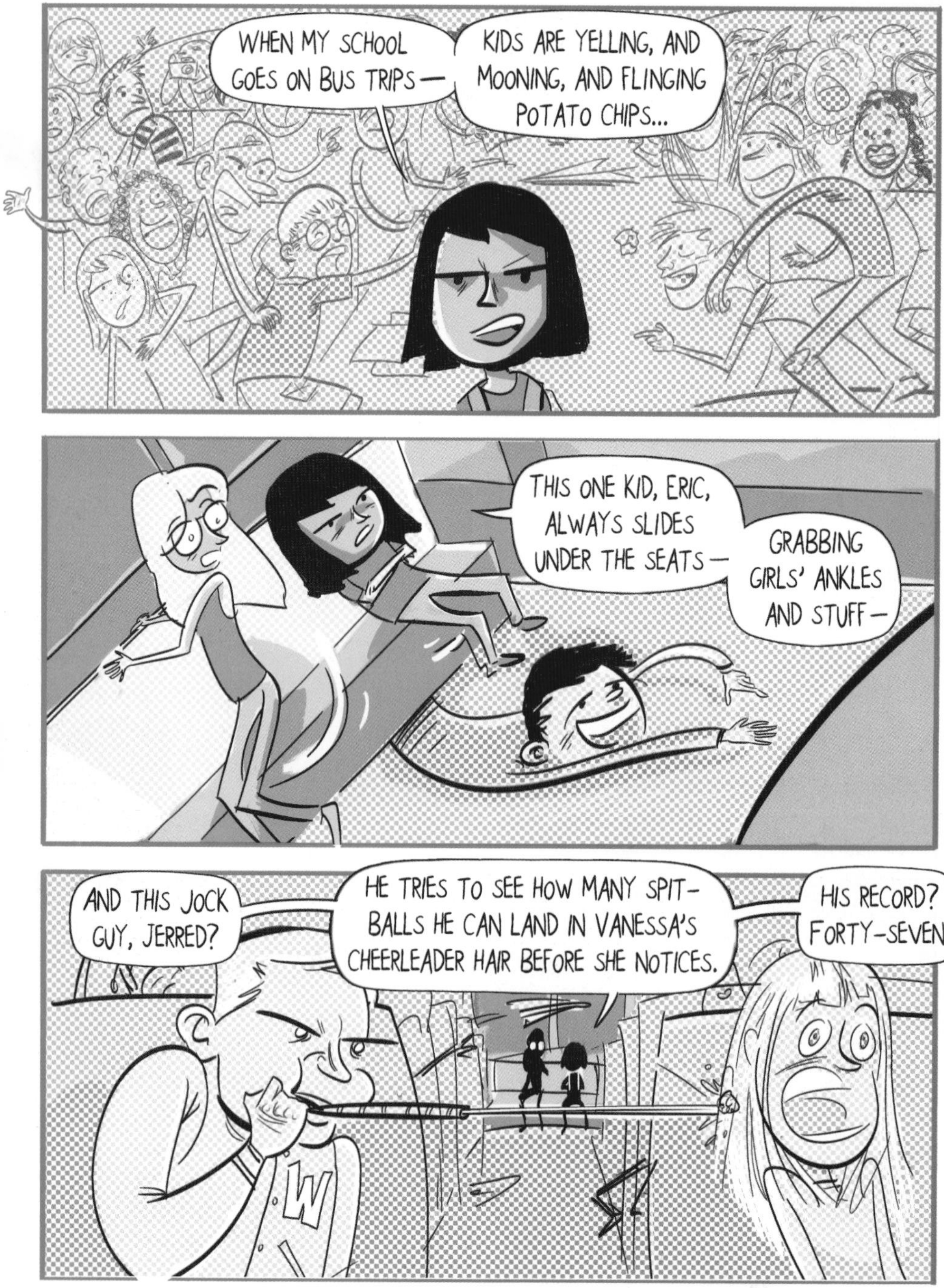
WHEN MY SCHOOL GOES ON BUS TRIPS—
KIDS ARE YELLING, AND MOONING, AND FLINGING POTATO CHIPS...
THIS ONE KID, ERIC, ALWAYS SLIDES UNDER THE SEATS—
GRABBING GIRLS' ANKLES AND STUFF—
AND THIS JOCK GUY, JERRED?
HE TRIES TO SEE HOW MANY SPIT-BALLS HE CAN LAND IN VANESSA'S CHEERLEADER HAIR BEFORE SHE NOTICES.
HIS RECORD? FORTY-SEVEN.
W

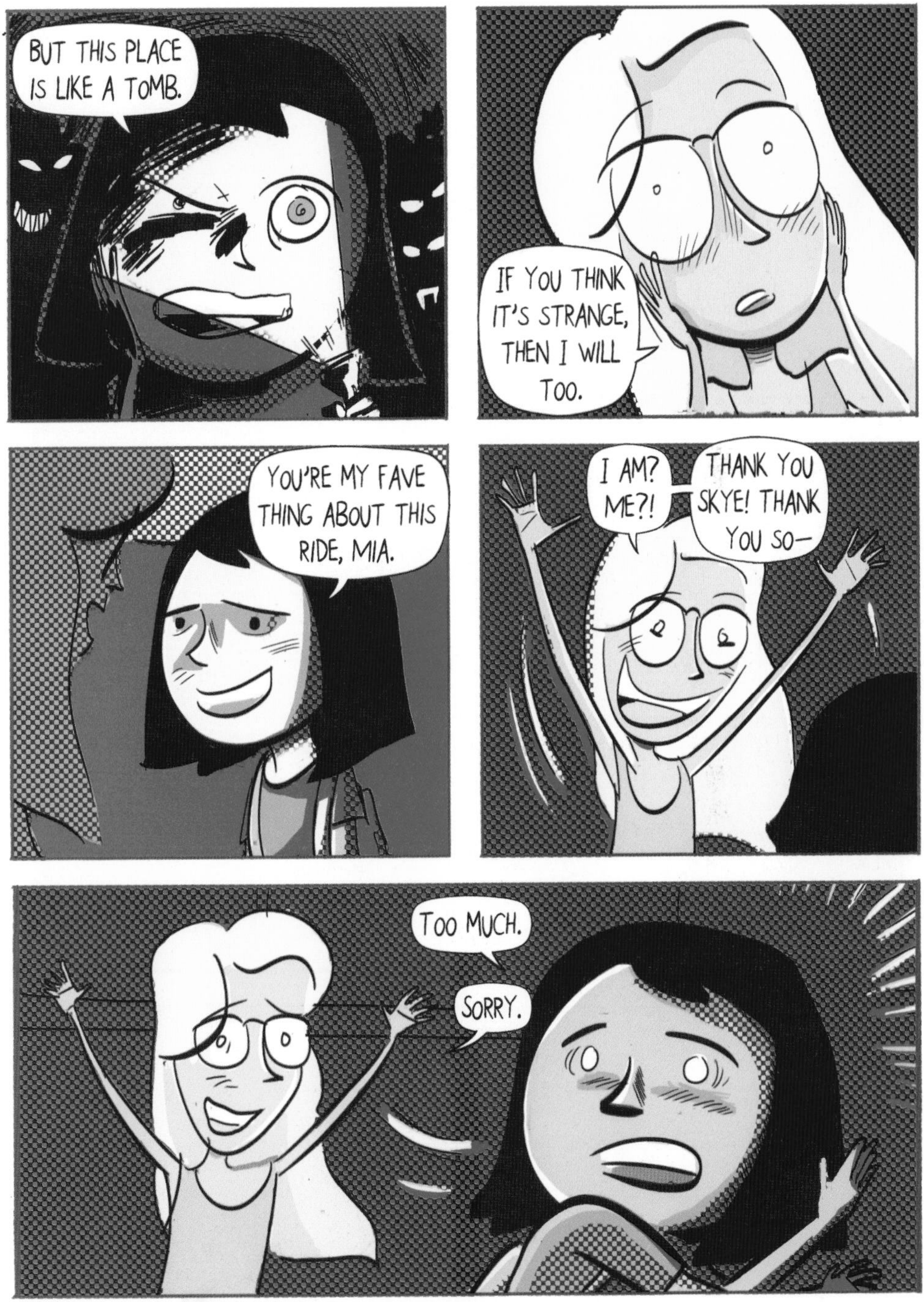

BUT THIS PLACE IS LIKE A TOMB.
IF YOU THINK IT'S STRANGE, THEN I WILL TOO.
YOU'RE MY FAVE THING ABOUT THIS RIDE, MIA.
I AM? ME?!
THANK YOU SKYE! THANK YOU SO—
TOO MUCH.
SORRY.

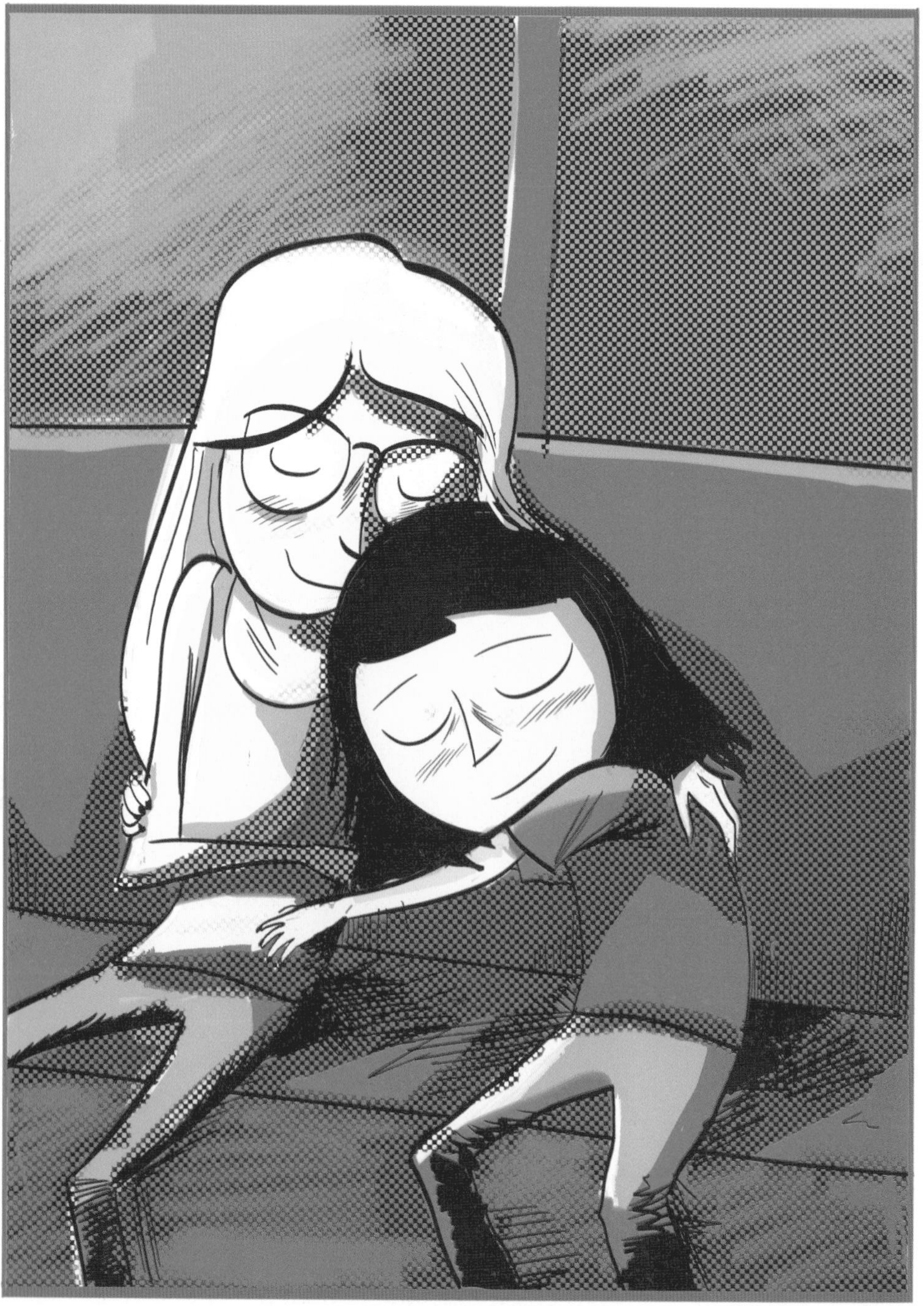

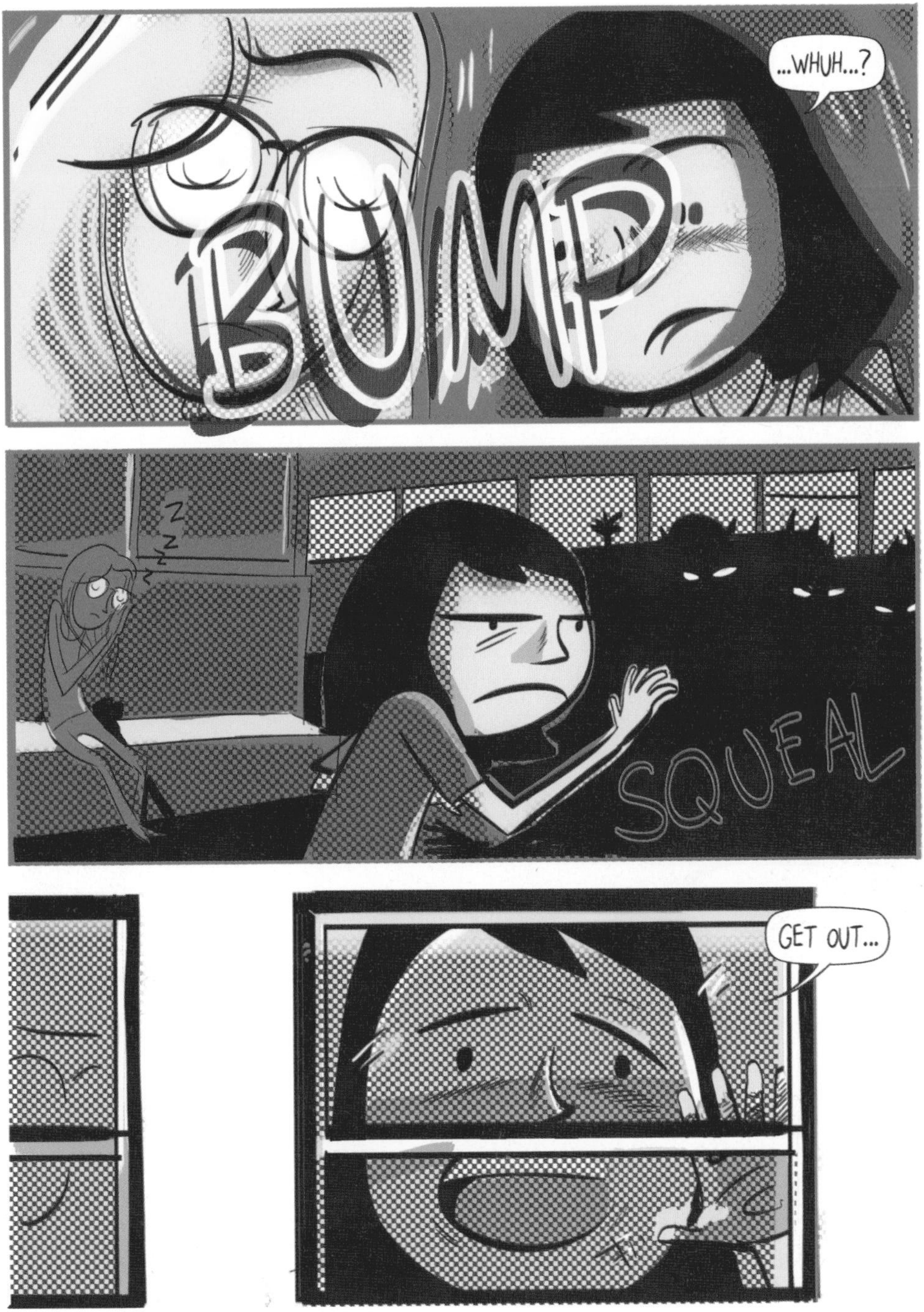
...WHUH...?
BUMP
SQUEAL
GET OUT...

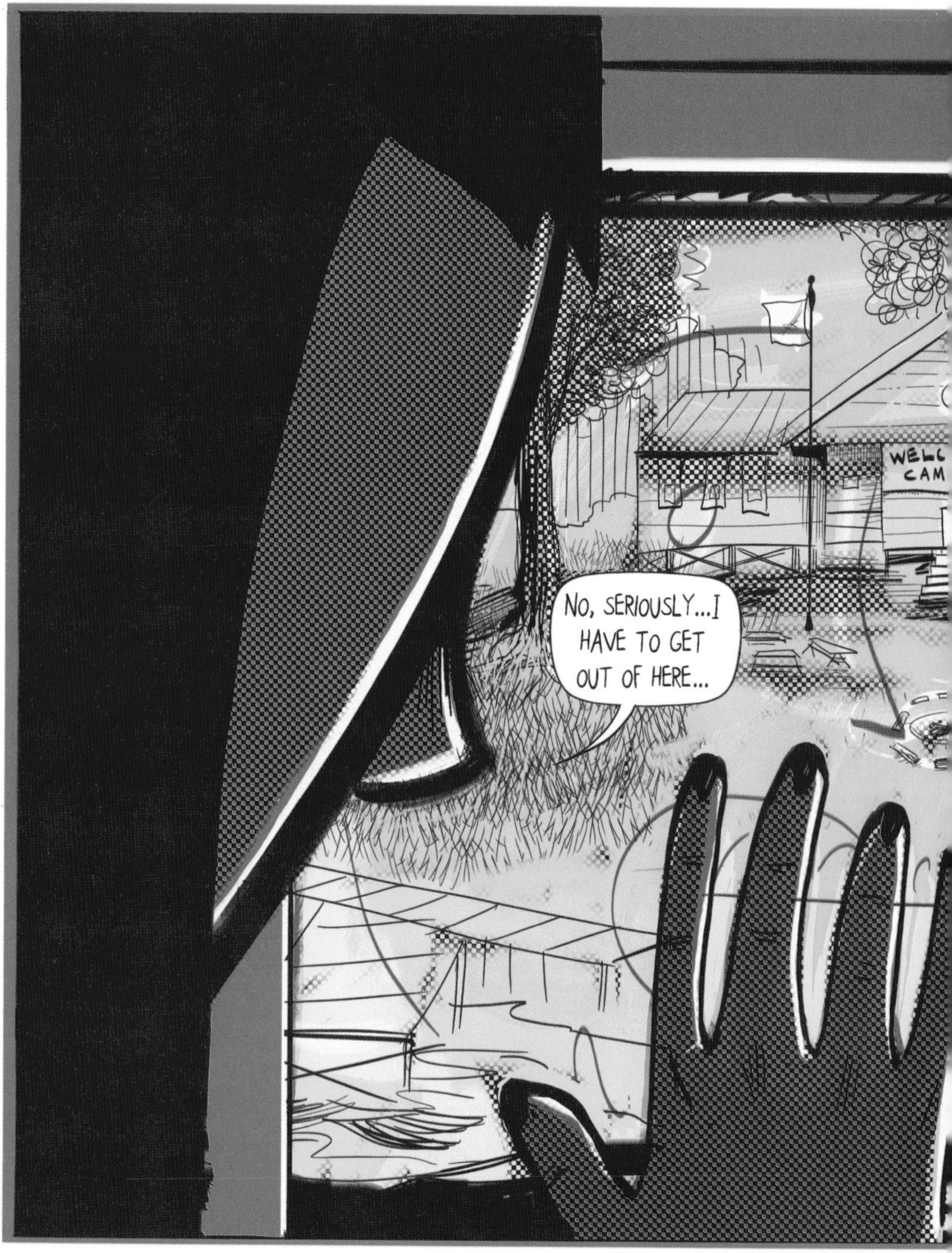
NO, SERIOUSLY...I HAVE TO GET OUT OF HERE...

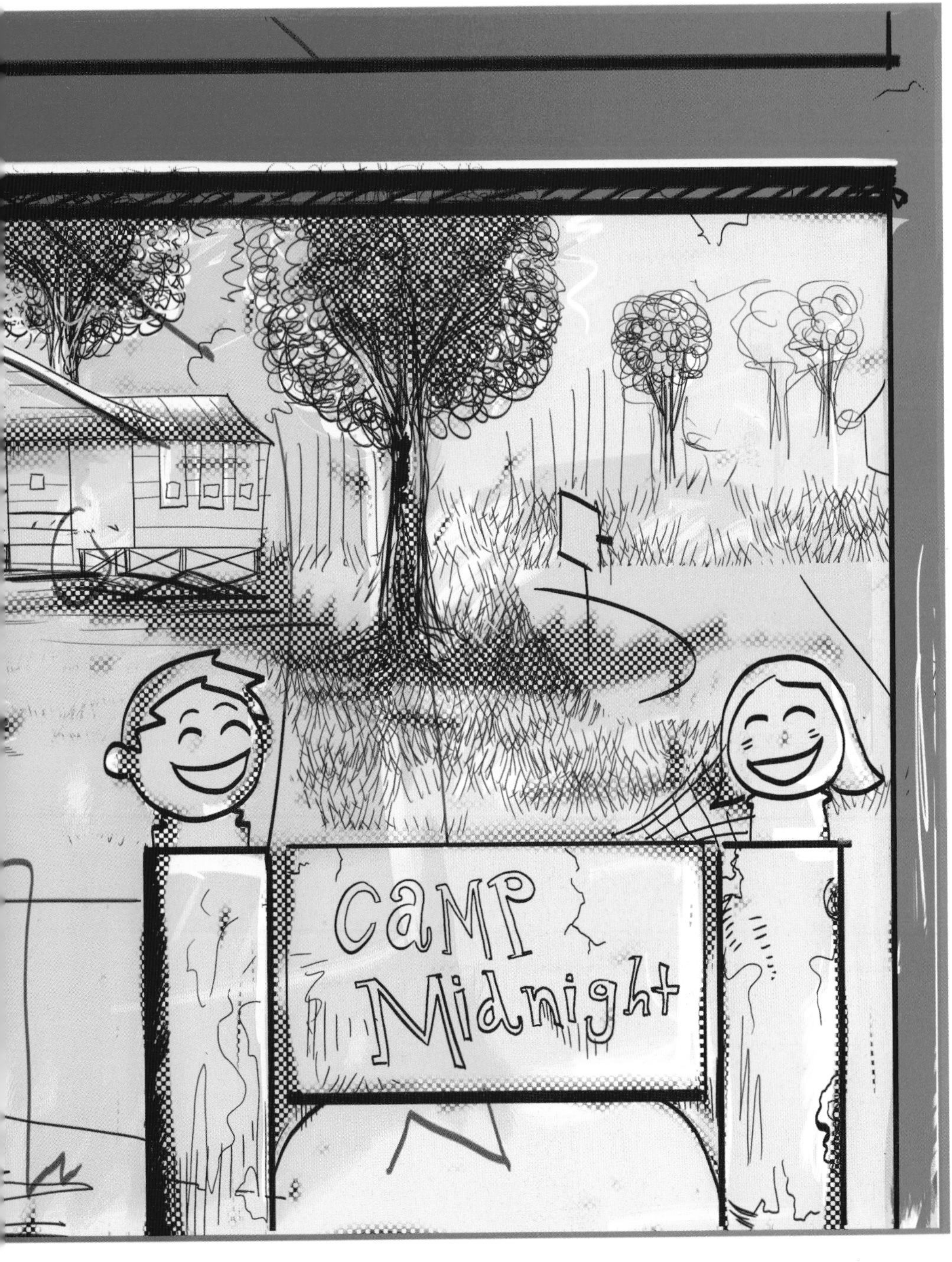
CAMP
Midnight

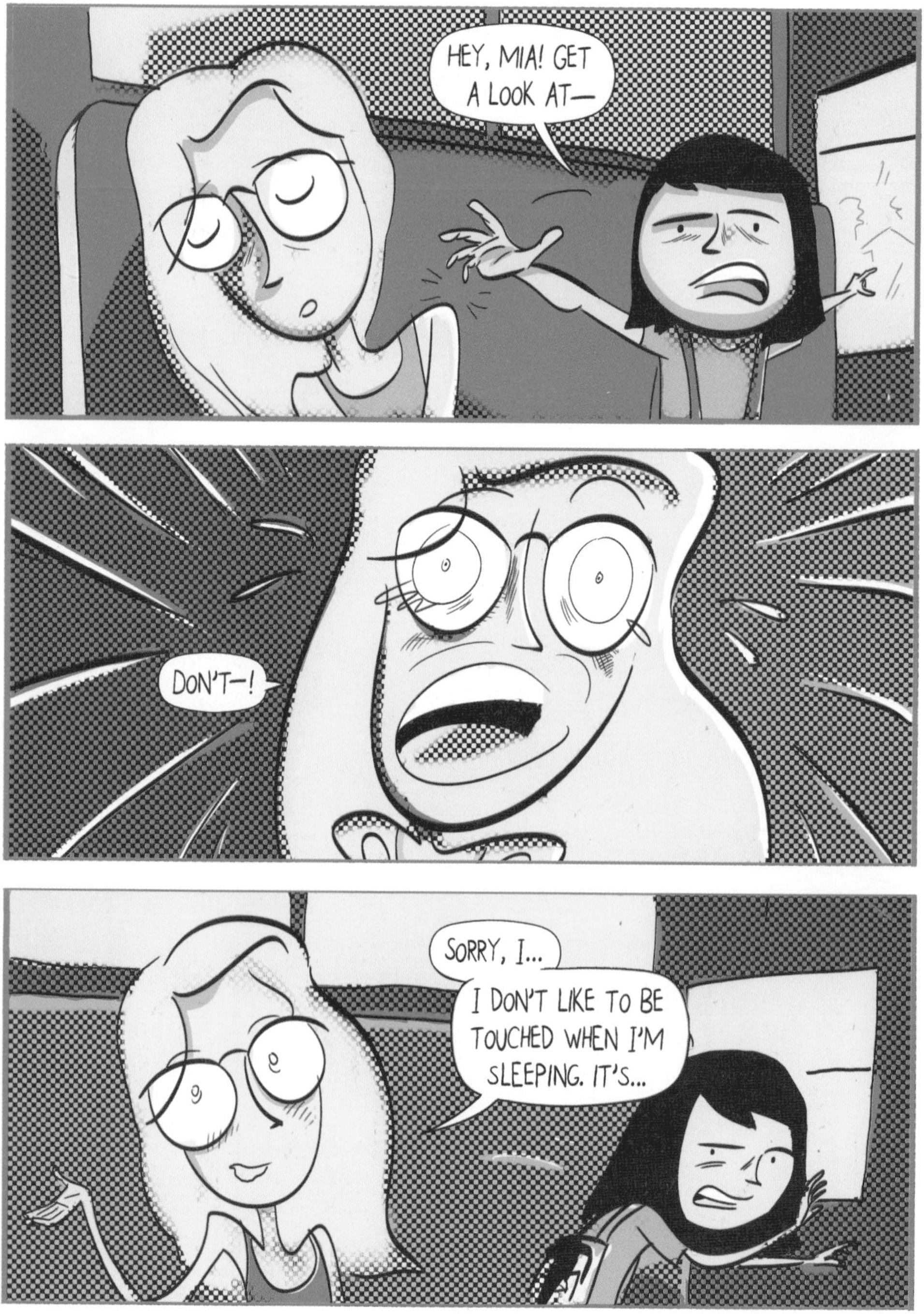
HEY, MIA! GET A LOOK AT—
DON'T—!
SORRY, I...
I DON'T LIKE TO BE TOUCHED WHEN I'M SLEEPING. IT'S...

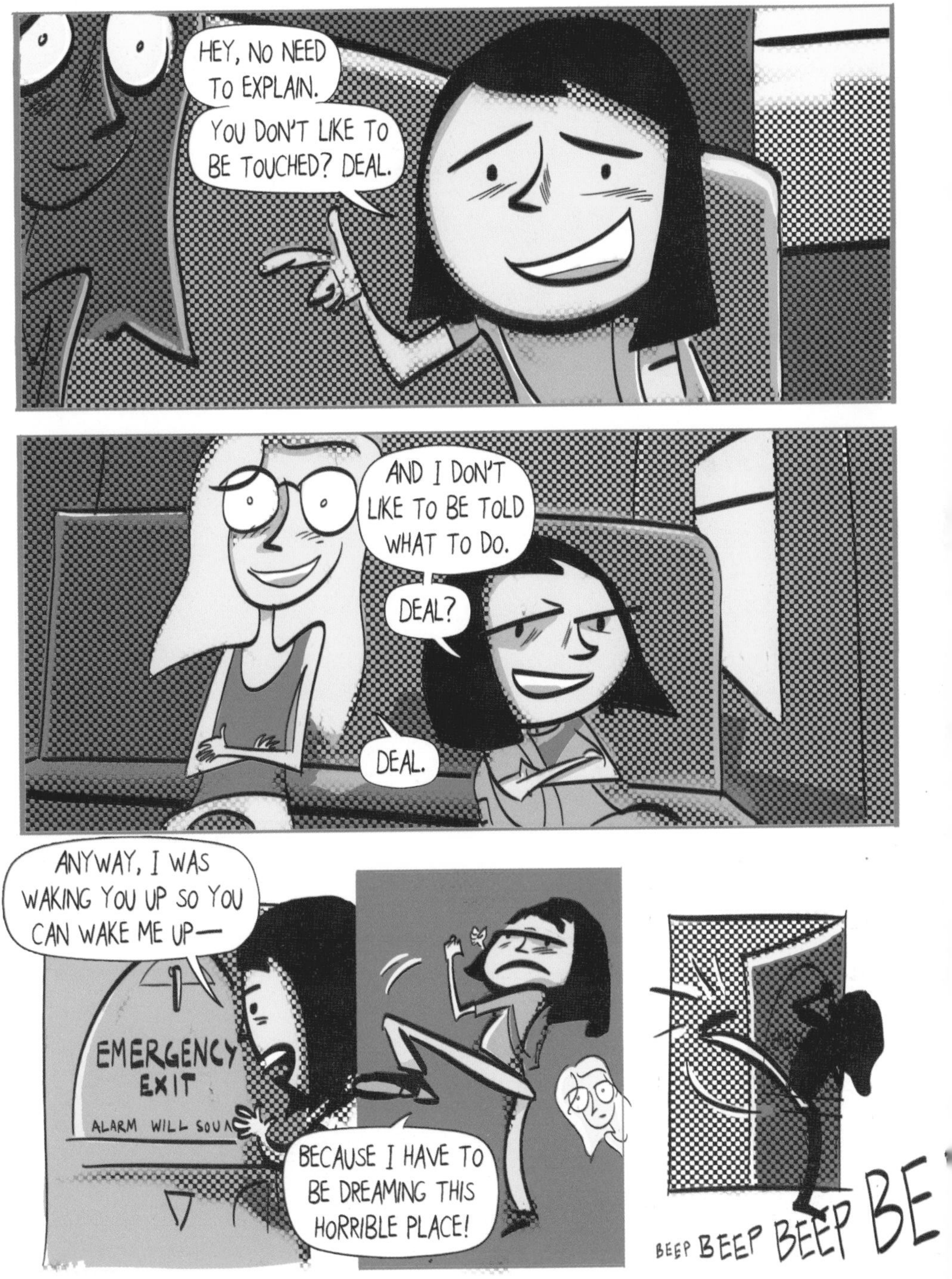

HEY, NO NEED TO EXPLAIN.
YOU DON'T LIKE TO BE TOUCHED? DEAL.
AND I DON'T LIKE TO BE TOLD WHAT TO DO.
DEAL?
DEAL.
ANYWAY, I WAS WAKING YOU UP SO YOU CAN WAKE ME UP—
EMERGENCY EXIT
ALARM WILL SOUN
BECAUSE I HAVE TO BE DREAMING THIS HORRIBLE PLACE!
BEEP BEEP BEEP BE

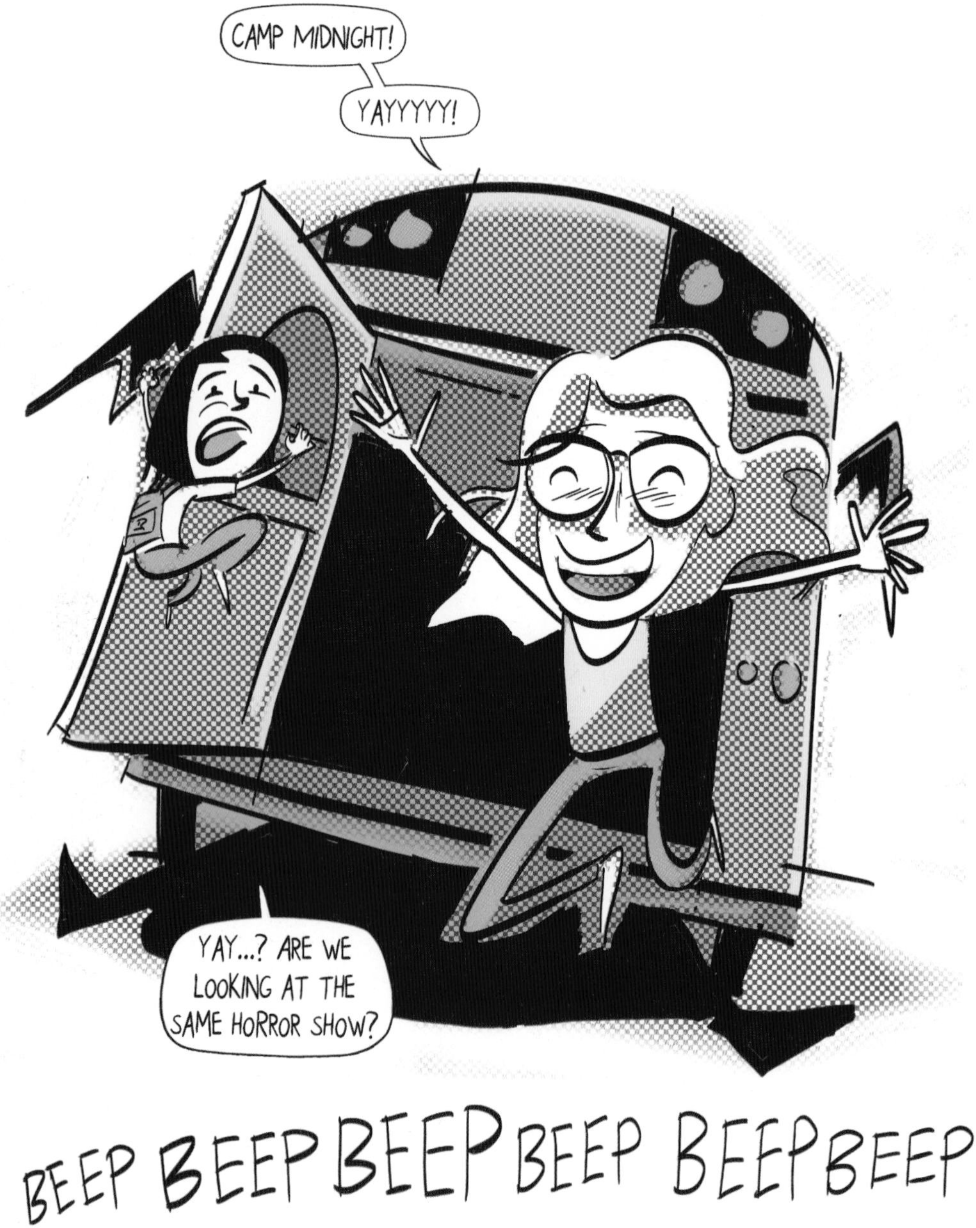
CAMP MIDNIGHT!
YAYYYYY!
YAY...? ARE WE LOOKING AT THE SAME HORROR SHOW?
BEEP BEEP BEEP BEEP BEEP BEEP

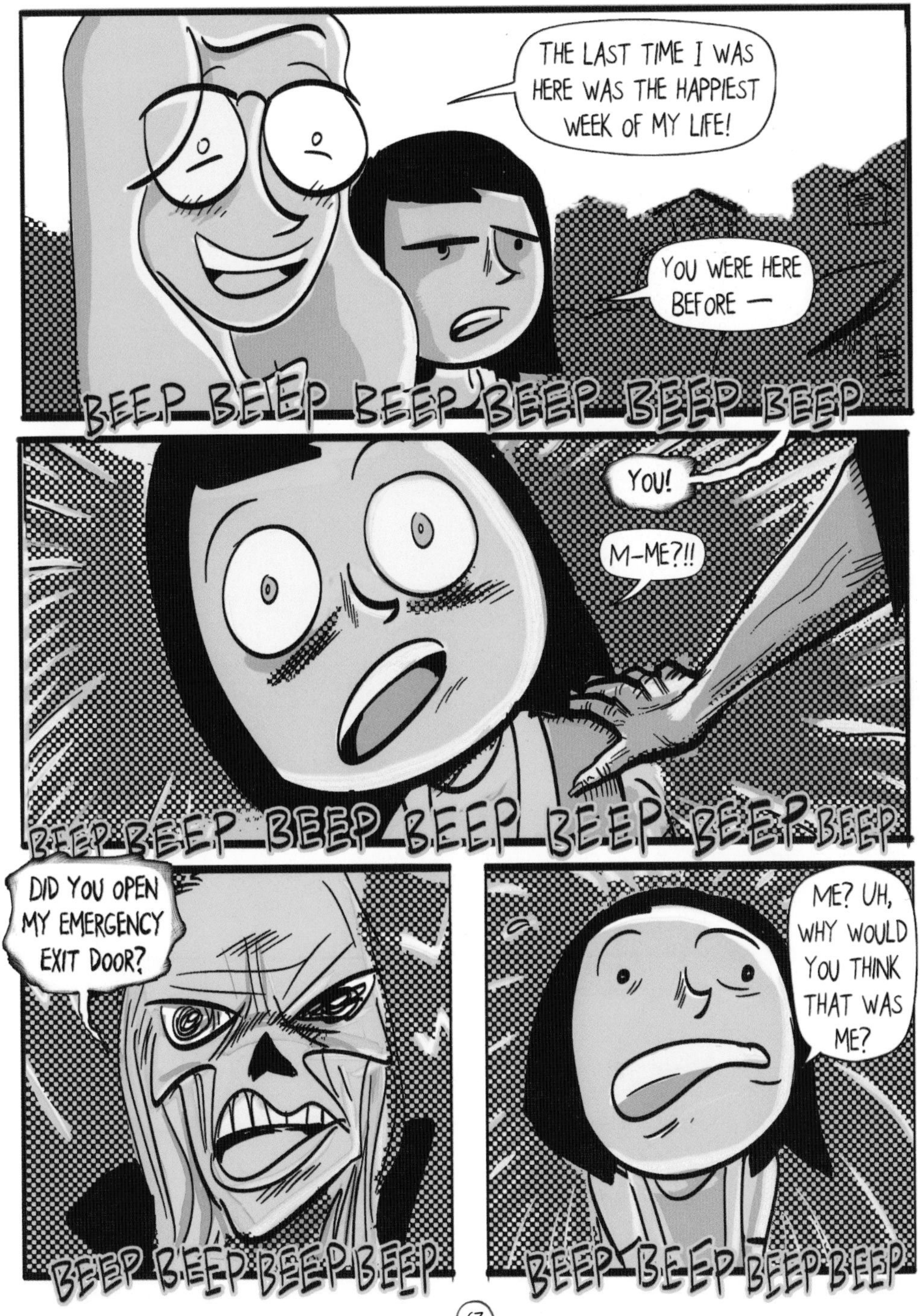
THE LAST TIME I WAS HERE WAS THE HAPPIEST WEEK OF MY LIFE!
YOU WERE HERE BEFORE —
BEEP BEEP BEEP BEEP BEEP BEEP
YOU!
M-ME?!!
BEEP BEEP BEEP BEEP BEEP BEEP BEEP
DID YOU OPEN MY EMERGENCY EXIT DOOR?
BEEP BEEP BEEP BEEP
ME? UH, WHY WOULD YOU THINK THAT WAS ME?
BEEP BEEP BEEP BEEP

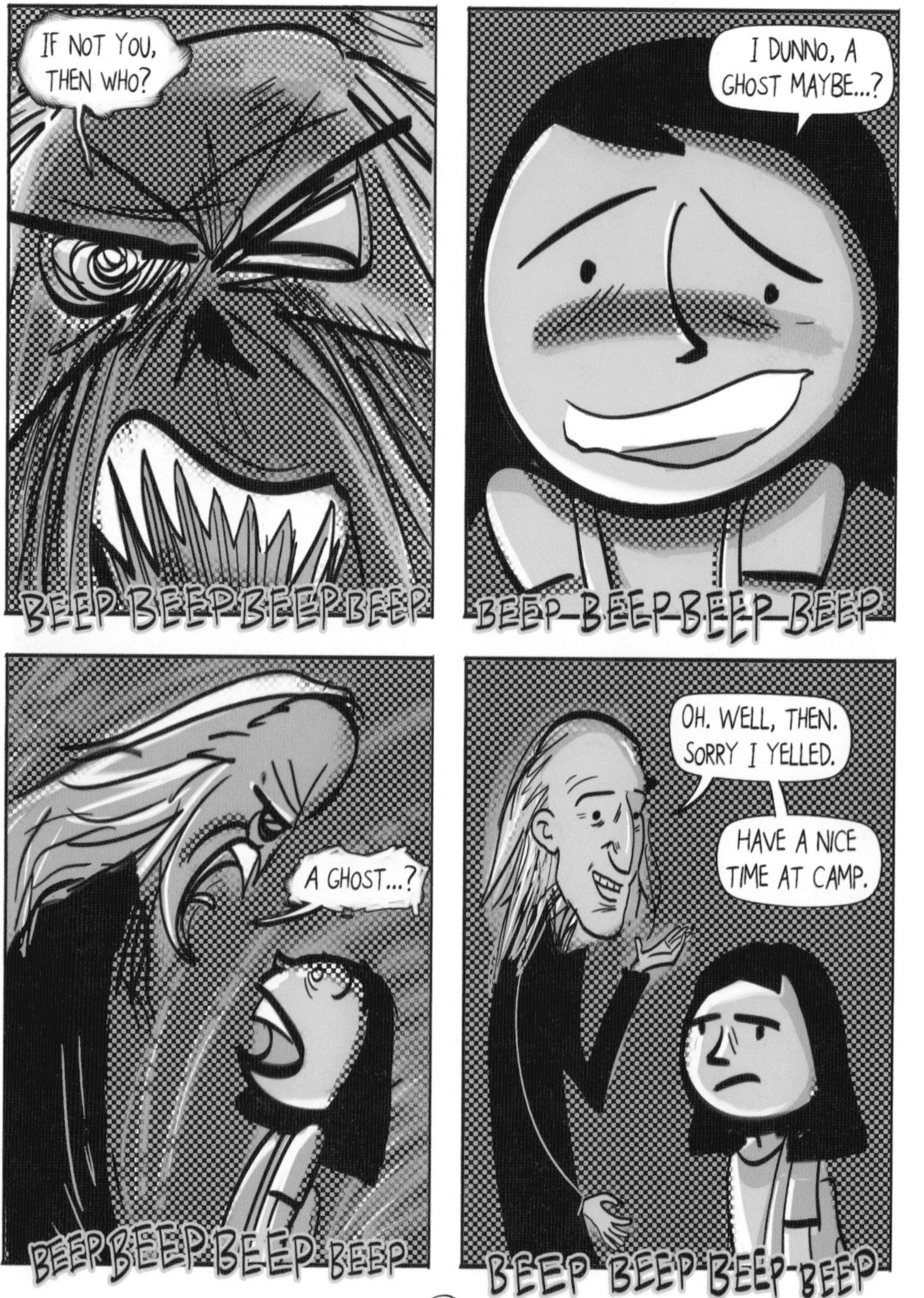
IF NOT YOU, THEN WHO?
BEEP BEEP BEEP BEEP
I DUNNO, A GHOST MAYBE...?
BEEP BEEP BEEP BEEP
A GHOST...?
BEEP BEEP BEEP BEEP
OH. WELL, THEN. SORRY I YELLED.
HAVE A NICE TIME AT CAMP.
BEEP BEEP BEEP BEEP

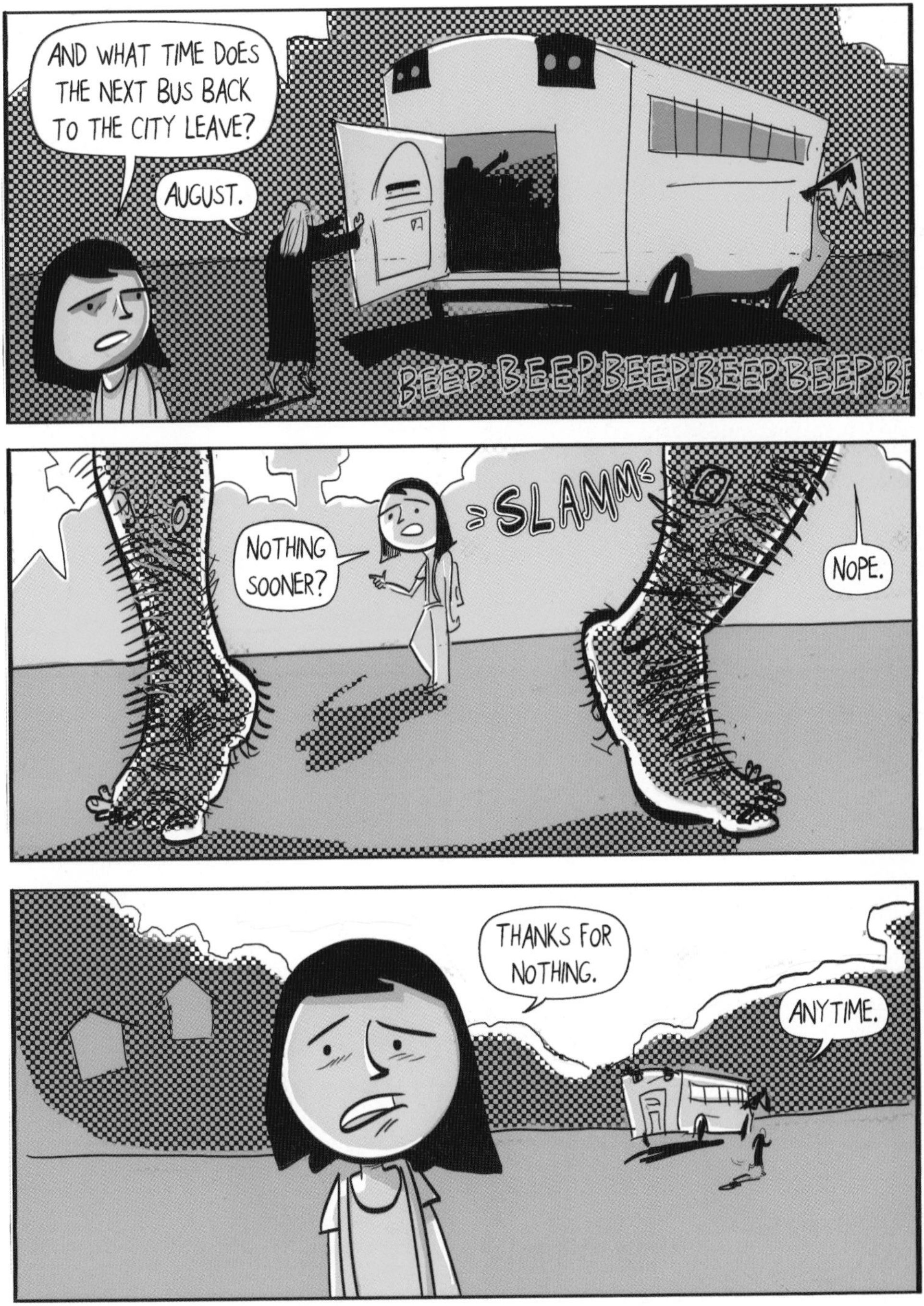
AND WHAT TIME DOES THE NEXT BUS BACK TO THE CITY LEAVE?
AUGUST.
BEEP BEEP BEEP BEEP BEEP BE
NOTHING SOONER?
SLAMM
NOPE.
THANKS FOR NOTHING.
ANYTIME.

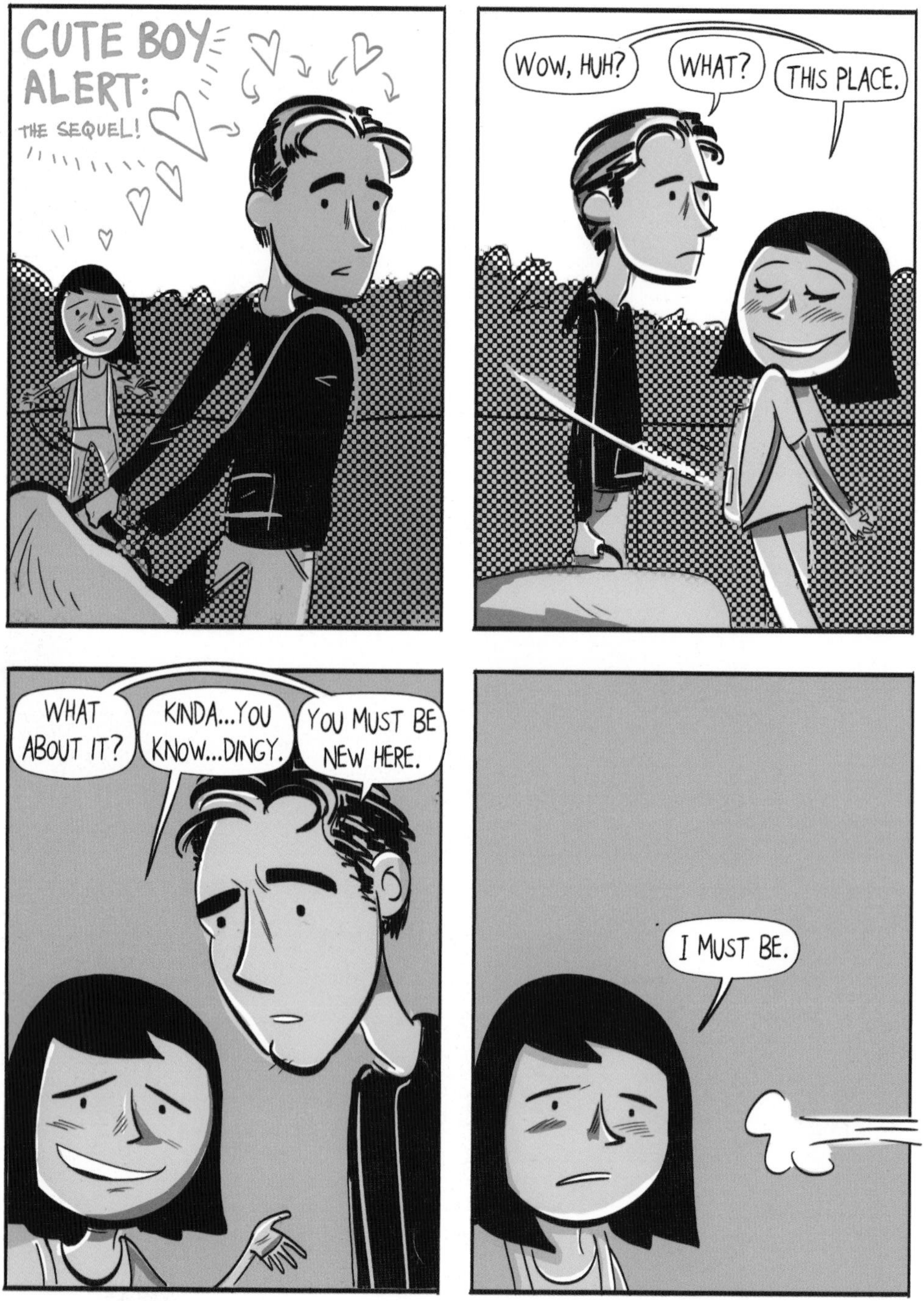
CUTE BOY ALERT:
THE SEQUEL!
WOW, HUH?
WHAT?
THIS PLACE.
WHAT ABOUT IT?
KINDA...YOU KNOW...DINGY.
YOU MUST BE NEW HERE.
I MUST BE.

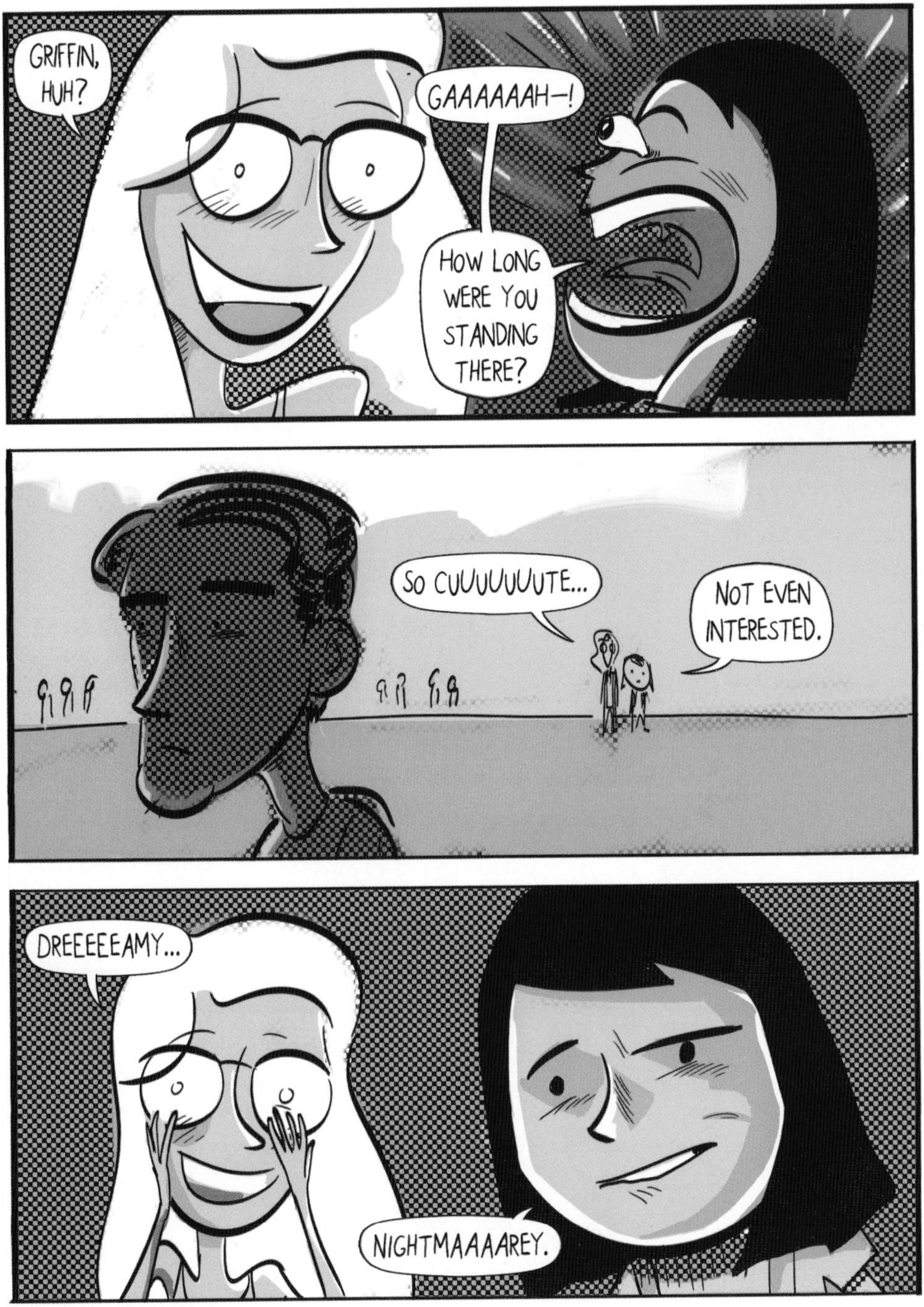
GRIFFIN, HUH?
GAAAAAAH—!
HOW LONG WERE YOU STANDING THERE?
SO CUUUUUUUTE...
NOT EVEN INTERESTED.
DREEEEEAMY...
NIGHTMAAAAREY.

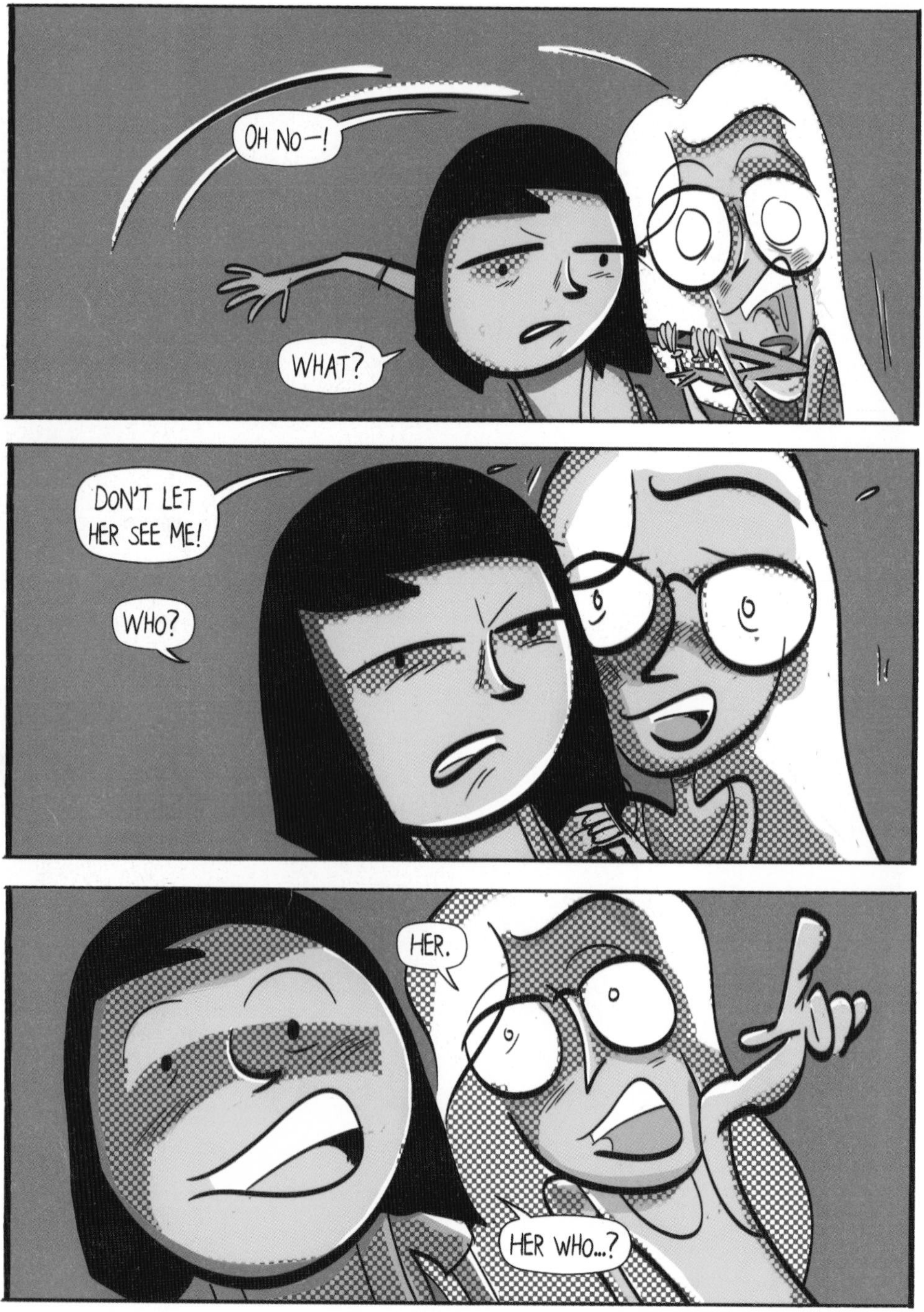
OH NO—!
WHAT?
DON'T LET HER SEE ME!
WHO?
HER.
HER WHO...?

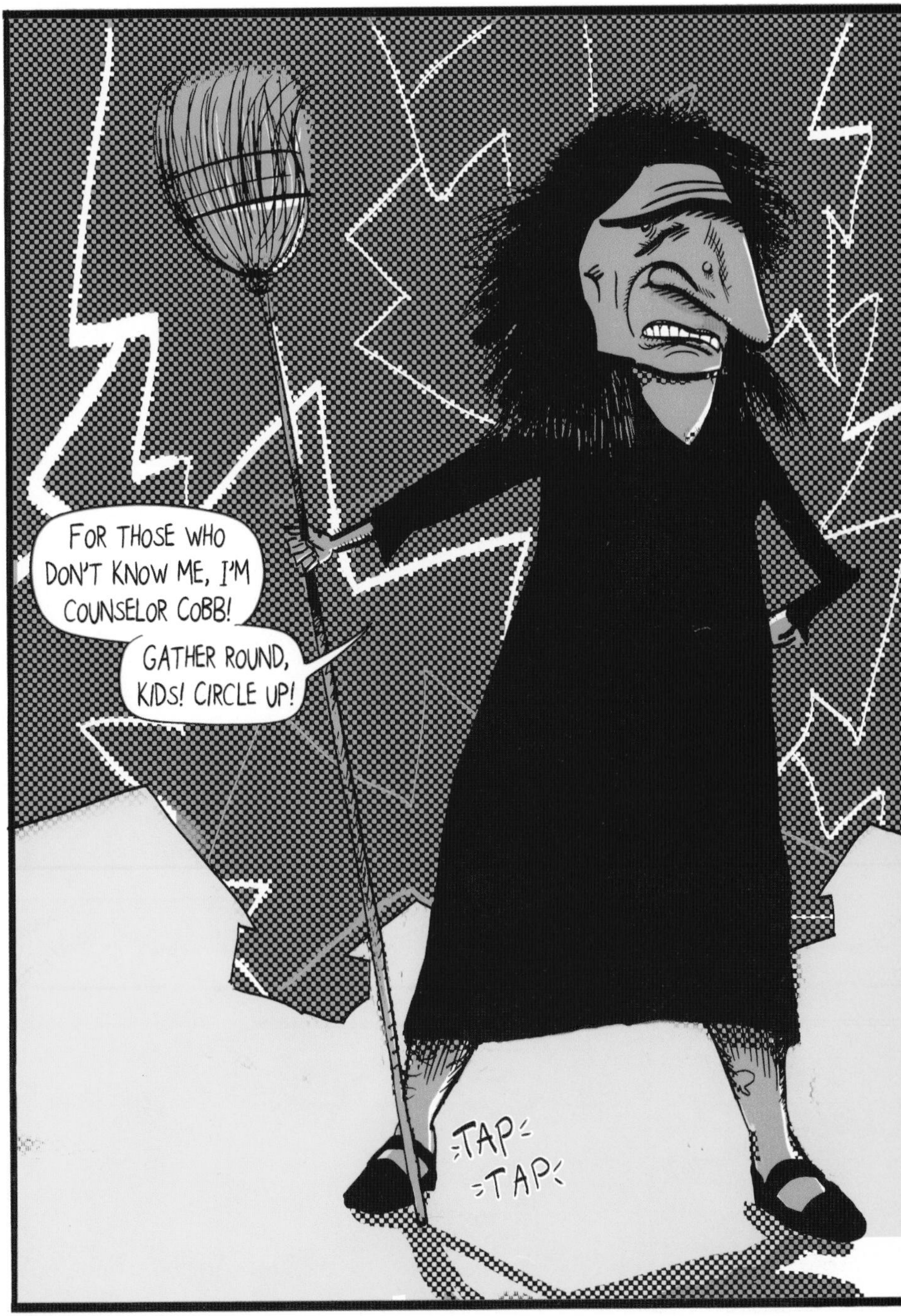
FOR THOSE WHO DON'T KNOW ME, I'M COUNSELOR COBB!
GATHER ROUND, KIDS! CIRCLE UP!
TAP
TAP

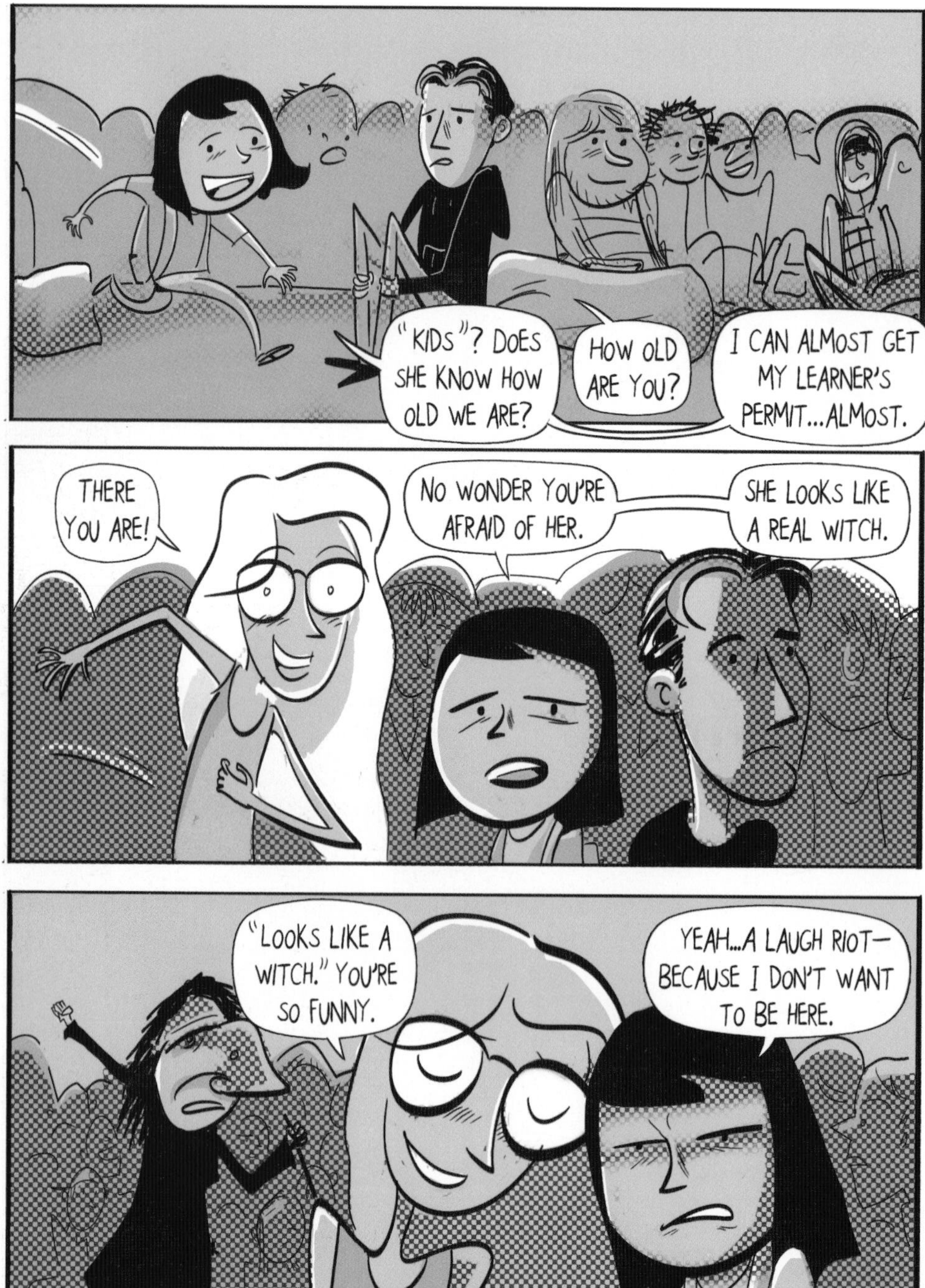
"KIDS"? DOES SHE KNOW HOW OLD WE ARE?
HOW OLD ARE YOU?
I CAN ALMOST GET MY LEARNER'S PERMIT...ALMOST.
THERE YOU ARE!
NO WONDER YOU'RE AFRAID OF HER.
SHE LOOKS LIKE A REAL WITCH.
"LOOKS LIKE A WITCH." YOU'RE SO FUNNY.
YEAH...A LAUGH RIOT—BECAUSE I DON'T WANT TO BE HERE.

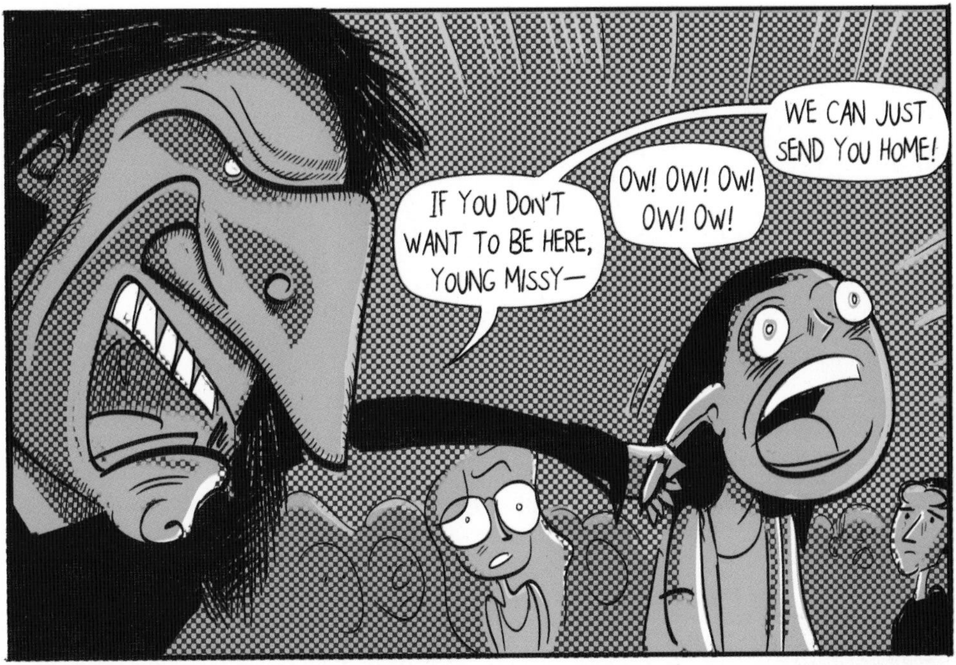
IF YOU DON'T WANT TO BE HERE, YOUNG MISSY—
OW! OW! OW! OW! OW!
WE CAN JUST SEND YOU HOME!

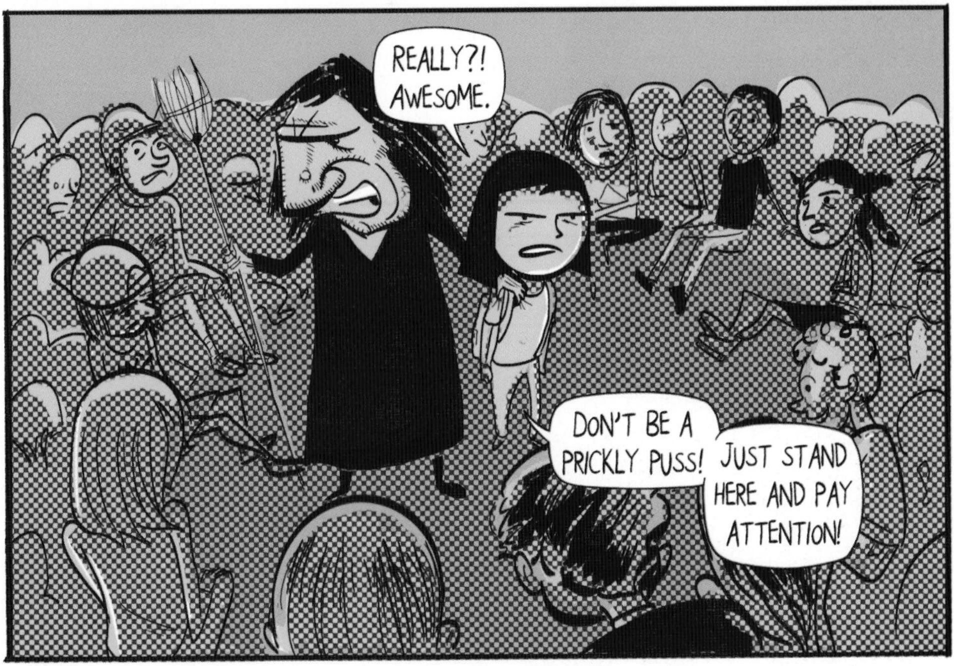
REALLY?! AWESOME.
DON'T BE A PRICKLY PUSS!
JUST STAND HERE AND PAY ATTENTION!

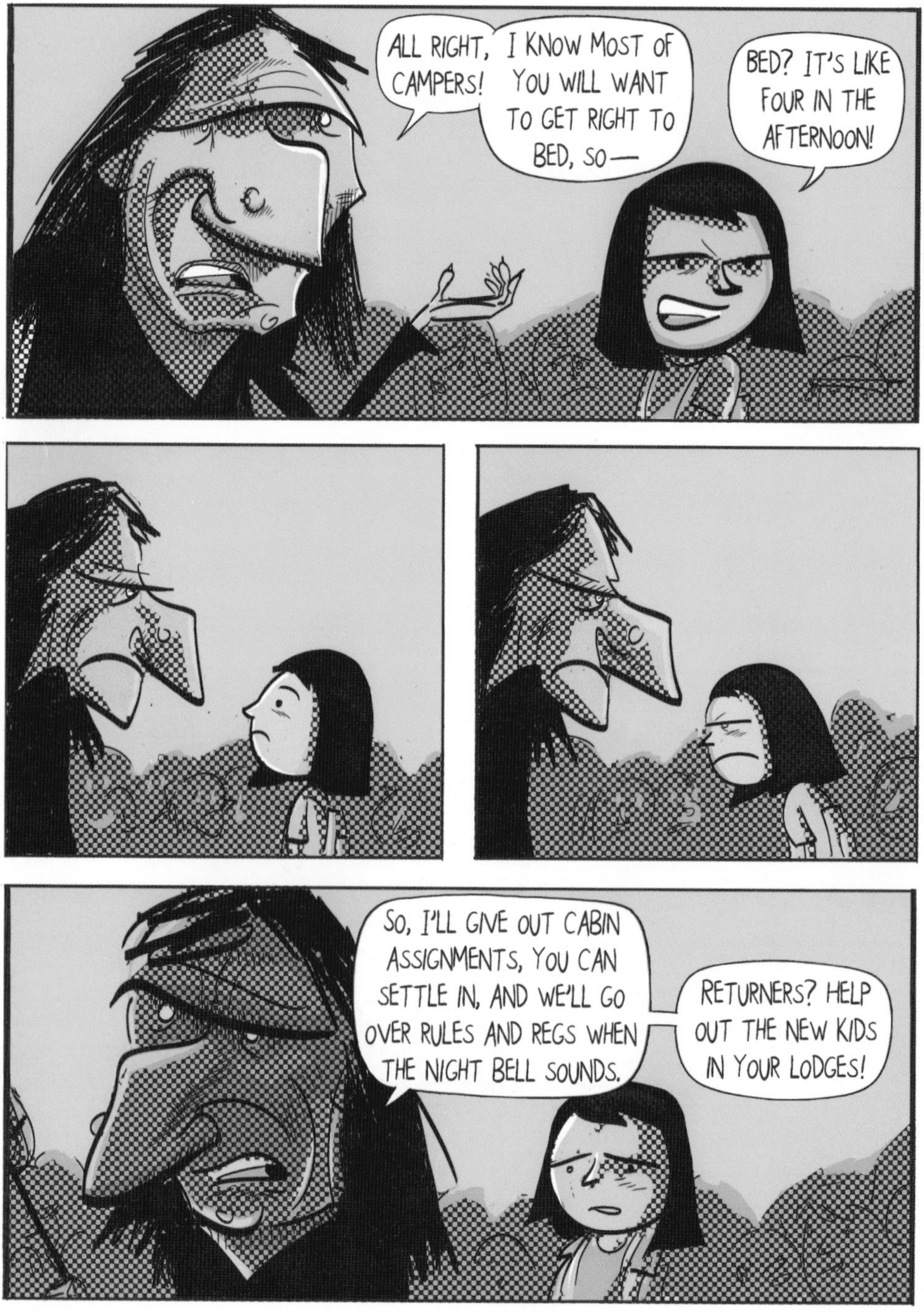
ALL RIGHT, CAMPERS!
I KNOW MOST OF YOU WILL WANT TO GET RIGHT TO BED, SO—
BED? IT'S LIKE FOUR IN THE AFTERNOON!
SO, I'LL GIVE OUT CABIN ASSIGNMENTS, YOU CAN SETTLE IN, AND WE'LL GO OVER RULES AND REGS WHEN THE NIGHT BELL SOUNDS.
RETURNERS? HELP OUT THE NEW KIDS IN YOUR LODGES!

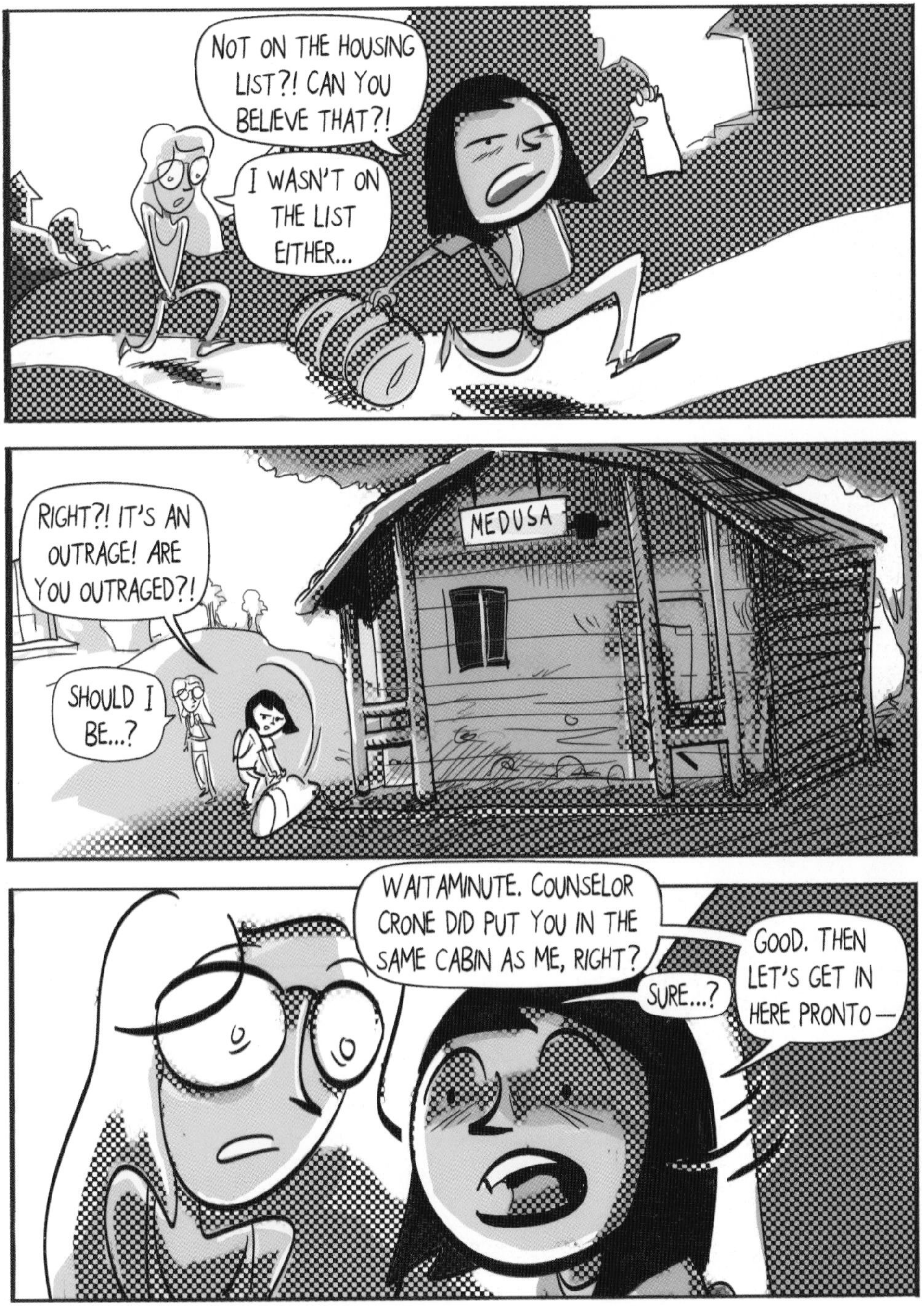
NOT ON THE HOUSING LIST?! CAN YOU BELIEVE THAT?!
I WASN'T ON THE LIST EITHER...
MEDUSA
RIGHT?! IT'S AN OUTRAGE! ARE YOU OUTRAGED?!
SHOULD I BE...?
WAITAMINUTE. COUNSELOR CRONE DID PUT YOU IN THE SAME CABIN AS ME, RIGHT?
SURE...?
GOOD. THEN LET'S GET IN HERE PRONTO—

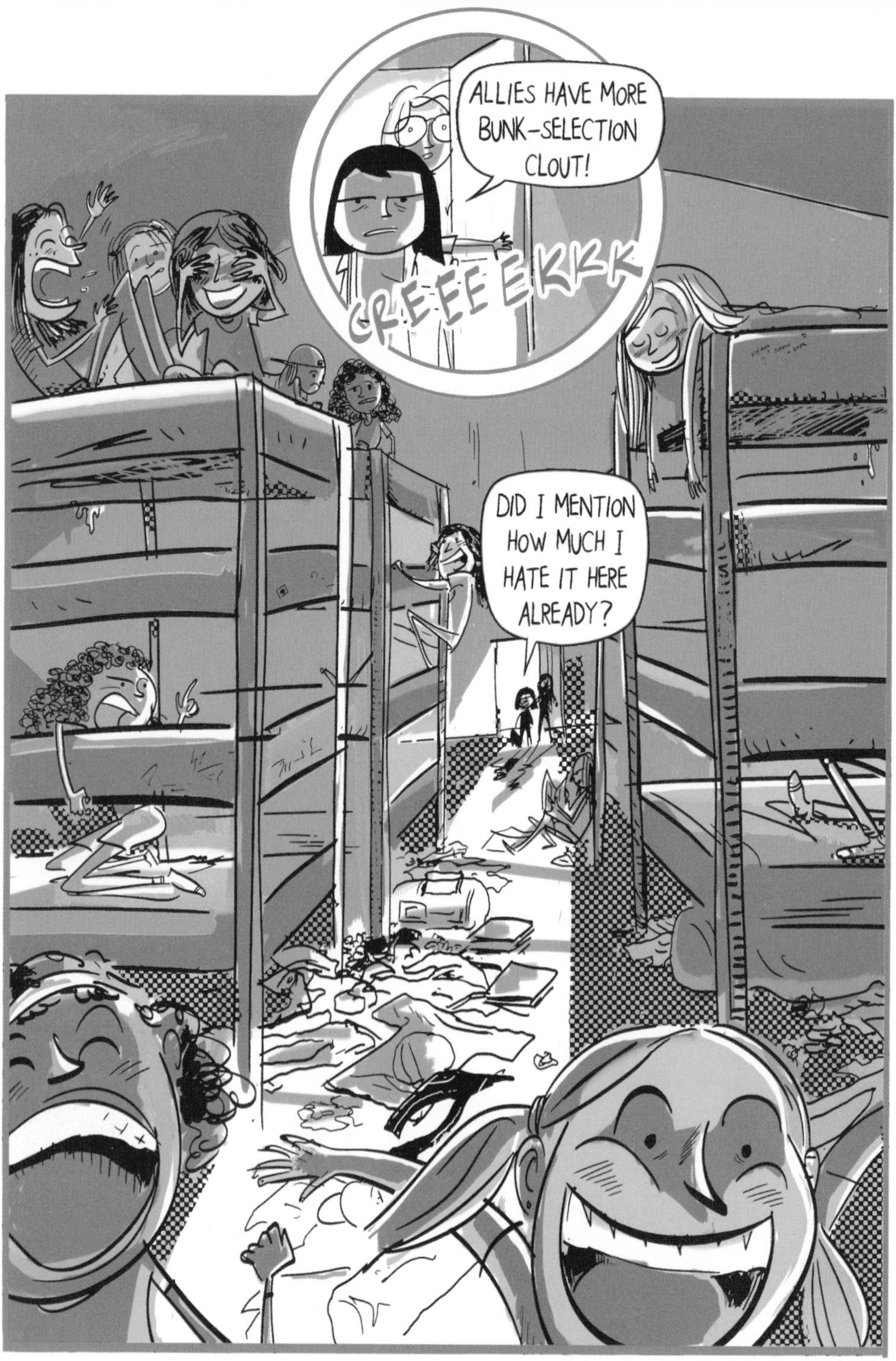
ALLIES HAVE MORE BUNK-SELECTION CLOUT!
CREEEEKKK
DID I MENTION HOW MUCH I HATE IT HERE ALREADY?

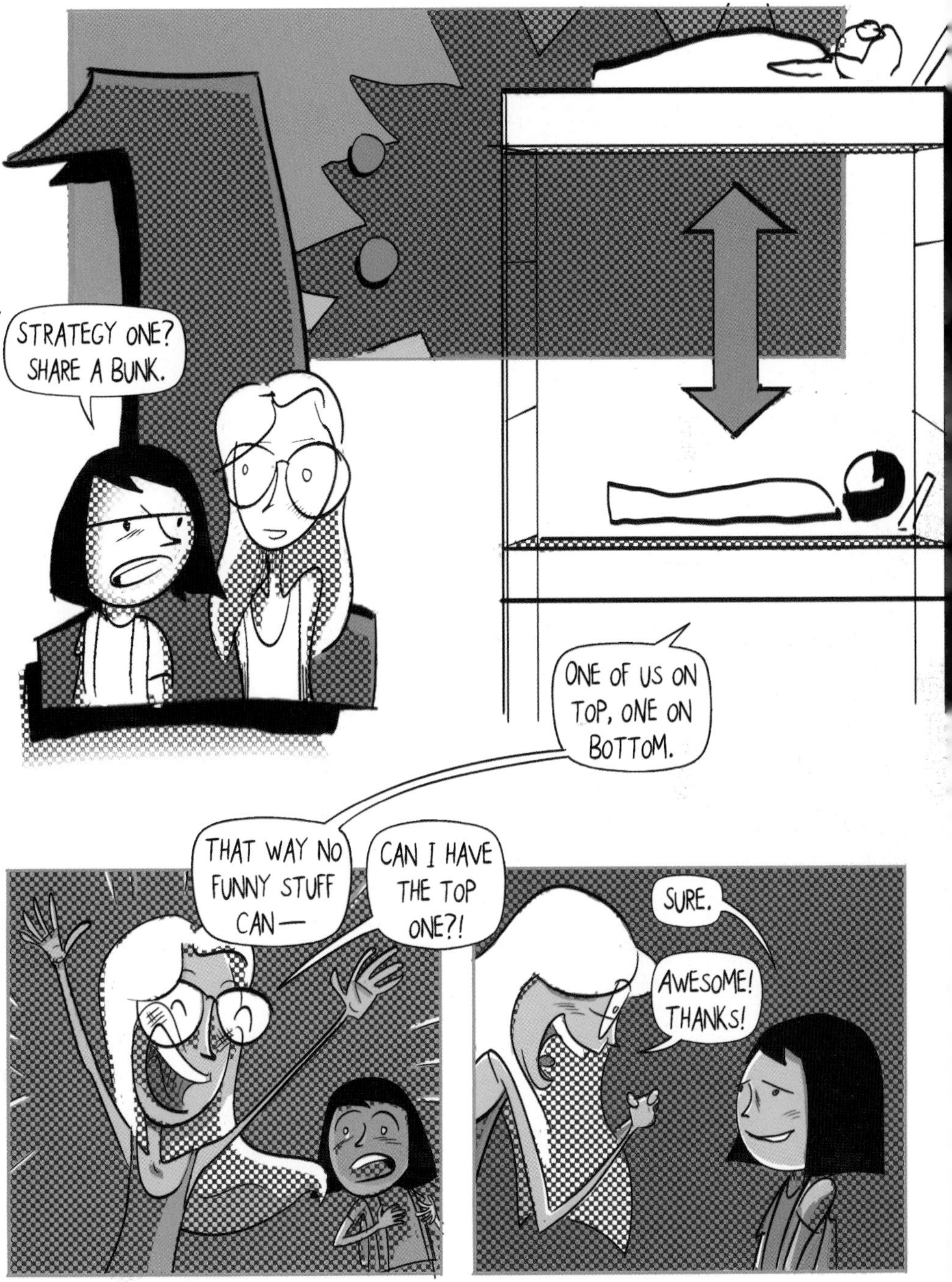
STRATEGY ONE? SHARE A BUNK.
ONE OF US ON TOP, ONE ON BOTTOM.
THAT WAY NO FUNNY STUFF CAN—
CAN I HAVE THE TOP ONE?!
SURE.
AWESOME! THANKS!

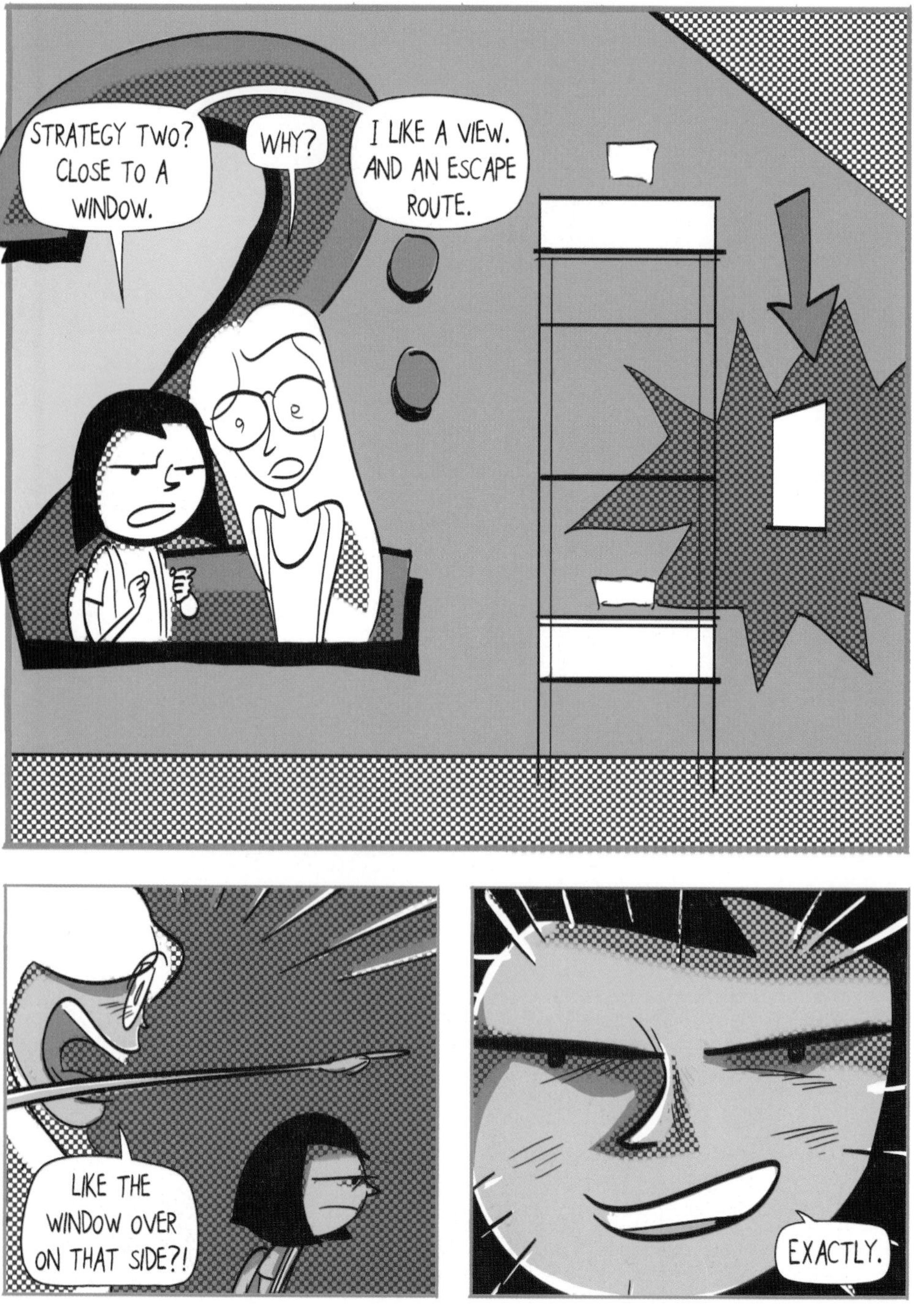
STRATEGY TWO? CLOSE TO A WINDOW.
WHY?
I LIKE A VIEW. AND AN ESCAPE ROUTE.
LIKE THE WINDOW OVER ON THAT SIDE?!
EXACTLY.

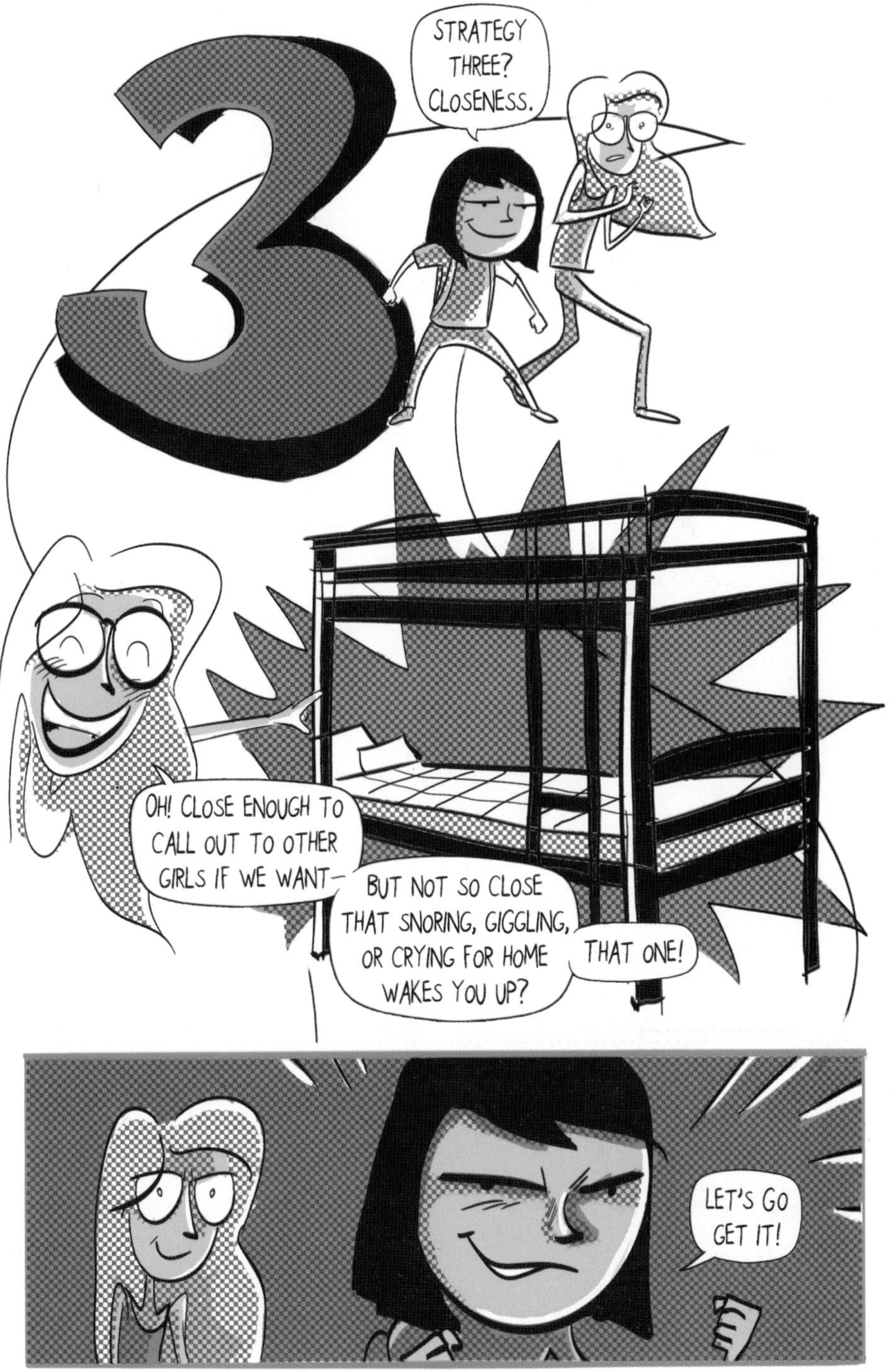
STRATEGY THREE? CLOSENESS.
OH! CLOSE ENOUGH TO CALL OUT TO OTHER GIRLS IF WE WANT—
BUT NOT SO CLOSE THAT SNORING, GIGGLING, OR CRYING FOR HOME WAKES YOU UP?
THAT ONE!
LET'S GO GET IT!

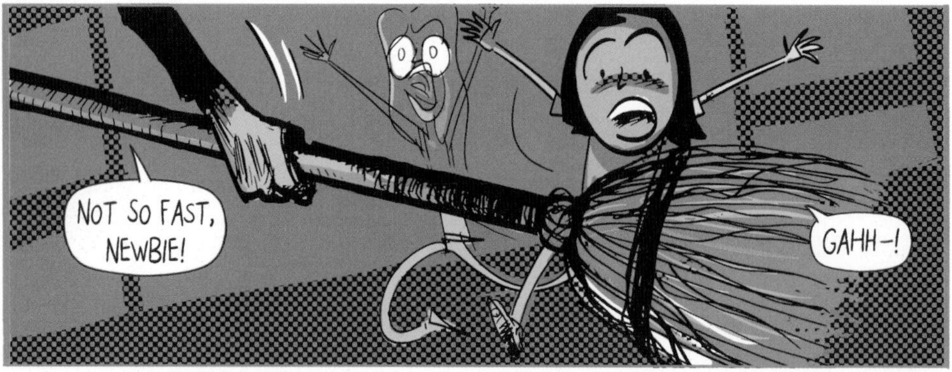
NOT SO FAST, NEWBIE!
GAHH-!

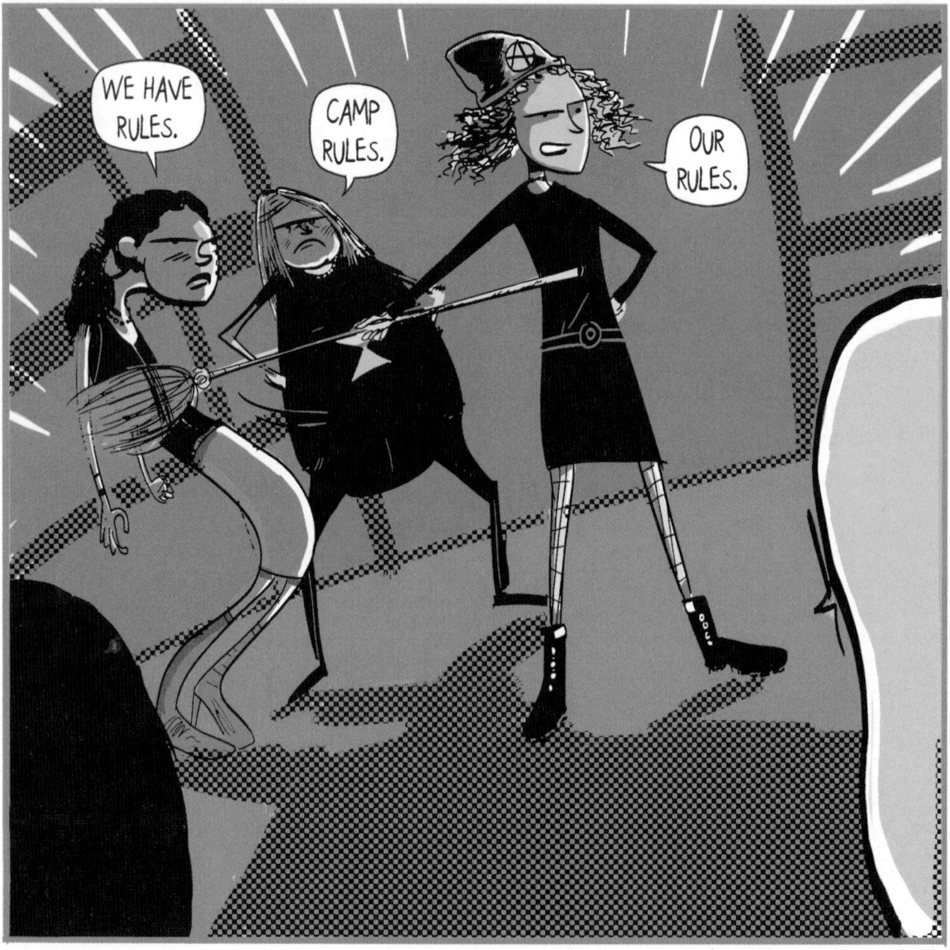
WE HAVE RULES.
CAMP RULES.
OUR RULES.

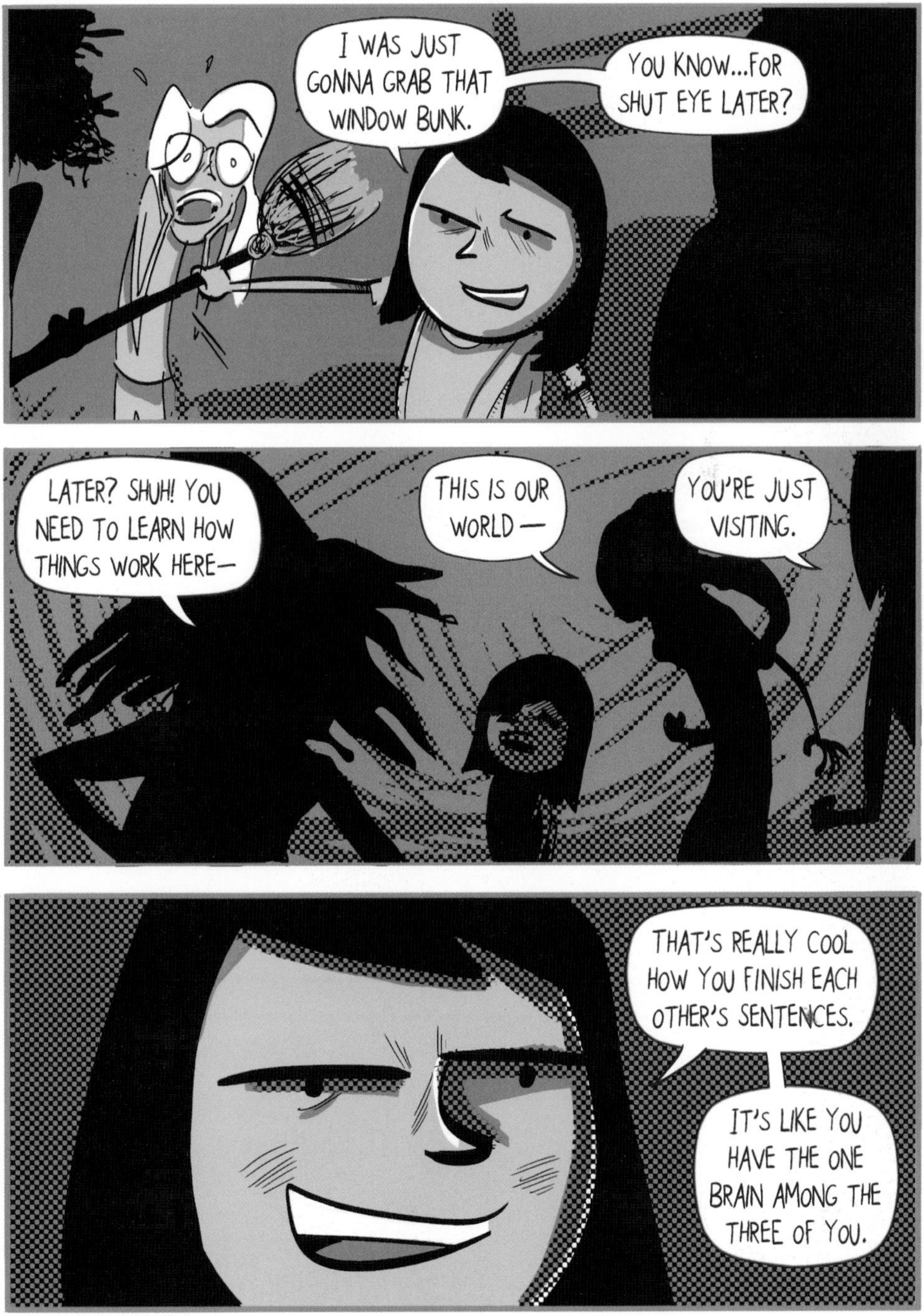
I WAS JUST GONNA GRAB THAT WINDOW BUNK.
YOU KNOW...FOR SHUT EYE LATER?
LATER? SHUH! YOU NEED TO LEARN HOW THINGS WORK HERE—
THIS IS OUR WORLD—
YOU'RE JUST VISITING.
THAT'S REALLY COOL HOW YOU FINISH EACH OTHER'S SENTENCES.
IT'S LIKE YOU HAVE THE ONE BRAIN AMONG THE THREE OF YOU.

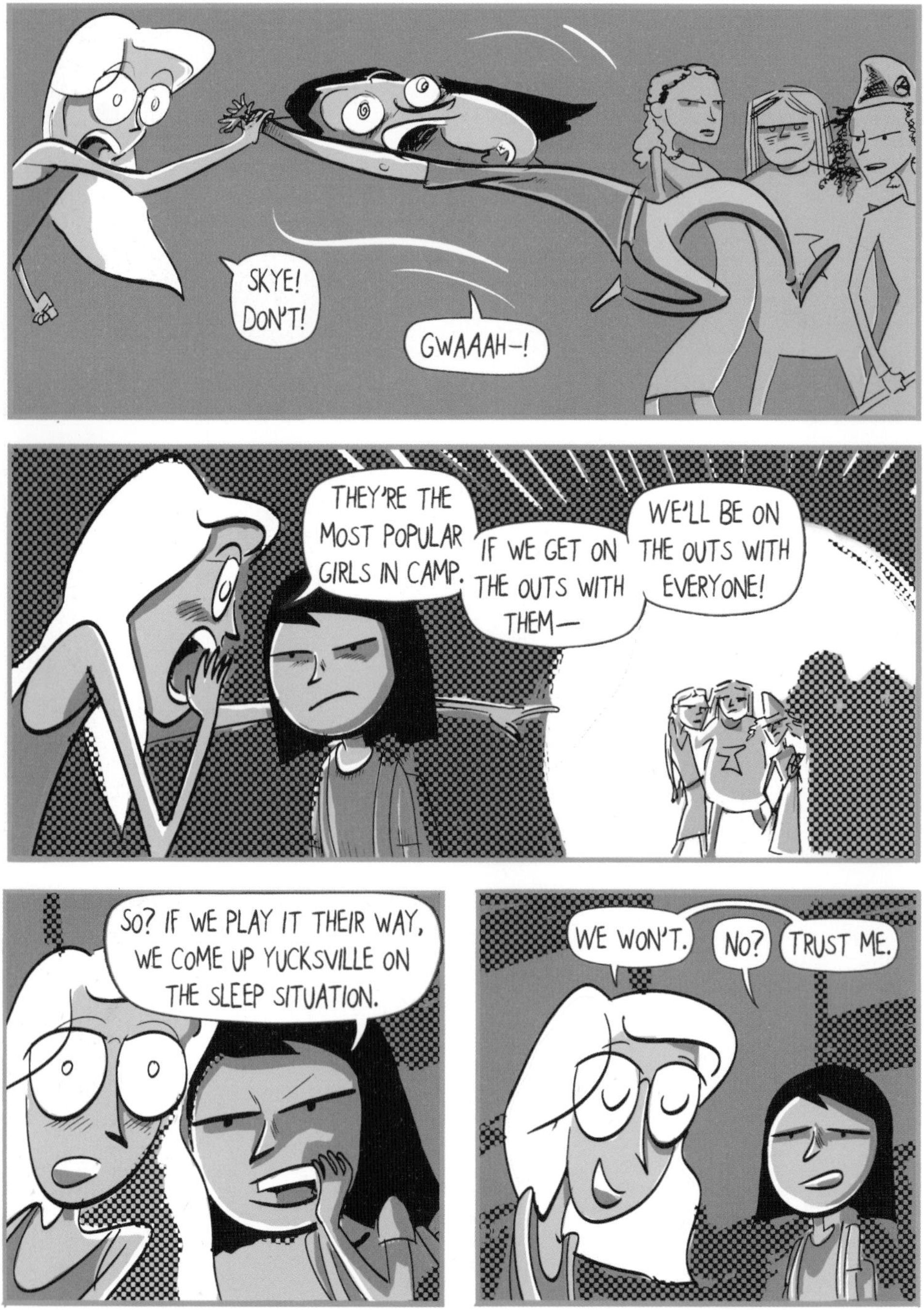
SKYE! DON'T!
GWAAAH–!
THEY'RE THE MOST POPULAR GIRLS IN CAMP.
IF WE GET ON THE OUTS WITH THEM—
WE'LL BE ON THE OUTS WITH EVERYONE!
SO? IF WE PLAY IT THEIR WAY, WE COME UP YUCKSVILLE ON THE SLEEP SITUATION.
WE WON'T.
NO?
TRUST ME.

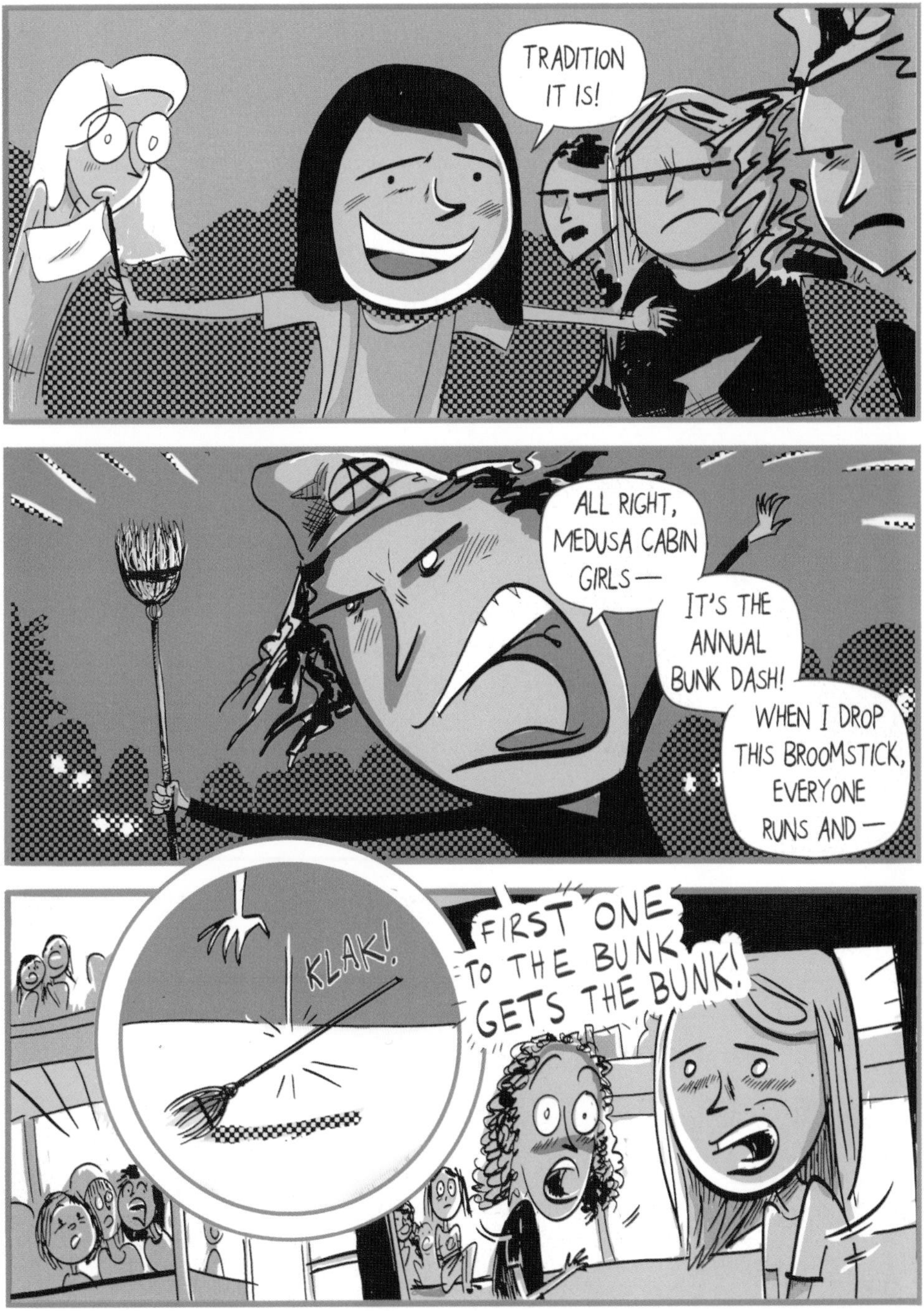
TRADITION IT IS!
ALL RIGHT, MEDUSA CABIN GIRLS—
IT'S THE ANNUAL BUNK DASH!
WHEN I DROP THIS BROOMSTICK, EVERYONE RUNS AND—
KLAK!
FIRST ONE TO THE BUNK GETS THE BUNK!

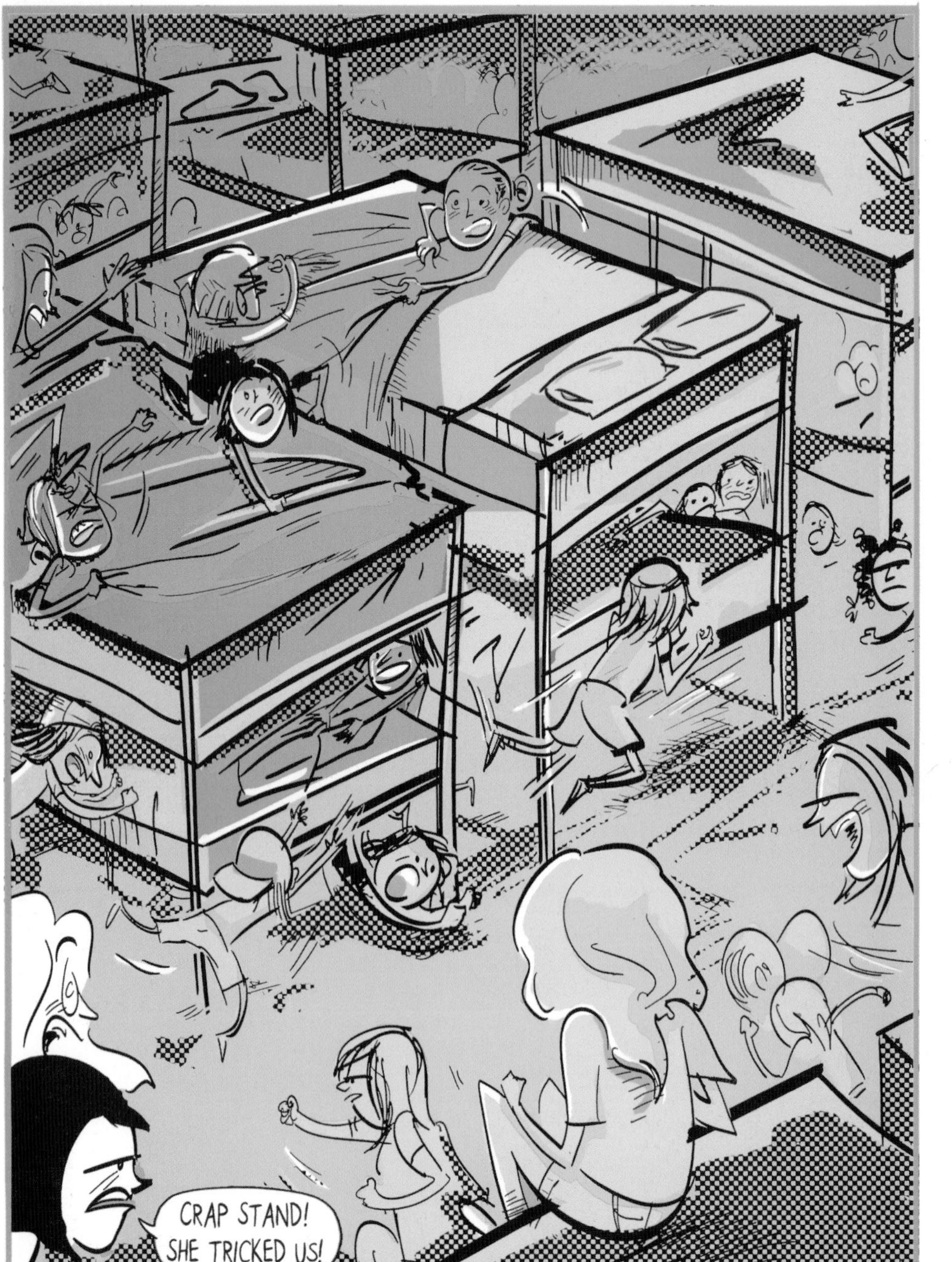
CRAP STAND! SHE TRICKED US!

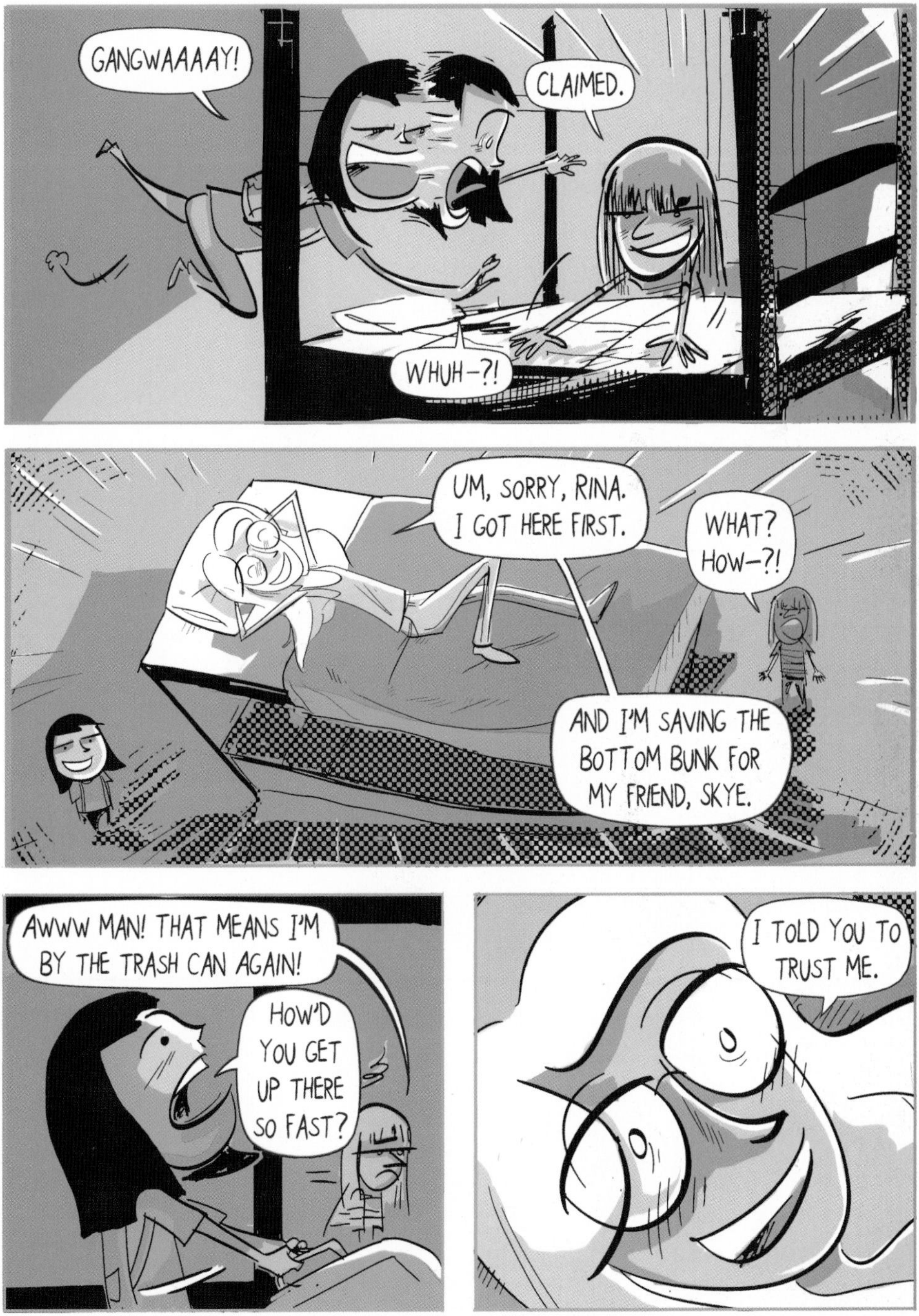
GANGWAAAAY!
CLAIMED.
WHUH-?!
UM, SORRY, RINA. I GOT HERE FIRST.
WHAT? HOW-?!
AND I'M SAVING THE BOTTOM BUNK FOR MY FRIEND, SKYE.
AWWW MAN! THAT MEANS I'M BY THE TRASH CAN AGAIN!
HOW'D YOU GET UP THERE SO FAST?
I TOLD YOU TO TRUST ME.

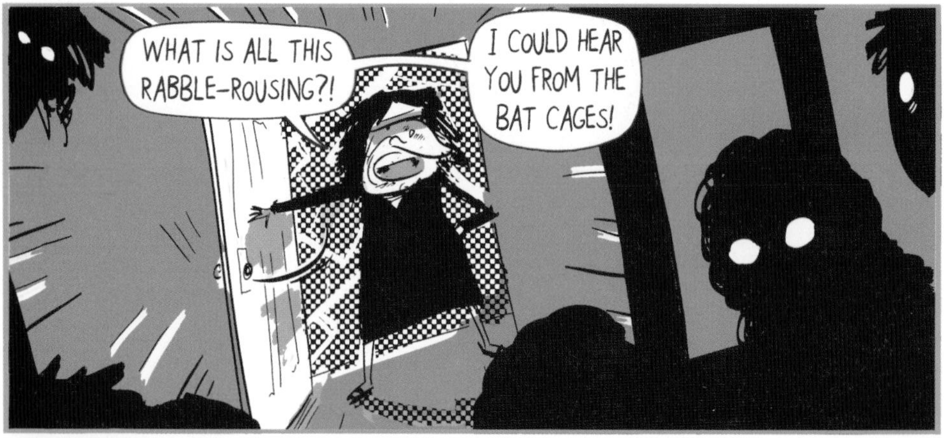
WHAT IS ALL THIS RABBLE-ROUSING?!
I COULD HEAR YOU FROM THE BAT CAGES!

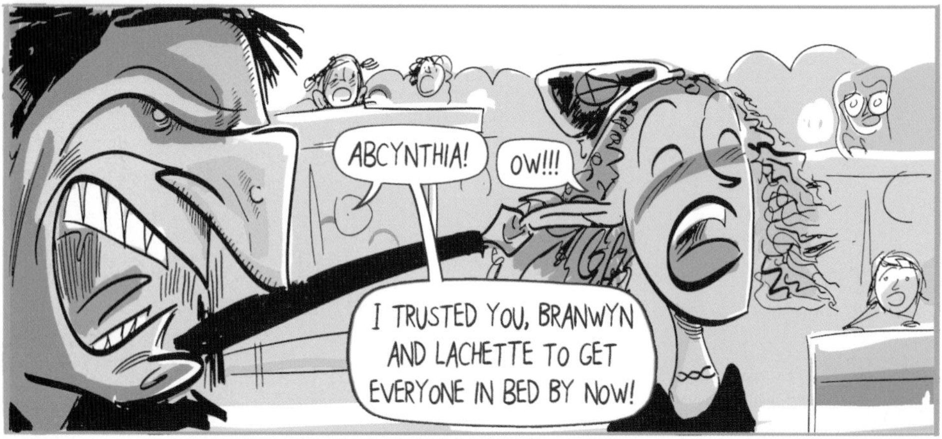
ABCYNTHIA!
OW!!!
I TRUSTED YOU, BRANWYN AND LACHETTE TO GET EVERYONE IN BED BY NOW!

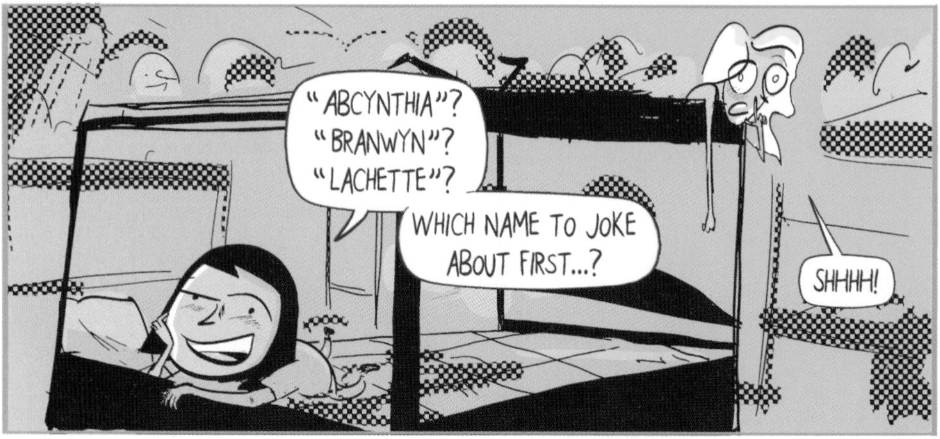
"ABCYNTHIA"? "BRANWYN"? "LACHETTE"?
WHICH NAME TO JOKE ABOUT FIRST...?
SHHHH!

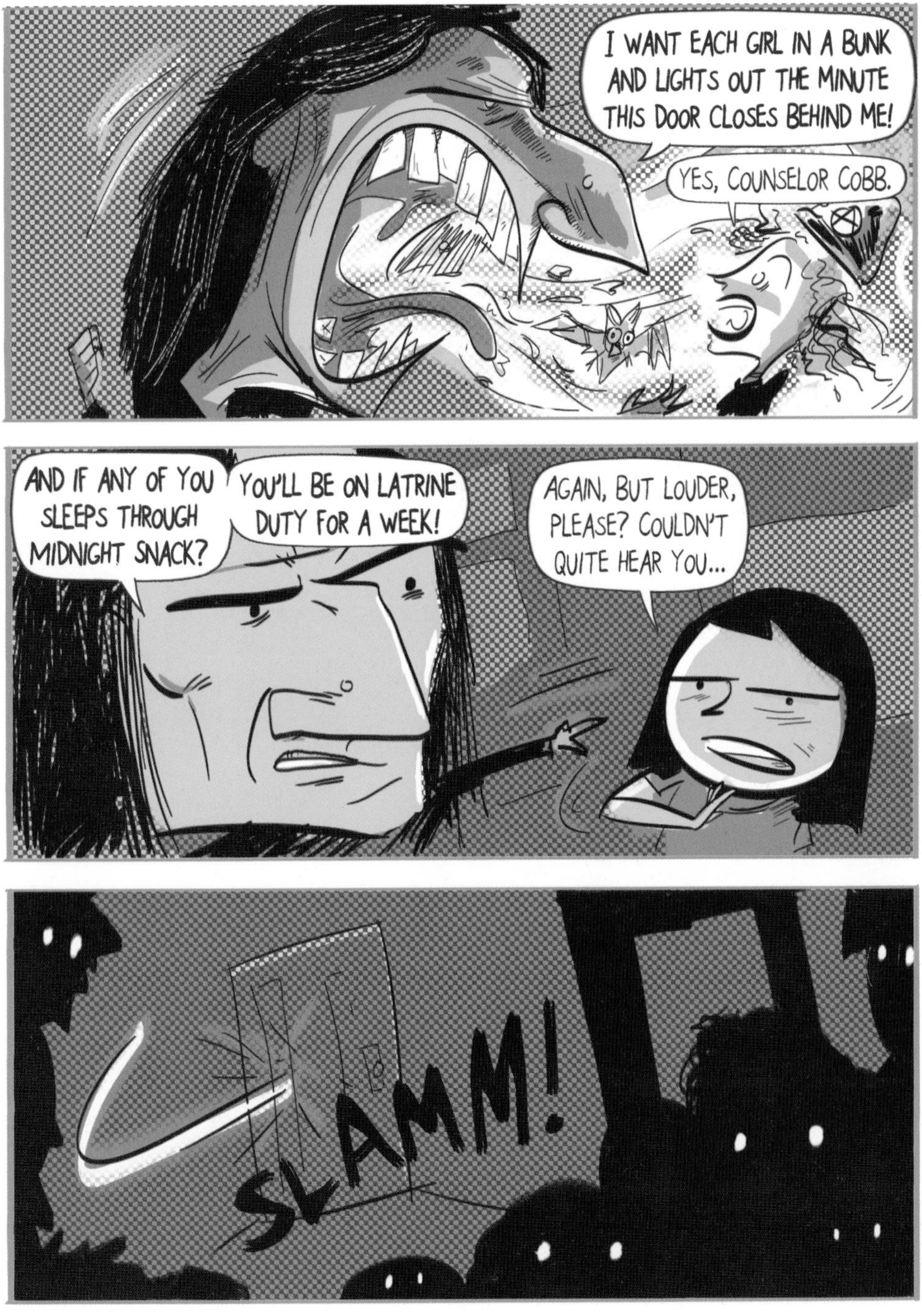
I WANT EACH GIRL IN A BUNK AND LIGHTS OUT THE MINUTE THIS DOOR CLOSES BEHIND ME!
YES, COUNSELOR COBB.
AND IF ANY OF YOU SLEEPS THROUGH MIDNIGHT SNACK?
YOU'LL BE ON LATRINE DUTY FOR A WEEK!
AGAIN, BUT LOUDER, PLEASE? COULDN'T QUITE HEAR YOU...
SLAMM!

REMIND ME TO SEE IF "CAMP BREATHMINTS" HAS ANY JOBS OPEN FOR OUR COUNSELOR FRIEND.
YOU AREN'T AFRAID OF HER?
BE QUIET.
YOU'RE GOING TO GET ME IN TROUBLE.
AND THAT WOULD BE THE WORST THING TO EVER HAPPEN?
OTHER THAN YOUR NAME?
SHHHHHHHH!
FINE. I'LL SLEEP.

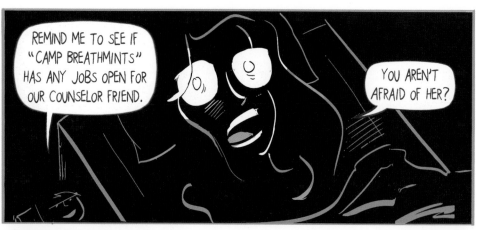

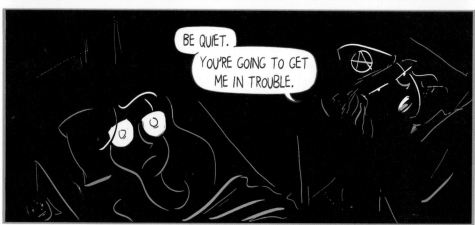

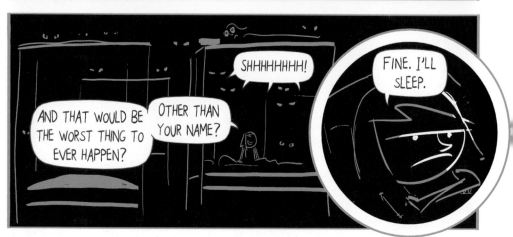

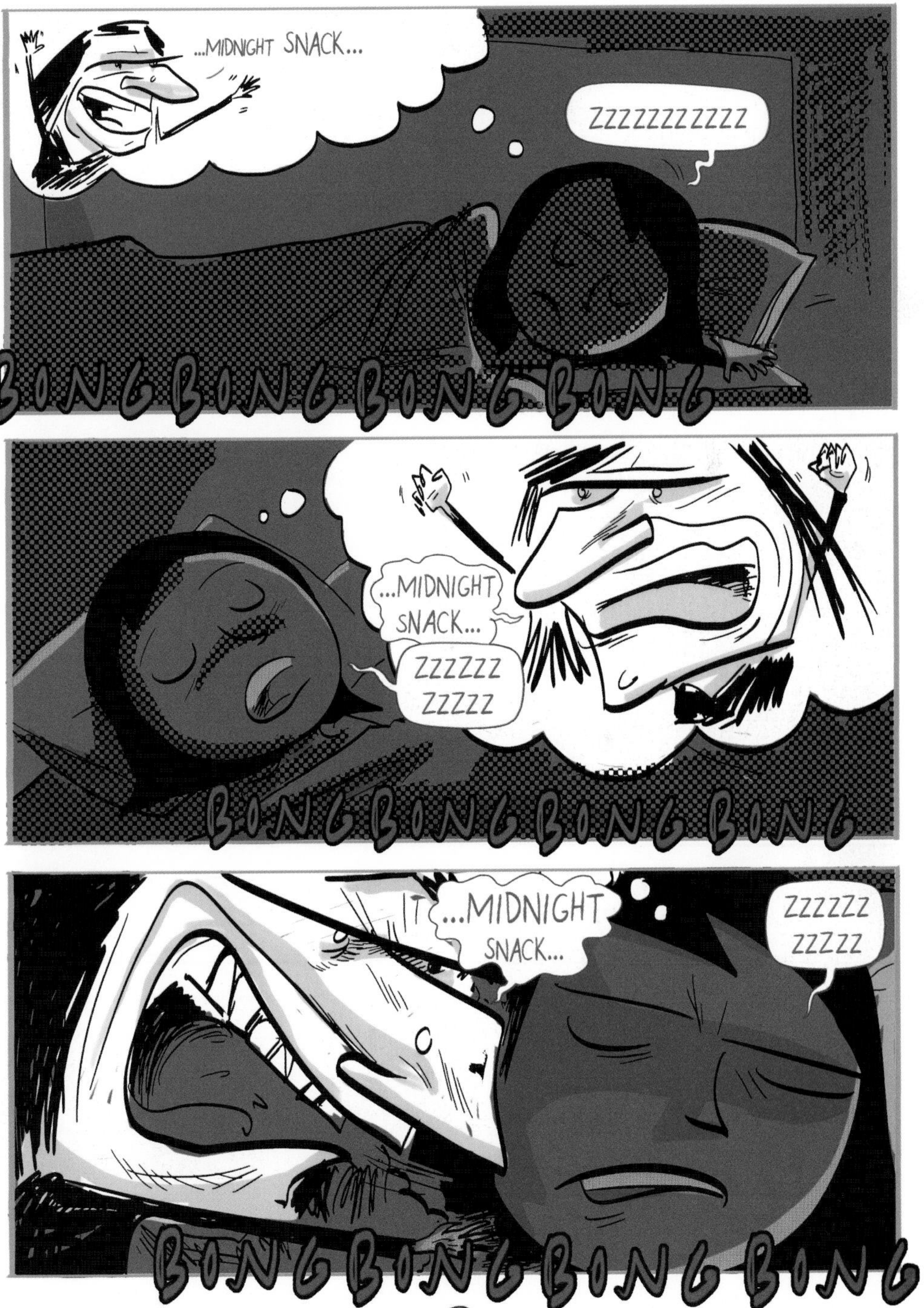
...MIDNIGHT SNACK...
ZZZZZZZZZZZ
BONG BONG BONG BONG
...MIDNIGHT SNACK...
ZZZZZZ ZZZZZ
BONG BONG BONG BONG
...MIDNIGHT SNACK...
ZZZZZZ ZZZZZ
BONG BONG BONG BONG

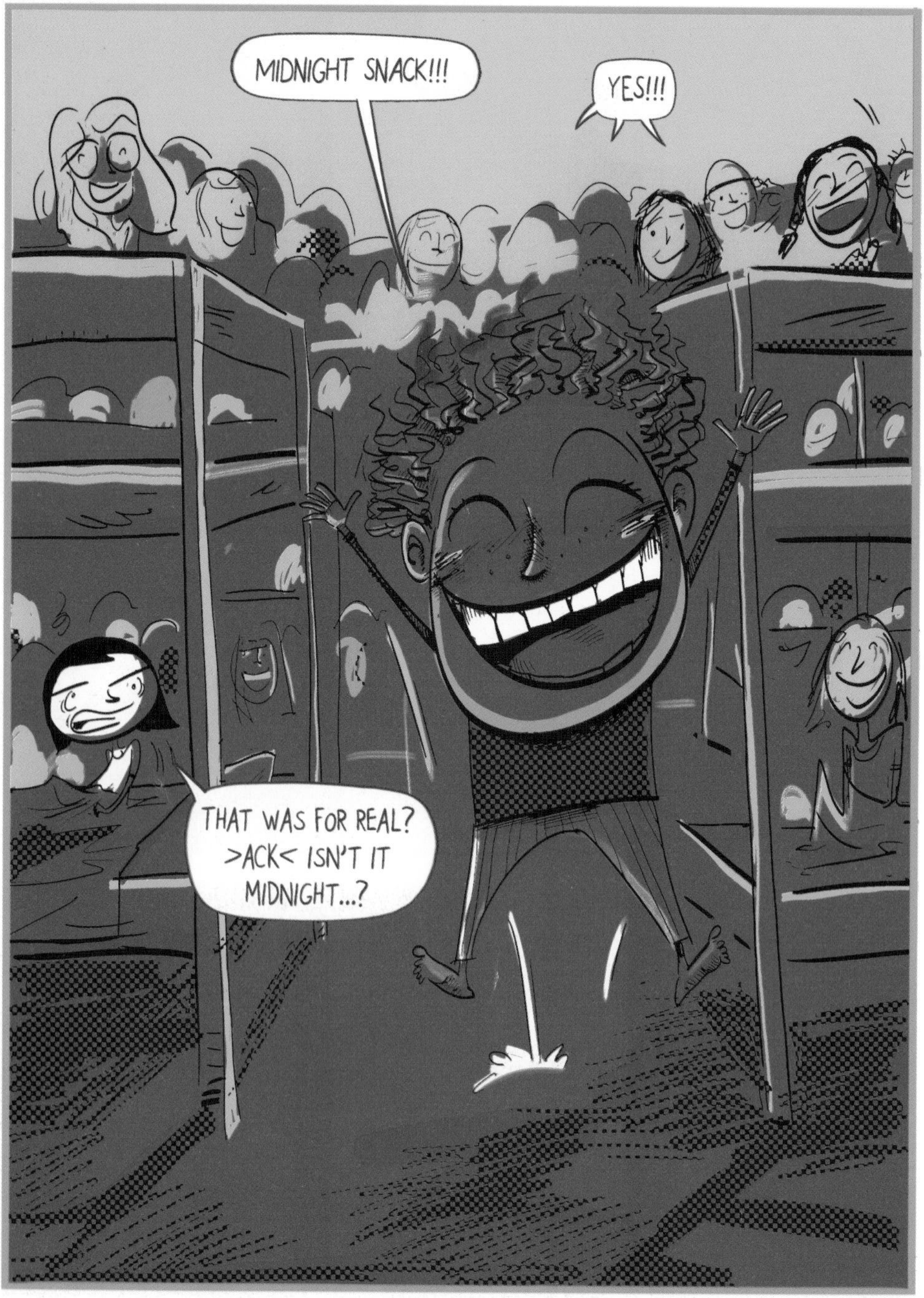
MIDNIGHT SNACK!!!
YES!!!
THAT WAS FOR REAL? >ACK< ISN'T IT MIDNIGHT...?

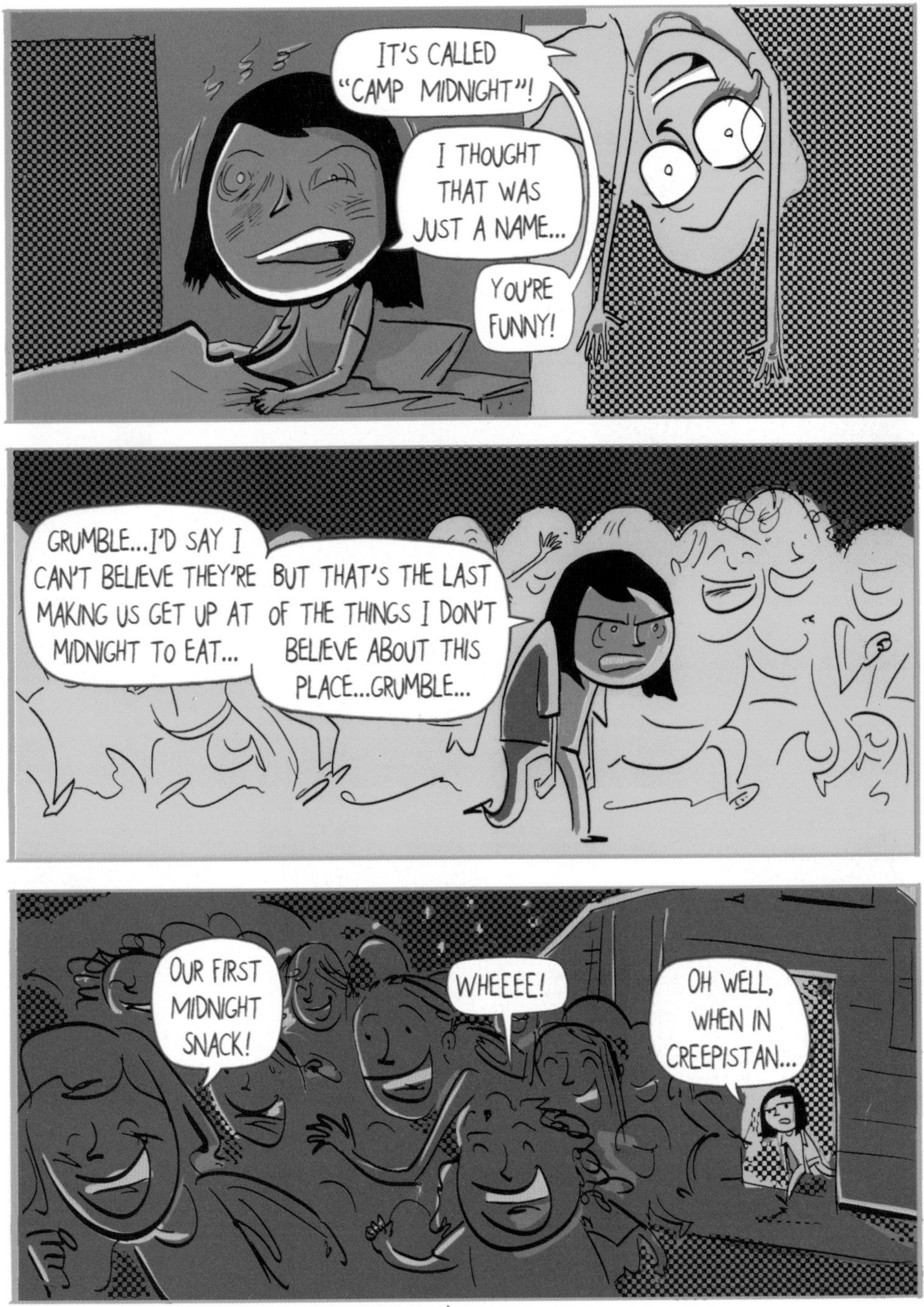
IT'S CALLED "CAMP MIDNIGHT"!
I THOUGHT THAT WAS JUST A NAME...
YOU'RE FUNNY!
GRUMBLE...I'D SAY I CAN'T BELIEVE THEY'RE MAKING US GET UP AT MIDNIGHT TO EAT...
BUT THAT'S THE LAST OF THE THINGS I DON'T BELIEVE ABOUT THIS PLACE...GRUMBLE...
OUR FIRST MIDNIGHT SNACK!
WHEEEE!
OH WELL, WHEN IN CREEPISTAN...

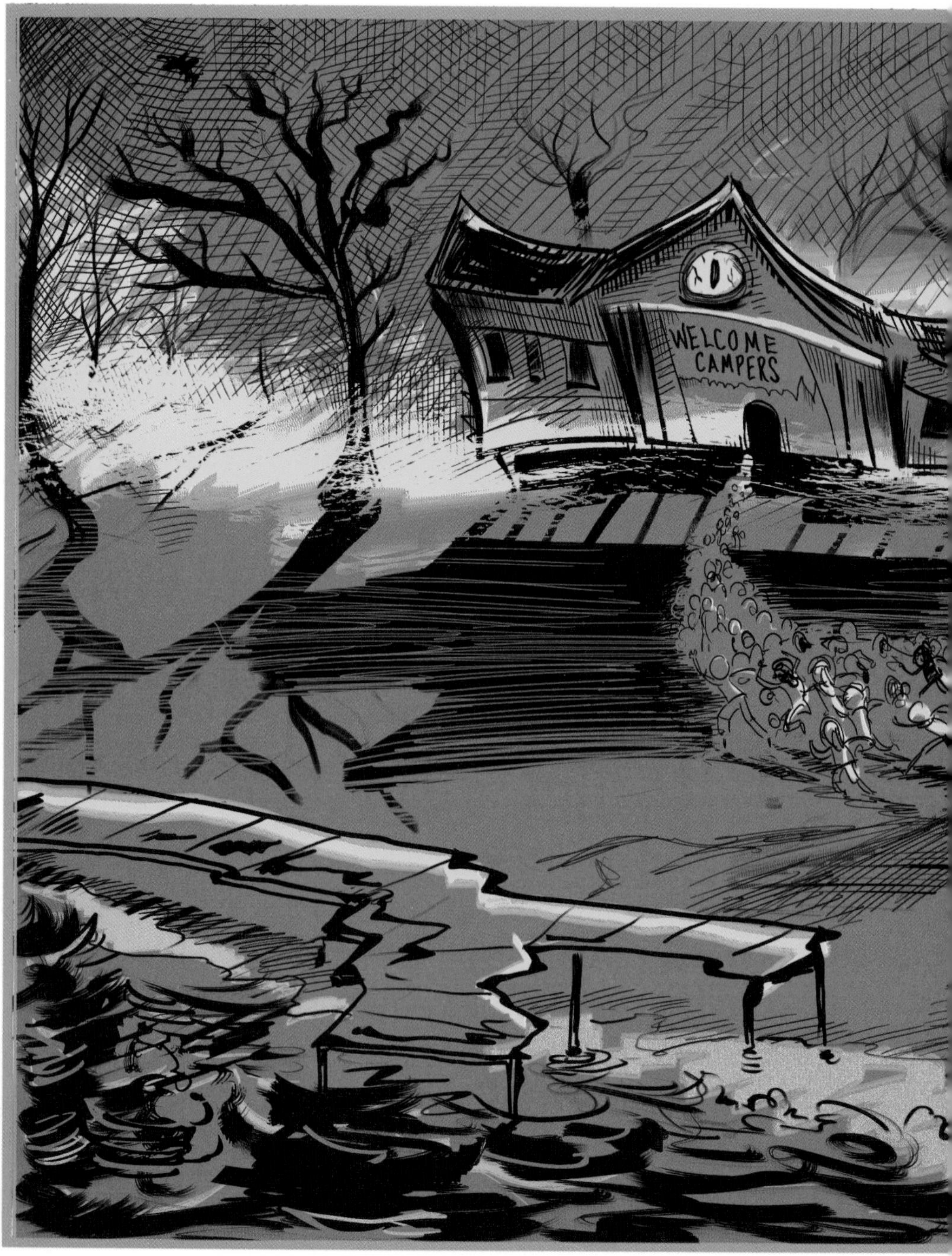
WELCOME
CAMPERS

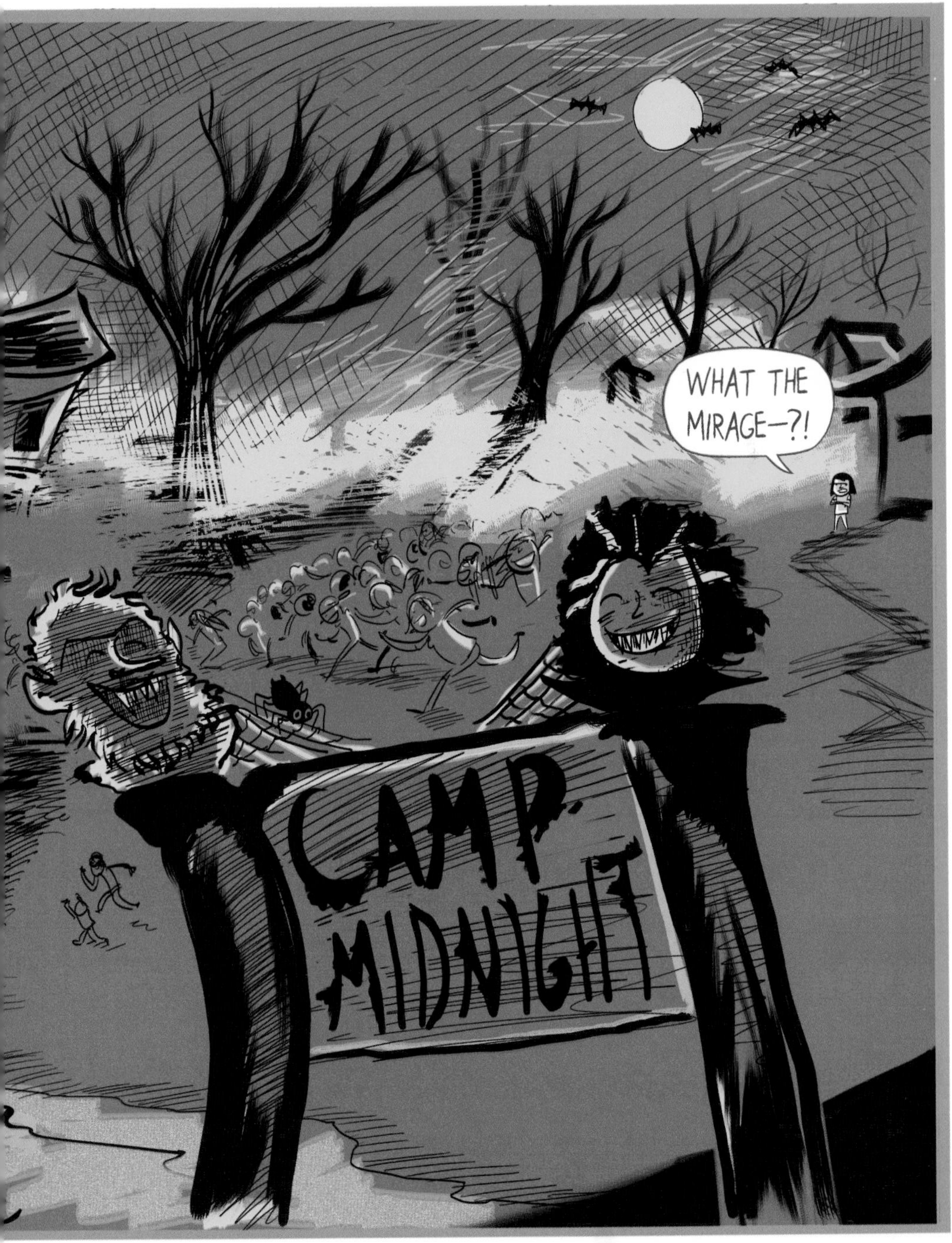
WHAT THE MIRAGE—?!
CAMP MIDNIGHT

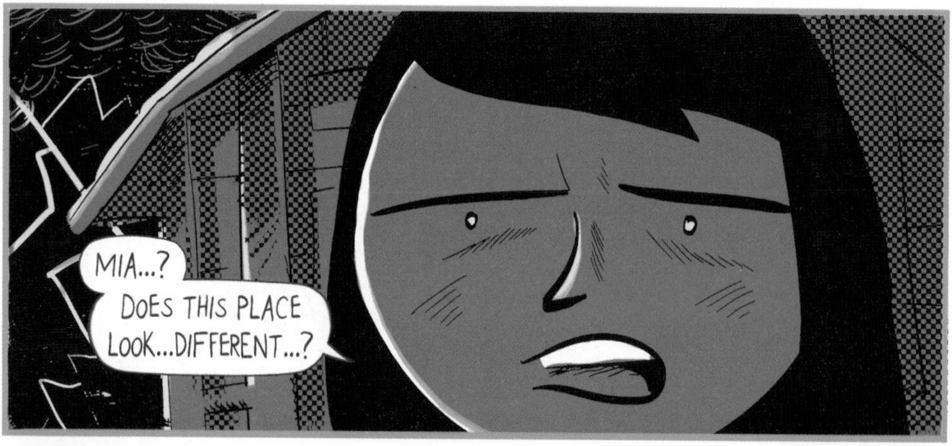
MIA...?
DOES THIS PLACE LOOK...DIFFERENT...?

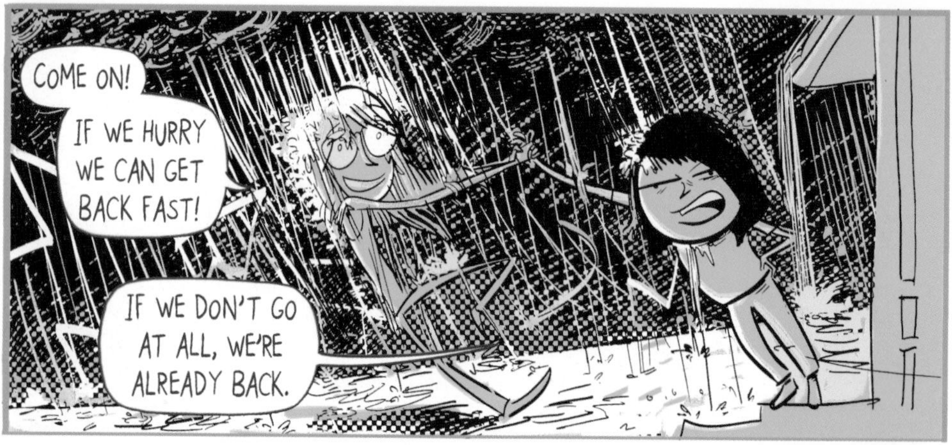
COME ON!
IF WE HURRY WE CAN GET BACK FAST!
IF WE DON'T GO AT ALL, WE'RE ALREADY BACK.

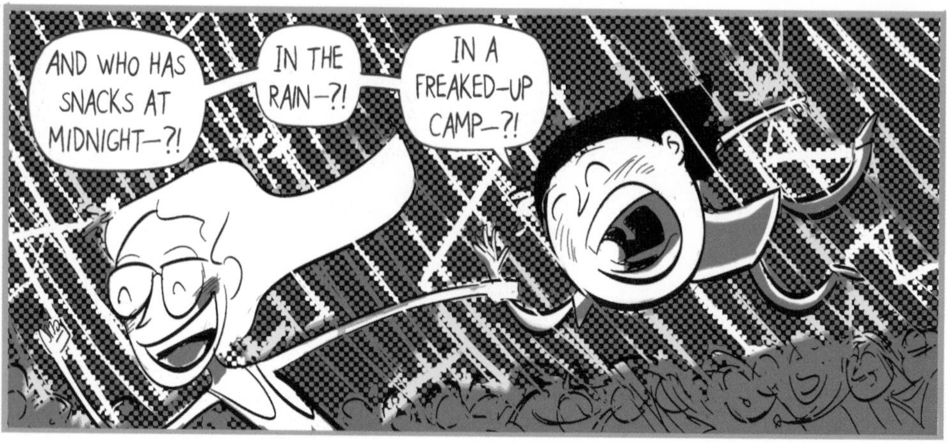
AND WHO HAS SNACKS AT MIDNIGHT—?!
IN THE RAIN—?!
IN A FREAKED-UP CAMP—?!

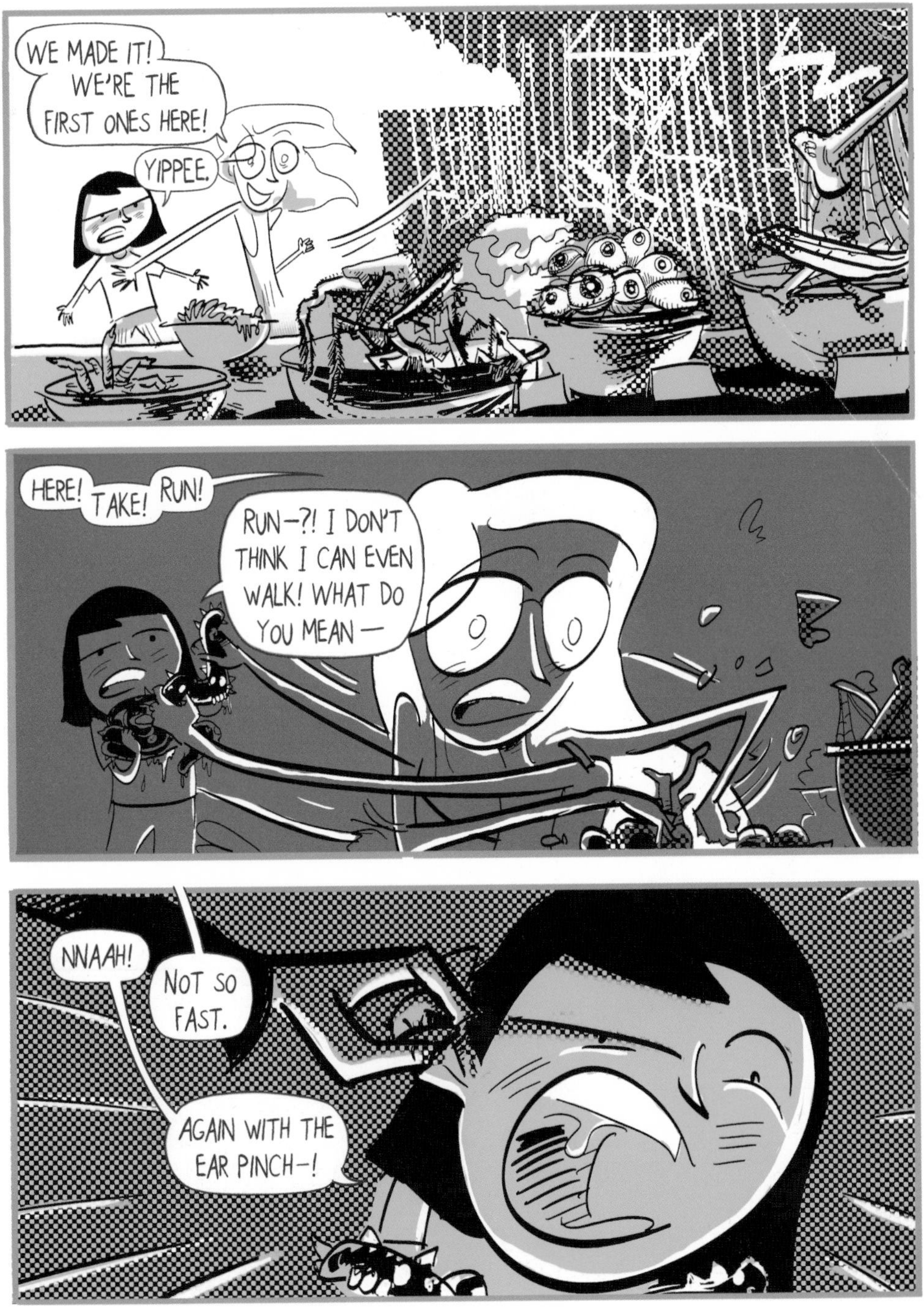
WE MADE IT! WE'RE THE FIRST ONES HERE!
YIPPEE.
HERE!
TAKE!
RUN!
RUN–?! I DON'T THINK I CAN EVEN WALK! WHAT DO YOU MEAN—
NNAAH!
NOT SO FAST.
AGAIN WITH THE EAR PINCH–!

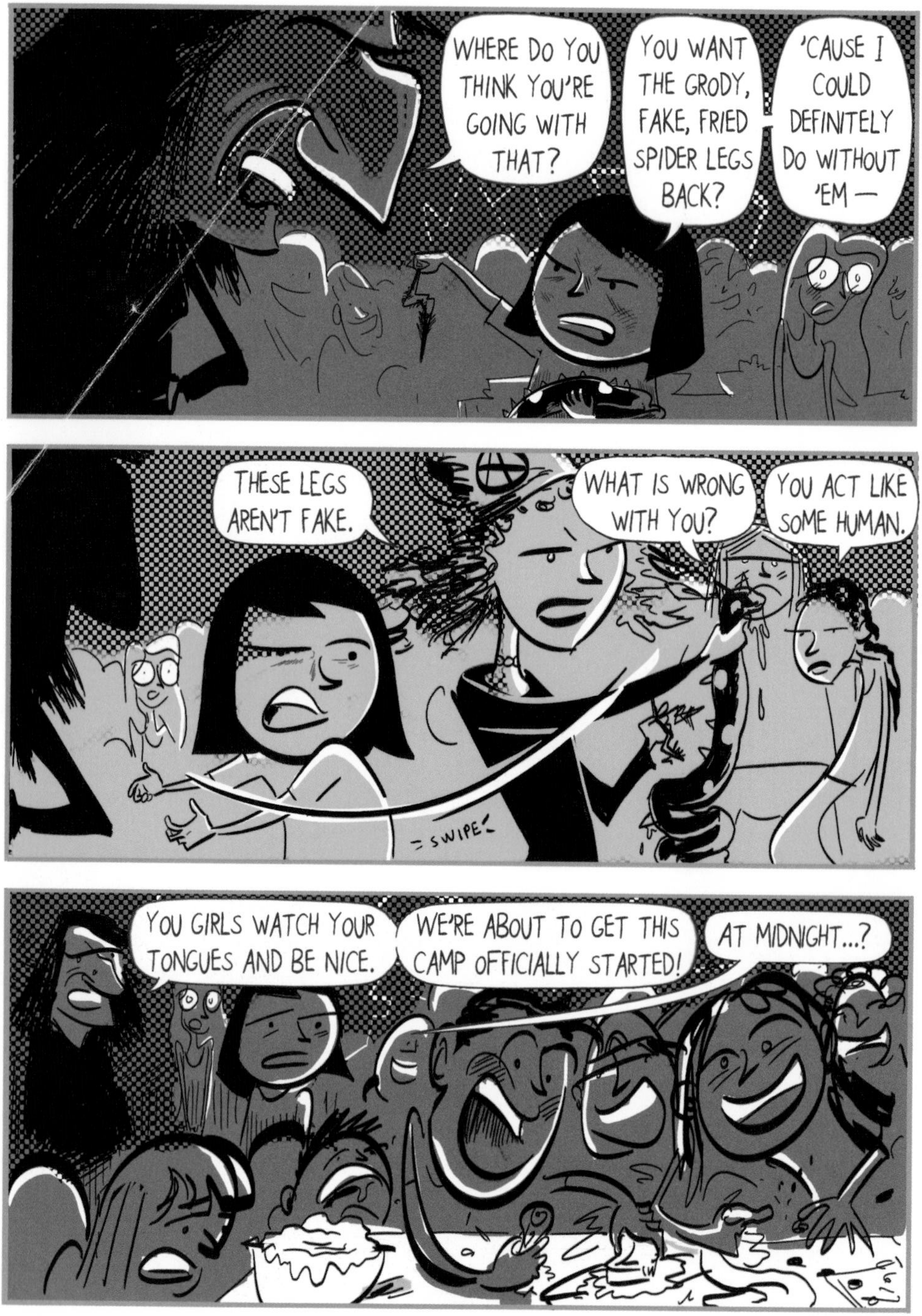
WHERE DO YOU THINK YOU'RE GOING WITH THAT?
YOU WANT THE GRODY, FAKE, FRIED SPIDER LEGS BACK?
'CAUSE I COULD DEFINITELY DO WITHOUT 'EM —
THESE LEGS AREN'T FAKE.
WHAT IS WRONG WITH YOU?
YOU ACT LIKE SOME HUMAN.
SWIPE
YOU GIRLS WATCH YOUR TONGUES AND BE NICE.
WE'RE ABOUT TO GET THIS CAMP OFFICIALLY STARTED!
AT MIDNIGHT...?

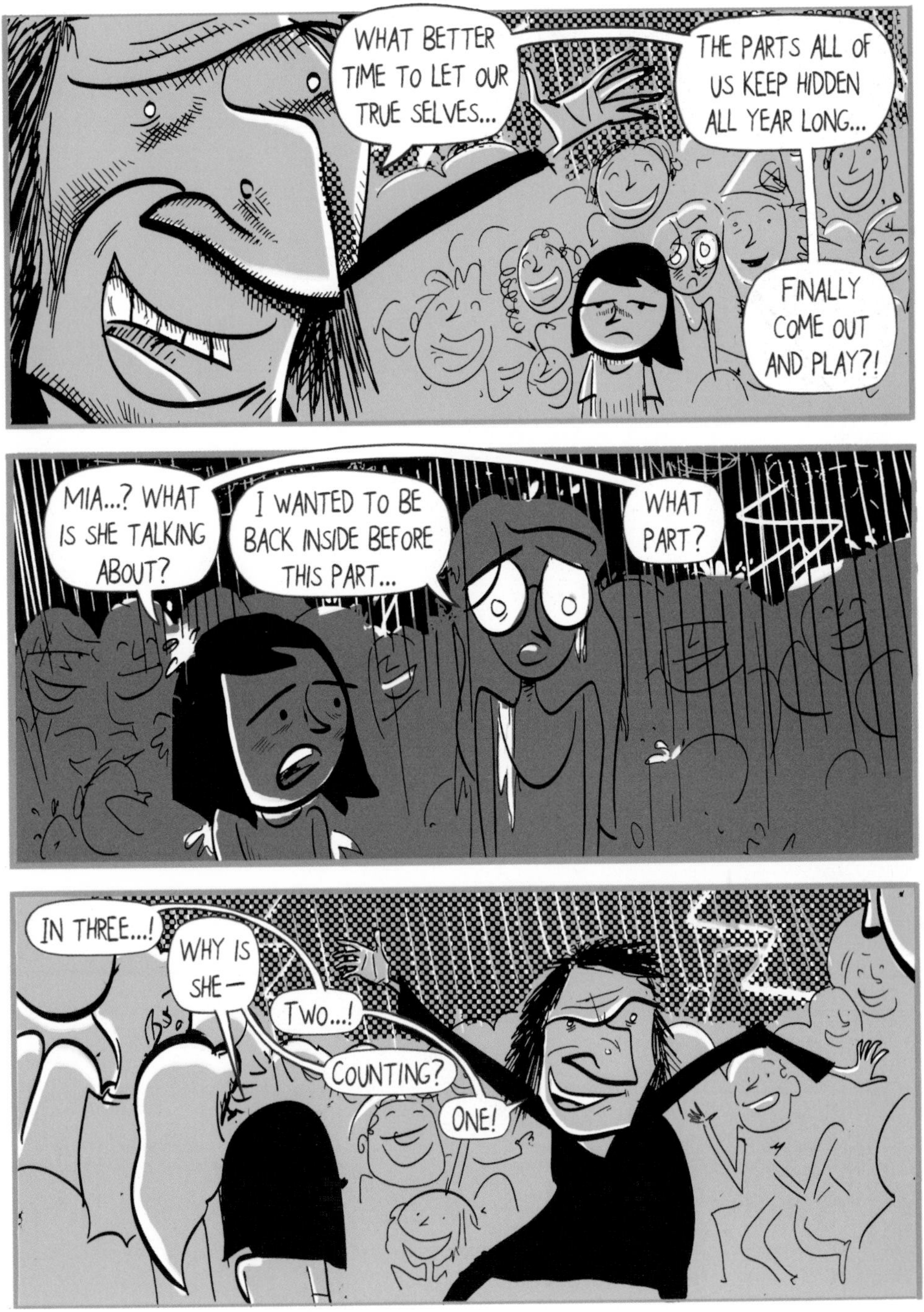
WHAT BETTER TIME TO LET OUR TRUE SELVES...
THE PARTS ALL OF US KEEP HIDDEN ALL YEAR LONG...
FINALLY COME OUT AND PLAY?!
MIA...? WHAT IS SHE TALKING ABOUT?
I WANTED TO BE BACK INSIDE BEFORE THIS PART...
WHAT PART?
IN THREE...!
WHY IS SHE—
TWO...!
COUNTING?
ONE!

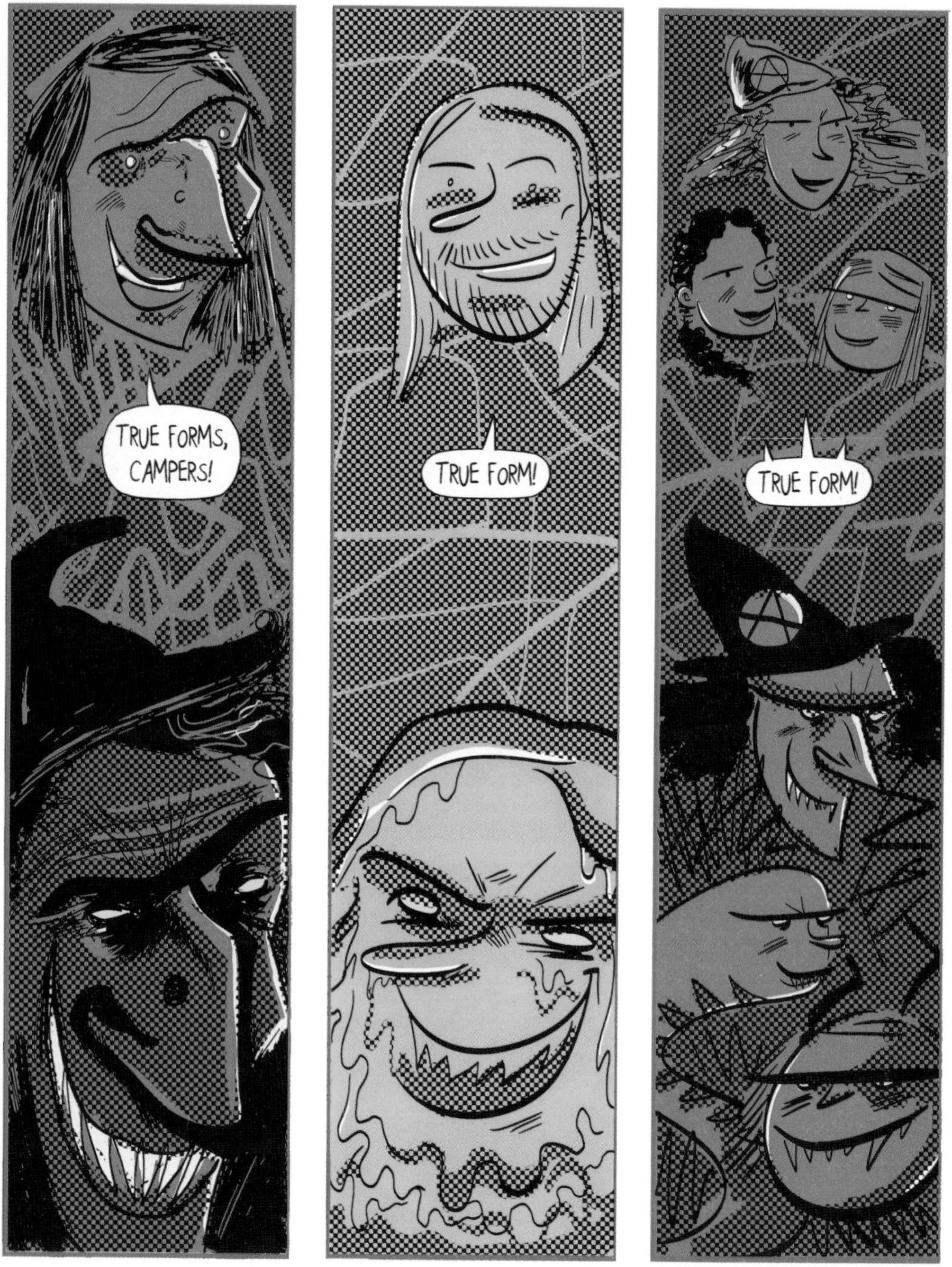
TRUE FORMS, CAMPERS!
TRUE FORM!
TRUE FORM!

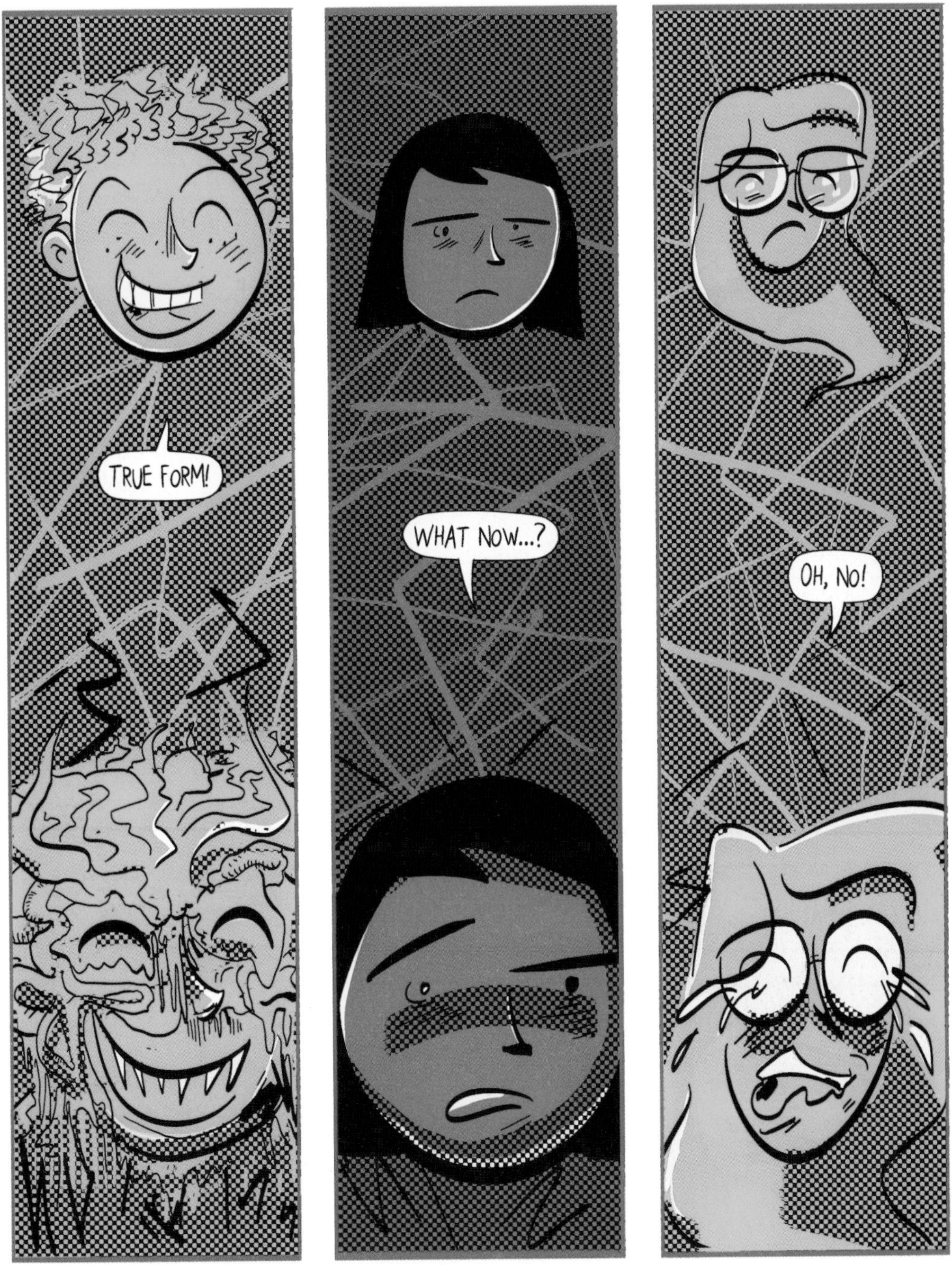
TRUE FORM!
WHAT NOW...?
OH, NO!

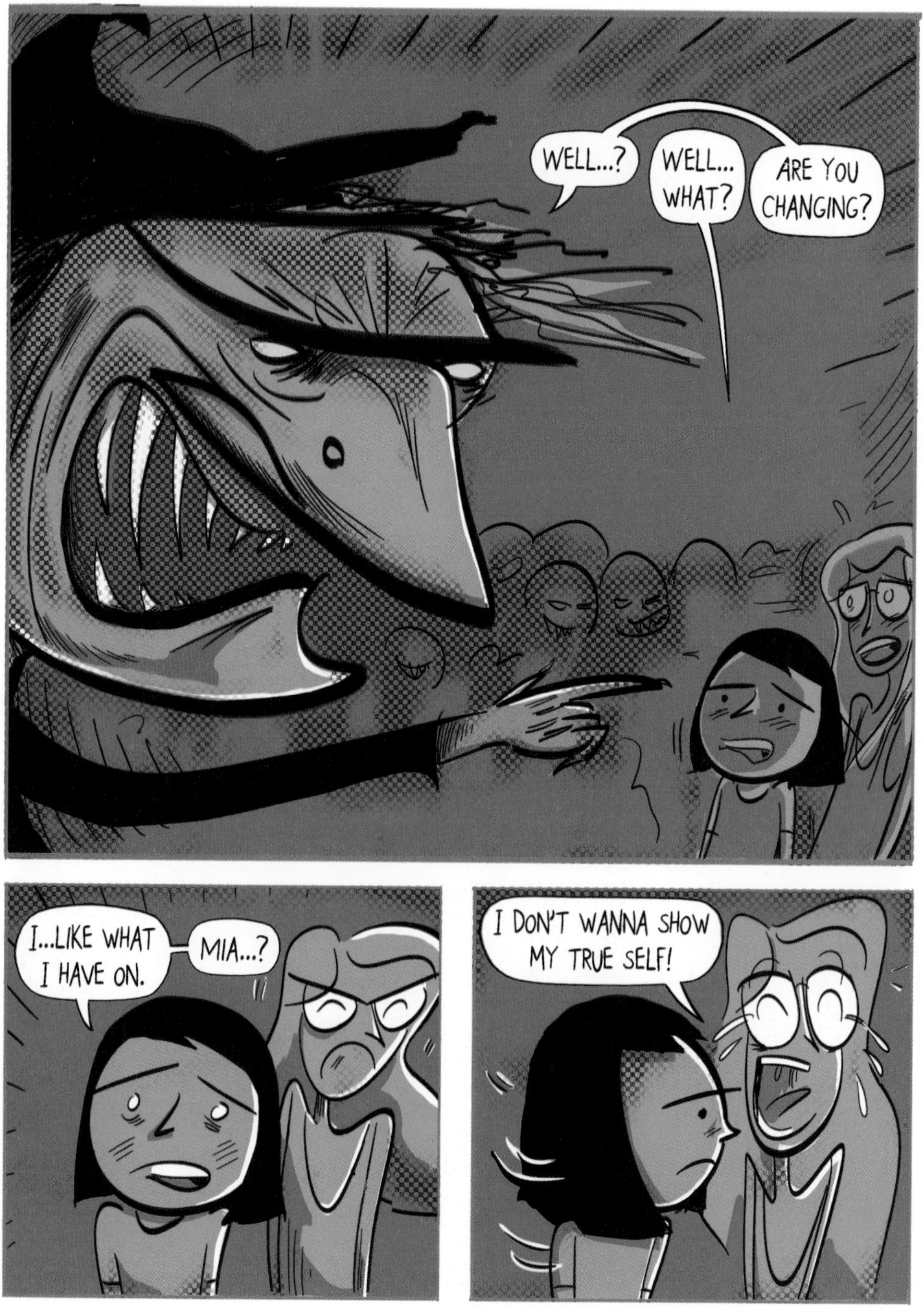
WELL...?
WELL... WHAT?
ARE YOU CHANGING?
I...LIKE WHAT I HAVE ON.
MIA...?
I DON'T WANNA SHOW MY TRUE SELF!

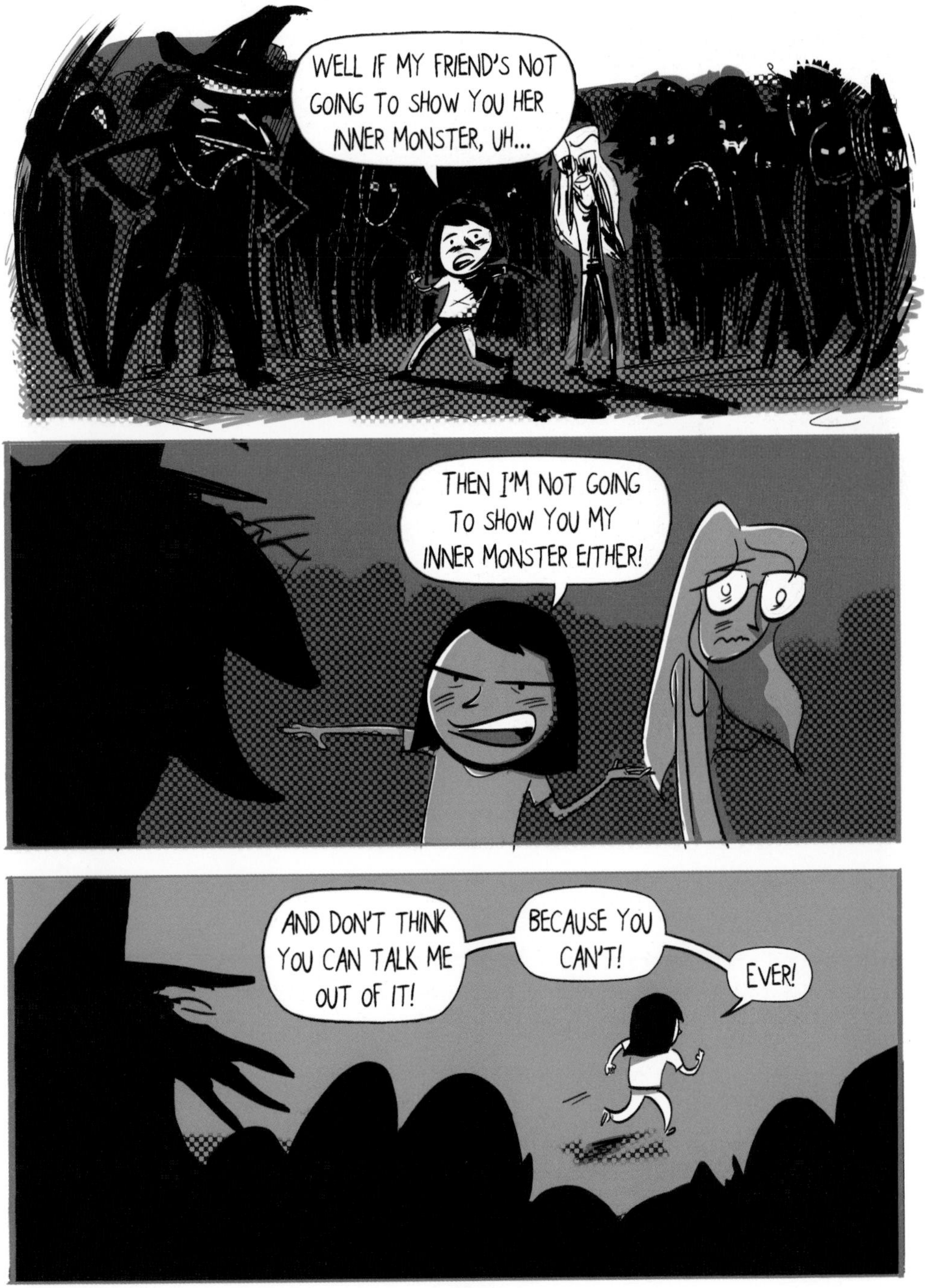
WELL IF MY FRIEND'S NOT GOING TO SHOW YOU HER INNER MONSTER, UH...
THEN I'M NOT GOING TO SHOW YOU MY INNER MONSTER EITHER!
AND DON'T THINK YOU CAN TALK ME OUT OF IT!
BECAUSE YOU CAN'T!
EVER!

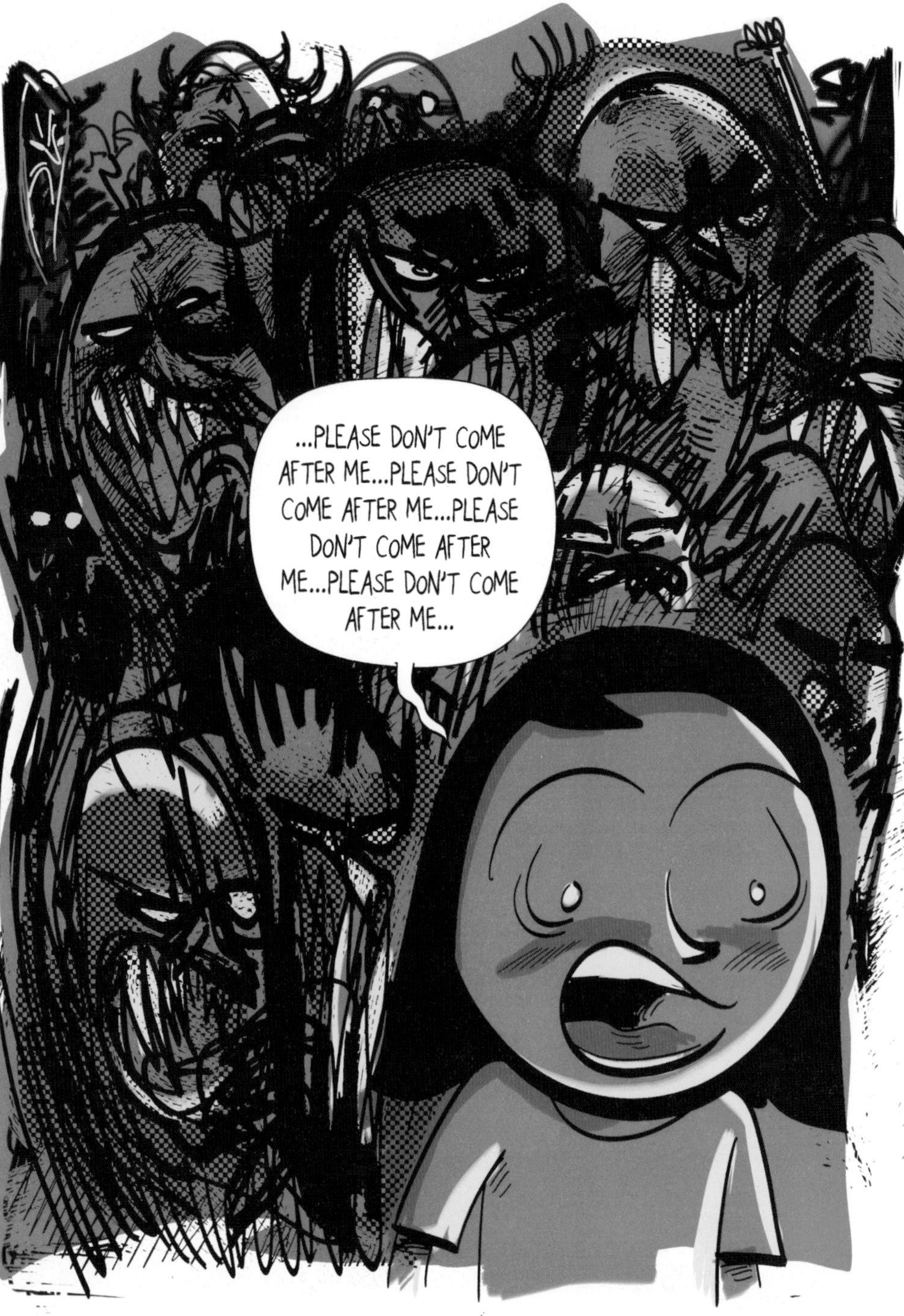
...PLEASE DON'T COME AFTER ME...PLEASE DON'T COME AFTER ME...PLEASE DON'T COME AFTER ME...PLEASE DON'T COME AFTER ME...

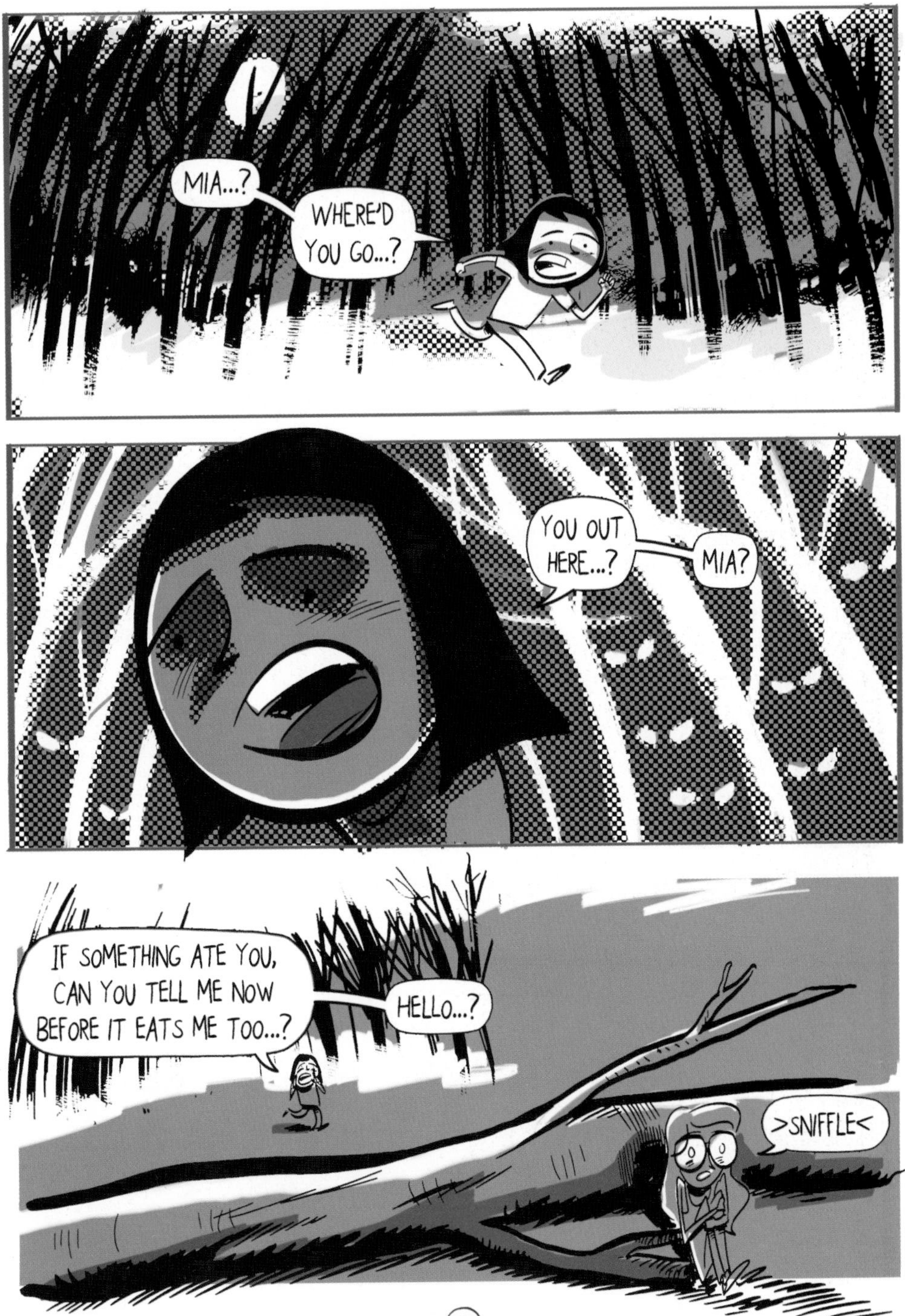
MIA...?
WHERE'D YOU GO...?
YOU OUT HERE...?
MIA?
IF SOMETHING ATE YOU, CAN YOU TELL ME NOW BEFORE IT EATS ME TOO...?
HELLO...?
>SNIFFLE<

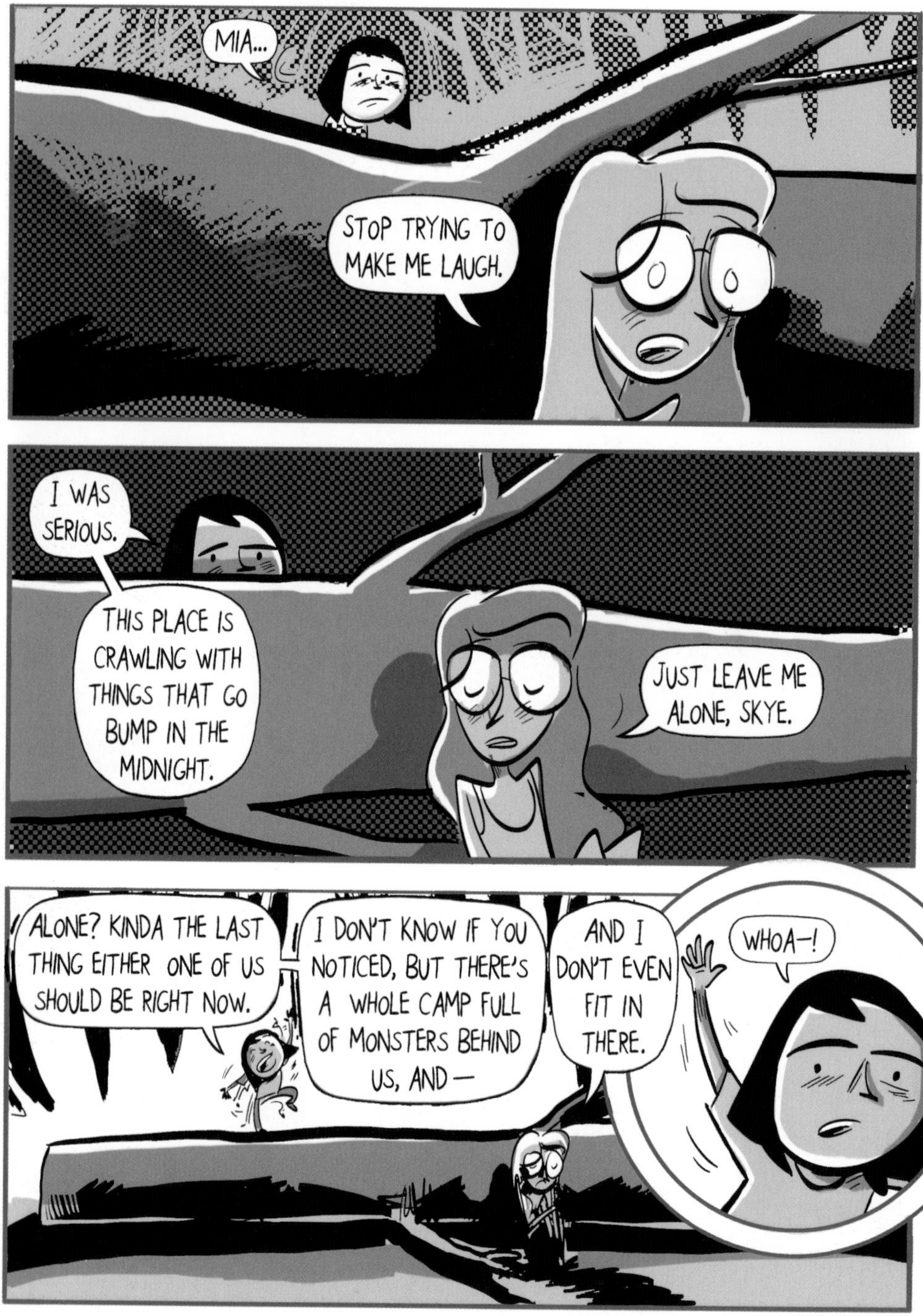
MIA...
STOP TRYING TO MAKE ME LAUGH.
I WAS SERIOUS.
THIS PLACE IS CRAWLING WITH THINGS THAT GO BUMP IN THE MIDNIGHT.
JUST LEAVE ME ALONE, SKYE.
ALONE? KINDA THE LAST THING EITHER ONE OF US SHOULD BE RIGHT NOW.
I DON'T KNOW IF YOU NOTICED, BUT THERE'S A WHOLE CAMP FULL OF MONSTERS BEHIND US, AND—
AND I DON'T EVEN FIT IN THERE.
WHOA—!

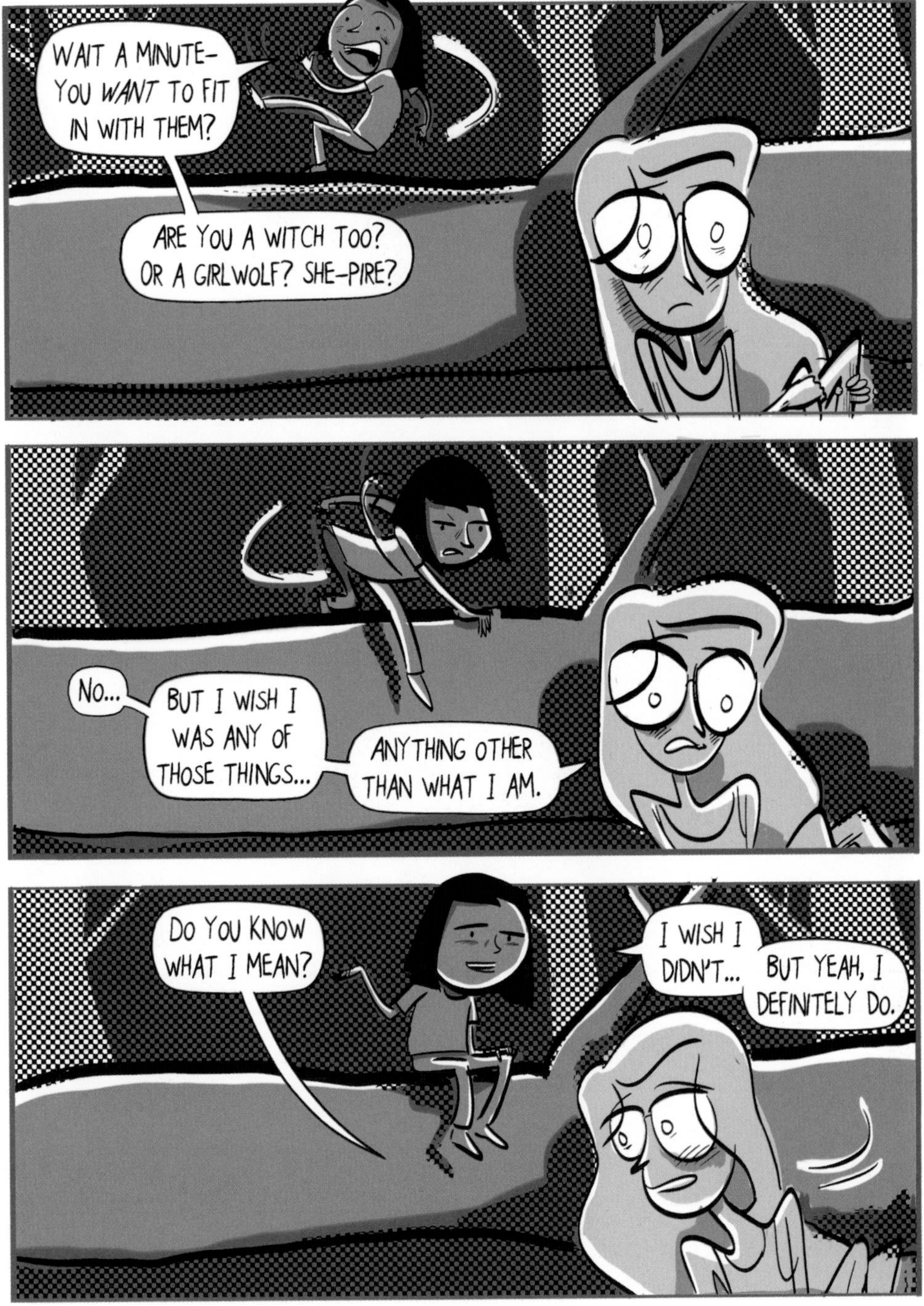
WAIT A MINUTE-
YOU *WANT* TO FIT IN WITH THEM?
ARE YOU A WITCH TOO? OR A GIRLWOLF? SHE-PIRE?
NO...
BUT I WISH I WAS ANY OF THOSE THINGS...
ANYTHING OTHER THAN WHAT I AM.
DO YOU KNOW WHAT I MEAN?
I WISH I DIDN'T...
BUT YEAH, I DEFINITELY DO.

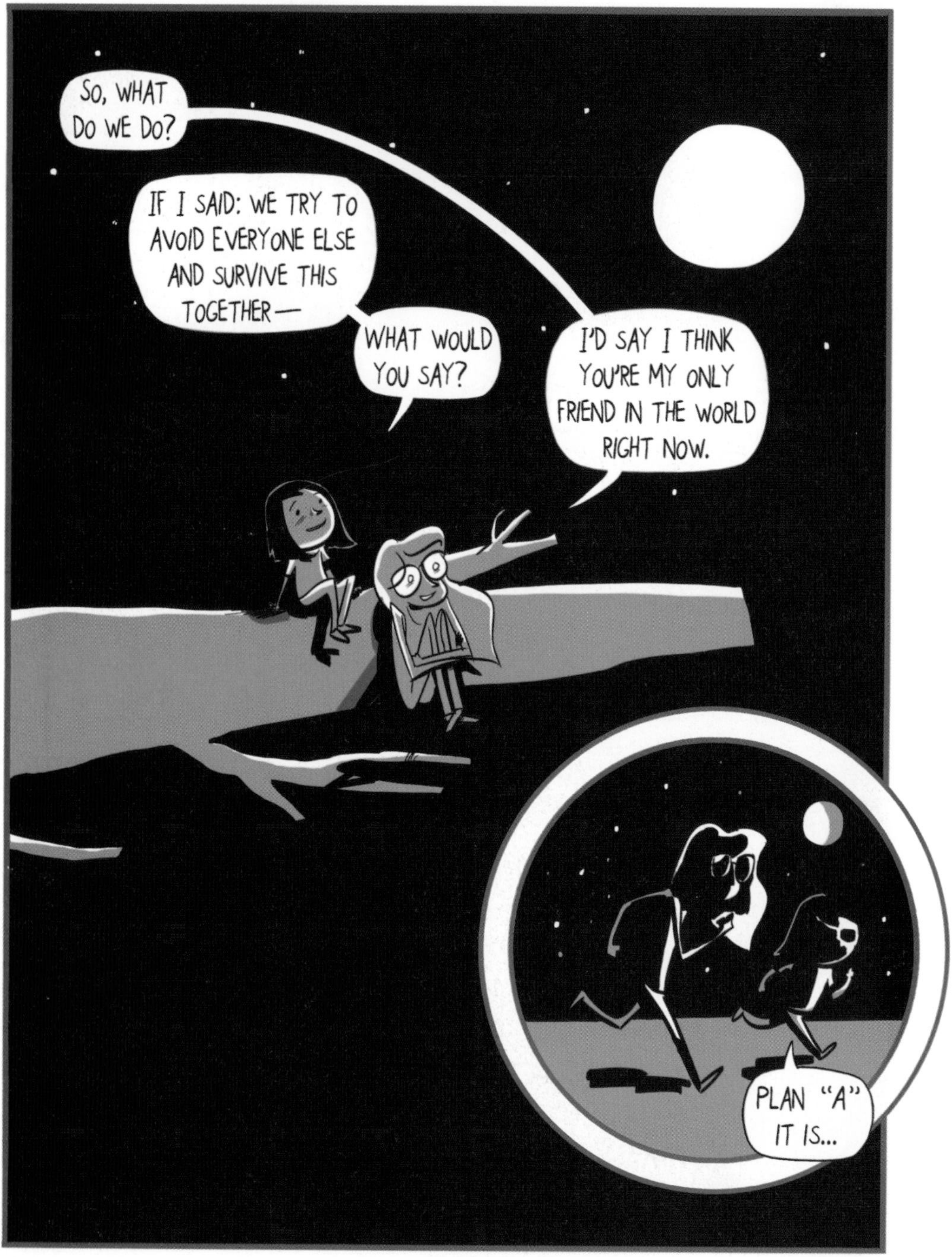
SO, WHAT DO WE DO?
IF I SAID: WE TRY TO AVOID EVERYONE ELSE AND SURVIVE THIS TOGETHER—
WHAT WOULD YOU SAY?
I'D SAY I THINK YOU'RE MY ONLY FRIEND IN THE WORLD RIGHT NOW.
PLAN "A" IT IS...

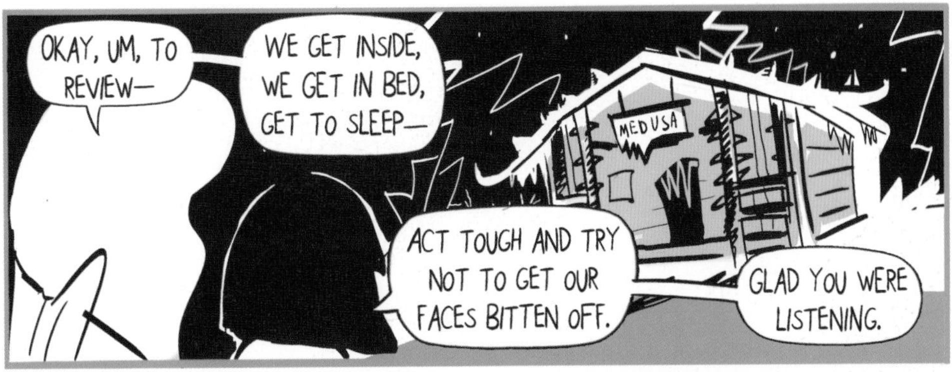
OKAY, UM, TO REVIEW—
WE GET INSIDE, WE GET IN BED, GET TO SLEEP—
MEDUSA
ACT TOUGH AND TRY NOT TO GET OUR FACES BITTEN OFF.
GLAD YOU WERE LISTENING.

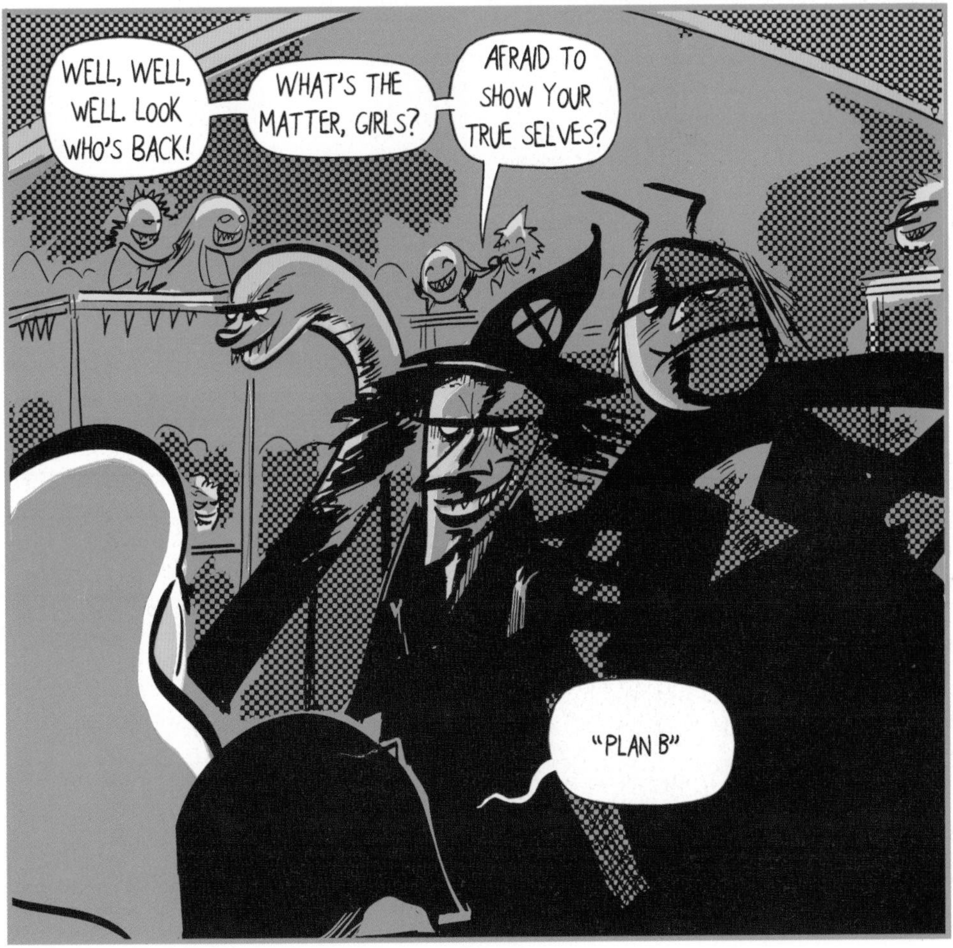
WELL, WELL, WELL. LOOK WHO'S BACK!
WHAT'S THE MATTER, GIRLS?
AFRAID TO SHOW YOUR TRUE SELVES?
"PLAN B"

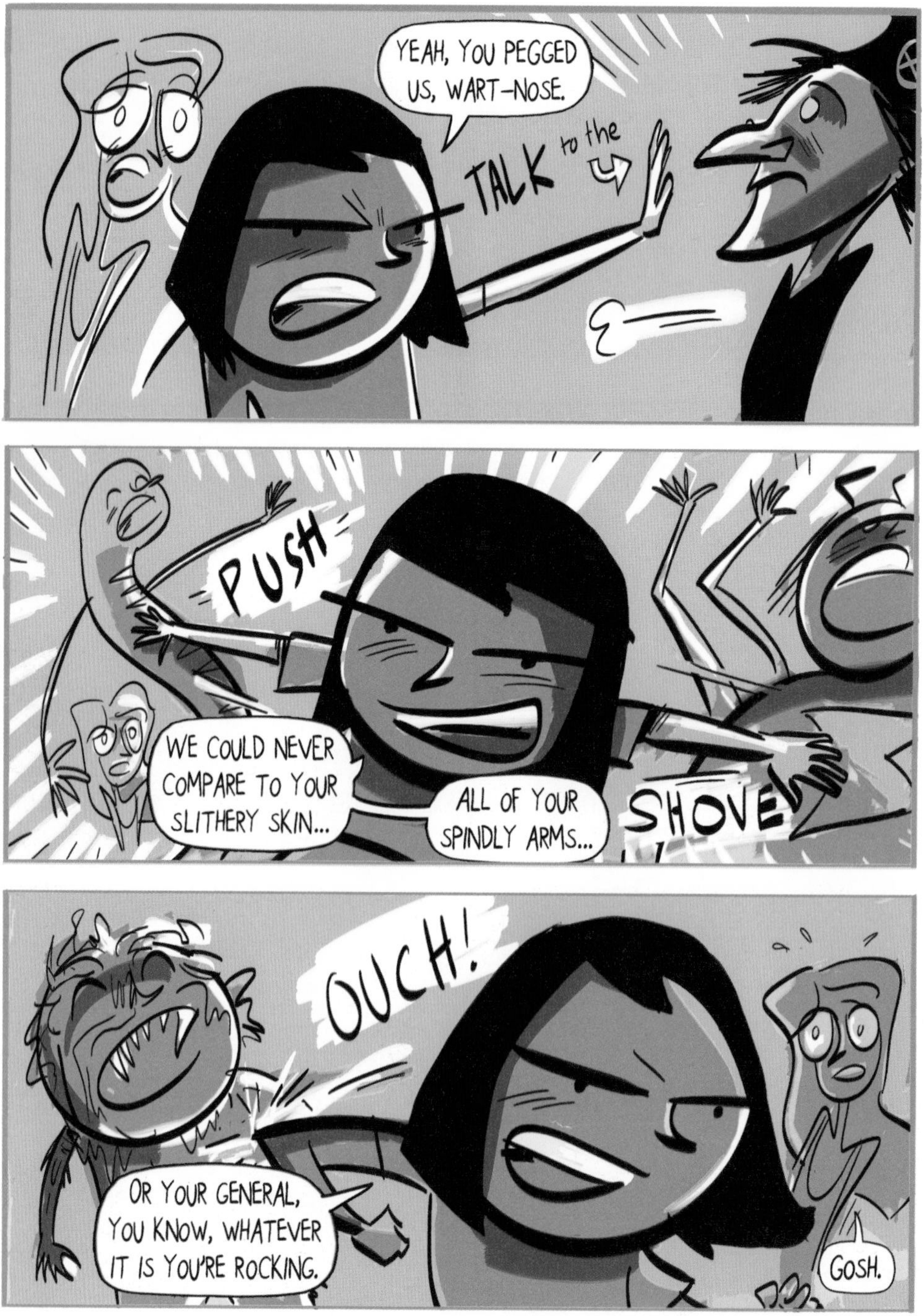
YEAH, YOU PEGGED US, WART-NOSE.
TALK to the
PUSH
WE COULD NEVER COMPARE TO YOUR SLITHERY SKIN...
ALL OF YOUR SPINDLY ARMS...
SHOVE
OUCH!
OR YOUR GENERAL, YOU KNOW, WHATEVER IT IS YOU'RE ROCKING.
GOSH.

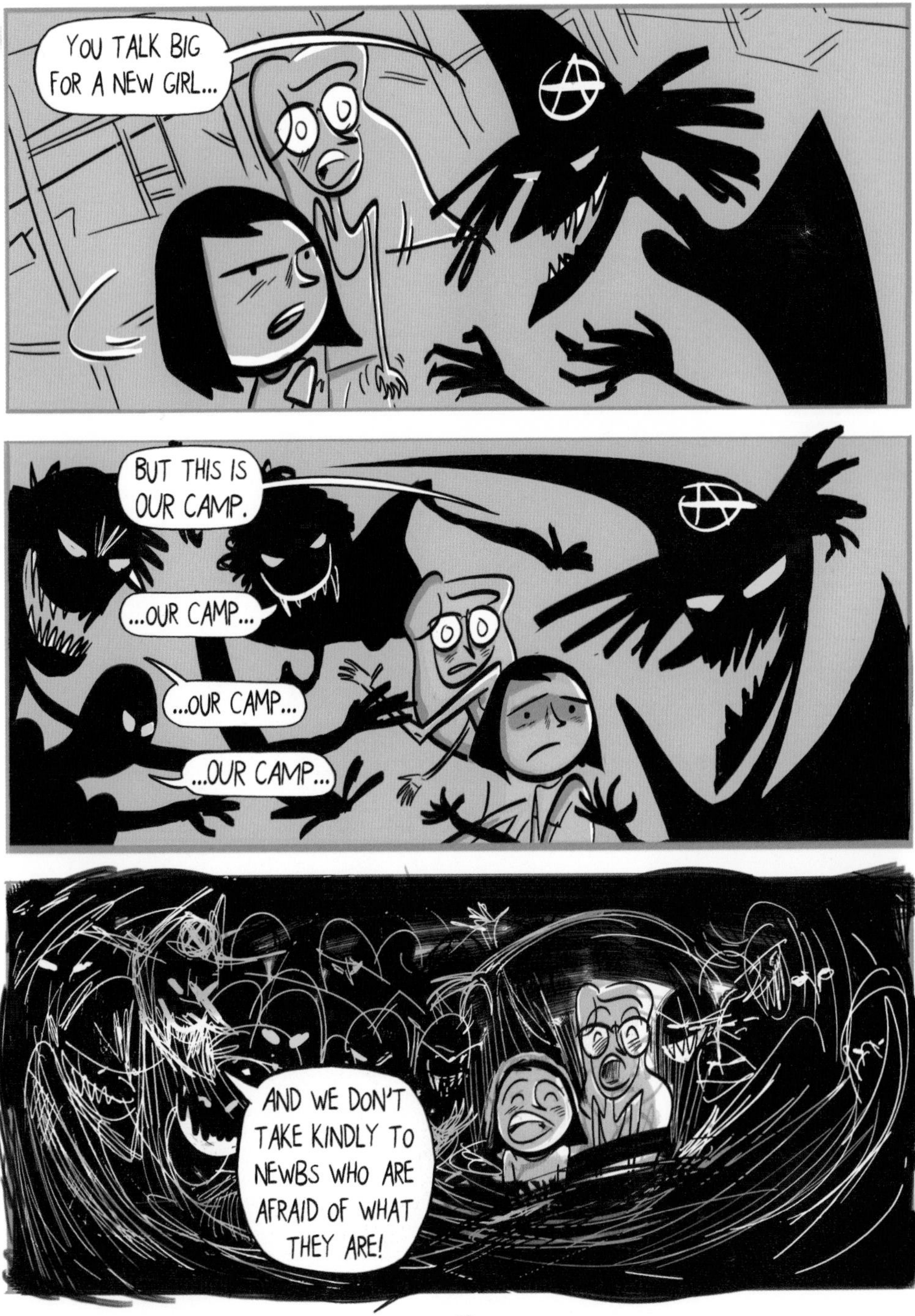
YOU TALK BIG FOR A NEW GIRL...
BUT THIS IS OUR CAMP.
...OUR CAMP...
...OUR CAMP...
...OUR CAMP...
AND WE DON'T TAKE KINDLY TO NEWBS WHO ARE AFRAID OF WHAT THEY ARE!

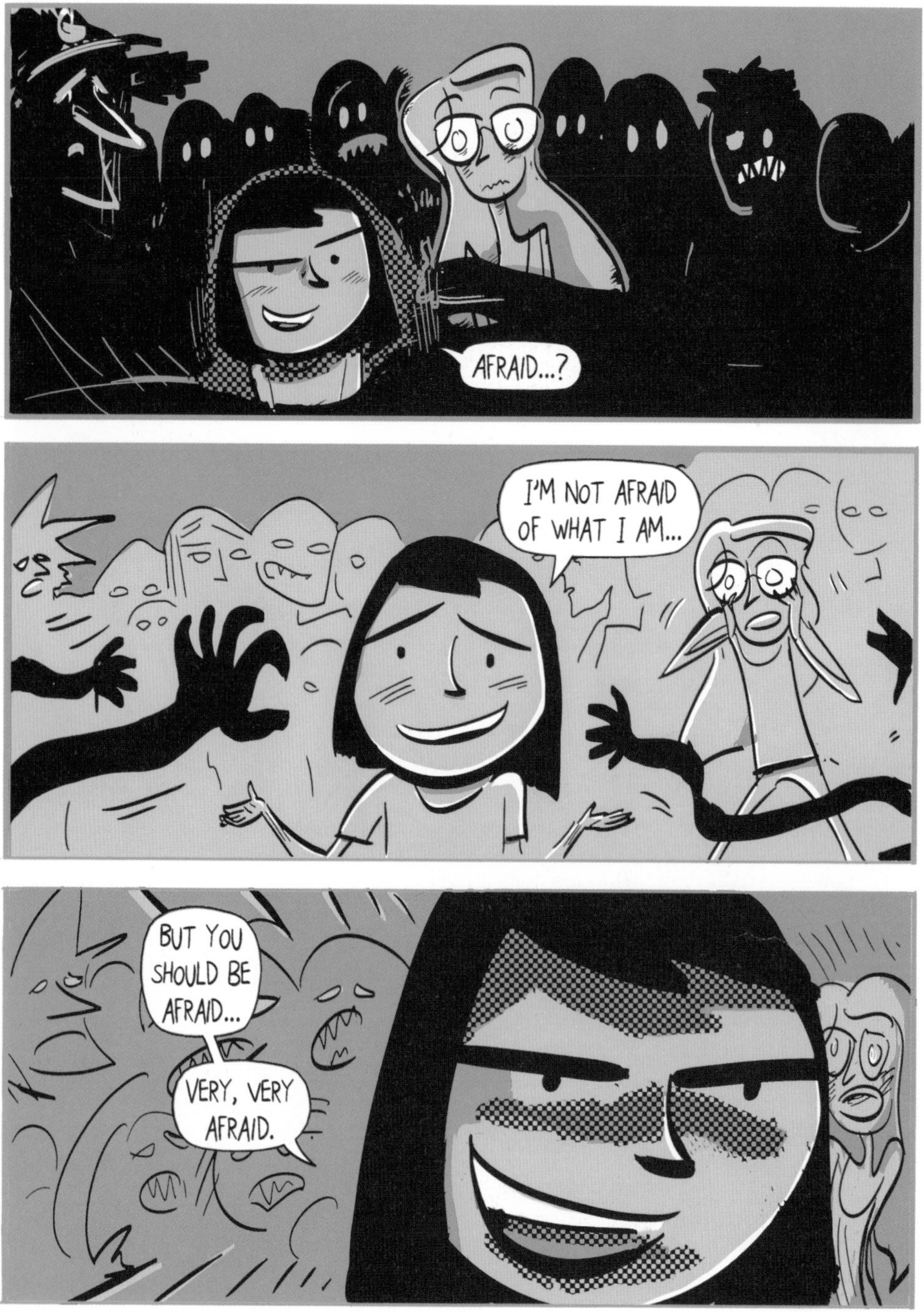
AFRAID...?
I'M NOT AFRAID OF WHAT I AM...
BUT YOU SHOULD BE AFRAID...
VERY, VERY AFRAID.

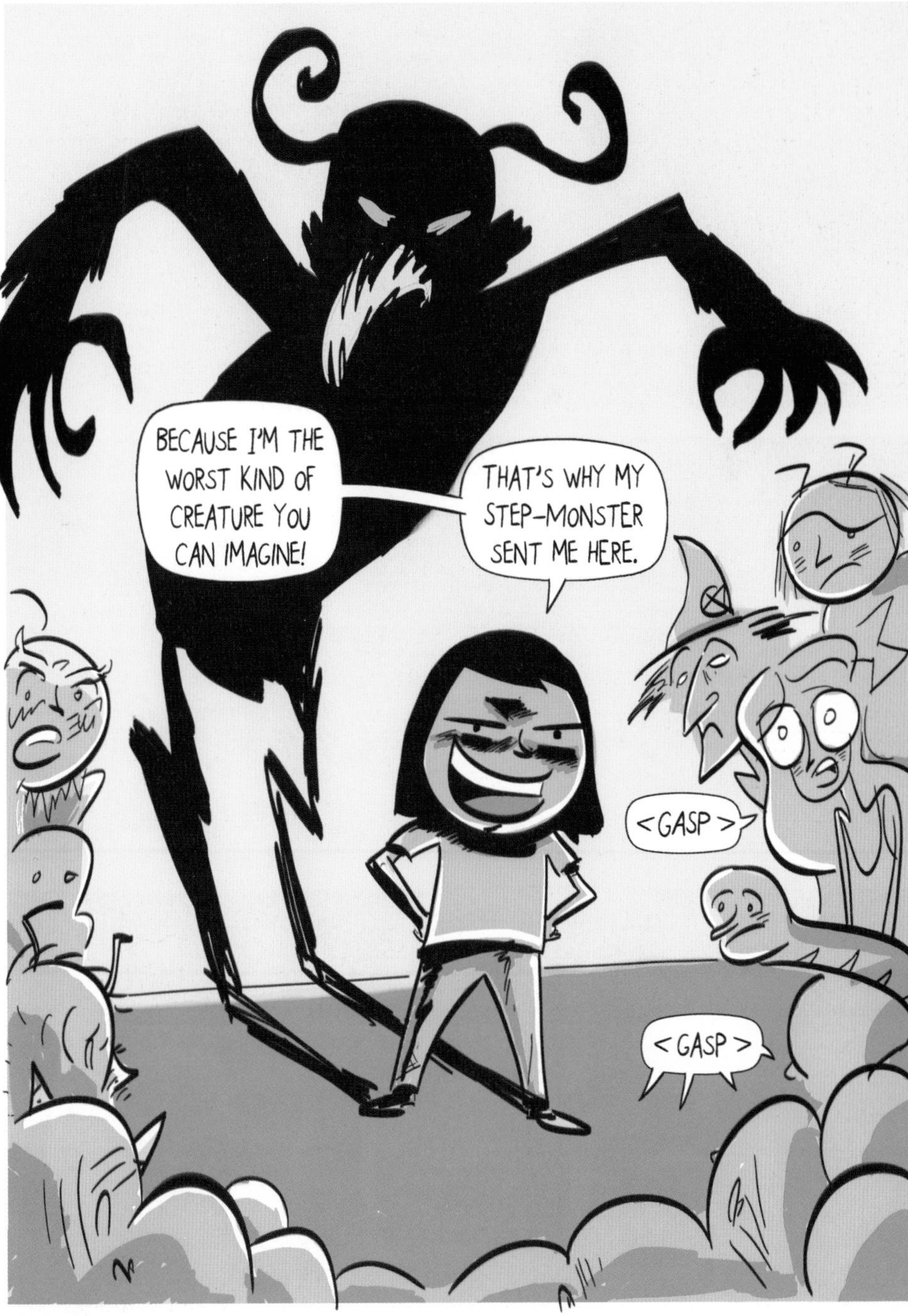
BECAUSE I'M THE WORST KIND OF CREATURE YOU CAN IMAGINE!
THAT'S WHY MY STEP-MONSTER SENT ME HERE.
<GASP>
<GASP>

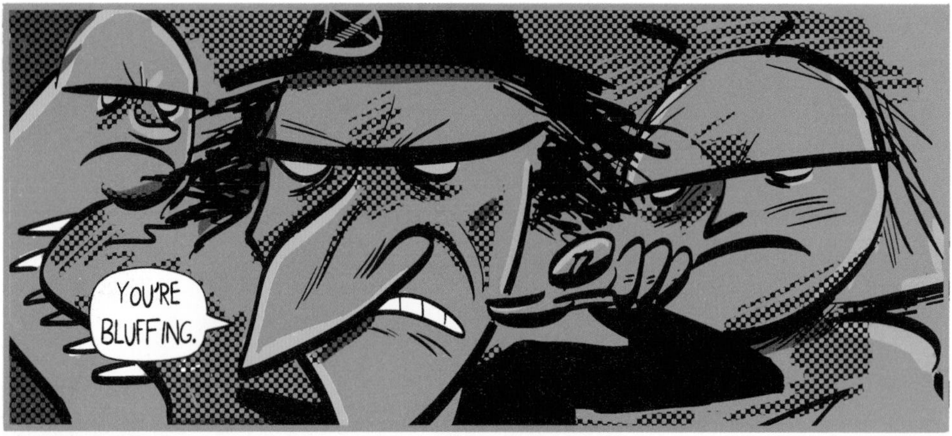
YOU'RE BLUFFING.

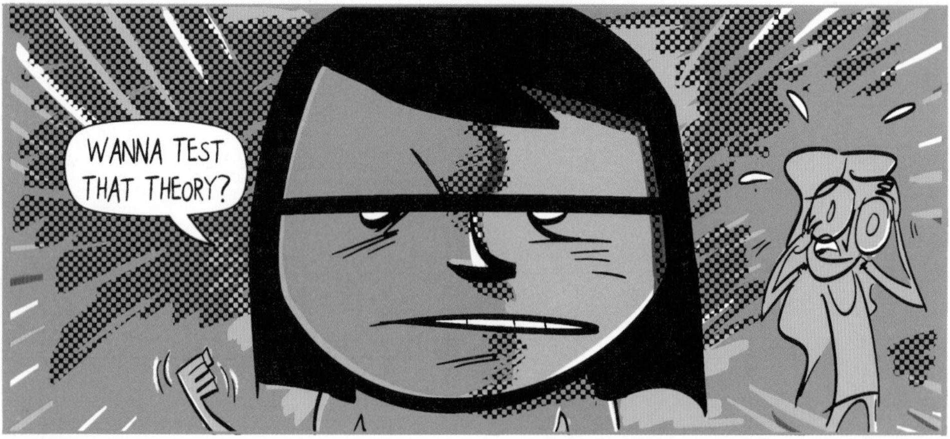
WANNA TEST THAT THEORY?

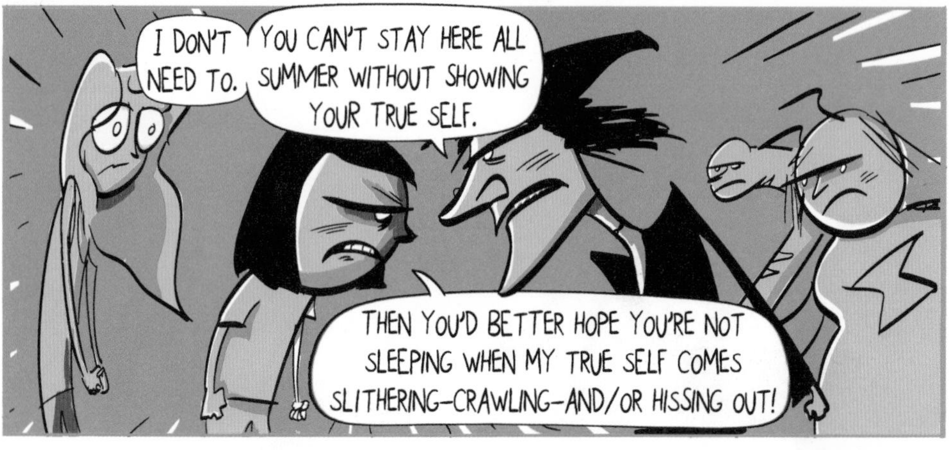
I DON'T NEED TO.
YOU CAN'T STAY HERE ALL SUMMER WITHOUT SHOWING YOUR TRUE SELF.
THEN YOU'D BETTER HOPE YOU'RE NOT SLEEPING WHEN MY TRUE SELF COMES SLITHERING-CRAWLING-AND/OR HISSING OUT!

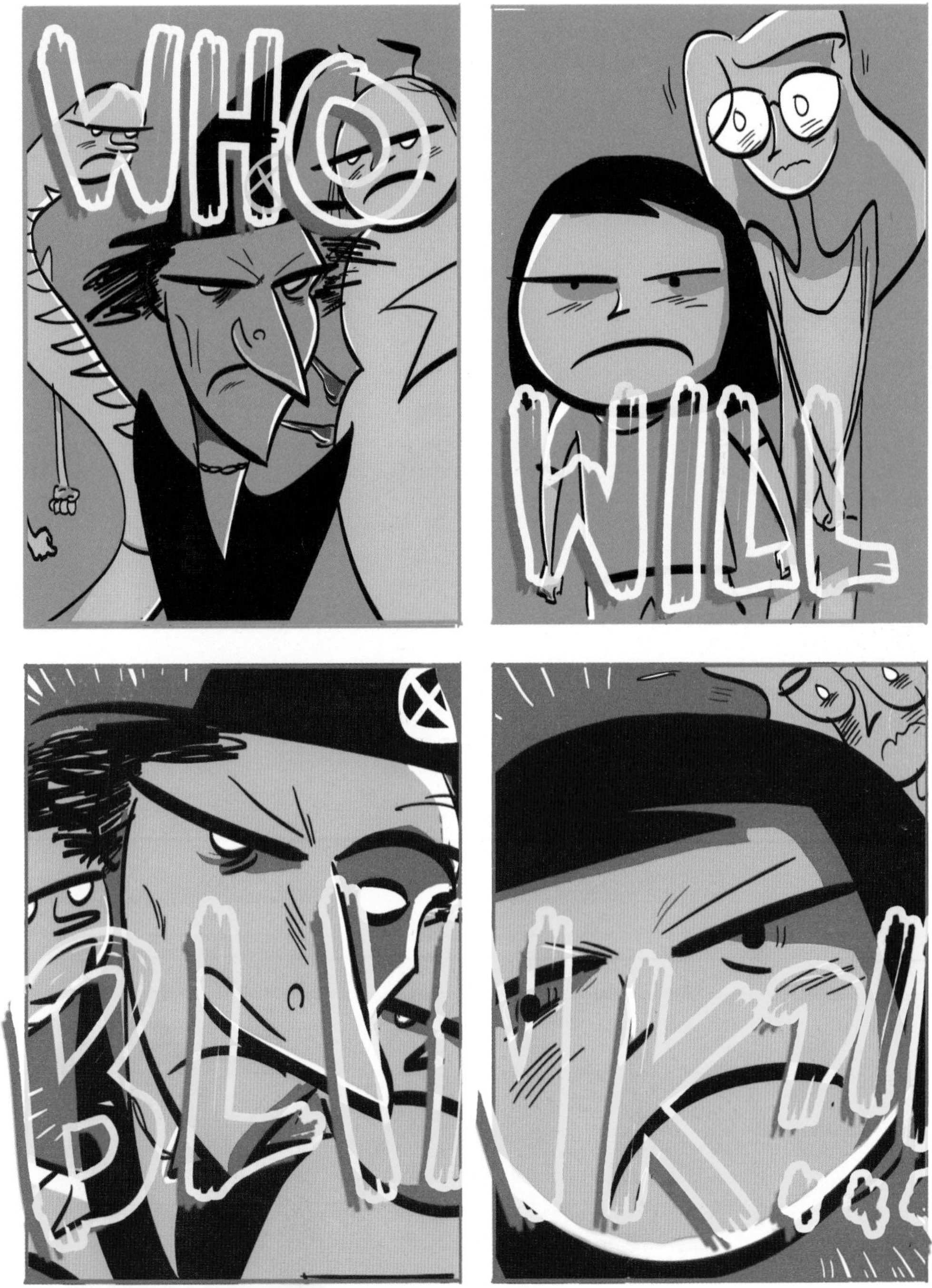
WHO
WILL
BLINK?

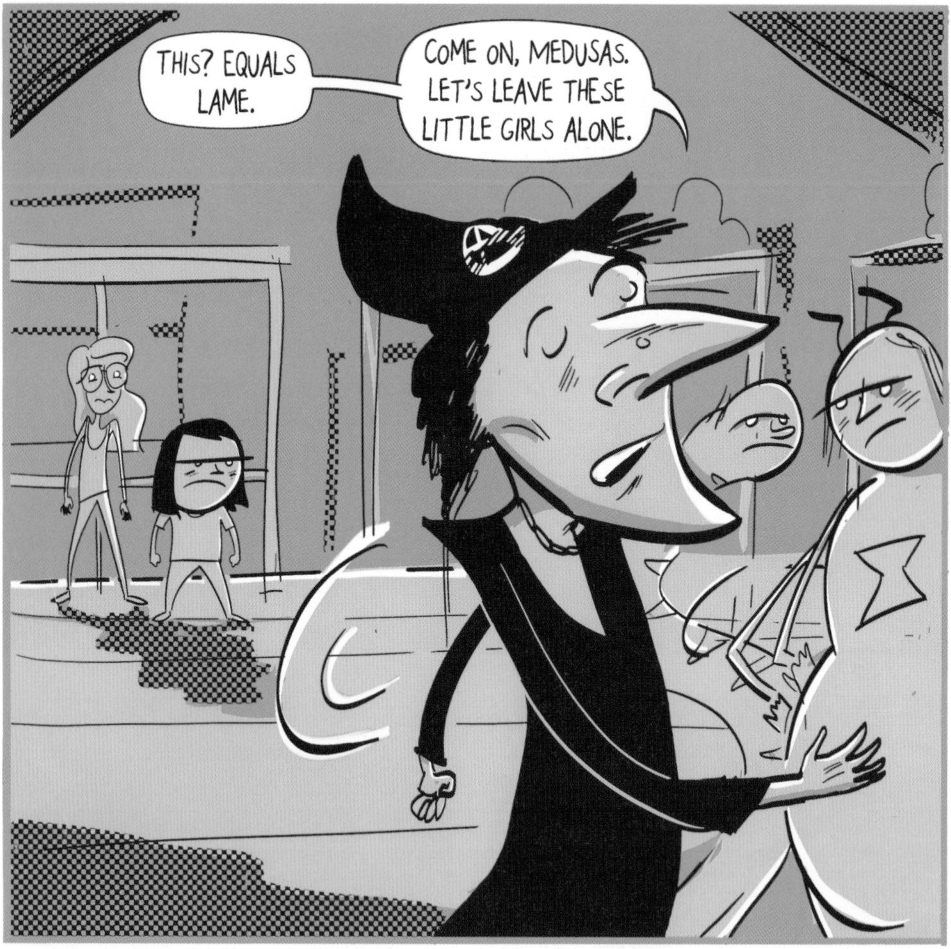
THIS? EQUALS LAME.
COME ON, MEDUSAS. LET'S LEAVE THESE LITTLE GIRLS ALONE.

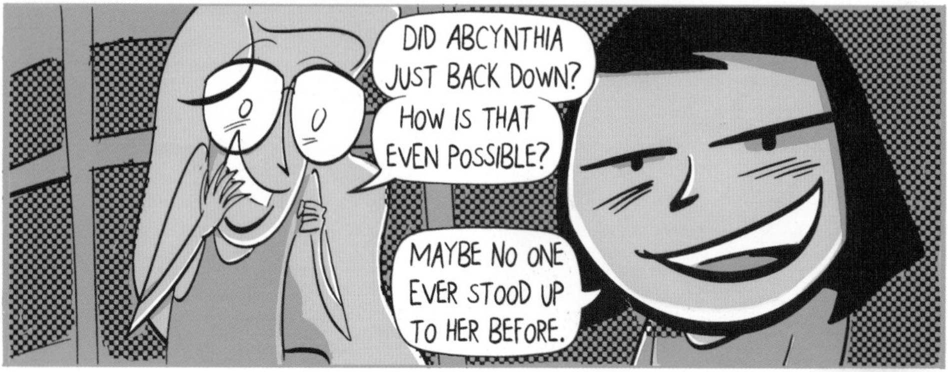
DID ABCYNTHIA JUST BACK DOWN?
HOW IS THAT EVEN POSSIBLE?
MAYBE NO ONE EVER STOOD UP TO HER BEFORE.

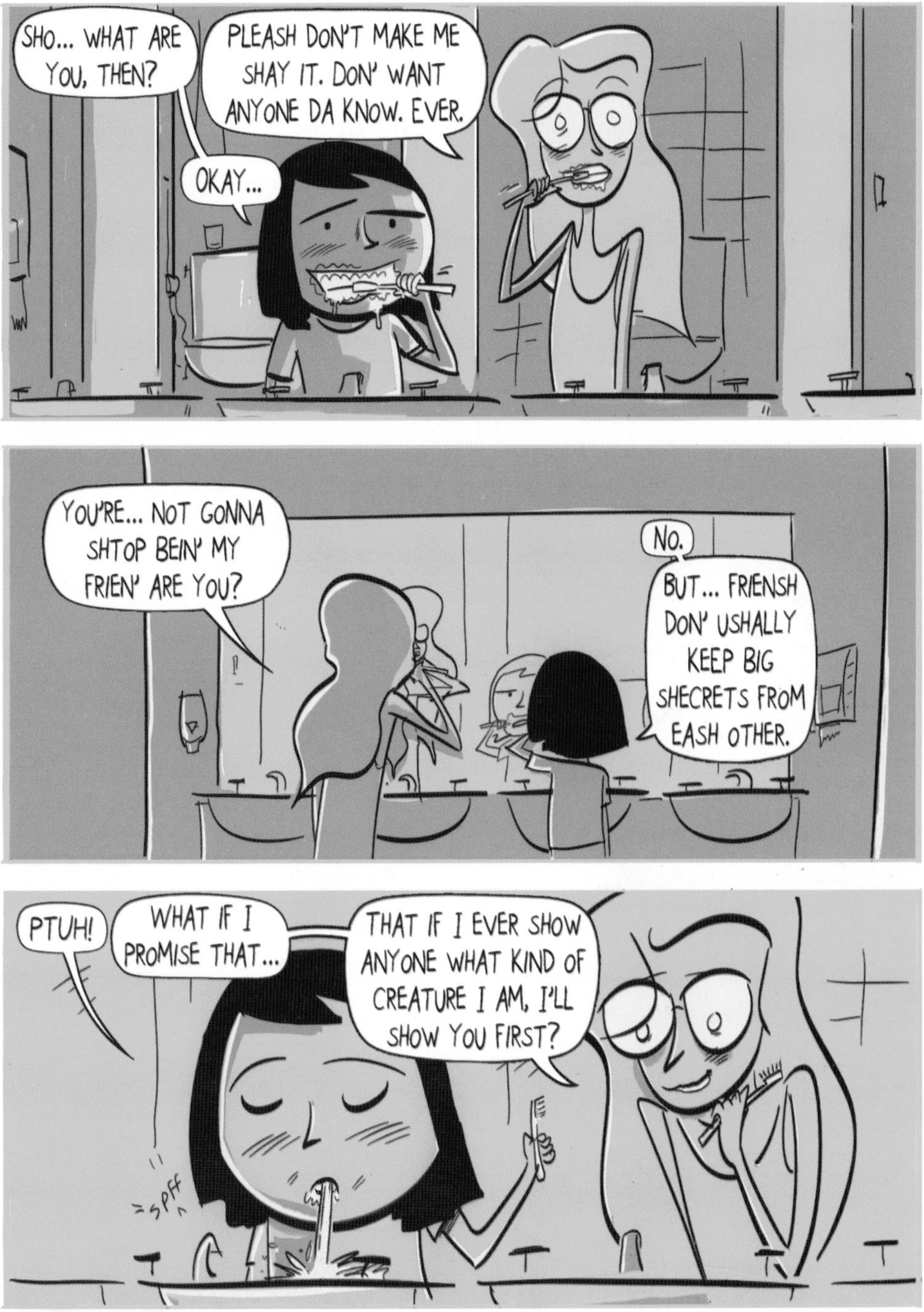
SHO... WHAT ARE YOU, THEN?
PLEASH DON'T MAKE ME SHAY IT. DON' WANT ANYONE DA KNOW. EVER.
OKAY...
YOU'RE... NOT GONNA SHTOP BEIN' MY FRIEN' ARE YOU?
NO.
BUT... FRIENSH DON' USHALLY KEEP BIG SHECRETS FROM EASH OTHER.
PTUH!
WHAT IF I PROMISE THAT...
THAT IF I EVER SHOW ANYONE WHAT KIND OF CREATURE I AM, I'LL SHOW YOU FIRST?
SPFF

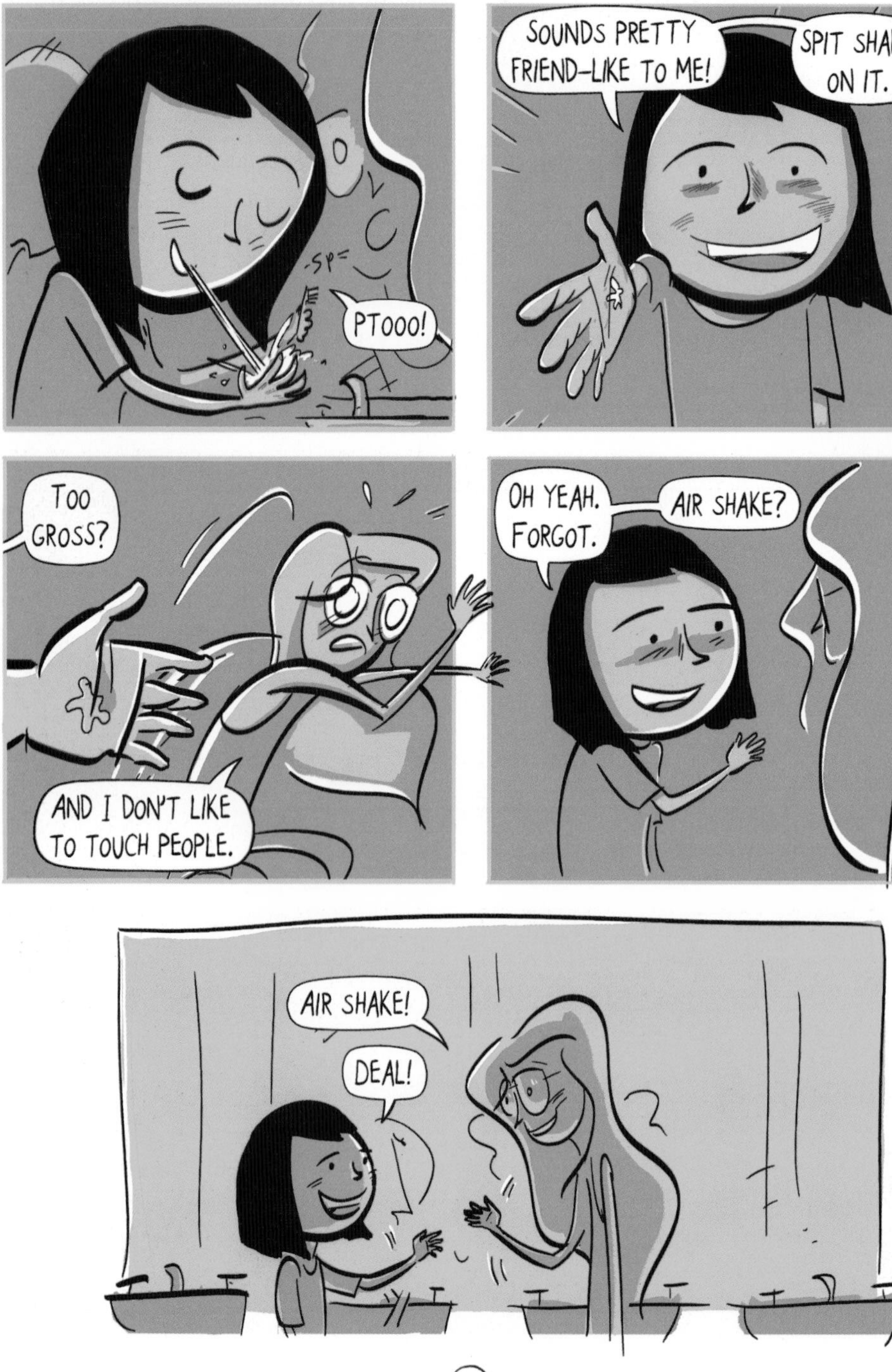
-SP=
PTOOO!
SOUNDS PRETTY FRIEND-LIKE TO ME!
SPIT SHAKE ON IT.
TOO GROSS?
AND I DON'T LIKE TO TOUCH PEOPLE.
OH YEAH. FORGOT.
AIR SHAKE?
AIR SHAKE!
DEAL!

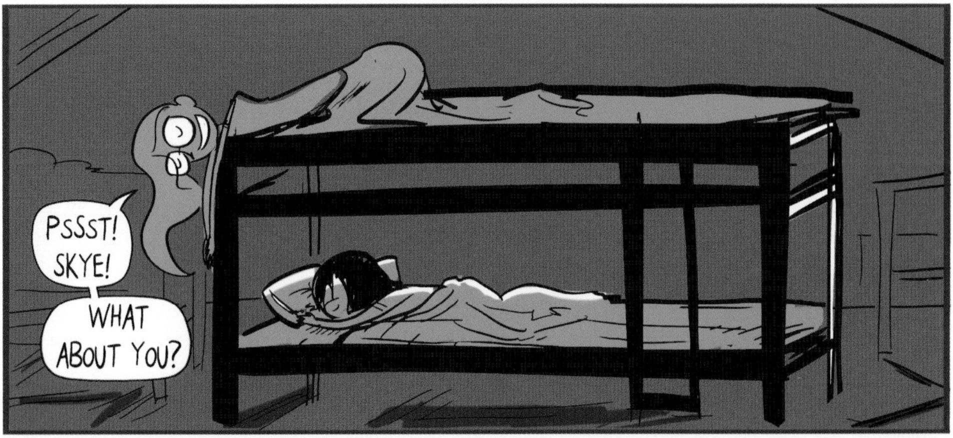
PSSST! SKYE!
WHAT ABOUT YOU?

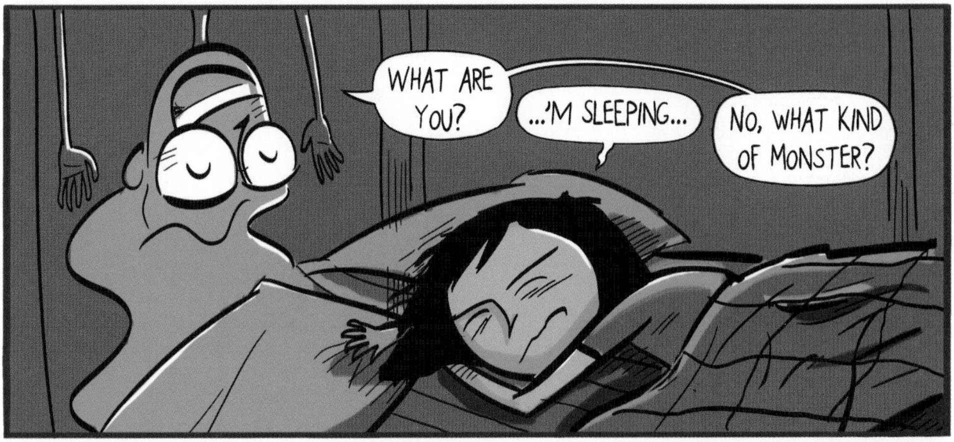
WHAT ARE YOU?
...'M SLEEPING...
NO, WHAT KIND OF MONSTER?

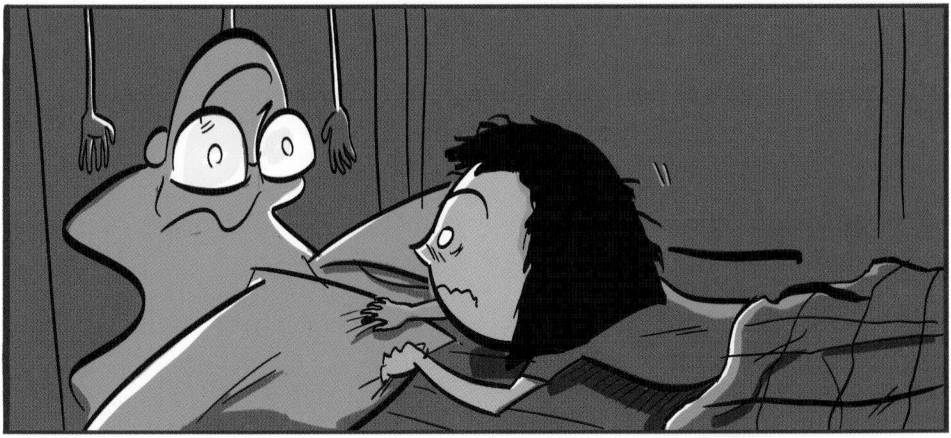

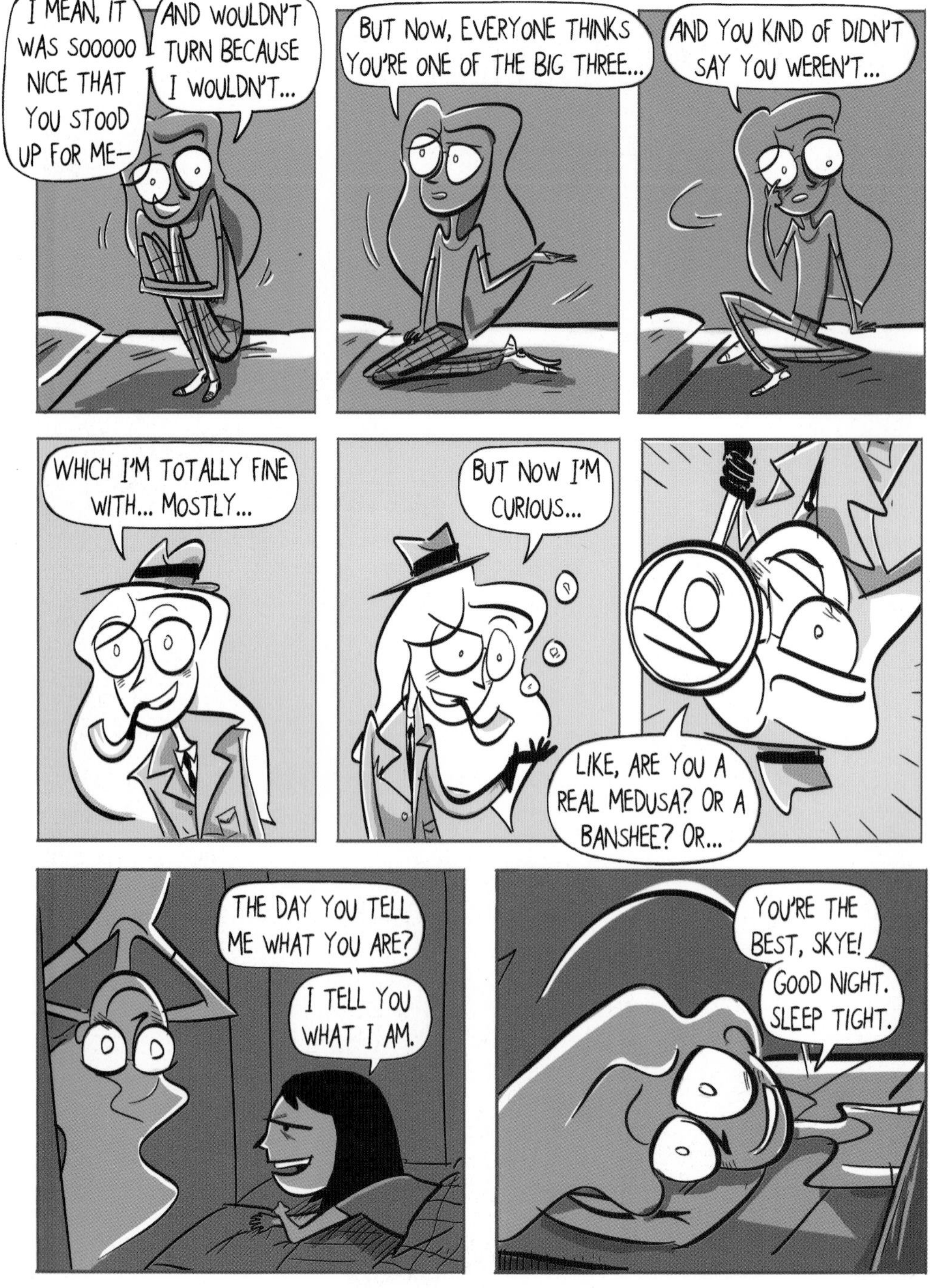
I MEAN, IT WAS SOOOOO NICE THAT YOU STOOD UP FOR ME–
AND WOULDN'T TURN BECAUSE I WOULDN'T...
BUT NOW, EVERYONE THINKS YOU'RE ONE OF THE BIG THREE...
AND YOU KIND OF DIDN'T SAY YOU WEREN'T...
WHICH I'M TOTALLY FINE WITH... MOSTLY...
BUT NOW I'M CURIOUS...
LIKE, ARE YOU A REAL MEDUSA? OR A BANSHEE? OR...
THE DAY YOU TELL ME WHAT YOU ARE?
I TELL YOU WHAT I AM.
YOU'RE THE BEST, SKYE!
GOOD NIGHT. SLEEP TIGHT.

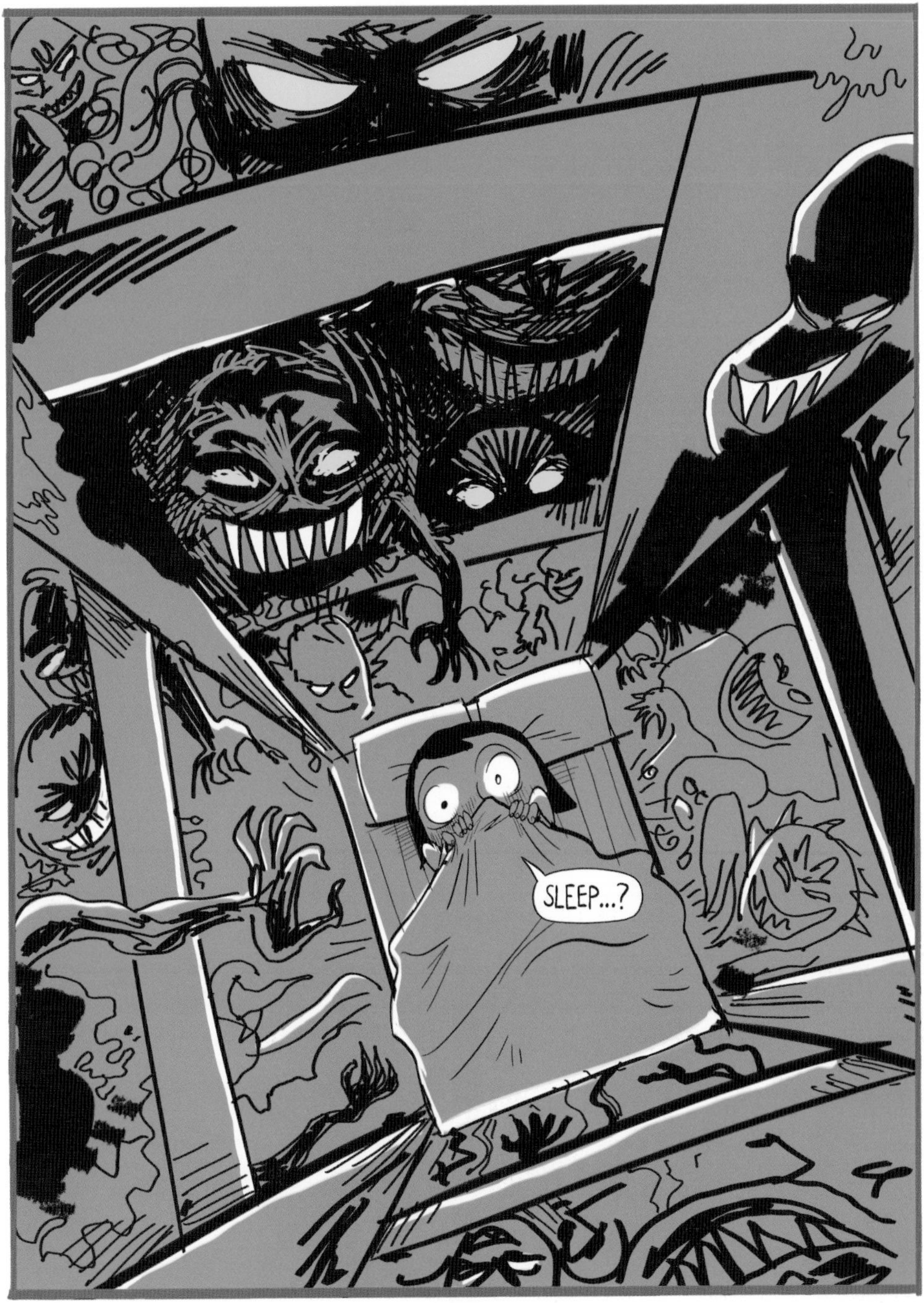
SLEEP...?

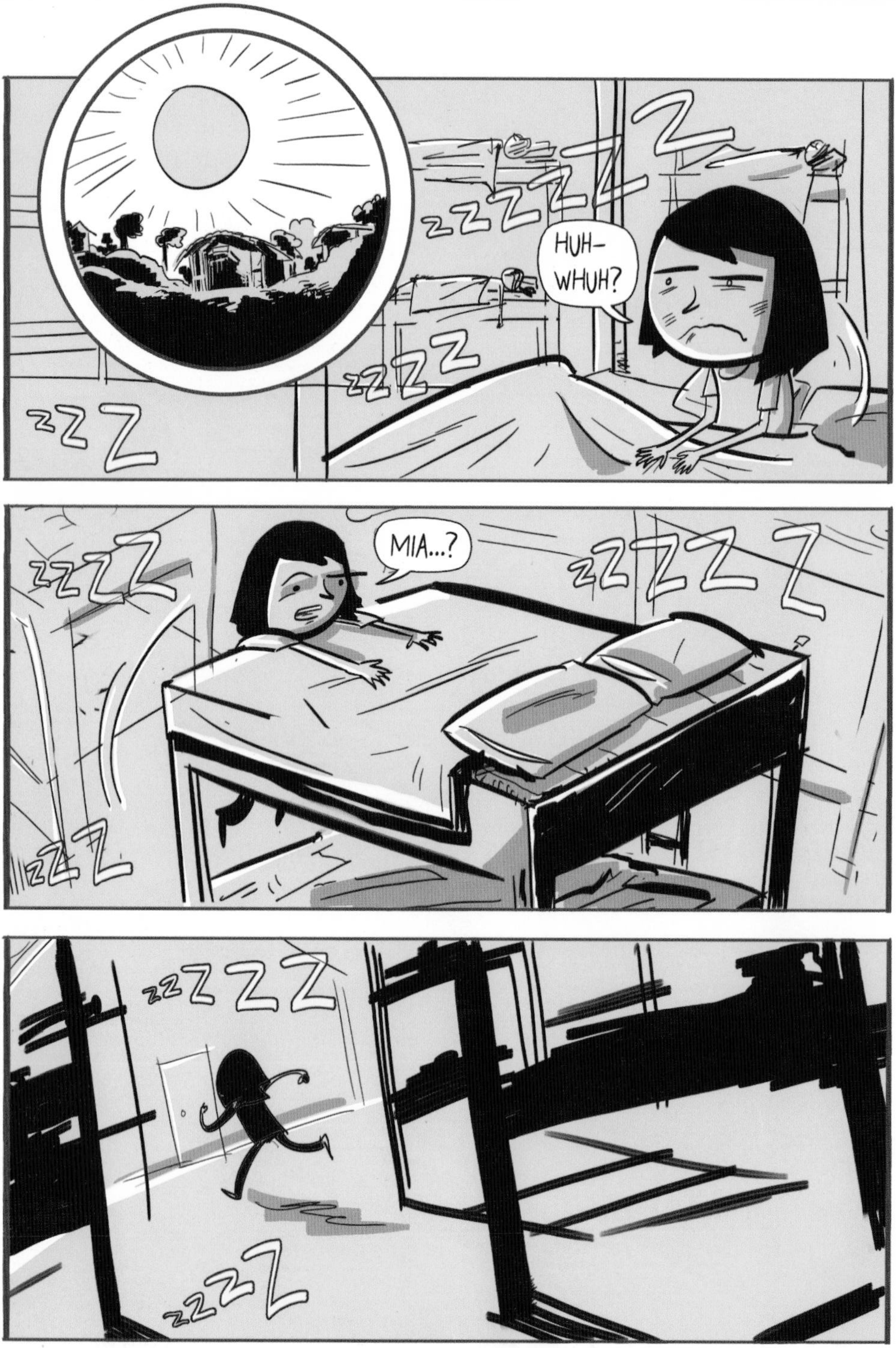
ZZZZZZ
HUH-
WHUH?
ZZZZ
ZZZ
ZZZZ
MIA...?
ZZZZZ
ZZZ
ZZZZZ
ZZZZ

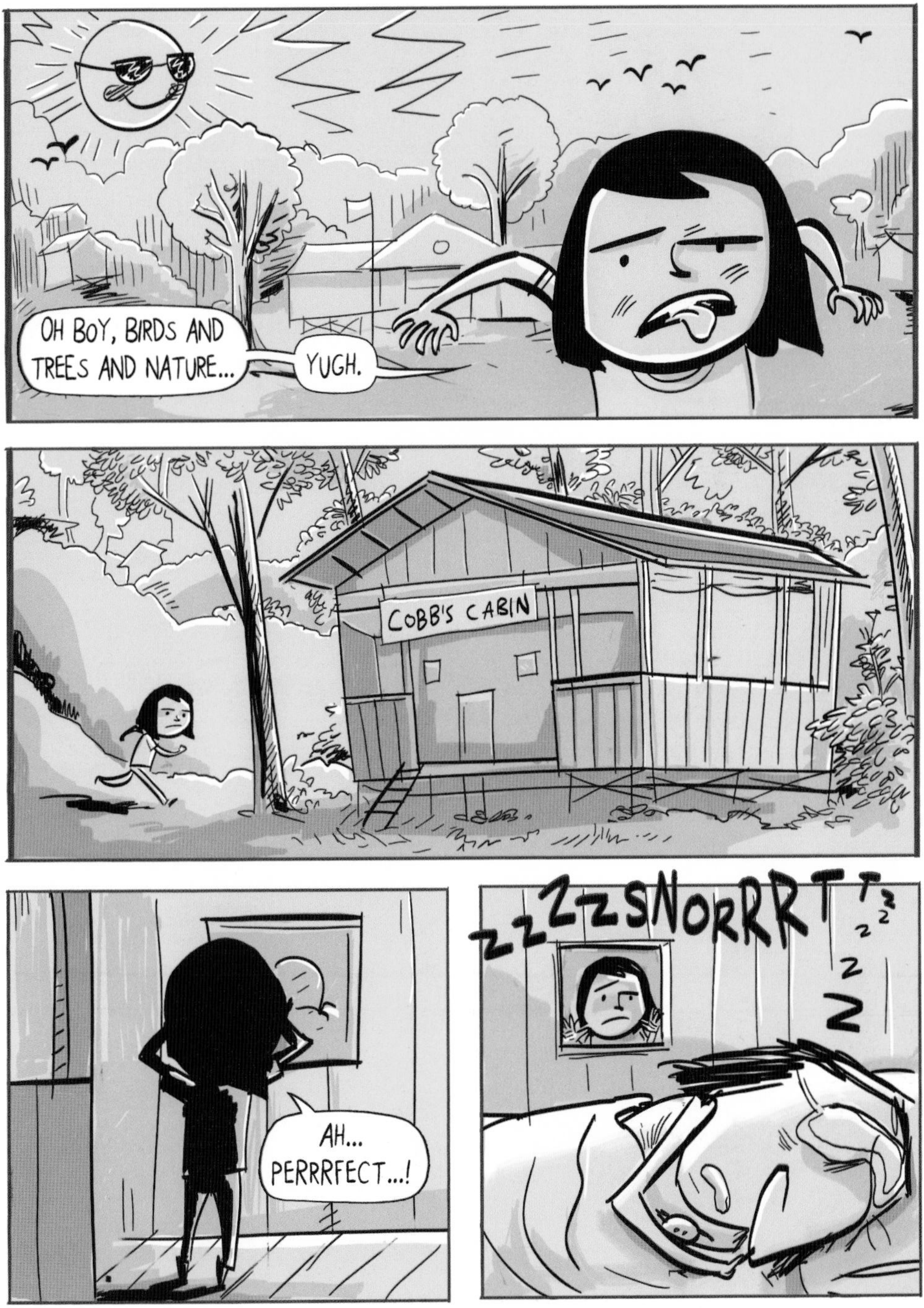
OH BOY, BIRDS AND TREES AND NATURE...
YUGH.
COBB'S CABIN
AH... PERRRFECT...!
zzZZzSNORRRRTzzzzZ

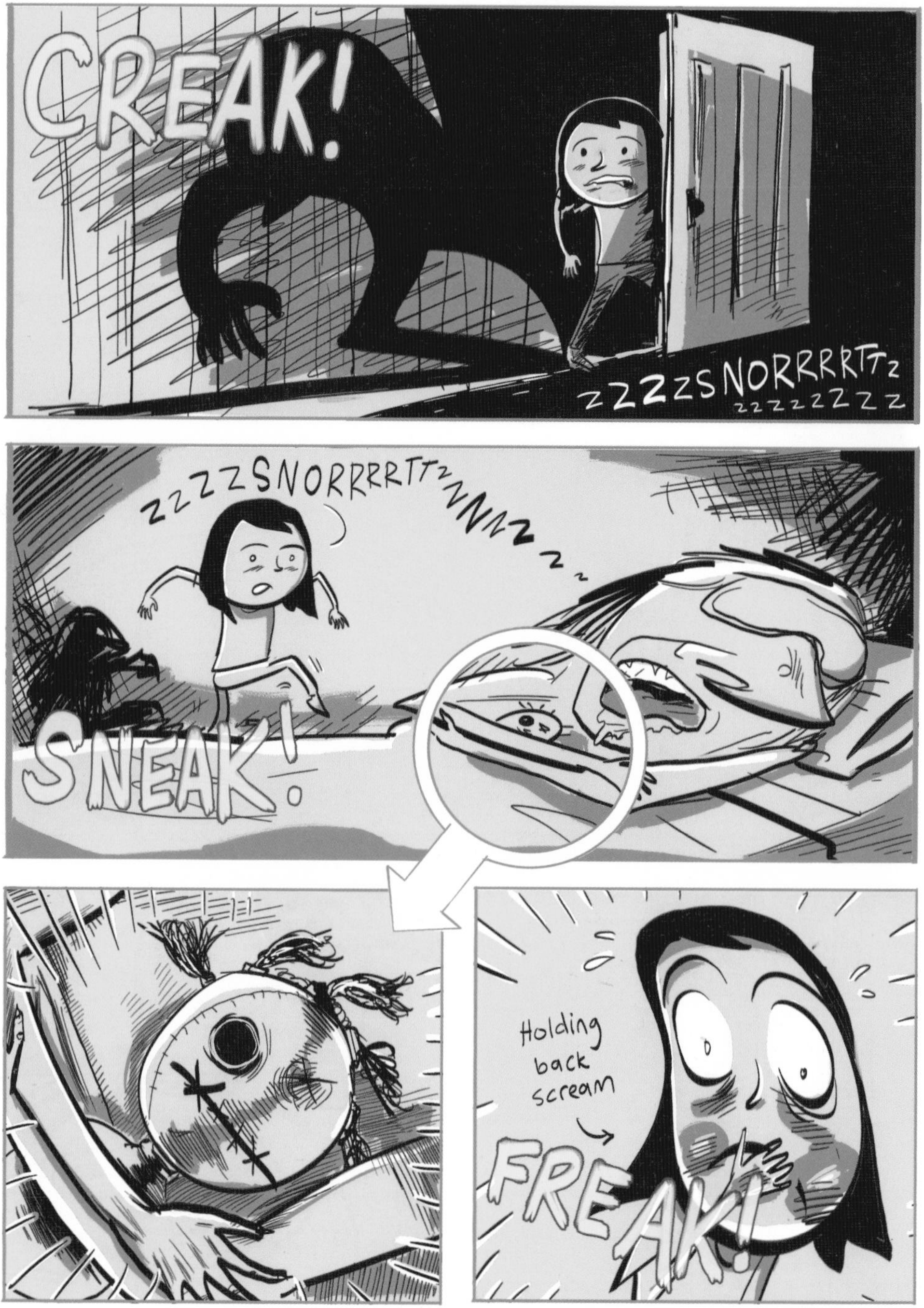
CREAK!
ZZZZSNORRRRTTZ
ZZZZZZZZ
ZZZZSNORRRRTTZ
ZZZZZZZ
SNEAK!
Holding back scream
FREAK!

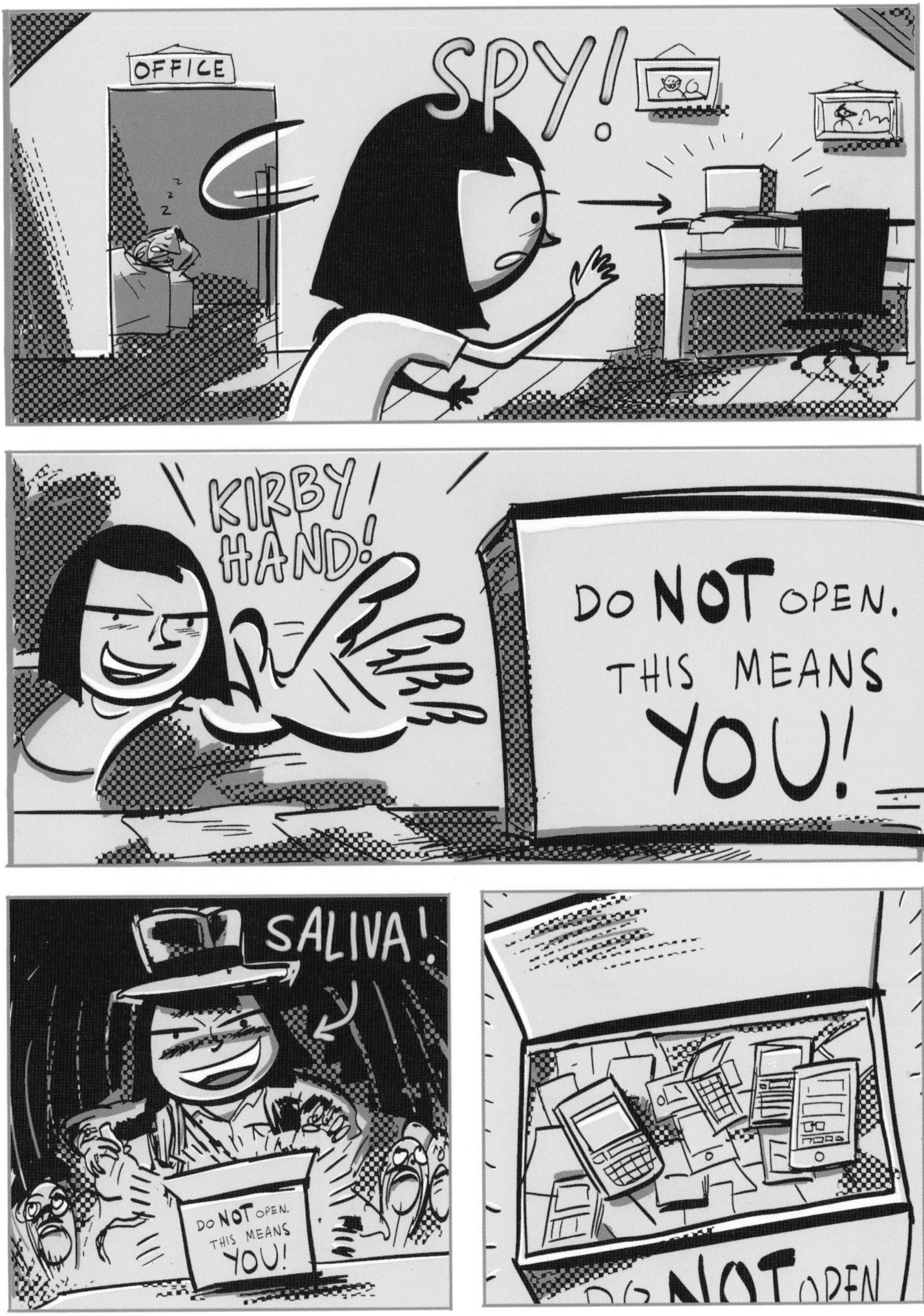
OFFICE
SPY!
KIRBY HAND!
DO NOT OPEN. THIS MEANS YOU!
SALIVA!
DO NOT OPEN. THIS MEANS YOU!

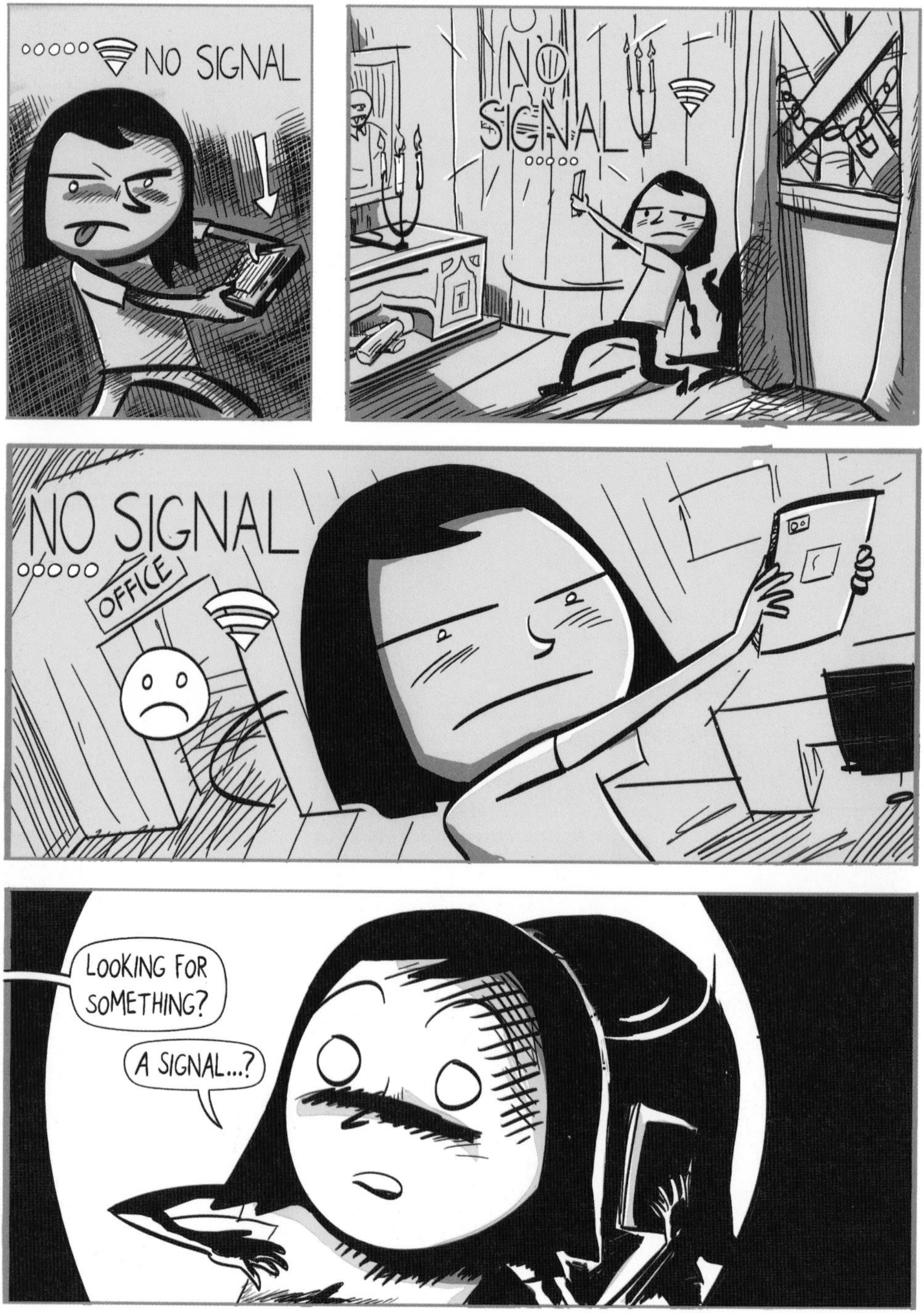
NO SIGNAL
NO SIGNAL
NO SIGNAL
OFFICE
LOOKING FOR SOMETHING?
A SIGNAL...?

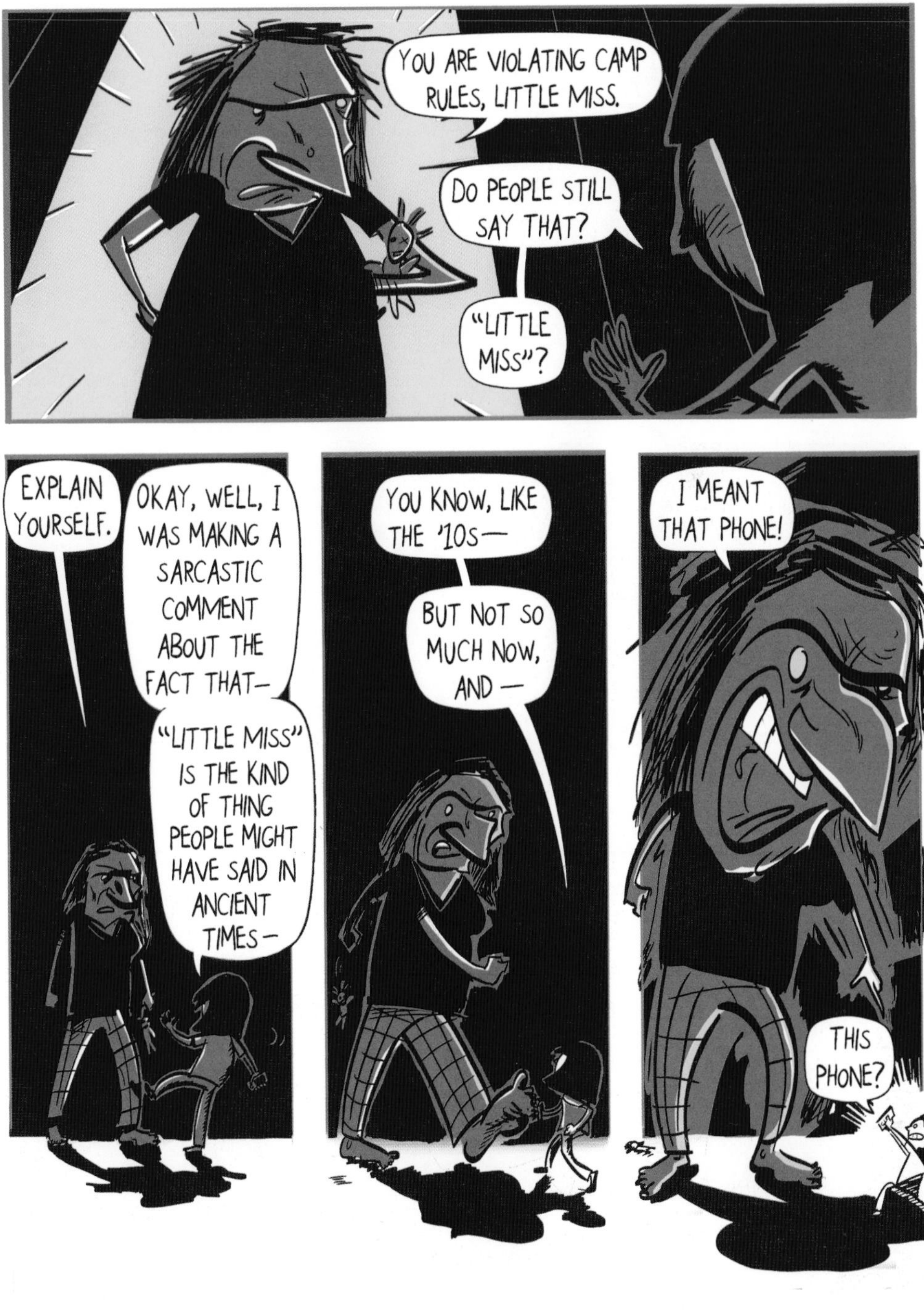

YOU ARE VIOLATING CAMP RULES, LITTLE MISS.
DO PEOPLE STILL SAY THAT?
"LITTLE MISS"?
EXPLAIN YOURSELF.
OKAY, WELL, I WAS MAKING A SARCASTIC COMMENT ABOUT THE FACT THAT—
"LITTLE MISS" IS THE KIND OF THING PEOPLE MIGHT HAVE SAID IN ANCIENT TIMES—
YOU KNOW, LIKE THE '10S—
BUT NOT SO MUCH NOW, AND—
I MEANT THAT PHONE!
THIS PHONE?

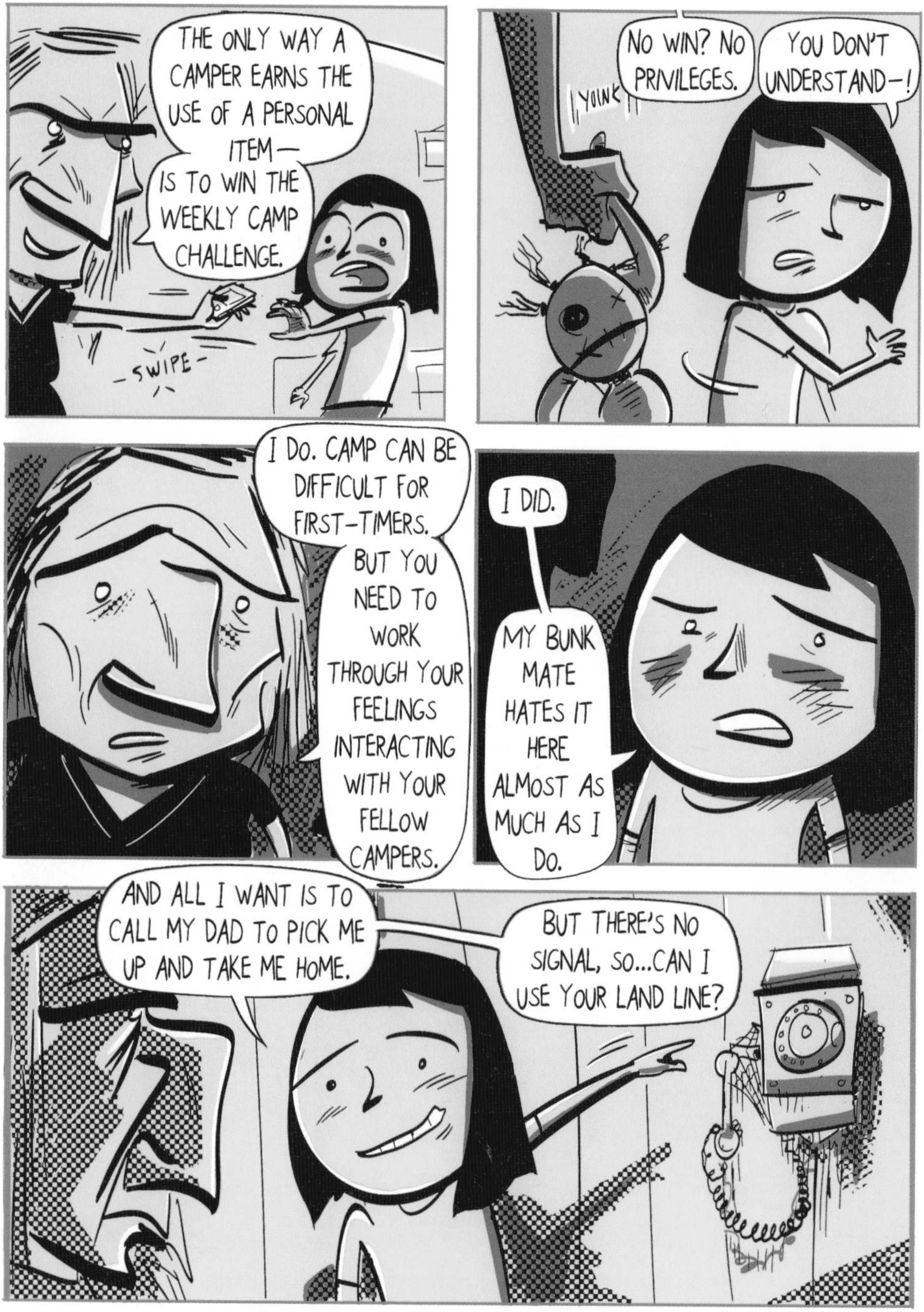
THE ONLY WAY A CAMPER EARNS THE USE OF A PERSONAL ITEM—
IS TO WIN THE WEEKLY CAMP CHALLENGE.
SWIPE
YOINK
NO WIN? NO PRIVILEGES.
YOU DON'T UNDERSTAND—!
I DO. CAMP CAN BE DIFFICULT FOR FIRST-TIMERS.
BUT YOU NEED TO WORK THROUGH YOUR FEELINGS INTERACTING WITH YOUR FELLOW CAMPERS.
I DID.
MY BUNK MATE HATES IT HERE ALMOST AS MUCH AS I DO.
AND ALL I WANT IS TO CALL MY DAD TO PICK ME UP AND TAKE ME HOME.
BUT THERE'S NO SIGNAL, SO...CAN I USE YOUR LAND LINE?

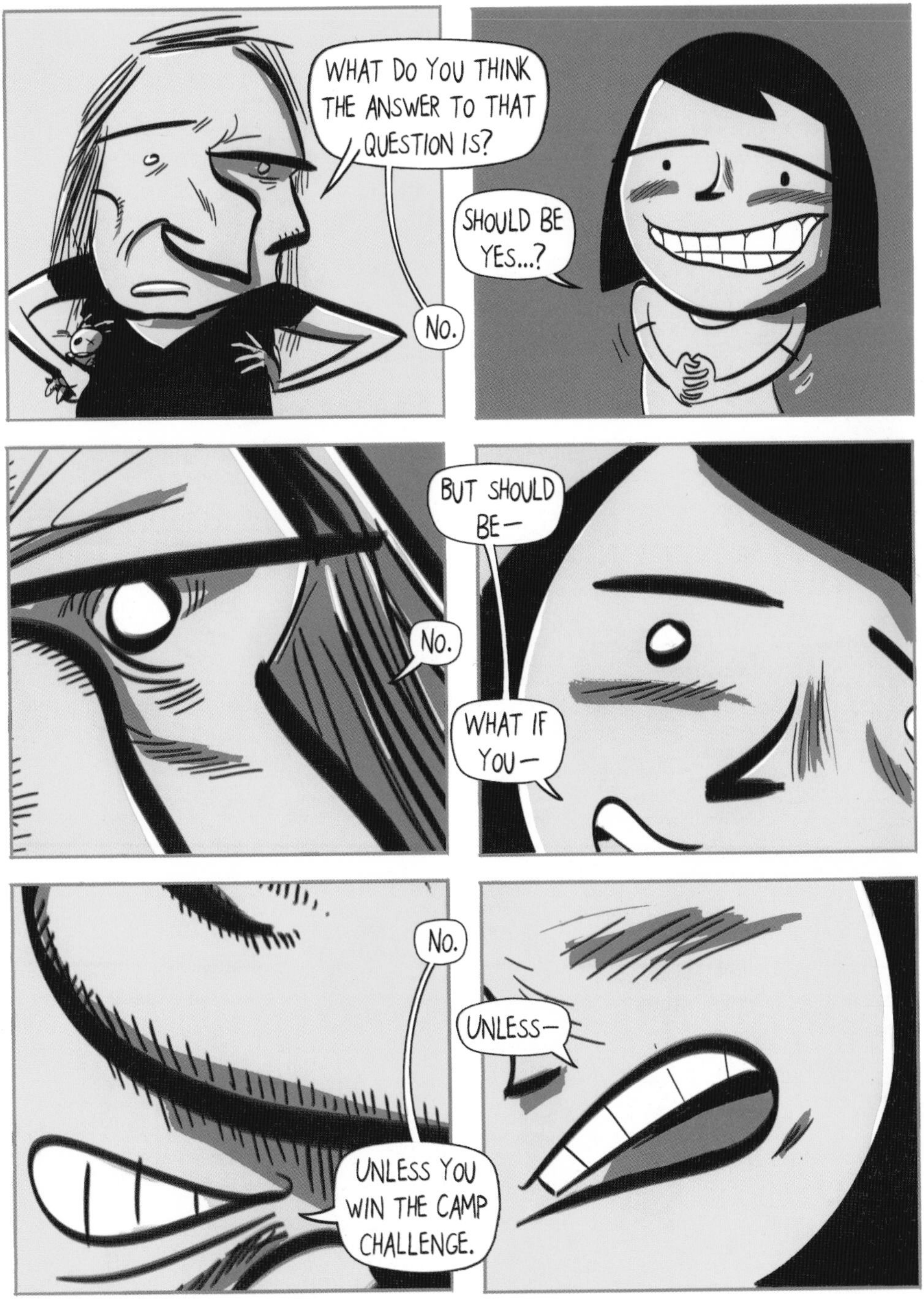
WHAT DO YOU THINK THE ANSWER TO THAT QUESTION IS?
SHOULD BE YES...?
NO.
BUT SHOULD BE—
NO.
WHAT IF YOU—
NO.
UNLESS—
UNLESS YOU WIN THE CAMP CHALLENGE.

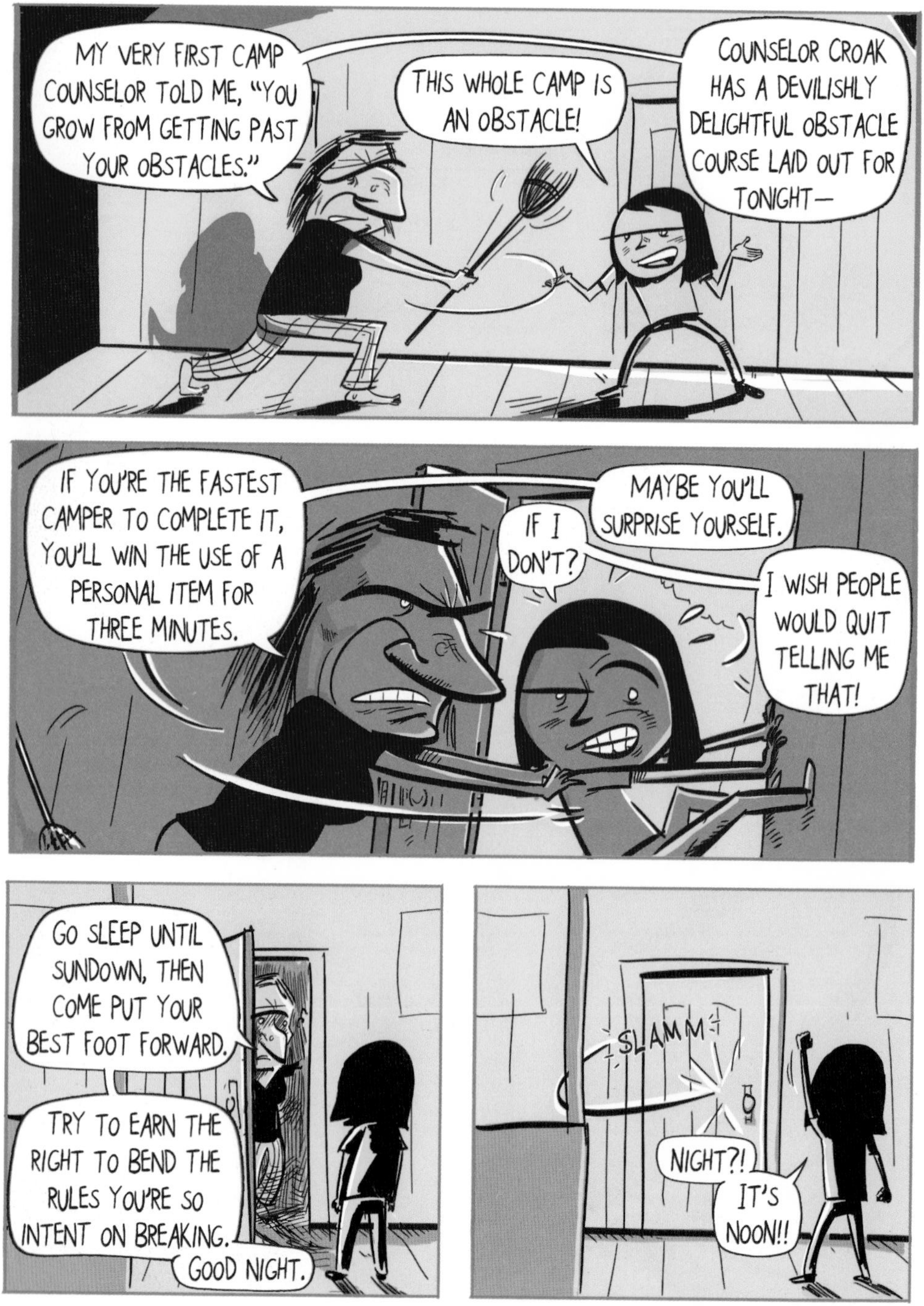
MY VERY FIRST CAMP COUNSELOR TOLD ME, "YOU GROW FROM GETTING PAST YOUR OBSTACLES."
THIS WHOLE CAMP IS AN OBSTACLE!
COUNSELOR CROAK HAS A DEVILISHLY DELIGHTFUL OBSTACLE COURSE LAID OUT FOR TONIGHT—
IF YOU'RE THE FASTEST CAMPER TO COMPLETE IT, YOU'LL WIN THE USE OF A PERSONAL ITEM FOR THREE MINUTES.
IF I DON'T?
MAYBE YOU'LL SURPRISE YOURSELF.
I WISH PEOPLE WOULD QUIT TELLING ME THAT!
GO SLEEP UNTIL SUNDOWN, THEN COME PUT YOUR BEST FOOT FORWARD.
TRY TO EARN THE RIGHT TO BEND THE RULES YOU'RE SO INTENT ON BREAKING.
GOOD NIGHT.
SLAMM
NIGHT?!
IT'S NOON!!

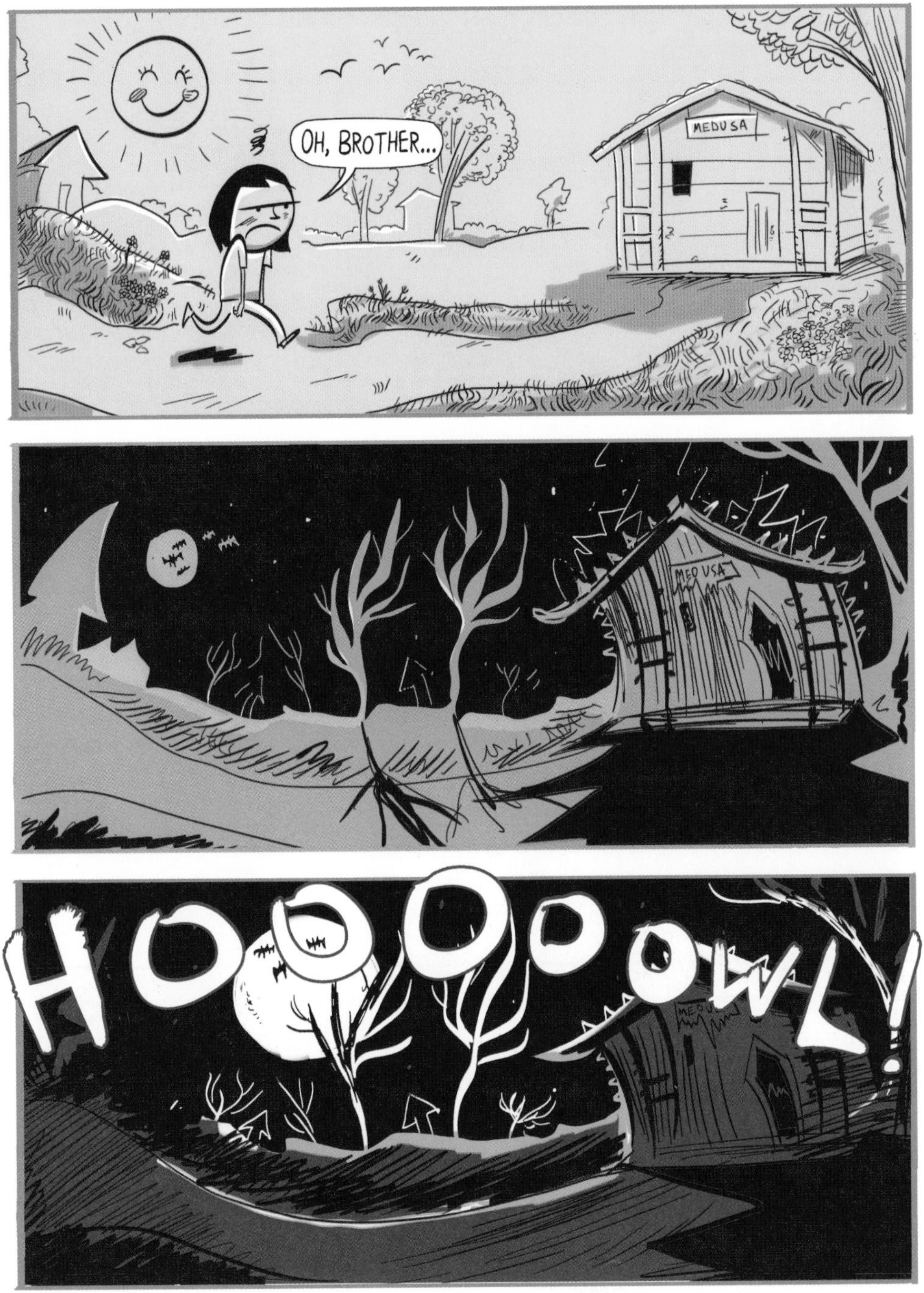

OH, BROTHER...
MEDUSA
MEDUSA
HOOOOOWL!

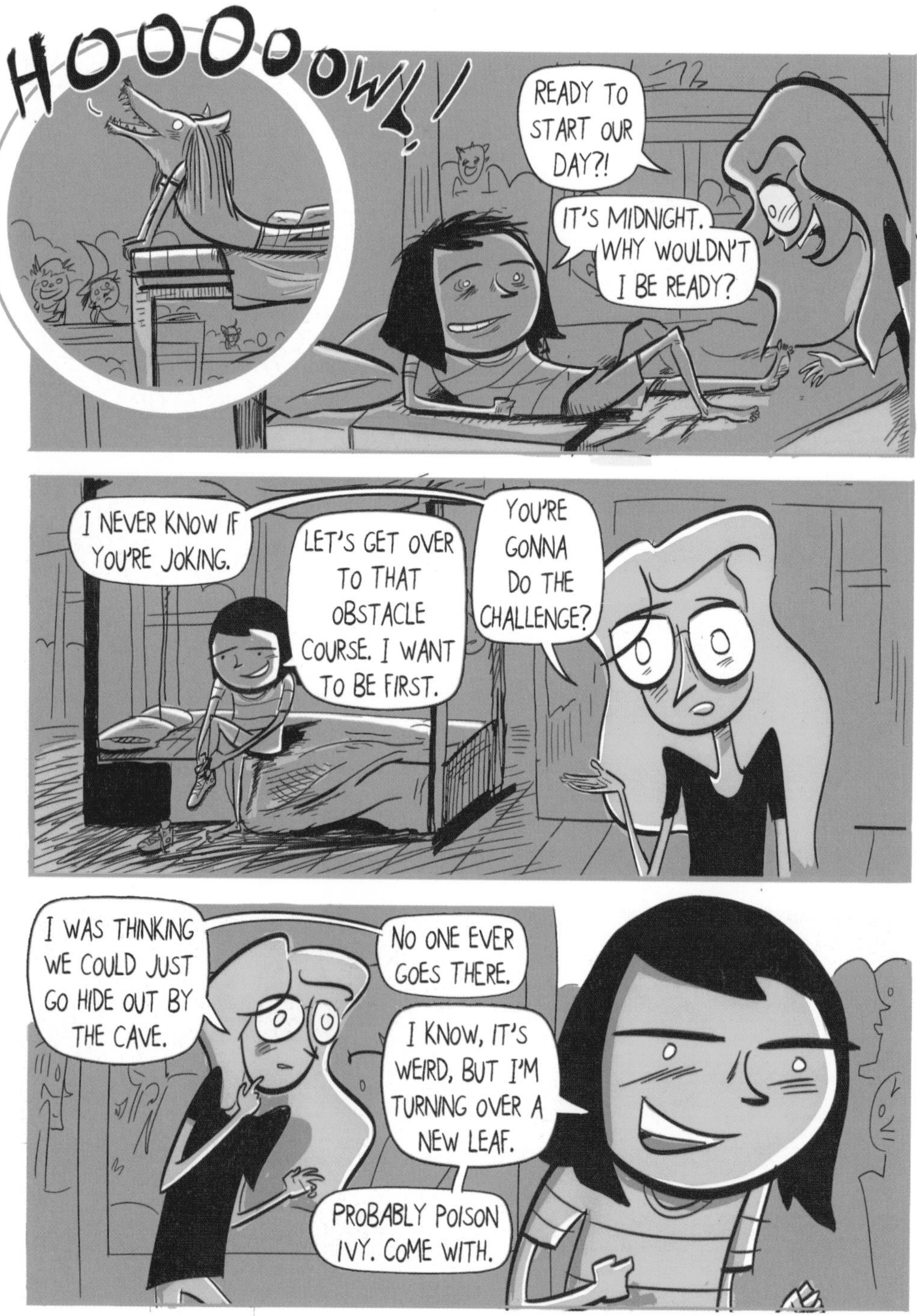
HOOOOoOWL!!
READY TO START OUR DAY?!
IT'S MIDNIGHT. WHY WOULDN'T I BE READY?
I NEVER KNOW IF YOU'RE JOKING.
LET'S GET OVER TO THAT OBSTACLE COURSE. I WANT TO BE FIRST.
YOU'RE GONNA DO THE CHALLENGE?
I WAS THINKING WE COULD JUST GO HIDE OUT BY THE CAVE.
NO ONE EVER GOES THERE.
I KNOW, IT'S WEIRD, BUT I'M TURNING OVER A NEW LEAF.
PROBABLY POISON IVY. COME WITH.

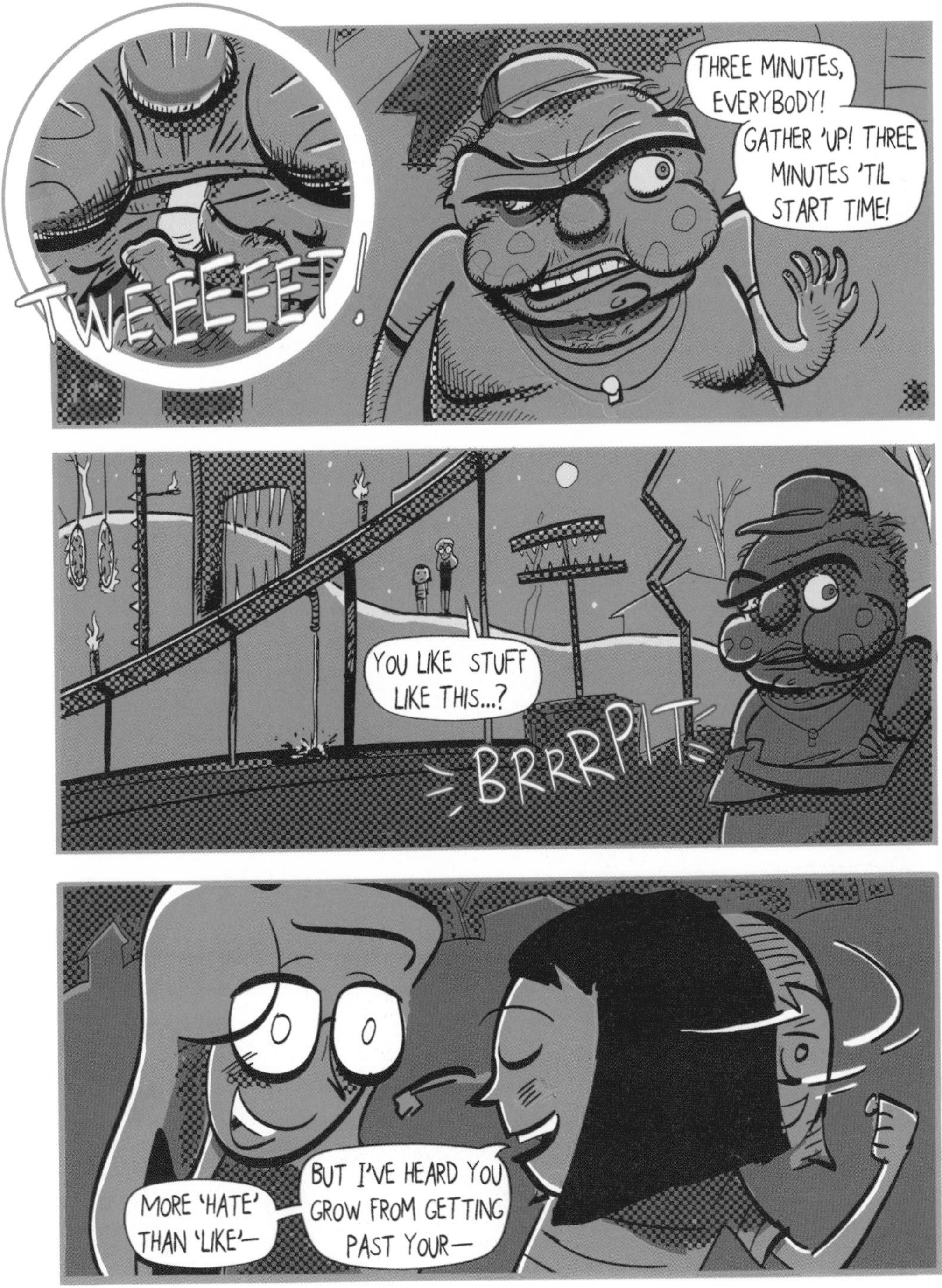
TWEEEEET!
THREE MINUTES, EVERYBODY!
GATHER 'UP! THREE MINUTES 'TIL START TIME!
YOU LIKE STUFF LIKE THIS...?
BRRRPIT
MORE 'HATE' THAN 'LIKE'—
BUT I'VE HEARD YOU GROW FROM GETTING PAST YOUR—

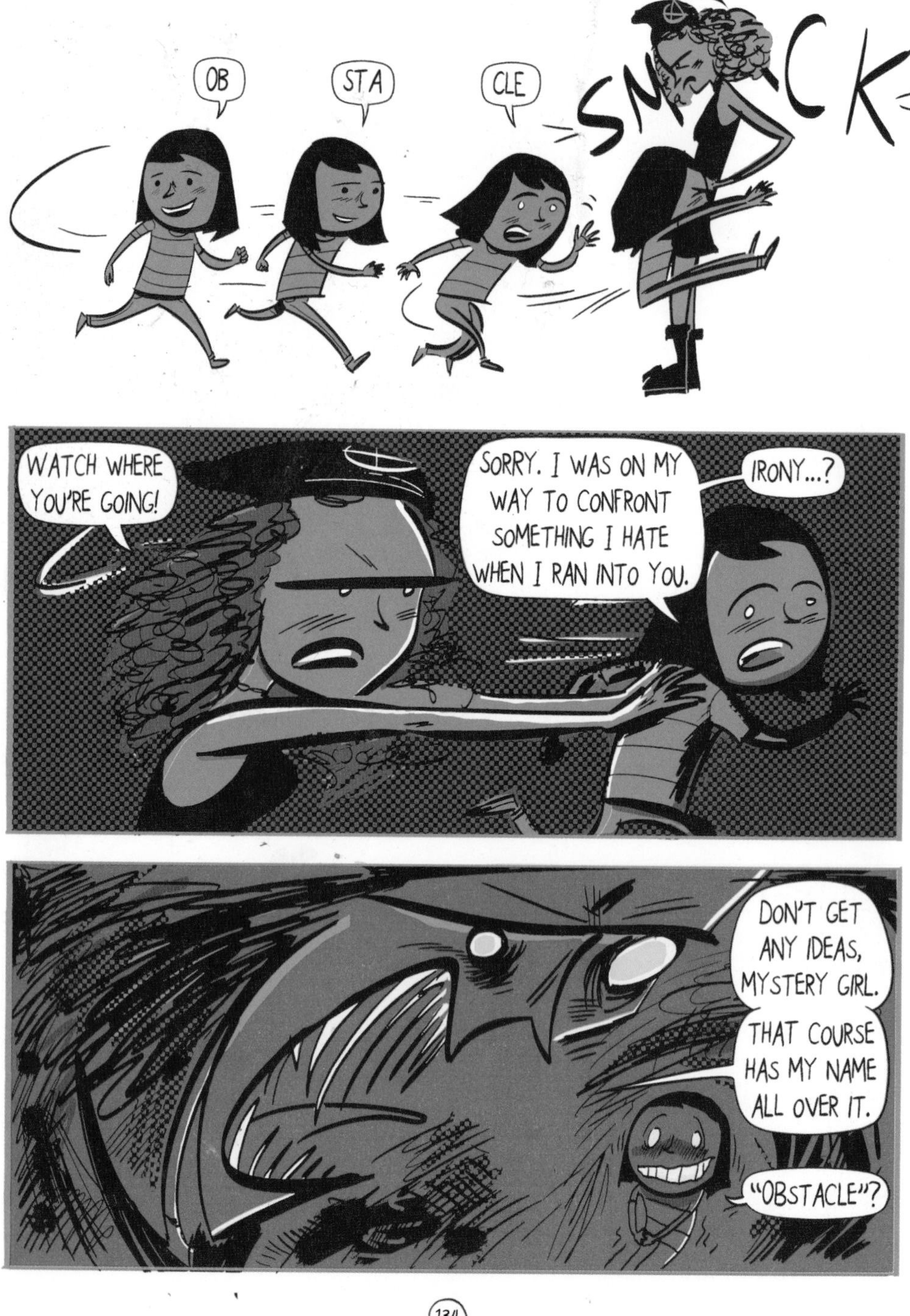
OB
STA
CLE
SMACK
WATCH WHERE YOU'RE GOING!
SORRY. I WAS ON MY WAY TO CONFRONT SOMETHING I HATE WHEN I RAN INTO YOU.
IRONY...?
DON'T GET ANY IDEAS, MYSTERY GIRL.
THAT COURSE HAS MY NAME ALL OVER IT.
"OBSTACLE"?

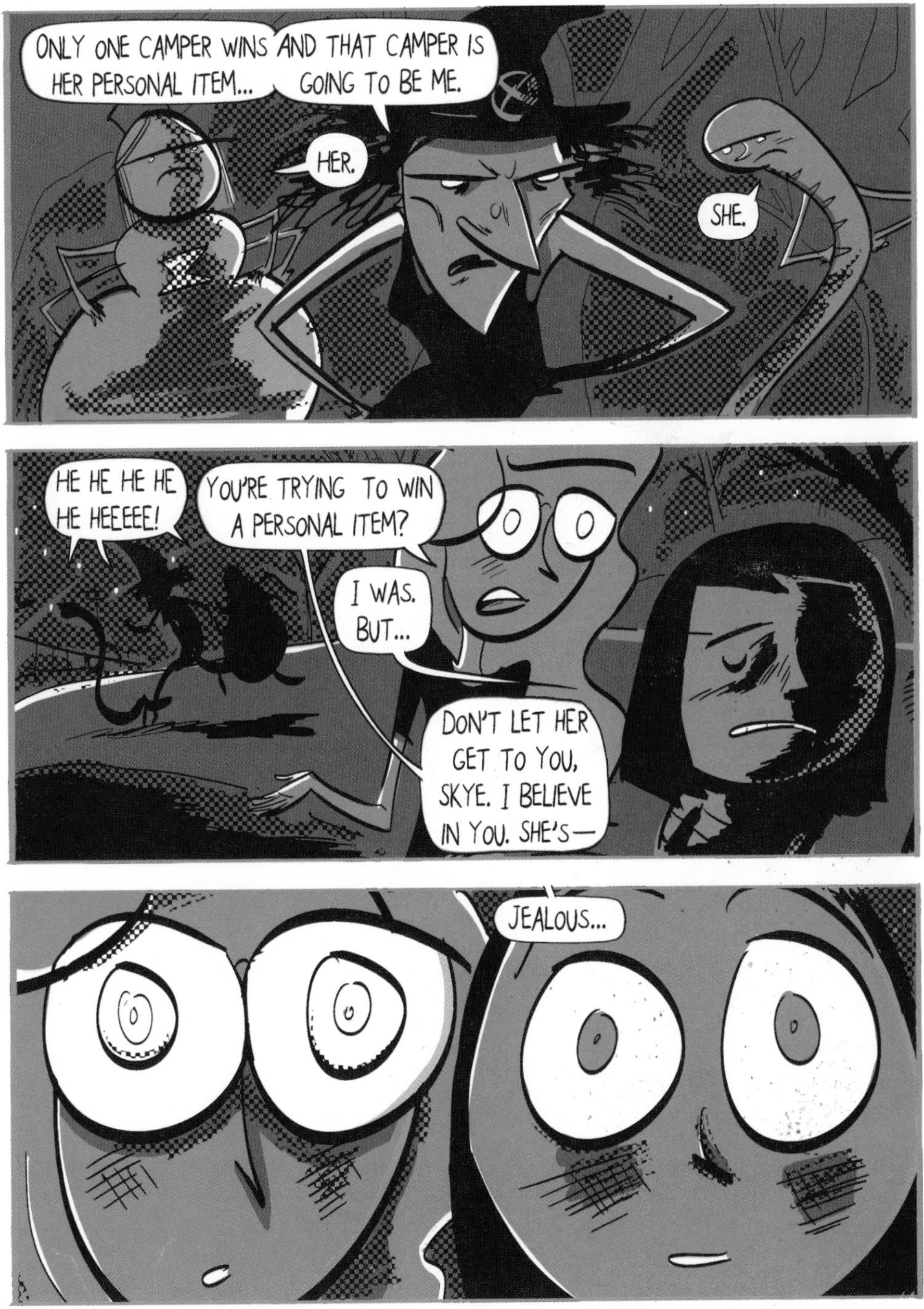
ONLY ONE CAMPER WINS HER PERSONAL ITEM...
AND THAT CAMPER IS GOING TO BE ME.
HER.
SHE.
HE HE HE HE HE HEEEEE!
YOU'RE TRYING TO WIN A PERSONAL ITEM?
I WAS. BUT...
DON'T LET HER GET TO YOU, SKYE. I BELIEVE IN YOU. SHE'S—
JEALOUS...

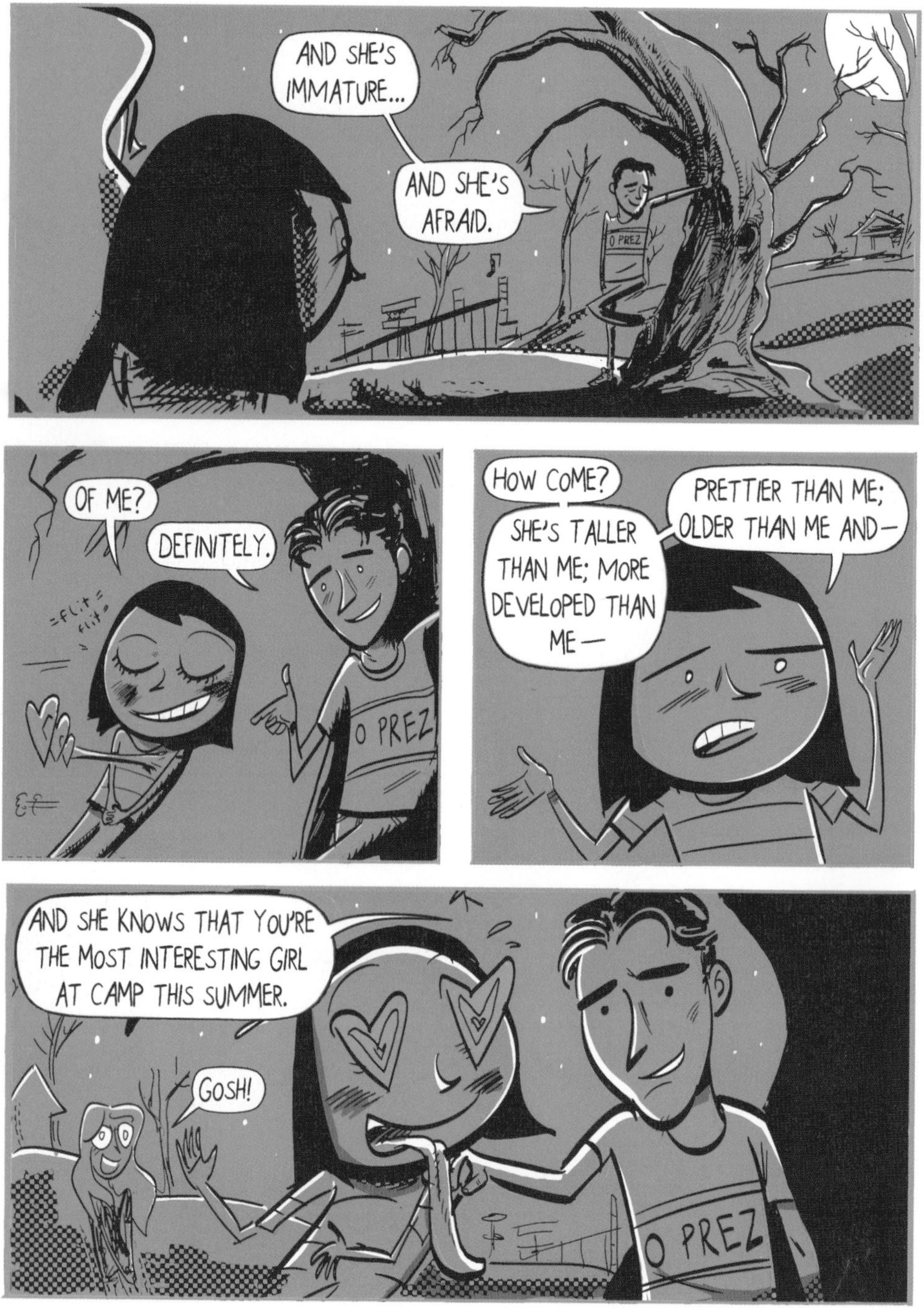
AND SHE'S IMMATURE...
AND SHE'S AFRAID.
O PREZ
OF ME?
DEFINITELY.
=flit= flit=
O PREZ
HOW COME?
SHE'S TALLER THAN ME; MORE DEVELOPED THAN ME—
PRETTIER THAN ME; OLDER THAN ME AND—
AND SHE KNOWS THAT YOU'RE THE MOST INTERESTING GIRL AT CAMP THIS SUMMER.
GOSH!
O PREZ

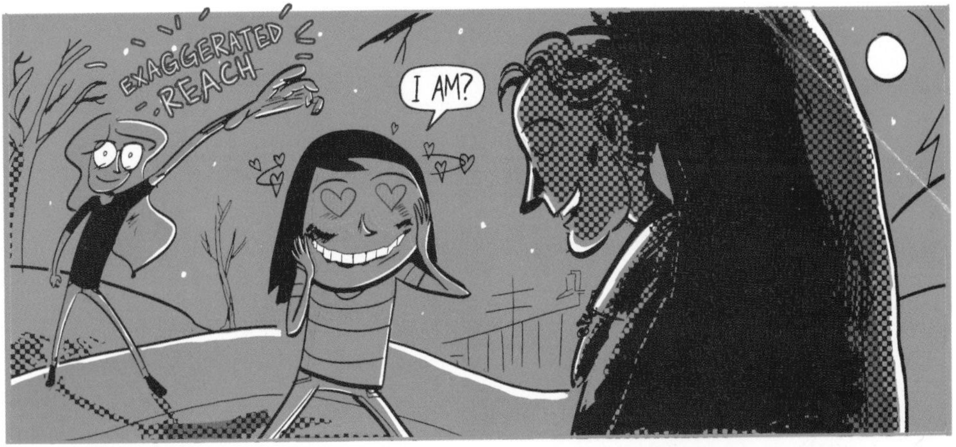
EXAGGERATED REACH
I AM?

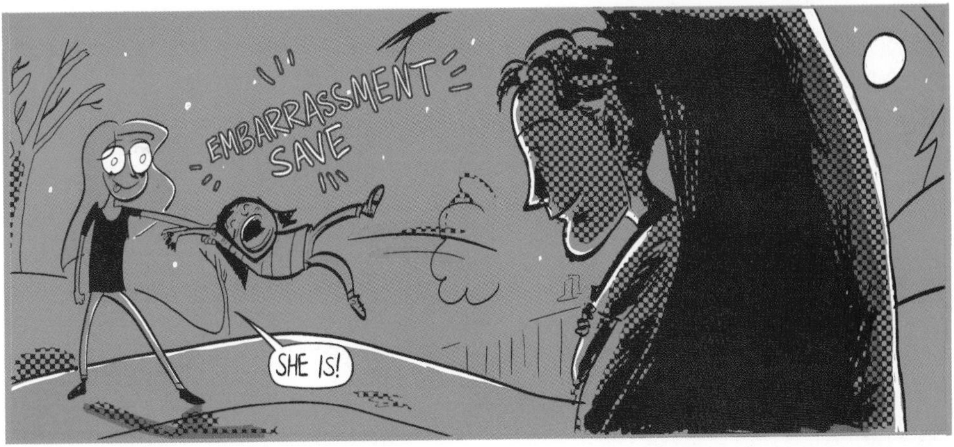
EMBARRASSMENT SAVE
SHE IS!

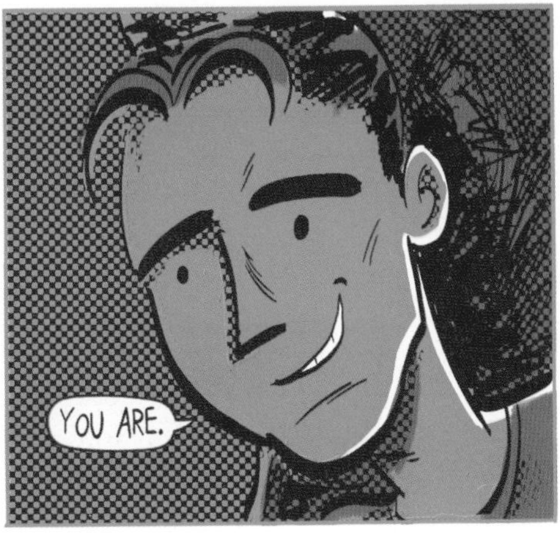
YOU ARE.

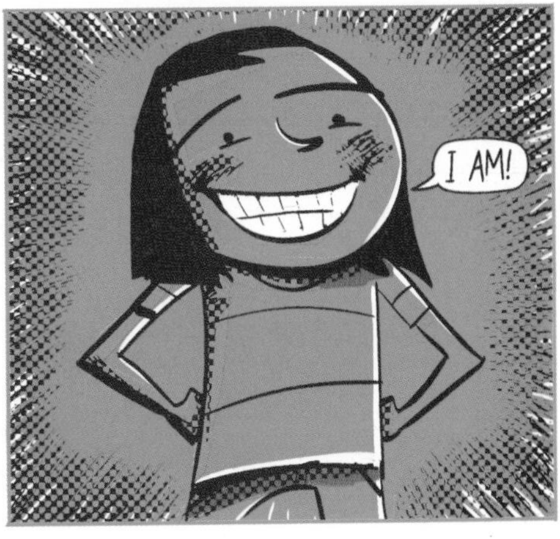
I AM!

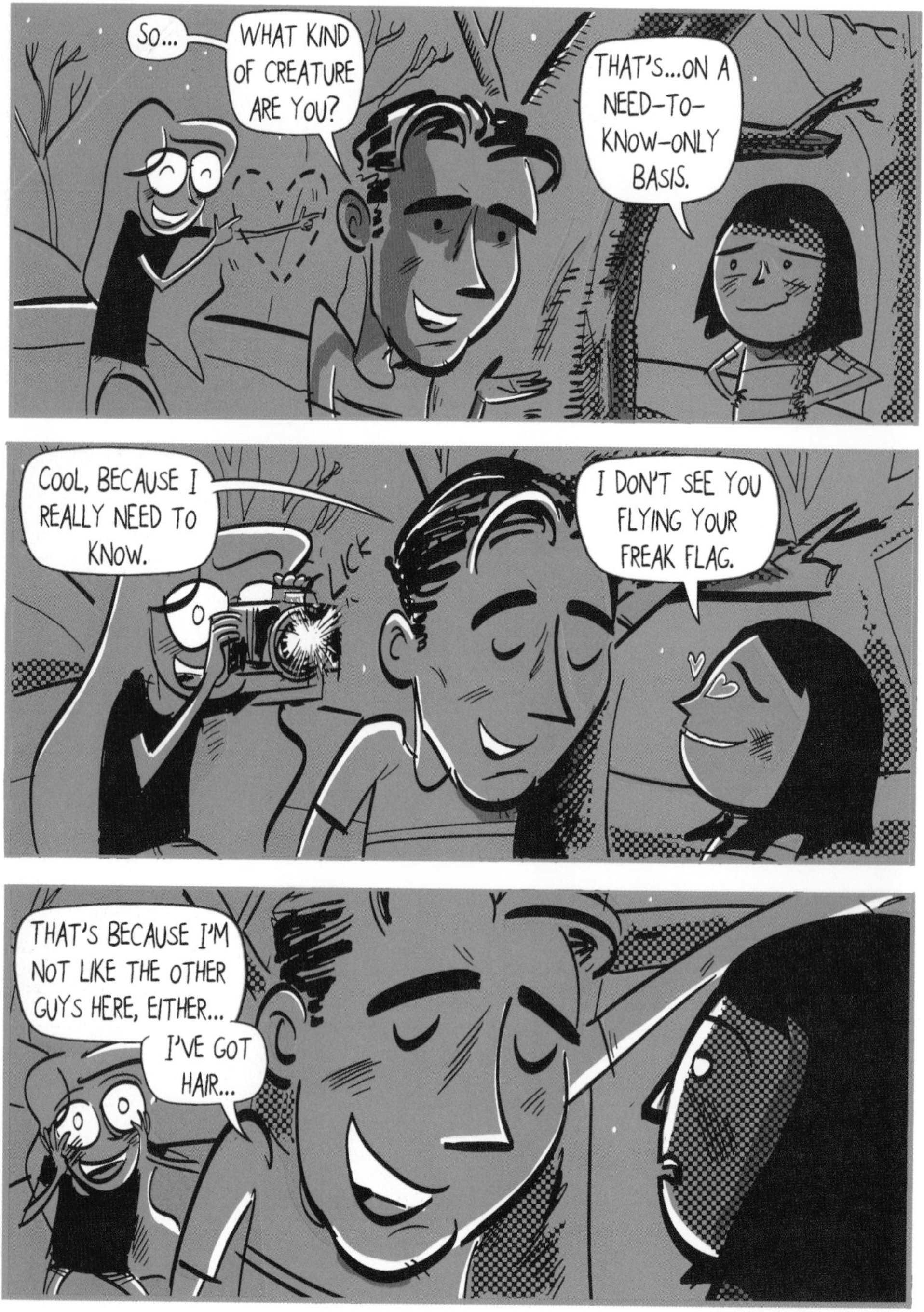
SO...
WHAT KIND OF CREATURE ARE YOU?
THAT'S...ON A NEED-TO-KNOW-ONLY BASIS.
COOL, BECAUSE I REALLY NEED TO KNOW.
CLICK
I DON'T SEE YOU FLYING YOUR FREAK FLAG.
THAT'S BECAUSE I'M NOT LIKE THE OTHER GUYS HERE, EITHER...
I'VE GOT HAIR...

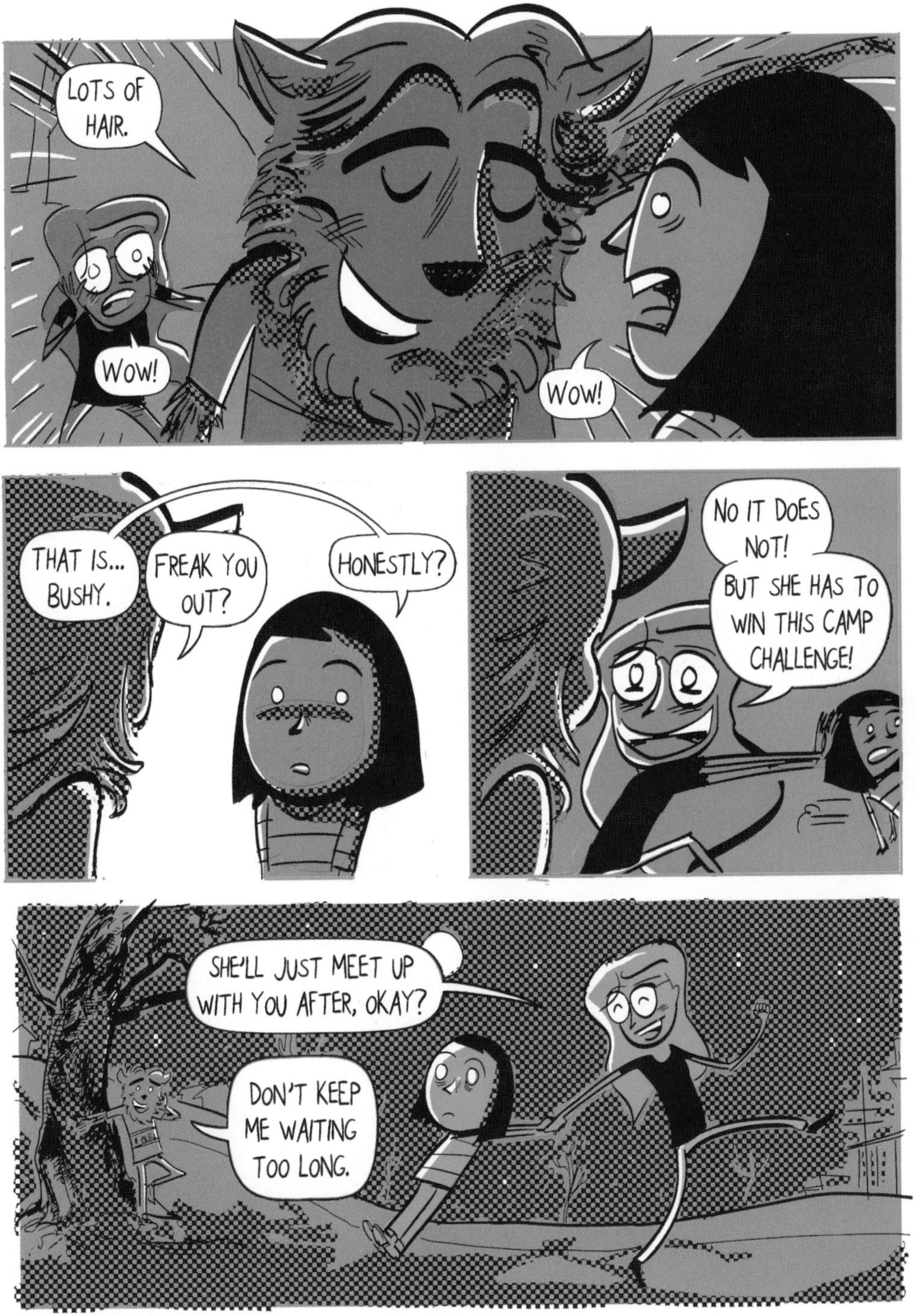
LOTS OF HAIR.
WOW!
WOW!
THAT IS... BUSHY.
FREAK YOU OUT?
HONESTLY?
NO IT DOES NOT!
BUT SHE HAS TO WIN THIS CAMP CHALLENGE!
SHE'LL JUST MEET UP WITH YOU AFTER, OKAY?
DON'T KEEP ME WAITING TOO LONG.

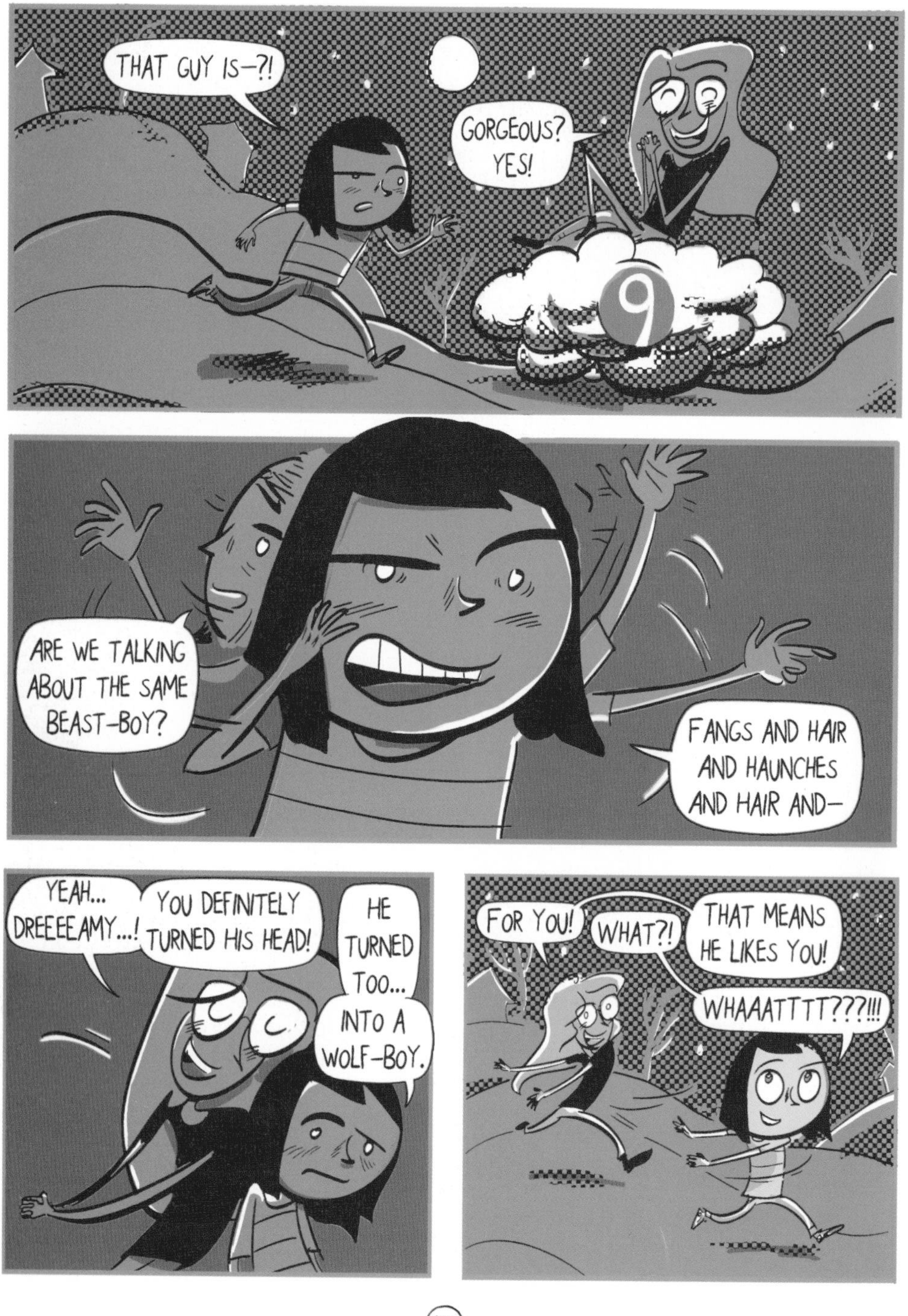
THAT GUY IS—?!
GORGEOUS? YES!
ARE WE TALKING ABOUT THE SAME BEAST-BOY?
FANGS AND HAIR AND HAUNCHES AND HAIR AND—
YEAH... DREEEEAMY...!
YOU DEFINITELY TURNED HIS HEAD!
HE TURNED TOO...
INTO A WOLF-BOY.
FOR YOU!
WHAT?!
THAT MEANS HE LIKES YOU!
WHAAATTTT???!!!

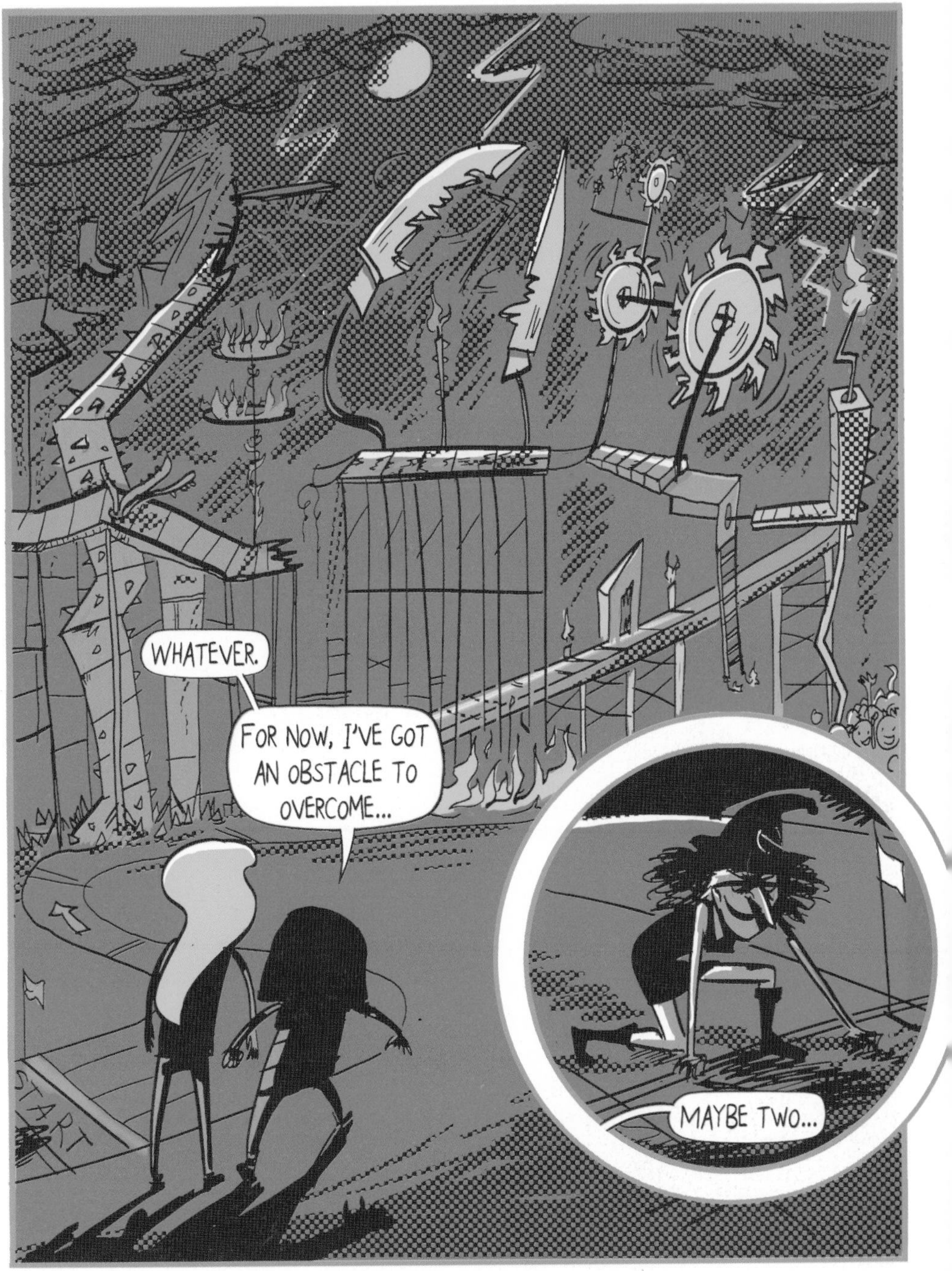
WHATEVER.
FOR NOW, I'VE GOT AN OBSTACLE TO OVERCOME...
START
MAYBE TWO...

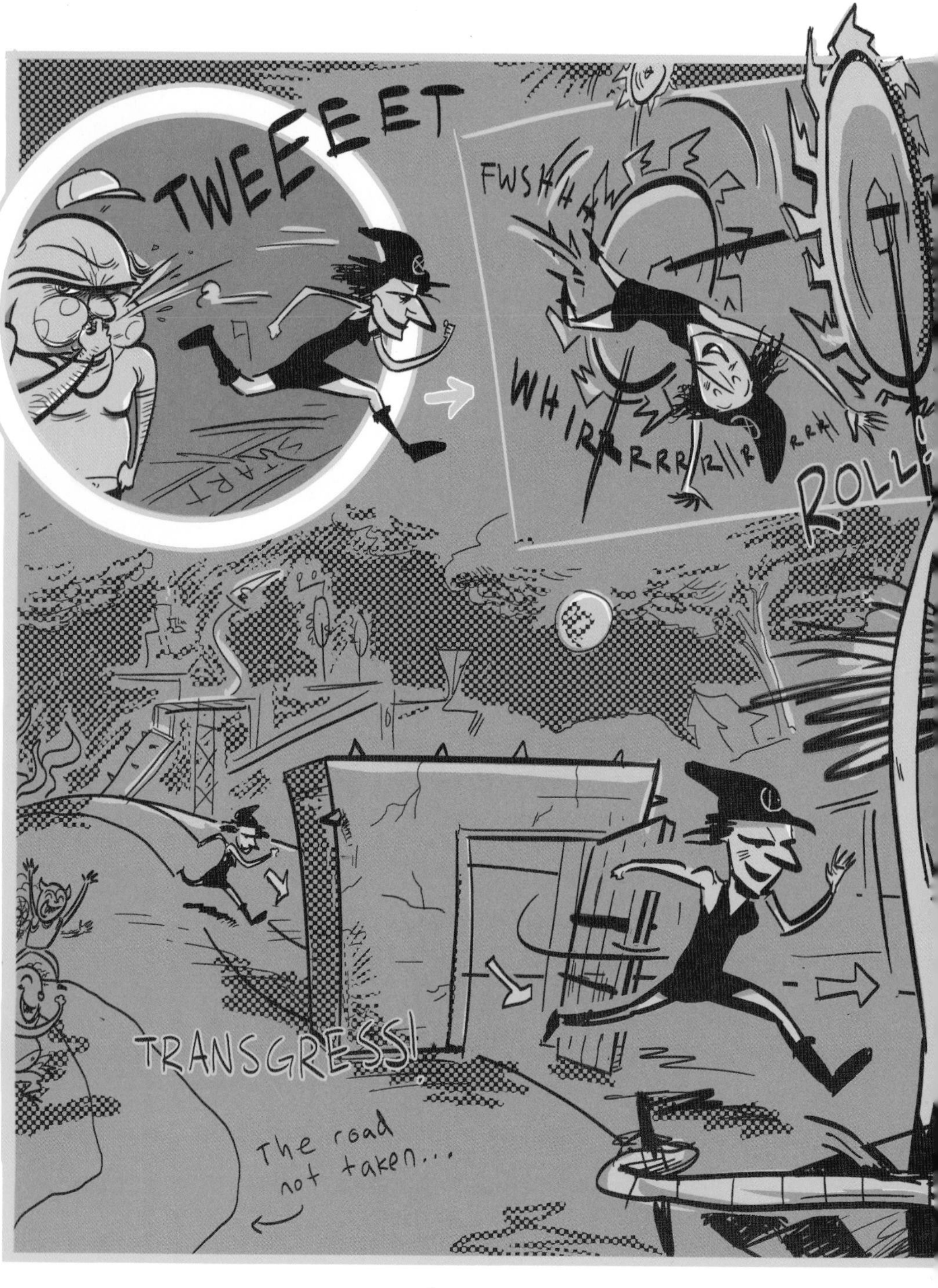
TWEEEEET
START
FWSHHH
WHIRRRRRRRRRRRR
ROLL!
TRANSGRESS!
The road not taken...

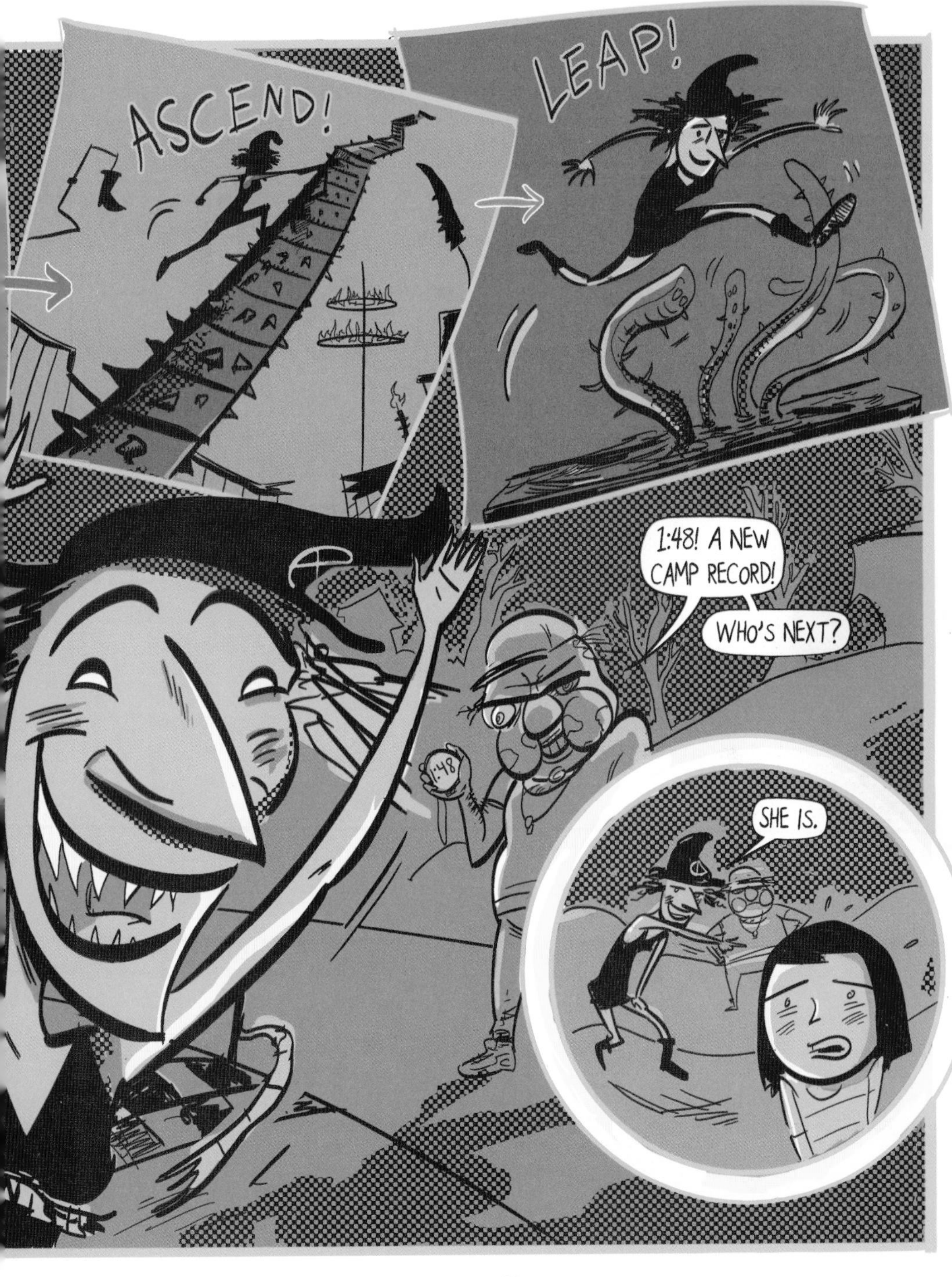
ASCEND!
LEAP!
1:48! A NEW CAMP RECORD!
WHO'S NEXT?
SHE IS.

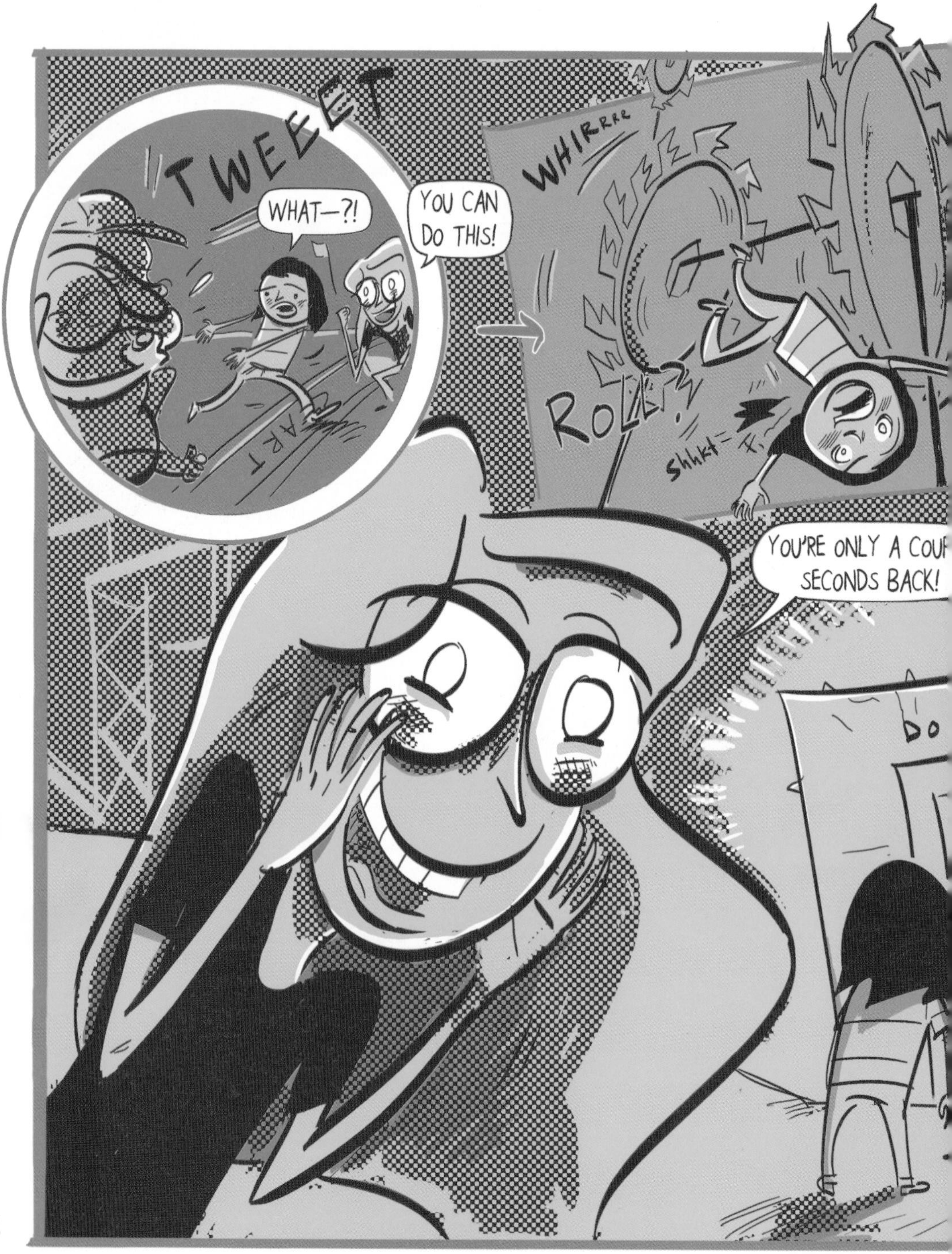
TWEEET
WHAT—?!
YOU CAN DO THIS!
START
WHIRRRR
ROLL!
SHHKT
YOU'RE ONLY A COUP
SECONDS BACK!

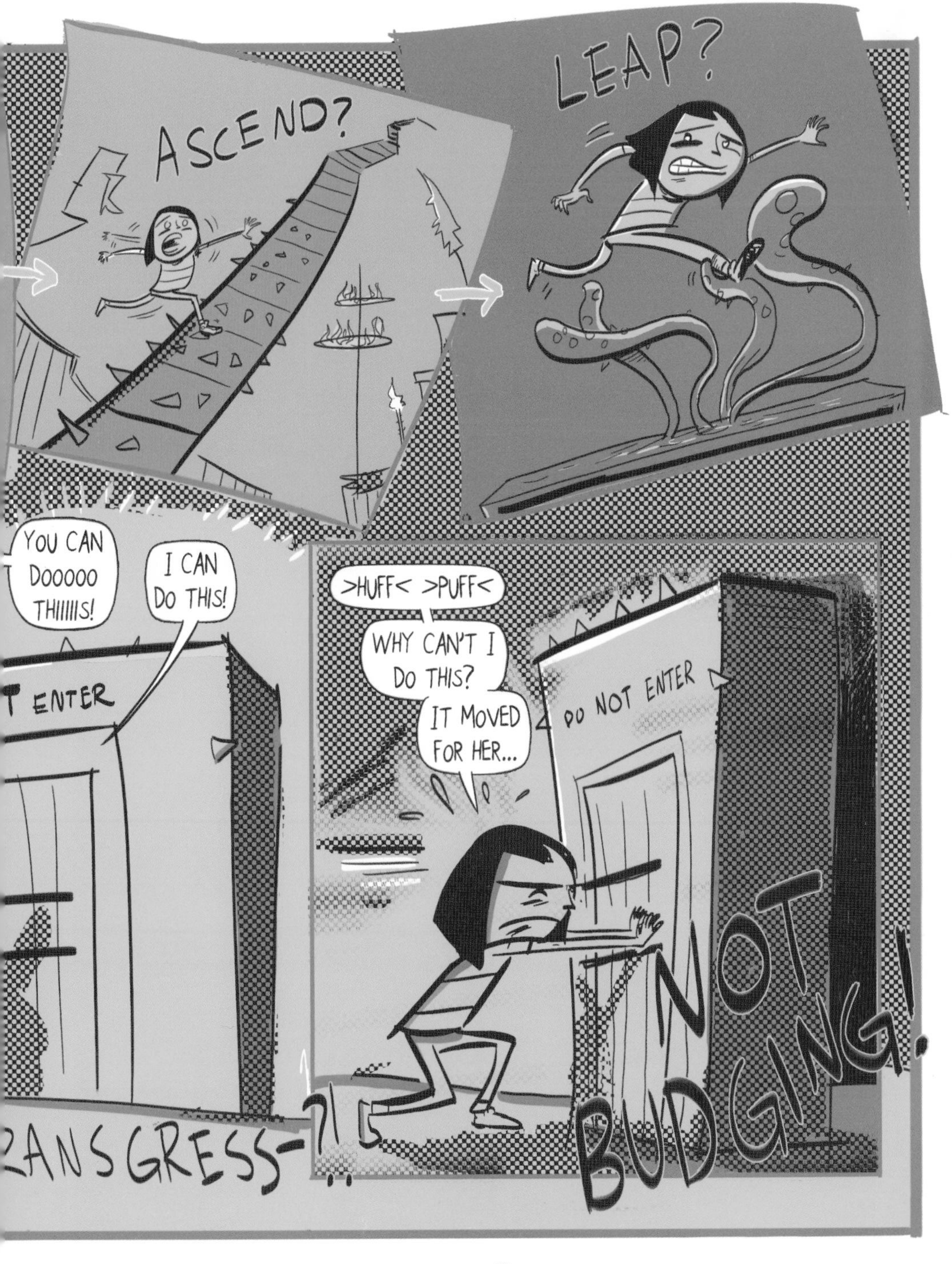
ASCEND?
LEAP?
YOU CAN DOOOOO THIIIIIS!
I CAN DO THIS!
T ENTER
ZANSGRESS-?!..
>HUFF< >PUFF<
WHY CAN'T I DO THIS?
IT MOVED FOR HER...
DO NOT ENTER
NOT BUDGING!.

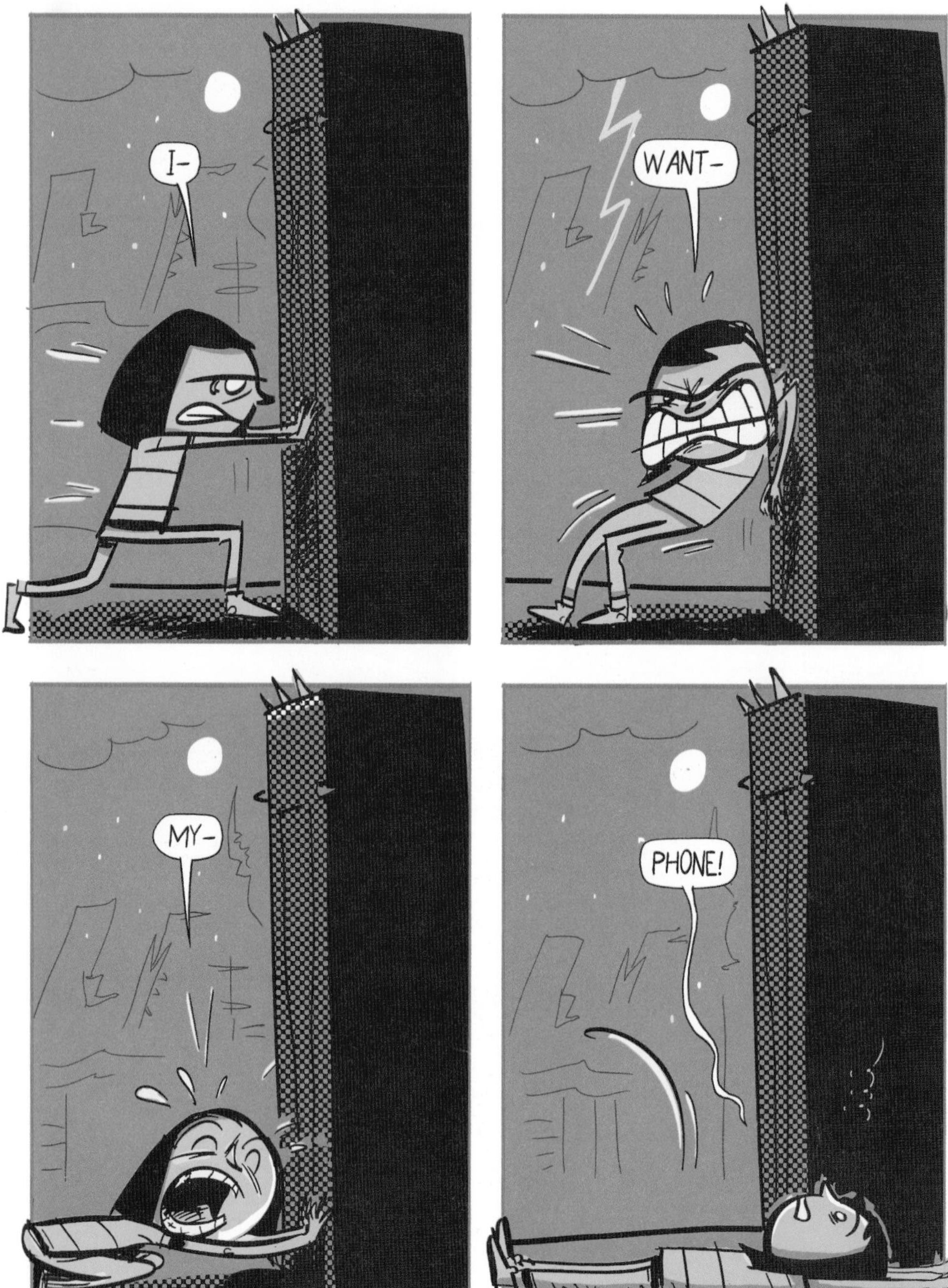
I-
WANT-
MY-
PHONE!

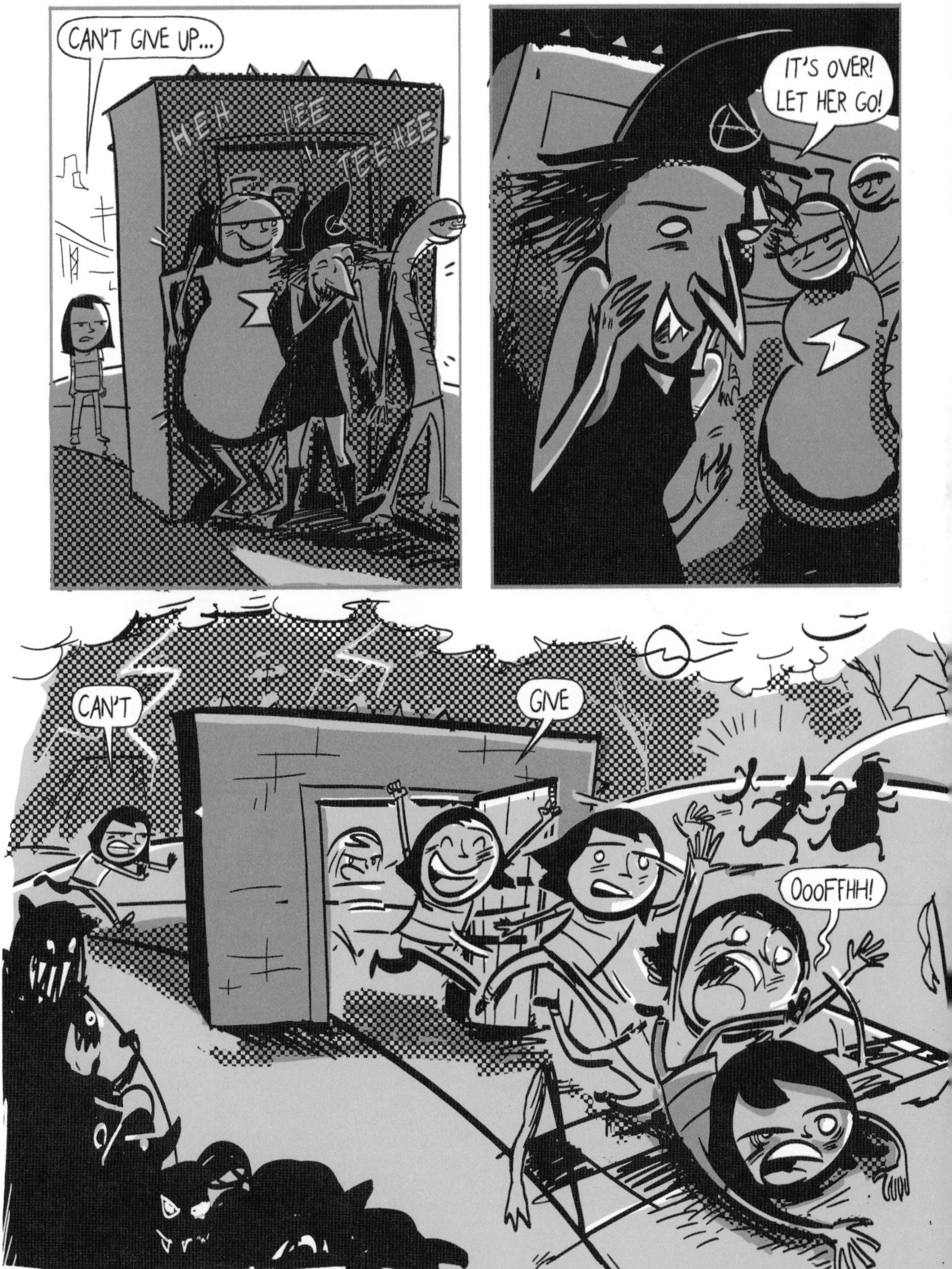
CAN'T GIVE UP...
HEH HEE TEE-HEE
IT'S OVER! LET HER GO!
CAN'T
GIVE
OooFFHH!

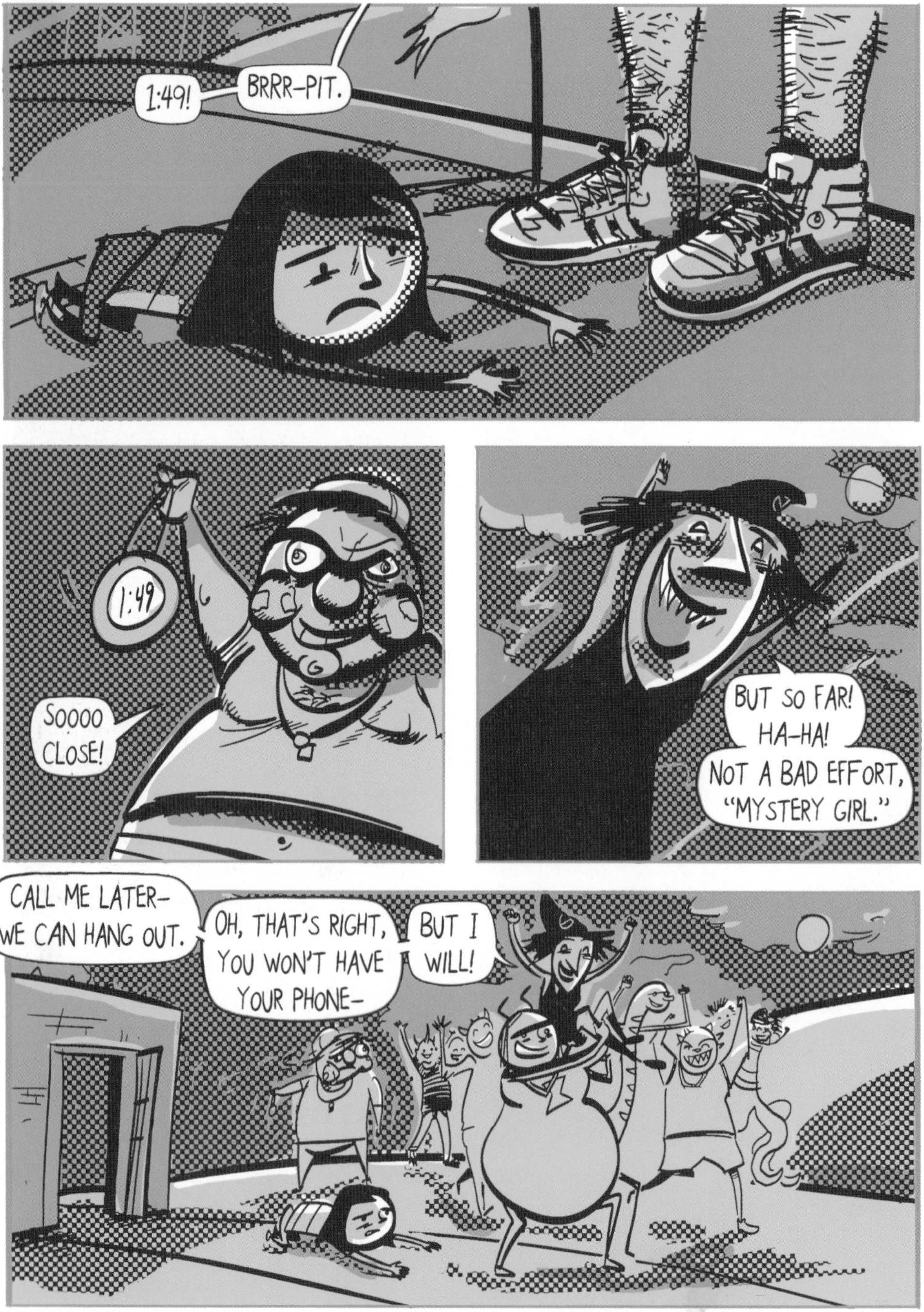
BRRR-PIT.
1:49!
1:49
SOOOO CLOSE!
BUT SO FAR! HA-HA! NOT A BAD EFFORT, "MYSTERY GIRL."
CALL ME LATER- WE CAN HANG OUT.
OH, THAT'S RIGHT, YOU WON'T HAVE YOUR PHONE-
BUT I WILL!

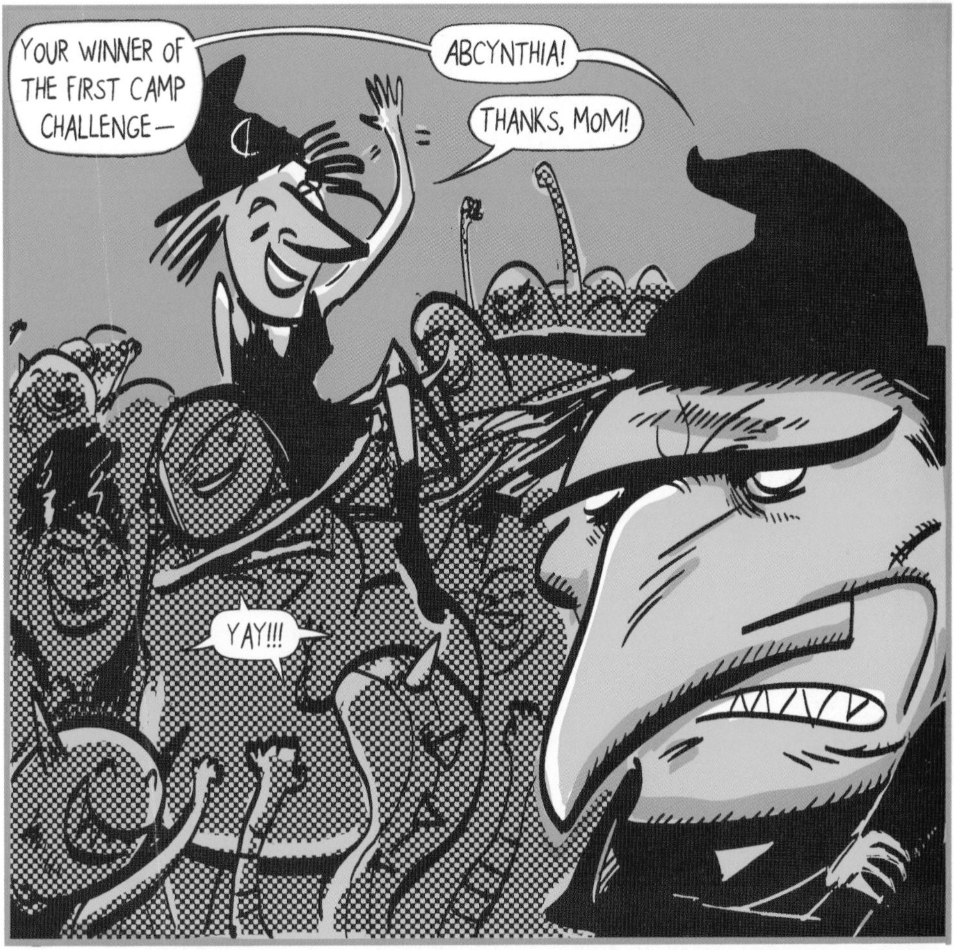
YOUR WINNER OF THE FIRST CAMP CHALLENGE—
ABCYNTHIA!
THANKS, MOM!
YAY!!!

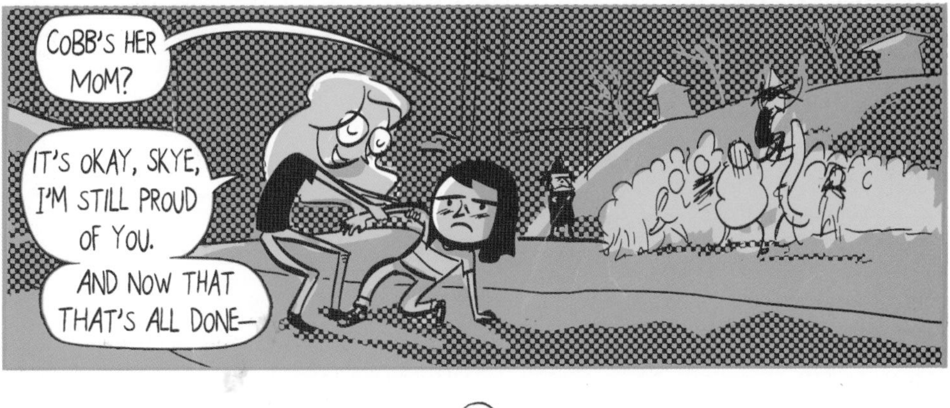
COBB'S HER MOM?
IT'S OKAY, SKYE, I'M STILL PROUD OF YOU.
AND NOW THAT THAT'S ALL DONE—

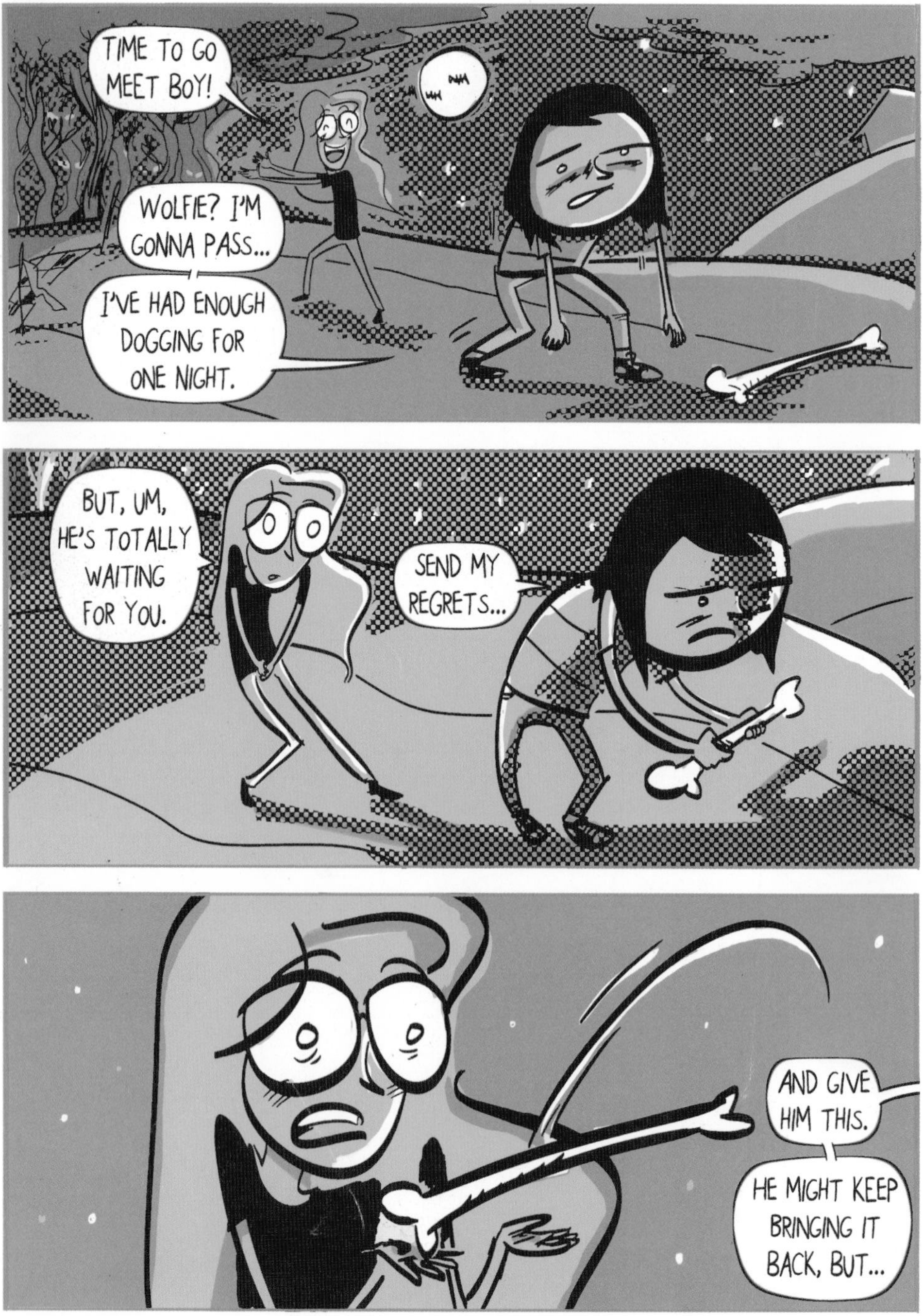
TIME TO GO MEET BOY!
WOLFIE? I'M GONNA PASS...
I'VE HAD ENOUGH DOGGING FOR ONE NIGHT.
BUT, UM, HE'S TOTALLY WAITING FOR YOU.
SEND MY REGRETS...
AND GIVE HIM THIS.
HE MIGHT KEEP BRINGING IT BACK, BUT...

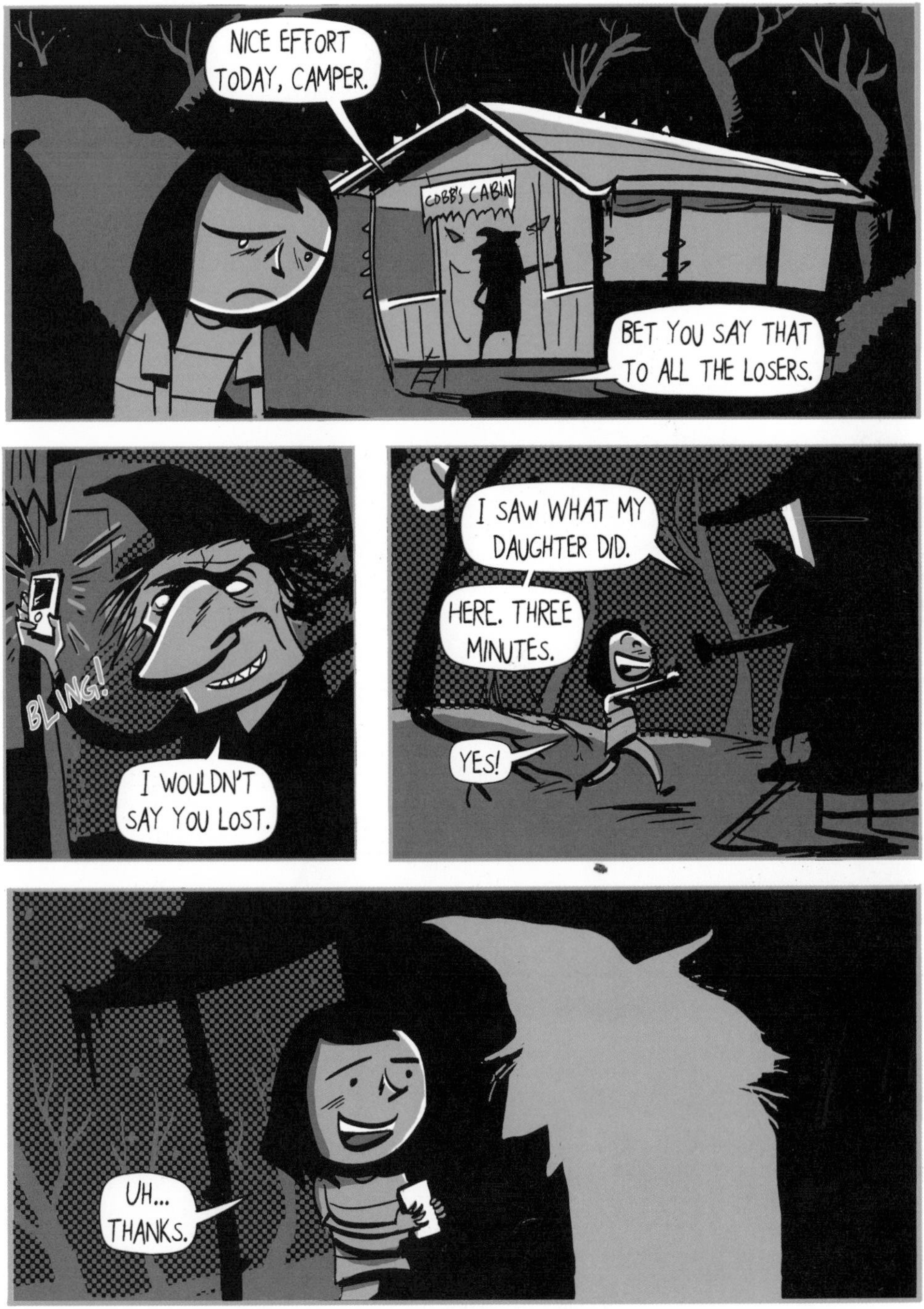
NICE EFFORT TODAY, CAMPER.
COBB'S CABIN
BET YOU SAY THAT TO ALL THE LOSERS.
BLING!
I WOULDN'T SAY YOU LOST.
I SAW WHAT MY DAUGHTER DID.
HERE. THREE MINUTES.
YES!
UH... THANKS.

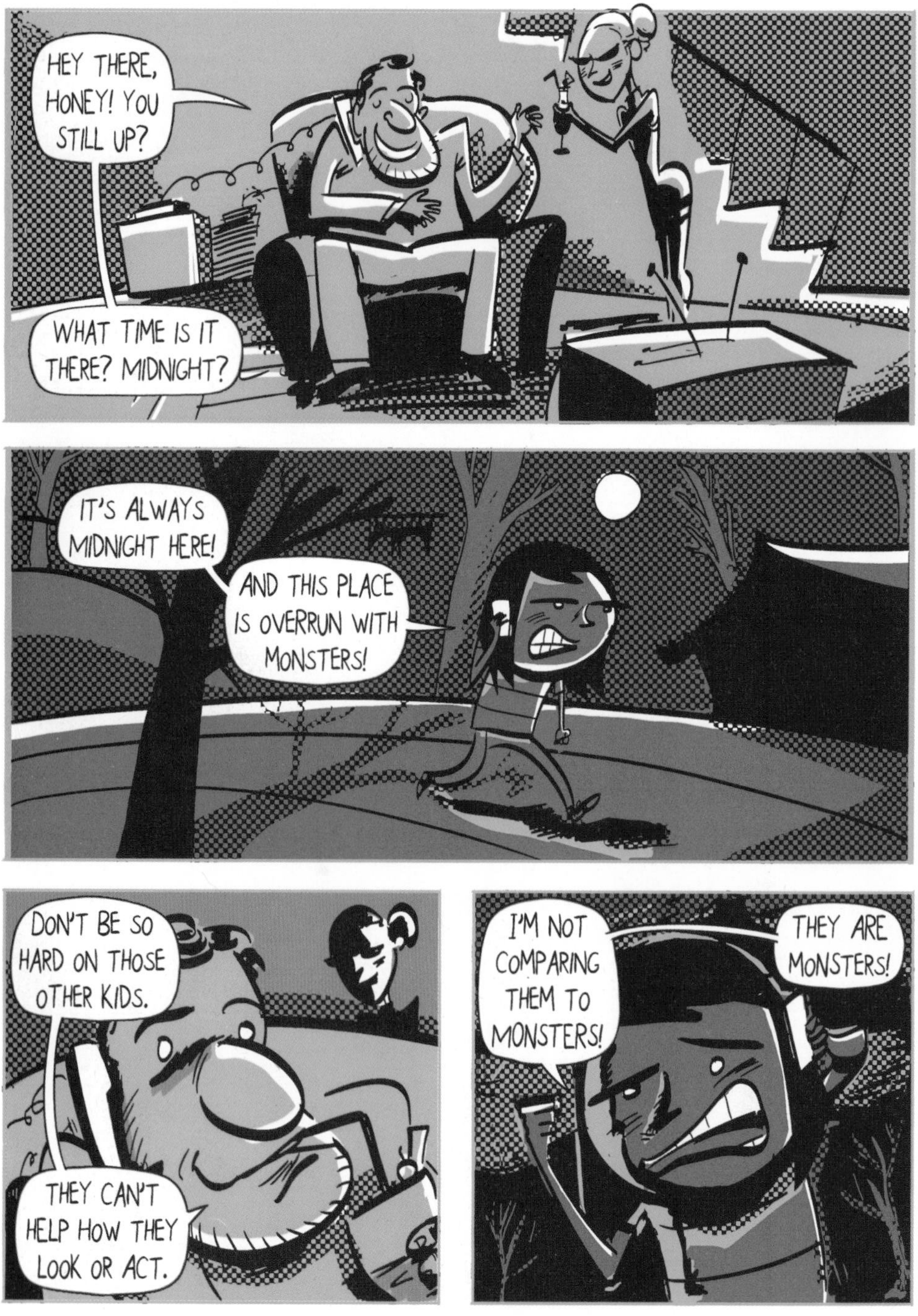
HEY THERE, HONEY! YOU STILL UP?
WHAT TIME IS IT THERE? MIDNIGHT?
IT'S ALWAYS MIDNIGHT HERE!
AND THIS PLACE IS OVERRUN WITH MONSTERS!
DON'T BE SO HARD ON THOSE OTHER KIDS.
THEY CAN'T HELP HOW THEY LOOK OR ACT.
I'M NOT COMPARING THEM TO MONSTERS!
THEY ARE MONSTERS!

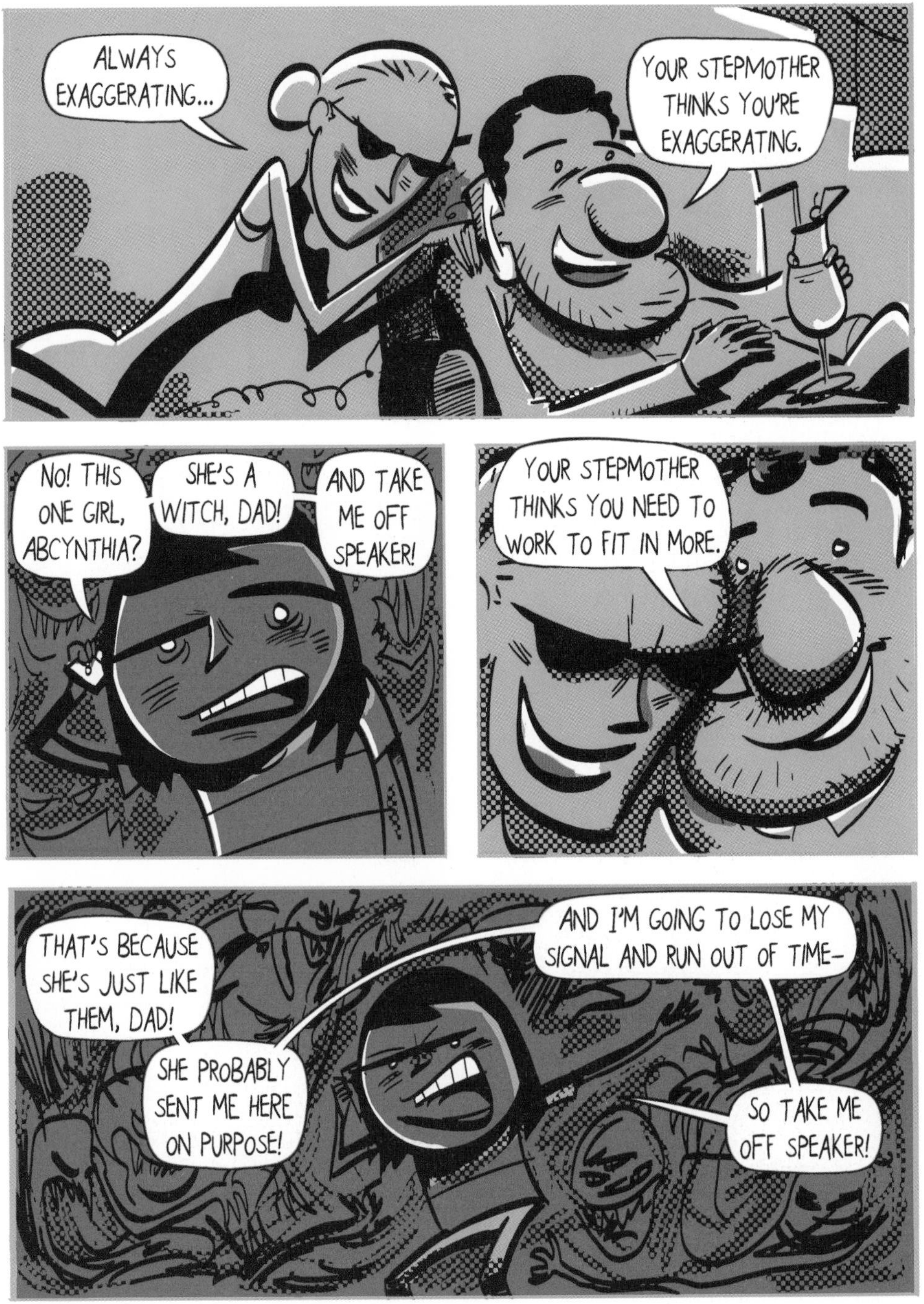
ALWAYS EXAGGERATING...
YOUR STEPMOTHER THINKS YOU'RE EXAGGERATING.
NO! THIS ONE GIRL, ABCYNTHIA?
SHE'S A WITCH, DAD!
AND TAKE ME OFF SPEAKER!
YOUR STEPMOTHER THINKS YOU NEED TO WORK TO FIT IN MORE.
THAT'S BECAUSE SHE'S JUST LIKE THEM, DAD!
SHE PROBABLY SENT ME HERE ON PURPOSE!
AND I'M GOING TO LOSE MY SIGNAL AND RUN OUT OF TIME–
SO TAKE ME OFF SPEAKER!

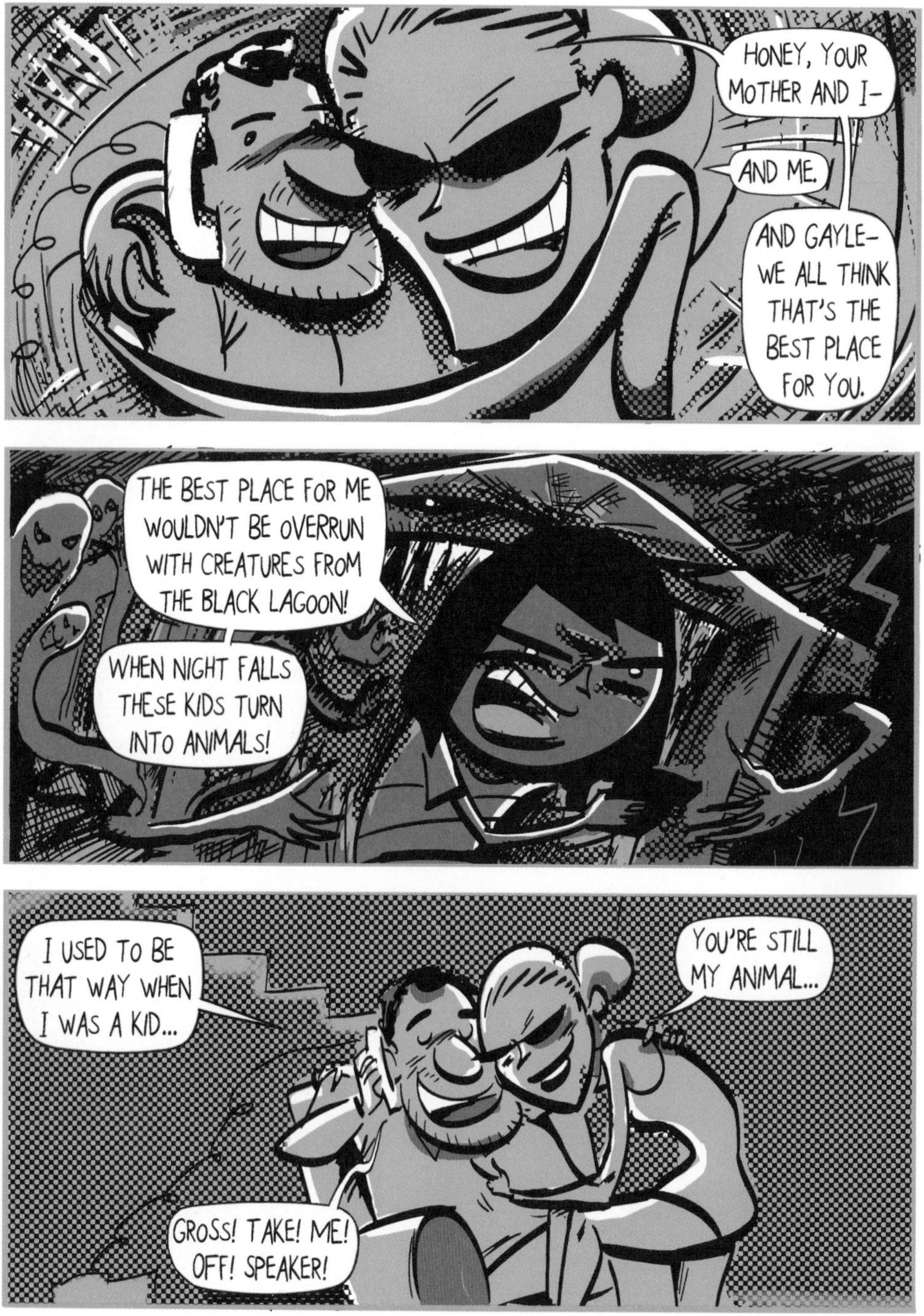
HONEY, YOUR MOTHER AND I-
AND ME.
AND GAYLE- WE ALL THINK THAT'S THE BEST PLACE FOR YOU.
THE BEST PLACE FOR ME WOULDN'T BE OVERRUN WITH CREATURES FROM THE BLACK LAGOON!
WHEN NIGHT FALLS THESE KIDS TURN INTO ANIMALS!
I USED TO BE THAT WAY WHEN I WAS A KID...
YOU'RE STILL MY ANIMAL...
GROSS! TAKE! ME! OFF! SPEAKER!

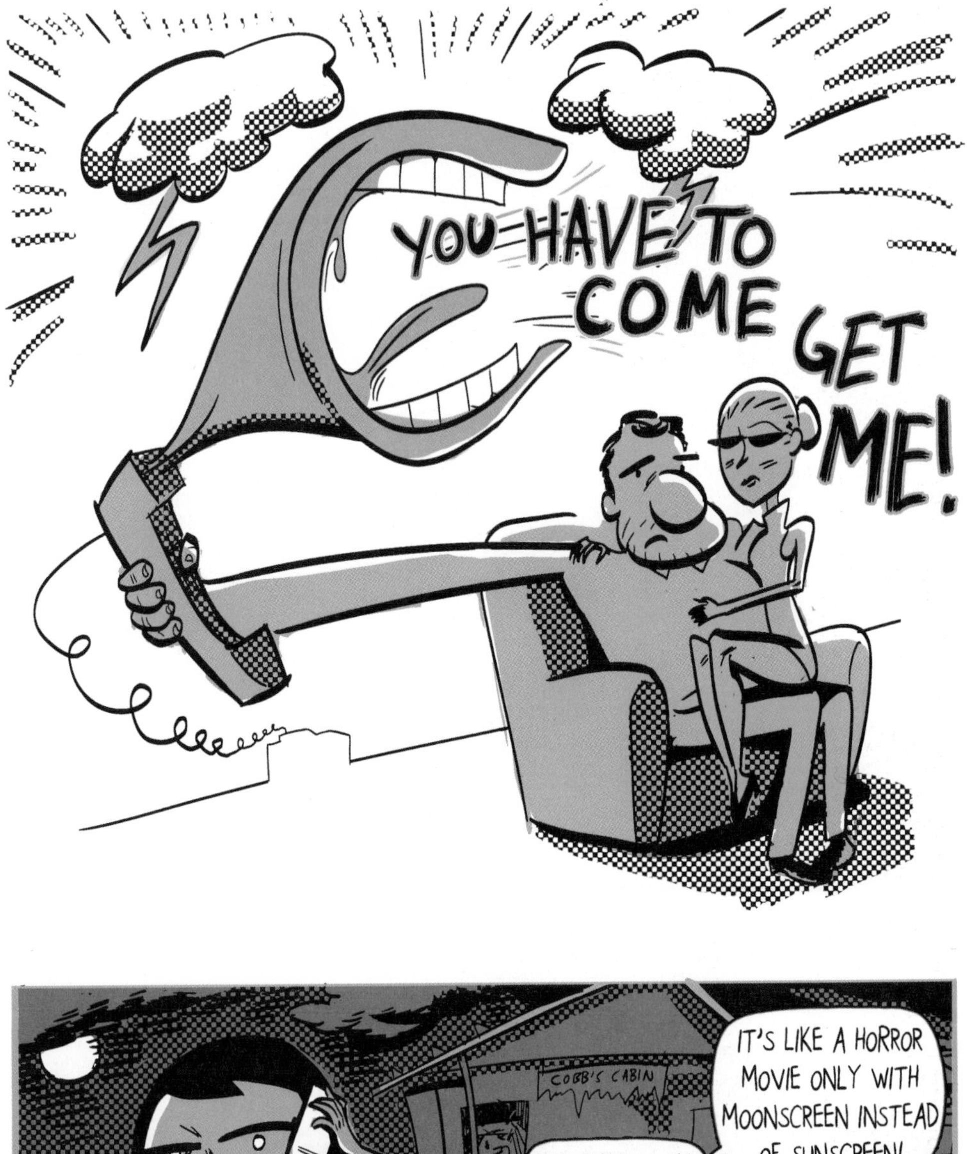
YOU HAVE TO COME GET ME!

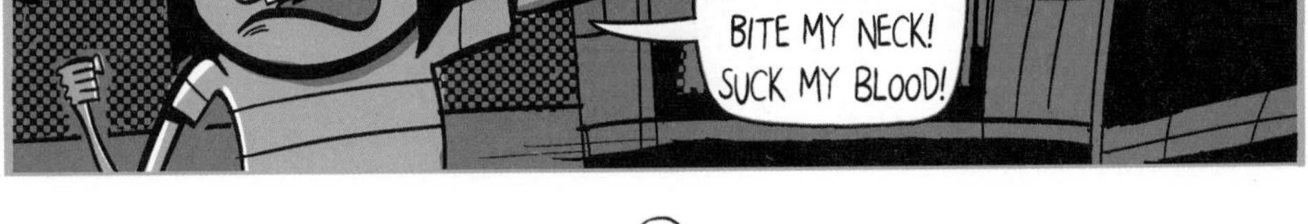
COBB'S CABIN
THESE KIDS WILL RIP ME TO PIECES! BITE MY NECK! SUCK MY BLOOD!
IT'S LIKE A HORROR MOVIE ONLY WITH MOONSCREEN INSTEAD OF SUNSCREEN!

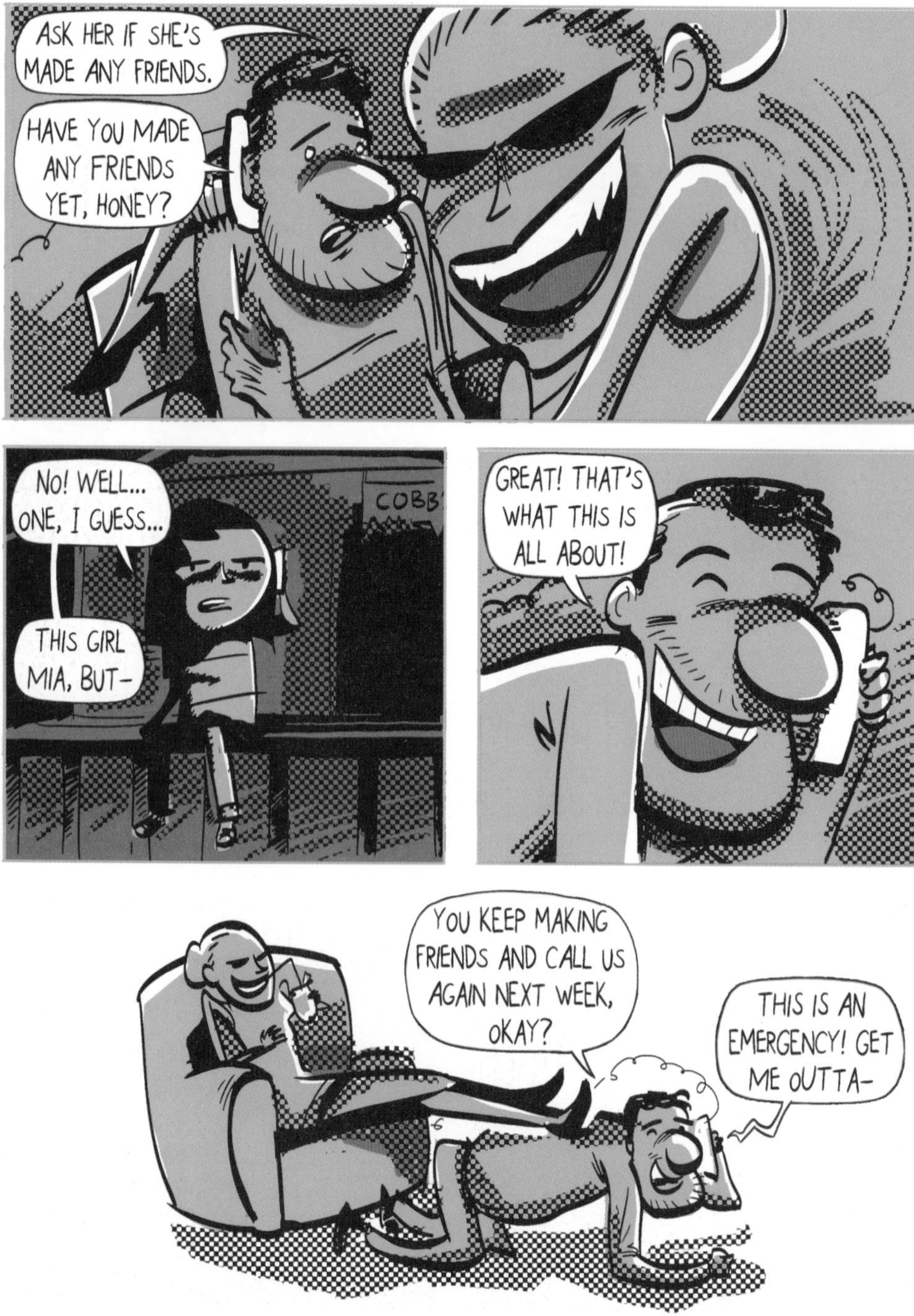
ASK HER IF SHE'S MADE ANY FRIENDS.
HAVE YOU MADE ANY FRIENDS YET, HONEY?
NO! WELL... ONE, I GUESS...
THIS GIRL MIA, BUT-
COBB
GREAT! THAT'S WHAT THIS IS ALL ABOUT!
YOU KEEP MAKING FRIENDS AND CALL US AGAIN NEXT WEEK, OKAY?
THIS IS AN EMERGENCY! GET ME OUTTA-

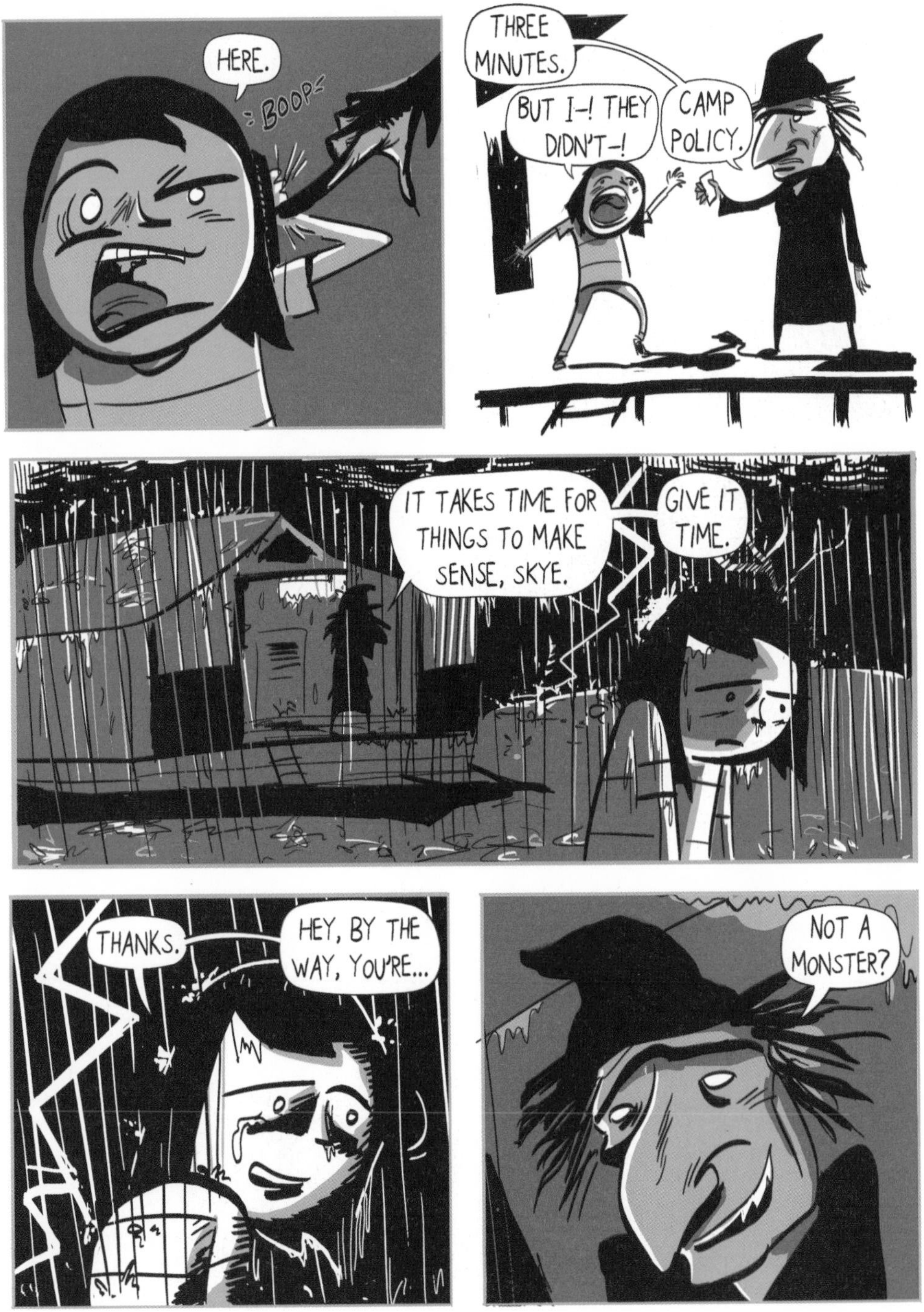
HERE.
BOOP
THREE MINUTES.
BUT I-! THEY DIDN'T-!
CAMP POLICY.
IT TAKES TIME FOR THINGS TO MAKE SENSE, SKYE.
GIVE IT TIME.
THANKS.
HEY, BY THE WAY, YOU'RE...
NOT A MONSTER?

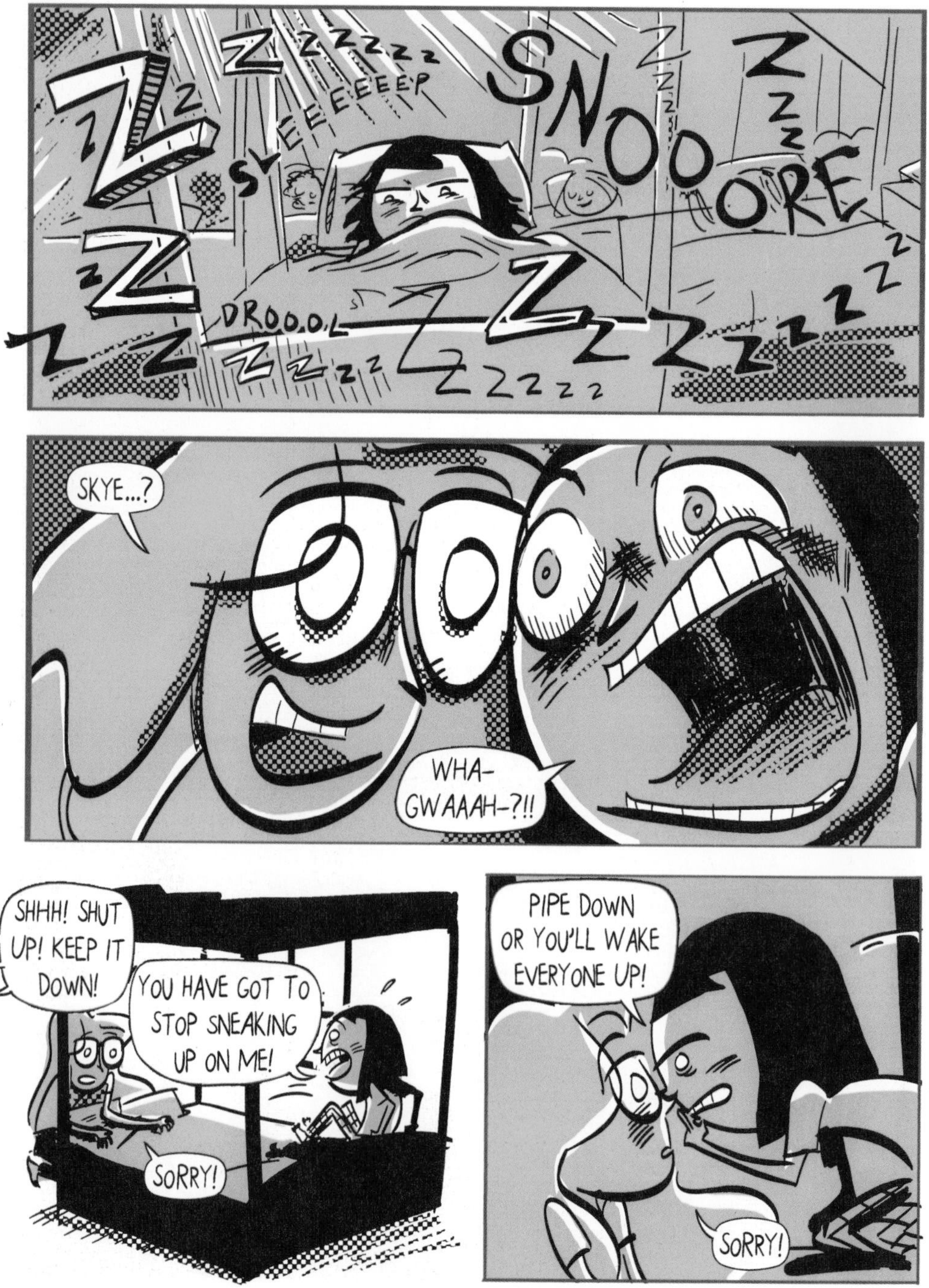

ZZZZZZZZ
SLEEEEEEEP
SNOOOORE
DROOOL
SKYE...?
WHA-GWAAAH-?!!
SHHH! SHUT UP! KEEP IT DOWN!
YOU HAVE GOT TO STOP SNEAKING UP ON ME!
SORRY!
PIPE DOWN OR YOU'LL WAKE EVERYONE UP!
SORRY!

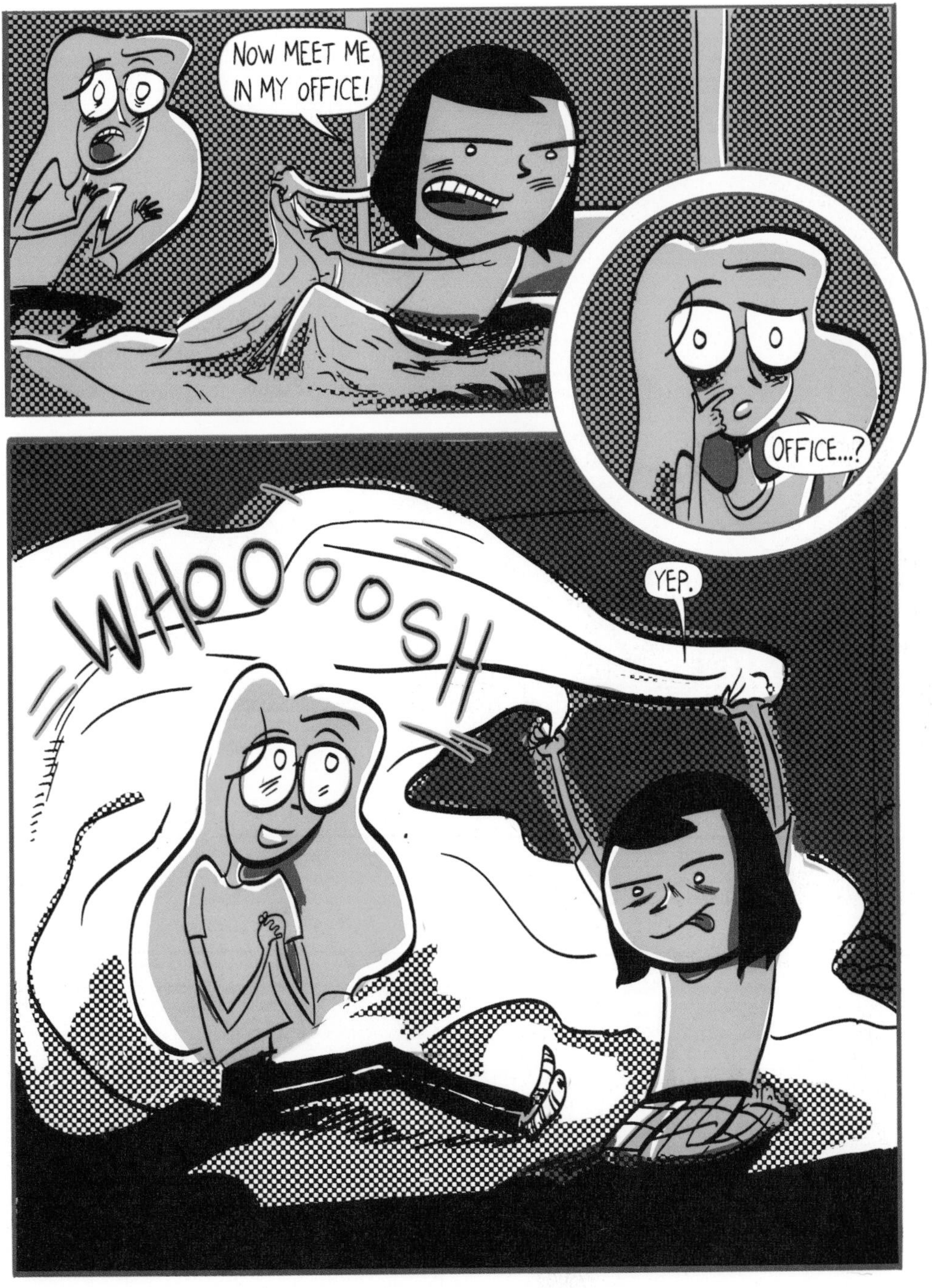
NOW MEET ME IN MY OFFICE!
OFFICE...?
WHOOOOOSH
YEP.

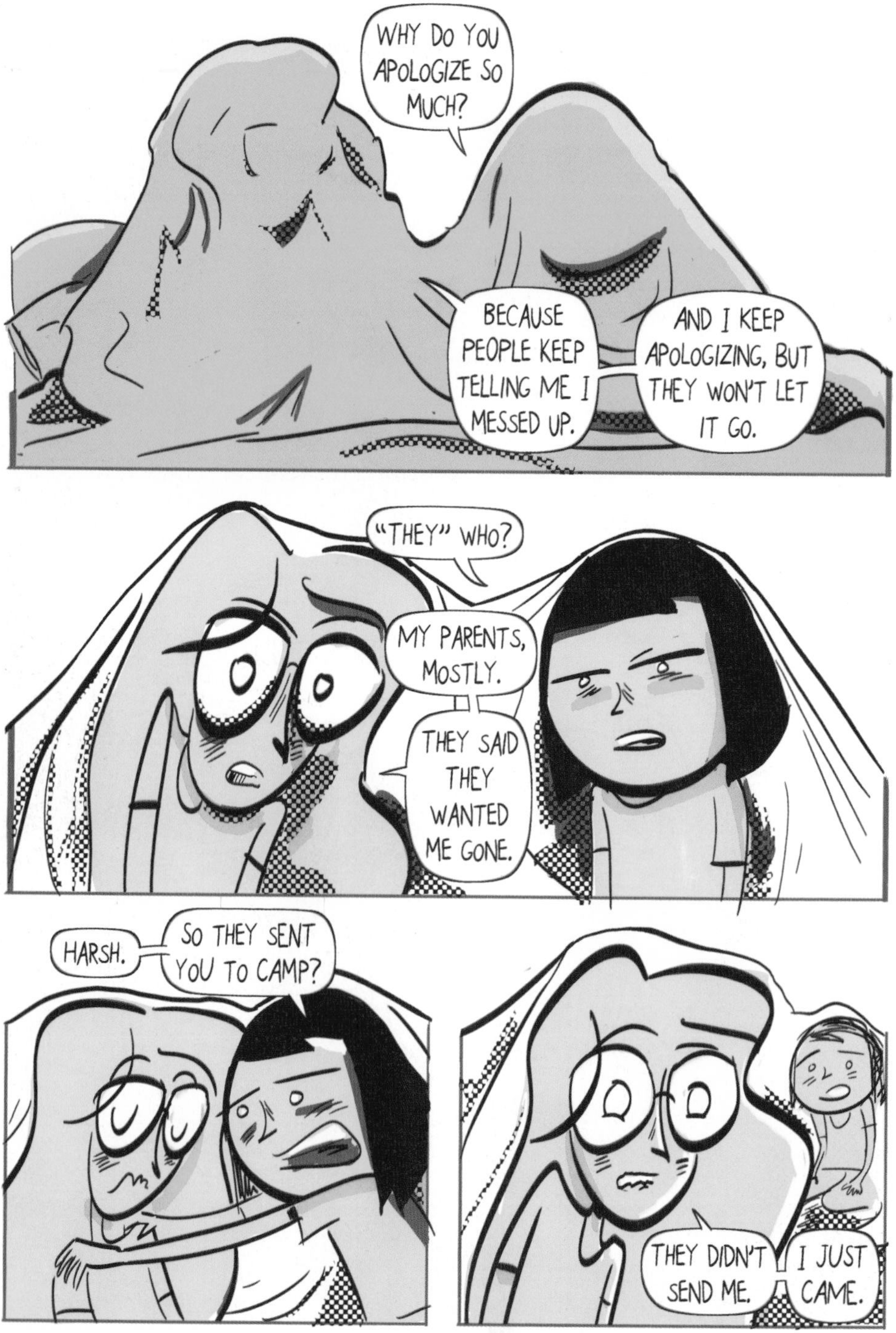
WHY DO YOU APOLOGIZE SO MUCH?
BECAUSE PEOPLE KEEP TELLING ME I MESSED UP.
AND I KEEP APOLOGIZING, BUT THEY WON'T LET IT GO.
"THEY" WHO?
MY PARENTS, MOSTLY.
THEY SAID THEY WANTED ME GONE.
HARSH.
SO THEY SENT YOU TO CAMP?
THEY DIDN'T SEND ME.
I JUST CAME.

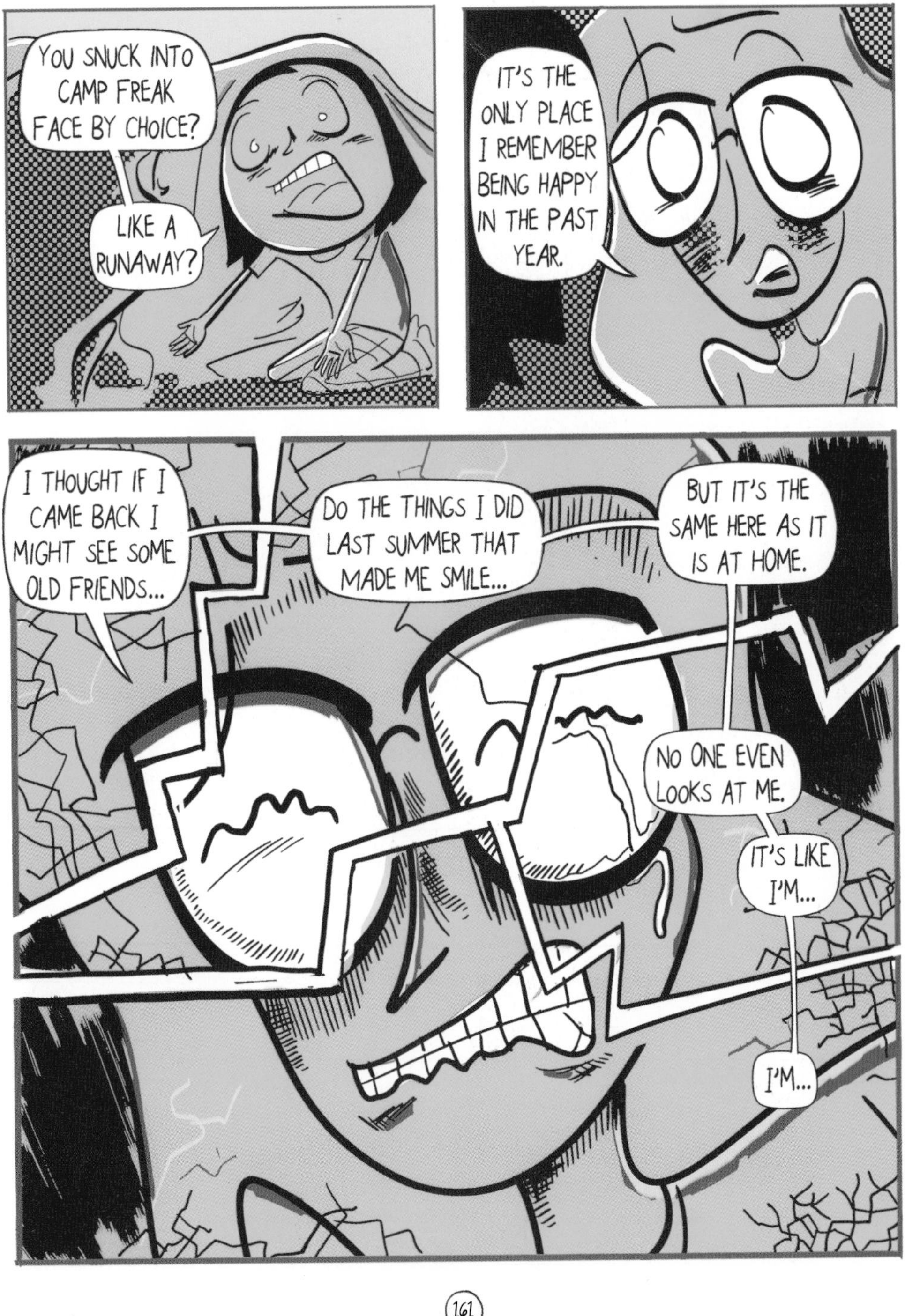
YOU SNUCK INTO CAMP FREAK FACE BY CHOICE?
LIKE A RUNAWAY?
IT'S THE ONLY PLACE I REMEMBER BEING HAPPY IN THE PAST YEAR.
I THOUGHT IF I CAME BACK I MIGHT SEE SOME OLD FRIENDS...
DO THE THINGS I DID LAST SUMMER THAT MADE ME SMILE...
BUT IT'S THE SAME HERE AS IT IS AT HOME.
NO ONE EVEN LOOKS AT ME.
IT'S LIKE I'M...
I'M...

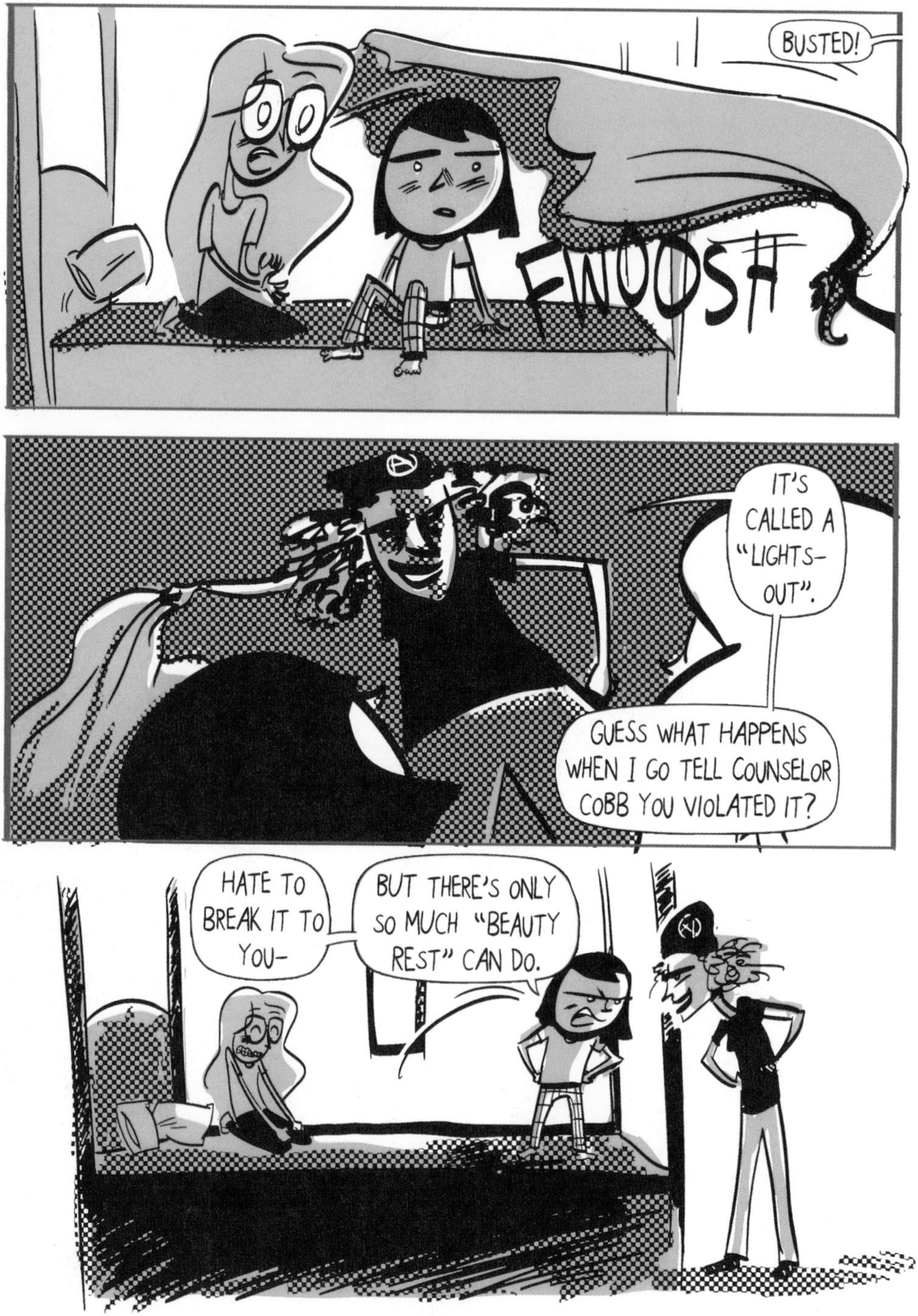
BUSTED!
FWOOSH
IT'S CALLED A "LIGHTS-OUT".
GUESS WHAT HAPPENS WHEN I GO TELL COUNSELOR COBB YOU VIOLATED IT?
HATE TO BREAK IT TO YOU-
BUT THERE'S ONLY SO MUCH "BEAUTY REST" CAN DO.

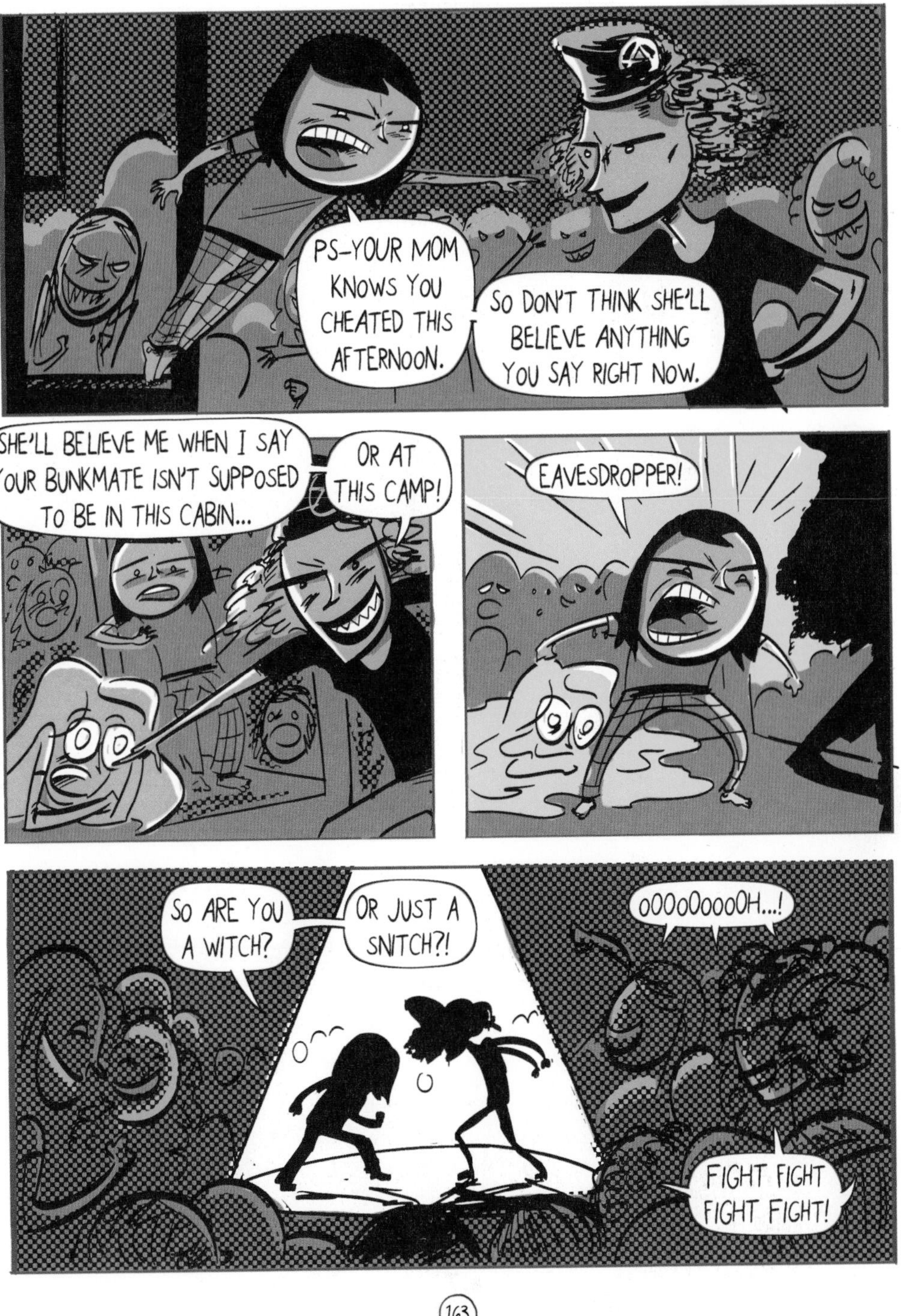
PS–YOUR MOM KNOWS YOU CHEATED THIS AFTERNOON.
SO DON'T THINK SHE'LL BELIEVE ANYTHING YOU SAY RIGHT NOW.
SHE'LL BELIEVE ME WHEN I SAY YOUR BUNKMATE ISN'T SUPPOSED TO BE IN THIS CABIN...
OR AT THIS CAMP!
EAVESDROPPER!
SO ARE YOU A WITCH?
OR JUST A SNITCH?!
OOOoOOOOOH...!
FIGHT FIGHT FIGHT FIGHT!

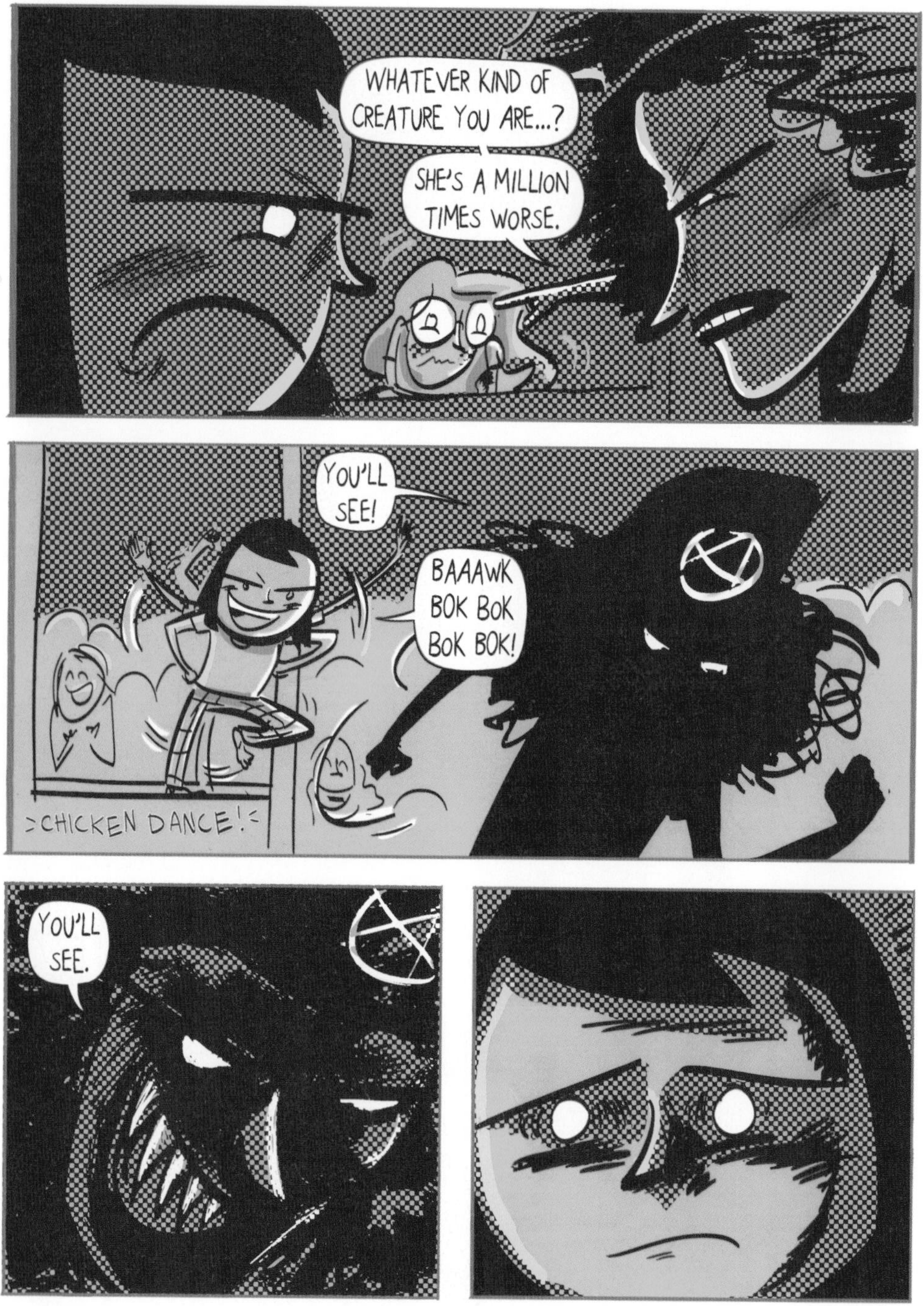
WHATEVER KIND OF CREATURE YOU ARE...?
SHE'S A MILLION TIMES WORSE.
YOU'LL SEE!
BAAAWK BOK BOK BOK BOK!
>CHICKEN DANCE!<
YOU'LL SEE.

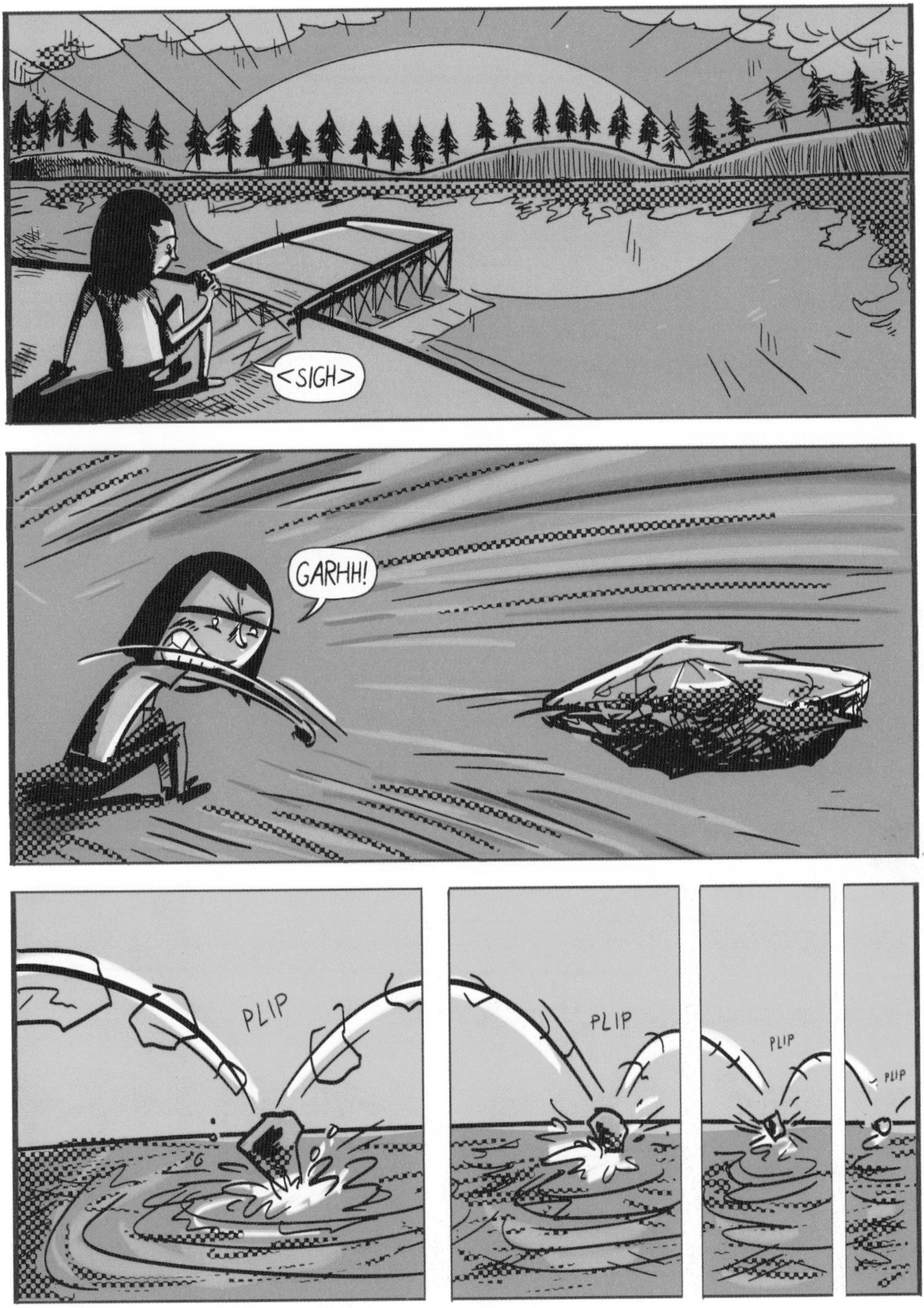

<SIGH>
GARHH!
PLIP
PLIP
PLIP
PLIP

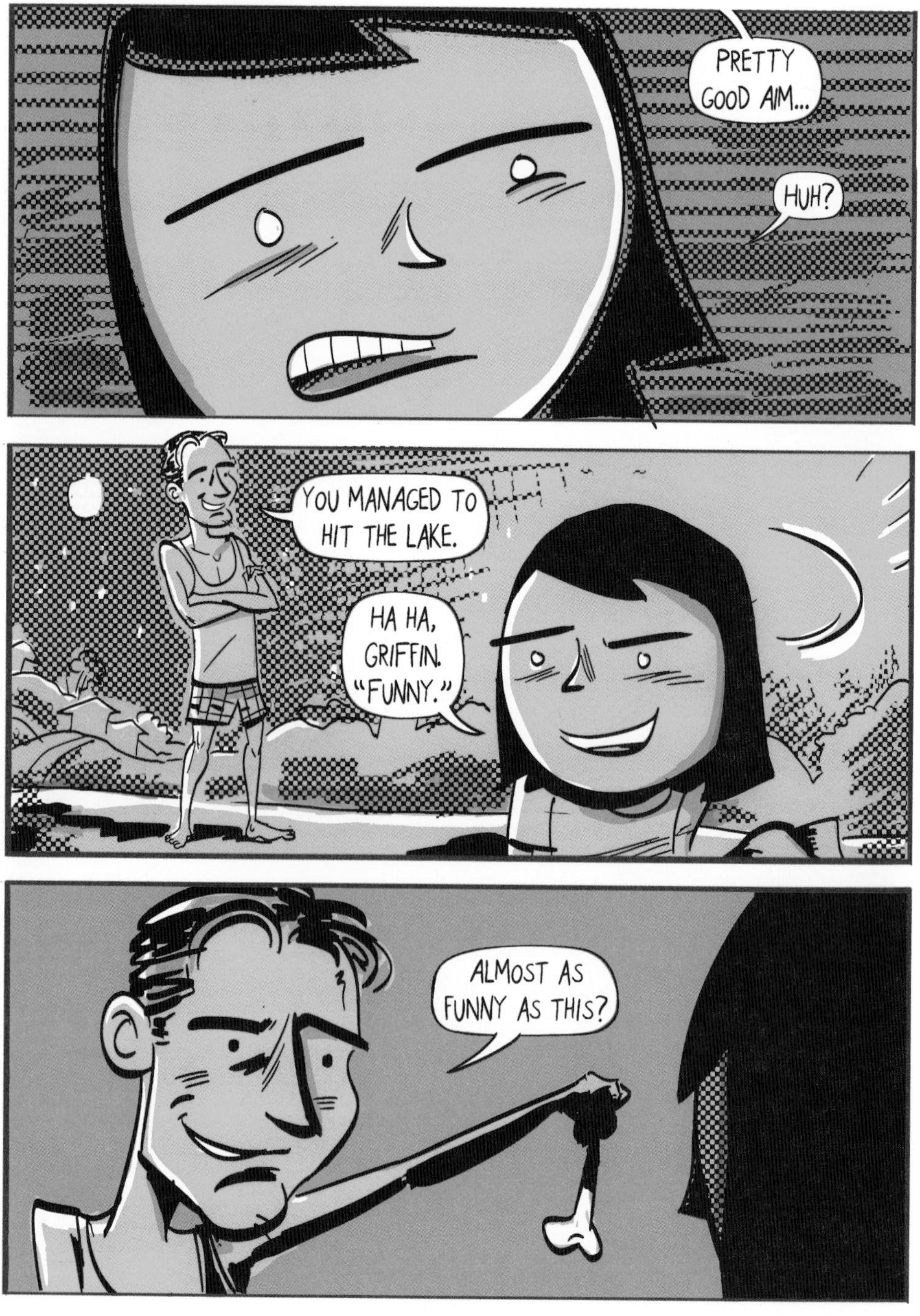
PRETTY GOOD AIM...
HUH?
YOU MANAGED TO HIT THE LAKE.
HA HA, GRIFFIN. "FUNNY."
ALMOST AS FUNNY AS THIS?

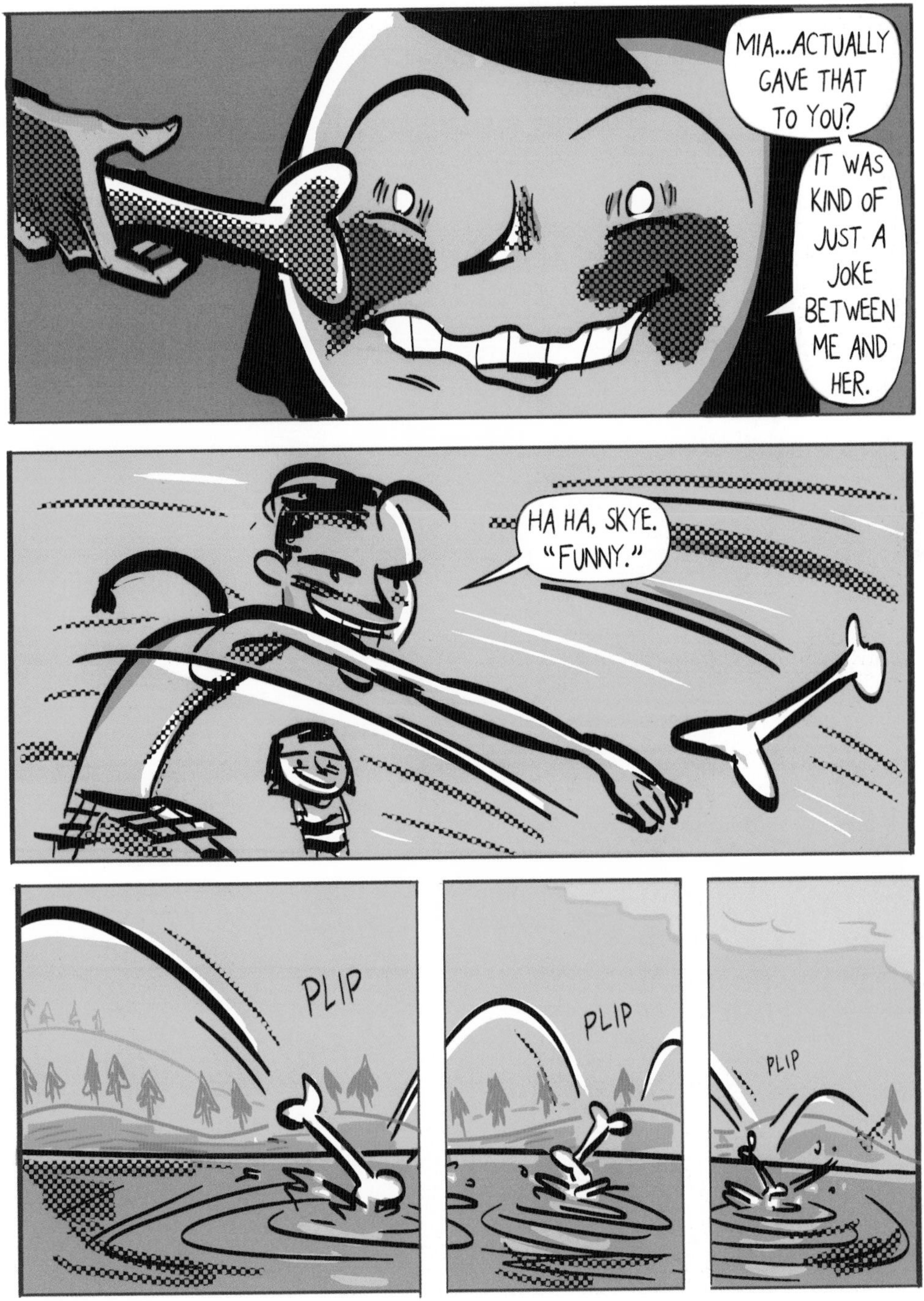
MIA...ACTUALLY GAVE THAT TO YOU?
IT WAS KIND OF JUST A JOKE BETWEEN ME AND HER.
HA HA, SKYE. "FUNNY."
PLIP
PLIP
PLIP

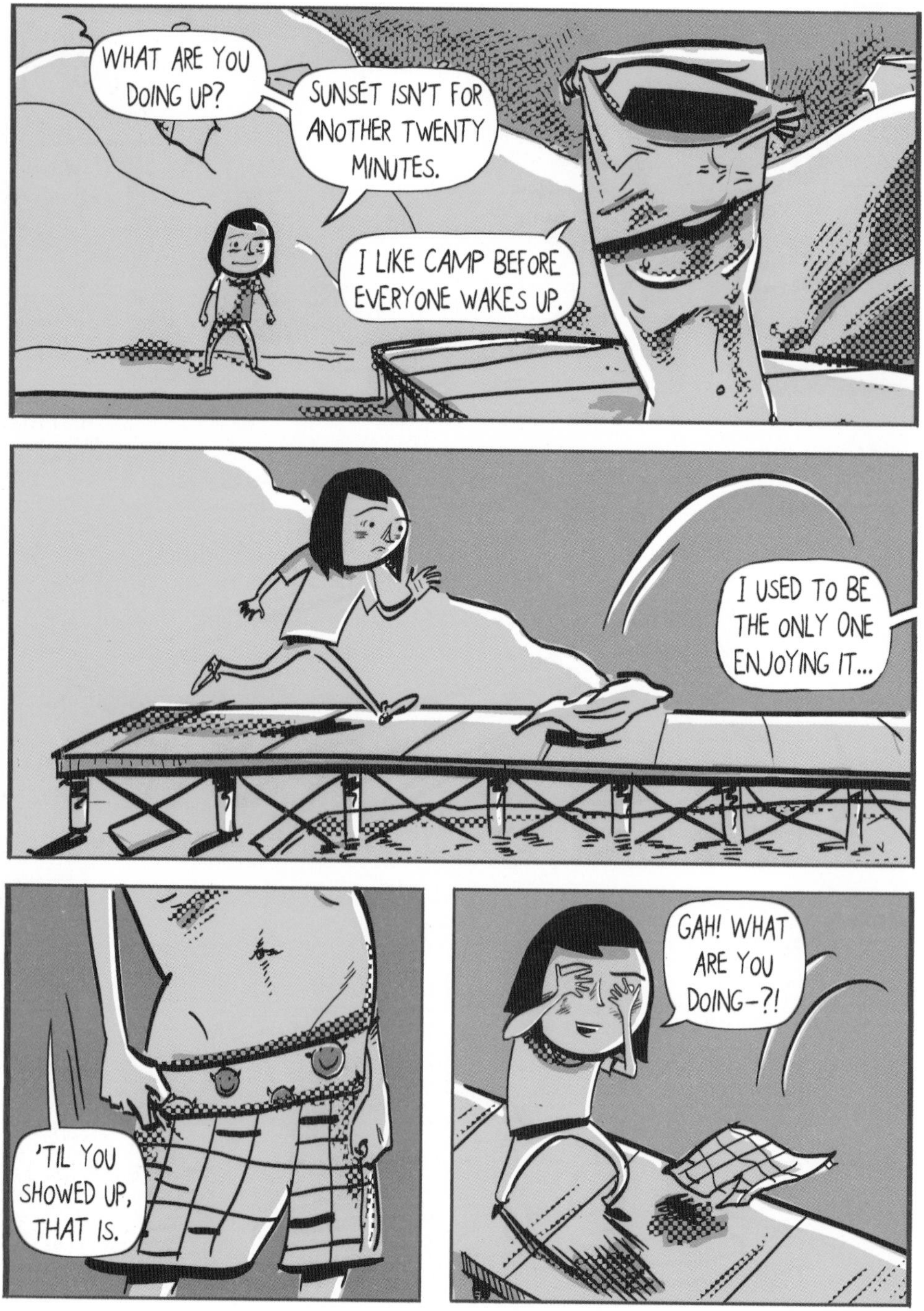
WHAT ARE YOU DOING UP?
SUNSET ISN'T FOR ANOTHER TWENTY MINUTES.
I LIKE CAMP BEFORE EVERYONE WAKES UP.
I USED TO BE THE ONLY ONE ENJOYING IT...
'TIL YOU SHOWED UP, THAT IS.
GAH! WHAT ARE YOU DOING-?!

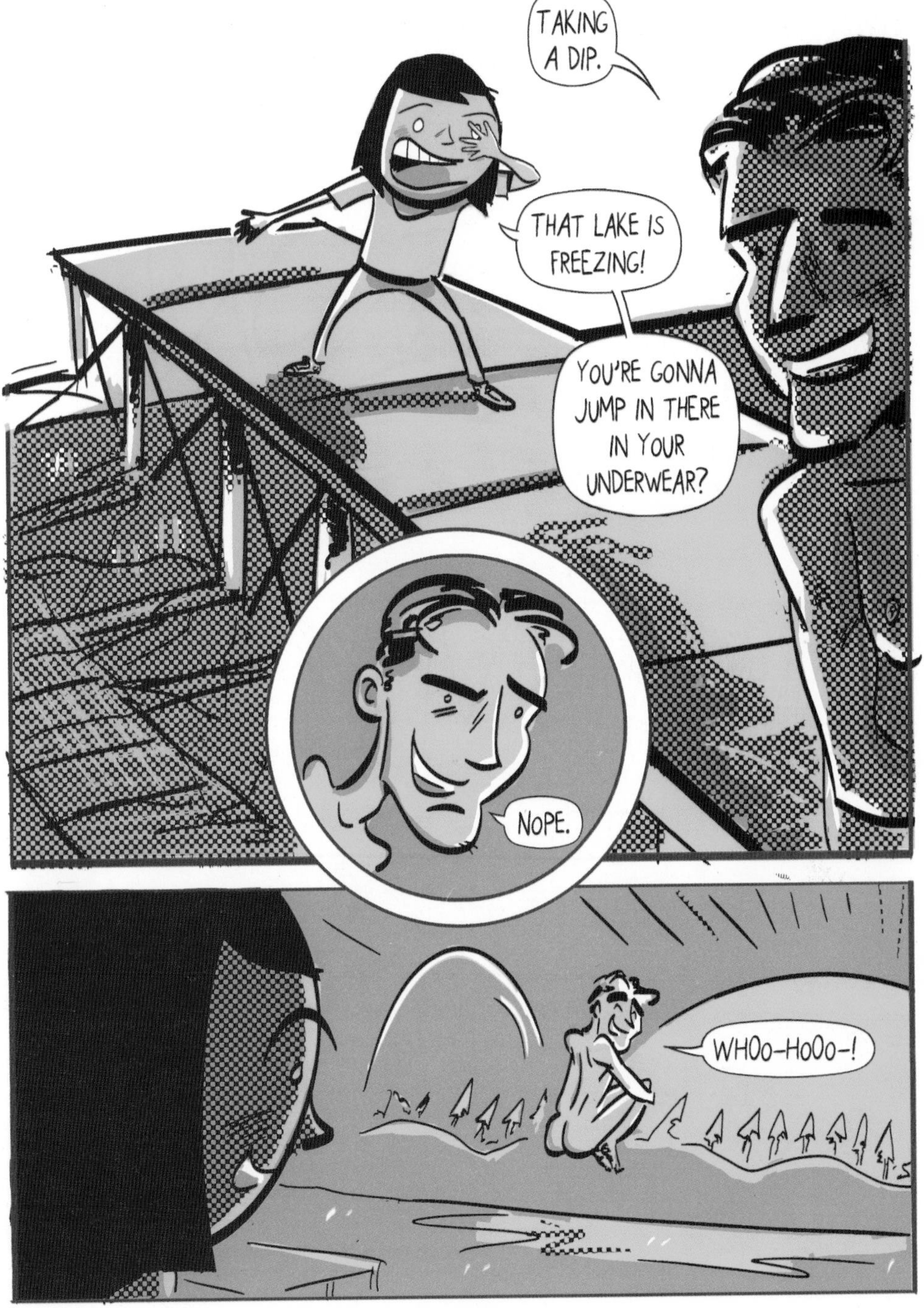
TAKING A DIP.
THAT LAKE IS FREEZING!
YOU'RE GONNA JUMP IN THERE IN YOUR UNDERWEAR?
NOPE.
WHOo-HoOo-!

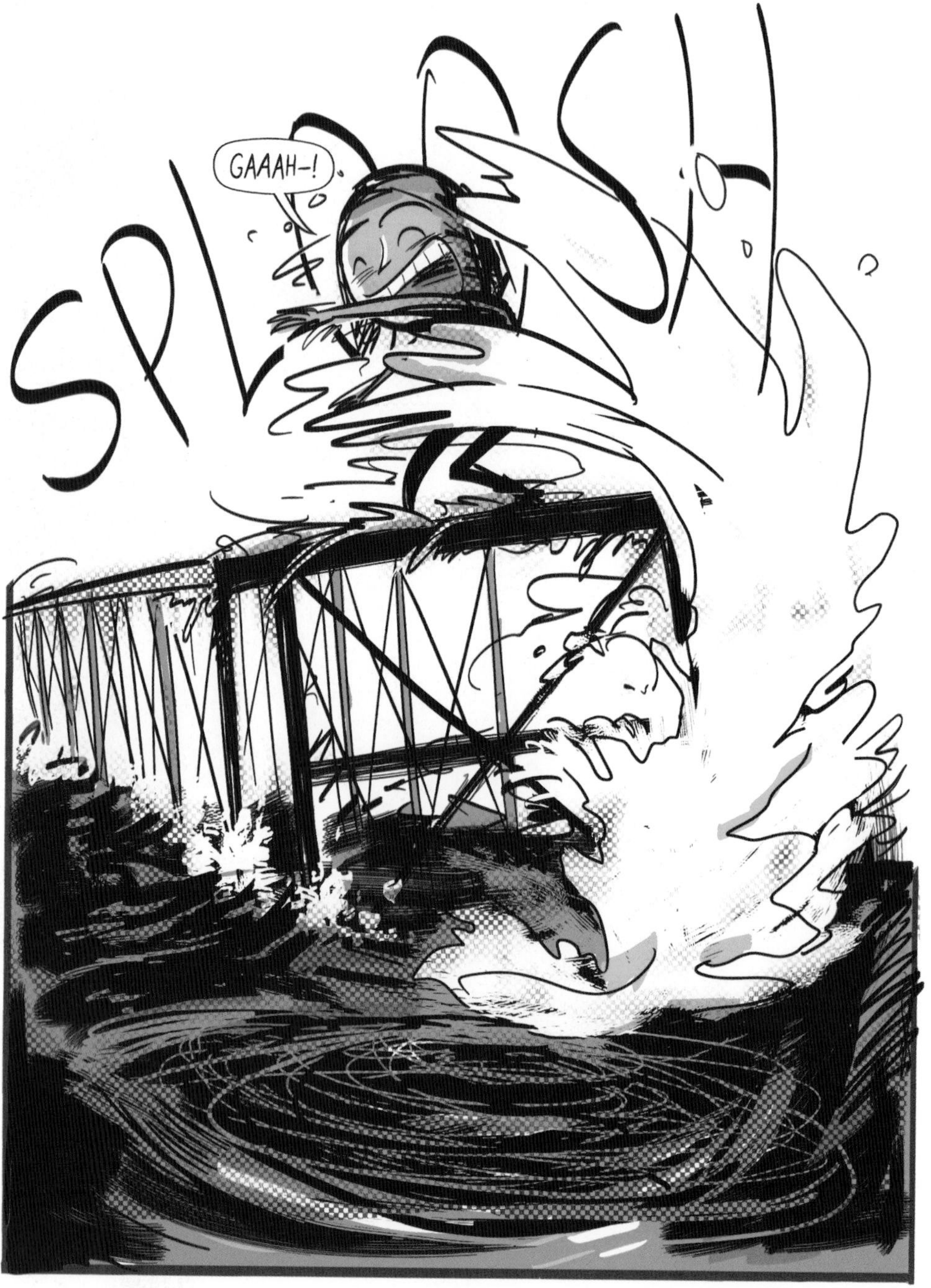
GAAAH-!
SPLOOSH

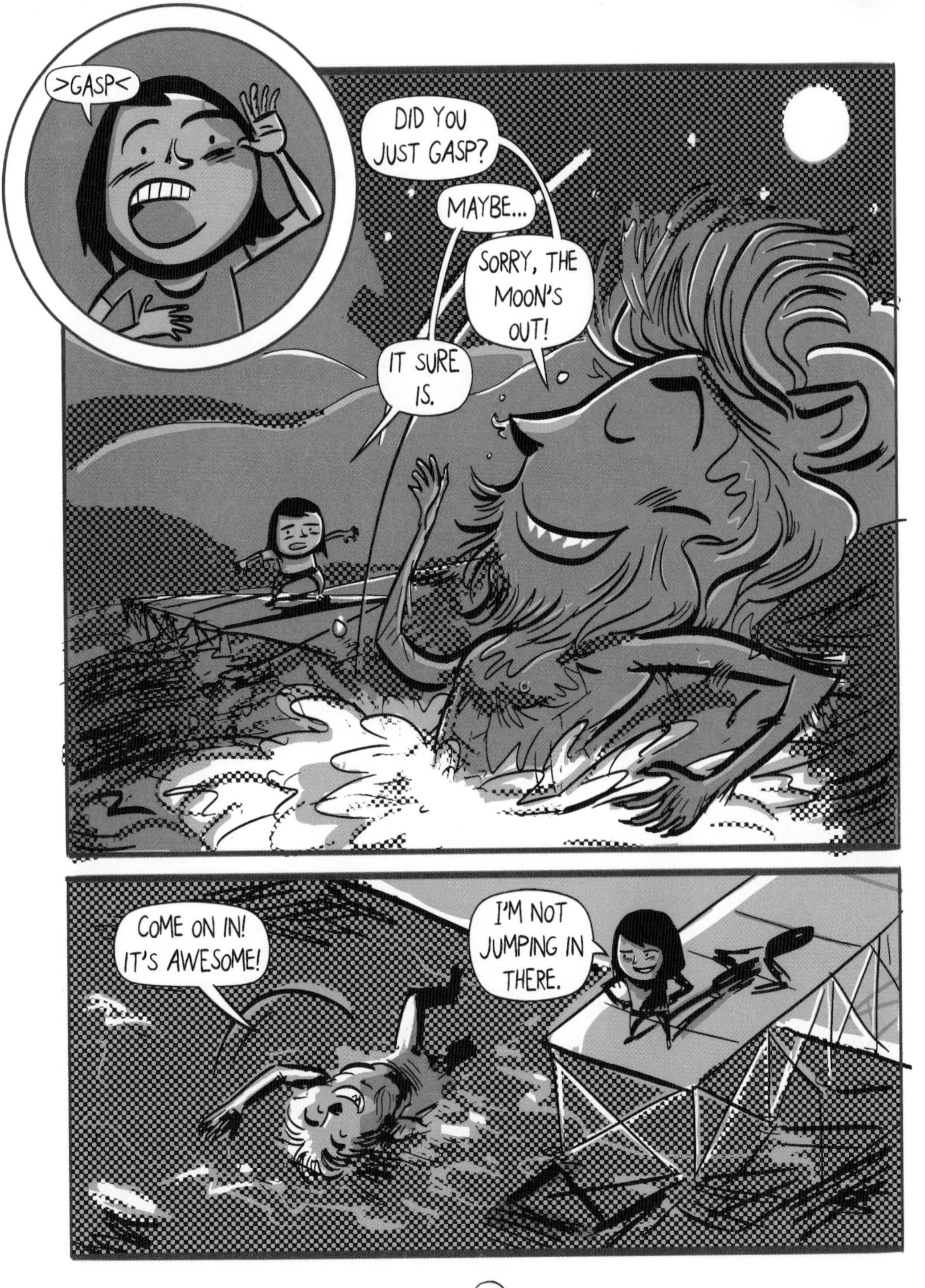
>GASP<
DID YOU JUST GASP?
MAYBE...
SORRY, THE MOON'S OUT!
IT SURE IS.
COME ON IN! IT'S AWESOME!
I'M NOT JUMPING IN THERE.

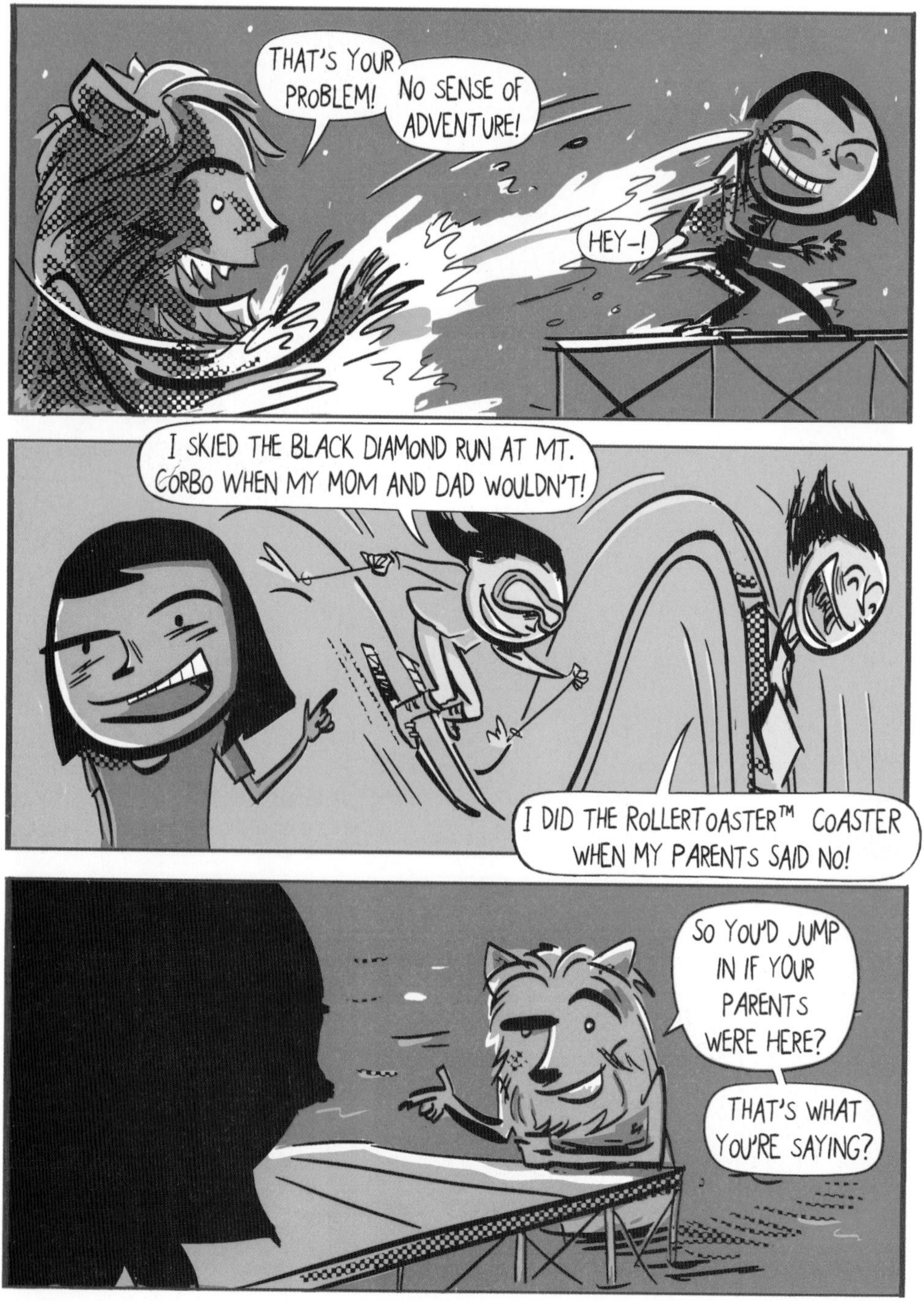
THAT'S YOUR PROBLEM!
NO SENSE OF ADVENTURE!
HEY–!
I SKIED THE BLACK DIAMOND RUN AT MT. CORBO WHEN MY MOM AND DAD WOULDN'T!
I DID THE ROLLERTOASTER™ COASTER WHEN MY PARENTS SAID NO!
SO YOU'D JUMP IN IF YOUR PARENTS WERE HERE?
THAT'S WHAT YOU'RE SAYING?

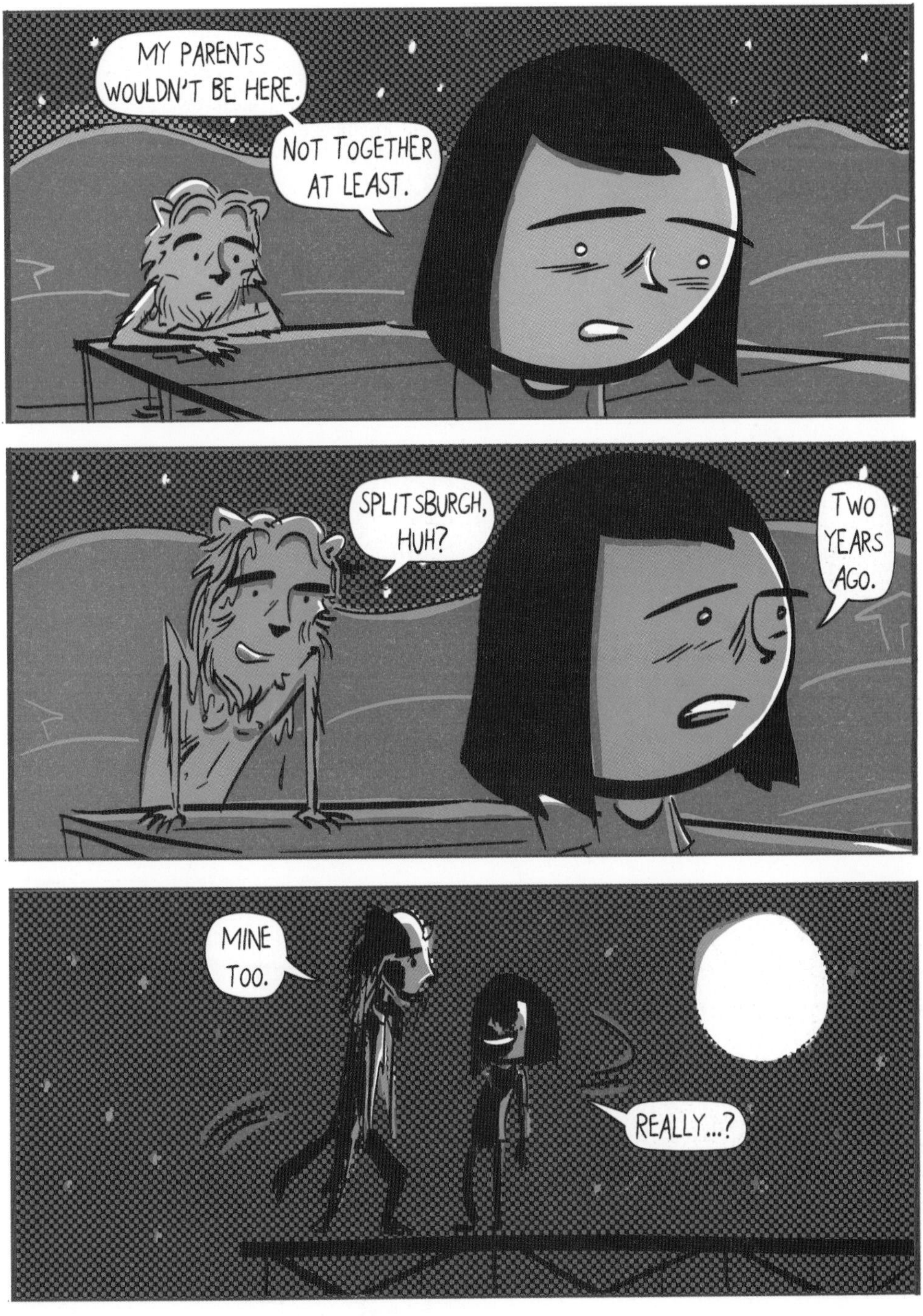
MY PARENTS WOULDN'T BE HERE.
NOT TOGETHER AT LEAST.
SPLITSBURGH, HUH?
TWO YEARS AGO.
MINE TOO.
REALLY...?

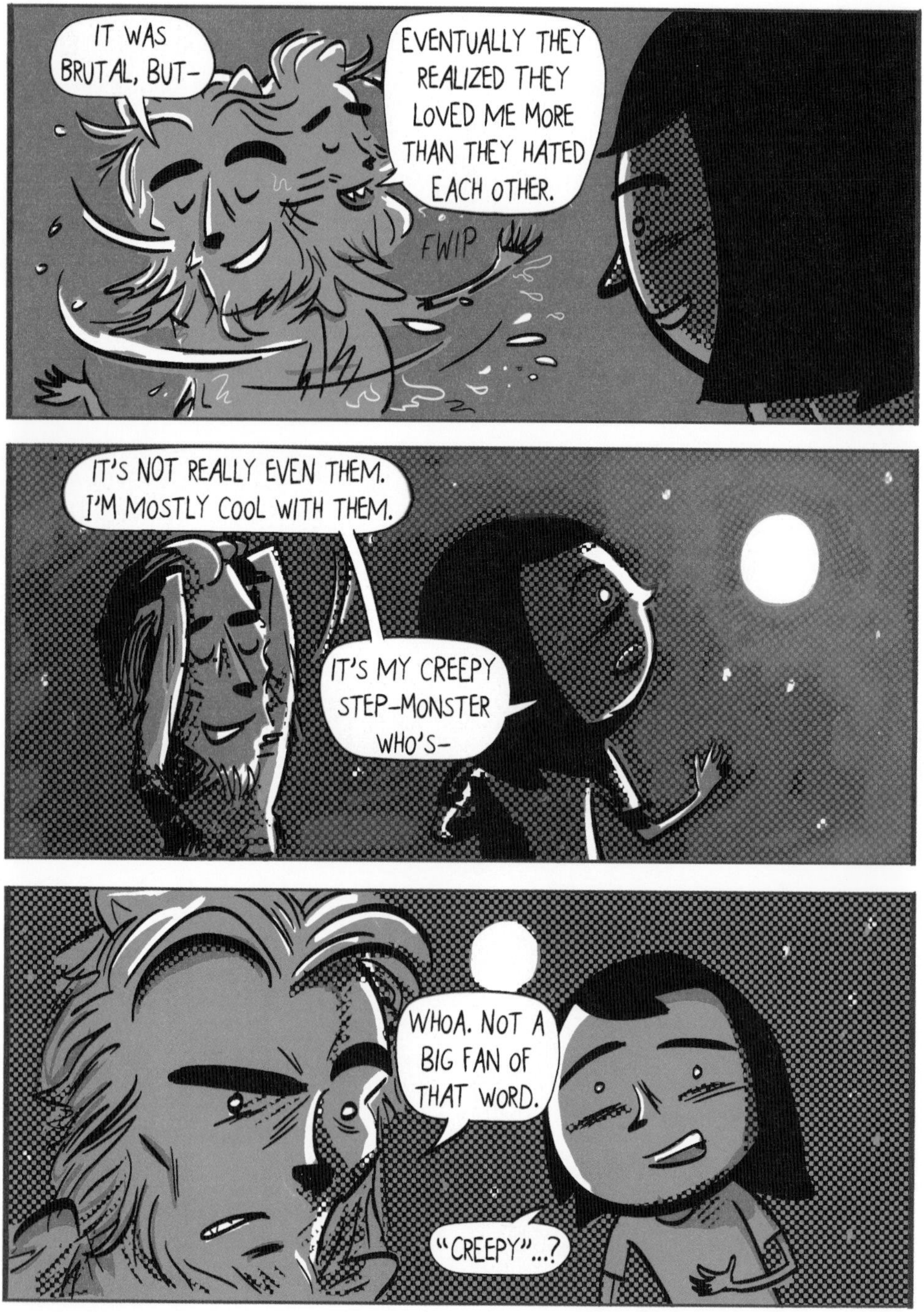
IT WAS BRUTAL, BUT-
EVENTUALLY THEY REALIZED THEY LOVED ME MORE THAN THEY HATED EACH OTHER.
FWIP
IT'S NOT REALLY EVEN THEM. I'M MOSTLY COOL WITH THEM.
IT'S MY CREEPY STEP-MONSTER WHO'S-
WHOA. NOT A BIG FAN OF THAT WORD.
"CREEPY"...?

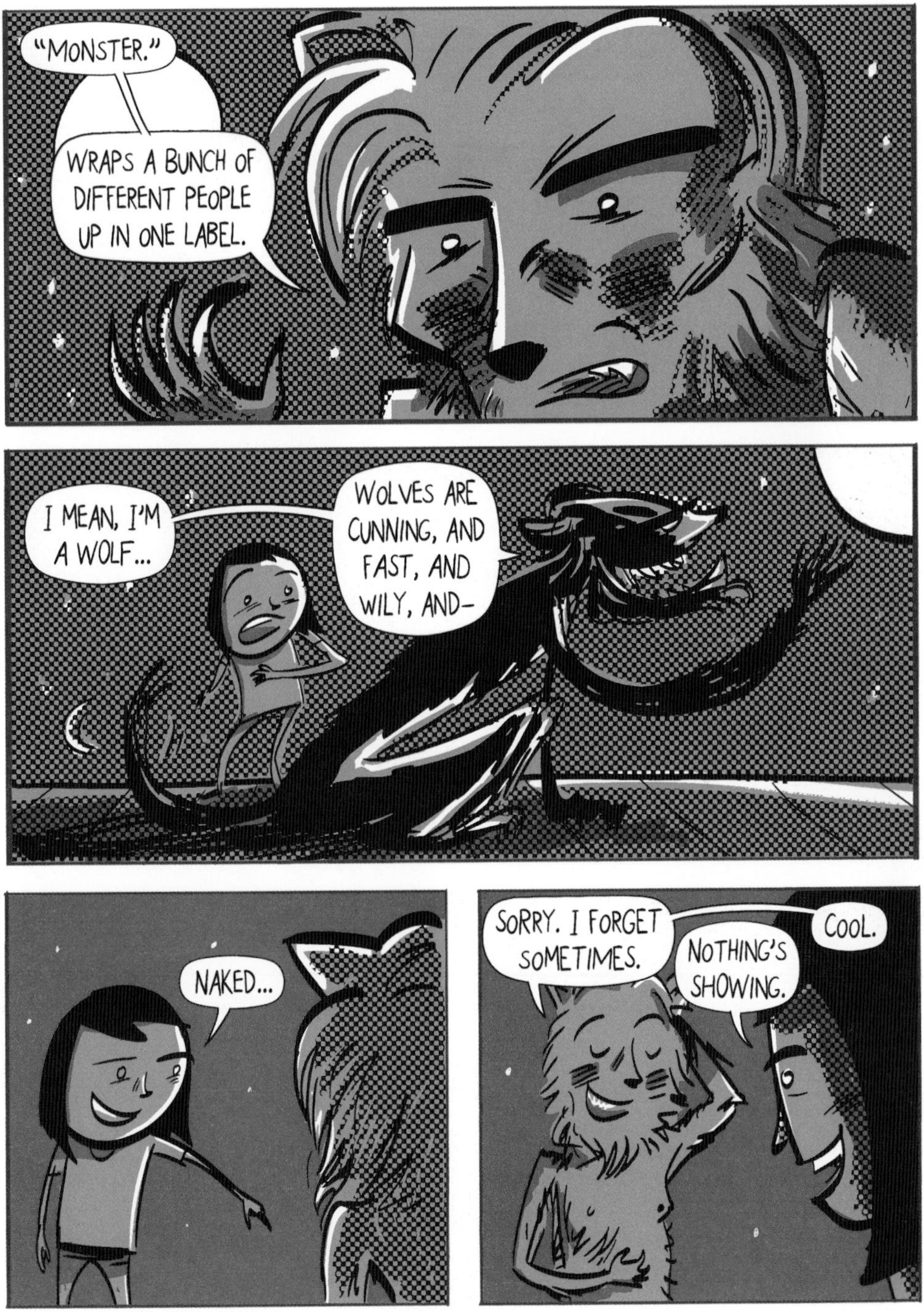
"MONSTER."
WRAPS A BUNCH OF DIFFERENT PEOPLE UP IN ONE LABEL.
I MEAN, I'M A WOLF...
WOLVES ARE CUNNING, AND FAST, AND WILY, AND-
NAKED...
SORRY. I FORGET SOMETIMES.
NOTHING'S SHOWING.
COOL.

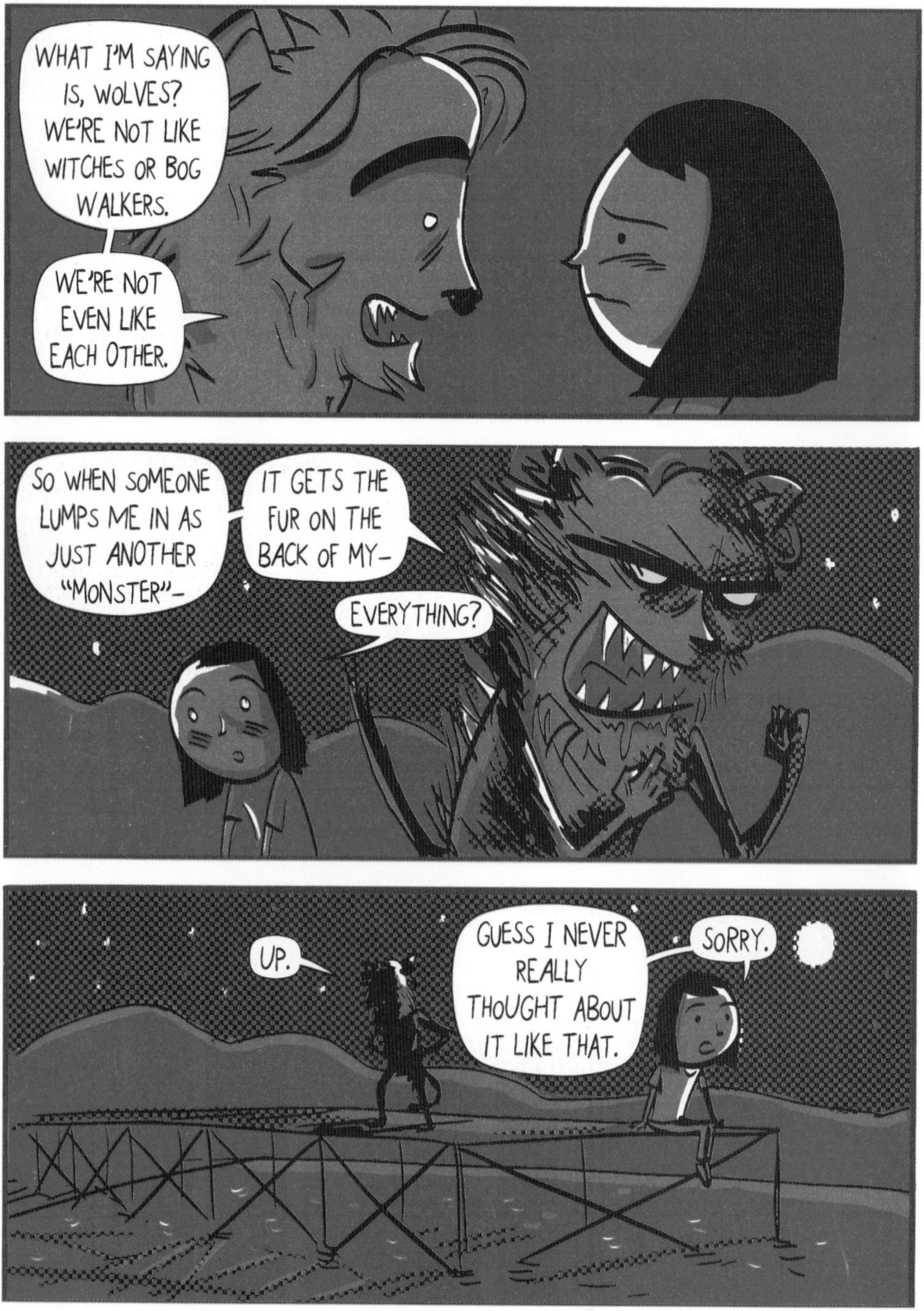
WHAT I'M SAYING IS, WOLVES? WE'RE NOT LIKE WITCHES OR BOG WALKERS.
WE'RE NOT EVEN LIKE EACH OTHER.
SO WHEN SOMEONE LUMPS ME IN AS JUST ANOTHER "MONSTER"–
IT GETS THE FUR ON THE BACK OF MY–
EVERYTHING?
UP.
GUESS I NEVER REALLY THOUGHT ABOUT IT LIKE THAT.
SORRY.

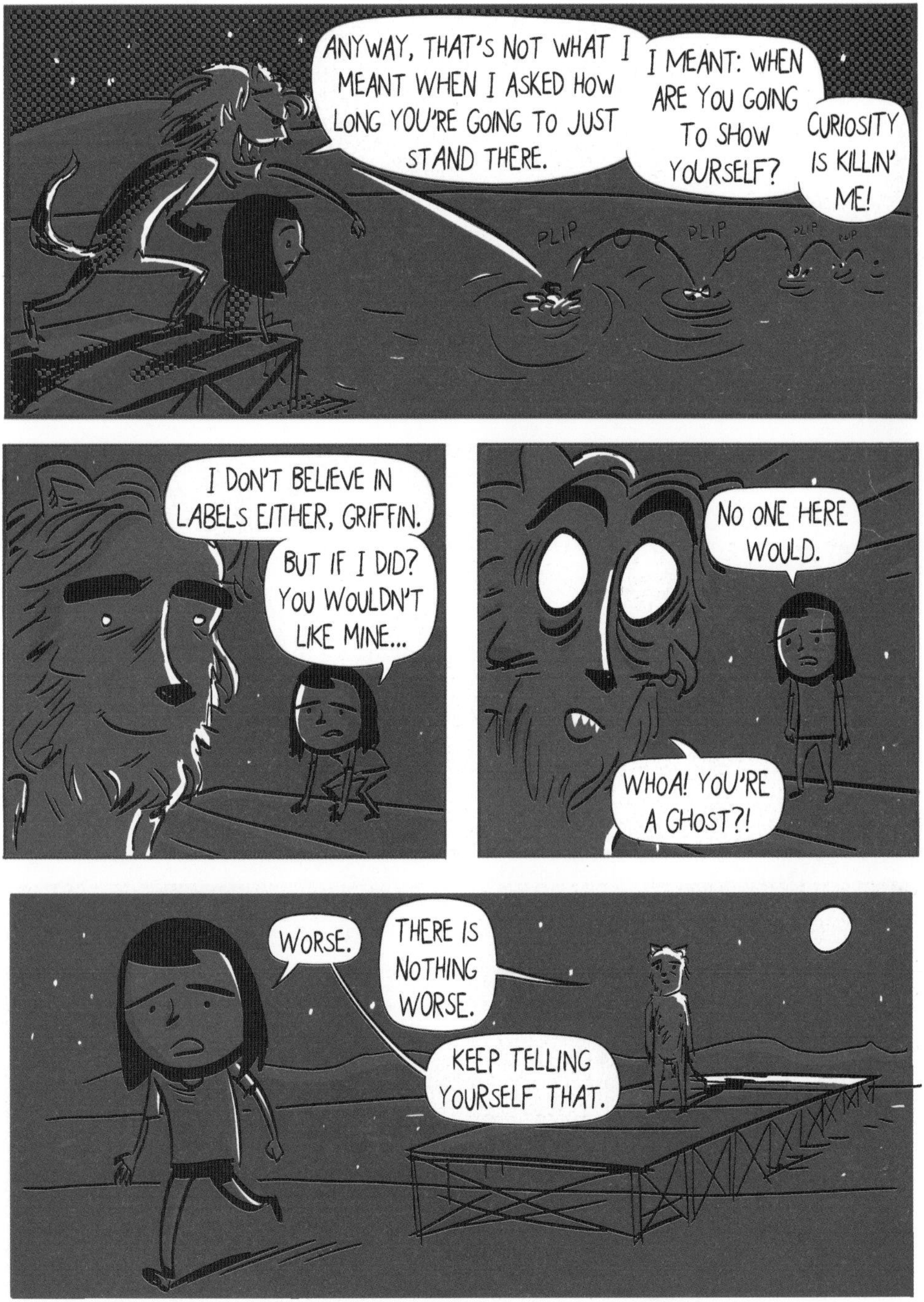
ANYWAY, THAT'S NOT WHAT I MEANT WHEN I ASKED HOW LONG YOU'RE GOING TO JUST STAND THERE.
I MEANT: WHEN ARE YOU GOING TO SHOW YOURSELF?
CURIOSITY IS KILLIN' ME!
PLIP
PLIP
I DON'T BELIEVE IN LABELS EITHER, GRIFFIN.
BUT IF I DID? YOU WOULDN'T LIKE MINE...
NO ONE HERE WOULD.
WHOA! YOU'RE A GHOST?!
WORSE.
THERE IS NOTHING WORSE.
KEEP TELLING YOURSELF THAT.

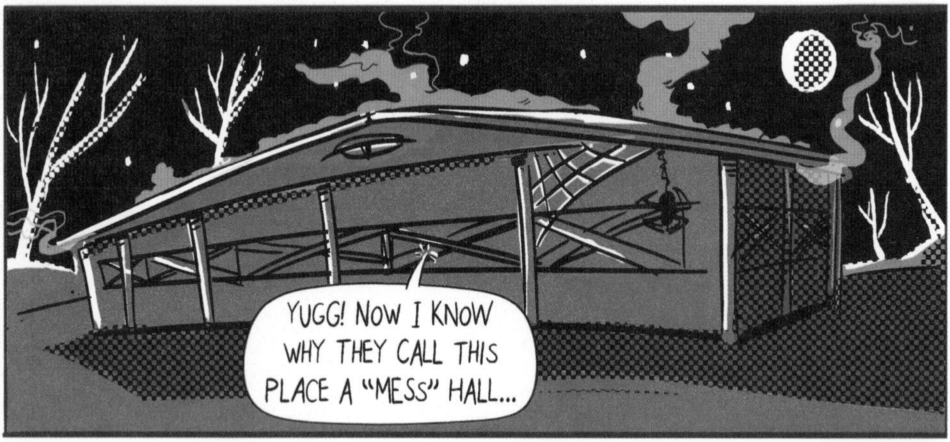
YUGG! NOW I KNOW WHY THEY CALL THIS PLACE A "MESS" HALL...

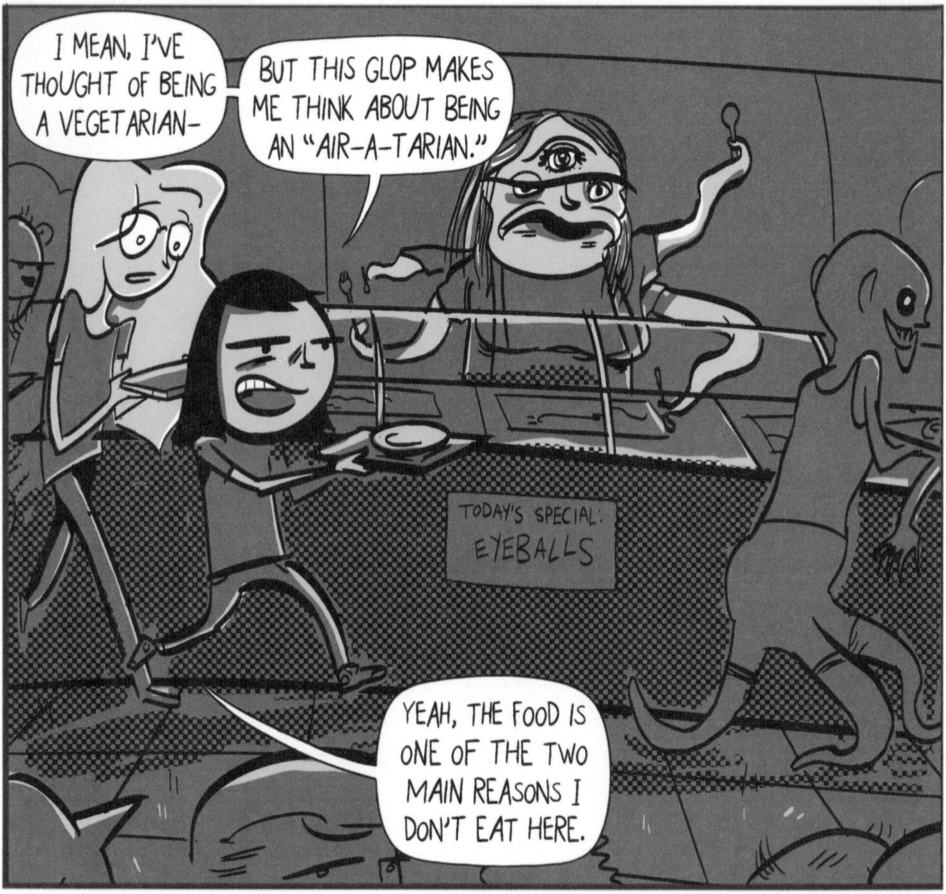
I MEAN, I'VE THOUGHT OF BEING A VEGETARIAN-
BUT THIS GLOP MAKES ME THINK ABOUT BEING AN "AIR-A-TARIAN."
TODAY'S SPECIAL: EYEBALLS
YEAH, THE FOOD IS ONE OF THE TWO MAIN REASONS I DON'T EAT HERE.

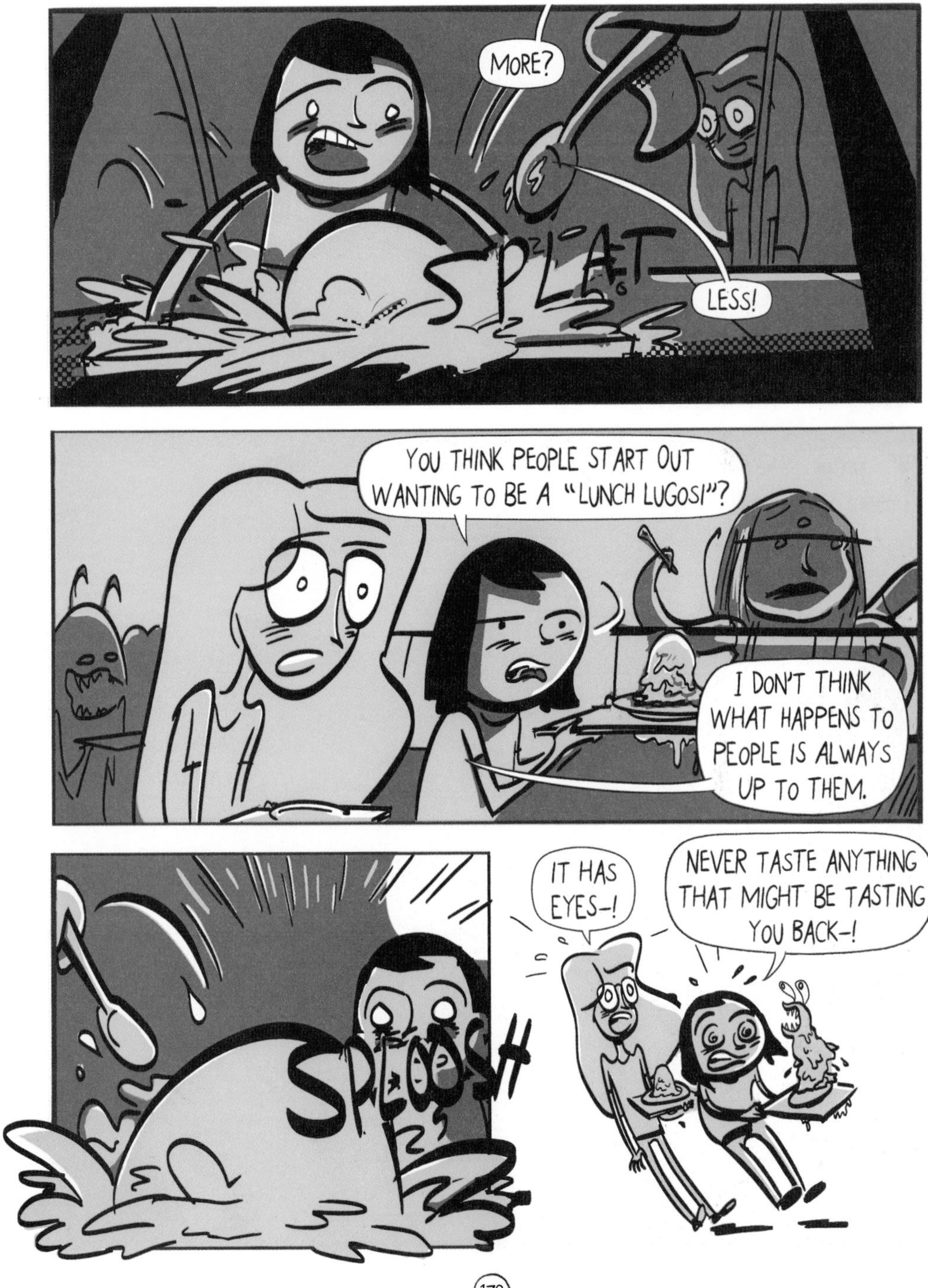
MORE?
SPLAT
LESS!
YOU THINK PEOPLE START OUT WANTING TO BE A "LUNCH LUGOSI"?
I DON'T THINK WHAT HAPPENS TO PEOPLE IS ALWAYS UP TO THEM.
SPLOOSH
IT HAS EYES-!
NEVER TASTE ANYTHING THAT MIGHT BE TASTING YOU BACK-!

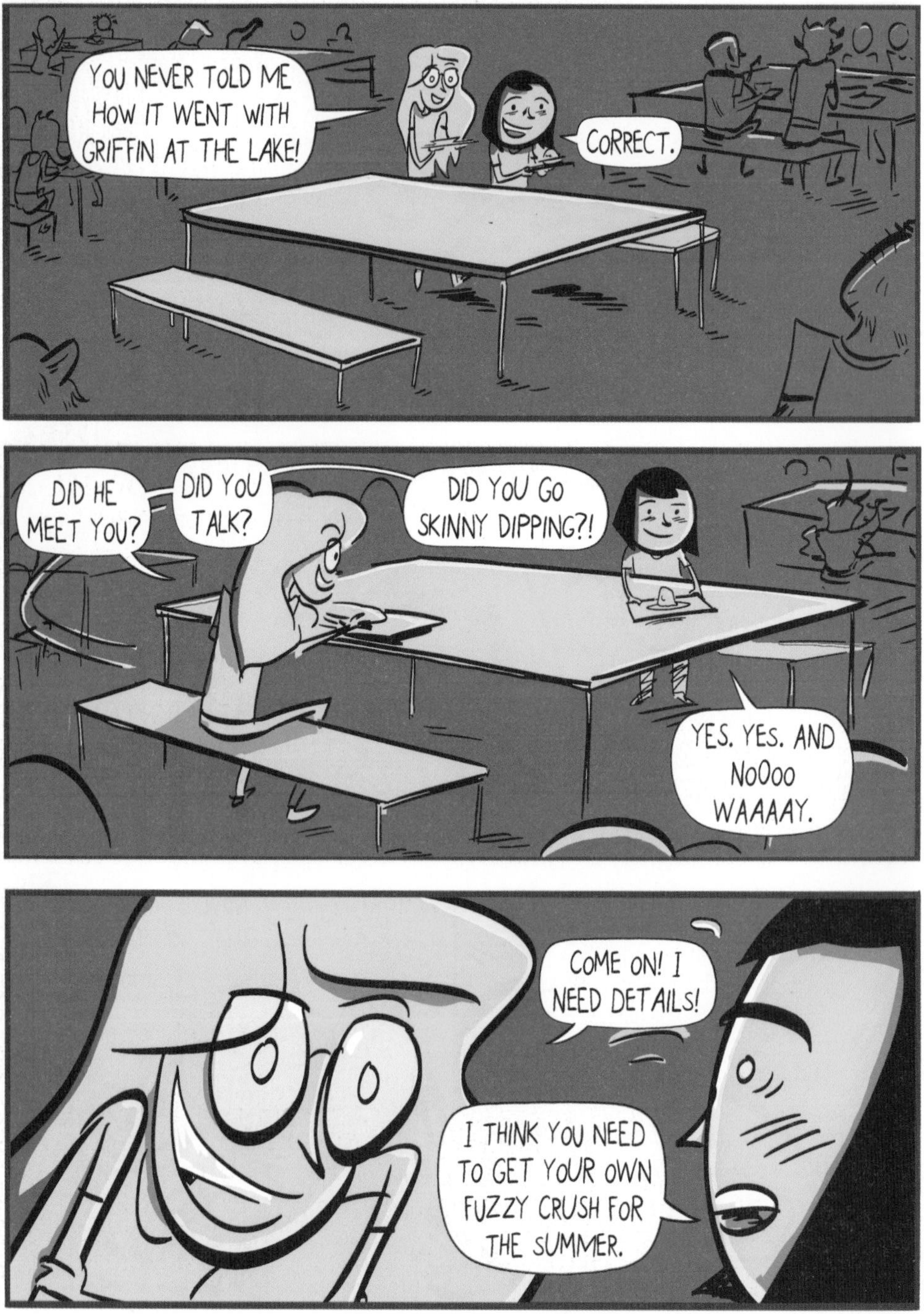
YOU NEVER TOLD ME HOW IT WENT WITH GRIFFIN AT THE LAKE!
CORRECT.
DID HE MEET YOU?
DID YOU TALK?
DID YOU GO SKINNY DIPPING?!
YES. YES. AND NoOoo WAAAAY.
COME ON! I NEED DETAILS!
I THINK YOU NEED TO GET YOUR OWN FUZZY CRUSH FOR THE SUMMER.

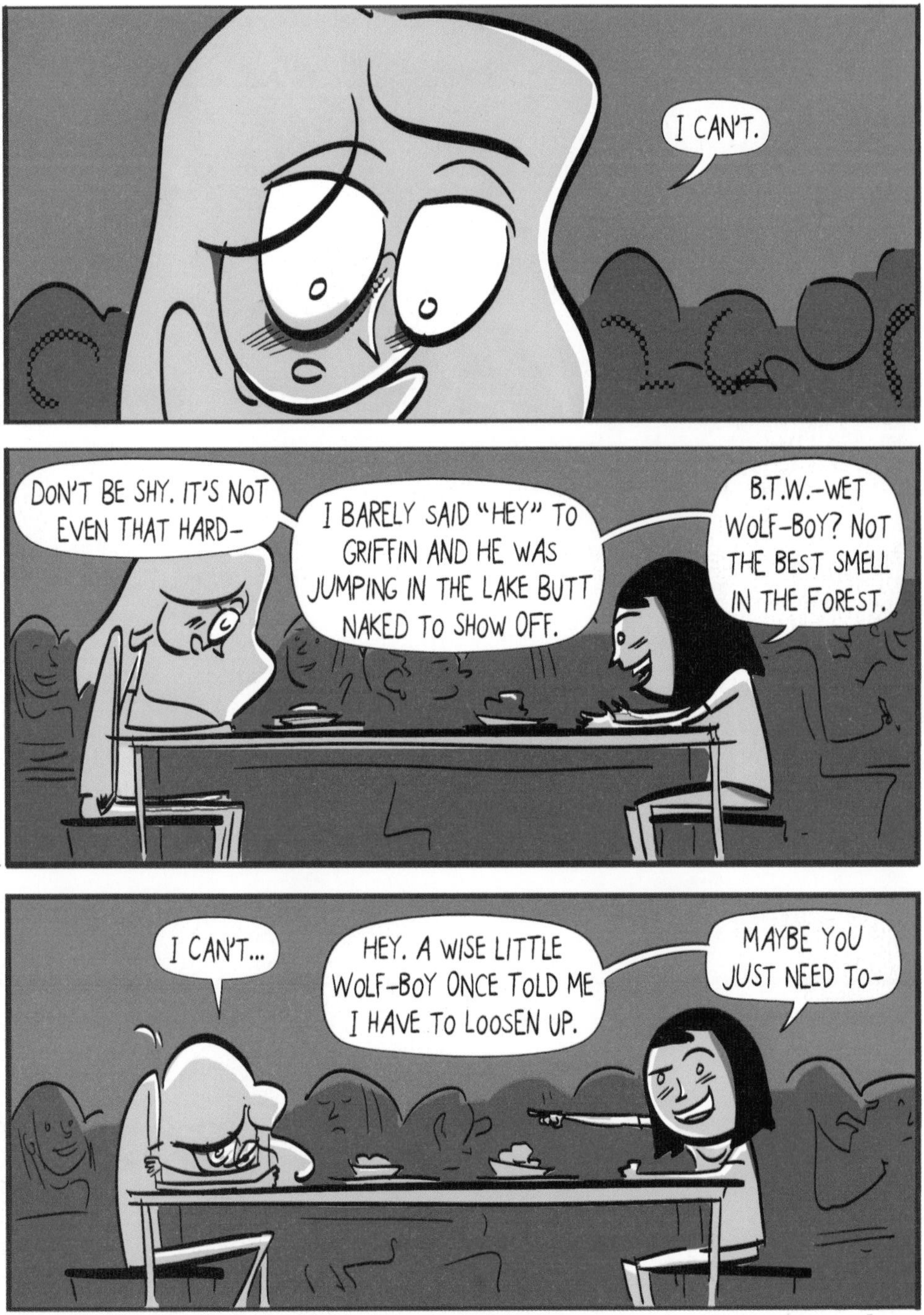
I CAN'T.
DON'T BE SHY. IT'S NOT EVEN THAT HARD-
I BARELY SAID "HEY" TO GRIFFIN AND HE WAS JUMPING IN THE LAKE BUTT NAKED TO SHOW OFF.
B.T.W.-WET WOLF-BOY? NOT THE BEST SMELL IN THE FOREST.
I CAN'T...
HEY. A WISE LITTLE WOLF-BOY ONCE TOLD ME I HAVE TO LOOSEN UP.
MAYBE YOU JUST NEED TO-

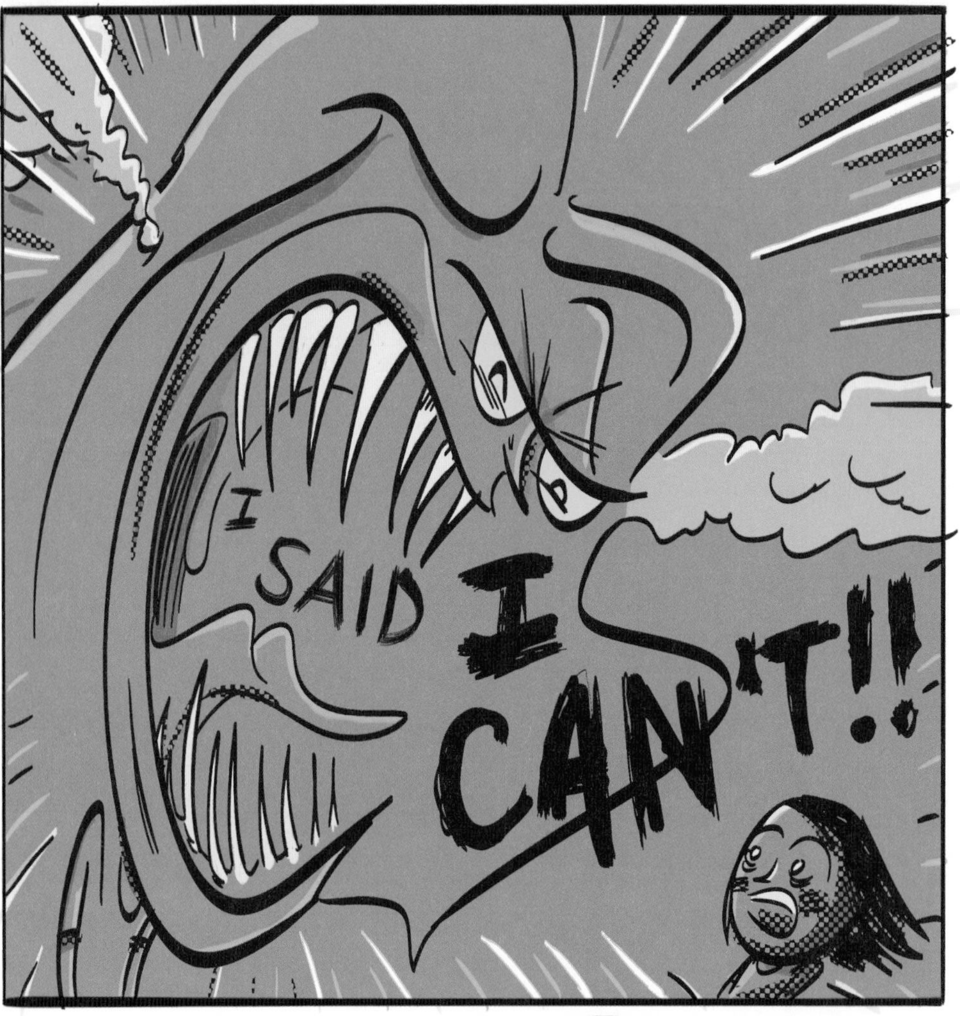
I SAID I CAN'T!!

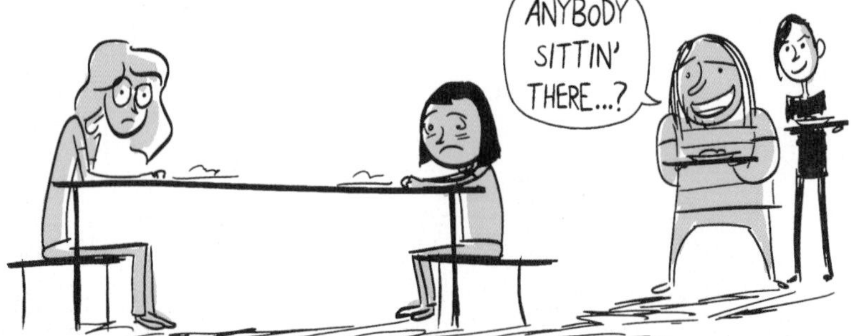
ANYBODY SITTIN' THERE...?

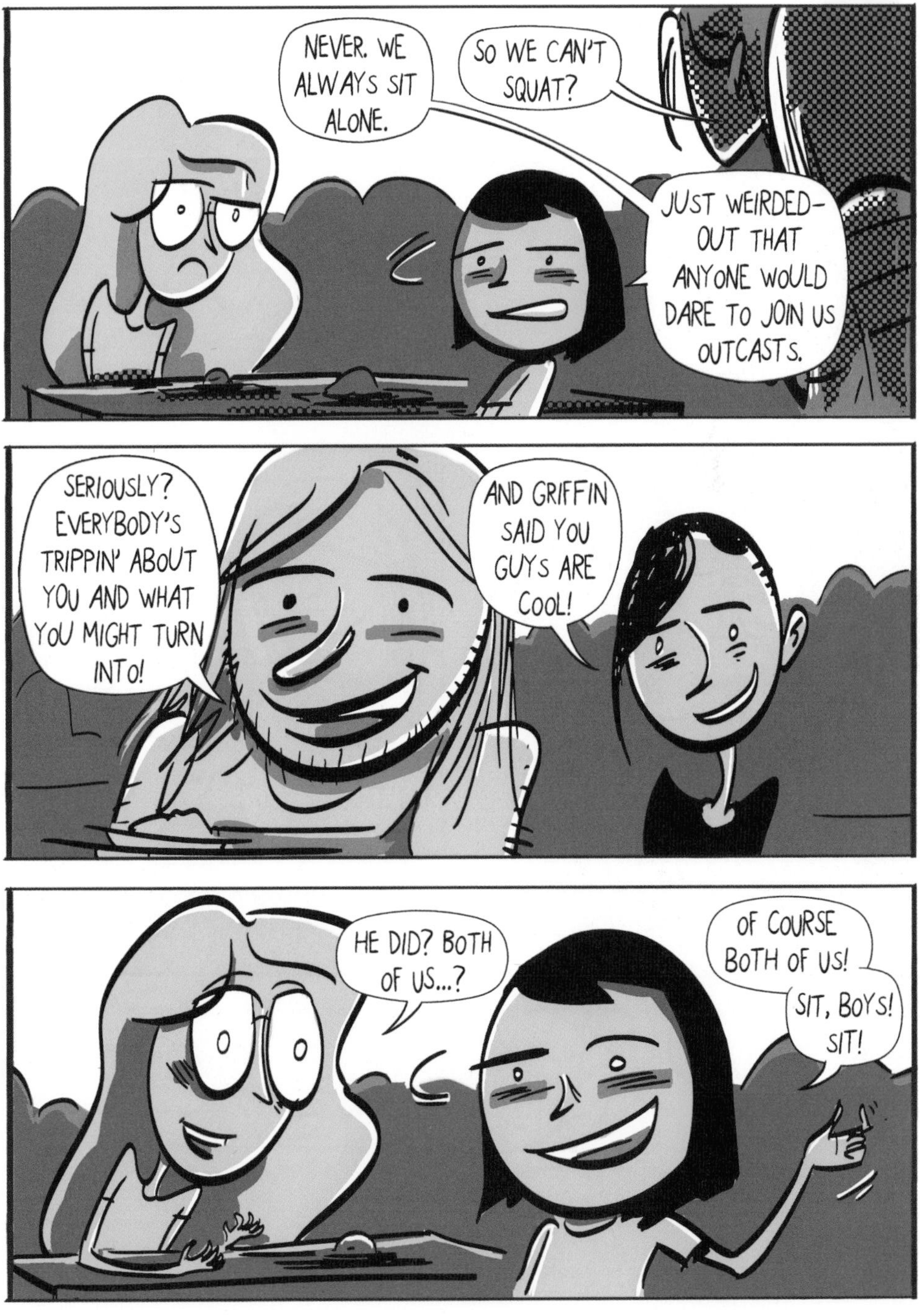
NEVER. WE ALWAYS SIT ALONE.
SO WE CAN'T SQUAT?
JUST WEIRDED-OUT THAT ANYONE WOULD DARE TO JOIN US OUTCASTS.
SERIOUSLY? EVERYBODY'S TRIPPIN' ABOUT YOU AND WHAT YOU MIGHT TURN INTO!
AND GRIFFIN SAID YOU GUYS ARE COOL!
HE DID? BOTH OF US...?
OF COURSE BOTH OF US!
SIT, BOYS! SIT!

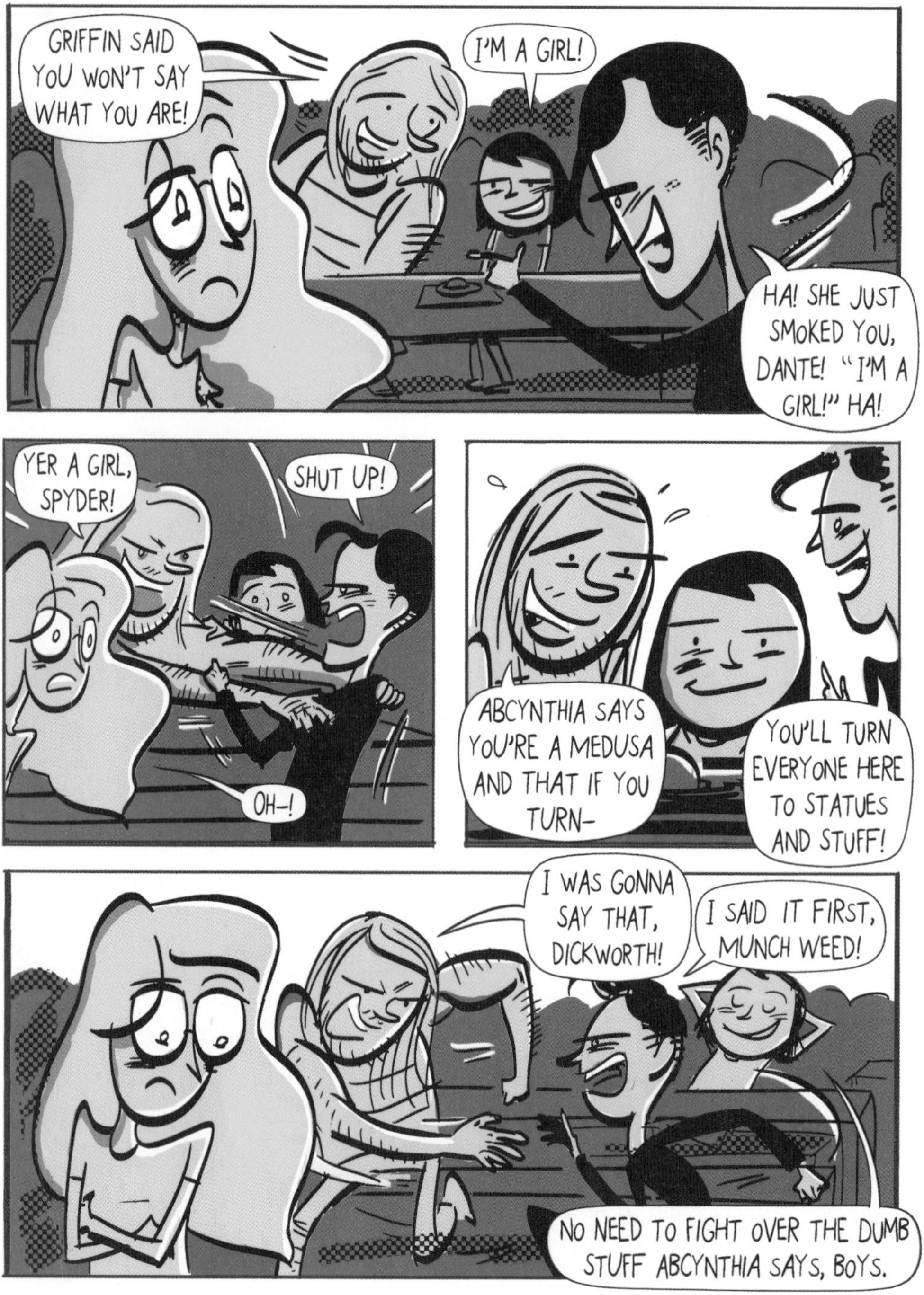
GRIFFIN SAID YOU WON'T SAY WHAT YOU ARE!
I'M A GIRL!
HA! SHE JUST SMOKED YOU, DANTE! "I'M A GIRL!" HA!
YER A GIRL, SPYDER!
SHUT UP!
OH-!
ABCYNTHIA SAYS YOU'RE A MEDUSA AND THAT IF YOU TURN-
YOU'LL TURN EVERYONE HERE TO STATUES AND STUFF!
I WAS GONNA SAY THAT, DICKWORTH!
I SAID IT FIRST, MUNCH WEED!
NO NEED TO FIGHT OVER THE DUMB STUFF ABCYNTHIA SAYS, BOYS.

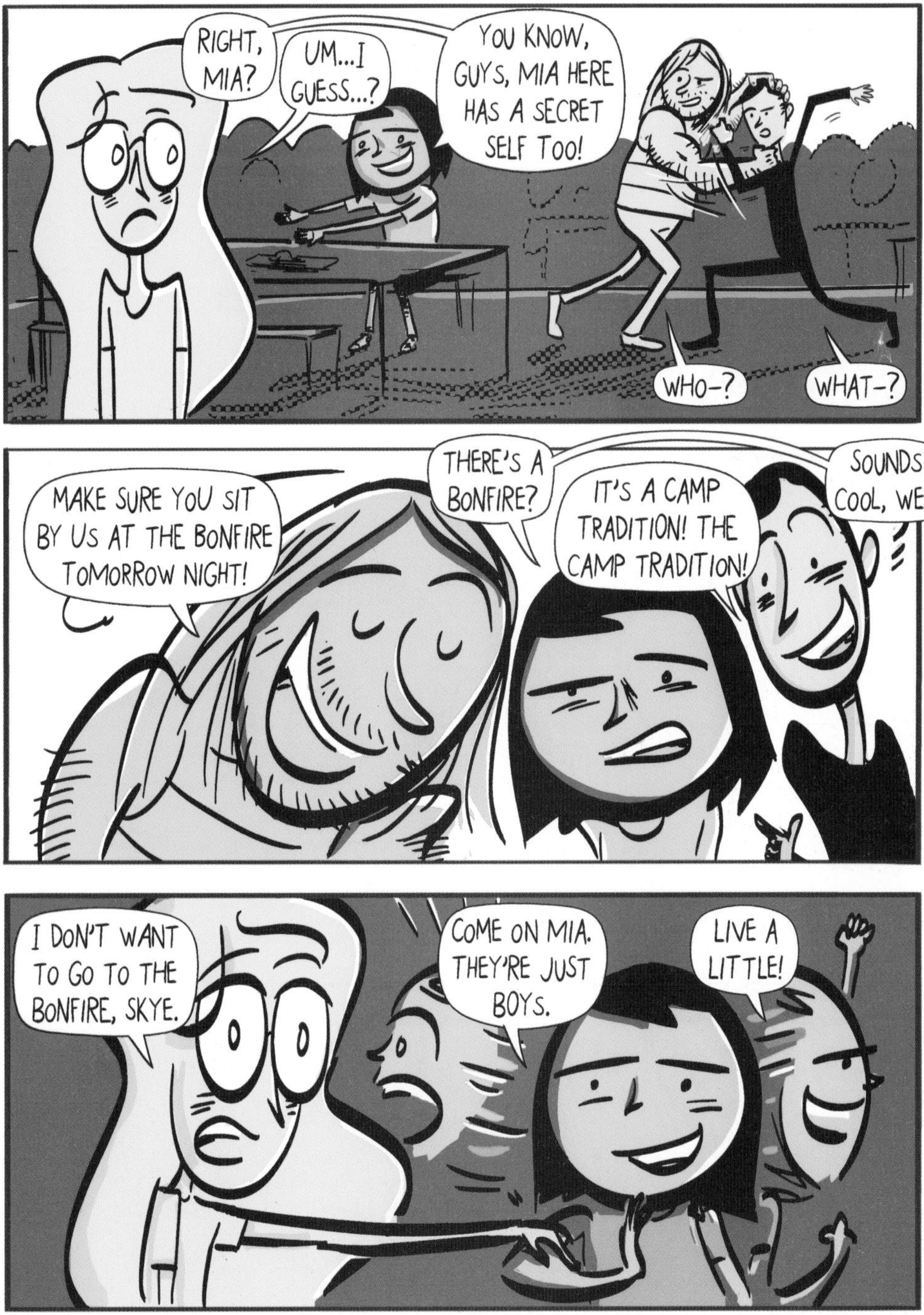

RIGHT, MIA?
UM...I GUESS...?
YOU KNOW, GUYS, MIA HERE HAS A SECRET SELF TOO!
WHO-?
WHAT-?
MAKE SURE YOU SIT BY US AT THE BONFIRE TOMORROW NIGHT!
THERE'S A BONFIRE?
IT'S A CAMP TRADITION! THE CAMP TRADITION!
SOUNDS COOL, WE-
I DON'T WANT TO GO TO THE BONFIRE, SKYE.
COME ON MIA. THEY'RE JUST BOYS.
LIVE A LITTLE!

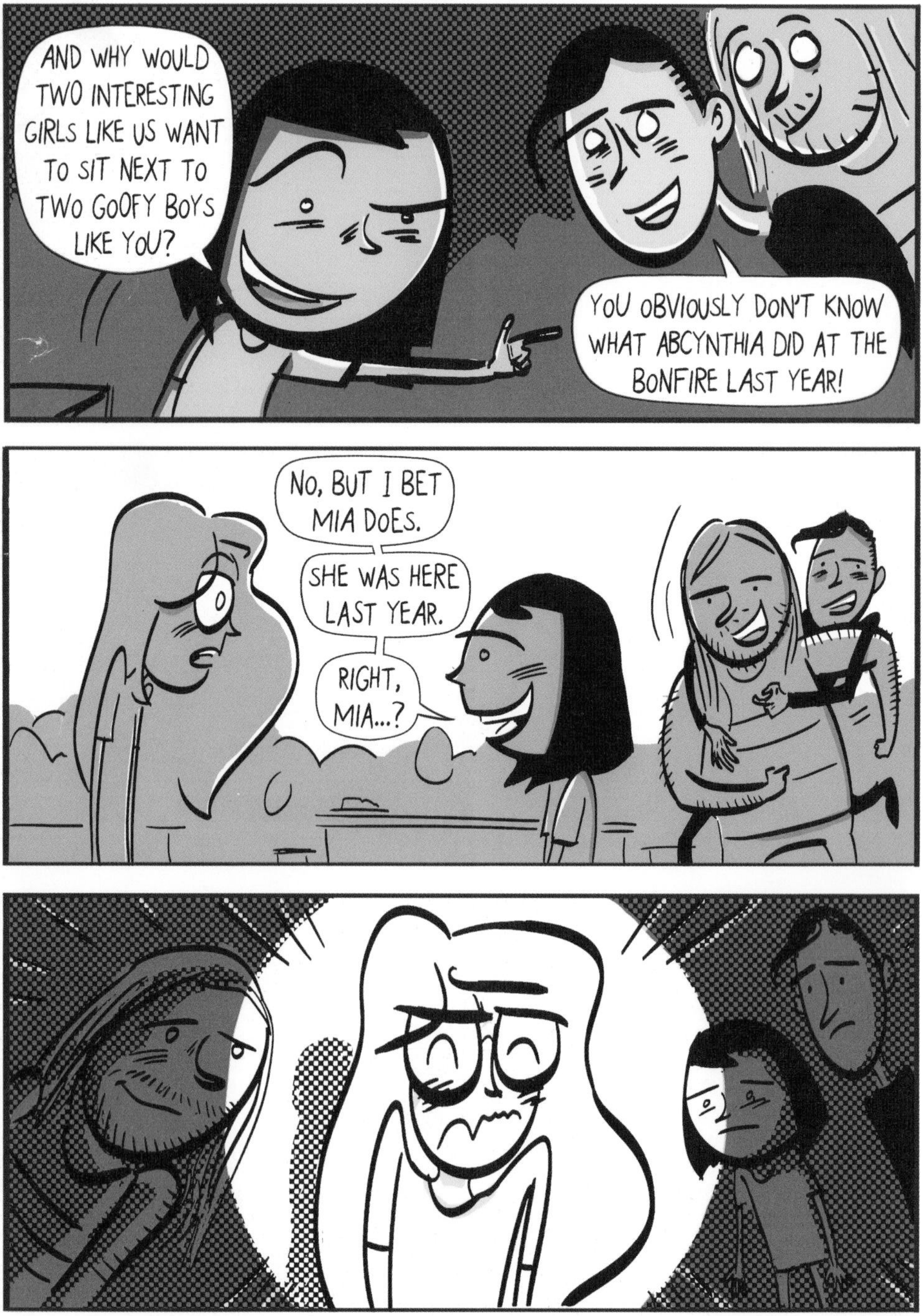
AND WHY WOULD TWO INTERESTING GIRLS LIKE US WANT TO SIT NEXT TO TWO GOOFY BOYS LIKE YOU?
YOU OBVIOUSLY DON'T KNOW WHAT ABCYNTHIA DID AT THE BONFIRE LAST YEAR!
NO, BUT I BET MIA DOES.
SHE WAS HERE LAST YEAR.
RIGHT, MIA...?

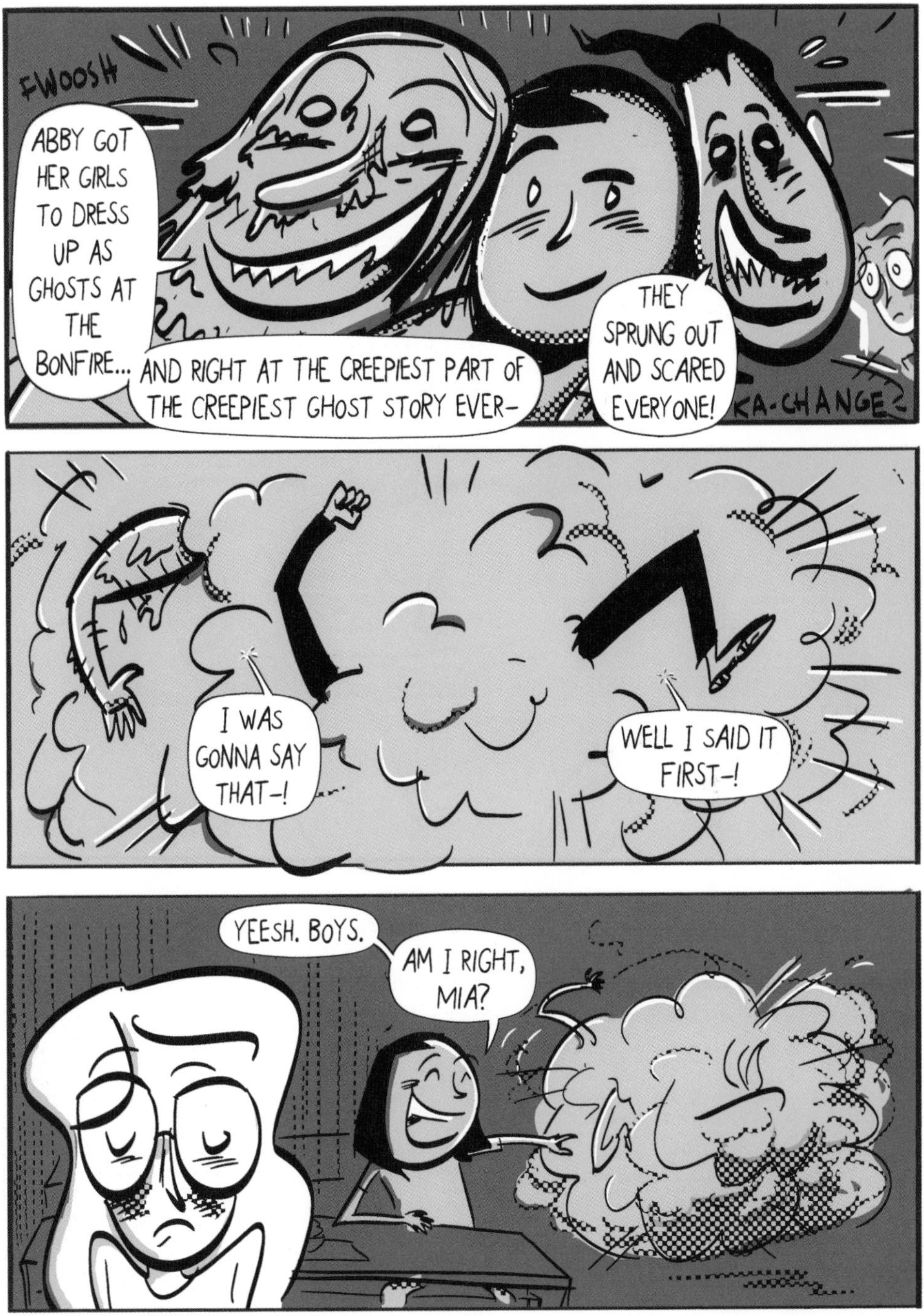
FWOOSH
ABBY GOT HER GIRLS TO DRESS UP AS GHOSTS AT THE BONFIRE...
AND RIGHT AT THE CREEPIEST PART OF THE CREEPIEST GHOST STORY EVER-
THEY SPRUNG OUT AND SCARED EVERYONE!
KA-CHANGE
I WAS GONNA SAY THAT-!
WELL I SAID IT FIRST-!
YEESH. BOYS.
AM I RIGHT, MIA?

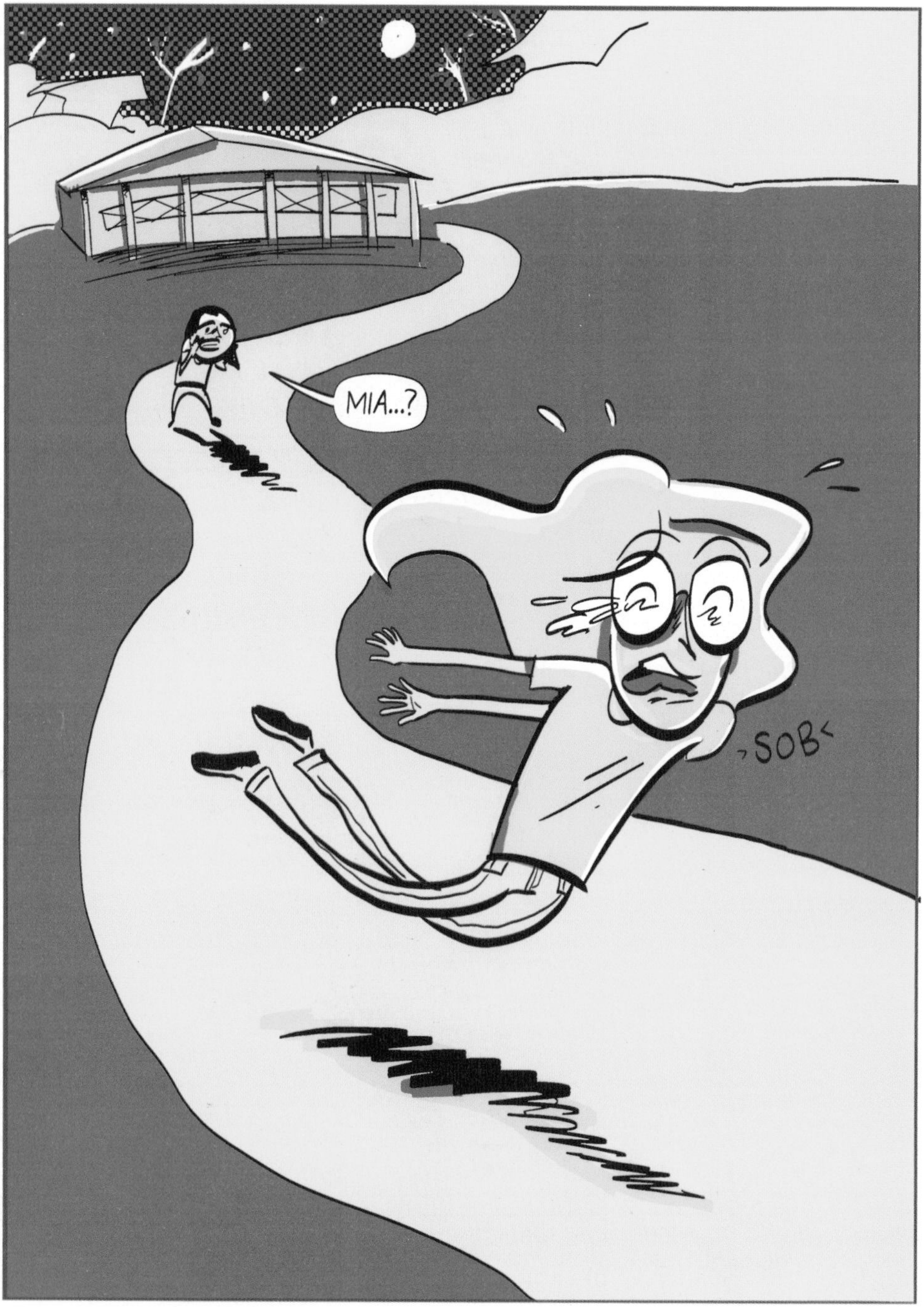
MIA...?
SOB

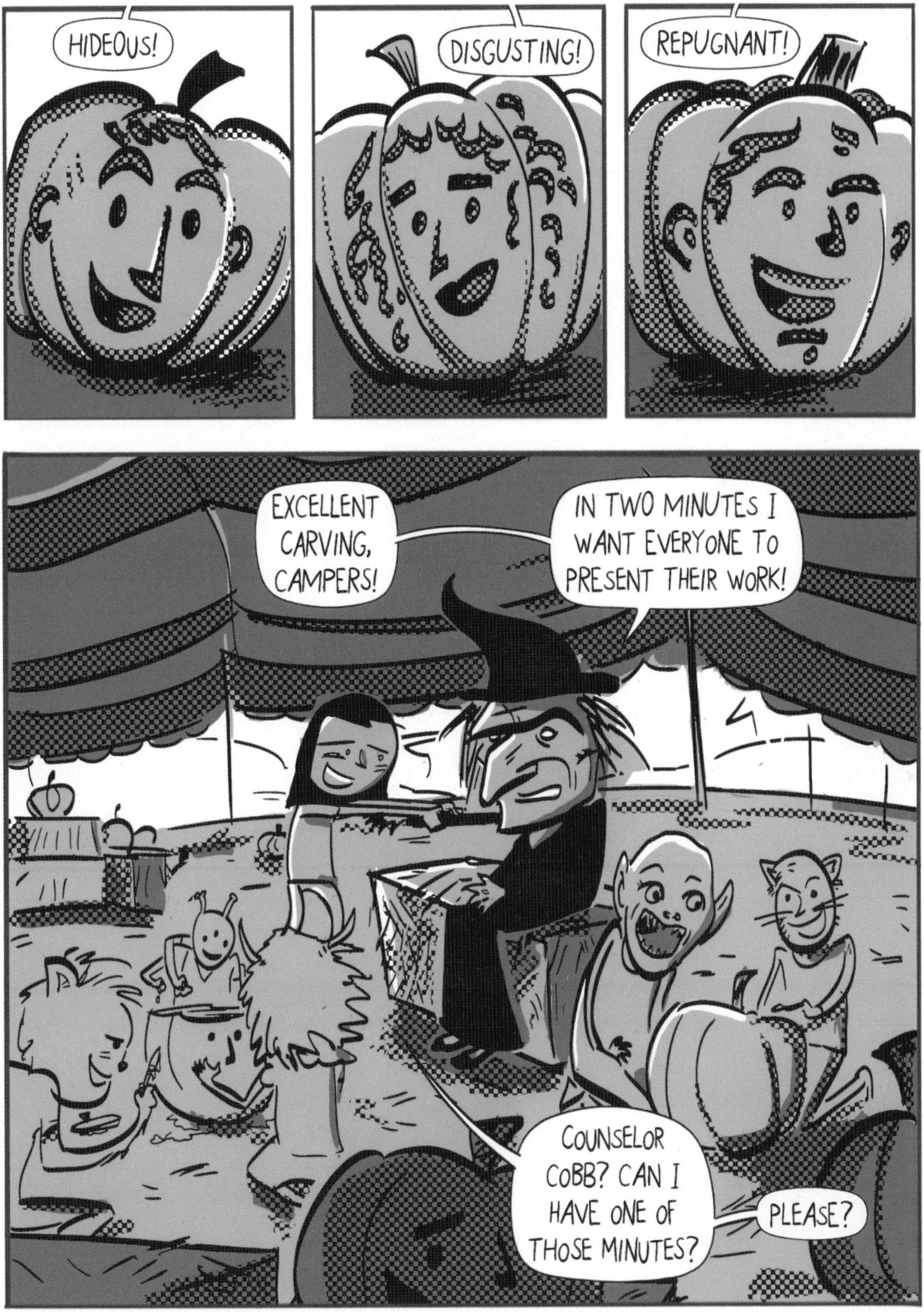
HIDEOUS!
DISGUSTING!
REPUGNANT!
EXCELLENT CARVING, CAMPERS!
IN TWO MINUTES I WANT EVERYONE TO PRESENT THEIR WORK!
COUNSELOR COBB? CAN I HAVE ONE OF THOSE MINUTES?
PLEASE?

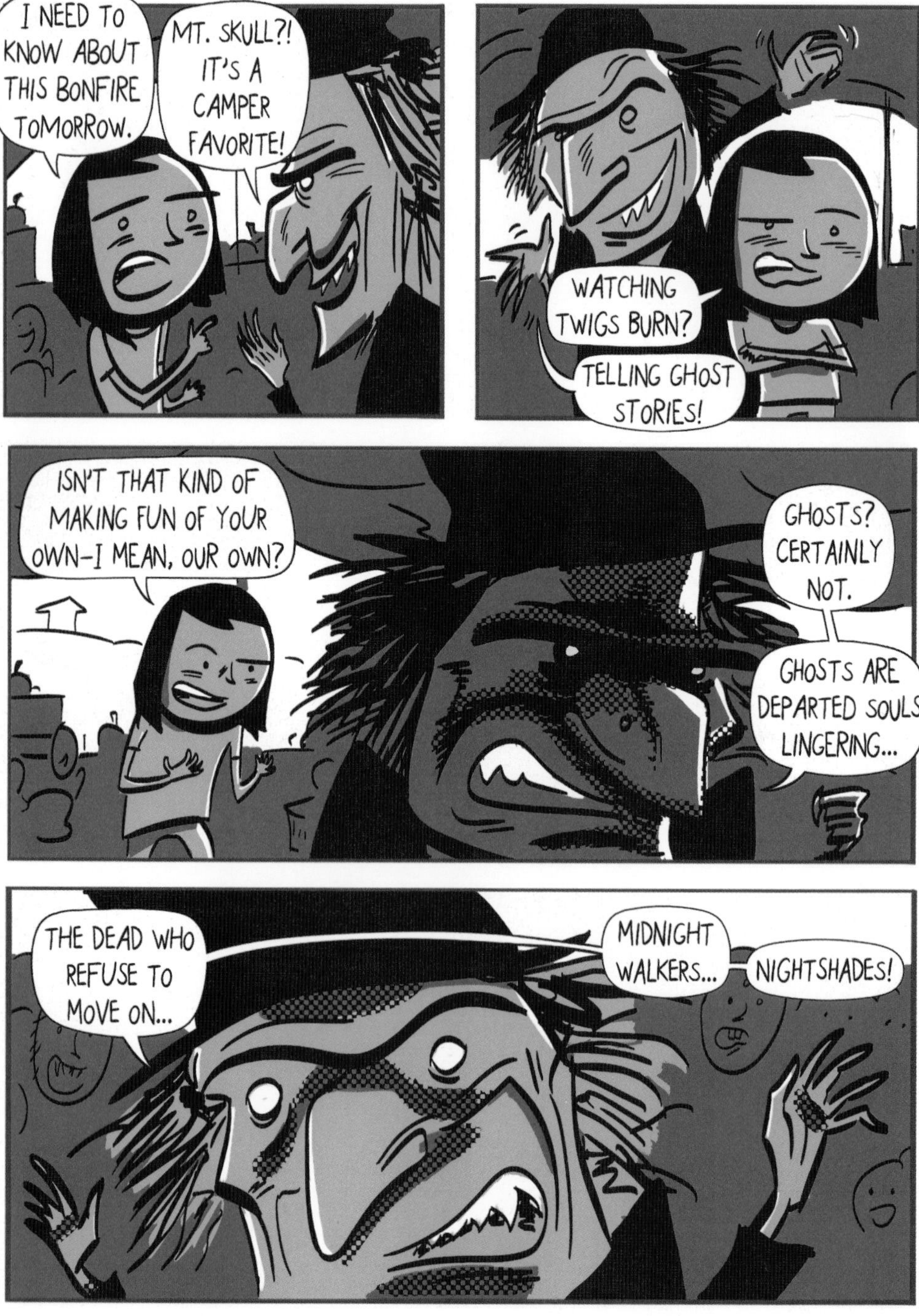
I NEED TO KNOW ABOUT THIS BONFIRE TOMORROW.
MT. SKULL?! IT'S A CAMPER FAVORITE!
WATCHING TWIGS BURN?
TELLING GHOST STORIES!
ISN'T THAT KIND OF MAKING FUN OF YOUR OWN–I MEAN, OUR OWN?
GHOSTS? CERTAINLY NOT.
GHOSTS ARE DEPARTED SOULS LINGERING...
THE DEAD WHO REFUSE TO MOVE ON...
MIDNIGHT WALKERS...
NIGHTSHADES!

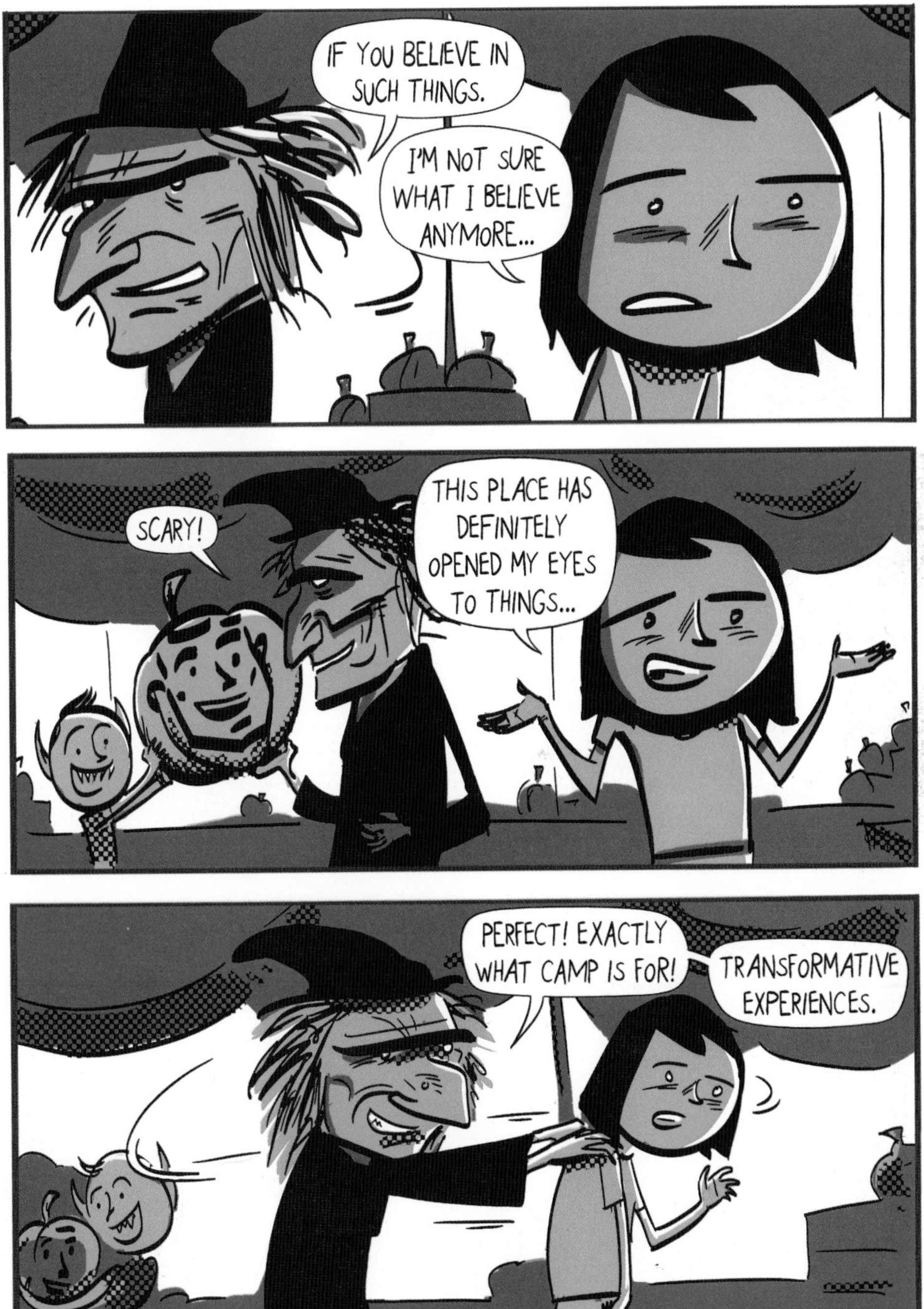
IF YOU BELIEVE IN SUCH THINGS.
I'M NOT SURE WHAT I BELIEVE ANYMORE...
SCARY!
THIS PLACE HAS DEFINITELY OPENED MY EYES TO THINGS...
PERFECT! EXACTLY WHAT CAMP IS FOR!
TRANSFORMATIVE EXPERIENCES.

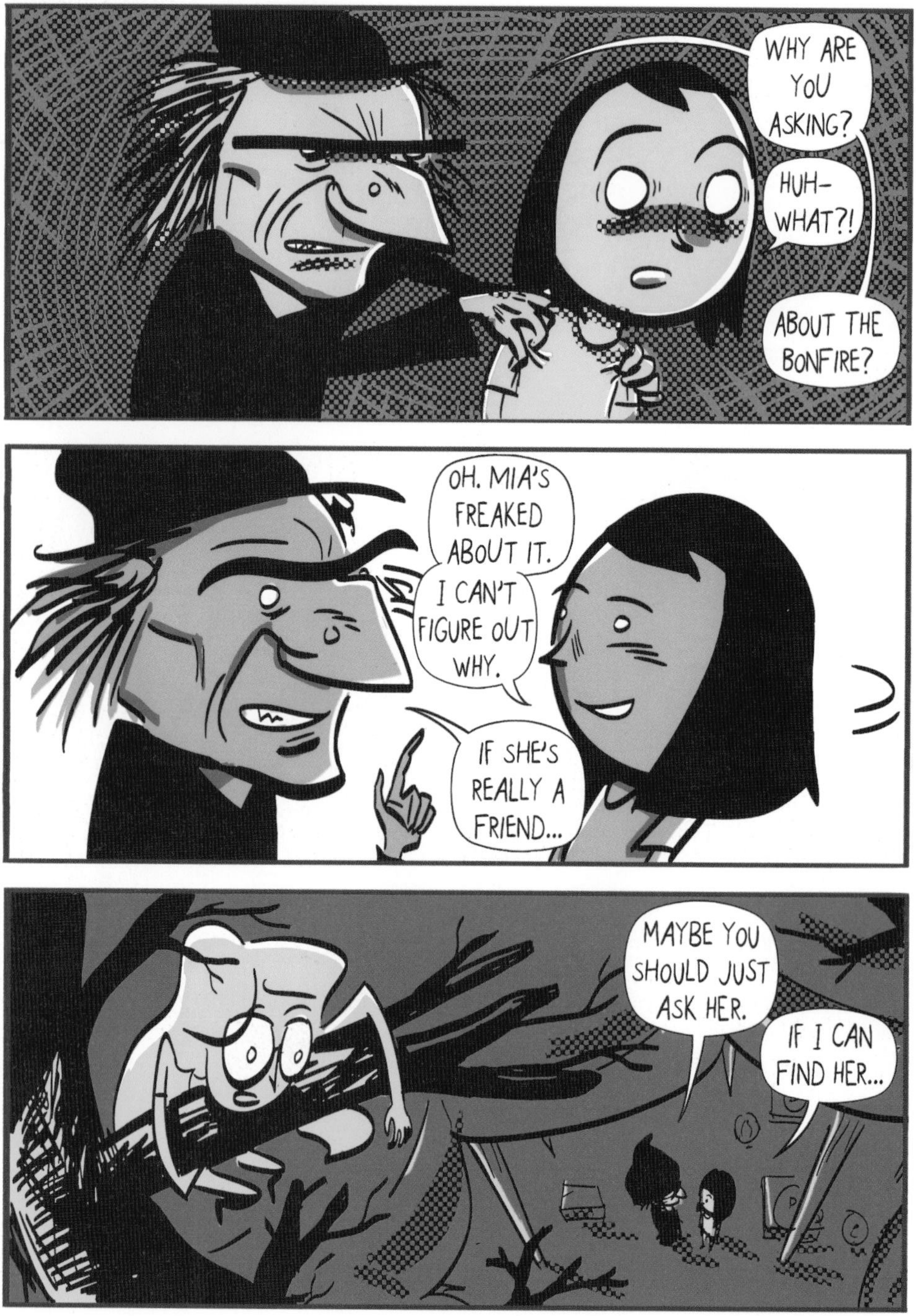
WHY ARE YOU ASKING?
HUH-WHAT?!
ABOUT THE BONFIRE?
OH. MIA'S FREAKED ABOUT IT.
I CAN'T FIGURE OUT WHY.
IF SHE'S REALLY A FRIEND...
MAYBE YOU SHOULD JUST ASK HER.
IF I CAN FIND HER...

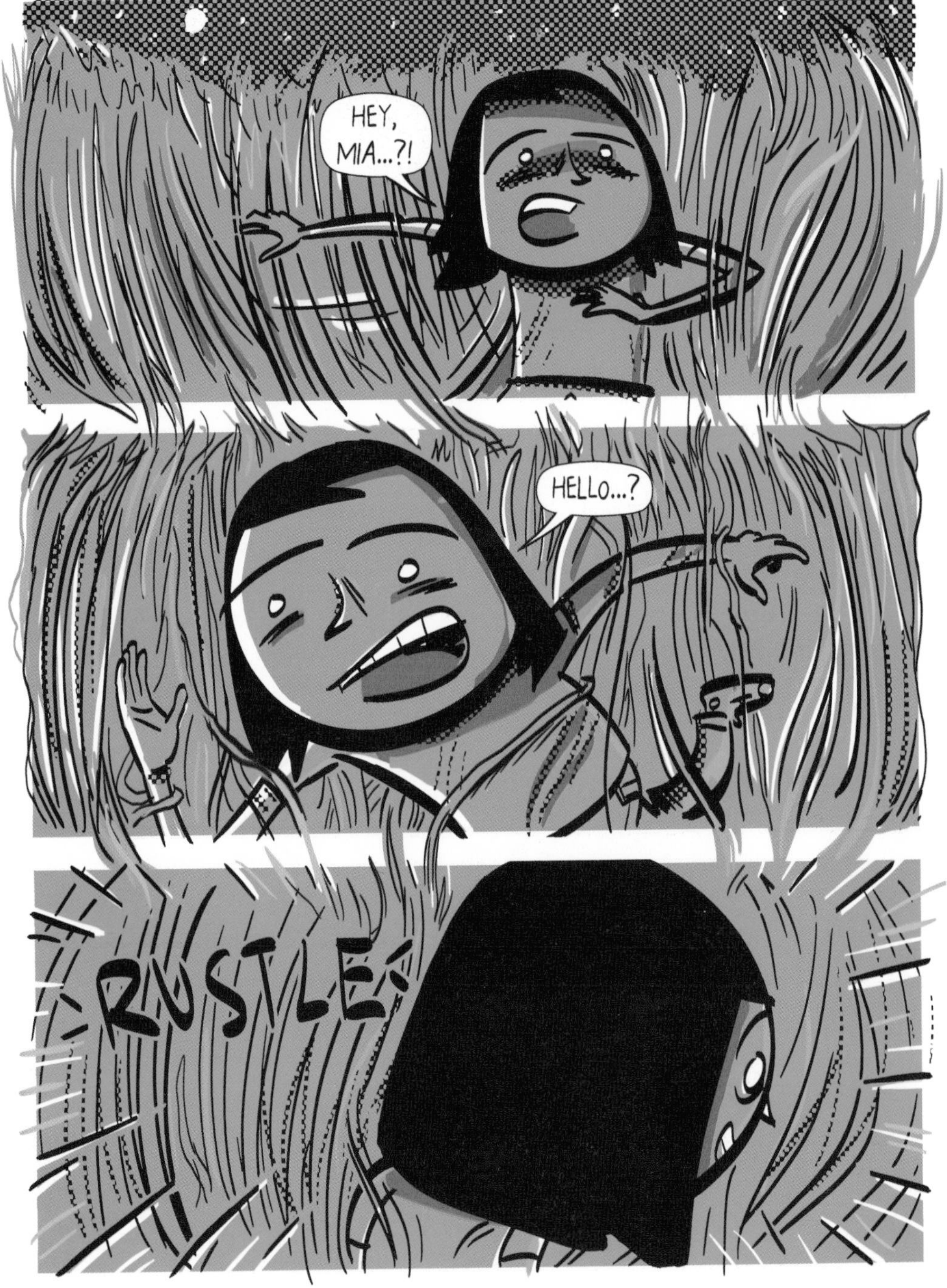
HEY, MIA...?!
HELLO...?
RUSTLE

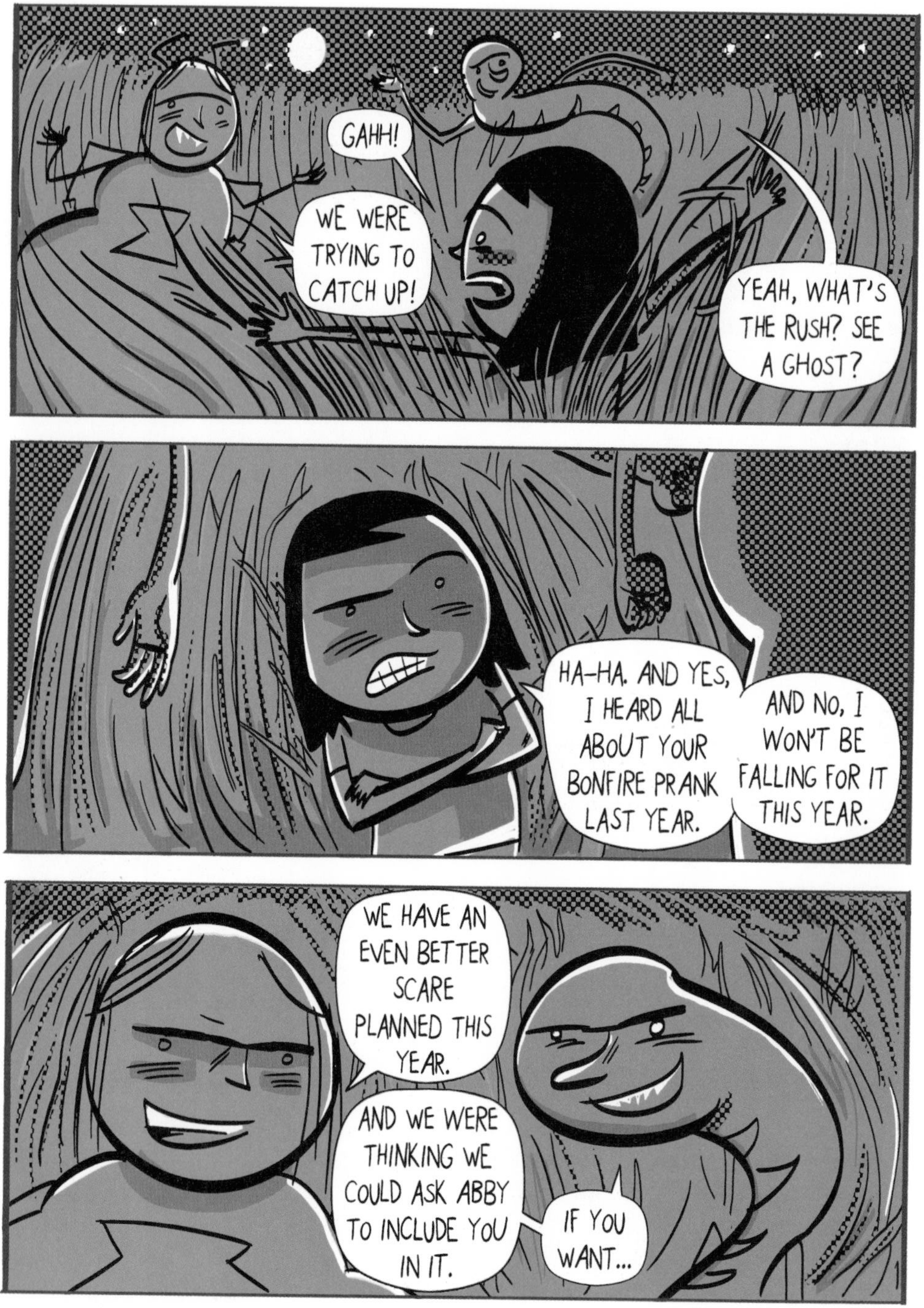
GAHH!
WE WERE TRYING TO CATCH UP!
YEAH, WHAT'S THE RUSH? SEE A GHOST?
HA-HA. AND YES, I HEARD ALL ABOUT YOUR BONFIRE PRANK LAST YEAR.
AND NO, I WON'T BE FALLING FOR IT THIS YEAR.
WE HAVE AN EVEN BETTER SCARE PLANNED THIS YEAR.
AND WE WERE THINKING WE COULD ASK ABBY TO INCLUDE YOU IN IT.
IF YOU WANT...

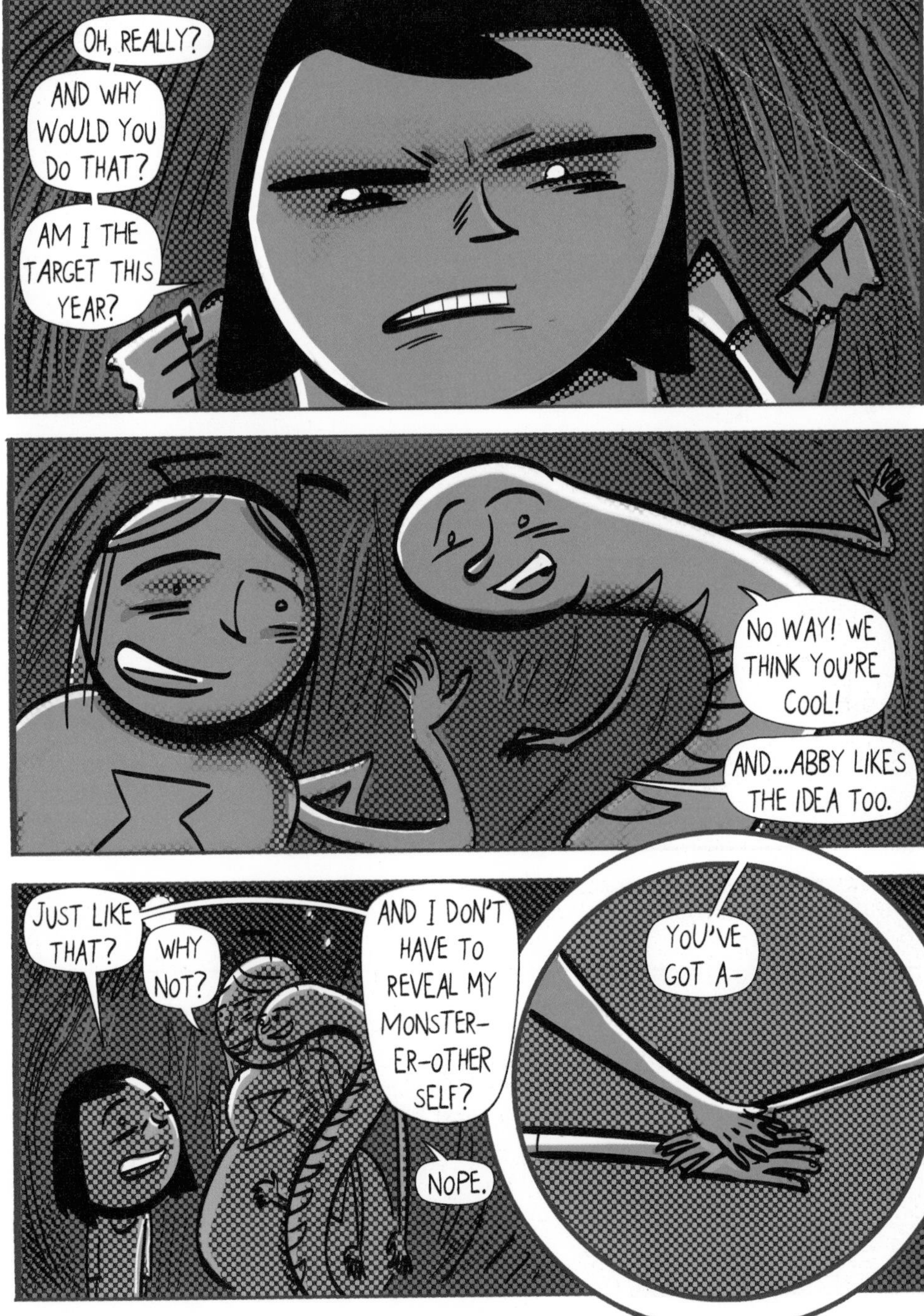
OH, REALLY?
AND WHY WOULD YOU DO THAT?
AM I THE TARGET THIS YEAR?
NO WAY! WE THINK YOU'RE COOL!
AND...ABBY LIKES THE IDEA TOO.
JUST LIKE THAT?
WHY NOT?
AND I DON'T HAVE TO REVEAL MY MONSTER-ER-OTHER SELF?
NOPE.
YOU'VE GOT A-

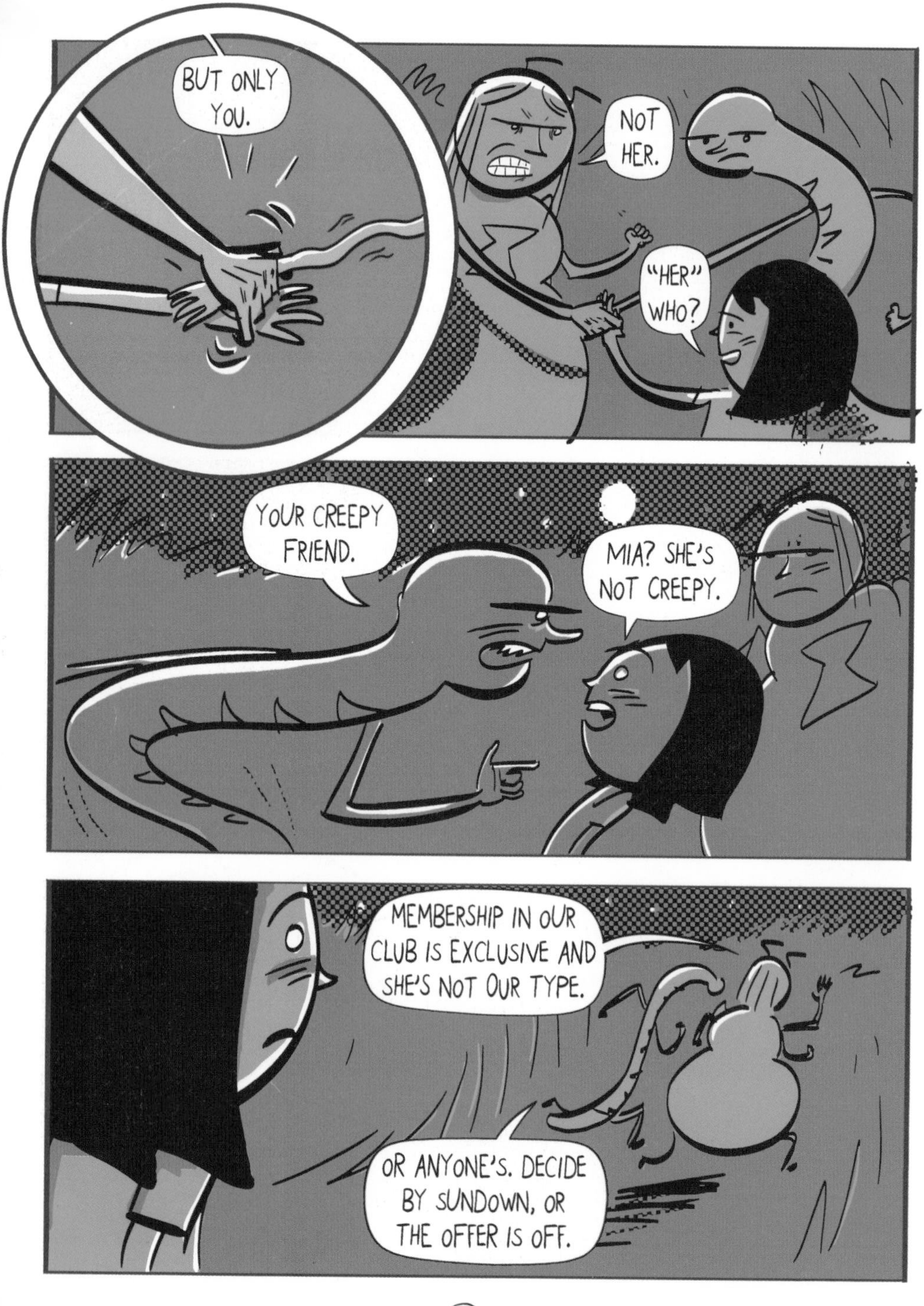
BUT ONLY YOU.
NOT HER.
"HER" WHO?
YOUR CREEPY FRIEND.
MIA? SHE'S NOT CREEPY.
MEMBERSHIP IN OUR CLUB IS EXCLUSIVE AND SHE'S NOT OUR TYPE.
OR ANYONE'S. DECIDE BY SUNDOWN, OR THE OFFER IS OFF.

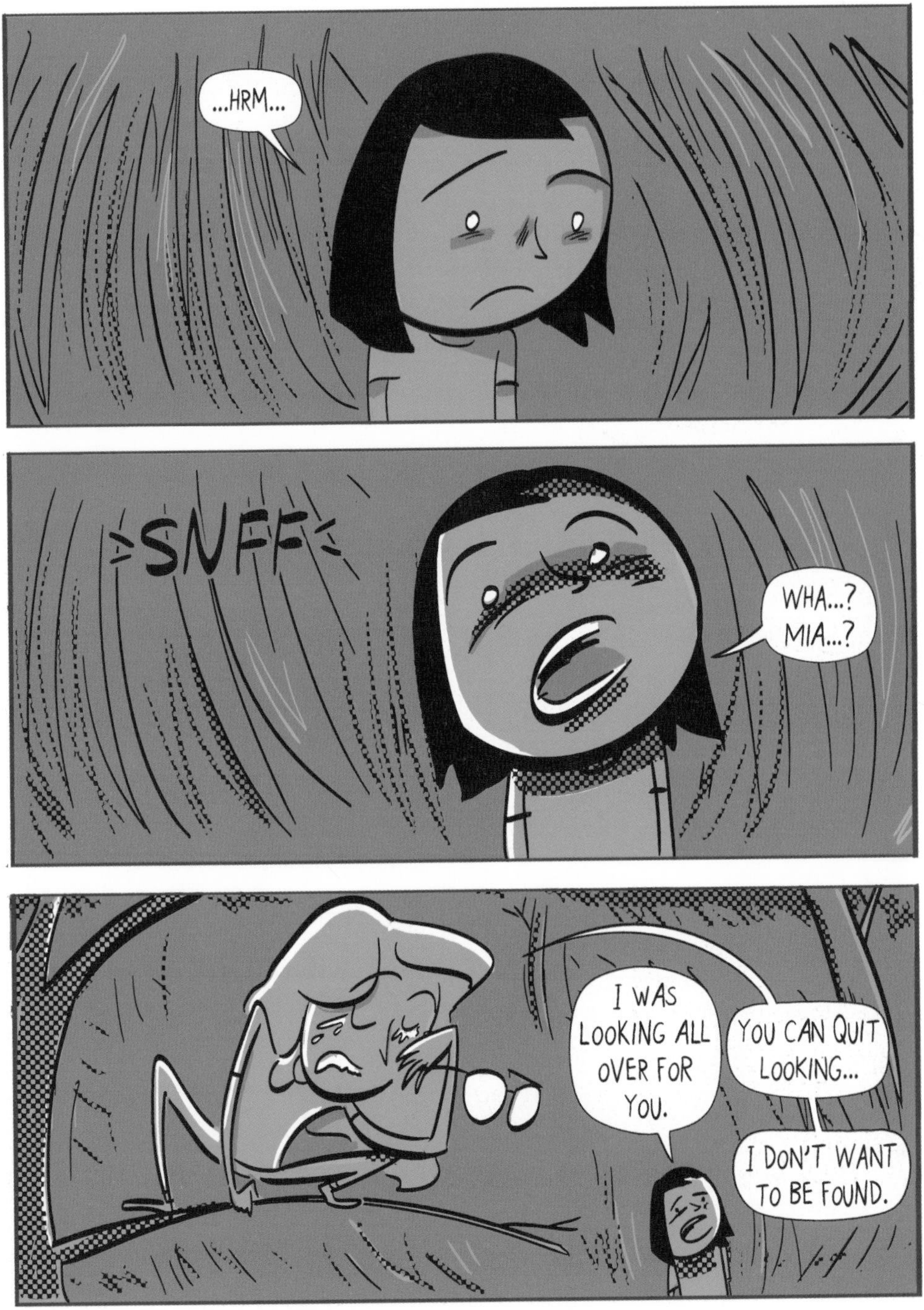
...HRM...
SNFF
WHA...? MIA...?
I WAS LOOKING ALL OVER FOR YOU.
YOU CAN QUIT LOOKING...
I DON'T WANT TO BE FOUND.

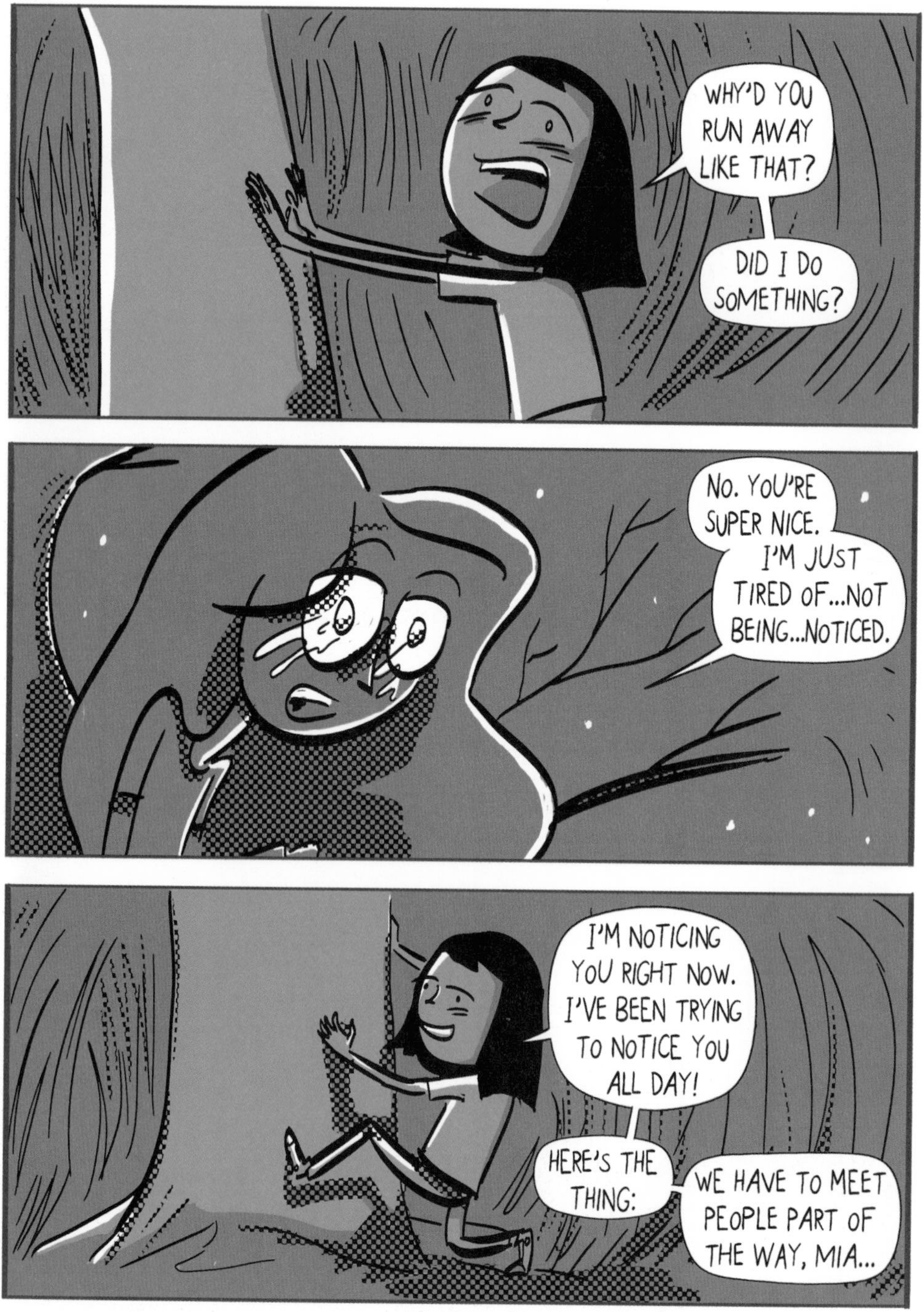
WHY'D YOU RUN AWAY LIKE THAT?
DID I DO SOMETHING?
NO. YOU'RE SUPER NICE.
I'M JUST TIRED OF...NOT BEING...NOTICED.
I'M NOTICING YOU RIGHT NOW. I'VE BEEN TRYING TO NOTICE YOU ALL DAY!
HERE'S THE THING:
WE HAVE TO MEET PEOPLE PART OF THE WAY, MIA...

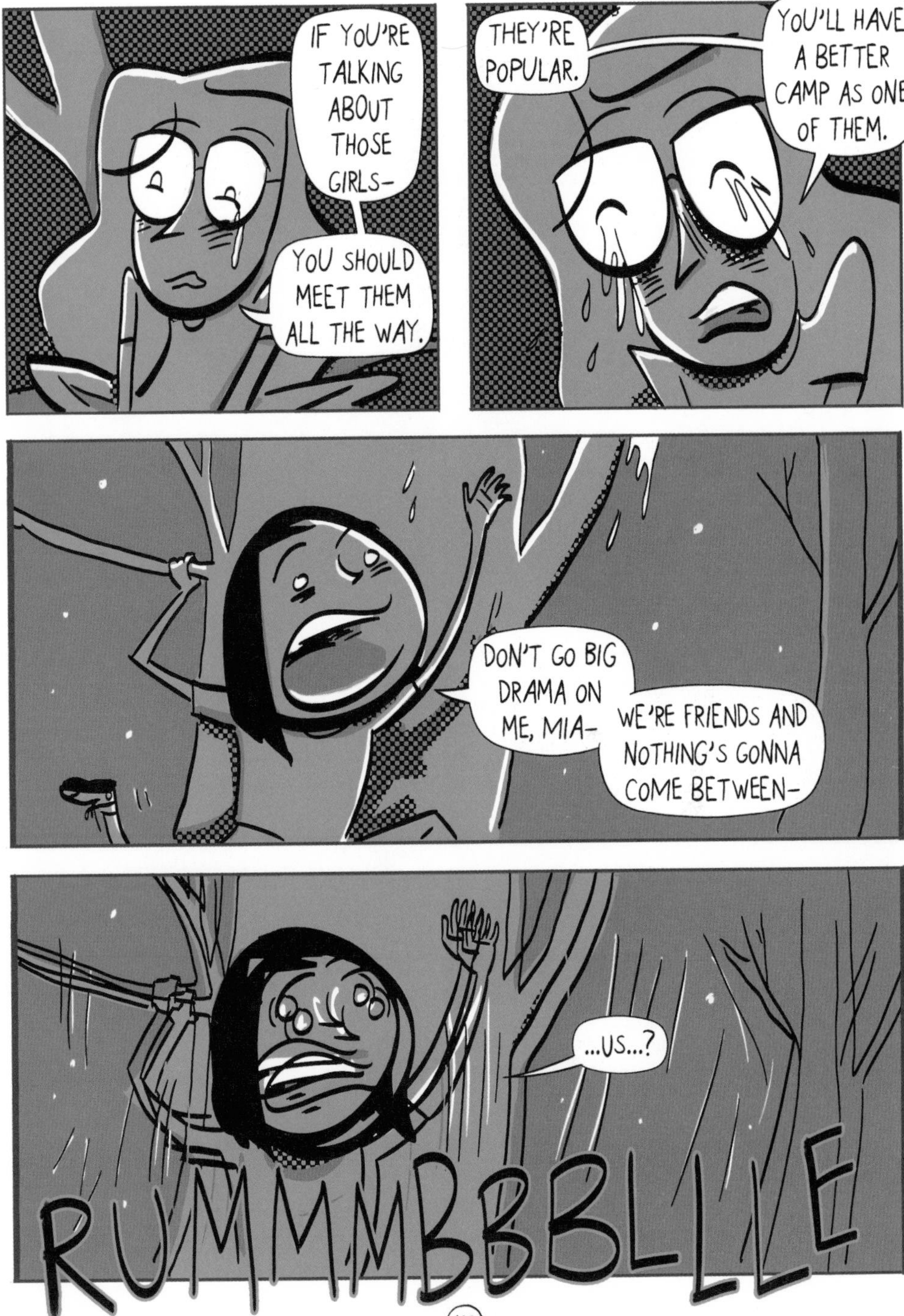
IF YOU'RE TALKING ABOUT THOSE GIRLS-
YOU SHOULD MEET THEM ALL THE WAY.
THEY'RE POPULAR.
YOU'LL HAVE A BETTER CAMP AS ONE OF THEM.
DON'T GO BIG DRAMA ON ME, MIA-
WE'RE FRIENDS AND NOTHING'S GONNA COME BETWEEN-
...US...?
RUMMMBBBLLLE

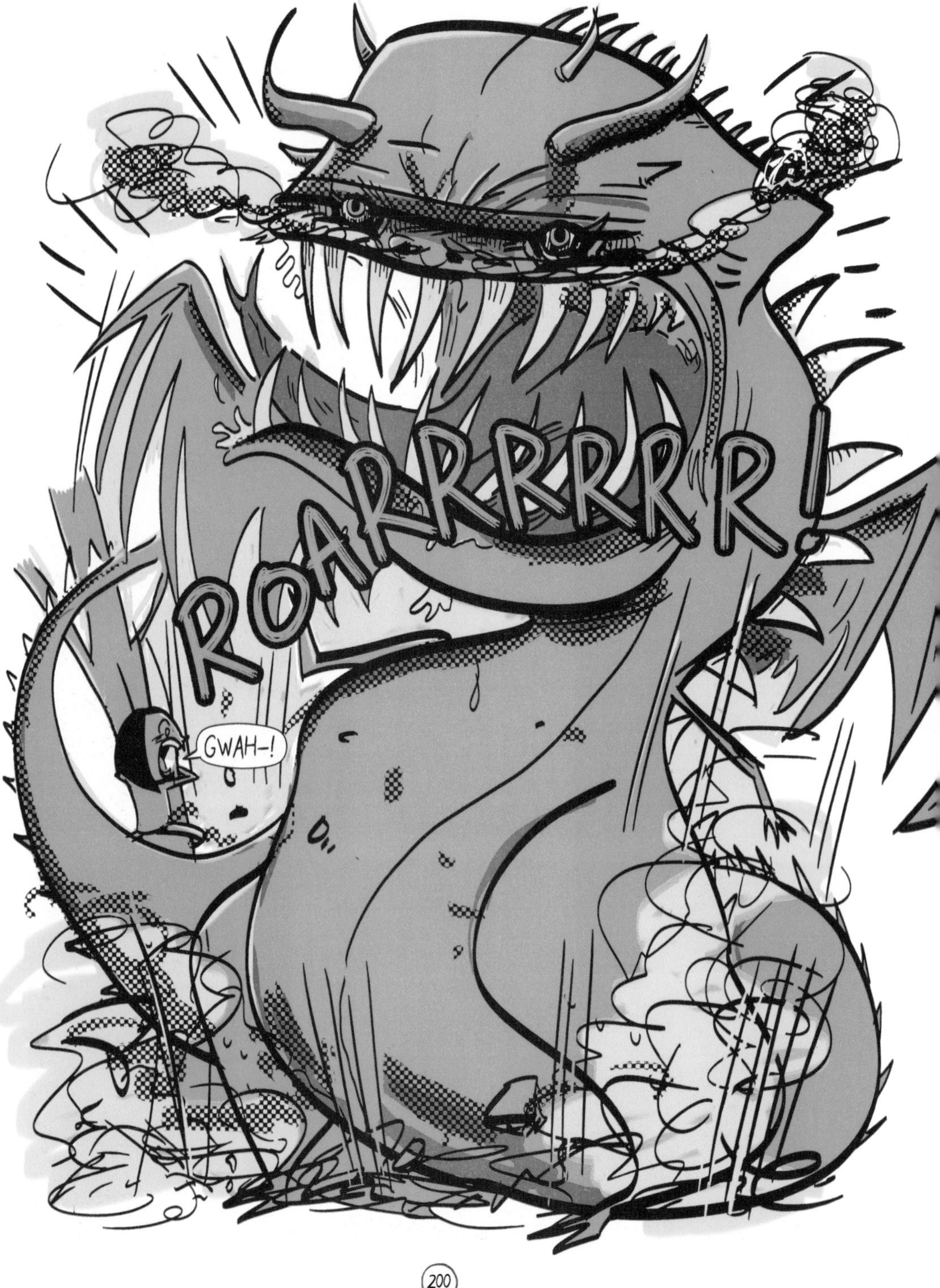
ROARRRRRR!
GWAH-!

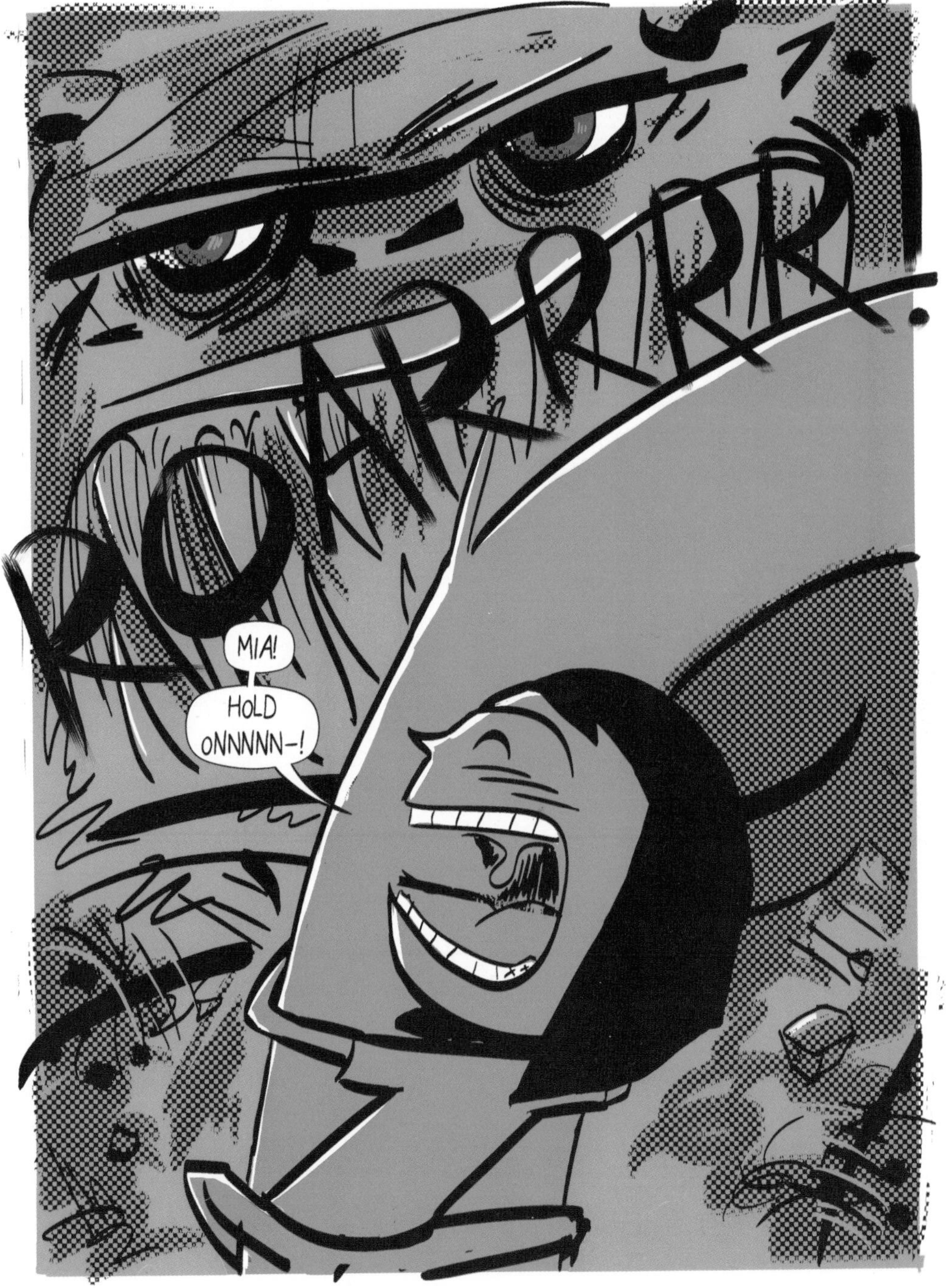
ROOARRRRR!
MIA!
HOLD ONNNNN-!

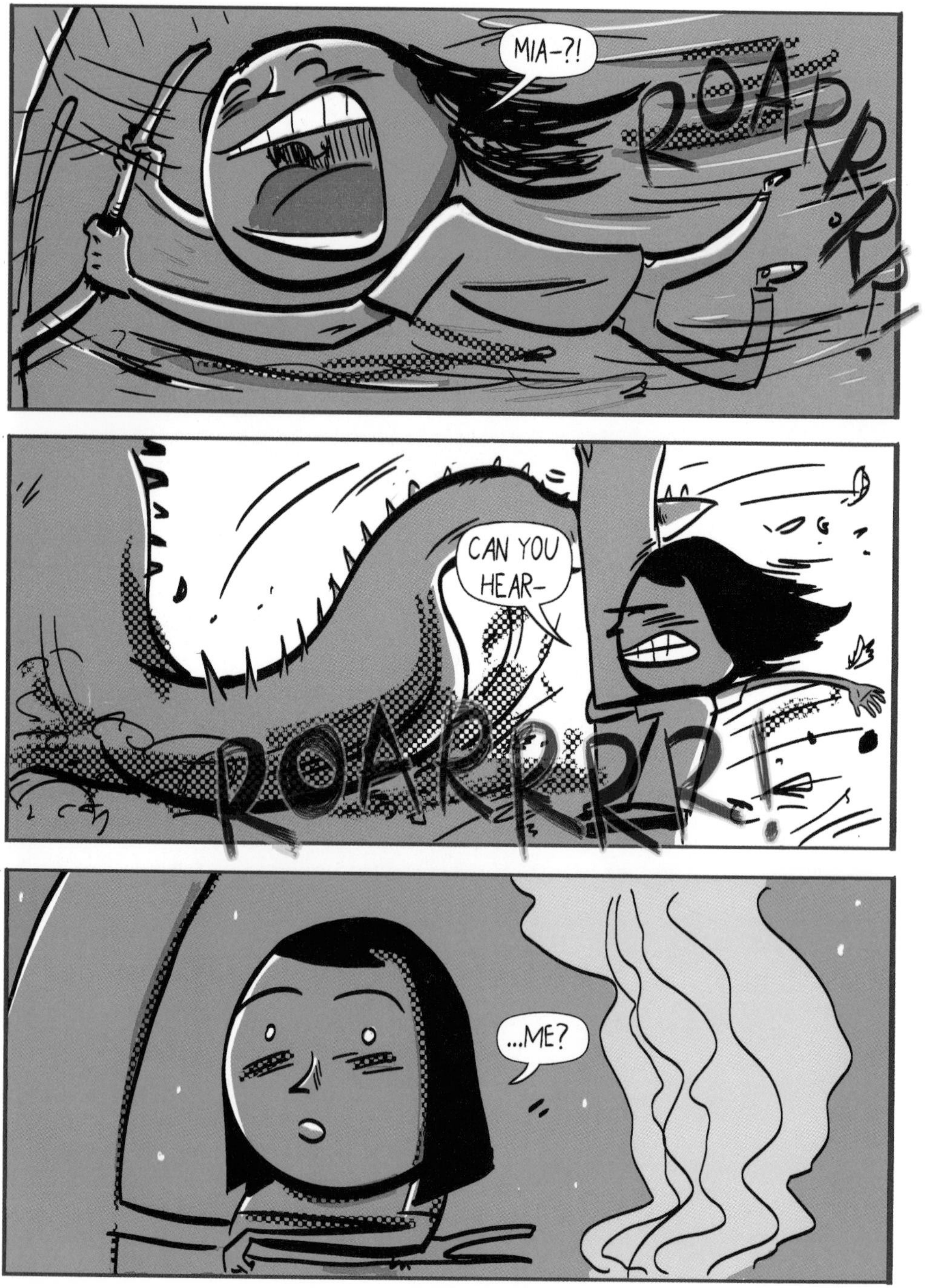
MIA-?!
ROARRR!
CAN YOU HEAR-
ROARRRR!
...ME?

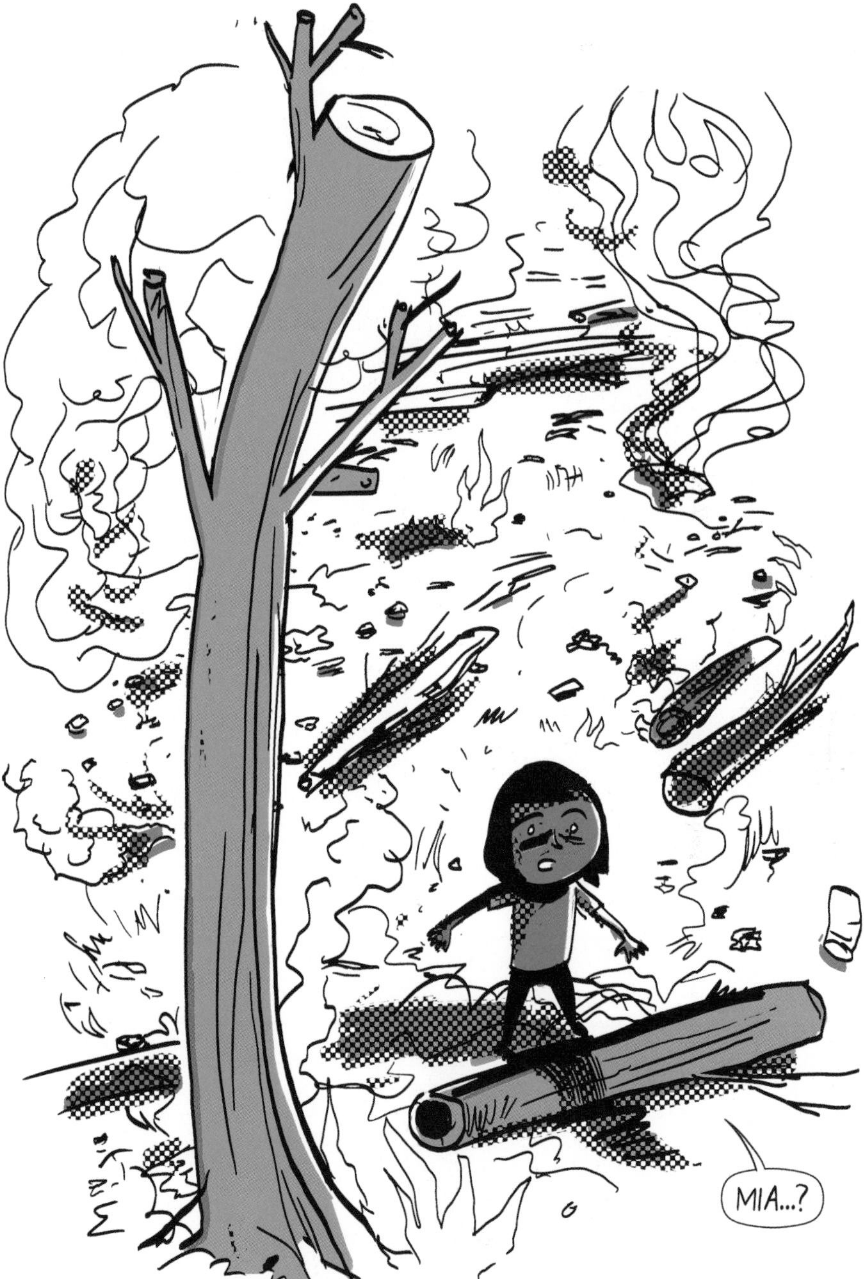
MIA...?

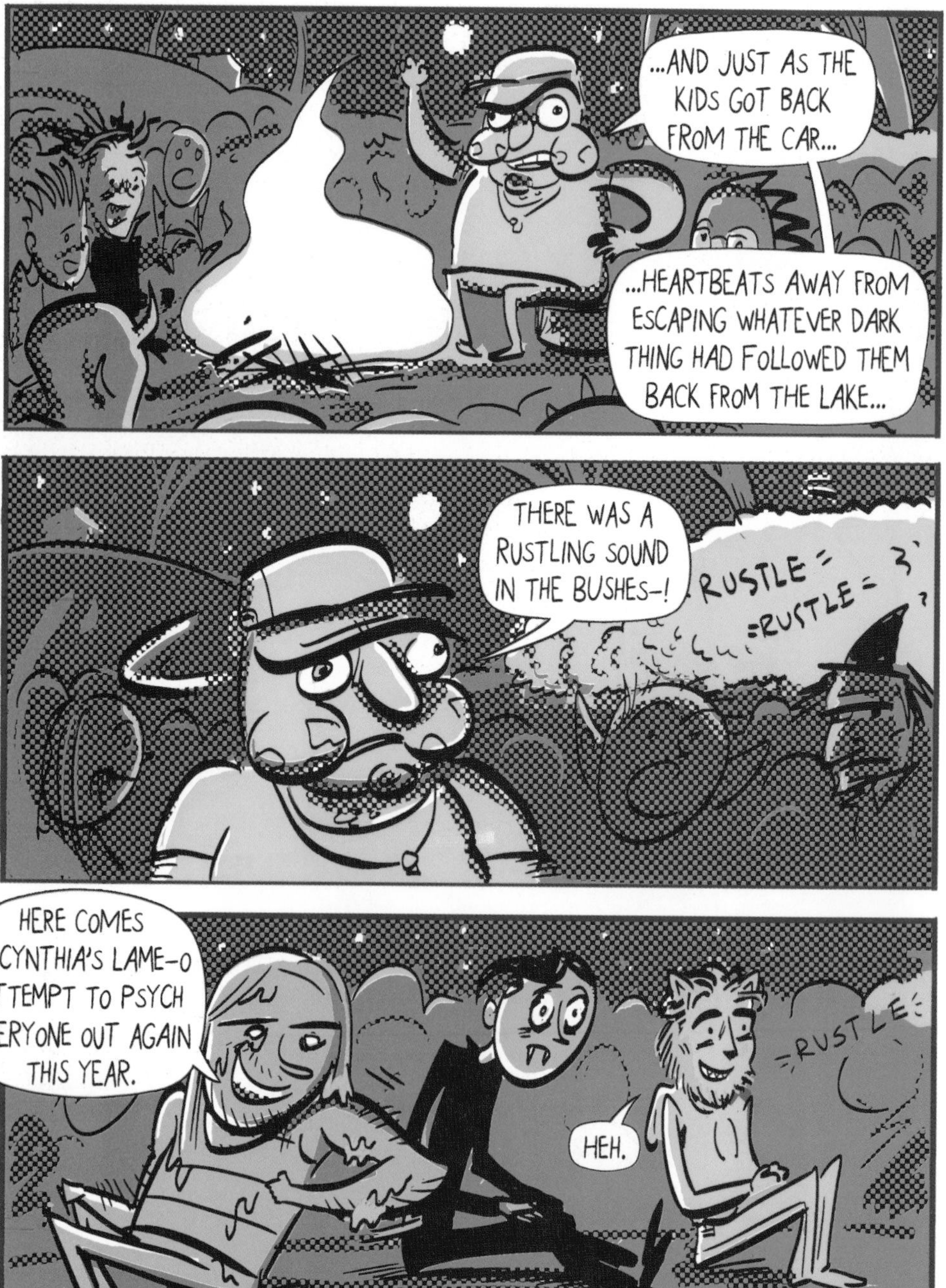

...AND JUST AS THE KIDS GOT BACK FROM THE CAR...
...HEARTBEATS AWAY FROM ESCAPING WHATEVER DARK THING HAD FOLLOWED THEM BACK FROM THE LAKE...
THERE WAS A RUSTLING SOUND IN THE BUSHES-!
RUSTLE
RUSTLE
HERE COMES ABCYNTHIA'S LAME-O ATTEMPT TO PSYCH EVERYONE OUT AGAIN THIS YEAR.
HEH.
RUSTLE

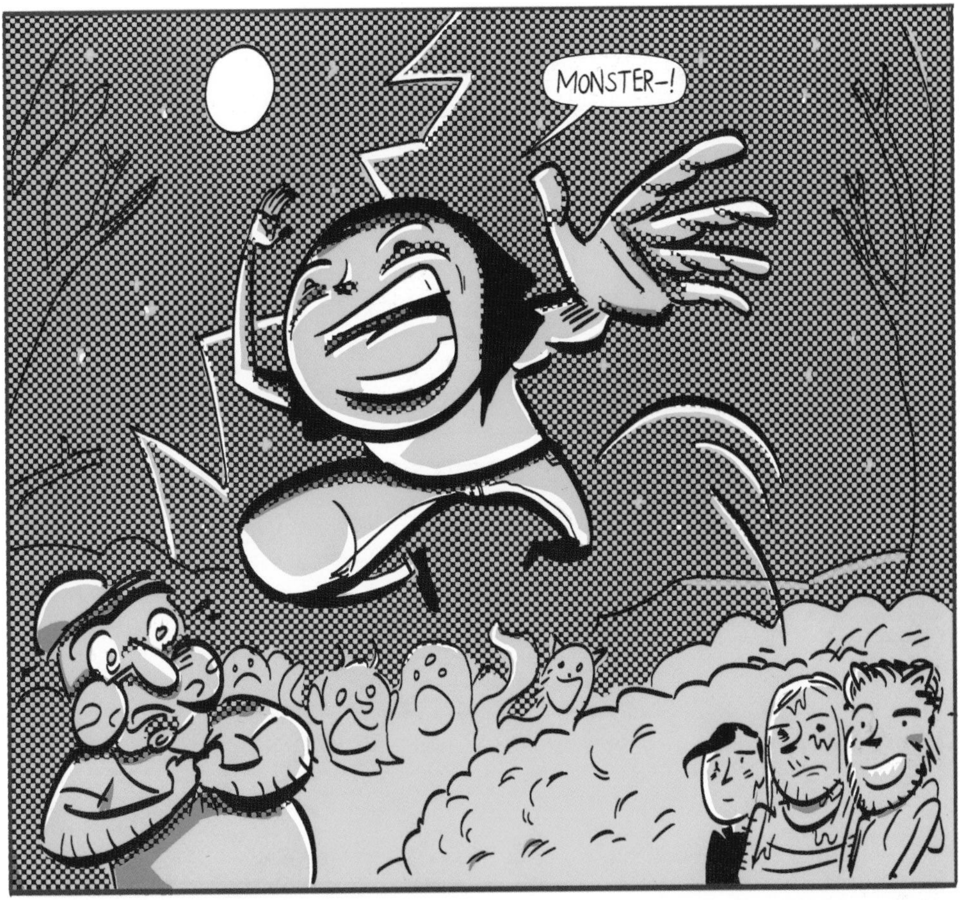
MONSTER-!

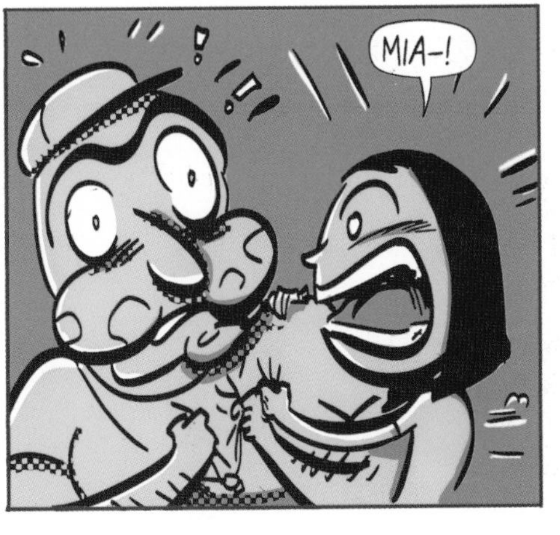
MIA-!

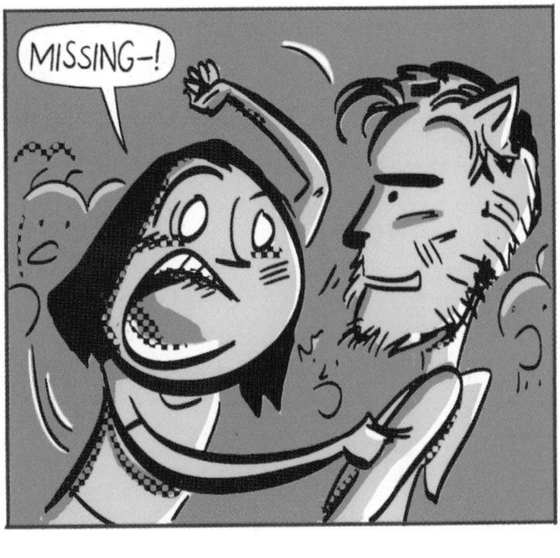
MISSING-!

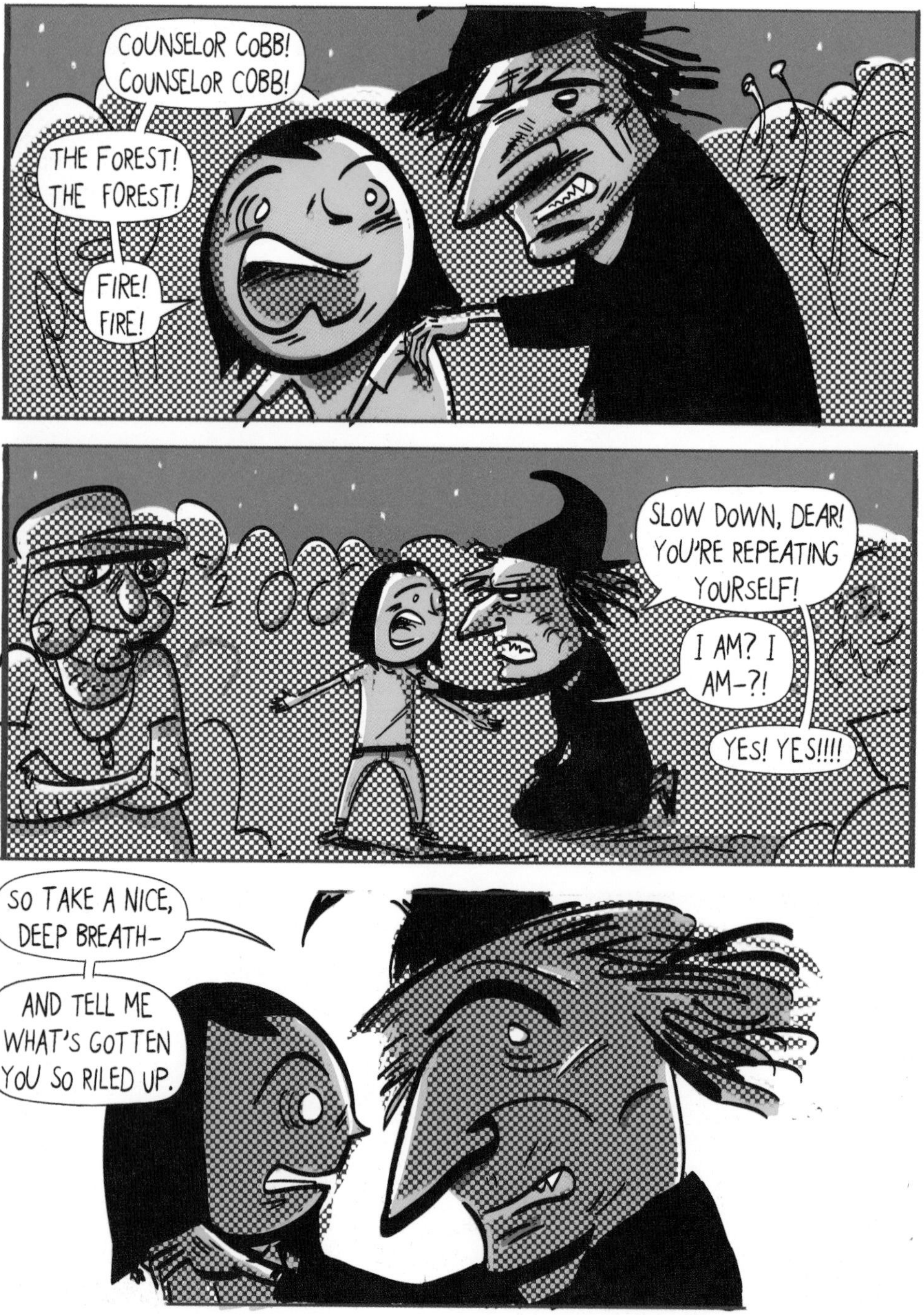
COUNSELOR COBB! COUNSELOR COBB!
THE FOREST! THE FOREST!
FIRE! FIRE!
SLOW DOWN, DEAR! YOU'RE REPEATING YOURSELF!
I AM? I AM-?!
YES! YES!!!!
SO TAKE A NICE, DEEP BREATH-
AND TELL ME WHAT'S GOTTEN YOU SO RILED UP.

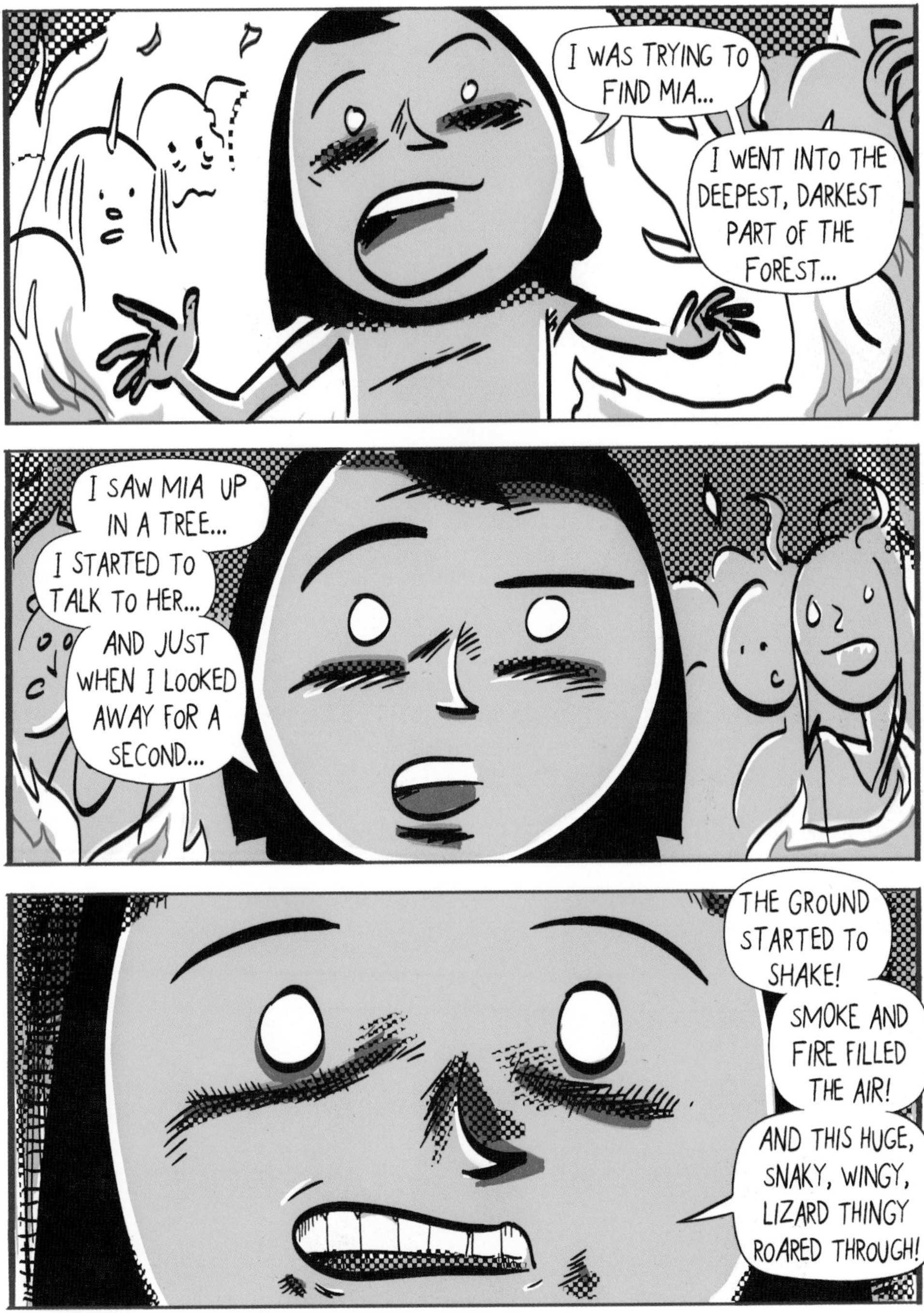
I WAS TRYING TO FIND MIA...
I WENT INTO THE DEEPEST, DARKEST PART OF THE FOREST...
I SAW MIA UP IN A TREE...
I STARTED TO TALK TO HER...
AND JUST WHEN I LOOKED AWAY FOR A SECOND...
THE GROUND STARTED TO SHAKE!
SMOKE AND FIRE FILLED THE AIR!
AND THIS HUGE, SNAKY, WINGY, LIZARD THINGY ROARED THROUGH!

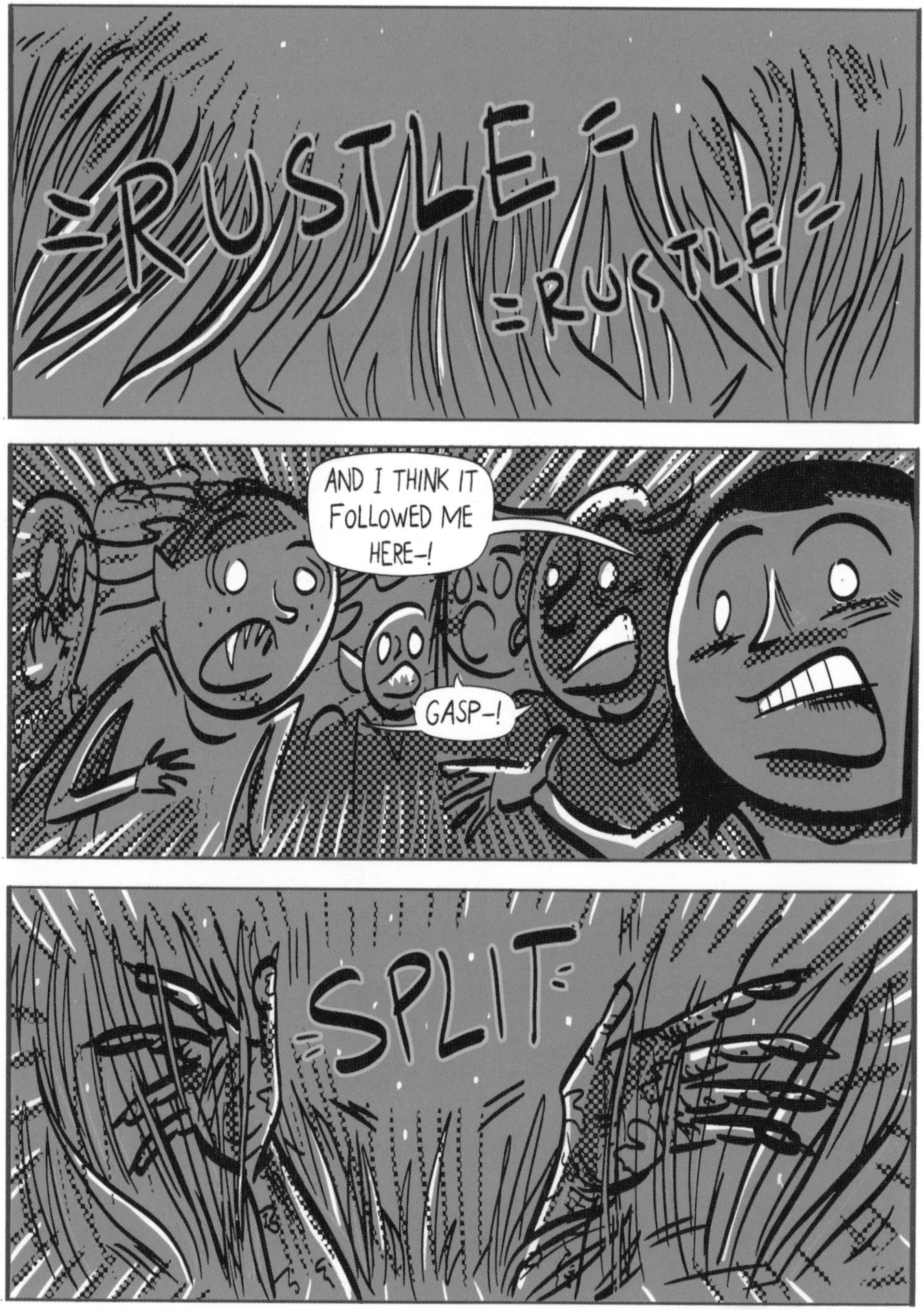
RUSTLE
RUSTLE
AND I THINK IT FOLLOWED ME HERE-!
GASP-!
SPLIT

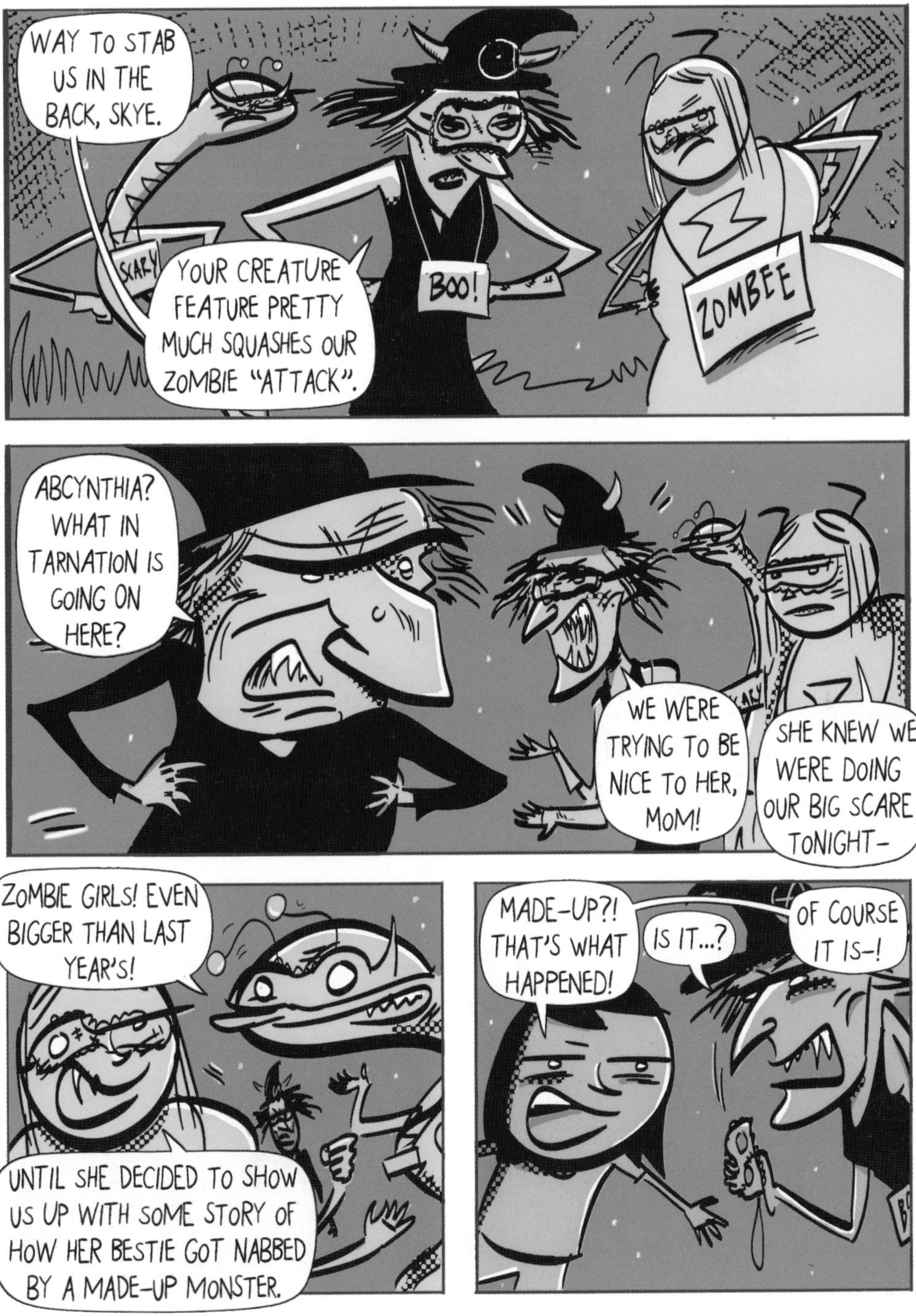
WAY TO STAB US IN THE BACK, SKYE.
YOUR CREATURE FEATURE PRETTY MUCH SQUASHES OUR ZOMBIE "ATTACK".
SCARY
BOO!
ZOMBEE
ABCYNTHIA? WHAT IN TARNATION IS GOING ON HERE?
WE WERE TRYING TO BE NICE TO HER, MOM!
SHE KNEW WE WERE DOING OUR BIG SCARE TONIGHT–
ZOMBIE GIRLS! EVEN BIGGER THAN LAST YEAR'S!
UNTIL SHE DECIDED TO SHOW US UP WITH SOME STORY OF HOW HER BESTIE GOT NABBED BY A MADE-UP MONSTER.
MADE-UP?! THAT'S WHAT HAPPENED!
IS IT...?
OF COURSE IT IS–!

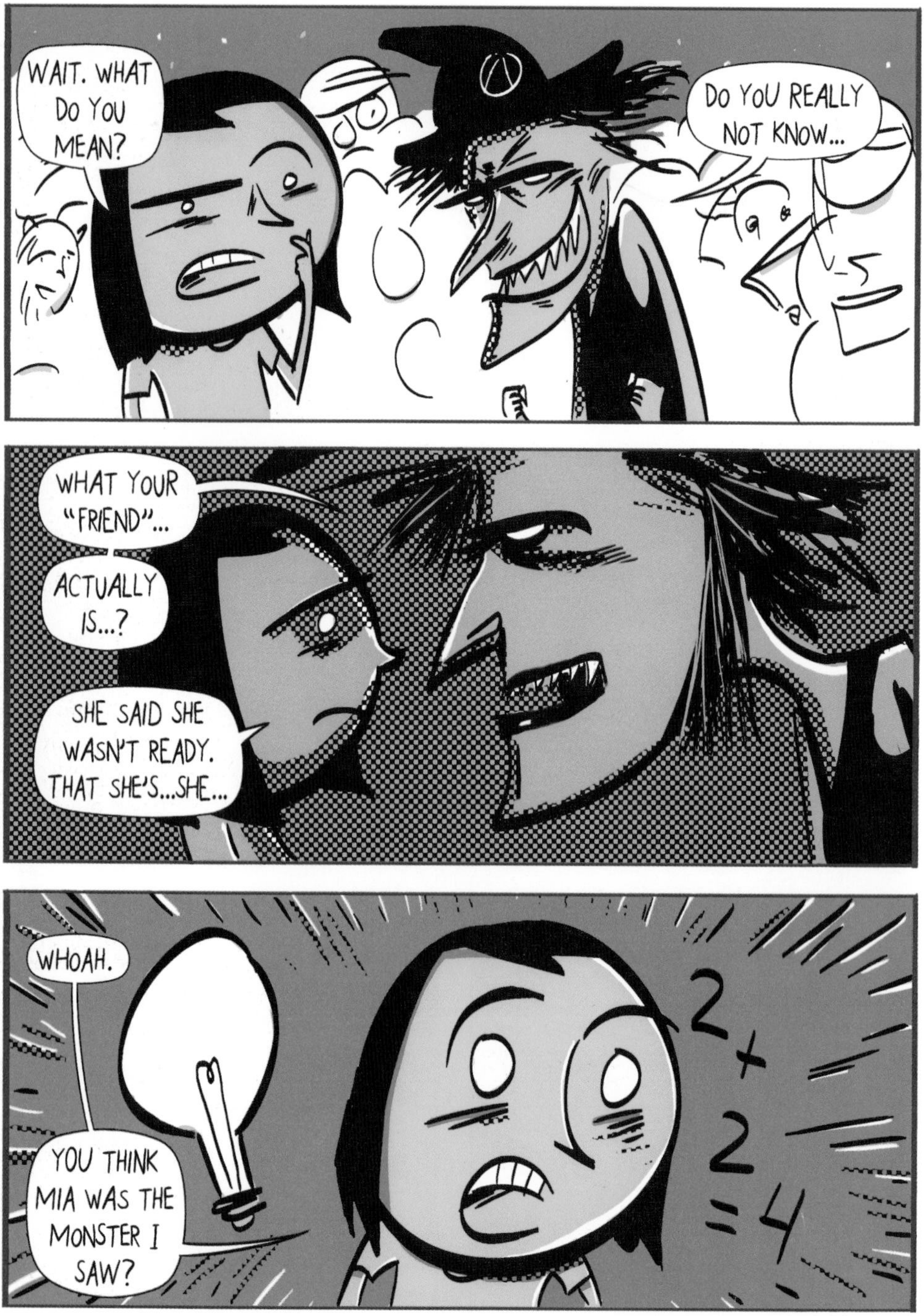

WAIT. WHAT DO YOU MEAN?
DO YOU REALLY NOT KNOW...
WHAT YOUR "FRIEND"...
ACTUALLY IS...?
SHE SAID SHE WASN'T READY. THAT SHE'S...SHE...
WHOAH.
YOU THINK MIA WAS THE MONSTER I SAW?
2 + 2 = 4

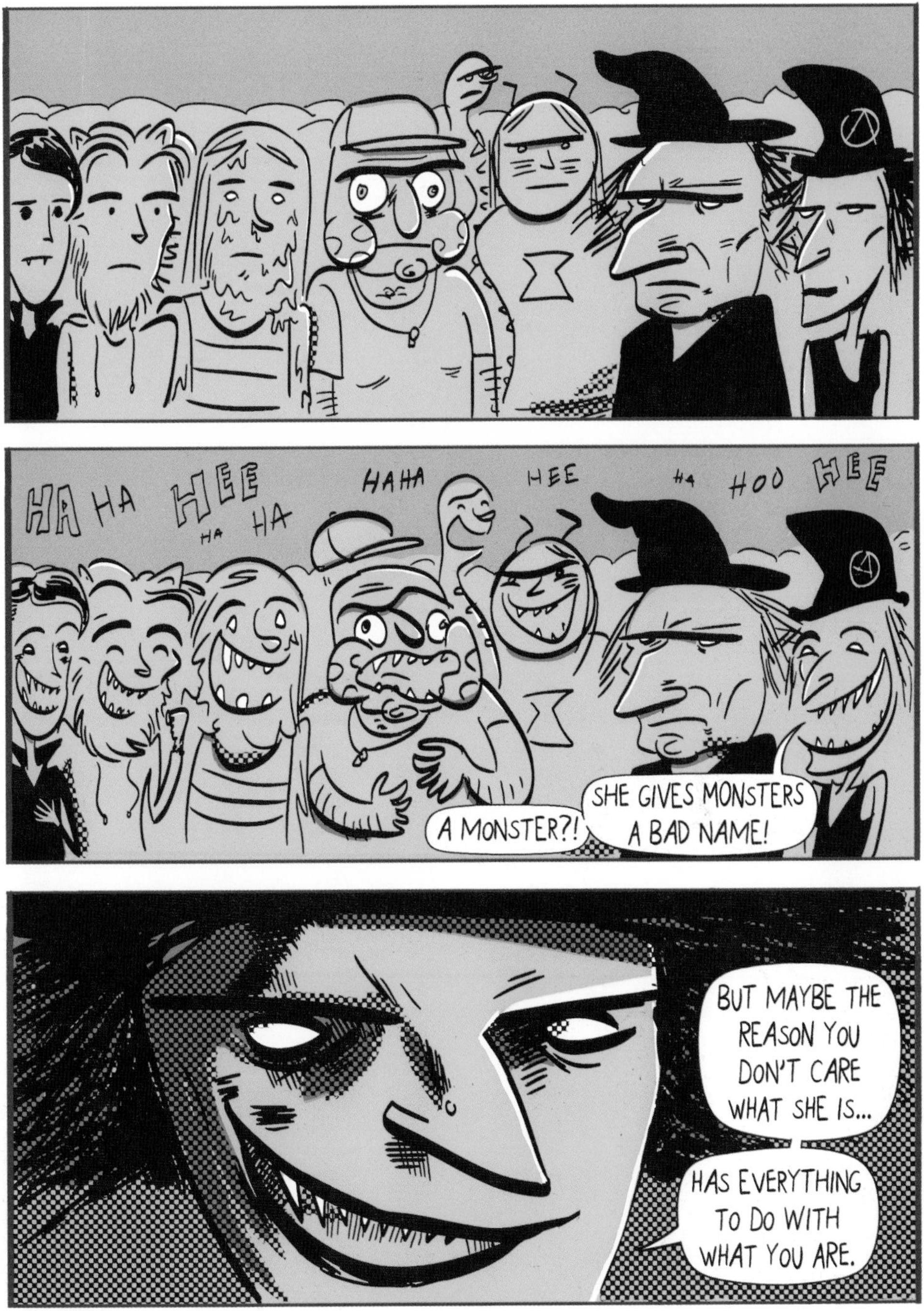
HA HA HEE HA HA HAHA HEE HA HOO HEE
A MONSTER?!
SHE GIVES MONSTERS A BAD NAME!
BUT MAYBE THE REASON YOU DON'T CARE WHAT SHE IS...
HAS EVERYTHING TO DO WITH WHAT YOU ARE.

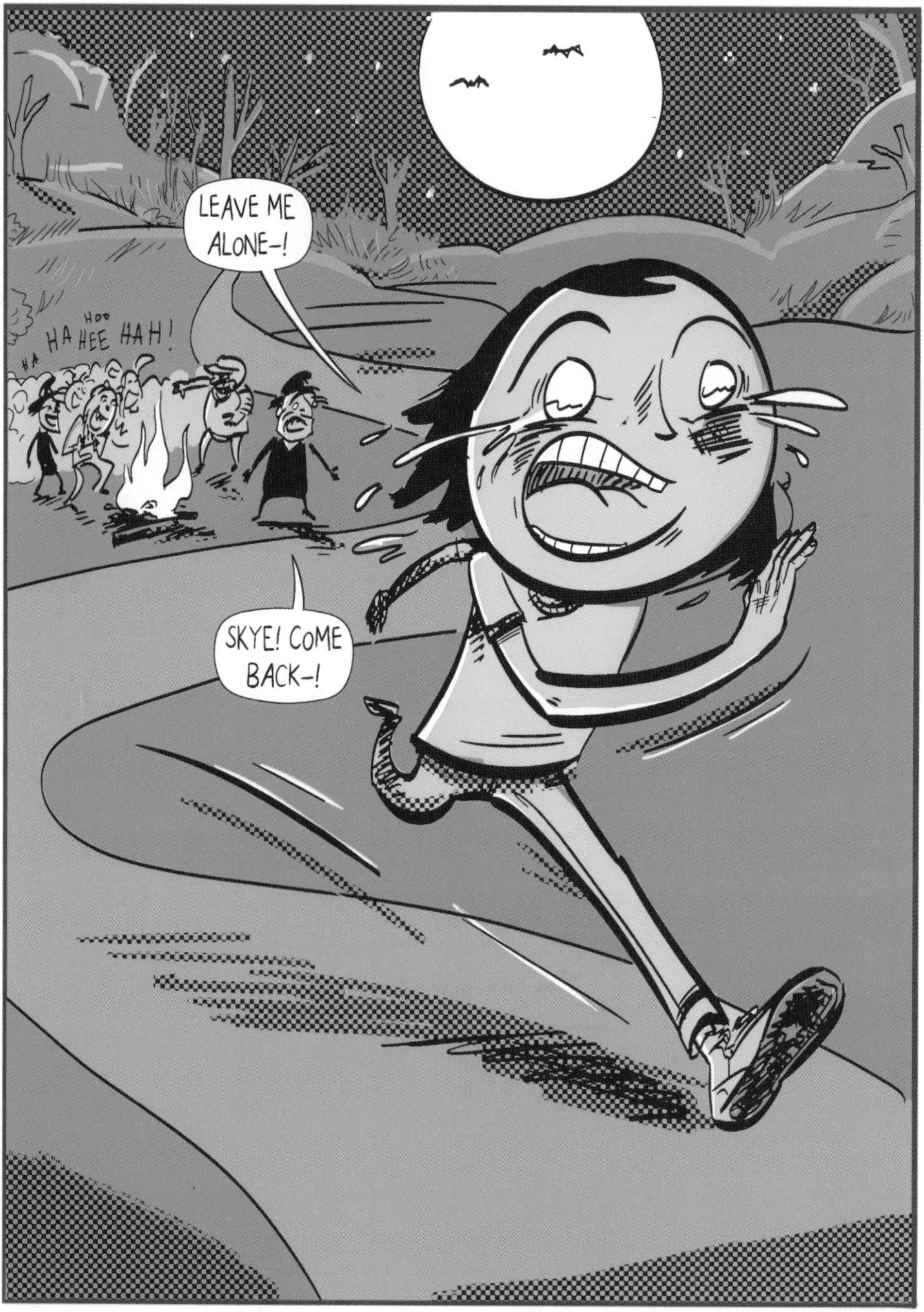
HA HA HOO HEE HAH!
LEAVE ME ALONE-!
SKYE! COME BACK-!

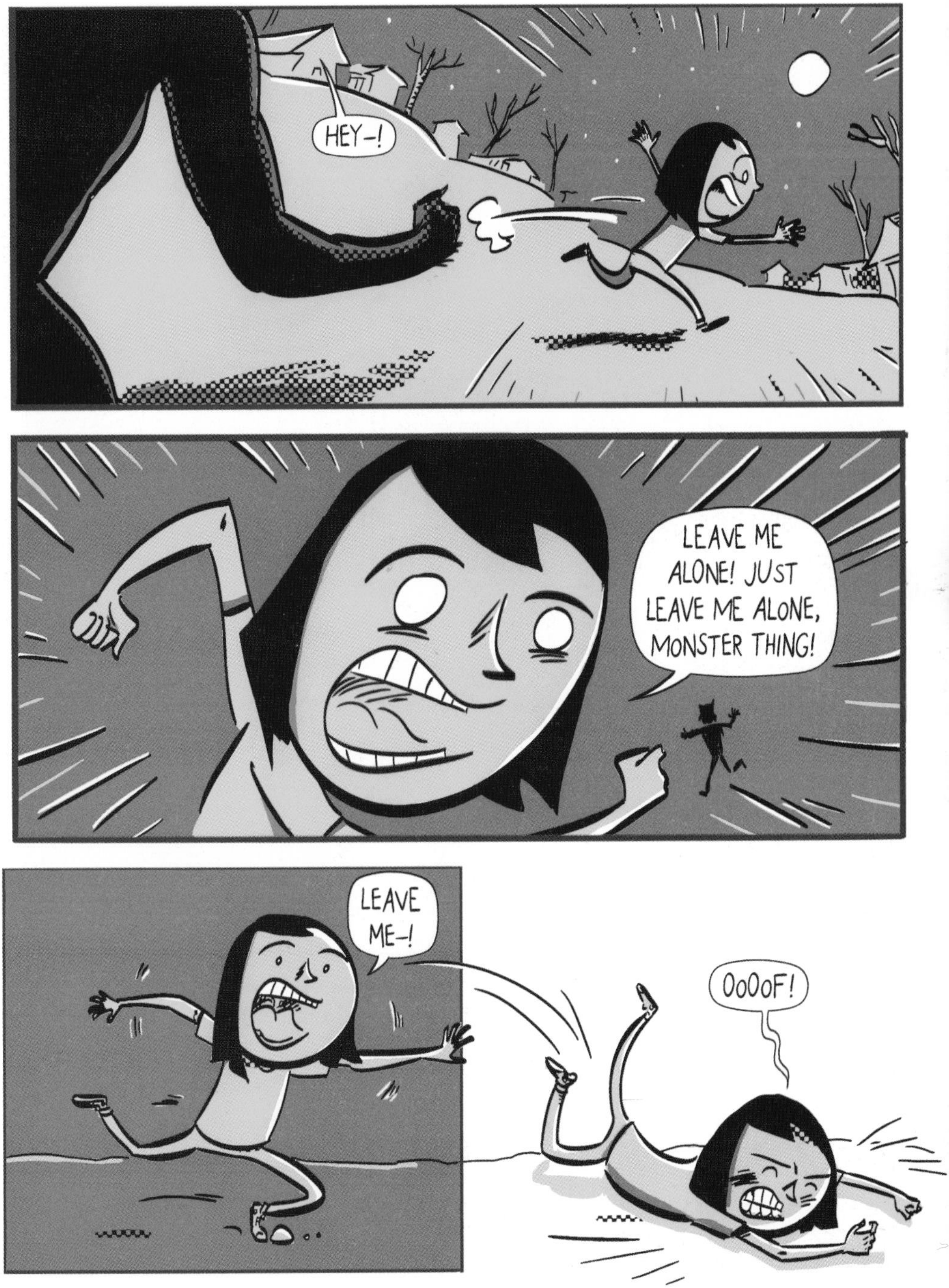
HEY-!
LEAVE ME ALONE! JUST LEAVE ME ALONE, MONSTER THING!
LEAVE ME-!
OOOOF!

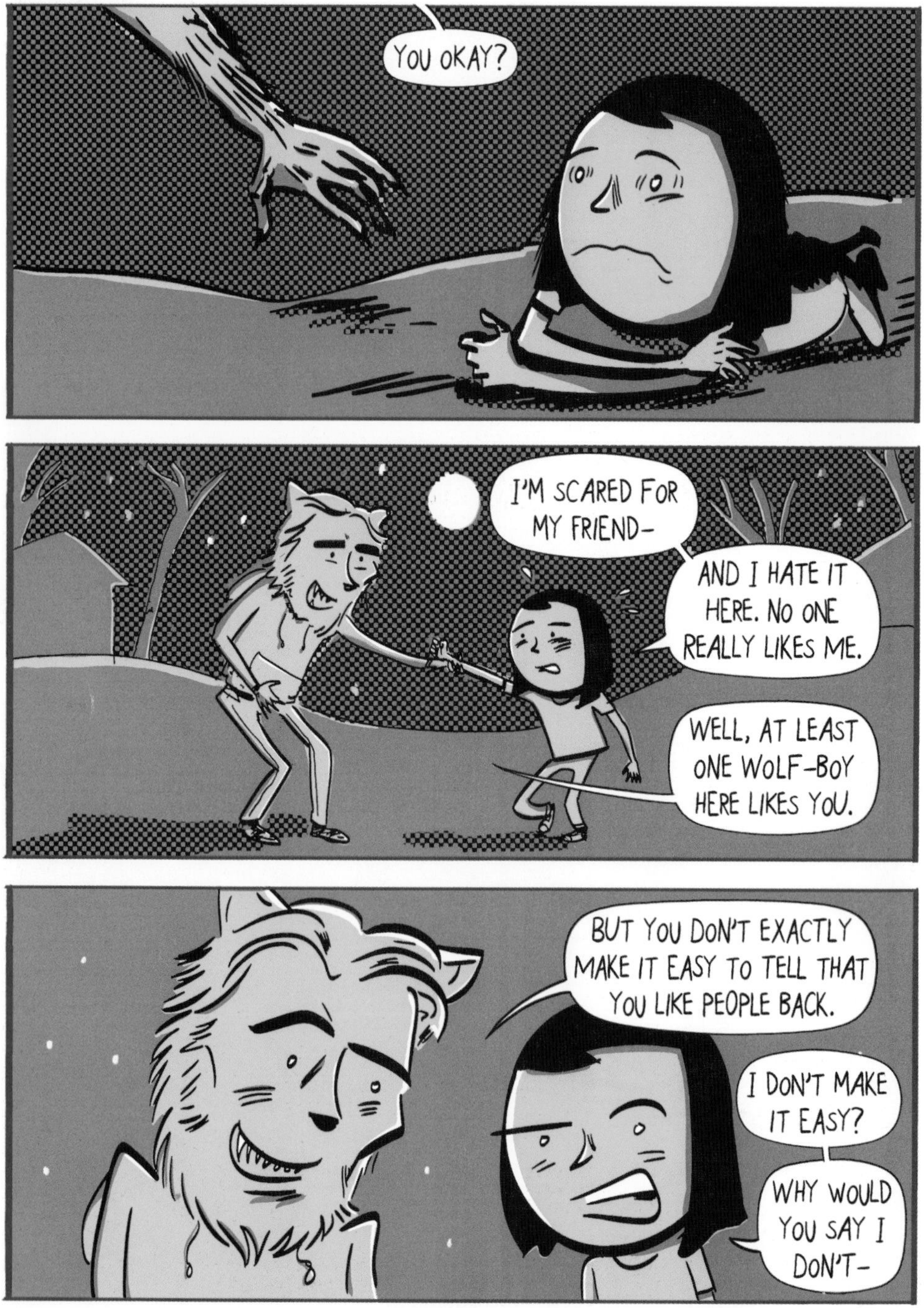

YOU OKAY?
I'M SCARED FOR MY FRIEND-
AND I HATE IT HERE. NO ONE REALLY LIKES ME.
WELL, AT LEAST ONE WOLF-BOY HERE LIKES YOU.
BUT YOU DON'T EXACTLY MAKE IT EASY TO TELL THAT YOU LIKE PEOPLE BACK.
I DON'T MAKE IT EASY?
WHY WOULD YOU SAY I DON'T-

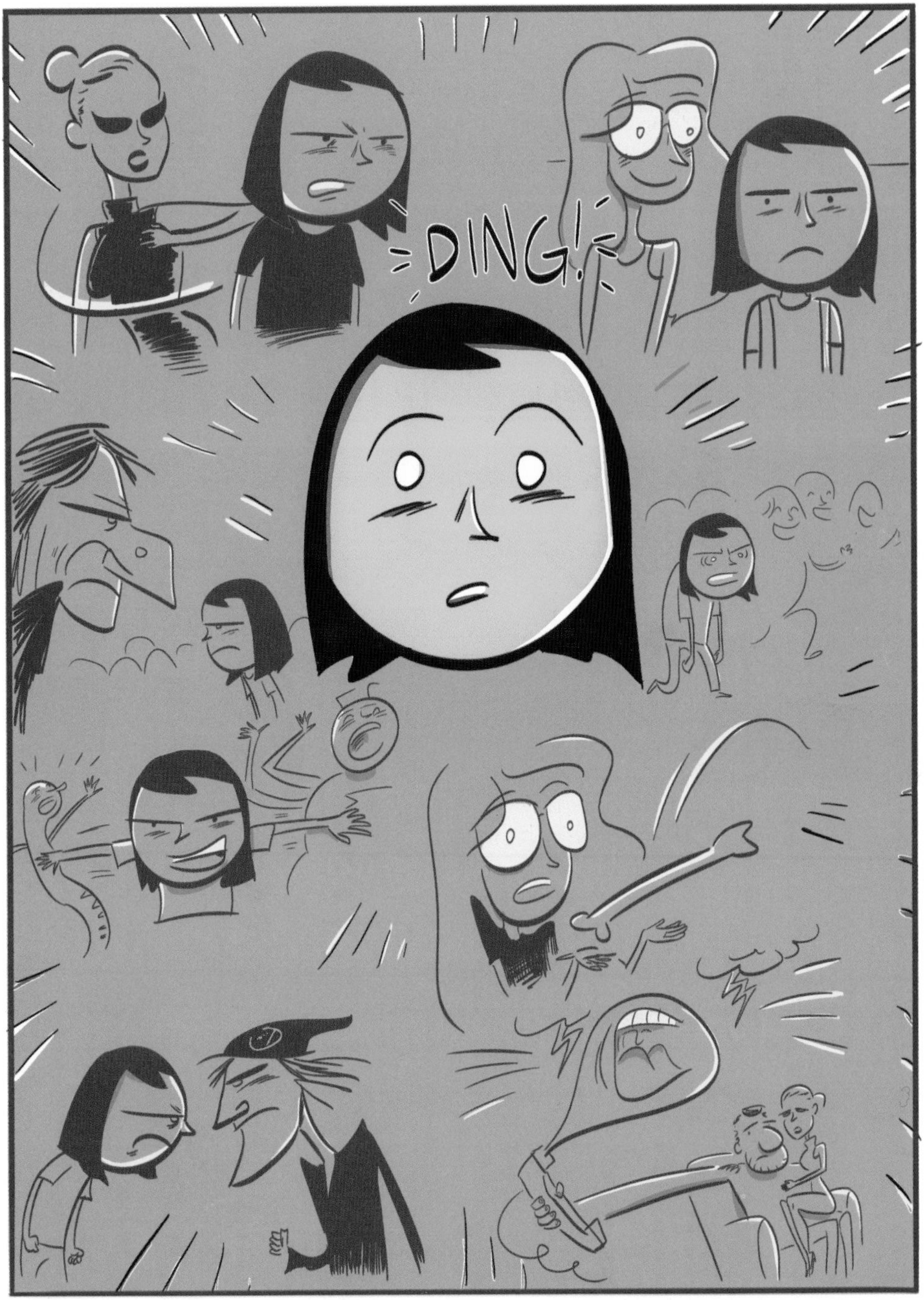
DING!

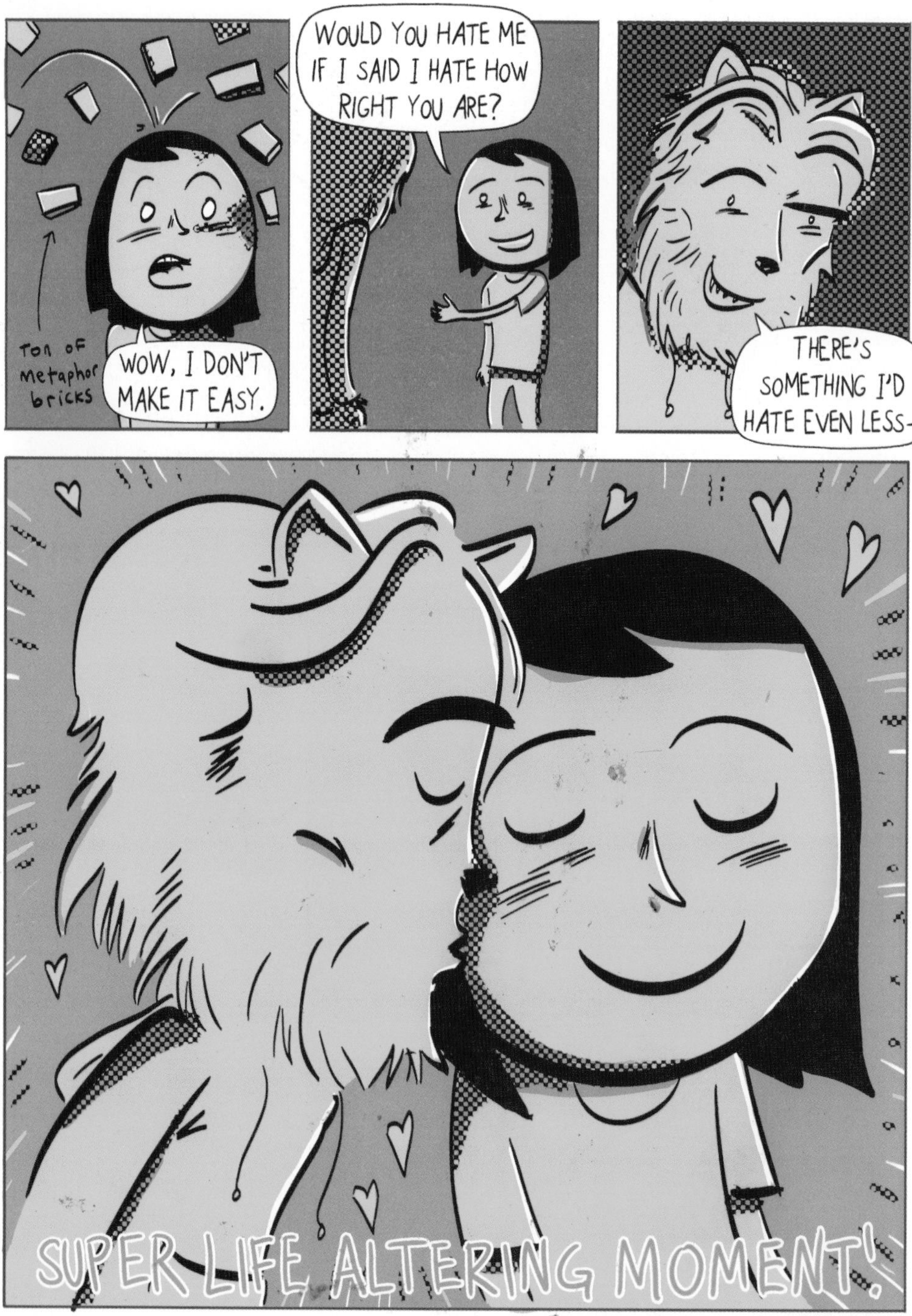
Ton of metaphor bricks
WOW, I DON'T MAKE IT EASY.
WOULD YOU HATE ME IF I SAID I HATE HOW RIGHT YOU ARE?
THERE'S SOMETHING I'D HATE EVEN LESS-
SUPER LIFE ALTERING MOMENT!

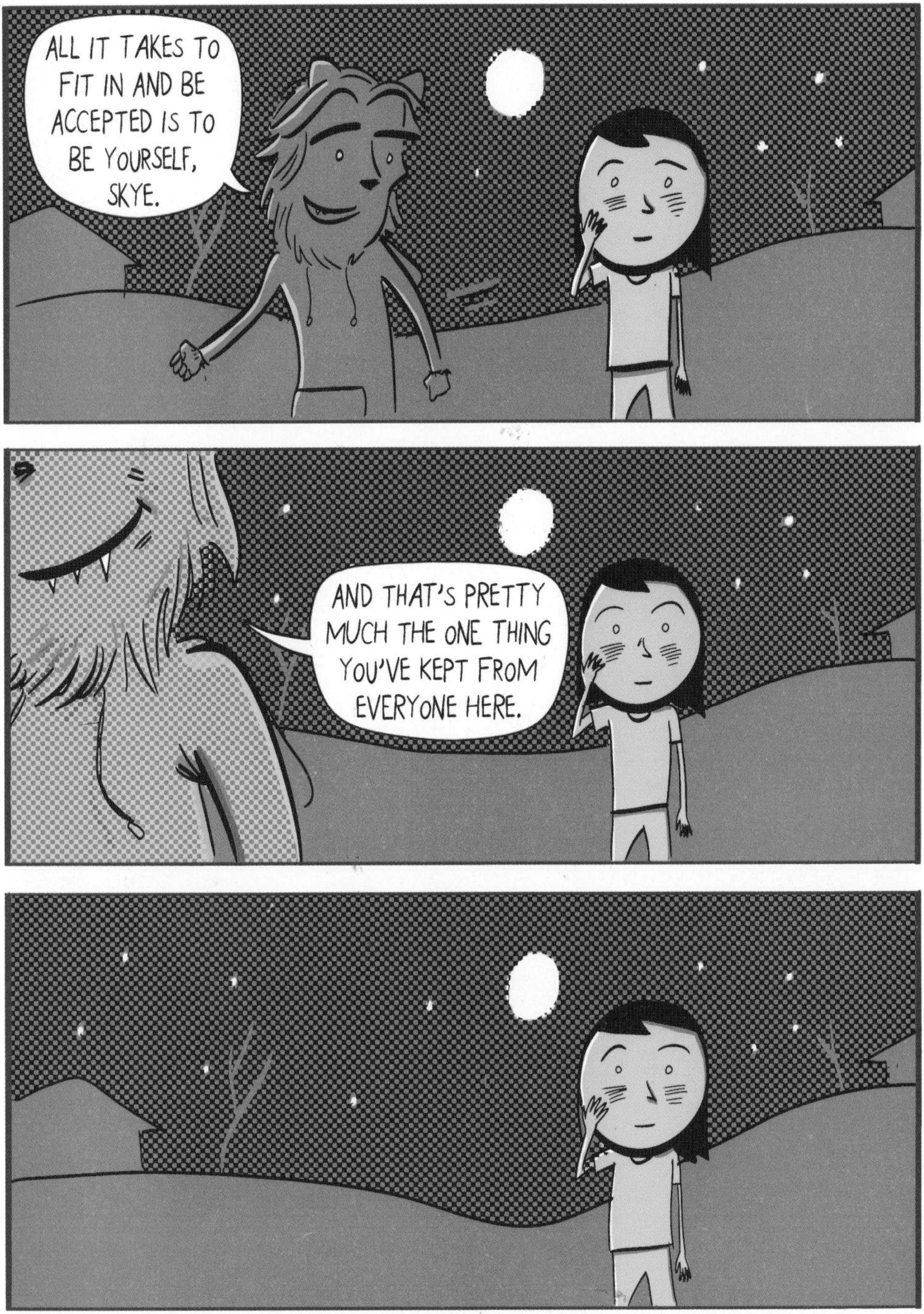
ALL IT TAKES TO FIT IN AND BE ACCEPTED IS TO BE YOURSELF, SKYE.
AND THAT'S PRETTY MUCH THE ONE THING YOU'VE KEPT FROM EVERYONE HERE.

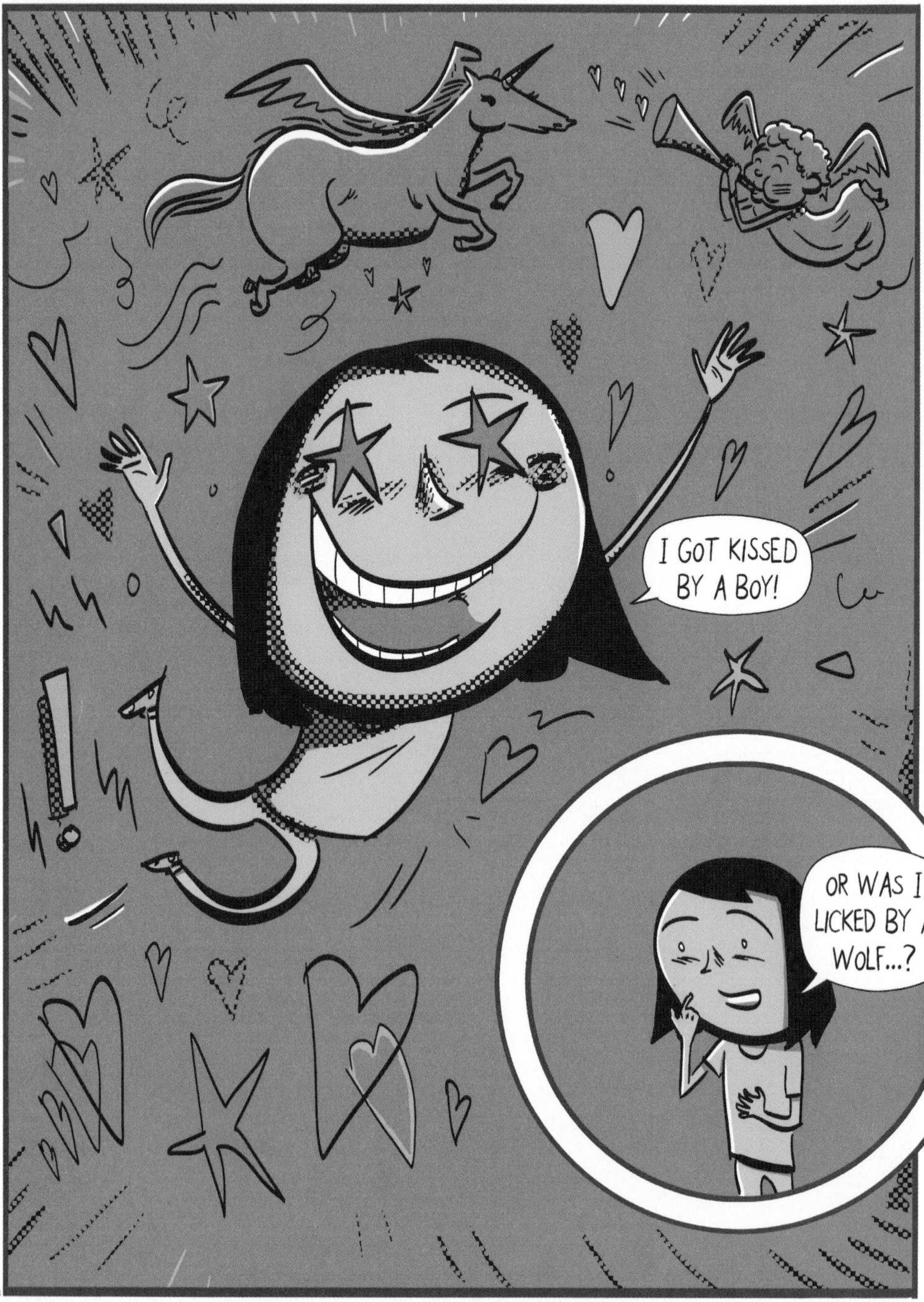
I GOT KISSED BY A BOY!
OR WAS I LICKED BY A WOLF...?

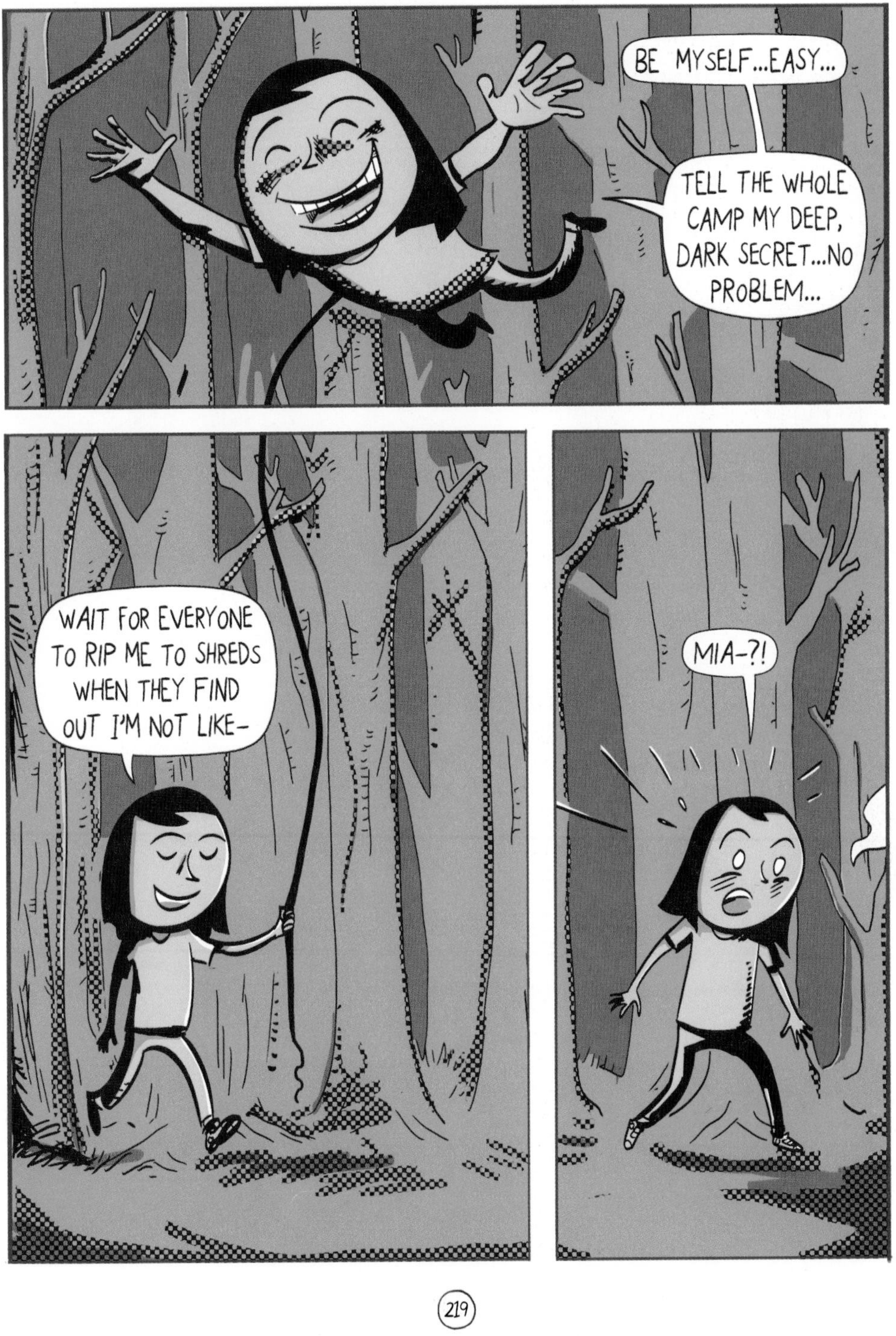
BE MYSELF...EASY...
TELL THE WHOLE CAMP MY DEEP, DARK SECRET...NO PROBLEM...
WAIT FOR EVERYONE TO RIP ME TO SHREDS WHEN THEY FIND OUT I'M NOT LIKE-
MIA-?!

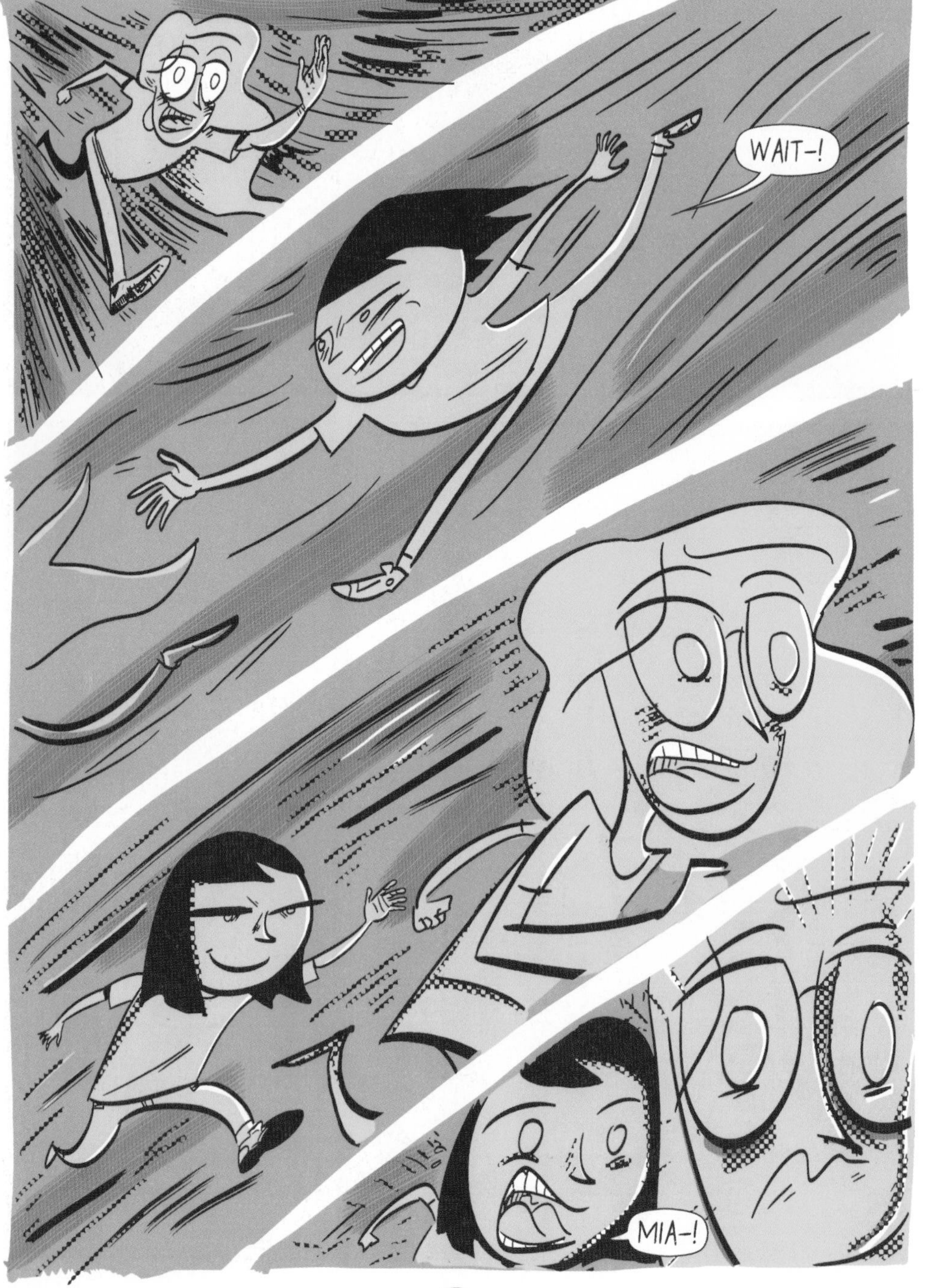
WAIT-!
MIA-!

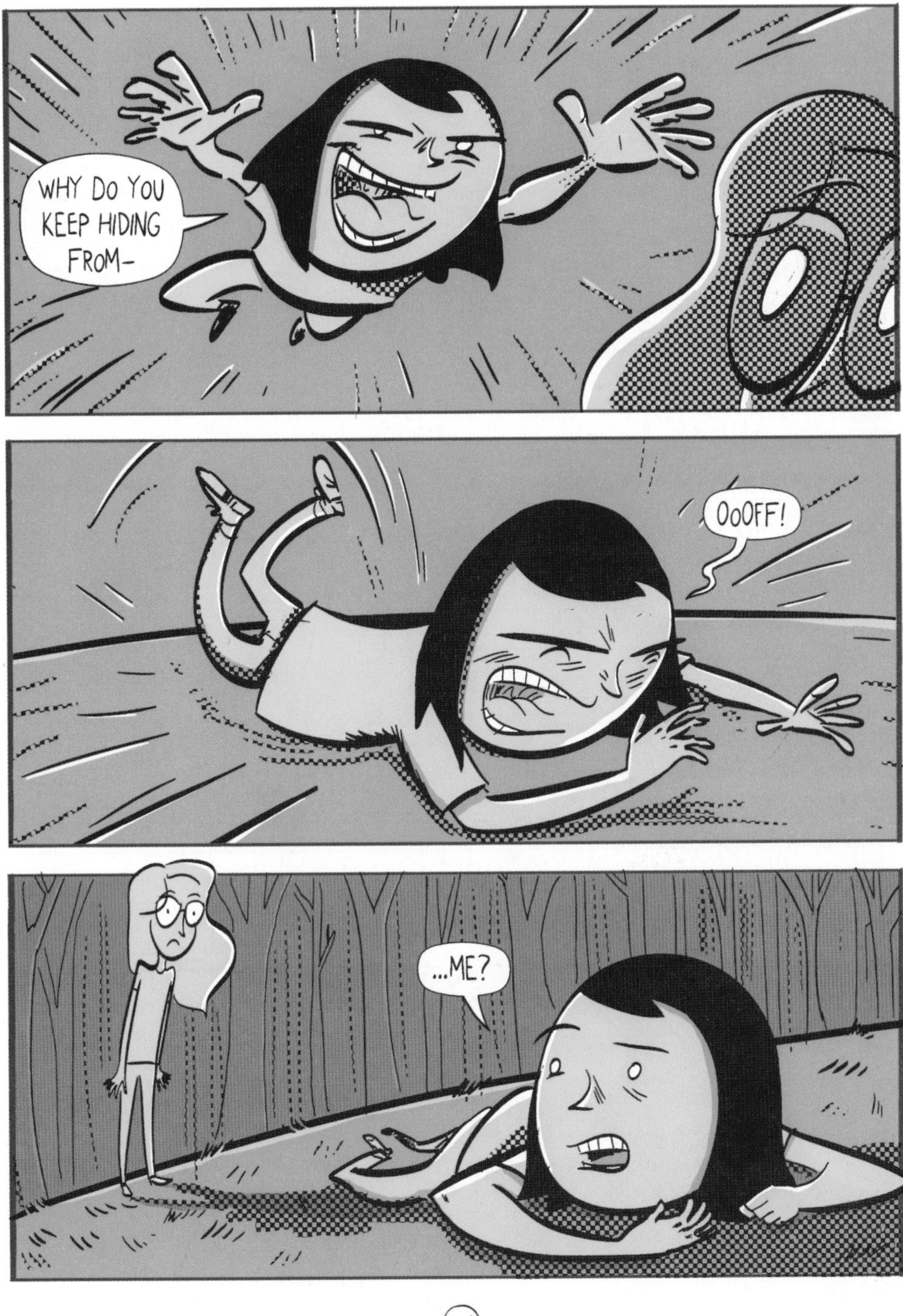
WHY DO YOU KEEP HIDING FROM-
OOOFF!
...ME?

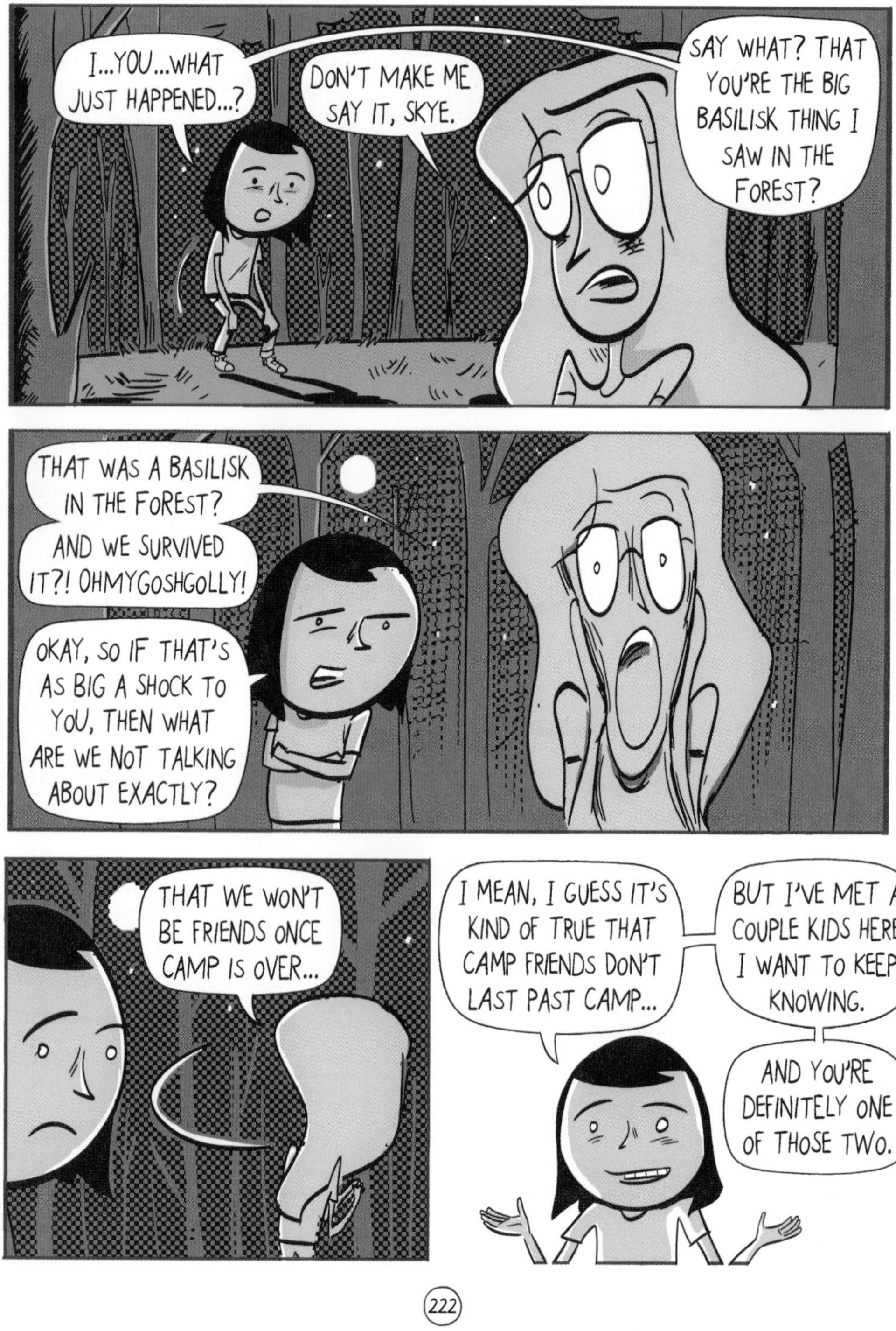
I...YOU...WHAT JUST HAPPENED...?
DON'T MAKE ME SAY IT, SKYE.
SAY WHAT? THAT YOU'RE THE BIG BASILISK THING I SAW IN THE FOREST?
THAT WAS A BASILISK IN THE FOREST?
AND WE SURVIVED IT?! OHMYGOSHGOLLY!
OKAY, SO IF THAT'S AS BIG A SHOCK TO YOU, THEN WHAT ARE WE NOT TALKING ABOUT EXACTLY?
THAT WE WON'T BE FRIENDS ONCE CAMP IS OVER...
I MEAN, I GUESS IT'S KIND OF TRUE THAT CAMP FRIENDS DON'T LAST PAST CAMP...
BUT I'VE MET A COUPLE KIDS HERE I WANT TO KEEP KNOWING.
AND YOU'RE DEFINITELY ONE OF THOSE TWO.

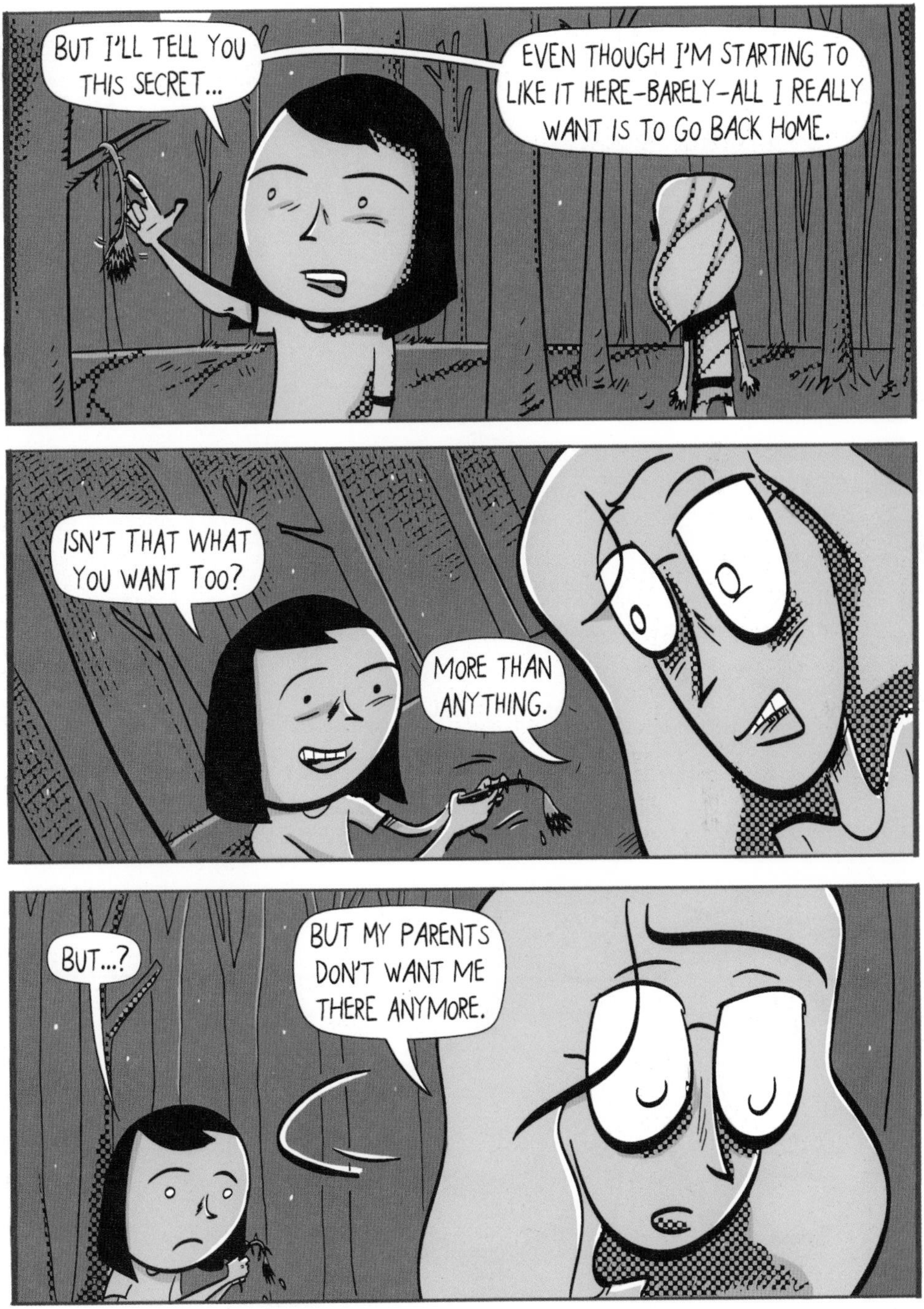
BUT I'LL TELL YOU THIS SECRET...
EVEN THOUGH I'M STARTING TO LIKE IT HERE–BARELY–ALL I REALLY WANT IS TO GO BACK HOME.
ISN'T THAT WHAT YOU WANT TOO?
MORE THAN ANYTHING.
BUT...?
BUT MY PARENTS DON'T WANT ME THERE ANYMORE.

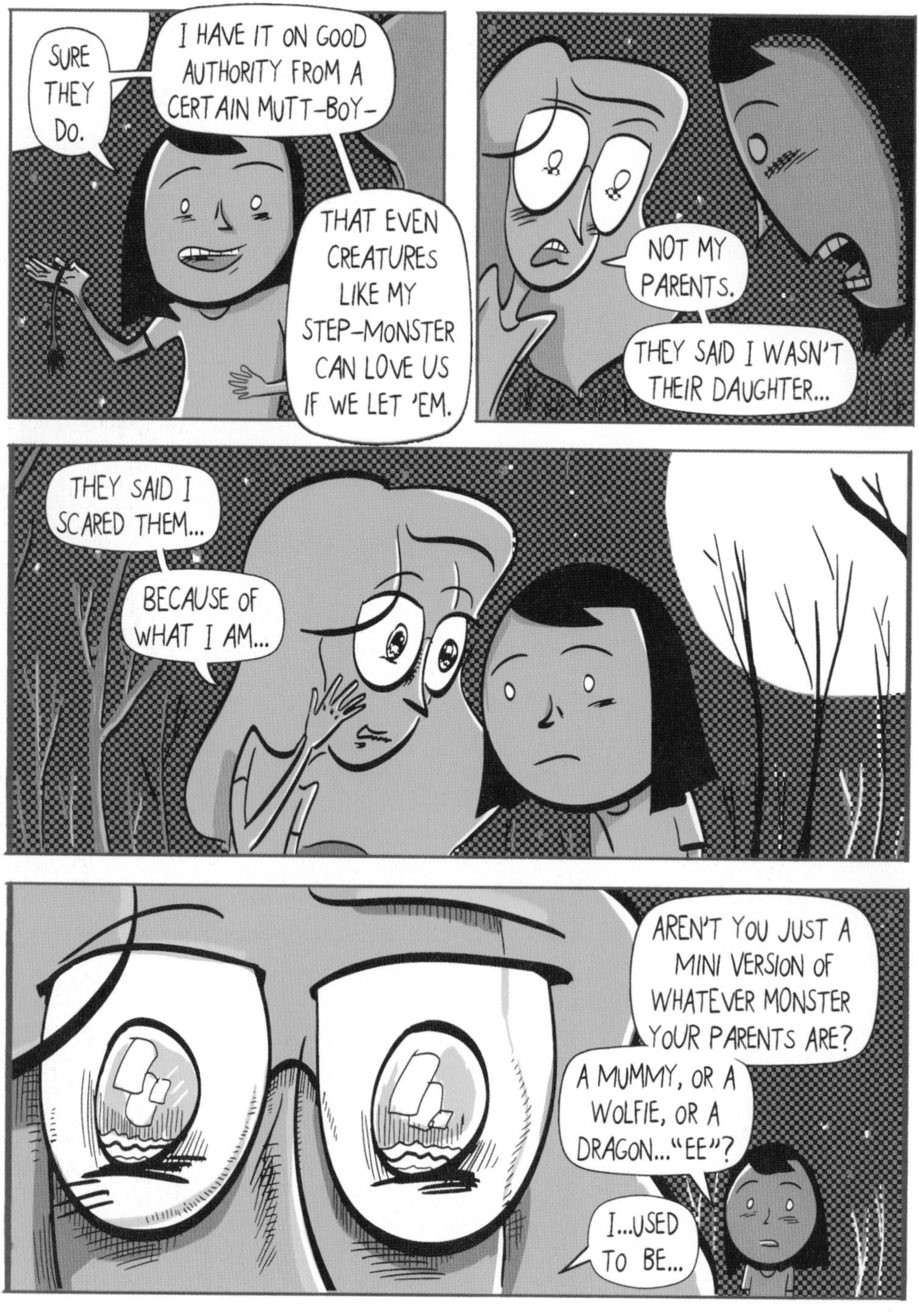
SURE THEY DO.
I HAVE IT ON GOOD AUTHORITY FROM A CERTAIN MUTT-BOY-
THAT EVEN CREATURES LIKE MY STEP-MONSTER CAN LOVE US IF WE LET 'EM.
NOT MY PARENTS.
THEY SAID I WASN'T THEIR DAUGHTER...
THEY SAID I SCARED THEM...
BECAUSE OF WHAT I AM...
AREN'T YOU JUST A MINI VERSION OF WHATEVER MONSTER YOUR PARENTS ARE?
A MUMMY, OR A WOLFIE, OR A DRAGON..."EE"?
I...USED TO BE...

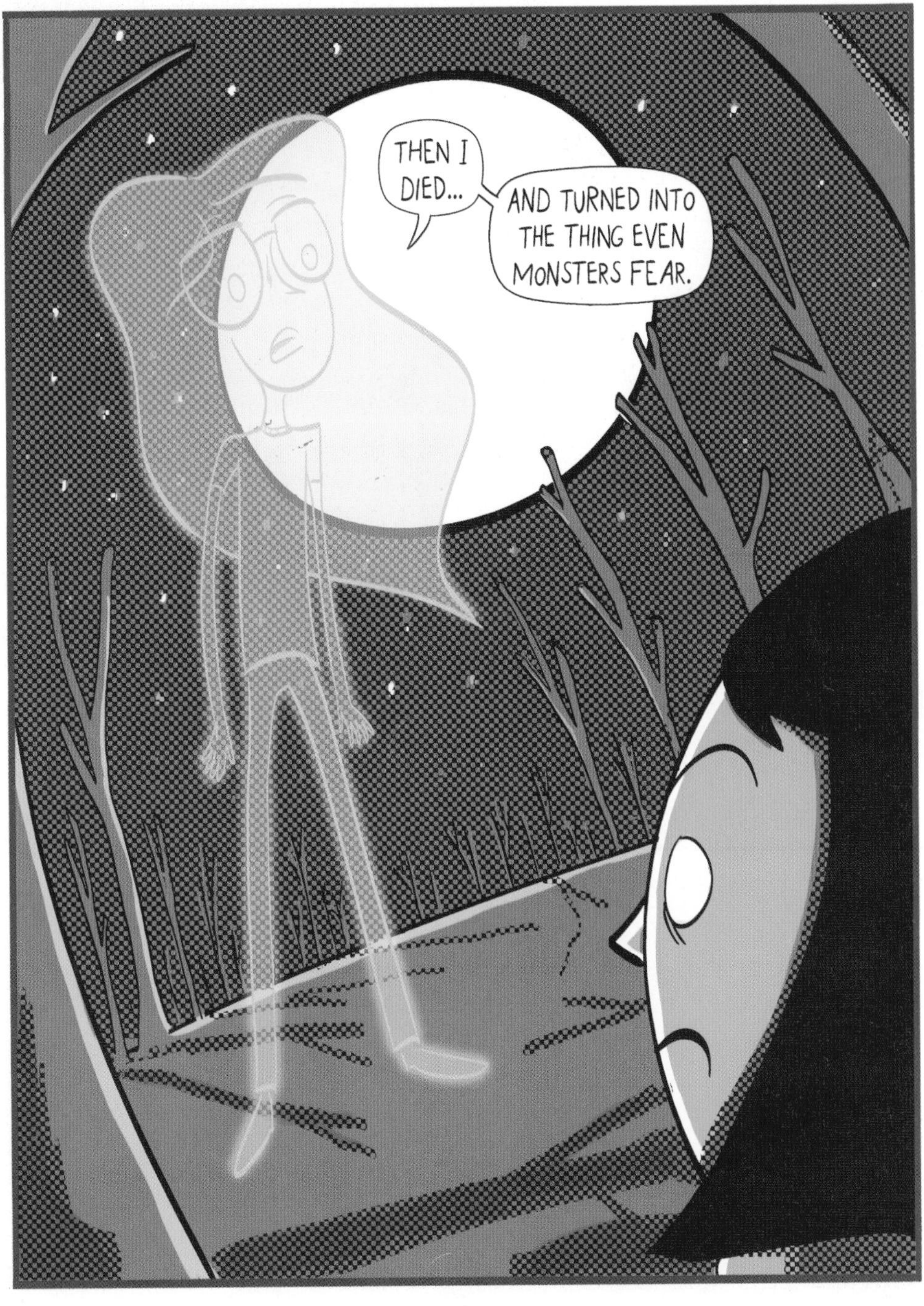
THEN I DIED...
AND TURNED INTO THE THING EVEN MONSTERS FEAR.

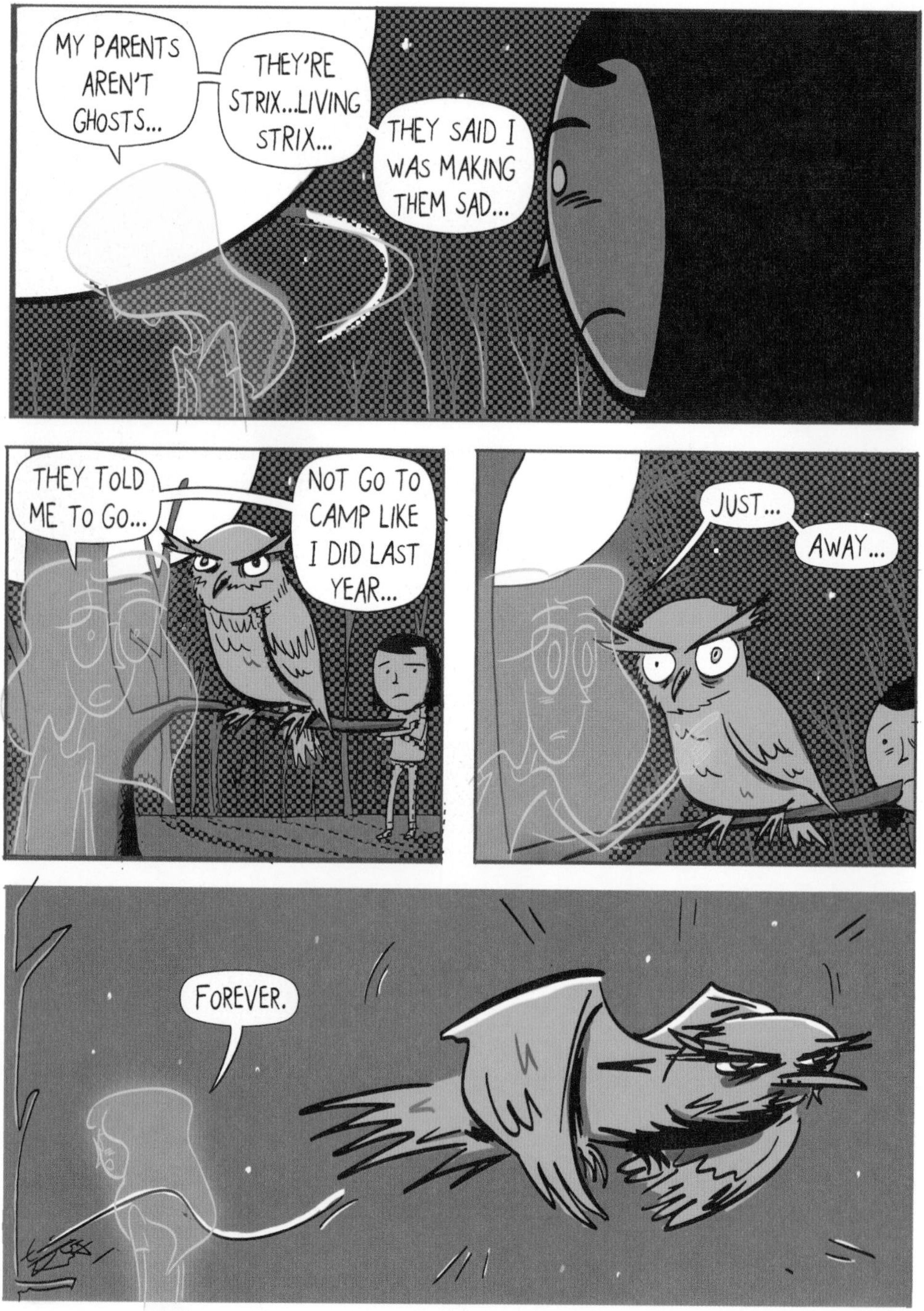
MY PARENTS AREN'T GHOSTS...
THEY'RE STRIX...LIVING STRIX...
THEY SAID I WAS MAKING THEM SAD...
THEY TOLD ME TO GO...
NOT GO TO CAMP LIKE I DID LAST YEAR...
JUST...
AWAY...
FOREVER.

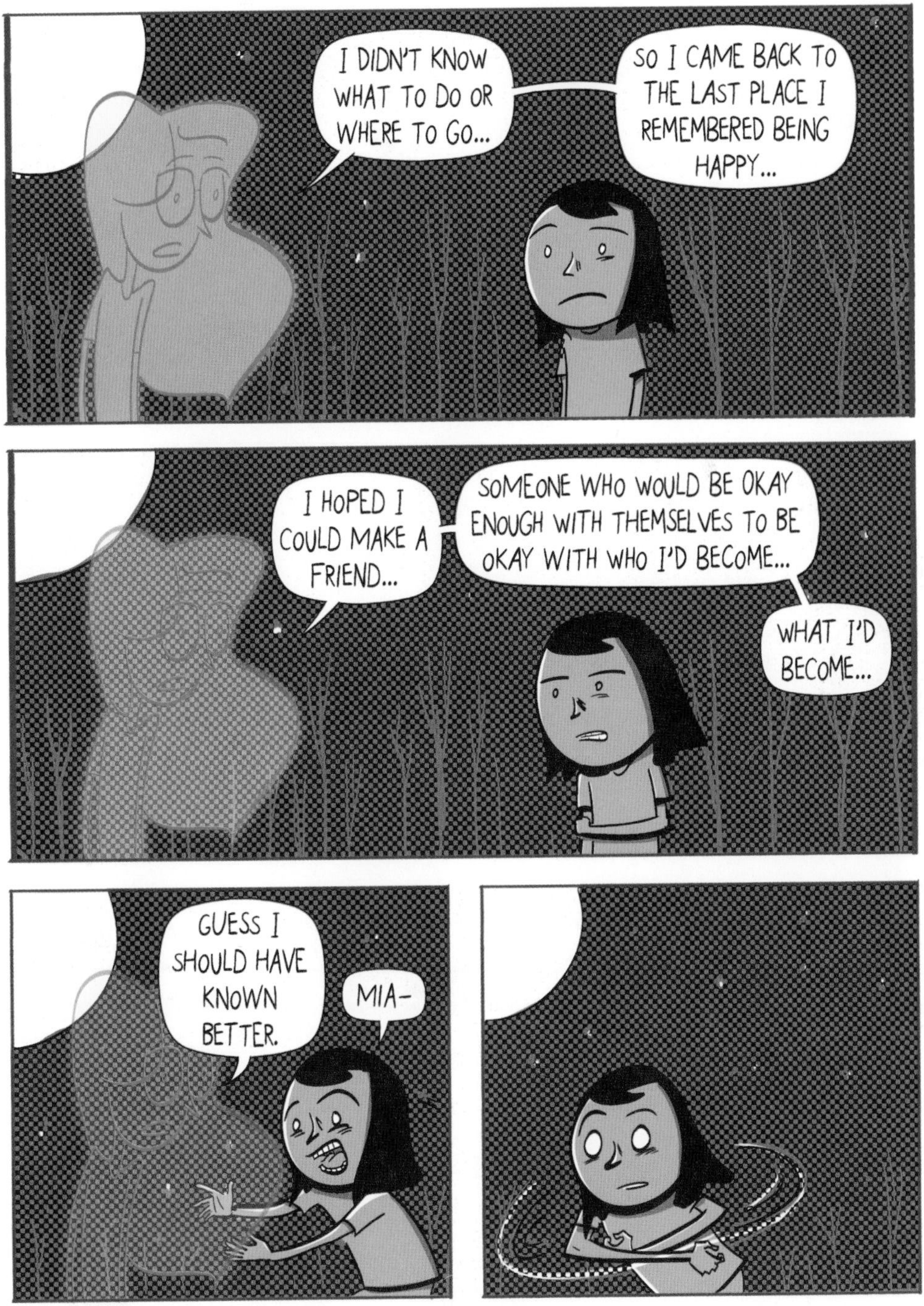
I DIDN'T KNOW WHAT TO DO OR WHERE TO GO...
SO I CAME BACK TO THE LAST PLACE I REMEMBERED BEING HAPPY...
I HOPED I COULD MAKE A FRIEND...
SOMEONE WHO WOULD BE OKAY ENOUGH WITH THEMSELVES TO BE OKAY WITH WHO I'D BECOME...
WHAT I'D BECOME...
GUESS I SHOULD HAVE KNOWN BETTER.
MIA-

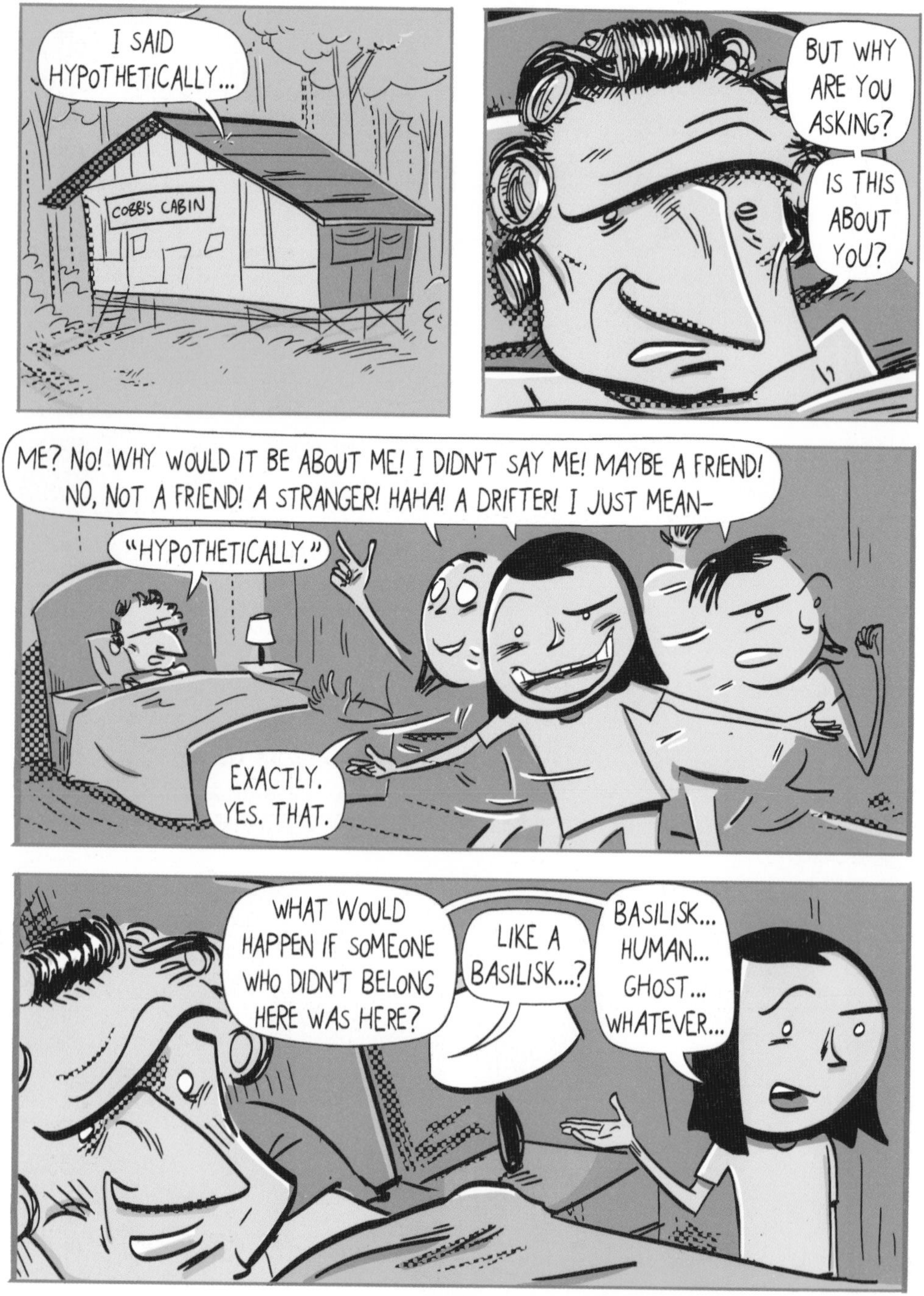
I SAID HYPOTHETICALLY...
COBB'S CABIN
BUT WHY ARE YOU ASKING?
IS THIS ABOUT YOU?
ME? NO! WHY WOULD IT BE ABOUT ME! I DIDN'T SAY ME! MAYBE A FRIEND! NO, NOT A FRIEND! A STRANGER! HAHA! A DRIFTER! I JUST MEAN–
"HYPOTHETICALLY."
EXACTLY. YES. THAT.
WHAT WOULD HAPPEN IF SOMEONE WHO DIDN'T BELONG HERE WAS HERE?
LIKE A BASILISK...?
BASILISK... HUMAN... GHOST... WHATEVER...

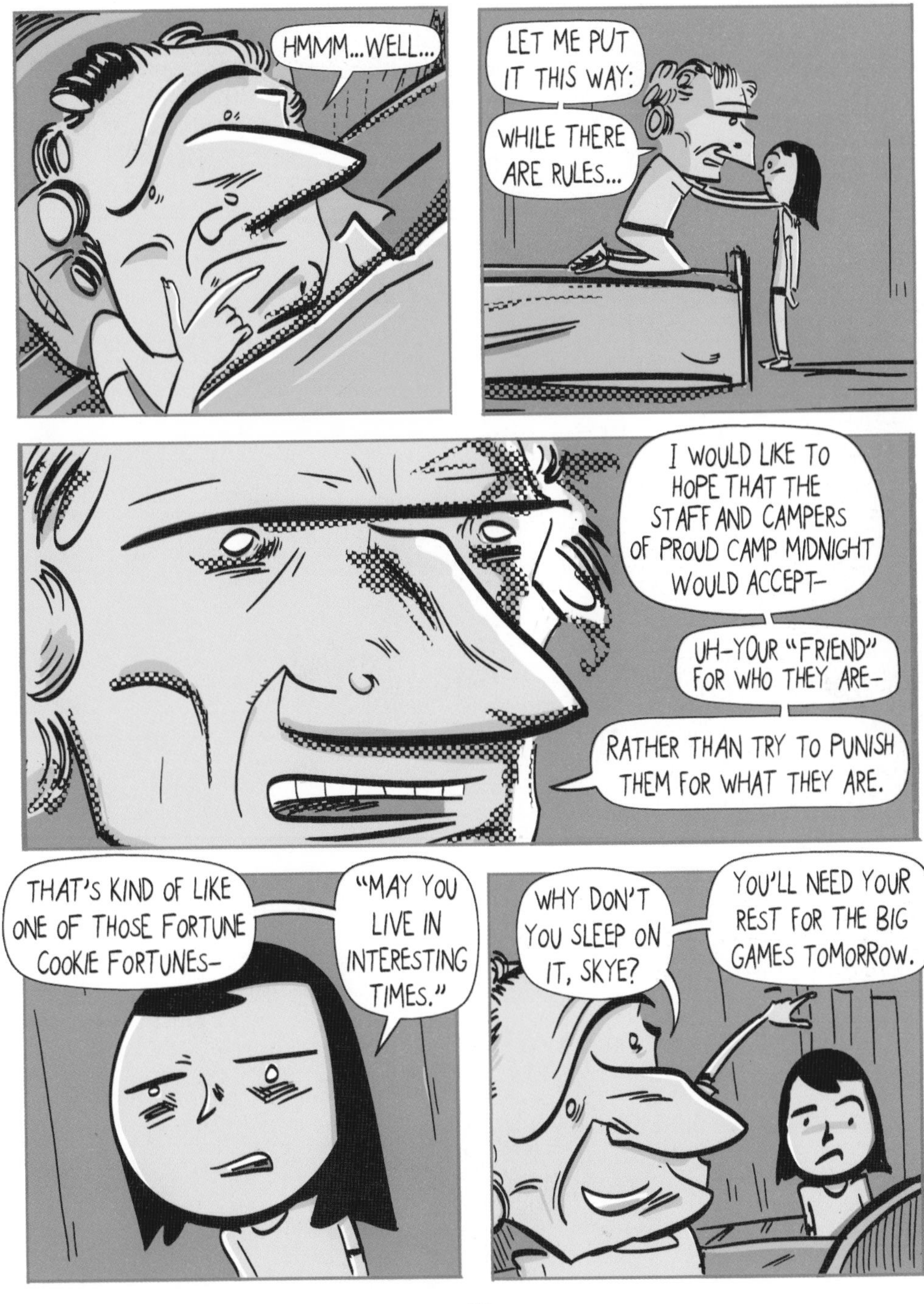
HMMM...WELL...
LET ME PUT IT THIS WAY:
WHILE THERE ARE RULES...
I WOULD LIKE TO HOPE THAT THE STAFF AND CAMPERS OF PROUD CAMP MIDNIGHT WOULD ACCEPT-
UH-YOUR "FRIEND" FOR WHO THEY ARE-
RATHER THAN TRY TO PUNISH THEM FOR WHAT THEY ARE.
THAT'S KIND OF LIKE ONE OF THOSE FORTUNE COOKIE FORTUNES-
"MAY YOU LIVE IN INTERESTING TIMES."
WHY DON'T YOU SLEEP ON IT, SKYE?
YOU'LL NEED YOUR REST FOR THE BIG GAMES TOMORROW.

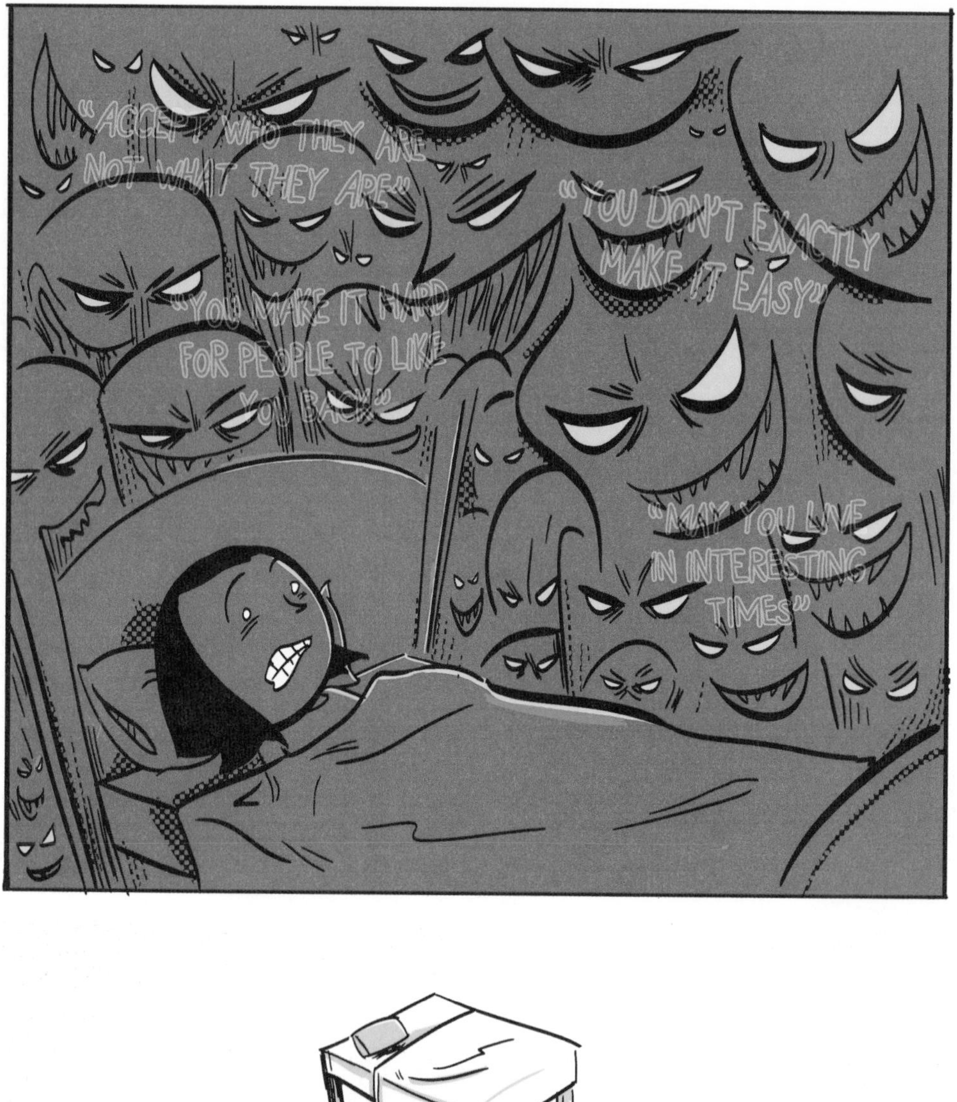
"ACCEPT WHO THEY ARE NOT WHAT THEY ARE"
"YOU DON'T EXACTLY MAKE IT EASY"
"YOU MAKE IT HARD FOR PEOPLE TO LIKE YOU BACK"
"MAY YOU LIVE IN INTERESTING TIMES"

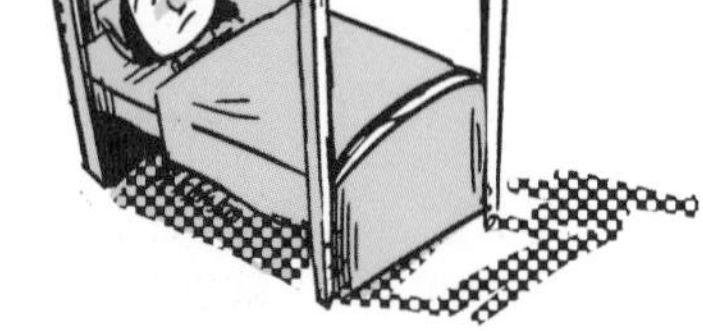

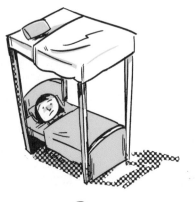

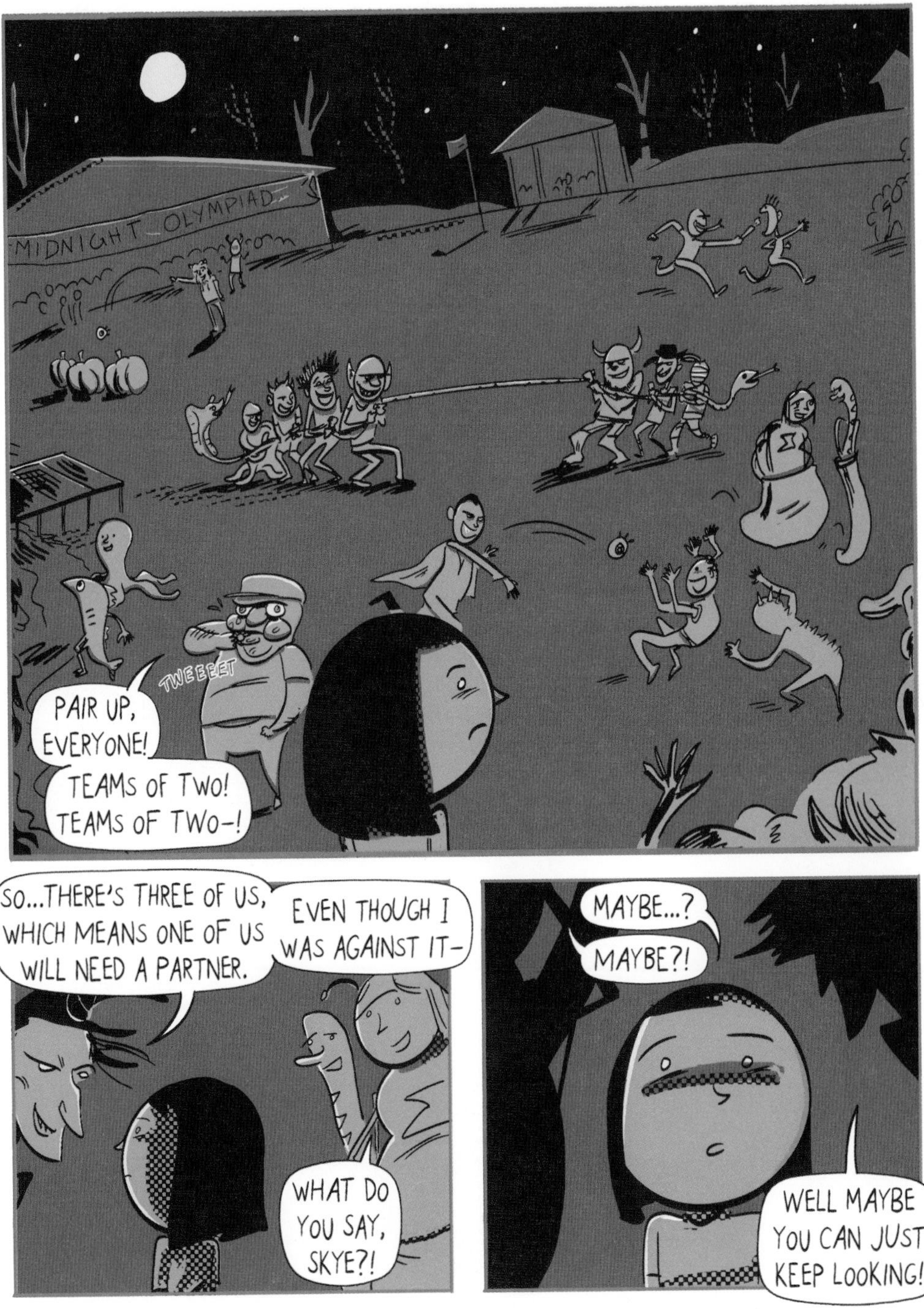
MIDNIGHT OLYMPIAD
TWEEEET
PAIR UP, EVERYONE!
TEAMS OF TWO! TEAMS OF TWO-!
SO...THERE'S THREE OF US, WHICH MEANS ONE OF US WILL NEED A PARTNER.
EVEN THOUGH I WAS AGAINST IT-
WHAT DO YOU SAY, SKYE?!
MAYBE...?
MAYBE?!
WELL MAYBE YOU CAN JUST KEEP LOOKING!

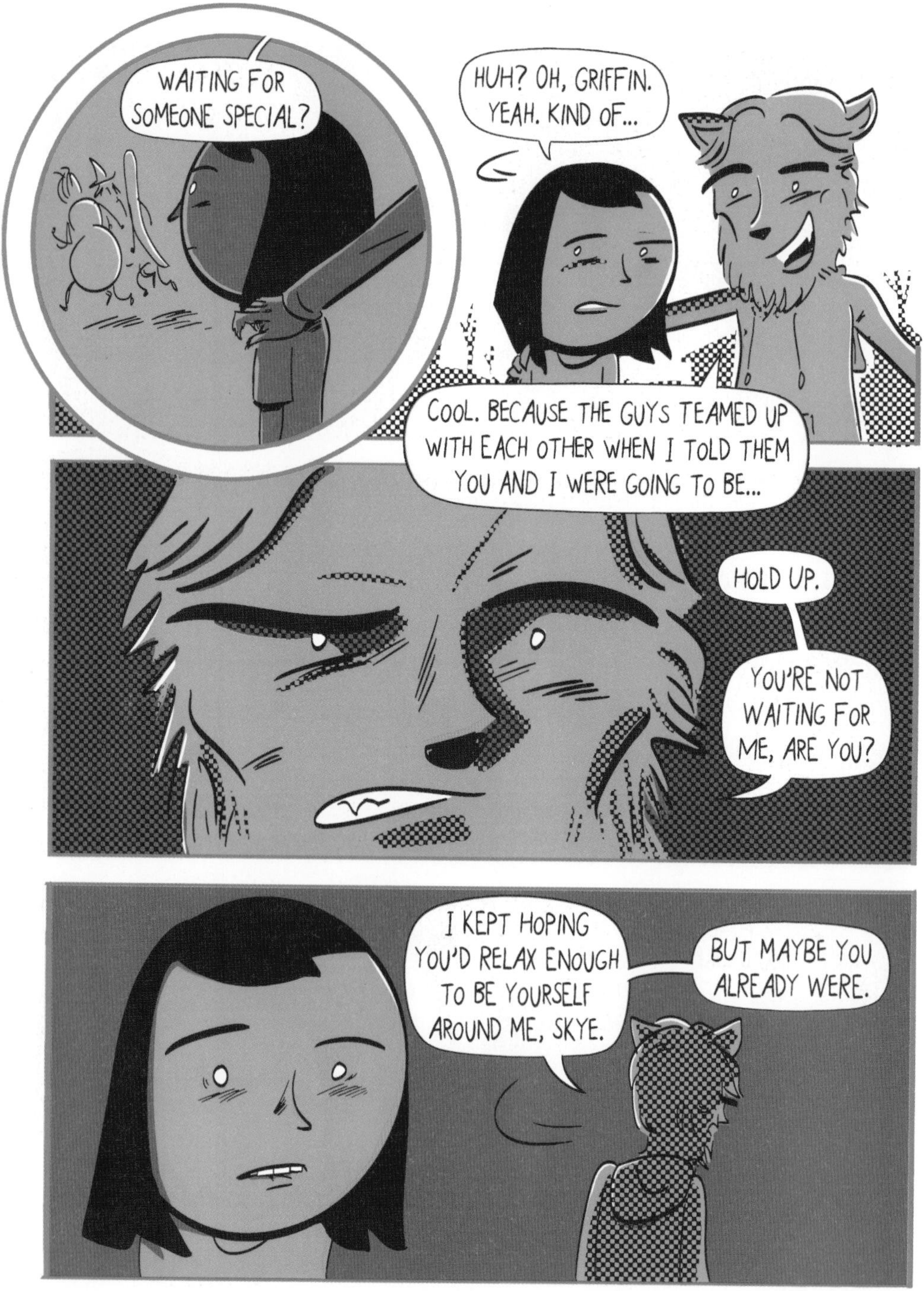
WAITING FOR SOMEONE SPECIAL?
HUH? OH, GRIFFIN. YEAH. KIND OF...
COOL. BECAUSE THE GUYS TEAMED UP WITH EACH OTHER WHEN I TOLD THEM YOU AND I WERE GOING TO BE...
HOLD UP.
YOU'RE NOT WAITING FOR ME, ARE YOU?
I KEPT HOPING YOU'D RELAX ENOUGH TO BE YOURSELF AROUND ME, SKYE.
BUT MAYBE YOU ALREADY WERE.

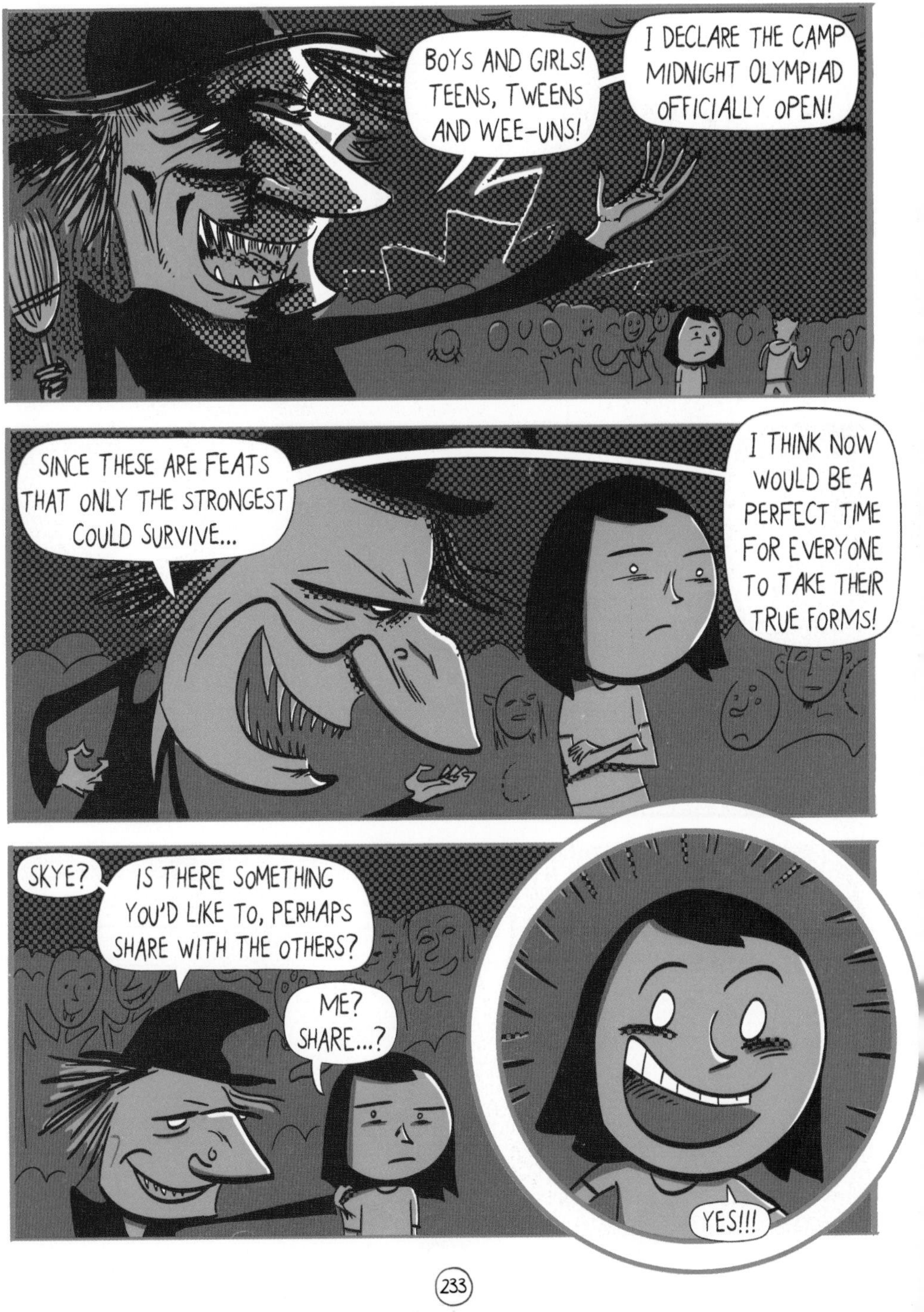
BOYS AND GIRLS! TEENS, TWEENS AND WEE-UNS!
I DECLARE THE CAMP MIDNIGHT OLYMPIAD OFFICIALLY OPEN!
SINCE THESE ARE FEATS THAT ONLY THE STRONGEST COULD SURVIVE...
I THINK NOW WOULD BE A PERFECT TIME FOR EVERYONE TO TAKE THEIR TRUE FORMS!
SKYE?
IS THERE SOMETHING YOU'D LIKE TO, PERHAPS SHARE WITH THE OTHERS?
ME? SHARE...?
YES!!!

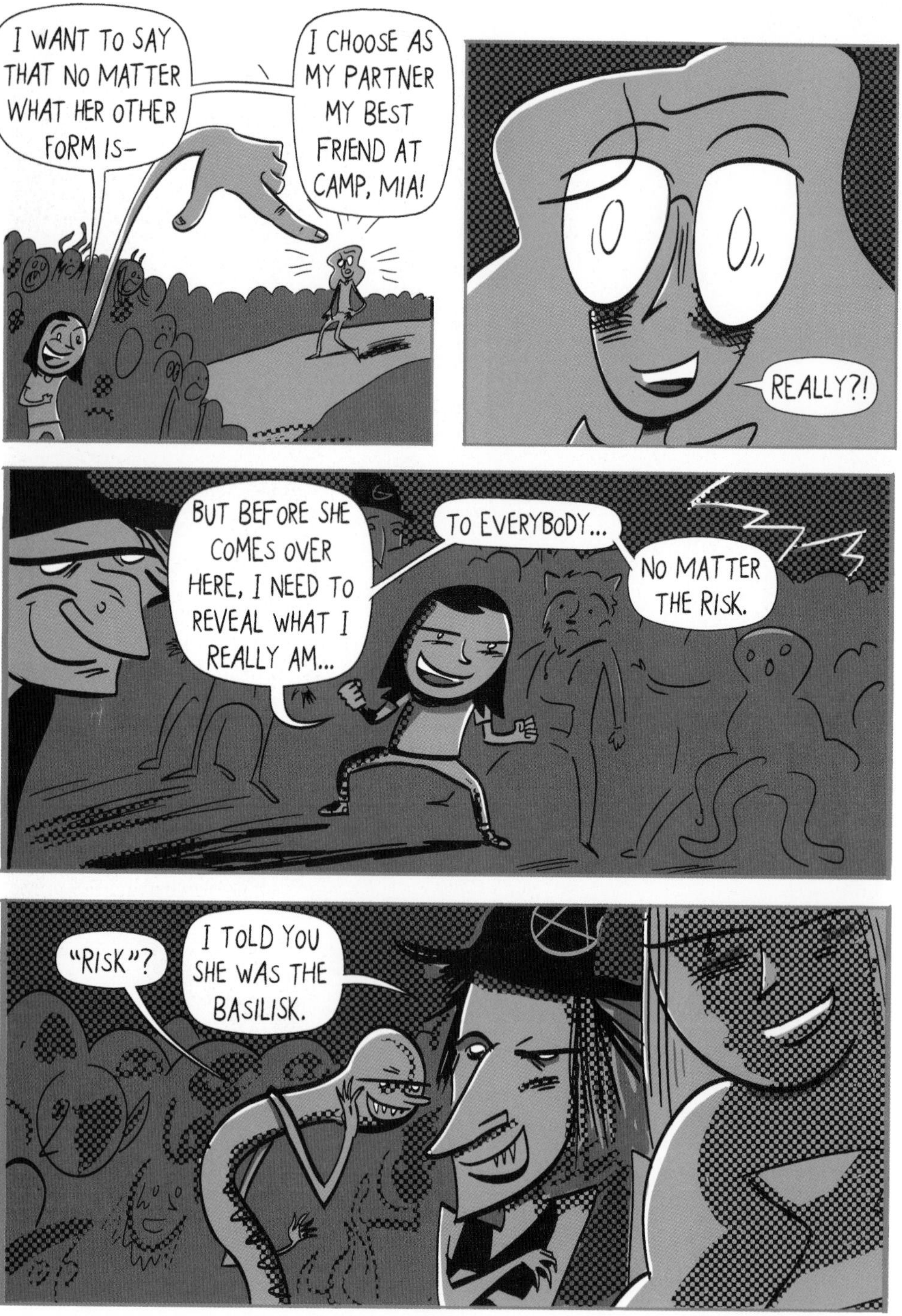
I WANT TO SAY THAT NO MATTER WHAT HER OTHER FORM IS-
I CHOOSE AS MY PARTNER MY BEST FRIEND AT CAMP, MIA!
REALLY?!
BUT BEFORE SHE COMES OVER HERE, I NEED TO REVEAL WHAT I REALLY AM...
TO EVERYBODY...
NO MATTER THE RISK.
"RISK"?
I TOLD YOU SHE WAS THE BASILISK.

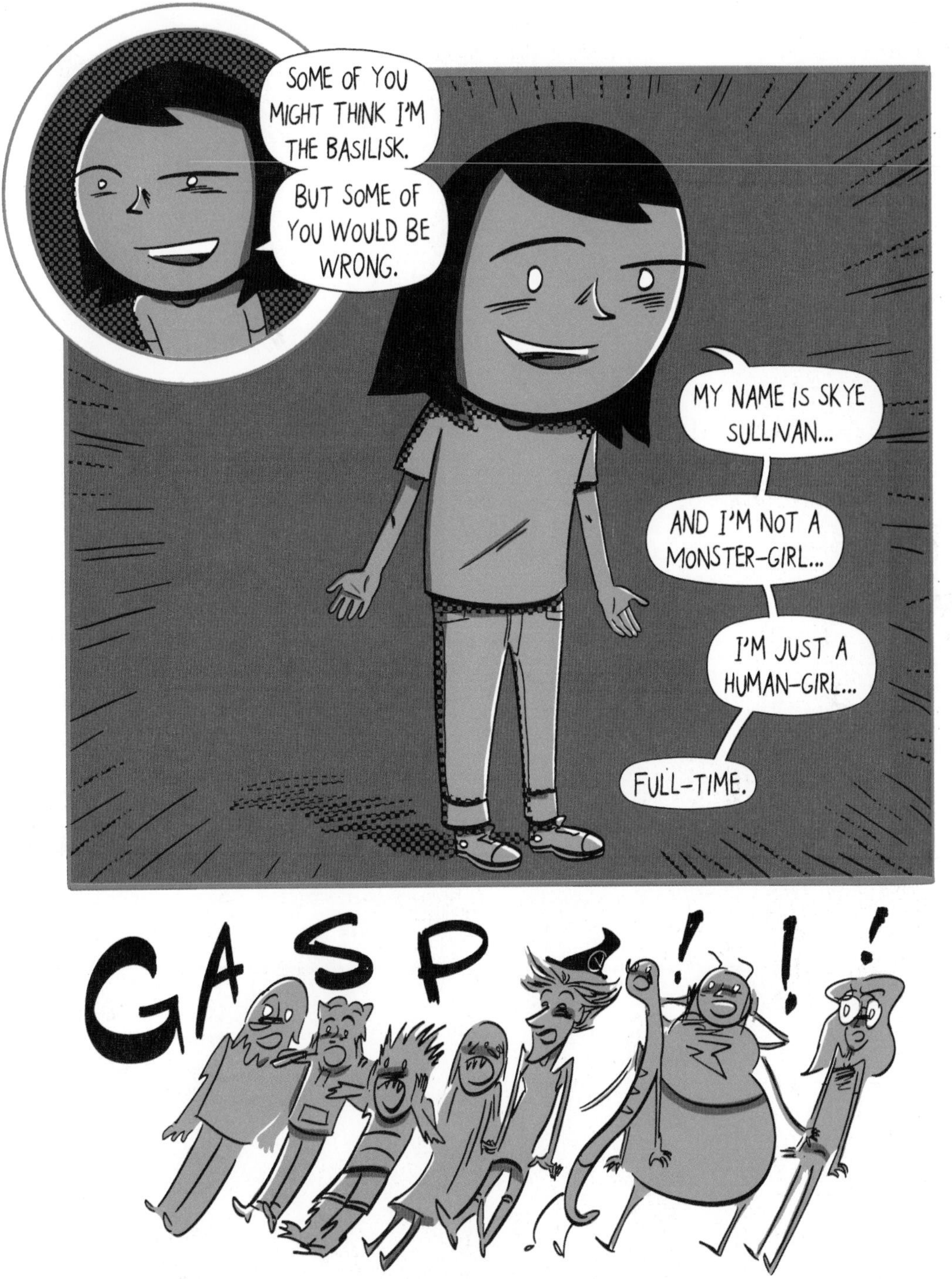
SOME OF YOU MIGHT THINK I'M THE BASILISK.
BUT SOME OF YOU WOULD BE WRONG.
MY NAME IS SKYE SULLIVAN...
AND I'M NOT A MONSTER-GIRL...
I'M JUST A HUMAN-GIRL...
FULL-TIME.
GASP!!!

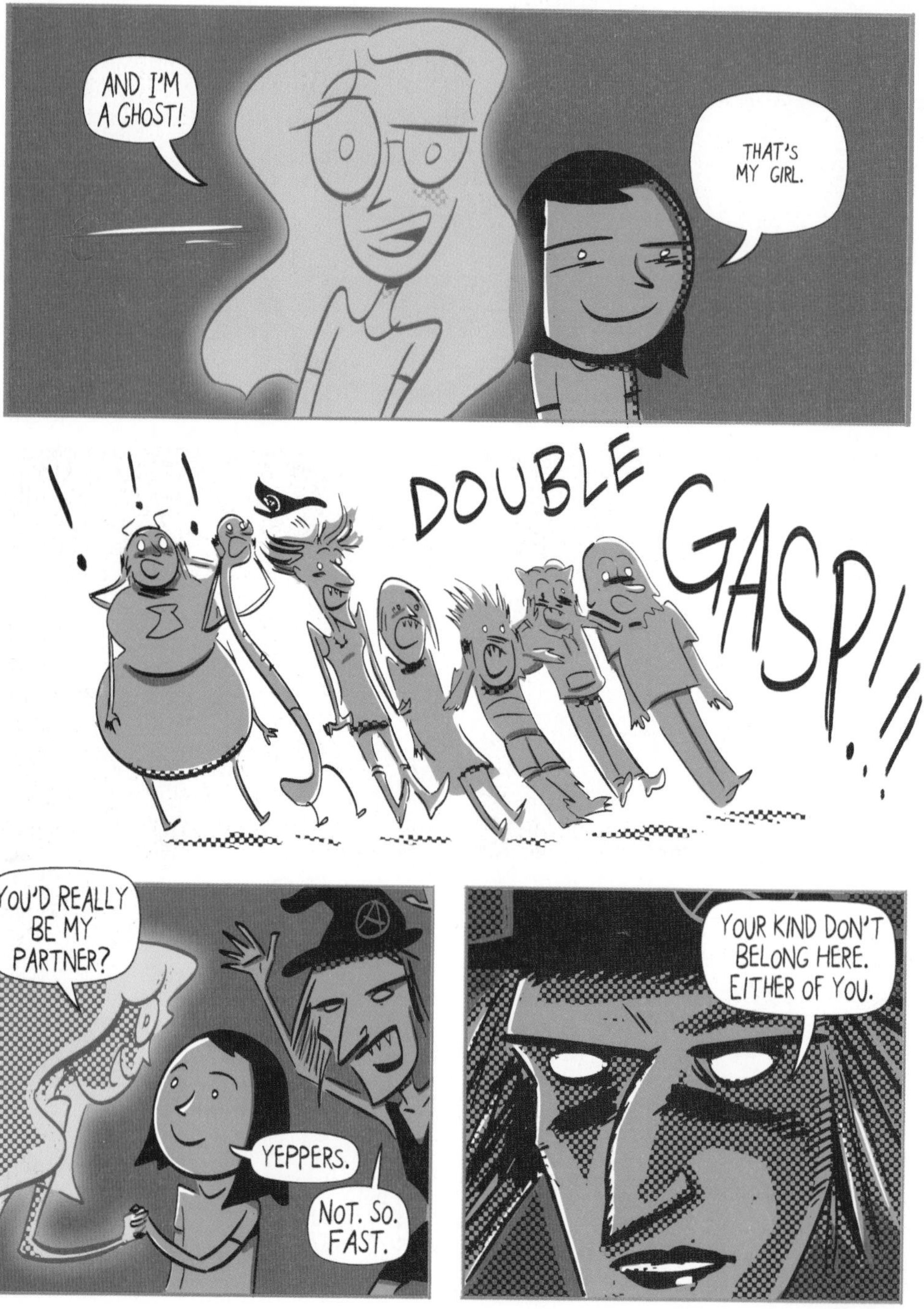
AND I'M A GHOST!
THAT'S MY GIRL.
! ! !
DOUBLE GASP!!!
YOU'D REALLY BE MY PARTNER?
YEPPERS.
NOT. SO. FAST.
YOUR KIND DON'T BELONG HERE. EITHER OF YOU.

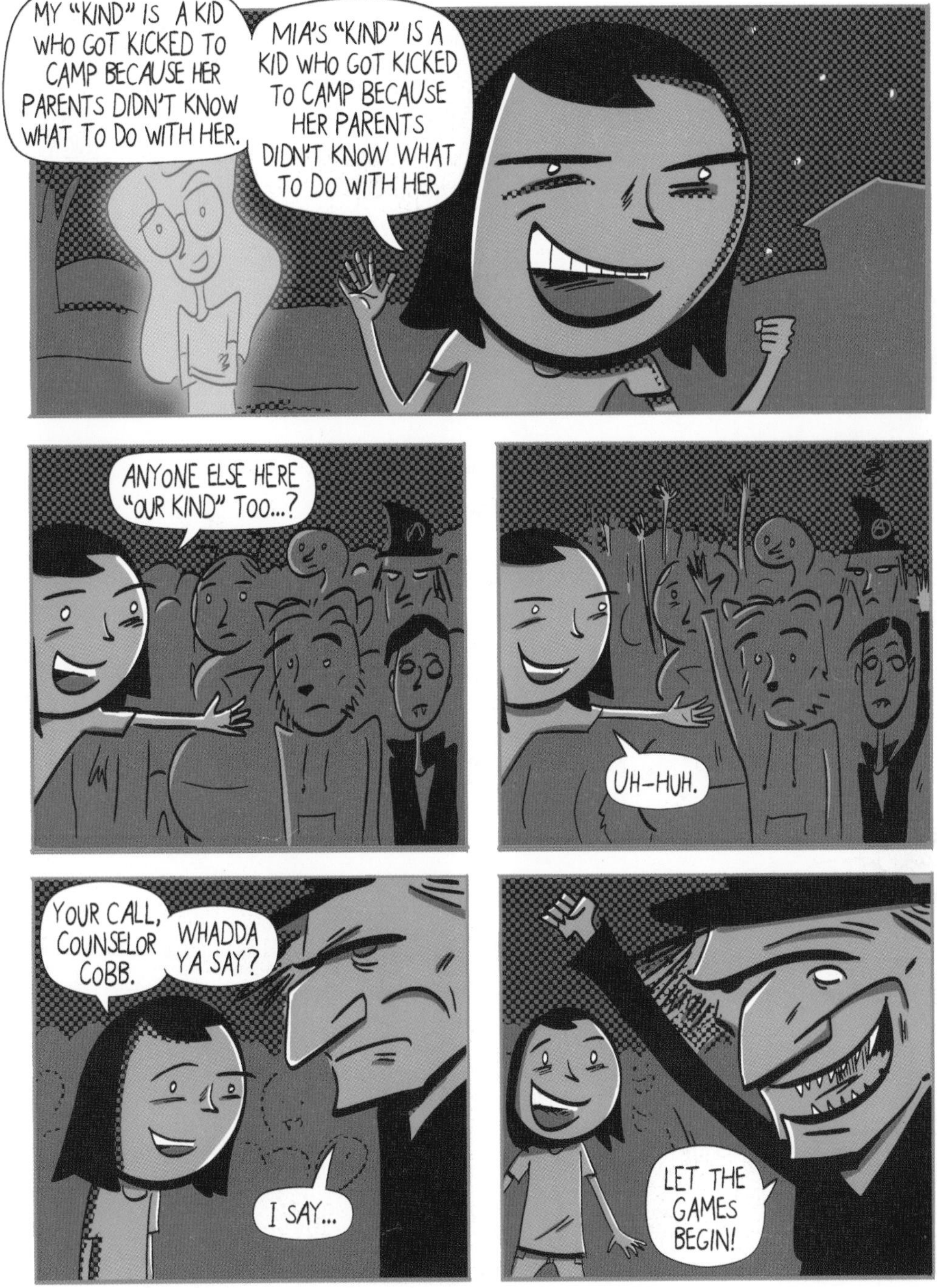

MY "KIND" IS A KID WHO GOT KICKED TO CAMP BECAUSE HER PARENTS DIDN'T KNOW WHAT TO DO WITH HER.
MIA'S "KIND" IS A KID WHO GOT KICKED TO CAMP BECAUSE HER PARENTS DIDN'T KNOW WHAT TO DO WITH HER.
ANYONE ELSE HERE "OUR KIND" TOO...?
UH-HUH.
YOUR CALL, COUNSELOR COBB.
WHADDA YA SAY?
I SAY...
LET THE GAMES BEGIN!

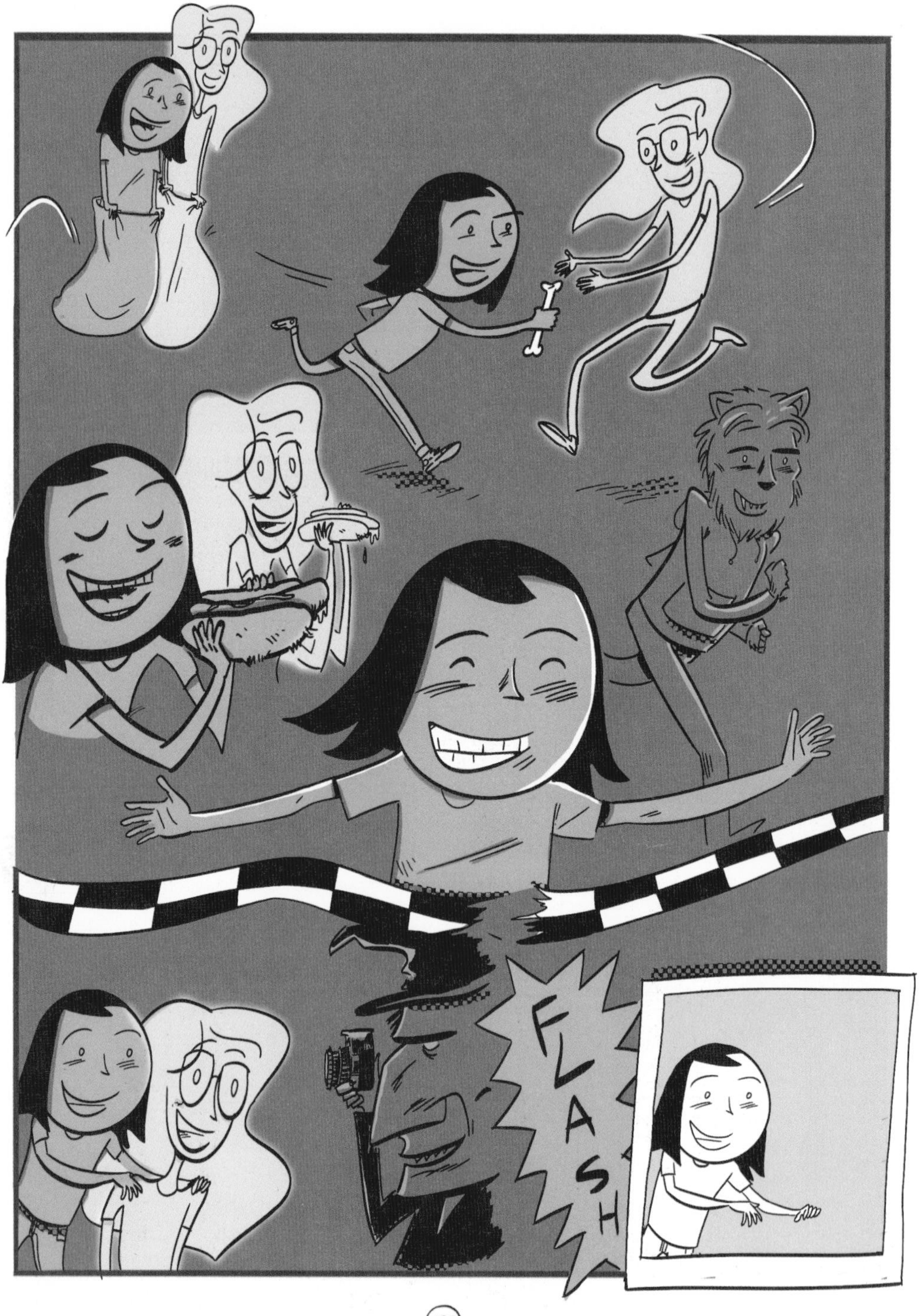
FLASH

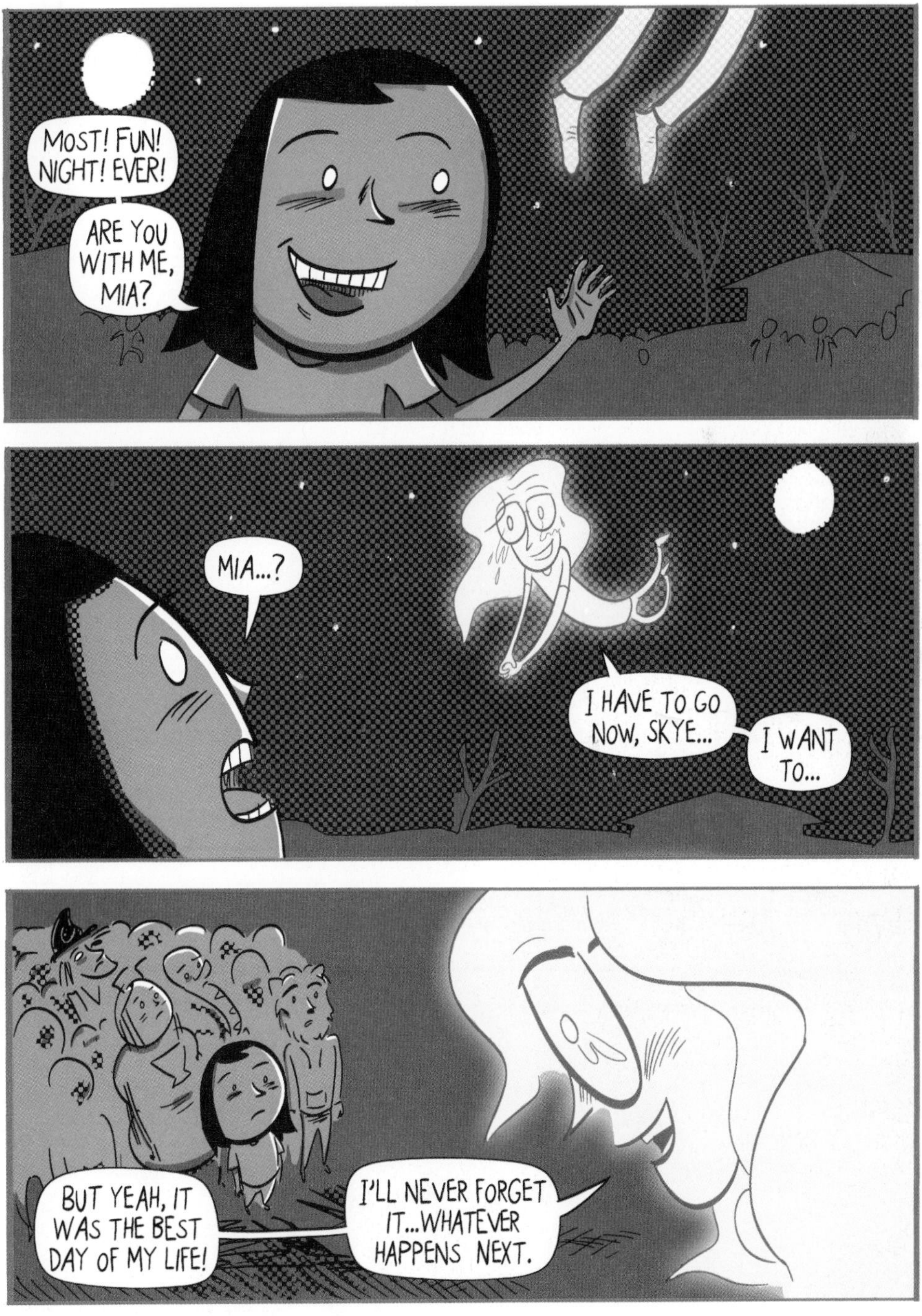
MOST! FUN! NIGHT! EVER!
ARE YOU WITH ME, MIA?
MIA...?
I HAVE TO GO NOW, SKYE...
I WANT TO...
BUT YEAH, IT WAS THE BEST DAY OF MY LIFE!
I'LL NEVER FORGET IT...WHATEVER HAPPENS NEXT.

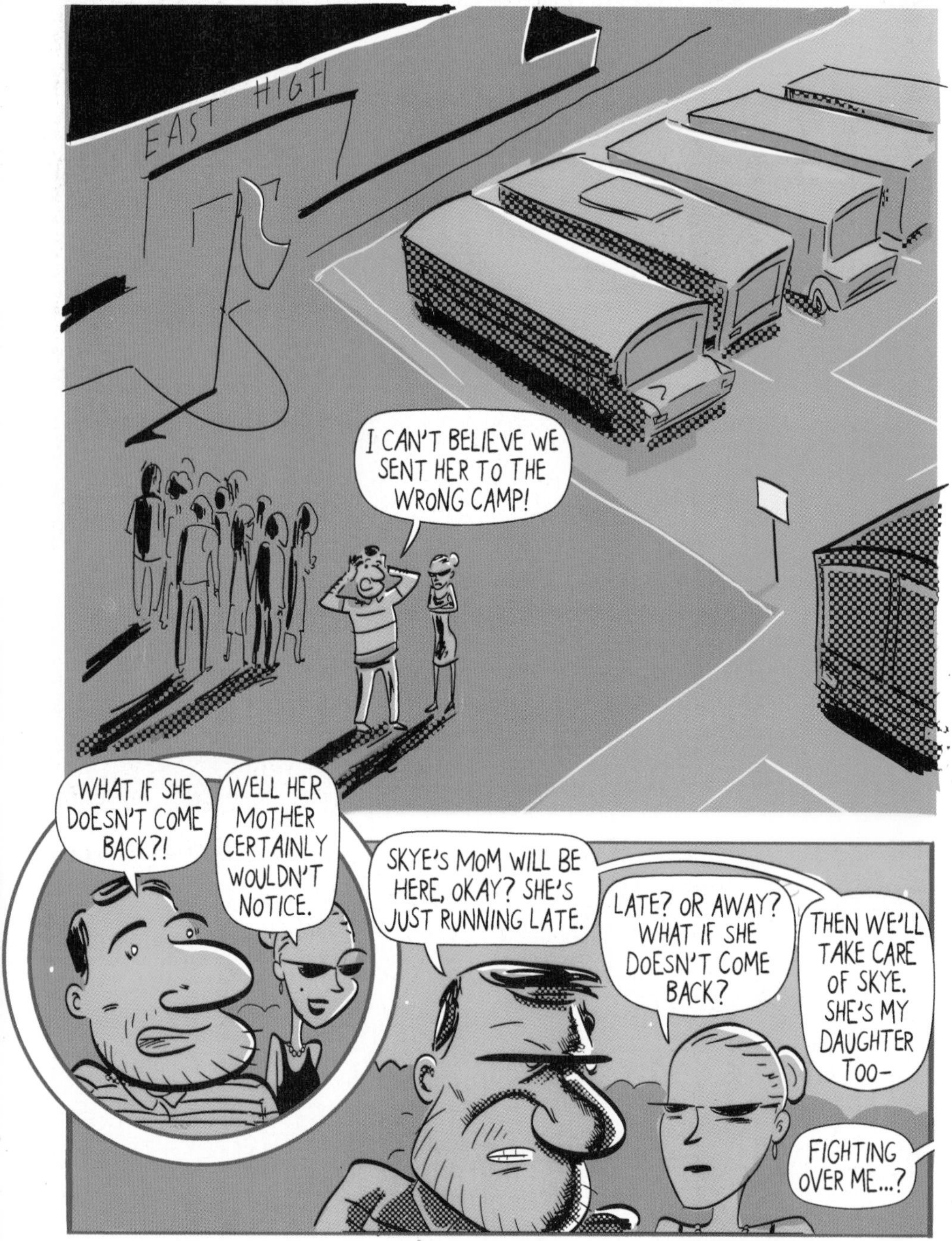
EAST HIGH
I CAN'T BELIEVE WE SENT HER TO THE WRONG CAMP!
WHAT IF SHE DOESN'T COME BACK?!
WELL HER MOTHER CERTAINLY WOULDN'T NOTICE.
SKYE'S MOM WILL BE HERE, OKAY? SHE'S JUST RUNNING LATE.
LATE? OR AWAY? WHAT IF SHE DOESN'T COME BACK?
THEN WE'LL TAKE CARE OF SKYE. SHE'S MY DAUGHTER TOO-
FIGHTING OVER ME...?

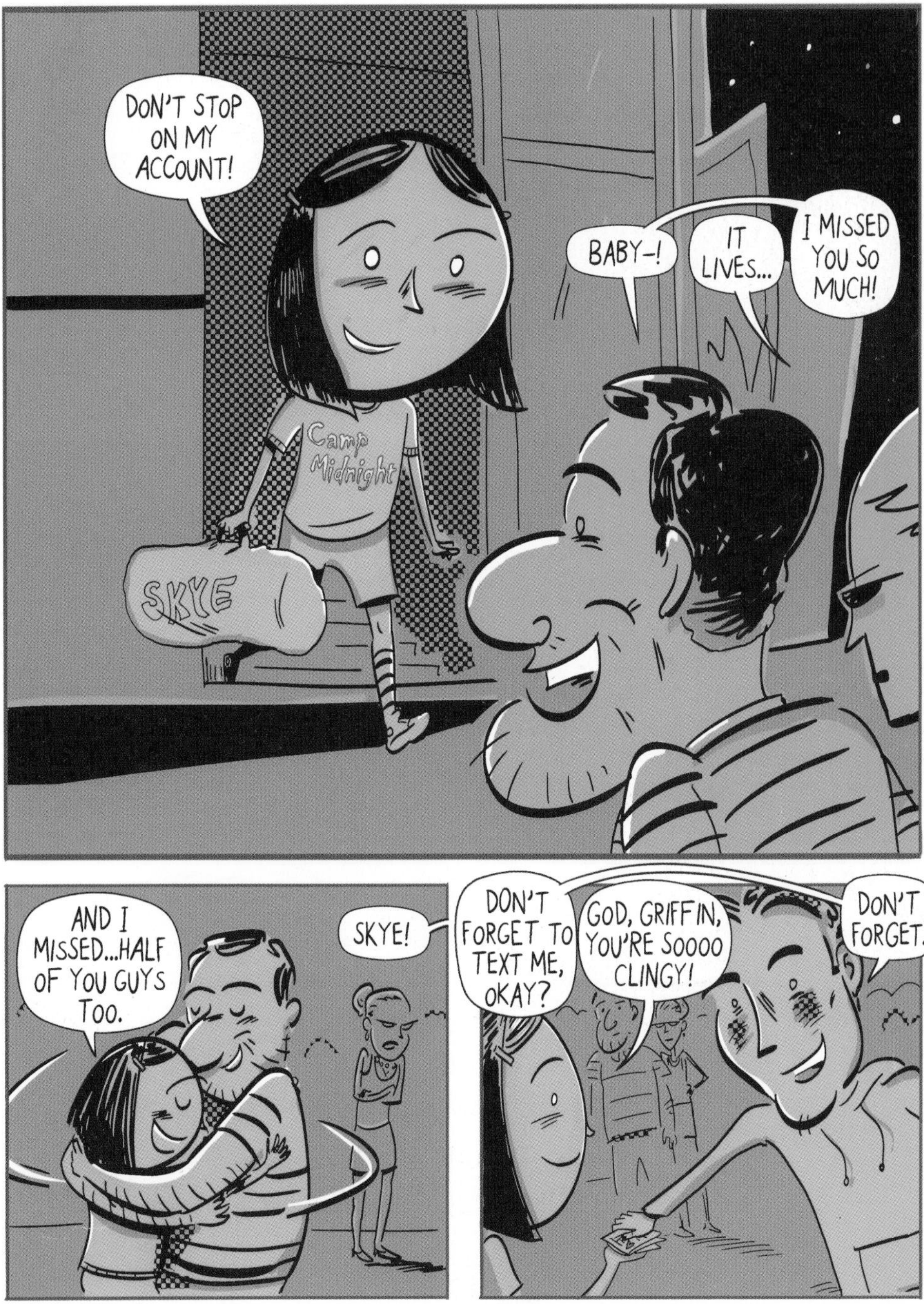
DON'T STOP ON MY ACCOUNT!
Camp Midnight
SKYE
BABY–!
IT LIVES...
I MISSED YOU SO MUCH!
AND I MISSED...HALF OF YOU GUYS TOO.
SKYE!
DON'T FORGET TO TEXT ME, OKAY?
GOD, GRIFFIN, YOU'RE SOOOO CLINGY!
DON'T FORGET.

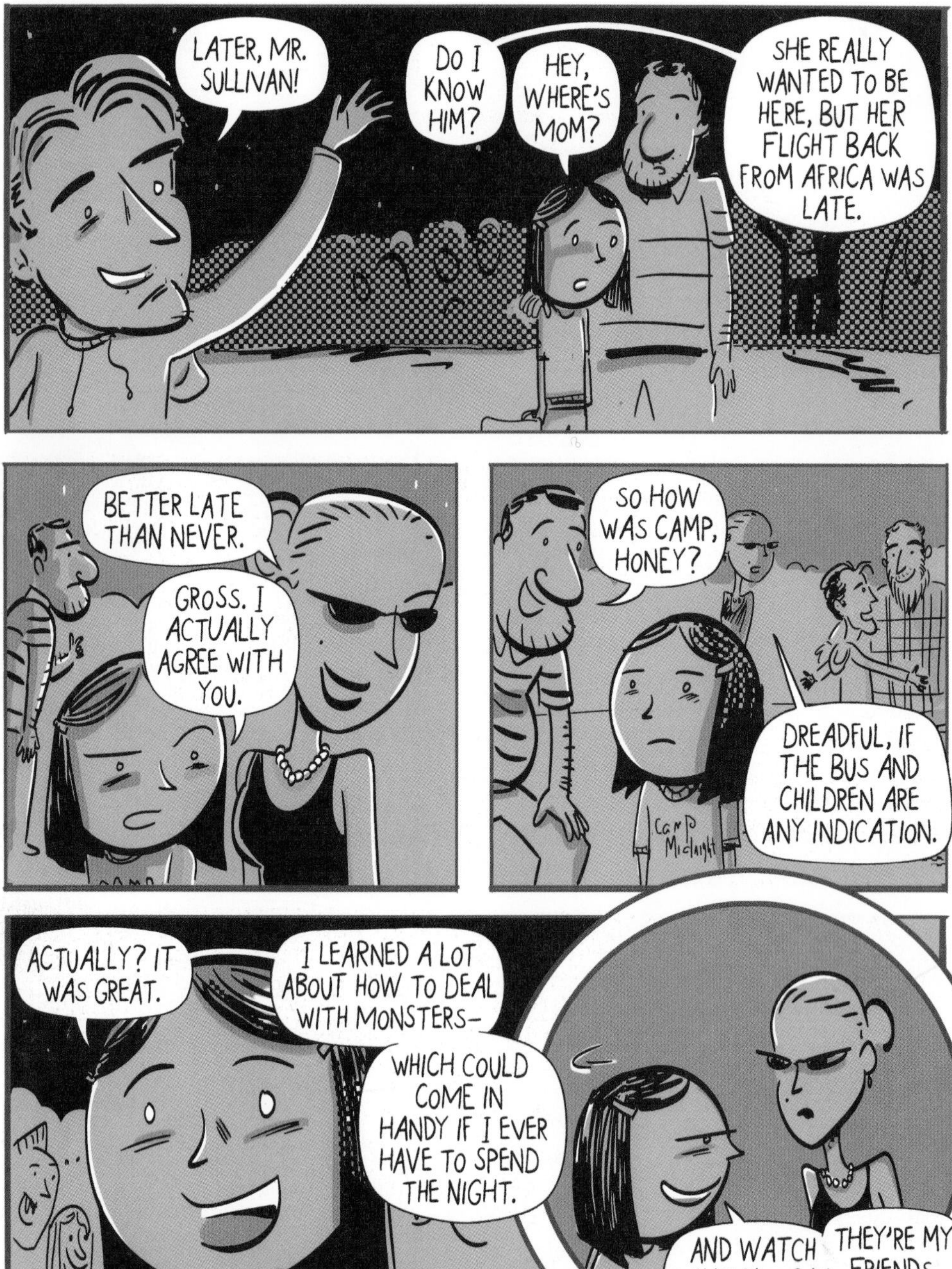
LATER, MR. SULLIVAN!
DO I KNOW HIM?
HEY, WHERE'S MOM?
SHE REALLY WANTED TO BE HERE, BUT HER FLIGHT BACK FROM AFRICA WAS LATE.
BETTER LATE THAN NEVER.
GROSS. I ACTUALLY AGREE WITH YOU.
SO HOW WAS CAMP, HONEY?
DREADFUL, IF THE BUS AND CHILDREN ARE ANY INDICATION.
Camp Midnight
ACTUALLY? IT WAS GREAT.
I LEARNED A LOT ABOUT HOW TO DEAL WITH MONSTERS–
WHICH COULD COME IN HANDY IF I EVER HAVE TO SPEND THE NIGHT.
AND WATCH WHAT YOU SAY ABOUT THOSE KIDS, GAYLE.
THEY'RE MY FRIENDS.

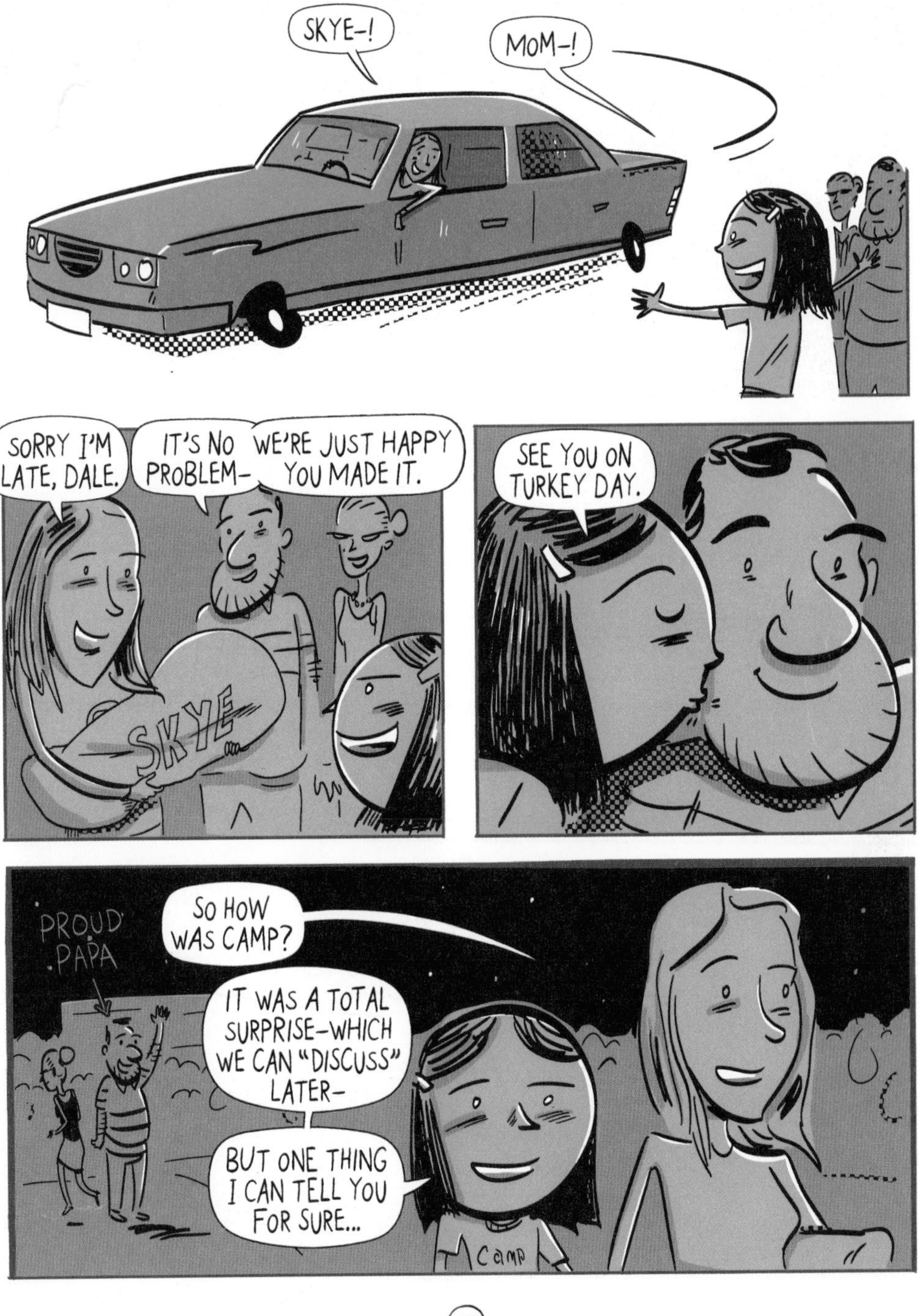
SKYE–!
MOM–!
SORRY I'M LATE, DALE.
IT'S NO PROBLEM–
WE'RE JUST HAPPY YOU MADE IT.
SKYE
SEE YOU ON TURKEY DAY.
PROUD PAPA
SO HOW WAS CAMP?
IT WAS A TOTAL SURPRISE–WHICH WE CAN "DISCUSS" LATER–
BUT ONE THING I CAN TELL YOU FOR SURE...
camp

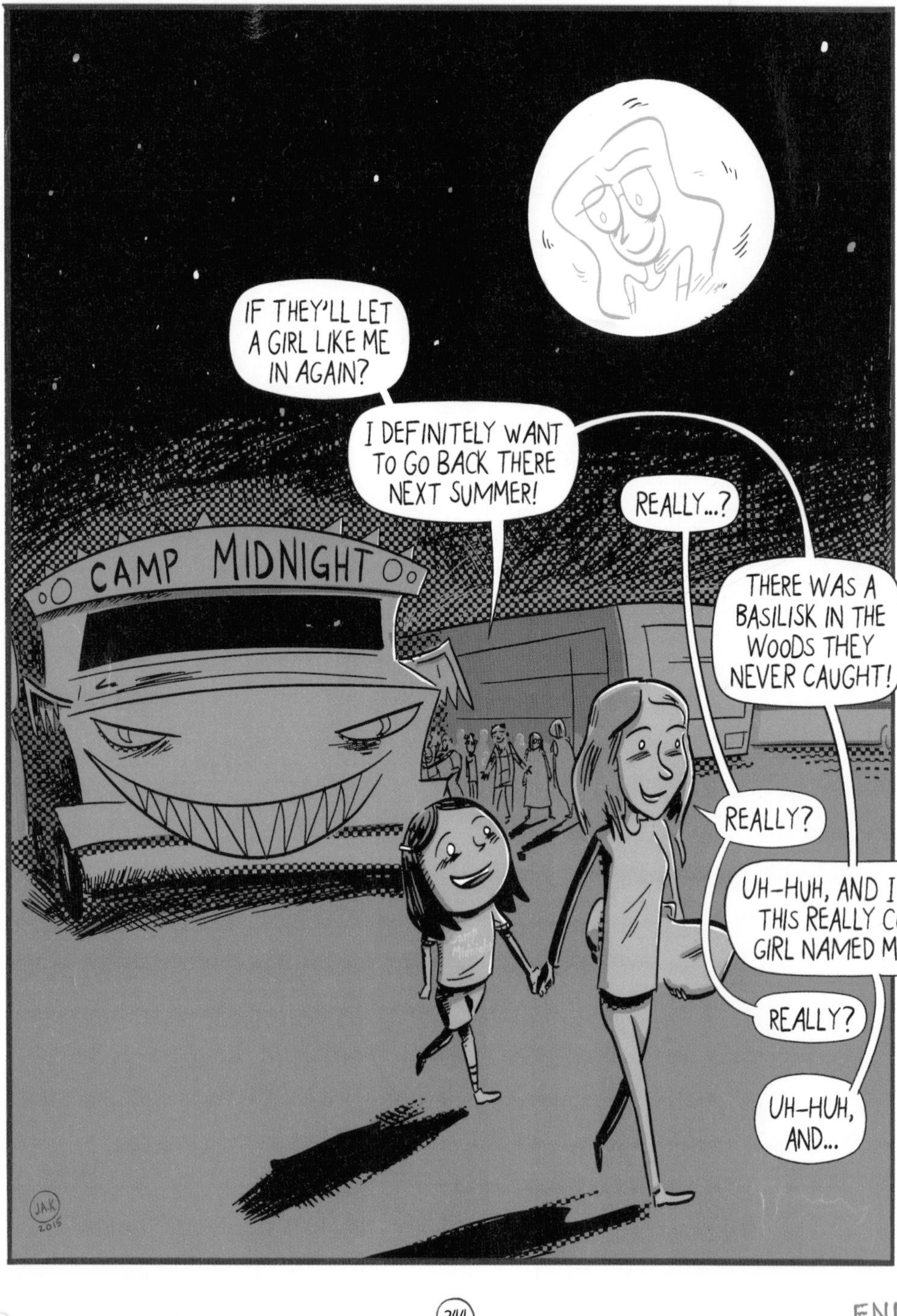
IF THEY'LL LET A GIRL LIKE ME IN AGAIN?
I DEFINITELY WANT TO GO BACK THERE NEXT SUMMER!
REALLY...?
THERE WAS A BASILISK IN THE WOODS THEY NEVER CAUGHT!
REALLY?
UH-HUH, AND I MET THIS REALLY COOL GIRL NAMED MIA...
REALLY?
UH-HUH, AND...
CAMP MIDNIGHT
JA.K 2015

END.

Steven T. Seagle is a comic book, cartoon, and TV writer and producer. He's a partner in a cool group of dudes called MAN OF ACTION. They created the Cartoon Network show BEN 10, and the team and characters for Disney's Oscar Winner BIG HERO 6, as well as a bunch of other fun stuff. The three things he remembers from camp are: hand dipping a candle, hitting his nose on a bunk bed post really hard, and how good the field at the foot of the big mountain smelled as he hiked across it.

Steve would like to thank Jason for agreeing to do this book with him and everyone at Image Comics for working so hard to get it out to the world.

Steve owes Daryl Sabara a HUGE thanks for introducing him to Jason!

Jason Adam Katzenstein is a cartoonist and TV animation writer. He's a member of a cool band called WET LEATHER where he plays keyboards and sings. He draws cartoons for the prestigious magazine The New Yorker and has also done illustrations for Newsweek and lots of other cool stuff. The three things Jason remembers from camp are staying up way too late with his friends, making really bad paintings, and feeling at home with being a dweeb for the very first time.

Jason would like to thank Steve for being a genius writer and collaborator, Image Comics for making his dreams come true, and his family and friends for loving and putting up with him.

Jason owes Daryl Sabara a HUGE thanks for introducing him to Steve!

MAN OF
action
ENTERTAINMENT

WWW.MANOFACTION.TV

IMAGE COMICS, INC.

Robert Kirkman - Chief Operating Officer
Erik Larsen - Chief Financial Officer
Todd McFarlane - President
Marc Silvestri - Chief Executive Officer
Jim Valentino - Vice-President
Eric Stephenson - Publisher
Corey Murphy - Director of Sales
Jeff Boison - Director of Publishing Planning & Book Trade Sales
Jeremy Sullivan - Director of Digital Sales
Kat Salazar - Director of PR & Marketing
Emily Miller - Director of Operations
Branwyn Bigglestone - Senior Accounts Manager
Sarah Mello - Accounts Manager
Drew Gill - Art Director
Jonathan Chan - Production Manager
Meredith Wallace - Print Manager
Briah Skelly - Publicity Assistant
Sasha Head - Sales & Marketing Production Designer
Randy Okamura - Digital Production Designer
David Brothers - Branding Manager
Ally Power - Content Manager
Addison Duke - Production Artist
Vincent Kukua - Production Artist
Tricia Ramos - Production Artist
Jeff Stang - Direct Market Sales Representative
Emilio Bautista - Digital Sales Associate
Leanna Caunter - Accounting Assistant
Chloe Ramos-Peterson - Administrative Assistant

IMAGECOMICS.COM